W9-CBV-352

FATAL PURSUIT

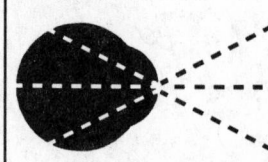

This Large Print Book carries the
Seal of Approval of N.A.V.H.

A BRUNO, CHIEF OF POLICE NOVEL

FATAL PURSUIT

MARTIN WALKER

THORNDIKE PRESS
A part of Gale, Cengage Learning

GALE
CENGAGE Learning®

Farmington Hills, Mich • San Francisco • New York • Waterville, Maine
Meriden, Conn • Mason, Ohio • Chicago

GALE
CENGAGE Learning

LIBRARY OF CONGRESS CATALOGING-IN-PUBLICATION DATA

Names: Walker, Martin, 1947 January 23- author.
Title: Fatal pursuit : a Bruno, chief of police novel / by Martin Walker.
Description: Large print edition. | Waterville, Maine : Thorndike Press, 2016. |
    Series: Thorndike Press large print mystery
Identifiers: LCCN 2016021377 | ISBN 9781410492098 (hardcover) | ISBN 1410492095
    (hardcover)
Subjects: LCSH: Large type books. | GSAFD: Mystery fiction.
Classification: LCC PR6073.A413 F38 2016b | DDC 823/.914--dc23
LC record available at https://lccn.loc.gov/2016021377

Published in 2016 by arrangement with Alfred A. Knopf, a division of Penguin Random House LLC

Printed in the United States of America
1 2 3 4 5 6 7 20 19 18 17 16

To my fellow grand consuls of the Consulat de la Vinée de Bergerac, a body established in 1254 by King Henry III of England to ensure and uphold the quality of the wines of Bergerac, and later established under French law by King Charles IV in 1322, and by the National Assembly of the French Republic in 1954

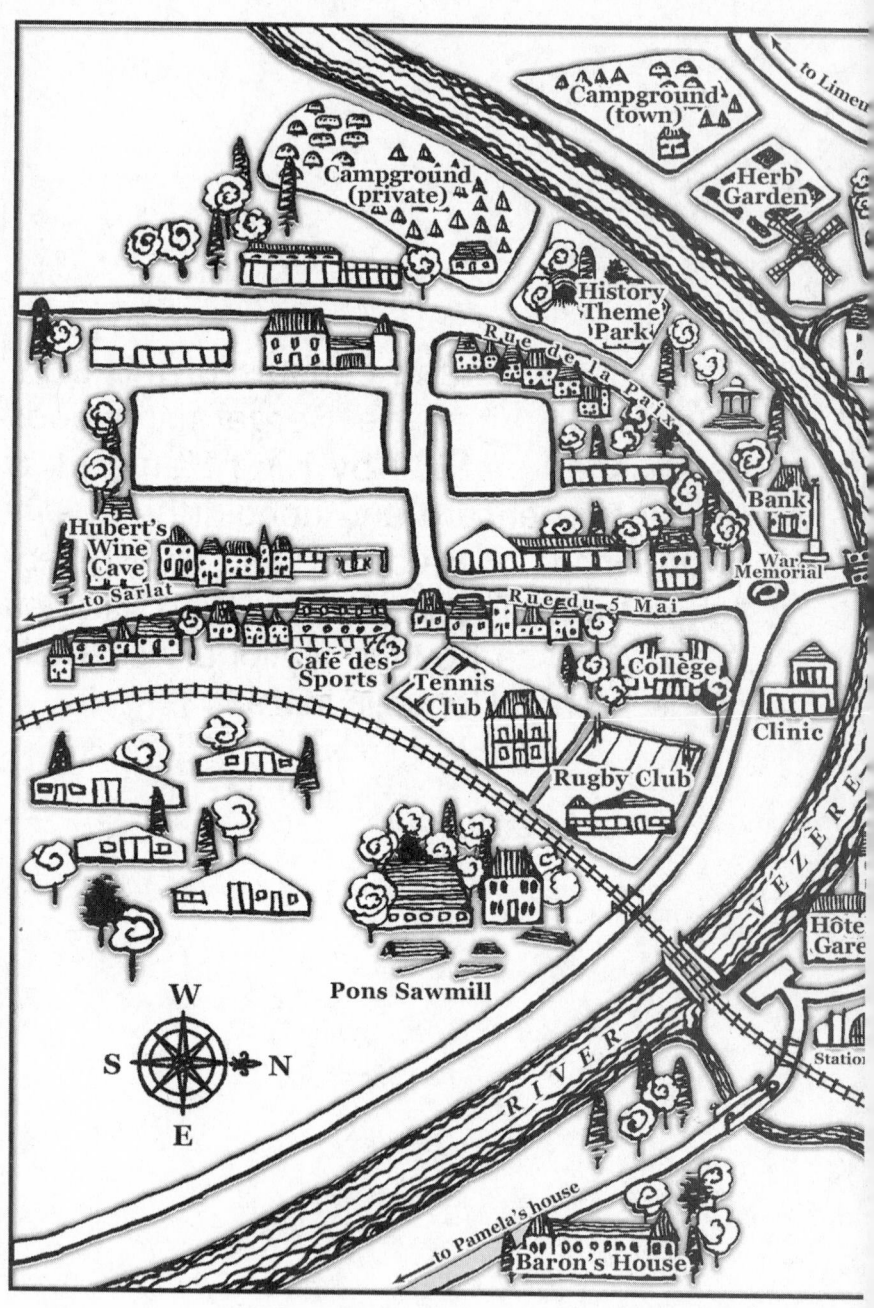

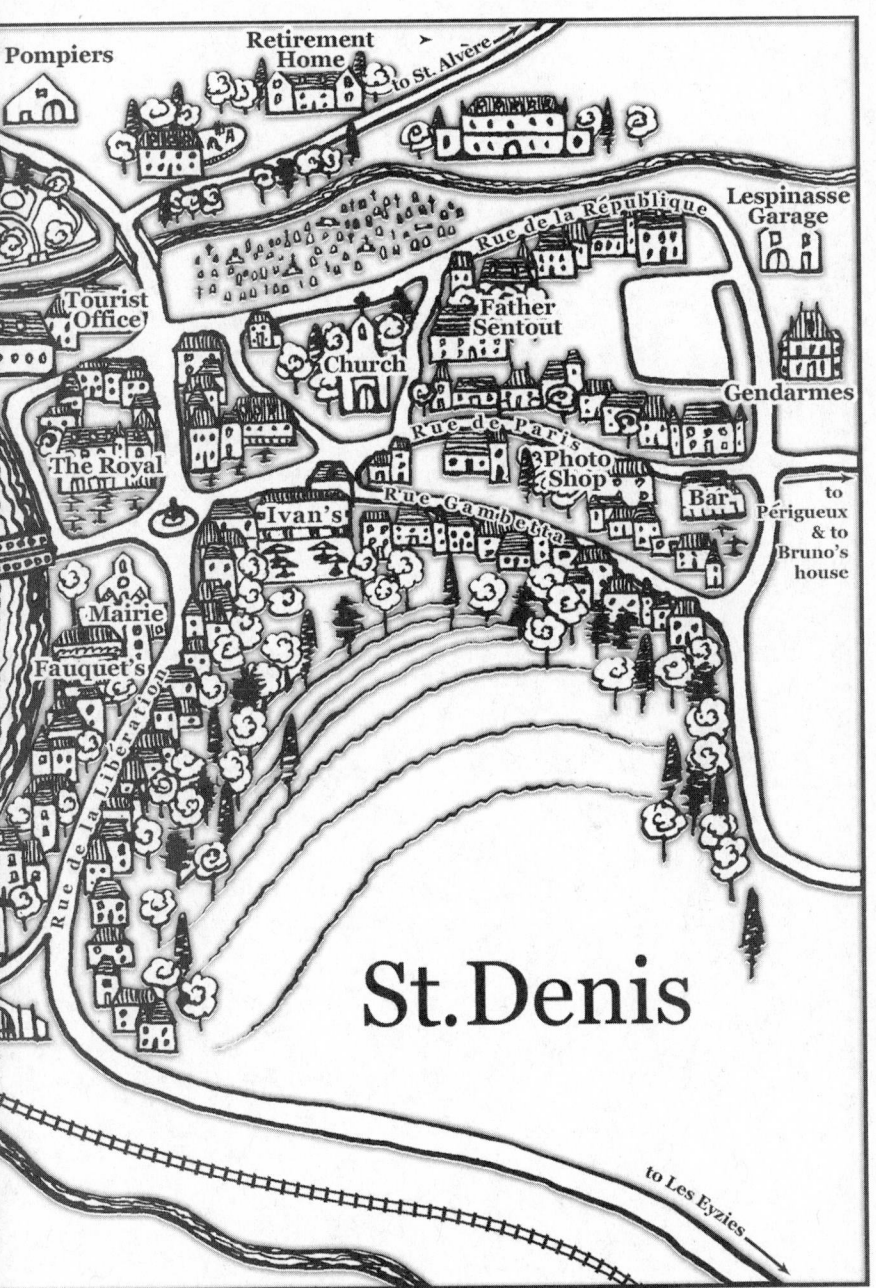

1

The lunar calendar said that the new moon made this a good day to plant broad beans, arugula and spinach, just as the previous days of a waning crescent moon were said to be the time to weed and to start a new compost heap. As Bruno Courrèges, chief of police of the small French town of St. Denis, planted the seeds he'd brought from his greenhouse, he wondered if this was some old wives' tale. Other gardeners he knew and trusted, prime among them the mayor of St. Denis, swore that the traditional ways of the lunar calendar worked for them, and there was no arguing with the quality of the generous crops they harvested. So when the mayor had given him a copy of the lunar almanac and advised him to try following its advice, Bruno thought he'd make the experiment. At the far side of his vegetable patch, his basset hound, Balzac, gazed at Bruno curiously, probably wondering why he was not allowed to play in this part of the garden.

"There is some science behind it," the mayor had insisted. "It's like the tides of the sea. The moon's gravity draws up the moisture in the soil when it's waxing and lets it down again when it's waning. So plant your aboveground vegetables when it's a waxing moon and your belowground ones when it's waning. It works for me."

The last of the seeds planted, Bruno used his watering can to sprinkle the ground and then stretched to ease his back, turning his face to the early morning sun. He'd picked the last of his vegetables when the moon had said the time was ripe, and some of them were already in the big stockpot he kept atop his wood-burning stove. Cooking a couple of quartered chickens with the carrots, onions and potatoes had made a plain but filling meal for his friends the previous evening. Now with some more vegetables and garlic and a pack of green lentils added, it would provide him and his dog with a hearty stew throughout the week.

Back in the house, Bruno heard his guests moving around upstairs in the new bedroom he'd built under the roof. He added some logs from his woodpile to the stove, closed the damper and then reopened it a notch. It would keep the place warm all day and let the stockpot cook slowly, the way he liked it. He poured the last of the previous evening's wine into the stew and added some hot water.

He wanted to clean his Land Rover and get to the tennis club early for the meeting and subsequent parade of classic cars, a new event in the calendar of St. Denis. His houseguests would get there on their own. Despite the work he had put into organizing the event, Bruno had never thought of himself as a car enthusiast. He did not read car magazines, and he seldom recognized the make of a new car until he saw its insignia. He put fuel in one end of his own vehicles and water in the other and expected them to function; they were merely tools to take people or goods from one place to another. He entrusted their repair and maintenance to experts and assumed they would be more or less efficient. He had driven many different vehicles, military and civilian. These days he mostly drove the utility police vans supplied to him by his employer, the mayor and council of St. Denis, or the aged Land Rover he had inherited from a hunting friend and for which he had developed a surprising affection.

The Land Rover was not a comfortable

vehicle to drive, built before the modern conveniences of adjustable seats, power steering and antilock brakes. Indeed, it was nearly twenty years older than Bruno. He had been surprised to learn this qualified it as a classic car. But it could go just about anywhere — cross rivers, climb the steepest and most muddy slopes and negotiate the most-rock-strewn trails through the woods where he hunted the region's abundant game. And it had never let him down. This was more than he could say for some of the fancy cars his friends drove, which seemed to require the skills of a computer expert as much as a traditional car mechanic. In his days in the French army, Bruno had driven jeeps, trucks, motorcycles and even the occasional armored car. He had a painful memory of the deafening and bone-shaking experience of driving an AMX-30, France's main battle tank, on the testing grounds at Saumur and had vowed never to repeat it. Forty tons was more than Bruno felt he could handle, particularly when the instructor had closed the driver's hatch so that Bruno's vision was limited to two narrow slits and a blurry periscope. Driving held little appeal for him ever since.

Bruno took little pleasure in driving fast and had been called to the scene of too many road accidents to push his limited skills. He had once been taken frighteningly fast around a course by a skilled rally driver, his friend Annette, a magistrate in Sarlat. She had skidded around bends, missed trees by inches and accelerated over the crests of hills in a way that Bruno's head repeatedly slammed against the roof of her specially equipped Peugeot. Bruno thought he had been saved from unconsciousness only by the helmet she had supplied. Such driving was not for him. Bruno's sole ambitions as a driver were to be competent and safe.

This morning Bruno skipped his usual morning run so that he could wash and polish the Land Rover. He had scrubbed the mud from the wheel wells and used a touch-up pen to cover the deeper scratches in the faded-green paint. He had wiped clean the canvas-covered seats and washed the windows, inside and out. He had swept out the dust and gravel from the interior. He had tidied up the rear, putting his tennis gear in one bag, his rugby boots and tracksuit in another and his all-weather garments and hunting clothes in a third.

He had washed the dog blanket that now nestled between the bags, where Balzac could rest while waiting for his master. A newly washed bowl and fresh water bottle stood ready for Balzac's refreshment. When Bruno drove, Balzac preferred to ride on the passenger seat where he could watch the road and landscape and, in the absence of a car radio, listen to Bruno sing. Other than his occasional attendance at church or on convivial evenings at the rugby club, Bruno had sufficient regard for the comfort of his fellow humans to reserve his singing for his Land Rover and his shower.

As Bruno, freshly showered and changed, drove into town, Balzac seemed to appreciate his owner's version of "Que Reste-t-il de Nos Amours?" Bruno tried to catch the breathy, almost-playful tones of the Charles Trenet 1943 original. For Bruno, no other version would do, although most French singers had made their own recordings, singing it too slowly or making it too sad, Bruno thought. His own mood when he thought of his past love affairs was of fond nostalgia rather than tragic loss. The memories made him grateful rather than despondent, so as Bruno pulled his unusually clean and gleaming car into the parking lot by the tennis club, he was pleased to see a familiar ancient Citroën *deux-chevaux*.

Pamela, its owner and the woman who had recently ended their affair, was standing nearby and admiring the baron's venerable 1958 Citroën DS, which still looked more modern than most of the vehicles on the road. The baron was leaning with one elbow on the roof of his car as he chatted with Pamela and gestured proudly at his second car, the old French military jeep that he used for hunting. It was being driven today by Sergeant Jules from the gendarmerie. Pamela waved and beckoned Bruno to join them as he let Balzac jump out of the car and scamper across to her. He waved back but went to greet his two houseguests, who had followed in their own car, and led them across the parking lot to meet his friends.

It was a fine turnout for the classic-car meeting, thought Bruno proudly, and a very international gathering. His English friend Jack Crimson was at the wheel of his white Jaguar Mark 2, his daughter, Miranda, beside him. Horst, a German archaeologist, was dressed for the part, wearing white gloves and a flat cap as he helped Clothilde, curator of the local prehistory museum, from the seat of her Porsche Speedster. A retired Dutch architect had brought his boxy DAF Variomatic, and someone else had an elderly Saab. Lespinasse from the garage was dusting his perfectly restored Citroën *traction-avant* from 1938, which was the oldest car of the gathering. To Bruno's eye the most striking vehicle was a white E-type Jaguar. From its passenger seat Annette was waving at him, a good-looking and fair-haired stranger at the wheel beside her.

"Meet George Young, an English friend," Annette said to Bruno as he approached, her hand on the young man's arm. "He's from London, where he runs a company bringing British drivers over to take part in French rallies and races. I met him at the Rallye des Remparts in Angoulême, and I persuaded him to bring his Jaguar to St. Denis for our parade. He's going to navigate for me at the rally tomorrow."

Her voice was animated, almost giddy, and she turned back with a shyly affectionate look at her companion as the two men shook hands, and then Bruno introduced his two guests from Alsace. It was about time Annette found herself a boyfriend, thought Bruno. The Englishman looked very suitable. He was about Bruno's height, slim but with powerful shoulders and a friendly smile. His French was fluent as he chatted to the couple from Alsace about his visit — he called it a pilgrimage — to the Bugatti collection at the Musée National de l'Automobile in Mulhouse, near their home.

From the corner of his eye, Bruno saw movement in the woods behind the tennis club and recognized a sullen, skinny teenager named Félix lurking in the trees. Félix was a truant who shunned the tennis and rugby lessons Bruno offered to the other students in the town's *collège.* He was the youngest child of two parents now well into in their fifties. The older siblings had long since left home, and the father had been unemployed for years. His mother, from a French island in the Caribbean, was a cleaning woman at the school. She had bequeathed to her son a skin just a shade or two darker than café au lait, which meant some cruel schoolmates sneered at him as a *métis,* a "half-caste." Félix had suffered a number of brushes with the law for shoplifting, petty vandalism and one case of joyriding in a stolen car. Bruno reminded himself to check on the boy's age; once he was sixteen, his next offense could mean juvenile detention. Bruno was disappointed that he'd never been able to straighten the boy out; he thought of Félix as one of his failures.

"Him again," said Yveline, commandant of the small gendarmerie in St. Denis, who had suddenly appeared at Bruno's side. She was in uniform. "You know we're going to have a lot of trouble with that kid."

"We already have," said Bruno. He gave Félix a stern stare, so the boy would know Bruno had his eye on him, before leading his friends to join a group congregating at a long trestle table set up in front of the club. One of the waitresses from Fauquet's café was serving croissants and *pains au chocolat* and dispensing coffee from two large thermoses to the gathering of drivers.

Bruno had chosen this spot for the cars to assemble, away from the main road and out of sight of the crowds who were expected to line the main streets for the parade. He had almost finished his coffee when two strikingly modern cars arrived. Fabiola was at the wheel of her new Renault Zoe electric car, and behind her came Alphonse, the town's only councillor from the Green Party, in his electric Kangoo van. Alphonse had persuaded the mayor to make a nod to the environment by welcoming electric cars into St. Denis's first Concours d'Élégance. That was the title Annette had dreamed up for what Bruno thought of simply as a vintage-car parade, one of the events marking the name day of St. Denis on October 9.

The idea had come from the baron over a rugby club dinner at the start of the year when the mayor had been thinking aloud about ways to extend the local tourist season beyond the summer months. The first idea had been a visitors' day at the town vineyard, then Stéphane had suggested a special rugby match, and Lespinasse had proposed a sports-car rally. That might usefully be combined with a vintage-car parade, suggested the baron, always keen to show off his splendid Citroën. Bruno had remained silent, knowing that whatever plans were made he'd be the one assigned by the mayor to turn them into reality.

It had been Xavier, the efficient deputy mayor, who had opened his diary and reminded his companions that the date fell on the weekend when the delegation from St. Denis's twin town in Alsace came for its annual visit. They came each year to commemorate the welcome the refugees from Alsace had been given in 1939 and 1940. The first came just after war had been declared in September 1939, when the French government evacuated to the Périgord the civilians from the regions near the German frontier. The following year, after the German reoccupation of Alsace and Lorraine, German settlers were moved in, and Alsatians of French stock were deported. Most of them came to the Périgord.

Inevitably, in the four years before France's liberation, friendships were forged and marriages took place, and after the war towns throughout Alsace twinned with those where they had been welcomed.

So the weekend of the town's name day now included a special market with stalls and vendors from Alsace, a rugby match with a team from Marckolsheim and a visitors' day at the vineyard followed by a feast. Lespinasse had arranged that St. Denis would at the same time host the regional heats for the French rally drivers' championship. Father Sentout had arranged a choral service for two choirs with his counterpart from Alsace, and Antoine the boatman had organized a fishing competition. Bruno had been assigned to coordinate it all and to arrange a fireworks display to round off the celebration. It was not what he had been trained to do in his course at the police academy, but this role as impresario of civic events gave Bruno great pleasure. It had also established a firm friendship with his Alsatian counterpart, Thomas, who with his wife was staying at Bruno's home for the weekend, just as Bruno had been their guest during his visits to Alsace for the twin-town reunions.

"I don't see Sylvestre," said Thomas, a

worried look on his weather-beaten face. "He's a friend from Marckolsheim, and we're counting on him to bring something very special for the parade. I hope he hasn't lost his way."

Thomas and his wife were devoted hikers, striding across the Vosges near their home most weekends and spending their summer vacations walking in the Alps. Bruno recalled with respect the pace they had set on a long day's hike from Colmar to Mulhouse on his last visit to Alsace. A few years older than Bruno, Thomas was trim and fit, a few centimeters taller than Bruno. His wife, Ingrid, looked equally healthy, despite the bottles of Alsace wine they had brought and downed at Bruno's dinner table the previous evening.

"I'd better give the drivers their briefing," said Bruno, looking at his watch. "It's almost time to begin."

Thomas pulled out his cell phone to call Sylvestre as Ingrid turned to embrace Fabiola and Pamela, whom she had met at Bruno's dinner the previous evening. Bruno took from his shoulder bag a sheaf of photocopies he'd made of the route the drivers would take through St. Denis and began handing them out. Each photocopy carried a number, indicating the order in which the cars would start.

"If I could have your attention," he began, using his parade-ground voice. "The route of our motorcade is clearly marked on your maps. Please set off in order of the number on your map. We'll go through the main streets before turning onto the quayside, where we'll park on the long stretch before the bridge. Please park as I do, facing the stone wall and with your back to the river. Leave enough space for people to walk all around the cars, and keep an eye on your vehicles in case kids try to climb in. I'll lead the way, so nobody should get lost. The baron will bring up the rear in his Citroën DS. And I'd like you to keep at least two car lengths' distance from the vehicle ahead."

As he finished, what looked like a furniture truck turned the corner, sounded its horn and pulled up on the street, too big to fit into the already crowded parking lot. Two young men in white overalls, white skullcaps and goggles jumped from the driving compartment, waved at the crowd and went to the rear of the truck. One opened the big double doors while the other pulled out a long ramp, lowered it to the ground and then clambered inside. Bruno heard the sound of a powerful engine being started,

dying with a ragged cough and then starting again. A large cloud of exhaust smoke
drifted from the rear of the truck, and then
a bright blue, open-topped racing car from
another era backed down the ramp.

The windshield was no more than four
inches in height and the hood took up two-
thirds of the car's length. The front wheels
and axle were at the very front of the
vehicle, ahead of the curved, flat radiator.
Leading back from the driver's seat, the
sides of the car curved in to form a pointed
rear that looked as sharp as an ax blade.
There were no mudguards above the wheels,
and a spare tire was attached to the car's
side with thick leather straps. The driver
revved the engine and unleashed a harsh
and potent roar before turning and driving
slowly to face the crowd that had been
stunned into silence. Bruno could read the
red badge on the arch-shaped radiator:
BUGATTI.

"Sylvestre always likes to make an entrance," Ingrid said drily once the throaty
roar of the engine had quieted. "That's the
one he bought last year. He paid seven
hundred thousand euros, and he says it's
worth a lot more now."

"A Type 35 from 1928, the car that made
Bugatti's name," said Thomas, something

close to reverence in his voice. "It was the only car of its day that could be driven both on the road and in Grand Prix races. And despite the name, it's a French car, designed and built in Alsace."

"It won every race going," said Young, Annette's friend, in a worshipful tone. "It took the world championship in 1926 and the Targa Florio five years in a row." He moved forward to help the driver from the cockpit and, as if suddenly released from bondage, the rest of the crowd surged forward to cluster around the small Bugatti.

"Welcome," said Bruno, introducing himself and handing the driver his photocopied map. "We're honored to have your car here. You're number nineteen, next to last in the parade. You'll follow the *traction-avant* and be just ahead of the DS."

"Thank you, and please call me Sylvestre," said the man in white, pushing his goggles back onto his brow. He looked to be in his thirties. He had bright blue eyes, a prominent nose and a firm jaw. The grip of his handshake was unnecessarily strong but his smile was affable.

"This is my friend, Freddy, he's from India," Sylvestre said, beckoning forward his companion, also in white overalls. "We're both glad to be here. My grand-

24

mother told me a lot about this place. She was born just outside St. Denis, and I thought this was a good opportunity to take a look at some property she left me." His expression was arrogant, almost haughty, as he gazed around at the crowd, before raising his voice to ask, "And which of these charming ladies would like to ride in the Bugatti with me?"

Sylvestre's eyes settled briefly on Fabiola, standing alone. "How about you, mademoiselle?"

"Thanks, but I'm driving my own car, the new Renault," she replied coolly. "We have electric cars in the parade."

"Excellent," said Sylvestre, and looked at Bruno. "In that case, would you have room for one more? I've got a Tesla in the back of the truck, and Freddy can drive it."

Suddenly he seemed aware of Félix, who had somehow pushed himself forward to stand at the side of the Bugatti and gaze reverently into the driving compartment.

"What about you, young man. Would you like to take a spin?" Sylvestre asked. And with what Bruno thought was an understandable glance of triumph at him, Félix clambered inside and seemed to glow with pride as he took his seat. He looked up at Sylvestre in awe.

Bruno had heard of the Tesla, an American-made electric sports car that ran on some revolutionary new battery, but he'd never seen one. Freddy clambered into the back of the big truck and backed out a sleek gray car. When Sylvestre turned off the Bugatti's engine, Bruno realized that the Tesla was utterly, eerily silent.

2

Shortly after the motorcade had ended and the cars were parked along the quayside, the crowds that had been cheering were now thronging noisily down the steps to the riverbank, when Bruno felt his phone vibrate. He could barely make out that Dr. Gelletreau was reporting a death. Bruno found his way clear of the crowds so he could hear more clearly.

The doctor told him that an elderly man in Savignac-de-Miremont had been found dead by his wife when she returned from visiting her sister. She had immediately called him. The doctor said the cause of death appeared to be a heart attack. The town wasn't in the commune of St. Denis, but, as a courtesy, Bruno took care of birth and death registration for the small neighboring communes, hence the call. He went in search of the mayor to explain why he had to leave and found him admiring the

Bugatti with the wide-eyed look of a little boy. Bruno entrusted his dog to Thomas and Ingrid and headed for the gendarmerie, where he had parked his official police van.

The commune of Savignac was composed mostly of farms, woods and meadows, its village tiny. There were barely a hundred people in the whole commune, so at some point almost every adult had to take his or her turn in being a member of the local council. Henri-Pierre Hugon, the dead man, had been serving his third term. That was why Bruno found his house easily. In rural areas, friends and neighbors erect at the home of each new council member a tall pole, bedecked with French flags and laurel wreaths and a sign saying HONOR TO THOSE WE ELECT. Bruno followed Dr. Gelletreau's directions until he saw the pole, its flags now somewhat faded, and turned in to see the doctor's elderly Citroën. The plump old man came to the door as Bruno pulled in.

"How goes the old-car parade?" Gelletreau asked, shaking hands. "I'm hoping I'll be in time to see them all. Somebody at the clinic told me there's one of those lovely E-type Jaguars. This shouldn't take long. Madame Hugon is bearing up very well. In fact she's making us some coffee. As soon as you've finished, I'll call the undertakers."

"Has he been dead long?" Bruno asked.

"He died in his study, and the light was on, so I think it was sometime yesterday evening," the doctor replied. "The central heating was on, which means the body temperature doesn't tell us much. I've been treating him for heart trouble for several years, since he was working in Périgueux. I've had him on beta-blockers, and he'd been very overweight as long as I've known him, even more than me. You knew him, didn't you?"

"Only to say hello to, mainly through SHAP, and I have a copy of his book at home," Bruno said. "He made his living as a researcher. I don't think I know his wife."

SHAP was the Society for the History and Archaeology of the Périgord, a body of local enthusiasts and scholars who held monthly meetings and organized lectures in a splendid sixteenth-century townhouse in the heart of Périgueux. The mayor had been a member for years and had encouraged Bruno to join, for which he was grateful. He tried never to miss the sessions and remembered with pleasure lectures he'd heard on the diet of the prehistoric peoples of the region, the development of medieval castle design and on that brief period in the

29

sixteenth century when Bergerac had been the capital of France, or at least of the Protestants rallying to King Henri IV. He'd also heard the dead man give a memorably dry lecture on Périgueux during World War II, during which few in the audience managed to stay awake. SHAP had helped Hugon publish his book, an encyclopedia of the members of the Resistance in the Périgord. Hugon had spent his life working as an archivist for the *département* and since his retirement had continued to visit the archives regularly in his new role as freelance historian and researcher. He was invariably neatly dressed, and Bruno had heard he was a meticulous worker with a good reputation among local lawyers and notaries.

"How old was he?" Bruno asked.

"He'd have been seventy-five next month. But he never exercised, always down in those gloomy archives. He lived a very sedentary life, and he was a smoker."

Once indoors, Bruno gave his condolences to Madame Hugon, accepted a cup of coffee and asked when she had found her husband.

"About an hour ago, when I got back, maybe it was a bit more than that," she said. Madame Hugon was dry eyed and com-

ded with an entry for July 30 of that year.
here was no sign of any current notebook,
st two virgin notebooks, ready for use.
The only item in the wastepaper basket
as an empty envelope from France Télé-
om. It was postmarked two days earlier, so
it had probably been delivered the previous
day. Bruno found a file for phone bills. In
the past two months there had been far
more calls than usual, including daily calls
to and from a mobile number that did not
feature in earlier bills. Bruno took out his
own phone and dialed the number, but an
automated reply said the number was no
longer available. That was odd. He called
the security line for France Télécom and
was told the number belonged to an unreg-
istered pay-as-you-go phone.

Bruno went back to Madame Hugon to
ask if she knew the password for the laptop.
She shook her head: nor did she recognize
the phone number. She added that her
husband had kept his diary and account
books in his desk, unless he was going to
the archives, when they'd be in his briefcase.

"They aren't there now," said Bruno.
"And there's no sign of the briefcase."

"Maybe he left them in the car," she said
with a shrug, not seeming much concerned.

The briefcase was in the car, but it con-

posed, with no sign of shock or grief. Her
hair was white, and she looked to be about
the same age as her husband but in much-
better health. Short and slim, she wore
lace-up flat shoes, a dark skirt and a light
blue blouse.

"I'd been at my sister's in Sarlat for a few
days. She has a new grandchild. My nephew
drove me back because he wanted to see
the old-car parade, and Henri had needed
the car while I was away. He was working
on a big research job and needed to go back
and forth to Périgueux and Bordeaux. I'd
left meals in the freezer for him."

Her nephew had dropped her at the house,
and she'd let herself in. The front door had
not been locked. She'd called for her husband, gotten no reply and found him dead
on the floor beside the desk in his study.
She had touched his cheek, found it cold
and called Dr. Gelletreau.

"You didn't call the *urgences*?" Bruno
asked. The *pompiers* of the St. Denis fire
brigade provided the local emergency service.

"There was no point. He'd obviously been
dead for hours. The doctor kept warning
him this might happen, but Henri never
listened." She shrugged and then looked at
Dr. Gelletreau. "He hadn't touched those

meals I'd left for him, and from the dishes he'd left in the sink it looks like he'd lived on steaks and fried potatoes, all those things you'd told him not to eat."

"I'm sorry for your loss," Bruno said. "I'd better take a look in the study. What was this big research job he was doing?"

"He'd been at it for a couple of months, five days a week. But he never told me what it was, just something about the war and the Resistance. But he said he'd make enough from it for us to have a nice vacation in the sun this winter. He used to get a hundred and fifty euros a day for his research work. I'd always wanted to see Morocco, and I was looking forward to it."

"Do you know who hired him?" Bruno asked. She shook her head, and Bruno did the math as Gelletreau led the way into the study, where the desk lamp was still lit. If Hugon had been working on a research project for two months he'd have earned six thousand euros, a tidy sum.

In the study, a chair had been overturned, and Hugon's plump body lay sprawled beside it, one leg partly under the desk. His right hand was clutching at his shirtfront, and his face looked as though he'd died in pain, his lips drawn back from his teeth. On his desk was a lamp, an old-fashioned

telephone, a blank messag___ ___en pencil lined up neatly beside it a___ T laptop computer. The printer was o___ u side table, switched off, with no prin the out-tray.

There was no sign of a diary or not__ that gave a clue to his research. The dra___ of the two filing cabinets against the were closed. Bruno slipped on a set evidence gloves and opened each drawer turn. Most of the files were organize alphabetically and seemed to reflect the names of the people included in his encyclo-pedia. One file marked "Current Projects" was empty. His bank statements showed no unusual activity, just his pension payments, reimbursements from medical insurance and some modest bank transfers from lawyers, presumably research fees. There was no sign of the six thousand euros. So where was the account book he would have to keep for tax records?

In the bookcase, filled with well-thumbed works of reference, there were two shelves filled with hardback notebooks, covered in black leather and much too big to fit into a pocket. Bruno leafed through them. Hugon's handwriting was neat and precise, and every entry was dated. They were filed in order. The last one on the bookshelf

tained only blank notepads, pens, a copy of the previous day's *Sud Ouest* and a half-empty pack of Royale cigarettes. Bruno went back to the body and found a wallet in the hip pocket. Inside were the usual identity, health and credit cards, along with five crisp, new two-hundred-euro bank-notes. Bruno asked where Hugon had kept his clothes and was shown to a wardrobe in the marital bedroom. He checked the pockets of the jackets and the bedside tables but found nothing.

"Was there any sign that anybody else might have been in the house while you were away?" Bruno asked Madame Hugon.

She shook her head. "Not that I noticed. We never had many visitors, except for my sister."

"Did you have any unusual visitors in recent days?" She shook her head. "Did he seem worried by anything?"

"Far from it. He was pleased to have this new research project. Henri liked it when he was busy. He was never one to hang around the house, and he didn't watch much television. There was nothing he liked more than poking around old archives, and getting paid for it was even better."

"Was he working very hard?" Gelletreau asked.

"More than usual. He was in his study until all hours, night after night. But that wasn't so unusual when he had his teeth into something. It was like when he was writing that book. But it didn't seem like it was a strain. It was work, but the kind of work he liked. It always cheered him up to be on the trail of something."

"Did he always work on the laptop, or did he work with documents?"

"Both. He had a big file of papers he'd collected, but he always had one of those black notebooks going as well."

"There's a file marked 'Current Projects' in the filing cabinet, but it's empty and the last entry in the latest black notebook was for sometime in July. So where's the one for August and September?"

"I don't know. Maybe he left it at the archives in Périgueux. They'd always let him leave stuff in a desk."

Bruno went into the kitchen and looked at the dirty dishes in the sink and piled up on the draining board, as if Hugon planned to leave them for his wife to wash on her return. There were four or five dinner plates, smeared with grease, some wineglasses and bowls that might have held soup or breakfast cereal.

"He used the good coffee cups; that's not

like him," she said, sounding surprised for the first time since Bruno's arrival. There were three dirty coffee cups beside the sink, all piled together as if they had been used at the same time.

"Did he drink much?" Bruno asked, eyeing three empty bottles of Bergerac red wine, an undistinguished brand that Bruno recognized from the local supermarket.

"He liked his glass of Ricard before dinner and red wine with his meals, just a glass or two. Dr. Gelletreau had told him to cut back on his drinking."

"How long were you away?" Bruno asked.

"Just the three nights."

"So he got through three bottles in three days. That seems like quite a lot for a man on his own."

She frowned, something like distaste in her expression. "I think he usually drank more when I wasn't here, just like he'd go back to his steaks rather than defrost those nice meals I made."

Gelletreau nodded sagely. "He was never what I'd call a good patient. You can give them all the advice in the world but if they don't want to take it . . ."

Bruno thanked Madame Hugon and asked her if she wanted him to call anybody, perhaps her sister or a priest? She shook her head, saying she'd already called her sister in Sarlat to tell her of the death, and her husband had never been a churchgoer. Once the undertaker had taken the body to the funeral home, she'd drive back to Sarlat and stay there.

"I might put the house on the market," she added.

In the garden, Bruno asked Dr. Gelletreau if he'd signed the death certificate yet.

"No, I was waiting for you to arrive," the doctor said, a little stiffly. Sometime earlier he'd been embarrassed after putting down "Natural Causes" on a death certificate when Bruno had later discovered that the victim had been murdered.

"I don't like this," Bruno said. "All that cash in his wallet, the disappearance of his diary and account book, those phone calls . . ."

"And the three coffee cups," said Gelletreau. "Still, I'm pretty sure it was a heart attack. You saw the way he was clutching his chest. It doesn't look much like a murder to me. Hugon was a heart attack waiting to happen. And he certainly died yesterday."

"So if his wife has an alibi from her family in Sarlat . . . ," said Bruno, thinking aloud.

"If that's the case you've got a real mystery on your hands, unless you've got another one of your hunches."

Bruno looked back at the house, pulled out his phone and called his friend Jean-Jacques, the chief detective for the *département,* to explain his suspicions.

"What does the doc say?" J-J replied.

"Heart attack, looks natural enough."

"And the wife? Does she think it was a natural death?"

"Yes. She found the body after staying with family in Sarlat for a few days, and she doesn't seem concerned. It's just me who thinks there's more to this than meets the eye."

"*Merde,* there's no sign of any struggle, the doctor and the widow aren't worried, and you know the state of my budget and what we have to pay to get an autopsy done. If it wasn't you saying this, Bruno . . ." J-J's voice trailed off. "Who's the doctor present? Is it Fabiola?"

"Dr. Gelletreau seems ready to sign the death certificate, citing cardiac arrest."

J-J grunted. "Well, we can always ask for a second opinion. See if you can persuade Fabiola to take a look at the body when the undertaker comes for it. If she thinks it's worth having an autopsy, I'll go along. By the way, have you heard anything from Isabelle?"

"Not lately," Bruno replied cautiously. In his own paternal way, J-J was almost as devoted as Bruno to Isabelle and claimed she was the best detective he'd ever trained. He'd never abandoned hope that Isabelle might one day give up her meteoric career, first in Paris and then with Eurojust in The Hague, and return to the Périgord to be his successor as chief detective.

"Word from Paris is that she's had some trouble in some big operation in Luxembourg, ruffling a lot of diplomatic feathers."

"That's news to me," said Bruno, making an effort to keep his voice neutral. He knew he would never stop caring about her. "But you know Isabelle, she'll find some way to turn it to her advantage."

"I thought maybe the brigadier might have said something," J-J said. "I know he's more in touch with you than with me, for which on the whole I'm very grateful. It always means trouble when he's around."

"I haven't heard from him for a while," Bruno replied. The brigadier, a senior figure in the Ministry of the Interior with wide-ranging responsibilities in security matters, had been Isabelle's boss before she transferred to Eurojust. "And diplomatic trouble sounds way above my pay grade."

"Probably above mine, too. Still, Isabelle

always trusted your hunches, and I've learned there's usually something to them," J-J said.

3

"This event has been a great success," said the mayor, leaning back in his chair with a glass of wine and staring contentedly at the crowded tables that filled the winery. "Our vintage cars made the TV news, thanks to that old Bugatti, and Fauquet's café was packed all day. And just look at this turnout tonight! We'll have to start doing this every year."

He raised his glass in thanks to his companions at the table, the same group that had devised the idea at the rugby club dinner. That means more work for me again next year, thought Bruno, clinking his glass against the mayor's, but he was pleased that the car show had brought in a crowd. Mauricette had told him her hotel had never before been full so early in the season. She'd devised a special offer for the weekend that had attracted the tourists who liked the idea of a winery dinner without the risk of being

Breathalyzed on a long drive home. And after the TV and radio publicity for the *concours,* a lot more people were expected the next day to watch the rally. Bruno had spent most of Friday checking on the safety barriers along the route, and once the rally was over he'd have to help the farmers pick up the hay bales they had placed at every corner.

At a sign from Julien, who ran the town vineyard, the mayor rose to his feet and went to the dais that stood in front of the stacked wine barrels at the end of the winery. There wasn't much space, with the drums, guitars and keyboard for that evening's music and dancing already in place. More barrels stood against the wall, and between them were long rows of tables and chairs, all filled with people who had paid twenty euros a head for the vineyard dinner of soup, pâté, roast duck, cheese with salad and a piece of walnut tart. As much wine as they wanted was included in the price of their meal, all of it from the town vineyard. Most of the diners had also bought tickets for the raffle, five euros for six chances to win. Tapping an empty bottle with a fork, the mayor called for silence and announced that the drawing was about to take place. The first prize was a case of a dozen bottles of the local wine, the second prize was six bottles, and there were three third prizes of two bottles each.

"Would our lovely ladies come forward, please, to draw the winning tickets?" the mayor said, and Fabiola, Annette and Florence joined him on the dais, Fabiola shaking her head in mock despair at the mayor's old-fashioned way of introducing them. He identified each of them as they joined him on the dais: Fabiola as one of the town's doctors, Annette as the local magistrate and star rally driver, and Florence as the science teacher at the *collège.*

"We didn't have teachers or doctors or magistrates like these when I was a boy," the mayor said. "But because we all want to wish Annette the best of luck in tomorrow's rally, I'll ask her to wait a little so she can draw the ticket for the first prize. Florence, please draw three tickets for the third prizes. And Fabiola will draw the ticket for the second prize."

The third and second prizes went to strangers, which was as it should be, thought Bruno, hoping that a tourist would also win the first prize. Each winner had been cheered by his and her neighbors at the various tables, but then a silence fell as Annette reached into the bucket to draw out the winning ticket. She read out the number.

"That's me," called out a male voice, and Bruno saw the Bugatti owner, Sylvestre, rise in his place and clasp his hands above his head in victory. Then he raised his voice to call across the tables to the mayor.

"Have another drawing. I donate my prize back to you." He paused and grinned around the winery. "I can't drink, I'm driving."

He sat down to a round of applause. Annette drew again, and this time Bruno cheered when his friend Ingrid rose to claim the prize. The mayor made a point of saying how pleased he was that the prize went to someone from their twin town in Alsace, adding that the visiting delegation would be at the St. Denis market the next morning, offering their wines and crafts and special foodstuffs.

"And then our local restaurants and producers will offer a food market in the main square after the end of the race, just as we do each Tuesday evening in July and August," the mayor went on. "There'll be roast chicken from rotisseries, hams grilled over open fires, snails, *moules frites,* along with salads, pizzas and apple pies, and wine from the town vineyard. So we'll hope to see you again tomorrow. Now it's time to dance."

He stepped down, and St. Denis's own rock band took its place on the dais. Lespinasse from the garage started with a drum roll. His son Édouard was on bass, Robert the singing architect on rhythm, and Patrick from the Maison de la Presse played lead guitar. Jean-Paul, the church organist, who was also the local piano teacher, climbed up to join them with his accordion around his neck and began with the theme from "Mon Amant de St. Jean." A classic from the bal musette dance halls of the 1930s and recently revived on one of the best-selling CDs in France, it was a song known to all present. Bruno led Florence to the dance floor and saw Fabiola and Gilles, Thomas and Ingrid, Annette and her Englishman, come to join them, and suddenly the floor was full. A cheer went up when the mayor joined them with his friend Jacqueline just as Robert was singing the line about how the girl knew the young man was lying to her, but she liked him anyway.

The music went on with the band's usual mix of Édith Piaf, sixties classics, Johnny Cash and Francis Cabrel numbers until Florence and Annette said they were thirsty and hauled the two men back to their table for more wine. Annette kept her hand in Young's as they sat, and Bruno wondered if Young knew that Annette was the daughter of an extremely rich and controversial financier.

"I'm so glad Sylvestre brought his Bugatti. It was the star of the show," said Annette, over the sound of the music. She gave Young a fond look. "How did you persuade him to come?"

"He didn't need much persuading," Young replied. "He told me he'd been planning to come down here to see some family property, and the chance of winning a Concours d'Élégance was too tempting to pass up. Even if nobody outside the Périgord has heard of the St. Denis *concours,* he reckons the title will raise the price of the Bugatti when he wants to sell it."

"If I had a car like that, I'd never let it go," said Florence so firmly that Bruno and the others turned to look at her. "I'm not really a car person, and I can't say I think of it as good to look at in a conventional way. It was too brutal, too arrogant, in the way it seemed to embody raw power, but it still struck me as extraordinarily beautiful." She paused, and then tossed her head and laughed, trying to shift the mood that she had suddenly made serious. "Anyway, I'd

47

be far too terrified even to think about driving some mechanical beast like that. But there was something very special about the way it sounded."

"A mere seven hundred thousand and it's yours," said Bruno, grinning. "I heard that was what he paid for it. I had no idea they were worth so much. How about that E-type of yours?" he asked Young. "What's that worth?"

"I got it years ago as a wreck for the equivalent of eight thousand euros, restored it myself, and now it's probably worth a hundred grand," Young replied. "I put years of work into it because that's the only way I was able to afford it. The old Porsche that was in the parade will probably be worth about the same. If you cleaned up that Land Rover, you'd get a pretty good price. What year was it built?"

"Nineteen fifty-four," said Bruno. He remembered Hercule, the friend who had bequeathed it to him, saying that he'd been in the French army, fighting in Vietnam, the year his Land Rover was made. Bruno knew that 1954 was a year of special significance for his friend, the year of the French defeat at Dien Bien Phu. Hercule had bought the vehicle decades later, when he'd taken his pension and settled down in the Périgord to hunt and raise truffles.

"Fully restored, you might get fifty or sixty thousand," said Young. "It's a booming market, now that the Arabs and Chinese are getting into classic cars. They want them as investments. Driving the cars is just the icing on the cake. That's how Sylvestre does so well with his auctions. He's already got a showroom in Dubai, and he's planning to open another one in Shanghai. I know he's expecting to get at least a million for his Bugatti, and I presume that's how he plans to finance his Chinese operation."

Florence rolled her eyes, and Bruno shook his head, stunned by the figures he was hearing.

"Is that how you got to know Sylvestre, through these classic-car sales?" Florence asked Young.

"In a way; I first met him at an auction in England a couple of years ago, but we've met since at several rallies. He's a very good driver, and unlike me he's got the money to pursue his hobby seriously."

Young explained that he'd first noticed Sylvestre bidding for a Ferrari Modena Spider. He himself had dropped out when the price reached a hundred thousand pounds, about a hundred and thirty thousand euros. The auction was held at the old

Goodwood racetrack, and it had gone down in history because a 1954 Mercedes Formula 1 racing car went for just under thirty million dollars, still the record for a public auction.

"The real money tends to be restricted to private auctions," Young added. "A Ferrari 250 GTO is supposed to have gone for over thirty million at a private auction in Italy, though it may just be rumor. Those private events are by invitation only, and I'm not on the list for any of those. Sylvestre gets invited to them, probably because of his Dubai connections."

"It makes my Land Rover seem cheap," Bruno said. "Are these classic-car sales the way Sylvestre made his money?"

"No, you have to start with a lot of money to get into the game. His family in Alsace is into property, and I gather they're very rich and own shopping malls and office blocks, but I don't know the details. We're quite friendly and usually have a drink or a meal together when we meet up or when Sylvestre comes to London, but I couldn't claim that we're close friends. He's a prickly type, a bit arrogant, but he certainly knows his way around cars."

"Talking about our neighbor Sylvestre?" came the voice of Bruno's friend Thomas,

Ingrid on his arm.

"We were just hearing about Sylvestre's car sales business," said Bruno, shifting his chair to give them room to sit down and reaching for the bottle. "Have another glass of wine."

"His family was very lucky," Thomas explained. "They were farmers, with land between Marckolsheim and Strasbourg, and just before war broke out in 1939 the French government bought some of the land to turn it into a military airfield. There was a court case because it was a compulsory purchase, and Sylvestre's grandfather had sued because the government offered too little money. After the war the air force still wanted the airbase and offered a deal by which it paid rent and promised that if it ever gave up the airfield Sylvestre's family could buy it back for the price that had originally been offered before the war. In the 1960s, when de Gaulle thought French security would depend on nuclear weapons, France began cutting back on conventional forces. Sylvestre's family got the land back cheaply, with a runway, hangars, underground fuel bunkers, offices and barracks.

"Strasbourg was then becoming one of the centers of the new European community and wanted a civilian airport," Thomas went on. "Sylvestre's father sold the airfield for many times more than he'd paid to buy it back. But he kept the rest of the land, thinking it was bound to increase in value."

"And it certainly did," Ingrid chimed in. "His heirs became one of the wealthiest families in Alsace. That's how Sylvestre can afford to spend seven hundred thousand on that Bugatti of his."

"That's nothing," said Young, taking out a smart phone from his shirt pocket. He tapped a few buttons and then held up the screen to show an extraordinary, gleaming black car with a hood that seemed to stretch out forever and the sweeping aerodynamic lines of the 1930s.

"*Mon Dieu,* it's beautiful," said Florence.

"This is the most expensive car of all time. What do you think it might be worth?" Young asked.

"Three million," Bruno suggested, plucking a figure from the air. Ingrid said five million, and Annette shook her head, saying she knew the price and their estimates would have to go a lot higher.

"Ten million," Florence suggested, laughing.

"Double that and then double it again," said Young. He suddenly looked solemn, as if this were serious business.

"What is it?" Bruno asked.

"It's another Bugatti, a model known as the Atlantic. Its real name is Type 57C, built in 1936. One of these was bought by the Mullin Automotive Museum in California for an undisclosed sum. The word is that it went for thirty-seven million. It's certainly the most valuable car of all time."

"That's insane," said Bruno, thinking it was almost obscene. "How can any car be worth that?"

"They made only four of them. One is owned by Ralph Lauren, there's the one in the museum, a third was destroyed by a train at a railway crossing, and another was lost somewhere in France during the war. It was being driven from the factory in Alsace to Bordeaux for safekeeping, but it never arrived, and nobody knows what happened to it."

"I agree with Florence," said Bruno, taking Young's phone and looking at the car more closely. "It certainly is beautiful. Is that the one in the museum?"

"No, that's the one owned by Ralph Lauren." He opened another photograph of the same car in silver-blue. "That's the one bought by the museum."

Bruno was about to ask about the one that was lost in the war when Fabiola and Gilles descended to haul them all back to the dance floor.

4

Bruno reined in at the top of the ridge and checked his watch as he waited for Fabiola to catch up on her old horse. He was meeting Thomas and Ingrid at Fauquet's café at nine for breakfast, but there was still time for a decent gallop before taking Hector back to the stables. He looked down at the familiar valley of the Vézère River, still shrouded in the early morning mist. The St. Denis bridge and the quayside where the vintage cars were parked on display were all somewhere beneath that gray cloud. Stray tendrils were rising like wisps of steam as the first, hesitant rays of the sun peeked above the ridge and began to warm the mist away. The spire of the old church and the houses that clambered up the hill seemed to float weightlessly in the sky. His horse and dog were still and silent as their eyes followed his gaze down into the valley until Balzac turned, hearing Victoria's hooves lumbering up the slope toward them.

"What did you think of Annette's young man?" Fabiola asked as she drew alongside and brought her horse to a halt. Victoria gave a curt neigh of gratitude, and Hector turned to rub the side of his head against hers. Sometimes Bruno thought the horses were more socially adept than many of the people he knew.

"Too soon to tell, but I liked him from the little I saw," Bruno replied. "He seemed good-natured and friendly, and he danced well. Apart from his passion for cars, that's about all I can say. But if Annette likes him, that's good enough for me."

"I think it's more than just liking him," Fabiola said. "Did you see how she looked at him? I hope it works out for her. But it won't be easy, her staying here in the Périgord while he's in London most of the time. I'm sure they can have thrilling reunions at rallies and car auctions, but you don't get to know a man that way."

Bruno looked at her with amused affection. "Gilles was in Paris and you were down here, but it worked out for you two."

"Gilles was ready to leave Paris and join me here. I don't think that's the case for Annette and George, and I don't want to see her hurt. Do you think he's ready to make some kind of commitment? Annette will need that."

"He drove all the way down here from London to be with her, so he's obviously more than just interested."

"That's not what I mean by 'commitment,' Bruno. You know what I'm talking about. She seems so much more interested than he is, and that imbalance is not reassuring. And he's not just good-looking, he's seriously handsome, the sort of man who's had lots of girls. Don't you think so?"

Among the many things that baffled Bruno about women was the time and effort they spent analyzing the love affairs of their friends. They seemed to make it all so complicated. Bruno liked to recall a scene from his favorite movie, *Les Enfants du Paradis,* when the actress Arletty turns to the tongue-tied young man who is besotted with her, lets her gown fall and says, *"L'amour, c'est si simple."* Bruno knew it was never quite so easy. There was an old Périgord proverb about love being like food: it changed with the time it spent cooking. But he could never see how it helped for others to pick endlessly over the passions and yearnings of their friends.

"It's early days for them," he said. "They met at the Angoulême rally this summer and again at the car show in Paris, so this is only their third meeting. He isn't even staying at her place."

"They haven't been to bed together yet," Fabiola replied. "She's nervous about that. Annette's not very experienced, and she thinks he is."

"That's for them to work out," said Bruno, and looked at her steadily. "Are you ready to ride on?"

"You aren't over your affair with Pamela," she said, ignoring his question.

"Nor is she, so that makes two of us," he replied, irritated and aware of a childish urge to have the last word. He certainly didn't want to pick over the bones of their parting to talk to Fabiola about his feelings. He touched his heels to Hector's flanks, and his horse sprang forward. Bruno could almost feel Hector's pleasure at being unleashed, bounding almost at once into a canter with Balzac lumbering along behind. Bruno pressed his horse to go faster, galloping to leave Fabiola's probing remarks in his wake and feel nothing but the wind in his face.

Forty minutes later, after stripping off his shirt to wash in the stable sink because there was no time to shower, Bruno walked into Fauquet's café. The clock on the *mairie* tower was striking nine, and the market stalls with the foods from Alsace were already busy. Some in the crowd were eating portions of *flammküchen,* thin slices of pastry covered with onions, bacon and melted cheese. Bruno's mouth began to water as his nostrils caught the aroma. Bruno was also tempted by another stall that was offering bowls of sausage chunks with choucroute and plastic glasses of Riesling. But he could see Thomas and Ingrid were already installed at a window table in the café. Before them were cups of coffee, the local newspaper and a basket of croissants and *pains au chocolat.* Ingrid was glancing through the weekly magazine of *Sud Ouest,* and Thomas handed Bruno the paper. It was already opened to a photograph of Sylvestre's Bugatti on the quayside, surrounded by a throng of people.

"The mayor will be pleased with all the publicity," said Thomas. He tore off a piece of his croissant to give to Balzac.

"I wonder if we'd have done so well if Sylvestre hadn't come with that old Bugatti," Bruno said, swallowing a mouthful of croissant and regretting that he hadn't bought some hot *flammküchen* for them all. But his friends probably got enough of that at home, he told himself as he caught sight of

59

Annette half running through the market to the café.

"Bruno, you've got to help," she said, bursting in. "George has got a terrible migraine, so he can't navigate for me, and I can't be in the rally without a codriver. I asked Yveline, but she's on safety duty with the rest of the gendarmes. Please, please, please, will you take George's place? I won't be able to enter the national rally unless I do well here today, and there's nobody else I can ask."

"I'm not nearly good enough to be a codriver," he said, half choking in surprise and with the effort of swallowing a half-chewed croissant. He drank from his glass of water. "I'm not qualified, Annette. What about Sylvestre?"

"I tried him, and he's competing with that Indian friend of his. And you don't have to drive, just navigate for me."

"Navigate?" he asked. "The rally track is clearly marked. You can't get lost."

"That's not what I mean. You navigate by telling me in advance of every bend and obstacle coming up." From her shoulder bag she took out what looked like two rolls of paper towels on wooden handles and brandished them at him. "I've got your track roll here. You just have to read it out so I know what's coming."

"But I've never done this," said Bruno. "And the last time I drove with you I got carsick."

"You'll be too busy concentrating on the scroll," she said. "Please, Bruno, this really means a lot to me."

He looked at the scroll, realizing that by turning the first wooden handle he could see line-by-line a detailed description of the road ahead. After the start of the rally, he read, there was an eighty-meter straightaway on tarmac, followed by a ninety-degree left turn onto gravel, then a forty-meter straight-away that led into a sixty-degree left turn into a dip with a bad camber . . .

He recognized the descriptions, having driven the track twice and walked parts of it when checking the hay bales that would protect the spectators.

"Did you make this roll with George Young?" he asked.

"I spent days on it before he arrived, driving the route with a tape recorder and then transcribing the tape onto my laptop and finding a printer that could make a continuous roll. All you have to do is read it out."

"I couldn't hear myself think when you drove me around that motor-cross track," he said. "You won't hear me."

"I've got microphones and headphones in the helmets. And I know the track almost by heart. But if I don't have a codriver, I'll be disqualified."

"I never thought of you as a man to turn down a damsel in distress," said Ingrid, grinning at him.

"Why turn down the opportunity for a new experience? You know you'll regret it if you say no," said Thomas, grinning as his wife had.

"And she'll never forgive you," said Ingrid.

"Right, I'll never forgive you," said Annette, laughing as Bruno looked from one face to another and rolled his eyes. She knew he'd have to say yes.

"Do I have time to finish my breakfast?" he asked.

"Five minutes. The rally starts at two, but they'll close the track at noon. Until then we can do test runs. We'll do one slowly so you get used to it, a second one at medium speed and then a third all out. By then you should have learned to handle the roll and judge when I need to hear your instructions."

"So simple," said Ingrid. "What could possibly go wrong?"

"Only the roll can go wrong," said Annette. "If you lose control of the paper, it

unravels and piles up all over the car and blocks my vision. I had that happen once, and it's not good. That's why you have to get some practice. I'll wait."

She folded her arms and stood at the end of the table, her jaw set and her eyes fixed on him but smiling at him expectantly. He was reminded of the first time he'd seen her, in the square outside the café in her first week in her new job, showing off out of sheer nervousness by driving too fast. Annette had gotten a parking ticket from him and a speeding ticket from Sergeant Jules. And she was only spared a charge of failing to stop for a pedestrian crossing when Florence realized it was her first job as magistrate and refused to press charges. And now she was a good friend who had learned to temper her own radical views and passion for the environment with a healthy respect for the customs and peculiarities of the Périgord. Bruno had come to respect her professionalism. And in an avuncular kind of way, which was a new sensation for him, Bruno was fond of her.

"This isn't your car," he said in the parking lot, looking at the unfamiliar white Citroën DS3 festooned with advertising stickers for motor oils and car accessories and a big garage in Sarlat. Annette opened the door to reveal internal roll bars forming a protective cage. "Where's your blue Peugeot?"

"This is my race car," she replied. "It's a turbo, borrowed from the Citroën garage in Brive. The owner's son, Fabrice, usually drives it, but he broke his leg waterskiing, so for once I'm being sponsored, which makes it my big chance to get into the national championship. That's why I need you. I can't give up this opportunity."

"What happened to Fabrice's navigator?"

"That would be me. That's why I'm being given his place."

Bruno took the helmet from the passenger's seat and eased himself into the car, feeling the high sides of the special rally seat enclose him. Annette climbed in her side and showed him how the double seat belts worked, straps over each shoulder and two more for the belt, meeting at a circular lock on his belly, like the one he recalled from parachute training in the army. He put on the helmet, and Annette leaned over again to adjust his microphone and plug the trailing wire into a socket between the seats. She did the same for her own audio feed and began a countdown test. He heard her perfectly and then did his own countdown, and she interrupted to say it was good.

"Now try unrolling this while we're parked," she said, putting the first roll into a bracket attached to the glove compartment. Between his feet was a second bracket, and she bent down to insert the main roll.

"Just turn the handles on the top roll to feed the paper and read out the instructions to me as they come," she said. "Keep your feet braced, and whatever you do, don't let your legs tear the paper or we're sunk. Try it."

It was easy enough, sitting in the parking lot, but she kept him practicing for twenty minutes before rewinding the roll, clicking in her own seat belts and then setting off for the start of the course on the road to Les Eyzies. Once on the dirt track, she kept her speed down, and Bruno had little difficulty controlling the paper roll. He even had time to glance up briefly at the route ahead, checking the instructions. The special seats and the double belts kept him securely in place, even when she began to pick up speed. The strain was on his neck, to stop his head from swinging from side to side as she accelerated out of the sharp bends.

"Okay," Annette said. "This time, don't touch the paper, just watch the road and get familiar with the track. I'll go fairly fast but nowhere near full speed."

She got onto the gravel track and shot away, moving slickly through second gear and into third before braking hard for the corner and then skidding as she stepped on the accelerator. Bruno felt stunned by the contrast between his own sense of the sedate pace he would take to drive this route and Annette's suicidal speed. Corners came up far too fast, and bends were whipped through so hard he felt the safety belts cutting into his flesh as they held him in place. Trees loomed before him, and he closed his eyes, sure that a crash was coming. Then somehow they were skidding sideways but still on the track, and he felt the panic rising again, certain that they were about to hit a pile of hay bales, and his neck was aching with the strain of keeping his head from jerking from side to side. He was meant to be learning the route, but his senses were too overwhelmed by fear and tension for anything to sink in.

Bruno gritted his teeth; he would have to get used to this. As the road climbed up into the woods around St. Cirq, he felt his reactions start to adjust to the much-higher speeds and to Annette's mastery of the car. He began to anticipate the corners and brace himself for the car's leap into the air when it crossed even the smallest ridge. He kept telling himself that Annette was completely in control when the rear of the car skidded sharply to one side. It was simply the way that she cornered.

"Let's do that one more time, without using the roll," he said, when she pulled up at the finish. He heard the breathlessness in his own voice. "I'm just starting to get the hang of this."

Without a word, Annette clicked a stopwatch on the dashboard and set off again at speed, but this time he felt ready, his senses catching up with the sheer pace at which the inputs were coming and his body anticipating the lurches as the g-forces tried to hurl him from side to side. Somehow his brain had learned that slamming into a tree was not inevitable and that Annette would hit the accelerator just as she went into the bend rather than wait until she was coming out of it. And he knew he was recognizing bends and corners, the short straightaways and the dips where the car bottomed out. The sense of panic was still there, but diminished. He felt he was back in control of himself.

"Okay," he said when Annette stopped again. "I think I'm ready to try it with the roll."

The next trip was worse. Bruno had almost no time to glance up at the route, and his eyes lost focus as the car bounced over bumps in the road and again when it seemed to take to the air as they went over even modest hillcrests. At one point when Annette braked very hard to go into a sharp right-hand bend, the g-force sent the paper ballooning out between his legs. Then Bruno briefly lost his place on the roll and realized he had to keep his thumb on the paper to mark each line as he read it. Somehow he got through to the end of the ride, and as Annette braked he closed his eyes and waited for his breathing to return to normal. His hands were trembling, and he felt exhausted from the intensity of the concentration.

"Not bad for a beginner, Bruno. That was under seventeen minutes," she said. "Now we'll do it again, only faster. If I'm going to win this thing, we'll have to do it in fifteen."

5

Two laps into the next training session, Annette distracted him by saying, "Someone very good is on our tail, and I think I know who it is. Hang on tight."

Bruno hadn't thought it was possible to go any faster, but Annette raised her pace. Still, he was starting to anticipate each place on the paper roll by the way she shifted gears and braked and by the direction of the g-force upon him at each bend. He learned to start reading out the next instruction as she accelerated out of each bend and to brace his legs to stop the paper from ballooning when the car briefly took flight as she topped each hill.

"He's very good," he heard Annette say as Bruno's tailbone made him wince when she slammed through a dip in the road. "He'll be the one to beat."

Bruno saw her eyes flick to the rearview mirror and was amazed that she could spare time or attention for anything but the road ahead. He felt he had never gone so fast in his life and had never heard anything louder than the roar of the engine as she pushed the tachometer into the red zone. But he kept up his commentary on the road ahead and felt he was beginning to know the route well enough to take the occasional brief glance at the road.

"That was our fastest yet," said Annette, slowing and braking to turn into the assembly area. "I think we'll be fine. How do you feel?"

"I feel very grateful we have air bags," he replied. "As long as they're working, I'll be okay."

She turned to him in surprise as the car drew to a halt. "They aren't working. We have to dismantle all the air bags for serious rally cars. Some of the jolts we take when we land after a hillcrest would trigger them."

Now she tells me, thought Bruno, trying to keep his face from revealing his dismay.

Half-a-dozen rally cars were already gathered, most of them with their hoods up, drivers leaning over their engines. Small knots of spectators were strolling around the cars, and Philippe Delaron, the local *Sud Ouest* correspondent, was taking photos, posing excited small boys against the cars.

"What about that car behind us?" Bruno asked.

"There won't be a car behind us in the rally. We race against the clock, not against one another. That would be too dangerous. Here they are now."

A white Volkswagen pulled up sharply beside them, two figures inside, unidentifiable in their crash helmets. The driver pulled off his helmet, and Sylvestre's face emerged.

"I didn't know you went in for this sport," Sylvestre said to Bruno while waving at Annette. He called across to her, "I bet you'll be the fastest woman on the circuit. But where's George?"

"He's sick," she replied calmly. "Bruno stepped into the breach. He's my secret weapon. Go too fast, and he'll give you a speeding ticket."

As Sylvestre smiled and drove off, Bruno's mobile rang. He had to release his seat belts to get to it and saw it was Fabiola.

"I'm at the funeral parlor, looking at the late Monsieur Hugon," she said. "I can't see much out of the ordinary. He's been dead at least thirty-six hours, maybe more. And the undertaker washed him down and cleaned him when he arrived, so there's no body waste to examine. There's some interesting irritation around the nose and mouth and in his throat. It could be no more than a cold, and he was certainly a prime candidate for a heart attack."

"Gelletreau was treating him for heart trouble," said Bruno.

"I'm not in the least surprised. In fact, I'd have been surprised if he wasn't being treated for it. He's very overweight and florid, so he must have had high blood pressure. There are nicotine stains on his fingers, so I assume he was a fairly heavy smoker. I found a bit of bruising that could well have happened when he collapsed. Are you sure this is a suspicious death?"

"No, I'm not sure, but there are some circumstantial things that worry me." Bruno explained his doubts about the absent file and notebook.

"I see." She paused and then said, "I presume you asked for an autopsy. What did J-J say?"

"He was reluctant but said to ask if you could take a look to see if you thought an autopsy was justified."

"Not so far, it isn't. But I'll take some swabs and get back to you. Will you be at the rally, watching Annette? I may see you there."

"You certainly will, and you may get a surprise." He laughed, closed the phone and looked at his watch. It was noon; there would be no more time for practice laps.

"Tell me what happens in the real race," he said to Annette.

"They already drew lots, and we go off fifth. That's good because the track and corners won't be too badly roughed up. There are twenty-four contestants, and we start at three-minute intervals. Those who finish first and second in this regional heat qualify for the national championship. Can I buy you some lunch? I need a sandwich."

"No, thank you. I think I'd lose it on the first turn."

"Make sure you drink some water, though. We need to meet up by one-thirty. Regulations require flame-retardant gear, just in case, so you'll need to change. I've got them in the back along with George's overalls, which should fit you. Can I drop you somewhere?"

"Drop me in town. Give me the clothes, and I'll change in the *mairie*. We can meet there later. I ought to show my face at the Alsace market first, just to say hello to the various stallholders. You could get something to eat there."

"Good idea, but stay away from the wine kiosk," she said with a smile. "I want you keeping all your wits about you, so not even a taste of Riesling, please. But I'll buy you a bottle after the race."

The midday sun was warm, and the square in front of the *mairie* was full of people gathered around the dozen or so stalls. Annette paused at one that was offering embroidery and lace, oven gloves and aprons with Alsace motifs. She bought a set of tea towels, murmuring to Bruno that she felt she ought to support them. Bruno leafed through a picture book at a stall run by the Alsace tourist board, recognizing one of the old concrete forts from the Maginot Line that he'd visited with Thomas and Ingrid. He pointed it out to Annette.

"That's just outside the town," Bruno said. "It's a museum now with a good account of the battle that took place there. The French held out for two days. You can see it had two turrets. The Germans knocked out one with artillery and the second with an attack by Stuka dive-bombers."

"I thought it was supposed to be impregnable," she said.

"Nothing is impregnable. The Germans

74

simply went around it and invaded through Belgium, while half of the French army was locked up in the Maginot Line, barely able to get involved in the war."

They walked on, glancing at a stall where Alsace sausages and cheeses were being sold. Bruno greeted his friend Stéphane, the cheese maker, who was tasting the wares while chatting with his visiting counterpart. The busiest stall was the one offering tastings of Riesling, Sylvaner and Pinot Gris. Bruno heard his name called. It was Thomas, who had been called in to help the stallholder cope with the demand.

"A glass for you, Bruno?"

He gestured at Annette behind him and called back, "Not when I'm driving."

Annette bought herself a *flammküchen*. Every table on Fauquet's terrace was taken, but Bruno bought two bottles of water, and he and Annette walked over to the stone balcony overlooking the river. She asked about Fabiola's call, saying it sounded like it could mean work for her or some other magistrate. It was too soon for that, Bruno said, but told her of his concerns over Hugon's death.

"Was that an overweight, elderly man, used to work for the archives in Périgueux?" she asked. Bruno nodded. "I knew him. We

75

hired him from time to time to do research on cases, tax issues mainly. He was a perfectionist and had a very good reputation. I can't imagine him not keeping all his notebooks up to date."

"His wife may have ditched them to try and avoid tax claims," he replied before drinking some water from his bottle. "But she was very open about what he was being paid for the latest job, and there were a thousand euros in his wallet. If she was worried about taxes, I think she'd have pocketed the money before I turned up."

"I hardly think she'd have been thinking about taxes if she walked in to find her husband dead. How long were they married?"

"Over forty years."

"And what was he working on?" asked Annette, finishing her *flammküchen* and pouring some of the water onto her hands before drying them with a paper napkin.

"It's not clear, but it had something to do with the war and the Resistance," Bruno said. "I'll try to find out what he was researching at the archives. Maybe that's where he left the missing file and notebook."

Bruno stood up as he saw the mayor heading toward him, waving to friends right and left as he bustled through the crowd. He began speaking from five meters away.

"I hear you're going to be taking part in the race, so good luck to you both, but a couple of things have come up," he said. He apologized to Annette and then took Bruno's arm and led him a few steps away, his voice dropping to a murmur.

"First, there's Jérôme's amusement park — he wants to buy some land from the town to enlarge the place and put in some new attractions. Could you go see him and get an idea if it's the kind of thing we should approve? He doesn't want to go to the expense of hiring an architect and getting a survey done if it doesn't have much chance of getting past the council.

"Another thing: that fellow with the Bugatti, Sylvestre Wémy, buttonholed me this morning to ask for my help regarding some property his grandmother left him. You know the place, that pretty *chartreuse* on the road to the St. Chamassy cemetery."

The term meant "charterhouse," but in this part of France it was used for a historic building that was larger than a manor house but not quite big enough to be called a château. It was usually a long, low building just one room wide with a single floor, although sometimes there were mansard windows to allow small bedrooms in the roof. Sylvestre wanted to turn the place into several expensive apartments and then sell them, the mayor explained. But the inheritance was divided between him and the St. Denis side of the family, and some kind of family feud had now developed. Sylvestre was hoping that the mayor might find some way to resolve matters, since St. Denis stood to lose the extra property taxes and the prospect of employment for gardeners and cleaners.

"You know the family, the Oudinots. He's a stubborn old devil. Could you go and see him, Bruno, and find out what the problem is from his side?"

Fernand Oudinot and his wife, Odette, were in their early sixties and still ran their farm raising ducks and geese; they also kept bees and ran a very productive walnut plantation. Bruno knew Fernand through one of the local hunting clubs, and he had a soft spot for Odette. She used her own honey and nuts to make the best *tarte aux noix* in the district; although she had shown Bruno how to make it, he could never get his pastry to turn out like hers.

"I'll find out what the problem is, but I don't want to get involved in a family quarrel," Bruno said. "I'm too attached to Odette's *tarte aux noix.*"

"So am I," said the mayor. "But I had a call from my colleague in Alsace, one mayor to another, asking if I could help. You know how it is."

Bruno nodded and said, "I've got to do this rally first, but I can talk to Sylvestre later and then see the Oudinots tomorrow. They're decent people. And I'll go and see Jérôme, too."

"There's no rush on the amusement park. If you could get us a preliminary report for the next council meeting, that would be fine." Returning to Annette, the mayor kissed her cheeks as he wished her luck in the race. "Just don't damage our town policeman. He's got too much to do."

"I'll do my best," she said, looking at her watch. "And now Bruno and I have to get into our driving clothes." They went into the *mairie* to change, Bruno using his office and Annette the ladies' room. They emerged in white Nomex overalls, all but their hands and faces covered in the material. They got some startled glances as they walked back to the car.

"I'm not sure I can operate that paper roll if I'm wearing gloves," he said.

"I'm the same — I hate driving with gloves. And don't forget to hit the stopwatch when we start because I'll have my hand on the gearstick."

They went through the ritual of shaking hands with the other drivers before getting into the Citroën, donning their helmets and heading for their place in the queue of cars lined up before the start. The lead car took off at the marshal's signal. Bruno felt his heart pounding as they rolled forward to the starting line. He looked across at Annette, wondering if he should wish her good luck, but settled for the all-purpose French word that team members exchanged at the start of a rugby match.

"Merde," he said.

"And *merde* to you," she replied, her voice sounding odd through the headphones. A second later the marshal's arm flashed down to release them. Bruno hit the stopwatch on the dashboard and was then rammed back into his seat by the acceleration, Annette taking off faster than ever before, and began reading from his roll.

"Eighty meters on tarmac then a ninety-degree left turn onto gravel." He remembered the phrases and the sequences as she slammed the car into a skidding turn.

"Forty meters straight to a sixty-degree left turn into a dip. Watch for the bad camber . . ."

And on it went, his body lifting and then

slamming back down, jerking from left to right. He tried to brace himself with only his feet, which were pressed hard against the bulkhead. Annette's hands were braced on the steering wheel, but his were occupied by the roll. He knew when the straightaways were coming and, from time to time, could risk a quick glance at the road.

"Ninety-degree right turn at the bottom of this slope and onto tarmac for two hundred meters . . ."

A blur of faces marked the turn, the people safely sheltered behind hay bales. They were waving, but because of his helmet he could hear nothing except the howl of the motor and the new thrust as the turbo kicked in. Then almost at once she was braking for the next bend, and he was telling her to watch for the tunnel after a thirty-degree right turn.

He almost lost it once when the paper ballooned up and he had to use his knees to hold it down in the well of the car, but he found his place just in time to warn Annette of the next bend.

"Beware of water in the dip at the bottom of this slope, then make an immediate ninety-degree left turn going into the S-bend . . ."

As she hammered the car around the

sharp turn, he was aware from the corner of his eye of another car on its side in the ditch along the side of the road.

Then they were through the S-bend and onto gravel, a short straight stretch rose steeply ahead, and then they seemed to sail through the air for a long second before slamming down and into a sixty-degree left turn with a bad camber. There were more faces and hay bales and a short straightaway with a banner over the road and a marshal holding a checkered flag. She went past him at high speed and began braking hard as Bruno hit the stopwatch. It read 15:08. Fifteen minutes and eight seconds. Annette had said they would have to beat fifteen minutes in order to win.

6

"Great job, you're in the lead," said a large, middle-aged man with a beard, opening Annette's door and hauling her out into an embrace. Beside him was a slender youth on crutches, one leg in a cast.

"Bonjour, Marcel . . . Bonjour, Fabrice," said Annette. She removed her helmet and turned to introduce Bruno, who was still trying to sort out the tangle of his paper roll. Finally he rolled it neatly back, took off his helmet, released his safety belts and clambered out. He felt light-headed, and his legs were still trembling from the strain of bracing them throughout the race. He leaned against the car and waved at the two strangers, not quite up to the expected handshakes and polite greetings.

"This is Bruno. He stepped into the breach when my navigator got sick. It's his first rally," Annette said. "Bruno, this is Marcel, the garage owner whose car this is, and this is his son Fabrice, who really should be driving."

"I don't think I could do that course in fifteen-eight," said the young man. "You were great." He looked at Bruno. "Your first ride? *Chapeau.*"

"It was the car," Annette said. "All that power, great brakes and perfectly tuned."

She turned to look at the large blackboard on which the times of each car were marked. They were mostly around 15:15, and one was 15:20. Fifteen-ten was the nearest to their time. Marcel handed Bruno a water bottle, and he drank, gratefully, aware of other drivers and navigators in overalls staring at him curiously. He recognized one of the drivers from a rugby match in Limoges, and another one waved at him, the son of one of the big winegrowers in Bergerac. Bruno waved his hand in return and then saw the slight figure of Félix edging through the crowd and looking shifty as he avoided Bruno's eye.

Another car jumped over the hill toward them and raced for the finish line. Fabrice clicked the button on his stopwatch and called across, "Fifteen-thirteen."

"That's Montjoie over there with the blond girl in the red jacket," said Marcel, pointing into the distance. "He made the national championships last year and he did fifteen-ten, so now you and Annette are the team to beat."

"It was all Annette," said Bruno. "I was just a passenger. Jesus, I feel too old for this sport."

"You're the cop in St. Denis," Marcel said. It wasn't a question. "Was this really your first race?"

"And my last," said Bruno.

"Not if you qualify in this heat," Marcel replied. "If you get into the national finals, it has to be with the same team that qualified."

Damn Annette, thought Bruno. She hadn't told him that. "No exceptions?" he asked, hopefully.

"Death, serious illness with a medical certificate, military orders, that's about it."

"Then I'll just have to hope there are faster cars to come."

"There's one who can beat you, maybe two more, and only two teams qualify."

As Marcel spoke, Annette came around to Bruno's side of the car to hug him. He knew her well but was momentarily startled as he remembered how small she was, the top of her head barely reaching his chin. Somehow in the course of the last few hours she seemed to have grown in his imagination as she demonstrated her mastery at the wheel.

Another car came across the finish line. This time the marshal at the blackboard wrote down "15:11."

"We're still leading," she said, looking up at him gleefully.

"Does that mean I can go and change?"

"Sorry, no. If there's a dead heat we might have to do it again. That shouldn't happen, though, because the marshals time us to tenths of a second."

Bruno was aware of his name being called and saw a group of his friends — Thomas and Ingrid, Gilles and Fabiola, Crimson and his daughter, Miranda, waving at him from behind the hay bales at the finish line and giving him a thumbs-up. He waved back, and then the mayor was at his side.

"I hear you're in the lead," he said.

"I'm counting on you to get me some military orders to save me from having to do this again," Bruno replied. "Apparently that's the only acceptable excuse, apart from death or serious injury. And shouldn't you be behind those protective hay bales with the others?"

"Rank has its privileges, Bruno. And here's the inevitable Philippe Delaron with his camera."

With the ease of a practiced politician, the

mayor insinuated himself into the photo for *Sud Ouest,* Annette between the two men, and then Philippe came forward with his notepad as another car came over the finishing line. The marshal had just finished writing "15:12" when he clutched at his waist and pulled out a mobile phone. He listened briefly and then shouted, "Ambulance," and began clanging a bell.

"Sector seven, the corner by the sawmill at Petit-Paris, a car's gone into a tree," he shouted at Ahmed moments later. Leaning out of the window of the *urgences* vehicle, Ahmed waved acknowledgment, put on his siren and roared off, not quite as fast as the rally cars but at a very impressive speed. Philippe ran to his own car and followed Ahmed, again at a speed that Bruno would have found terrifying before today. Lespinasse followed in his tow truck.

"Don't worry," Annette said to Bruno. "You saw the roll bars and security cages in the car. It's unusual for anyone to be hurt."

"In that case we ought to install them in every car that's built," Bruno said. He'd seen the results of too many car crashes in his years as a policeman.

The marshals halted the remaining cars that were waiting in line for their own runs. There were only half a dozen still to go. Last in line was Sylvestre's Volkswagen. To Bruno's surprise, Sylvestre was the navigator, and his Indian friend Freddy was at the wheel. As he looked, Sylvestre turned, caught his eye and gave a casual wave before rolling down the window and calling for Annette. She strolled across, bent to listen, smiled and backed away with a wave.

"He was just paying us a compliment on our run," she said when she returned.

"I'm surprised he's not driving," said Bruno. "He seemed like the kind of man who'd like to be in the driver's seat. And he seemed pretty quick when he caught up with us this morning."

"Sylvestre is very good, but Freddy's better. He came in second in last year's desert rally in Qatar. That's a big international event with serious prize money. And a team is a team — either one can drive. The navigator is formally known as the codriver. That's why I could race after Fabrice broke his leg."

"And I gather that you're stuck with me if we do qualify," said Bruno.

"I doubt that we will. Fifteen-eight isn't really good enough. And the best we can hope for is to qualify in second place. Freddy's bound to win. Even if he weren't such a top driver with a big corporate sponsor, he's going to be the last car to race, which means he knows what time he has to beat. That's a real advantage."

"What do you mean 'a big corporate sponsor'? What has that to do with how he races?"

She gestured at a large truck in the parking lot across the road with a big VW logo on its side. "That's his support team with mechanics, spare parts and different sets of tires for the various conditions. There's even a guy with a radio to tell him the times of the drivers who set off just ahead of him. These rally championships are big business, Bruno. Marcel isn't paying for this car himself; he's got Citroën behind him. You must have seen the Citroën advertising after they won the world rally championship. Victories sell cars."

Bruno nodded, understanding that he was involved in something much bigger than he'd assumed when Annette had first appealed to him that morning. There was big business here and serious money, a great deal of organization and a whole subculture built around the rallies.

Suddenly, electronic feedback howled across the assembly area as the marshal at the blackboard started speaking into a bullhorn. He adjusted it, and the howl died.

"No injuries," he said. "Driver and codriver are unhurt. The car cannot be driven, so number seventeen is scratched. The race resumes."

"What about the cars that were already on the track before the crash?" Bruno asked Annette.

"They'll have been waved down by the marshals, and now they'll have to come back and run again, once the tow truck has cleared the route."

Marcel came up to them, his mobile phone at his ear. He said "Thanks" into the mouthpiece and then looked solemnly at Annette.

"I'm not sure you're going to qualify," he said. "I have a friend stationed on the course with a stopwatch. Number eighteen, Rostand, from Toulouse, was two seconds ahead of your time at the halfway point. Villeneuve from Cahors, number nineteen, matched your time. They're two good drivers, both in Citroëns like yours, and then there's the VW team."

"And it usually helps to run again," said Annette, looking crestfallen. Marcel shrugged.

"Come on, let's take a stroll, see our friends," said Bruno, taking Annette's arm. "Until all the results are in, there's nothing we can do but wait."

Reluctantly, she followed across the assembly area to the hay bales where their friends were gathered with steaming mugs. Bruno could smell cinnamon and cloves.

"I know it's not cold, but Miranda thought it would be fun to make some mulled wine," said Crimson, holding up a large thermos. "You're in the lead, so you deserve some."

"Thanks, but not yet," said Annette. "If there's a dead heat we may have to race again, and there are some very good drivers to come."

"This is my first time at one of these rallies," said Gilles. "I'd never realized how popular they are. There are hundreds of people here and around the course. We had trouble finding a place to park."

As he spoke, the marshal brought up the next car to the starting line and waved the flag to commence the run. Now Sylvestre and Freddy were no longer last in line; the three cars that had interrupted their runs because of the crash had returned to take their places at the rear. Bruno heard Fabiola and Miranda asking Annette what had happened to her English codriver, the three women drifting away to one side to talk among themselves. Good, thought Bruno, it will distract Annette from watching the clock.

"Do you know your face was absolutely white when Annette pulled up after her race?" Gilles asked. "You looked like you were going to be sick."

"I very nearly was," Bruno replied. With half an ear he could hear the women murmuring. He could pick up only individual words and phrases, like "migraine" and "handsome" and "serious" and "up to him." They were evidently talking about Annette's new boyfriend.

"You've no idea how fast it felt from the passenger seat," Bruno said to Gilles and Crimson. "Make sure Annette doesn't tempt Fabiola into taking up the sport. She drives fast enough already."

The next car started badly, wheels spinning as the driver used too much throttle. He must have lost a second or two.

"That's why it's good to be one of the early ones," Annette called across to Bruno. "The start is getting chewed up. We'll have to watch that if we're told to race again."

"Where did Annette learn to drive like that?" Crimson asked.

"Madagascar, when she was working for Médecins Sans Frontières," said Bruno, thinking that the mulled wine smelled very inviting. "But I think she has a gift; it seems to come naturally to her."

At three-minute intervals, the remaining cars took off, a little slower than the earlier ones, the drivers cautious after seeing the first wheelspin. Then they began to come over the hill to the finish line. The first one was clocked at 15:10, the next one was 15:09, and then Freddy in his VW was just 15:03, beating Annette's time by five seconds. The VW pulled over, and Sylvestre and Freddy clambered out, their fists pumping the air, and ran to embrace each other at the front of their car.

Annette was still in second place, but then the last car passed the finish line, timed at 15:08. The marshals began to confer. Annette had one hand to her mouth, the other hand clutching Fabiola's arm. Her eyes were opened enormously wide. Bruno felt himself being caught up in her excitement. Would they have to race again?

Sylvestre strolled across to join them. Bruno shook his hand and murmured congratulations. Annette was now bouncing up and down on her toes as she waited for the marshals to do something. Finally one of them turned to the blackboard. Annette's name remained in second place as the marshal filled in the tenths of a second.

93

Annette had been timed at 15:082. Her rival for the vital second place came in at 15:084.

"We did it!" she screamed and turned to jump into Bruno's arms, her small body trembling with emotion as she planted a smacking kiss on his cheek. "We're in the national championship!"

Bruno forced himself to smile as he hugged her and pretended to be delighted, although inside he felt a foreboding that was mixed with dismay. Once had been more than enough. Their friends clustered around slapping them on the back and cheering. Philippe Delaron was taking more photos.

"Thanks," Bruno said to Crimson. "I hope there's enough of that mulled wine left in the thermos for me to have a glass or two. In fact, give me two glasses; there's someone I should talk to."

He took the glasses across to Sylvestre, who was leaning against his VW, eyes closed and head back, enjoying the last of the autumn sun.

"Congratulations again," said Bruno, and handed him a glass. "Where's your partner?"

"Freddy is in the marshals' tent doing the paperwork." He took the wine, sniffed it, sipped and then nodded his thanks.

"I heard from the mayor that you're hav-

ing some problems with your property here, and he's asked if I could look into it, see if we could help."

"I'd be very grateful," Sylvestre said, his manner suddenly businesslike. "It's because of one of those foolish family feuds that's made worse by jealousy. My grandmother had a brother, and they shared the family property here when their parents died. It's a pleasant little château with about fifteen hectares of land. Since my grandmother moved to Alsace when she married, she couldn't use the farm, and she agreed with her brother to split the estate. She got the *chartreuse* and garden, and her brother, my great-uncle Thibaut, got all the land. She didn't bother to get a formal easement from her brother giving her a right-of-way onto the property."

Bruno nodded sympathetically, thinking he could guess what was coming.

"It was fine as long as Thibaut was alive, but when Thibaut's son Fernand learned that our side of the family was becoming wealthy through property investments, relations cooled a bit. When my grandmother died, it got worse. Fernand asked for the return of some of the family furniture she brought to Alsace when she got married. Naturally we discussed it the next time we came down here one summer to stay at the house. We were very polite and friendly, but we said no. Our grandmother had wanted the furniture to stay with her grandchildren. The family feud began, and pretty soon it started to escalate. You know Fernand keeps geese?"

Bruno nodded. "So do I, just a couple. They're pretty common in the countryside around here."

"Yes, but they're very noisy. When we said no, Fernand moved a couple hundred geese to within about five meters of the back of our house, on land that was his. They started cackling just after dawn, and it went on until nightfall. That was the end of our vacation, and for about ten years we didn't bother coming down here. But on principle we determined to keep the house. We paid the taxes, and then five years ago my mother came down for the twin-town reunion, staying at a hotel. She went to see the house and hired a local company to come and do maintenance, repaint the place, repair the roof and so on. She tried to see Fernand, but he wouldn't let her into his house.

"Two years ago, I came down with her and saw the possibility of converting the house into three really nice residences, selling them and washing our hands of the place and of the other branch of the family. My mother refused. It was her family inheritance. She died last year, and I telephoned Fernand to invite him to the funeral, but he slammed the phone down on me. Then I wrote to him, saying what I proposed and that I'd send the builders in, put a swimming pool where the vegetables used to be and fix up the garden. He wrote back saying he had no objection to any building works I proposed. So I wrote thanking him and went ahead, putting over a hundred thousand euros into the conversion. When I came down this time with Freddy, I parked the car, unpacked and went to see Fernand, hoping that we'd be putting the feud behind us."

"But it didn't work out like that."

"No, he met me on his doorstep, didn't invite me in, and then gave me a nasty smile as if he'd been looking forward to this moment. He asked how I intended to sell any of these conversions when he wouldn't allow any of the new buyers to cross his land to get to the place. That was when I found out there was no right-of-way."

"He can't stop you from getting access to your land."

"He doesn't have to. I can use a small and very narrow dirt track. But I can't sell the residences as luxury holiday homes if that's the only way in. And then this morning, Fernand fired the second barrel. The geese are back."

7

When Annette came back from the caravan the race marshals were using as an office, she was hanging on to the arm of George Young, who was beaming, evidently delighted at her success. He seemed to have recovered from his migraine, if that was what caused him to miss the race, and shook Bruno's hand to congratulate him.

"This calls for a celebration," he said. "My treat — but you'll know better where we can go around here, Bruno."

Bruno scratched his head. On Sunday evenings out of season, Ivan's bistro was closed, and there was not much choice in St. Denis beyond the local pizzeria. But Young was right; Annette was entitled to a celebration. Bruno had planned to make dinner for his guests from Alsace, a simple meal featuring some of his homemade pâté, followed by his vegetable stew, cheese and salad, all accompanied by the big round *tourte* of country bread he'd picked up from the bakery that morning. But Annette's success deserved better than that. Had it been anyone else, Bruno would have called on Maurice, a local duck farmer, and picked up some fresh foie gras to fry very fast in its own fat and serve with a sauce of honey and balsamic vinegar. But although she was no longer a vegetarian, Annette drew the line at foie gras. Maybe he could call the baron and see if he'd caught any trout that day.

"Didn't the mayor say there was going to be a special *marché nocturne* tonight, in honor of the race?" Annette asked. "I'm sure lots of the other drivers will be there, so I wouldn't mind going."

"I've never been to one," said Young. "Let's do it."

The idea for a night market had started just up the road in the hilltop village of Audrix, where the local farmers were invited on Saturday evenings in summer to sell their produce from stalls erected around the village square, which the *mairie* filled with tables and benches for the public. It had begun modestly with pâtés, salads and strawberries, foie gras and cheeses, a stall that grilled steaks and lamb chops and another selling wine by the bottle. It proved

100

highly popular with the locals as well as tourists and quickly expanded to include *haricots couennes,* beans cooked with pork rind, as well as *pommes frites,* omelettes and soups. Then a local farm began offering snails in their shells with butter and garlic, and the *mairie* rebuilt the village's old stone baking oven in the center of the square to produce fresh bread and pizzas. By the end of the first season, local bands and singers were performing, there was a donkey cart to take children around the village, and it was hard to find a place at the tables. By the second year, half the villages of the Périgord were offering similar events.

St. Denis, never a village to rush into things, watched and waited. Bruno and the mayor and their friends sampled the other markets, observed what worked and what didn't and carefully planned their own version. They didn't want loud rock music, since they had learned that the diners liked to hear themselves talk. They decided to offer folksingers, jazz groups and balladeers until ten o'clock, and then a disco took over so the people could dance. Bruno and the mayor had tasted the cheap plonk sold at inflated prices in other markets, so they insisted on offering only good local wines and kept a close eye on the prices. With the local butcher they set up a proper barbecue that produced steaks, lamb, chicken and fish. Huge cauldrons were brought in to cook *moules marinières* and paella. Bruno persuaded his friend Stéphane to bring his cheese stall, the Vinhs to offer their Asian food, and Fauquet to keep his café open until midnight and to make vast quantities of his own ice cream.

They had brought Florence into their plans from the beginning, since she had persuaded the local education authorities that the best way to teach environmental sciences was to have schoolchildren run their own small farm at the *collège*. It was doing well enough to provide the night market with eggs, chickens, tomatoes, zucchini and lettuces. Florence also insisted on proper plates, glasses and cutlery rather than plastic forks and paper plates and arranged for the use of the *collège*'s industrial dishwashers. The older schoolchildren earned pocket money for setting up the tables and benches in the town square. Since Florence reckoned that there was not much use in the children growing food if they didn't know how to prepare it, she had set up a voluntary cooking class in the *collège* kitchens after school hours. So the children had their own stall offering the pâtés, lemon tarts, apple pies and brownies they had made.

Bruno was proud of the town's night market and happy to agree to Annette's request. "It's a warm enough evening," he said.

"And it's going to be a spectacular sunset," said Young, looking at the scattered low clouds in the west, already touched with pink and gold as the sun began its slow decline.

"We arrange those specially for occasions like this," came a new voice, and Yveline joined them, embracing Annette and adding her own congratulations. She was in her gendarme uniform, with the two white stripes of a lieutenant on her shoulders. "You'll have to show me how to drive like that."

"Please don't," said Bruno. "My nerves couldn't stand it." He introduced her to George Young as Annette's friend, to make it clear he'd be joining them. "Are you on duty this evening, or can you join us at the *marché nocturne* in town?"

"I'm on duty, but I can take a meal break, and I'd probably take a stroll around the market anyway." She glanced at Bruno's fire-retardant driving clothes, smiling as she raised an eyebrow. "Will you change into

103

your uniform, or will you be eating disguised as a snowman?"

"You're right, I've got to change, but first I'd better call my houseguests to tell them where we'll be having dinner. You'll enjoy meeting my friend Thomas, Yveline. He's another *flic,* municipal police like me."

"Merde," she said, rolling her eyes in mock horror. "Just what we need, another cop like you."

After calling his friends, Bruno steered Young toward Monique's, the new wine bar on the rue de Paris, to wait while he and Annette changed in the *mairie.* As they came out, they ran into Florence, who was supervising her pupils as they unloaded crockery and cutlery along with some of their pies and pâtés from the back of her car. Annette invited her to join their table for dinner.

"I'd love to. Another of my pupils is babysitting my kids this evening," Florence replied. "But I may have to be up and down a bit, since I'm supposed to keep an eye on the youngsters."

"I may have to take a turn at barbecue duty," said Bruno, glancing across to where Valentin, the town butcher, was manning the grill. The tables in the square were beginning to fill, and Florence and Yveline sat at one to reserve spaces for them all. Annette and Young went to collect plates, glasses and cutlery from the stall run by Florence's pupils. Bruno bought a bottle of white wine and another of red from Raoul at the town vineyard's stall and took them to the table where Thomas and Ingrid had just arrived. He introduced them to Yveline and went to place an order for the meat.

Young joined Bruno at the barbecue, carrying plates and insisting on paying the bill. "I've ordered a small steak and a lamb chop for each of us, but chicken for Annette," Bruno said.

When they returned to the table with the loaded plates, the baron had joined them, bringing a double portion of mussels cooked in white wine for the table to share. Yveline had already bought salad and *pommes frites* for everyone, and Florence had ordered apple pies for dessert. Bruno, who enjoyed the way these night markets always seemed to expand beyond the original guests to create an unexpected fellowship in which all shared the food, poured the wine and offered a toast to Annette. Thomas went for more wine, and Ingrid came back from Stéphane's stall with some goat cheese and Cantal.

"What's it like, being married to a policeman?" Florence asked Ingrid. "Do you worry about what might happen to him?"

"Of course," Ingrid replied. "But it's what he wants to do or, rather, he did, until these new rules and management systems came in with Sarkozy. Now they have targets and quotas for arrests, and Thomas agrees with Bruno that's no way to judge police efficiency. He's thinking of taking early retirement."

"He's not the only one," Yveline chimed in. "They're turning us into not much more than traffic cops. That's not why I joined the gendarmes. It's all right for Bruno; he works for the mayor, who likes the way Bruno operates. He hardly ever has to make an arrest."

"That can work in a small town like St. Denis, where I know everybody," said Bruno. "It wouldn't work in a big city."

On the stage, Arlette, a newcomer to St. Denis who had recently joined the *mairie* as an accountant, was adjusting the microphone as she settled on a stool and began to play some classical guitar music. Yveline was asking Young if there was much theft in the antique-car business, and Florence was telling Annette about the latest efforts of the *collège* computer club to design a video game they hoped to sell. The sun was setting, streaks of rosy pink and red alternating with the scattered lines of cloud, and the old stone of the *mairie* had turned into a rich gold. It was that brief moment of twilight before someone turned on the lamps over the diners, and Bruno murmured to himself one of his favorite words.

"*Crépuscule,*" he said as he looked at the red sheen of the setting sun on the bend of the river, not aware that he had spoken aloud until the baron repeated it back to him.

"*Crépuscule,* one of the loveliest words in our language, for one of the loveliest times of day just as it gives way to night," the baron said softly, gazing at the shifting planes of red and crimson light on the river. "Sitting here, with wine and food and surrounded by friends as generations must have done before us in this very place, makes all the world's troubles seem very far away. Sometimes I imagine the prehistoric people sitting here on the riverbank, sharing their roast mammoth or whatever it was, and watching the sun go down just like us."

He raised his glass. "I drink to them, whoever they were."

"I never thought of you as such a romantic," said Bruno.

"When you get to my age, you'll realize

that we men are the real romantics. Women are much more practical; they have to be." The baron paused, turning his head to look at the stage. "Who is that girl playing guitar? She's good."

Bruno explained, and as he spoke, Arlette ended the piece, put down her guitar and picked up a lute. She was a tall, slim young woman but seemed to have a wiry strength. She was shy, usually playing with her head bowed so her face was hidden by long wings of straight, dark hair. She bent to raise the microphone higher and announced she intended to play an old medieval song by one of the troubadours of the region, Bertran de Born, a twelfth-century knight who had been lord of the castle of Hautefort. She began to pick out a delicate but haunting melody on the lute.

Suddenly to the surprise of all at the table, Young rose to his feet and began to sing in a fine tenor voice, in a language that Bruno could not understand although it seemed distantly familiar. He heard the baron mutter that it was Occitan, but then all fell silent as Young sang through to the end, Annette gazing up at him entranced and then bursting into applause, in which other tables joined. Ingrid called out "Bravo," and Valentin the butcher banged his tongs against the grill and demanded an encore.

"Another?" Arlette called down to him from the stage.

"Mon chan fenisc ab dol et ab maltraire," Young called back, and she nodded and began to play again, a slower song that sounded like a lament.

Bruno had applauded politely with the rest, but while he respected the antiquity of the music and the tradition it represented, it was not much to his taste. Young sang well, and it was interesting to come across a man whose main interest was cars who also had this side to his character. Annette clearly delighted in it and in Young, but except for their common interest in motor sports he seemed an unlikely partner for her. Annette was fair-haired, slim and pretty in the way of a little girl. She looked much younger than her years and had a shy, almost-timid manner until you got to know her. Bruno would have thought Young was the type to be attracted to a more dramatic, assertive kind of woman, one of those leggy blondes who liked fast cars and discos. Maybe he was misjudging Young, but again Bruno wondered if Young knew of Annette's father's wealth.

"Where did you learn that?" Annette asked as Young sat down, kissing him on his cheek. "You were brilliant."

"I read Romantic languages at university, and Bertran de Born was required reading," Young said, laughing as he picked up his wineglass. "I'm not a great fan, all that glorifying of wars and battles and how he loved to fight and see men die. One of his poems was about Richard Lionheart, to tell him there was too much peace about and it was time for some more slaughter."

"We have an early start tomorrow to get back to Alsace, so for us it's time for some sleep," said Thomas, rising. "Thank you all for a very fine weekend, and you are always welcome to visit us."

8

After saying good-bye the next morning to Thomas and his wife before they set off on the long drive home to Alsace, Bruno was in his office going through routine paperwork when his desk phone rang. He put aside a circular from the office of the prefect of the *département* on police exceptions to the thirty-five-hour workweek, thinking there were many weeks when he worked twice that much, picked up the phone and recognized the voice of the manager of the local supermarket.

"Another shoplifting case, caught on the security camera," Bruno heard. "You can probably guess the identity of the kid who did it?"

"Félix again?" Bruno asked with a sigh.

"Right, and as you know, it's not his first time. We're holding him here in my office with our security guy, and we'll wait for you."

"I have to contact his father first, then the youth services people. You know the rules for juveniles, whatever your cameras might show."

"I know these damn rules only too well, Bruno. You're never going to straighten these kids out if you baby them."

"Come off it, Simon. You've got the lowest shoplifting rate in the *département*. I'll be there as soon as I can. What was he stealing?"

"A set of stereo headphones."

To double-check on Félix's age, Bruno first went to the dusty room filled with old files that the mayor called his archives and pulled out the large ledger that recorded the town's births and deaths. He saw that Félix would not be sixteen for another ten days and, as Bruno suspected, he had to be treated as a minor. He returned to his office and called the youth services in Périgueux, but no one was available to talk to him. The receptionist said he should use someone from the social services at his own *mairie* to sit in for the preliminary questioning.

Bruno sat back, considering. The rules on dealing with minors were strict, and on the whole Bruno thought they made sense. If this case was going anywhere, a magistrate would have to be called in, and the magistrate who usually dealt with juvenile cases was Annette, as the most junior in the office. He called her and explained. Her office was in Sarlat, but she was in a meeting with a lawyer in Les Eyzies. She could join him at the supermarket within the hour.

Félix's father wasn't at home, but Bruno knew he could find him in a local café that had offtrack betting and TV sets permanently tuned to horse racing. He rounded him up, and along with Roberte from the *mairie* they headed for the supermarket. A discreet door at the side of the row of checkout counters led to a staircase and the office upstairs.

Félix was slumped on a chair in the corner of the room. He was wearing jeans that were too short for him, an old denim jacket and a T-shirt. The sneakers on his feet had seen better days, one sole repaired with duct tape. The security man, Bertrand, whom Bruno knew from the rugby club, was standing over the boy. He was wearing a single earphone in one ear with a flesh-colored wire leading from it and disappearing under his collar. That was new, thought Bruno. Simon, the manager, was behind his desk. Four TV screens on the wall showed images from the security cameras. A fifth TV stood on a filing cabinet.

Félix looked up at the new arrivals, his lip curling in a sneer at the sight of his father and Bruno. Bruno tried to remember what it had been like to be almost sixteen and to have no money when prosperous school-mates were buying CDs and fashionable clothes and seemed to have endless supplies of one-franc pieces to put into pinball machines.

"You should be at school, Félix," he began after the usual greetings. "Would you like to tell me what happened?"

Félix shrugged and turned away to look out of the window.

"Answer the policeman, you little jerk," said Félix's father, stepping forward aggressively. Bruno put a restraining hand on his arm.

"Simon, do you have a statement?" he asked.

"Mine and our security guard's statement are already typed up, signed and witnessed," said Simon, handing the neat sheets of paper across his desk, briskly confident in his familiarity with the procedure. "You realize that I have no latitude in these cases. Company policy is that all shoplifters must be pursued to the limit of the law. And it's not the first time with this kid. I've made a copy of the videotape for you, but let's take a look at it."

The TV screen on the filing cabinet flickered into life, showing a washed-out image of the aisle with CDs, DVDs and electronic equipment.

"We have one fixed camera here and another for the alcohol, since they're the two high-value zones. The other cameras are on swivels so they can monitor different aisles," Simon explained. "The boy came in just as we opened at eight-thirty, when there's always a bit of a rush, as he well knows. He probably thought he could slink out without us spotting him."

"I wanted to get to school," said Félix in a low voice, the first time he had spoken. He was looking out the window at the parked cars as if these proceedings had nothing to do with him. His arms were folded protectively across his chest.

The screen showed a modest throng of shoppers walking along the main aisle and then a thin youngster peeling off and going into the electronics aisle, straight to a section with stereo headphones. He pulls down three or four, examining them in turn. Then he turns his back on the camera while appearing to replace the headphones and walks quickly to the end of the aisle and turns left past the microwaves and coffee-making machines.

"I was watching the camera, spotted Félix and thought he was behaving suspiciously," said Simon, reading aloud from his copy of his written statement. Bruno recognized the wording. It came straight from the template given to all the store managers by the company's legal office.

"So I used the radio to alert Bertrand, the security guard, who was standing by the entrance. When Félix walked through the checkout without paying, Bertrand stopped him and asked him to come to the office. The boy tried to run out of the store, but Bertrand caught him by his jacket, and these headphones fell from under his arm where he'd hidden them. The retail price is thirty-nine euros and ninety-nine cents. Bertrand then made a citizen's arrest, and we called you at once."

"Anything to say, Félix?" Bruno asked.

"Ask him why I took that brand of headphones," said the boy, still gazing at the world beyond the window.

"Why do you think he took that brand?" Bruno asked.

Simon shrugged. "Maybe he liked the color. I don't know."

"Is it the best brand or the most expensive?"

"No, it's a midprice model. Some are over a hundred euros."

"Why did you take that brand, Félix?" Bruno asked.

"Because that was the brand I used to have, earphones that I bought here a week ago with money that I earned chopping wood. Ask my mother, she can confirm that."

His father grunted something that might have been agreement. Bruno knew that Félix's mother worked weekends cleaning houses, as well as cleaning at the *collège* during the week. He could imagine that the boy's only pocket money would come from odd jobs he found through his mother.

"So what happened to your old earphones?"

Félix continued to stare out the window. "Tell him to ask his son."

The plot thickens, thought Bruno. Simon's son, Tristan, was the same age as Félix and in the same class at the *collège.* Tristan was big for his age, a forward on the school rugby team and strikingly good-looking with clear skin, curly fair hair and very long eyelashes. When he began playing rugby, his mother had badgered Bruno about the game being too rough and could Bruno guarantee that his handsome features would not get damaged. But Tristan's manners did not match his looks. He was brash, noisy and inclined to throw his weight about. Bruno had warned him several times about dirty play, and he'd noticed that while most of the good young rugby players seemed popular with the local girls, Tristan was an exception. They steered clear of him. Bruno looked quizzically at Simon, who was blushing.

"Let's talk privately," Bruno said, and led Simon out into the corridor and then into the staircase where they would be out of hearing.

"Could Tristan be involved in this in some way?" he asked. "I'm trying to understand why Félix said we should ask him about the earphones."

"I don't see how," Simon replied, but he wouldn't meet Bruno's eyes.

"Has Tristan got earphones of his own?" Bruno pressed.

"Yes, a much-better set, he got them for his birthday." Simon paused and then sighed. "But I confiscated them last week because he wasn't doing his homework." He looked up at Bruno. "When they get to that age, it's not easy to discipline them."

Bruno nodded sympathetically. Simon was a slim man, shorter than Bruno, and about the same height as his wife. She was a burly woman, an aggressive tennis player with a loud voice who seemed to change her hairstyle and color almost every week. Their son took after her, rather than Simon. Tristan was already bigger than his father and probably stronger.

"So if I went to the *collège,* do you think it's possible that I'd find Félix's earphones on Tristan?"

"Look, Bruno, this kid Félix has been in trouble with the law before. My son has never been caught doing anything wrong. You'd have no right to do that, none at all."

"I know your son. I'm his rugby coach, and I've seen him behaving badly on the field too many times. It's not just that Tristan seems to have little idea of fair play; he's cost us more penalties than anyone else on the team. It's very unusual for anyone to be sent off in *collège* games, but it happened to him twice last season. You know I've threatened to drop him from the team unless he starts to control himself?"

"No, I didn't know that," Simon said, sounding tired and sad. Again he wouldn't look at Bruno.

"Do you think your son is a bully?"

"It's just his age, high spirits; he'll settle down."

119

"Let's hope you're right," Bruno said. "But it looks to me as if your son took Félix's headphones, and Félix came in today to replace them from the store run by Tristan's father. He might even have seen it as a kind of justice. Does that sound plausible to you?"

"It was still shoplifting, and anyway, the procedure has started. We can't drop it now."

"Of course you can. I can take care of Bertrand and Roberte. Even if you go ahead, Félix is still a few days short of sixteen. As far as the law is concerned, he's a juvenile, so nothing is going to happen to him, except that the very word 'justice' will leave a nasty taste in his mouth. But he's not going to get off lightly. I'll go back in there, take him home with his dad, put the fear of God into him and search his room. If there's any more evidence of shoplifting, I'll throw the book at him."

"What about Tristan?"

"You're his dad, that's up to you," said Bruno. "But if you want to go ahead and press charges against Félix, I think I've got reasonable cause to haul your son out of his classroom and, if I find those headphones, that would be a case of theft, probably theft with threats of violence. And your son has passed his sixteenth birthday, so in the eyes of the law he's an adult. Do you really want me to do that?"

Simon closed his eyes, his mouth working. He seemed about to speak but then stopped himself and clenched his jaw.

Bruno decided to use his last weapon. He spoke so quietly that it was almost a whisper. "I don't think your wife would like that."

Simon closed his eyes again and took a deep breath and looked at Bruno and shrugged. "Okay, I'll drop the charges. And I'll pay for the headphones. But if that kid ever comes in this store again, we'll film his every move."

"You're right," said Bruno, knowing it was time to leave Simon with some shred of self-respect. "And I'll make sure Félix knows that. And we both know you're doing the right thing, Simon. You're a good man." Bruno slapped him gently on the shoulder. "I'll take him off now and search his room and make sure he never gives you reason to regret this."

"Regret what?" came a familiar voice and the sound of high heels on stairs as Annette appeared. She was wearing her usual working uniform of a dark blue suit and a white blouse buttoned to the neck, a black leather briefcase in one hand.

"Bonjour, Bruno," she said, kissing him on both cheeks and holding out her hand to Simon. "Monsieur," she said.

"Congratulations on your success in the rally, mademoiselle," Simon said. "I saw the report in the paper today. But your photo did not do you justice."

"Whereas mine showed me scared to death," said Bruno, smiling. "I think we're almost done here, Annette. Simon here, the store manager, has decided not to proceed with charges against the boy. But I thought you and I should at least visit his home and see if there is any evidence there of other thefts. I can explain the details as we drive."

He led the way back to Simon's office, introduced Annette, thanked Bertrand and Roberte and said he'd drop Roberte back at the *mairie* now that the magistrate was present. No need, she said, she'd take the opportunity to do some shopping. Félix was staring wide eyed at Annette, as if awed to be in her presence. He must know about her success in the rally, Bruno thought. He took Bertrand aside and said the store manager would explain the agreement he'd reached with Bruno. Bertrand nodded his okay. Bruno turned back to inform Félix and his father that he and the magistrate were going to search Félix's room at home. He showed everyone out into the corridor, picking up the set of headphones from Simon's desk and slipping them into his pocket as he said to Simon, "Since you're paying for them . . ."

Bruno took Félix's father in his police van, and Annette followed with Félix. Bruno used the drive to explain that he'd persuaded the store to drop charges on account of Félix's age but on the condition that there was no other evidence of shoplifting.

"He's a handful, that kid," said his father, lighting a cigarette as they drove. He had lit one earlier as soon as they were out of the supermarket. Bruno plucked it from his hand and threw it out of the partly open window. "Not in a police van," he said. The man shrugged, coughed and opened the window fully to spit. "His mother can handle him, but he never listens to me."

"Maybe that's because you don't have a job and you're never at home, always in the café," said Bruno.

"There aren't any damn jobs, not for someone my age, not anymore."

"Your wife finds work to do, and so does Félix. Lots of old people would pay a few euros to get their wood chopped, their gardens taken care of."

123

"Is this about me or about my son?"

"Both. If your son is getting into trouble, and we both know it's not the first time, it's your job to take an interest. You could steer him back onto the straight and narrow, set him a good example. What was your job when you worked?"

"Storeman at the sawmill, until they closed it. I had that job for nearly thirty years, ever since I came out of military service."

"Which unit were you in?"

"Infantry, One Hundred Tenth Regiment, based in Germany at Baden-Baden."

Bruno had been based there for a few months after finishing basic training, before he went on the course for the combat engineers. There had been over fifty thousand French troops stationed there at the time, including the headquarters of two army corps before the army finally withdrew from German soil in 1999.

"Not a bad posting," said Bruno. "Did they give you conscripts the extra money for being outside of France?"

"Not much, but yes, a few of those deutsche marks. I remember a bar we used to go to, Chez Hannes, it was called, run by a big German guy who'd been in the Foreign Legion, always ready to tell a few war stories. He'd been in Indochina and Algeria."

"I've been there," Bruno said, remembering. "If I remember rightly, Hannes was as bald as a badger, but he had one of those big handlebar mustaches, and he'd sing 'Le Boudin' when he got drunk."

"That's right, the old legionnaires' marching song. *Putain,* I can see the old bastard now with all those tattoos on his arms." He laughed, his eyes lively as he remembered. "Hard as nails, Hannes was. You should have seen him throwing people out when there was a fight. I wouldn't have wanted to be on the wrong end of one of his punches."

They drew up outside Félix's home, an old public-housing block of four stories and no elevator.

"Did you ever tell Félix about those days, what it was like when you were young and in the army? He'd probably be interested."

The old man looked sideways at Bruno, then nodded grudgingly before climbing out of the car and lighting another cigarette. Bruno sighed as Annette parked behind him. He'd talk to the manager of the old folks' home, see if there were any odd jobs that could be found for an old soldier.

Félix had a small room to himself. It contained a single bed, a small chest of drawers, an old card table and a chair. The floor was covered in old linoleum, holes in it patched with duct tape. Two hooks on the back of the door provided the only place to hang clothes. There were no photos of pop groups or pinups on the walls, only an array of photos of sports cars and horses taken from magazines. There was no laptop, no radio, and Bruno knew Félix was one of the few *collège* students with no mobile phone. The room smelled stale with an overlay of dirty socks. Bruno checked the drawers and found T-shirts and threadbare underwear, another pair of jeans. One drawer contained about a dozen apples. There were some cores in the wastepaper basket. On the card table was a pile of schoolbooks and beside them two old issues of *Cheval Magazine,* lacking their covers. Bruno looked up; they had been stuck to the wall with sticky tape.

"Obviously he likes horses and cars," said Annette, looking around. She closed the door behind her. "Are you going to tell me what happened here? I'm called to a shop-lifting case with a juvenile, and suddenly it's all dropped when I know that manager is supposed to demand legal action."

Bruno explained and brought out the headphones. "Do you think I should give them back to him?"

126

"No, I think you should get the bully to return Félix's own phones. In the circumstances, you're pushing your legal rights in searching this boy's room. If the father hadn't allowed you inside, I think I'd have stopped you. And I don't see any evidence of other shoplifting here, except maybe those apples."

"You're right. But this kid is going to get into more trouble unless somebody sets him straight, and pretty soon. The next time he gets into trouble, he'll face juvenile detention," Bruno said. Annette made a face, evidently disapproving of the tougher new laws Sarkozy had brought in.

"I've never been able to get through to the boy, not through rugby or tennis or anything else, and I don't think his dad has much of a relationship with him," Bruno went on. "Félix is a loner, scrawny, not big for his age, with no friends that I know of, a bit of a victim."

"If he'd been arrested, we could have gotten him assigned to community service," Annette said. "That might have helped, gotten him started on something that might lead to a job and a bit of self-respect. But now that the case has been dropped, there's no cause to arrest him."

Bruno nodded thoughtfully. "I'm wondering if these pictures of horses tell us something. Maybe we could steer him into work that way."

"You mean Pamela's riding school? It's worth a try." She looked around the drab room, sadly. "*Mon Dieu,* how the other half lives."

9

Fernand and Odette Oudinot lived in a cottage that had in the old days belonged to one of the farmworkers employed by the owners of the *chartreuse*. With a lot of hard work they had transformed it into a welcoming and attractive home. They had turned the attic into a large bedroom with its own bathroom, and downstairs they had knocked down walls to make two large rooms, a huge kitchen and a separate dining room, where Bruno had often been a guest. They had also created a large archway into the connecting barn, where in the past tobacco plants had been dried. The lower part of the barn was now a vast living room, twelve meters long and five meters wide. Its large and double-glazed windows gave spectacular views down the slope where Fernand kept a small herd of cows. Fernand had done most of the conversion work himself. Upstairs were three guest rooms, each with its own bathroom.

At the other side of the large vegetable garden and far enough removed to be almost out of earshot was another barn, where the geese, ducks and chickens were kept at night. Beyond them stood a *pigeonnier,* a tall tower that still housed pigeons for the family pot, a large pond and then two hectares of land where the birds roamed free. Then came the orchards and the walnut plantation, and just over the brow of the slope was the *chartreuse* that belonged to Sylvestre.

The whole place was a tribute to the ability of the farmers of the Périgord to adapt. It was hard to make a living from ducks and geese alone, so Fernand's dairy cows brought in a little extra money, and the calves he raised were known to produce the best veal in the district. And in the summer, the three guest rooms were rented out by the week for farm vacations. The guests ate with Fernand and Odette, roamed the farm and enjoyed the countryside. Odette cared for her bees and cooked endlessly, making jams and her splendid pies and tarts to sell in the market along with her honey. From her vegetable garden came strawberries and zucchini, tomatoes and eggplants, peppers and every other vegetable Bruno could think of. What wasn't eaten by the paying guests was pickled, preserved and put into jars to be sold in the market in winter. And with all of this, Odette still found time to cultivate the daffodils that made the hillside dance in spring and the roses that she'd trained to wind prettily around the doors and windows of her cottage. It made a splendid palette of colors in summer with the sunflowers that flanked the guests' barn and a lower meadow filled with wildflowers where her bees and hosts of butterflies dallied and feasted.

Fernand and Odette had made their home and their farm into one of the better-known places in the Périgord. Hardly a tourist brochure was printed without a photo of their ducks and geese in the shadow of the *pigeonnier* or their garden with the rose-covered cottage behind. It was every city dweller's fantasy of the French countryside and the rural heritage that most French people still held dear and to which every French politician paid homage. The mayor's own campaign brochures featured him smiling as he picked tomatoes in Odette's garden or sat on the terrace helping Fernand shell walnuts. This was the image of La Belle France and a promise that some core of that grand tradition was still to be seen and enjoyed.

"Bonjour, Bruno," Odette said, wiping her hands on an apron and advancing to kiss him on both cheeks. A plump and motherly woman, Odette had rosy cheeks as round as two little apples. She smelled of flour and jam and good cooking. Behind her on the giant stove were four large copper pots, each bubbling with black currants, and on the kitchen table an army of empty jam jars waited to be filled. *"Tu as mangé?"*

Bruno grinned at the traditional farm welcome, the eternal question "Have you eaten?" It was an invitation as much as a welcome, and Bruno loved to eat in this friendly home, staring down at the grazing cows and the ducks and geese waddling among them.

"I'm on duty today, so I can't stay, Odette, much as I'd like to," he said. "Is Fernand around?"

She directed him to the workshop, a lean-to attached to the barn for the ducks and geese. Fernand was using a small circular saw to cut logs for the winter and stacking them neatly under the eaves of the barn. When he saw Bruno, he pushed his protective goggles up onto his bald head, shook hands and said with his bright blue eyes glinting, "Time for a *p'tit apéro*? I keep a bottle here that Odette's not supposed to know about. You can tell me about the race you were in. I saw it in the paper."

"Not this time, Fernand. It's business, although very unofficial. The mayor got a call from a mayor in Alsace about this trouble with your cousins over the *chartreuse.* He's tied up today with the regional council meeting or he'd have come himself, but he asked me if there's anything we can do to help."

"It's a family thing," Fernand said. "I can't say I'm happy about the way it's built up, but I don't want to see the big old family house turned into some fancy place for rich tourists."

"You have a few tourists here yourself."

"Yes, but what we do is tourism on the farm; ecotourism, they call it these days. The kids get to play with the ducks and chickens, see the cows and calves, pick vegetables for their lunch — it's educational. The Alsace part of the family wants to do something very different, make a fortune by selling off these luxury apartments. It's crazy; this is the countryside, not the heart of Paris. Besides, there's some bad blood built up between us over the years."

"How do you mean? I thought you and your aunt, Sylvestre's grandmother, agreed to divide it, she got the *chartreuse* and you got the land."

"Yes, but we had a verbal agreement that we'd try to keep it all together in the family, not start selling it off. The Alsace family used to come down here every year, and we'd light the fires, air the beds, take care of the garden, get a meal ready to welcome them."

"What went wrong?"

"It was money, of course. When our parents died — they died within three weeks of each other — there was this land and there was a fair bit of money saved up. I was underage, but I wanted to stay with the farm, so my aunt agreed to let Jeannot, our neighbor, take me on as an apprentice, and he and I farmed this land together. The idea was that I'd take over the farm when I came of age. That was fine, just what I wanted, but then she came to me and asked if she could use the money to invest in some business project that she and her husband had back in Alsace. She promised to pay me back, with interest, and got a *notaire* to make it all legal."

"And did she pay you back?"

"Oh yes, in cash and right on time, but she paid me only three percent interest a year at a time when inflation was roaring away. And she used our money, my money, to help her new family buy back the aerodrome, which eventually made them millionaires. I'd just married Odette, and I had a fight with my aunt at the wedding when I said I wanted to be paid what the money was worth before the inflation, as well as the interest. That was when it started. She said a deal is a deal, and there was nothing in the contract about inflation. Anyway, it went on from there, me and Odette struggling to build this farm up and make ends meet, while she and her family up in Alsace were buying fast cars and fancy clothes. And she took all the family furniture, although half of it was mine."

"What would it take to settle this?"

"They've got all the money in the world. It wouldn't hurt them to let me have the *chartreuse,* as compensation for all the money I lost through inflation, and the interest I lost along with it. I sat down one night and worked it all out, using the government's own inflation figures. Last time I looked, it was close to half a million euros they owe me. And I'm not asking for anything that's not mine by right. So if they think they can make some more money from this place, they'll have me and my rights to reckon with. And it's not just me;

it's our Martine. All this will be hers when Odette and I are gone, and I'd like her to have the *chartreuse.*"

Bruno nodded. Martine was a late child, probably now in her thirties, who'd gone to the lycée in Périgueux and then to university in Bordeaux and got some high-powered job in Paris.

"Is she still in Paris?" Bruno asked, thinking she might be prepared to reach some sensible settlement with Sylvestre.

"She's based in England now, got her own business helping French companies get established in London. She's doing very well, employs three or four people," Fernand said proudly. "She was always good with languages."

"Didn't she get married, must be ten years ago or more, just about the time I got here and took this job?"

"She married a colleague from Paris, but it didn't last. I never took to him. She's divorced now, no kids, more's the pity. Odette can't wait to be a grandmother. And I'm not getting any younger. I'd love to have a grandson take this place over one day."

"Do you see much of her?"

"She's here now, just came for the week on one of those discount flights from London that come into Bergerac. Only cost her fifty euros, there and back. She's off seeing friends in Périgueux, but she'll be back for dinner. Come and join us. You'll like her."

Bruno had to decline, citing a previous engagement. He left his car outside the cottage, and Fernand led the way through the walnut plantation.

"I saw the parade of old cars the other day, but I was sorry we missed your race. We were having lunch with friends in Rouffignac. But I saw that white Jaguar again as we were driving there. It raced right past me."

"The E-type?" Bruno asked. "Are you sure?" That was Young's car. Why was he driving around when he was supposed to have been laid low by a migraine? Maybe he wasn't as attached to Annette as she seemed to think.

"Oh yes, and it was the same driver, the fair-haired young man."

They walked on over the brow of the hill. Strolling through the geese to the wire fence Fernand had erected just a few meters from the rear of the *chartreuse,* Bruno saw the building had two wings enclosing a large courtyard with a handsome old tree in its center. About thirty meters beyond the archway that led into the courtyard was a separate gatehouse. The main house was

137

about fifty meters in length, with mansard windows in the roof.

"Sylvestre turned each wing into a separate house, and he plans to keep the gatehouse for himself," said Fernand, over the noise of the geese. "I've fenced off his land from mine, so you'll have to walk around from here and get to his house by the dirt path that leads off from the road." He opened a small gate in his fence to let Bruno out of the enclosure for the geese and back into the walnut plantation.

"Any message for him?" Bruno asked.

"Tell him to restore to me what his family owes, and I'll remove the geese and sell him an easement for an access road. I'll even put up with him living in the gatehouse."

Bruno continued alone on a pleasant stroll through the trees and out to the single-lane road of tarmac. The potholes in the road suggested heavy use by trucks coming with building materials for Sylvestre's conversion. The path that led off to the *chartreuse* was muddy and narrow, marked by ruts that had been filled in with gravel. Trees and bushes on each side had been battered by the truck traffic. Nobody interested in a luxury home would want to arrive this way. And the closer Bruno approached, the louder the cackling of the geese.

Once past the path, Bruno whistled in admiration and pulled out his mobile phone to take some photos. To his left was the two-story gatehouse with a four-by-four vehicle outside. It was about the size of Bruno's own cottage, big enough for at least two generous bedrooms upstairs. Straight ahead was the stone archway leading into the courtyard with another four-by-four vehicle parked in the shade of the central tree. The *chartreuse* itself was a fine building, with two white pillars supporting a porch above the main door, tall French windows to either side and mansard windows on the floor above. The barns to each side of the courtyard had also been given tall French windows, and the walls of local stone had been cleaned and repainted.

As he advanced he saw to his right an all-weather swimming pool with a sliding glass roof where somebody was swimming laps. Behind the pool stood a handsome stone *pigeonnier* just beyond a terrace. A long stone building, evidently newly built and topped with solar panels, seemed to be the pool house. Expensive deck chairs lined the length of the pool. On a terrace between the pool and the house stood a large wooden table and chairs where Sylvestre was sitting with a dark-haired woman in jeans, an off-white cotton sweater and very large sunglasses. As he approached, Bruno saw a tall, slim bottle that signaled an Alsace wine on the table, along with green-stemmed glasses and a large ashtray.

"Bonjour, Bruno, this is an unexpected pleasure," said Sylvestre, rising and speaking loudly above the geese. "Do you know my cousin, Martine? Will you join us in a glass of Riesling?"

"I'm glad to see at least two members of the family are talking," he said and turned to Martine. "I've just been to see your mother and father. He's very proud of you and your career in London."

"Did he add that he can't wait for me to drop it all and start giving him grandchildren?" she replied, an edge to her voice as she stretched out a lazy hand to be shaken.

She took off the sunglasses and gave him a lopsided smile. Her voice was lower than he'd expected and her accent pure Parisian. Her dark hair fell gracefully to her shoulders from a side parting. Bruno guessed it had been expensively cut. She wore no makeup, except perhaps for something subtle that made her eyes look striking. They were her father's eyes, bright blue and twinkling. She had a wide, full mouth, perfect cheekbones

and an imperious nose that some would
have found too large for her face. Bruno
thought it gave her character. Her legs were
long and her shoulders broad. He noticed
she was wearing flat shoes of the kind
people wore on yachts in glossy magazine
ads. She could be a model herself.

"Your father said something about want-
ing grandchildren to leave the farm to, and
he's right to be proud of it and the business
he's built with your mother. But I think
everybody's inheritance could be improved
if the two wings of the family could reach
an agreement," Bruno said. "The mayor is
hoping that can happen because he likes
Sylvestre's project. He thinks it will bring
more tourists and maybe a few more jobs
for local people."

"The *mairie* is already enjoying the new
property taxes I'm paying," said Sylvestre.
He gave a short, barking laugh. "If anybody
can reach a settlement, it will be me and
Martine."

"You've made the place look great," said
Bruno. "I wish you luck, and if I can help in
any way . . ."

"Thanks, but let's not talk of that now."
Sylvestre poured a glass of wine and pushed
it across to Bruno. "I don't think you were
there the other day after the parade when

141

we got talking with your doctor and that Green council member, Alphonse, about electric cars. He was wondering if I could help organize a special race for them in the Vézère Valley. Martine is in public relations, and she's been sharing some ideas she has about getting sponsorships to make it happen."

"I imagine your Tesla would start as the favorite," said Bruno. "Talking of that car, where is it?" He looked around.

"There's no way I'd bring it up that rutted path. The truck with the Tesla and the Bugatti is in the secure parking lot of that logistics company in Le Buisson. I hired the Range Rover to get into my property and to get around." Sylvestre gestured to the vehicle parked in the courtyard behind him. "Alphonse said he'd talk to the mayor, and he called me this morning to say the mayor is interested in the idea."

"The mayor has become an enthusiast after the *concours* and yesterday's rally," said Bruno as a splash came from the pool and Freddy hauled himself out. He was thin and wiry, a mass of black hair tumbling down from his chest and into his trunks. He grabbed a towel from one of the deck chairs, put on a terry-cloth robe and came to shake hands before excusing himself to go and change.

"You're a brave man," said Bruno. "It's too late in the year for me to go swimming in the open air."

"The pool is heated by those solar panels," said Freddy, in good French but with an accent Bruno didn't recognize.

"How are you enjoying the Périgord?" Bruno asked. "Is this your first visit?"

"I like it a lot, all those old castles. And it's very green, a pleasant change after living in the Emirates. Excuse me, I should go and change."

He nodded courteously and left, and Bruno noticed that he headed for the gatehouse rather than the main building.

"Perhaps I could come and see you about the electric-car-rally idea," said Martine. "My father tells me you're the mayor's right-hand man."

"No, that's his deputy, Xavier, the *maire-adjoint,*" said Bruno. "I'm just the municipal policeman, but I'd be happy to make an appointment for you to see the mayor. It's this family feud that I'm here for. You two seem to get on well, and your father seems to be open to some kind of financial settlement —"

"He is," said Martine, smoothly interrupting. "But every time he meets Sylvestre, all the old family resentments come out, and he starts demanding the return of a grandfather clock and some bed of my great-great-grandmother and talking about historic inflation rates. If there's a deal to be made, Sylvestre and I will do our best to reach it, and then it will be up to me to sell it to my father."

"Which way did you come here?" Sylvestre asked, and Bruno explained how he'd walked through the woods from Fernand's home.

"So he didn't steer you the other way around, where you'd have seen a perfectly good road that goes around his walnut trees and comes out by my swimming pool. That's the logical way to get here, but he's fenced it off."

"The law gives you a minimum right of access to your property," said Bruno. "You could turn that rutted path into a decent gravel road, and it would make for a handsome approach."

" 'Minimum' is the word, not even two meters wide, and since it's not my land I can't make it into a paved or tarmac road. Still, I'm going to put down the gravel. But that doesn't solve the problem of the geese. Even with double glazing and earplugs, they wake me at dawn, and it goes on all day. It's enough to drive me crazy. I'd never be able to sell any of these apartments."

"That reminds me of a tourist who came to the *mairie* to lodge a complaint about the house he'd rented for a week," said Bruno. "It was just on the outskirts of St. Denis, and the people in the houses on each side kept chickens. The tourist wanted me to find some way to silence the cockerels who woke him at dawn every day."

"What did you say?" Martine asked. She'd been raised in the country herself and sounded amused.

"I asked him why he'd come to the French countryside where cockerels were to be expected. And he should count himself lucky that the neighbors didn't raise geese or donkeys."

"Peacocks are the worst of all," she said. "Their screams sound like someone's being murdered." She turned to Sylvestre. "Don't worry, I won't suggest my father get some peacocks — as long as you're prepared to be reasonable. In the meantime, just to show goodwill, I've brought you a peace offering."

Sylvestre sat up when she reached into her shoulder bag and brought out a sheaf of photocopies of handwritten pages that looked as if they came from a private journal or diary.

"It's about that Bugatti you're interested in," she said. "It's the unpublished memoir of an RAF bomber pilot shot down in 1941 and rescued by someone driving a car that sounds like the car that obsesses you. When the airman died, his family sent his unpublished memoir to the Imperial War Museum in London. I'd been working with them on getting French sponsors to help promote a new exhibition about French escape routes for downed pilots, which is how I heard about it."

She handed the pages across to Sylvestre, who took them as if receiving some holy relic and began quickly scanning the pages.

"Is this about the Bugatti that disappeared in the war when being driven to Bordeaux?" Bruno asked.

She looked at him in surprise. "You know about it, too?"

"I just heard about this lost Bugatti at the dinner that followed the Concours d'Élégance. Some people were talking about the most valuable cars in the world. I didn't know it was that famous."

"I'd never heard about it until I was doing some business with the new Bugatti headquarters in London, and Sylvestre let them borrow his old sports car for the launch of their showroom," she said. "Once I heard his name, I realized that we were cousins, even though we were on opposite sides of the family feud, and I introduced myself. We agreed to meet for lunch, and he told me of his interest in the lost Bugatti."

"This airman says he was hit by flak after bombing the Michelin plant in Clermont-Ferrand, lost an engine, and the crew had to bail out," said Sylvestre, lifting his head from the pages, his eyes alight with excitement. "He was picked up by someone in a black Bugatti who didn't give his name but was in his mid-forties and said he'd been a pilot in the First World War. He drove very fast and dropped the airman at a château where the family spoke English. They got him in touch with some people who had access to an escape route to Spain over the Pyrenees. He says it was called the PAT, after a British naval officer named Pat O'Leary who had helped to start it."

"Any route from Clermont-Ferrand to Bordeaux would probably have come through this region," said Bruno.

"A man in his mid-forties who drove fast, a pilot in the Grande Guerre — that could be Robert Benoist," said Sylvestre. "He won the French, British and Italian Grand Prix, and he went on to win Le Mans and run the Bugatti racing team. Who else would they trust to get the Bugatti to Bordeaux?"

He turned to his cousin, his eyes shining. "This is amazing, Martine. I won't forget this."

10

Back in town, Bruno turned down the rue de la Paix and pulled into the parking lot by the river that served the amusement park. Bruno had long considered it an eyesore. At the far end of the park was a stretch of scrubland, almost a field, between the windmill and the camping site farther downriver. That would be the place to park cars, tucked well back so they didn't spoil the view of the river from the other bank. Whatever Jérôme said about his plans for expansion, changing the parking area was going to be Bruno's first recommendation to the mayor.

Bruno had visited the place twice, once as a new arrival in St. Denis and more recently when he had taken Florence and her young children there as a treat to ride the carousel, to eat sausages smothered in mild mustard and ketchup inside a baguette and to watch him win each of them a stuffed animal at the popgun range. She had ignored the children's pleas to see the burning of Joan of Arc and the guillotine beheading Marie Antoinette, the park's two more renowned attractions, and marched them into the water garden to eat their sausages and paddle in the shallow streams. When Bruno saw the burning at the stake, he had been mildly impressed, thanks mainly to the clothes worn by the figure of Joan. They were fashioned from a special kind of paper that burned furiously with a bright flame, like the blond wig that ignited in a suitably dramatic manner as a bell tolled, black smoke poured out, and the visitors were wheeled out to make room for the next batch.

"They're banning Joan," said Jérôme when Bruno went into his office. "They've been at me for years about it, first for the smoke and then for the asbestos that we used to make the model. And now the new prefect is pro-Green, so I'm sunk. I have to think of something else, and I remembered something my father always wanted to do."

A burly man in his forties with a long, thin nose and a salesman's easy patter, Jérôme was a member of the town council who was usually at odds with the mayor over anything that might increase his taxes. The mayor in return kept an eye on any of Jérôme's more imaginative plans for new exhibits and had memorably vetoed the scheme to reenact a Black Mass being performed on the naked form of one of King Louis XIV's mistresses.

"My dad dreamed it up in the seventies, when I was still a kid, and the small farms around here were closing down or being brought together into bigger units with tractors, and all the old rural life was disappearing. Dad thought people would like to see how it used to be, so he had this idea to recreate a nineteenth-century village with its schoolroom, blacksmith, apothecary and basket weaver, people dressed in period costumes, making knives and spinning wool and weaving cloth on looms."

"I think the mayor would prefer that to the Black Mass," said Bruno as Jérôme unrolled a large blueprint that more than covered his desk.

"I'd put a waterwheel in here in a little cut I'd make in the riverbank and use that to grind corn, then we could sell both the flour and the old-fashioned bread we'd make. At the far end beyond the windmill, I'd have an old-fashioned farm with ducks, geese and chickens, a petting zoo for the kids with some sheep and dwarf goats and a display of traditional farm implements,

151

including horse-drawn ones. My dad had already started collecting some. We'd have a restaurant called the Old Farmhouse Kitchen, and I want to start a brewery. I'd keep the existing amusement park, minus poor old Joan, of course, and build this new village on that land beyond the windmill. We just use it now for storage. What do you think?"

"I think the mayor will like it. I certainly do, and it sounds like it means some new jobs in season."

"About five or six jobs, probably, but if it works well, it could be more. The thing is, Bruno, we can promote it as educational, which would mean school groups coming here and bringing in business outside the school holidays."

"You'll need more parking space. Could you use some of that land beyond your windmill, over by the campsite but on the side near the road rather than the river?"

"That makes sense. Yes, why not?"

"Just two more questions," said Bruno. "How are you going to replace Joan of Arc, and how do you get that effect on Marie Antoinette's neck when her head rolls into the basket?"

"For Joan, I'm going to build an exhibition of nineteenth-century clothes with a small photo studio attached so people can dress up and have their photos taken — singly, couples, the whole family. But Marie Antoinette is a trade secret."

"Come on, Jérôme. I worked out that you have a small pump in there that shoots out the fake blood, but it's the neck that interests me."

"It's spaghetti in tomato sauce behind a sheet of glass, but don't you agree it looks good? I came across it in England when I went over for a rugby international. I saw people eating it on toast in a café and couldn't believe my eyes. Spaghetti and toast — those English will eat anything. And they sell it in cans. But as I looked, I thought it was just the thing for Marie's neck, so I brought some cans back."

Bruno took his leave, telling Jérôme to drop off a copy of the plans at the *mairie*. His working day was over, his horse needed exercising, and he needed to pick up his dog. And tonight was the regular weekly dinner with his friends. He found himself smiling as he drove up the familiar road, imagining their reaction when he told them of Jérôme's use for tinned spaghetti.

Even though his affair with Pamela was over, Bruno always enjoyed the approach to what he still thought of as Pamela's house, even though she no longer lived there. Gilles and Fabiola had bought it, and Bruno still kept his horse, Hector, in the adjoining stables along with the old mare, Victoria. And his dog, Balzac, often spent the day there with Hector, whom he'd known since he was a puppy. Gilles was waiting for him, the horses already saddled. Hector nuzzled at Bruno, expecting his usual apple. Bruno gave it to him as he stroked Hector's smooth neck. Balzac put his paw on Bruno's foot by way of greeting, and Bruno gave him a biscuit. The basset hound wolfed it down and then darted around the horses' legs, eager for his customary run. Bruno donned his riding boots and hat as Gilles explained that Fabiola would meet them at Pamela's riding school where there was a new horse she might buy. Gilles had just started learning to ride, so Bruno checked the saddle girths and kneed each horse gently in the stomach so he could tighten the straps a notch. They set off side by side at a sedate walk, Balzac trotting ahead.

"Do you remember Annette's English boyfriend talking about the Bugatti the other night, the one that's worth millions?" Bruno asked. "Something has come up that might make a story for you." He explained what he had learned from Sylvestre about the downed British airman and his handwritten memoir.

"Robert Benoist?" Gilles exclaimed. "I've heard of him, a hero in both world wars and a Resistance leader. I'm pretty sure he was arrested and shot. They held a special race in his name in the Bois de Boulogne in Paris after the war. There's a plaque about the race in the Bois. I'd better go and see Sylvestre; it's the kind of story *Paris Match* loves."

Gilles had taken a buyout at the magazine after getting a book contract and deciding to leave Paris to be with Fabiola, but he still wrote articles for them as a freelancer.

"Ready to start riding?" Bruno asked. "We'll start with a trot and then go into an easy canter along the firebreak."

He set off, holding Hector back from the gallop he was expecting and glanced back to see Gilles riding well. Balzac was trotting at Bruno's side, looking up from time to time as if waiting for the pace to pick up. Bruno now loosened the rein and let Hector canter up the shallow slope that led to the forest and the long firebreak that would take them to Pamela's riding school. At the start of the firebreak, he reined in.

"Wait a few seconds after I set off and let

Victoria set her own pace. She's too old for gallops, but Hector's impatient for his run." Bruno's horse was tossing his head, eager to go, but Bruno kept him circling until he saw Gilles understood. Balzac was already fifty meters ahead, looking back to see if Bruno was coming. "I'll rein in at the far end and wait for you. We're in no hurry, so there's no need to rush."

He loosened the reins, bent down in the saddle and let Hector bound forward, moving almost at once into a stretching run that swiftly became the gallop he and his rider had been waiting for. The trees blurred away on each side, and Bruno narrowed his eyes against the rush of wind as Hector's hooves drummed on the turf. Within seconds, Balzac was passed and left behind, and Bruno felt the familiar strain in his thighs as he bent far forward, his rump clear of the saddle and his horse moving as if he could run forever. All too soon the end of the firebreak loomed ahead, and he sat back in the saddle, taking deep breaths as Hector slowed. He turned to see Gilles cantering easily in the distance with Balzac bouncing valiantly along beside the horse. As they came closer, Bruno smiled at the way Balzac's ears flapped like some primitive set of wings.

"You're riding well," Bruno said. "You're better than me when I was a beginner. Pamela says you have a natural seat."

"I certainly enjoy it. I just wish I'd started when I was younger."

They walked the horses down the bridle trail that came out on the ridge above Pamela's new place and paused, looking down at the half-dozen children on ponies walking around the sand-floored ring. Miranda sat on her white mare in the middle of the ring as she watched them circle. Pamela was in the paddock, standing by a low hedge over which two older youngsters were taking turns jumping.

"It looks busy," said Gilles. "And Fabiola's here already; there's her car, though I don't see her."

"Probably trying out the new horse," said Bruno, looking down at the freshly painted doors and windows of the office and stables. The old house Pamela had bought along with the riding school still looked down at heel, but Bruno could see men working in the emptied swimming pool repairing the leaks, and the shutters on the *gîtes* gleamed with new paint. There was a lot of work to be done to get the *gîtes* ready for the next tourist season, and for the moment Pamela and Miranda along with her children would all be living in the main house. Bruno admired the courage of the two women, each of them determined that her hard work and energy could make a success of what had been a failing riding school. Pamela had a good track record, having made a success of renting out her *gîtes* at her former house. Miranda had her father's money behind her, which didn't hurt.

As Bruno and Gilles walked their horses past the apple orchard toward the stables, they heard a shout and saw Fabiola cantering toward them on a dappled gray mare with a distinctive, darker mane. The mare was smaller than Victoria, Bruno saw, probably a good size for Fabiola. She reined in alongside them and edged her mare forward alongside Gilles so she could reach over and touch his hand.

"I'd try to kiss you, but I think we both might fall off," she said. "You, too, Bruno, consider yourself kissed. How was your ride?"

"Wonderful, perfect autumn weather, a good gallop, and Gilles is riding well. How's the mare?"

"Perfect, but I'm not sure I can afford the asking price until we pay the mortgage on the new house," Fabiola said. "We might have to wait until next summer when we start getting some money from the rentals. They want four thousand for her. She's six years old, a Spanish horse, Andalusian but bred in France. Pamela thinks she can get the price down a bit, and then I might be able to afford it.

"Enough of that," she went on. "Bruno, I've got some good news, well, maybe not good, but you'll be pleased to know I'm recommending an autopsy on Monsieur Hugon. I've already told J-J."

"That's great. Thanks very much," said Bruno.

"The autopsy might not tell us much because, if it's what I think it is, detection after this amount of time won't be easy," she went on. "I've asked J-J for a forensic check on the room where the body was found."

"What do you think it was? Poison?"

"It's possible, only possible, that cyanide was either put into his drink or sprayed straight into his face. But it's not easy to be sure. Cyanide traces dissipate very fast after death, and then human tissue can produce cyanide gas as part of the decomposition process."

"What kind of drink? Could it have been coffee?" Bruno recalled the three dirty coffee cups beside the sink. Madame Hugon

159

had said they were her favorite cups and had been surprised that her husband had used them. Could he have been killed by his visitors?

"Yes, indeed," Fabiola went on. "Half a gram of potassium cyanide is usually fatal, and in crystallized form, mixed with sugar or artificial sweetener, the victim is unlikely to detect it. You don't need much, less than the amount of salt you'd put on your *pommes frites.* Or it could be delivered by a spray, which could be indicated in this case by the irritation around the victim's nose and mouth."

"Isn't cyanide a controlled substance?" Gilles asked. "You can't just go into a pharmacy and buy it."

"No, but it's used a lot in the metals industry and in electroplating and by some photographers. I can think of several work-shops and garages in town that would prob-ably have it. You even find it in some fertil-izers," she said. "And it isn't hard to make for anybody with a basic knowledge of chemistry. I could make enough for a fatal dose from heating green almond shells and then running the hydrocyanic gas that's released through a solution of baking soda. It would be even stronger if I excluded air when I heated the shells and replaced it with an inert gas like helium or nitrogen. I could even do it through heating polyurethane. Some fire victims actually die of cyanide poisoning from the polyurethane in a mattress."

Bruno stared at Fabiola, stunned by the contrast between what she was saying and the bucolic scene around him, the autumn countryside and the laughter of children in the riding ring, the snorting of the horses and Balzac's busy foraging beneath the apple trees.

Fabiola followed his glance and added, "You could even make cyanide from apple seeds, if you had enough of them. One of my teachers in medical school had a grisly sense of humor and used to talk of ways to commit the perfect murder. Cyanide was his top choice, especially for anyone with heart or respiratory problems. It works by stopping the body from processing oxygen."

"Why is it hard to detect?" Bruno asked.

"It breaks down so fast. The usual toxicology tests don't work too well just one day after death, and they're almost useless after two days. If Hugon drank it in coffee, we might get an indication from signs of burning in the esophagus or stomach. If he was killed by a spray, then we'll have to use a new technique, by looking at his liver cells with a biomarker called ACTA, which stands for 'aminothiazole and carboxylic acid.' We don't have that capability in the Bergerac lab, so the body would have to be shipped to Bordeaux."

"What made you think of cyanide?" he asked.

"I found a trace of potassium on the nasal hairs and something else that I think might be DMSO, dimethyl sulfoxide. DMSO is a terrifyingly efficient way of carrying cyanide into the body, so efficient that it's known in chemistry labs as liquid death. That's why I recommended an autopsy and a full forensic check of the room where the man died."

Bruno's mind was racing. Who had a motive to kill Hugon? His wife was in the clear; her alibi in Sarlat had been confirmed. Bruno had spent part of the afternoon on the phone with the Périgueux archives and the Resistance archives at the Centre Jean Moulin in Bordeaux, trying to trace the subjects of Hugon's research. In Périgueux, it turned out, Hugon had been working on property tax records and files for registered foreigners in the *département* in the prewar years. In Bordeaux, he'd called up files covering the earliest years of the Resistance, from 1940 until the end of 1942, when German forced-labor requirements sent floods

162

of young Frenchmen fleeing into the Maquis, hiding in the woods. In both places, Hugon was well known enough that he was allowed to roam at will through the stacks, so not all his searches could be traced.

"So are you going to buy the horse or not?" Gilles asked, jerking Bruno from his thoughts.

"Yes, if Pamela can get the right price, or if we can reach an agreement that we buy her jointly, put her to a stallion, and then I get the mare, and Pamela gets the foal." Fabiola turned to Bruno. "Pamela plans to buy mares so she can grow the herd more cheaply than by buying new horses."

They rode down to the stables to greet Pamela and Miranda, and by the time they had unsaddled and brushed down the horses, Crimson had arrived in his old Jaguar with the baron. They carried the half case of wine they had brought into the old house and put it on the kitchen table next to the baron's old iron cooking pot, which was sitting in a box of hay to keep it warm. Beside it were stacked two cans of the baron's homemade pâté, a large apple pie and a wooden platter crammed with small round *cabécous* of goat cheese, a wedge of Stéphane's Tomme d'Audrix and a cylinder of English Stilton that Crimson had bought on his last trip to London.

The dinner to be prepared was a new ritual that had begun when Pamela and Miranda had first moved to the riding school, and Bruno, Florence, Fabiola and the baron had taken turns bringing dinner for the two women. The evenings had been so enjoyable that now each week they held a similar dinner, with each of the friends taking turns to provide the food and wine. This evening was the baron's turn to feed all eight of them, and since Crimson claimed to be a hopeless cook, he provided the wines from his well-stocked cellar.

They were now so accustomed to preparing the meal that they fell automatically into their usual roles. Fabiola polished the wineglasses and set the table, and Miranda's father decanted the wines he'd brought before starting to slice the big, circular *tourte* of fresh bread. The baron opened his cans of pâté, explaining that he'd brought one of venison and one of rabbit. Pamela went to the vegetable garden to pick lettuce for the salad while Bruno and Gilles took the big plastic *bidons* to the spring that burbled from the hillside to bring back some water. Meanwhile Florence and Miranda bathed their children and prepared them for bed, but they would eat with the adults before

164

heading upstairs to snuggle into the old feather beds that had come with the house.

It was the kind of evening that Bruno most enjoyed. It felt like being part of a family, with friends and good food, the presence of children, even when they squabbled, and the comforting knowledge that this had taken place last week and the week before that. Above all, he could expect to be with these same people the following week and uncounted weeks ahead. Strange, he thought, that they never ran out of things to talk about: local politics, the economics of riding schools, the merits of local vineyards and the best way to prepare various dishes.

As he and Gilles staggered back with the now-heavy *bidons,* Bruno thinking how to run a pipe system down to the house from the hillside, they ran into Pamela with her lettuces. He asked her to wait a moment when they reached the house and explained his concern for young Félix and his interest in horses. Could she find a use for the youngster around the stables, perhaps in return for riding lessons?

"If he's prepared to muck out the stables, I certainly could, but he doesn't sound like an attractive youth or even particularly trustworthy," she replied. "Still, bring him round, and I'll take a look at him. How's he going to get here?"

"I'll take care of that," Bruno said. He'd taken some garden waste to the *déchetterie* that weekend and seen an old bicycle that Jacquot, the custodian of the recycling center, had salvaged. He'd found it to be in working order and put it to one side. Bruno had already called Jacquot to say he had a use for it.

Inside the large kitchen, where Crimson had lit a fire in the elderly wood-burning iron range that stood against one wall, the baron was explaining to the freshly bathed children the art of making a cassoulet *périgourdin.*

"Down in Toulouse they think they know about cassoulet, but we know better," he was saying as he lifted the lid on the pot to let them smell the rich aroma. Four pairs of young eyes hung on his every word. "A real cassoulet has to contain stuffed neck of duck and some duck sausage, and I like to add some *manchons* of duck as well because my grandmother always put those small pieces of duck into hers. A cassoulet is always based on white beans with onions and tomatoes. It's fine to add some ordinary pork sausage as well, as long as it's been made with plenty of garlic, but without the duck it's just a pale shadow of a true cassoulet. It also needs to cook very slowly, which is why I made it this morning and left it cooking in the haybox all day."

"Time to eat," called Pamela, putting out a bowl of cornichons to go with the pâté. Bruno stared at her with affection and admiration as they took their places. Crimson poured them each a glass of white Bergerac from Château Montdoyen, and Miranda gave the children water from the spring. Pamela picked up the large serving spoon, and Florence began passing her the children's plates.

"This cassoulet smells magnificent, Baron," Pamela said. "Bon appétit, everyone."

11

The next morning, after an early ride with Hector, Bruno picked up the elderly bicycle from the *déchetterie* and arrived shortly after eight at the project where Félix lived. He walked up the stairs with Balzac at his heels and tried the bell. He heard no sound of ringing, and no one came to the door, so he began knocking. After a moment Félix's mother opened it, wearing a wraparound apron over her working clothes, and invited him in for coffee.

"I heard you sorted things out for Félix at the supermarket," she said, leading him into a cramped kitchen before putting the kettle on and washing a bowl at the sink. Even after all the years in St. Denis, she still spoke with a West Indian accent. "Thank you, we don't seem able to do much with him."

"Unless you do, he's going to get into real trouble," Bruno said as she spooned a coffee-chicory mixture into the bowl from a jar and poured in boiled water, followed by a splash of milk. "I saw from the pictures in his room that he seems to like horses."

"Horses and cars, anything mechanical, but it's mainly cars he likes. I sometimes think he only likes the horses because it gives him something to talk about with his dad, but he's always liked animals. He's one of those boys who collects stray dogs. They always follow him home, but we could never afford to keep one." She looked down at Balzac and smiled. "Would your dog like a bowl of water?"

"Yes, please," he said, knowing that people with little money took pride in offering something to others. "That would be very kind."

She washed another bowl at the sink, filled it with water and bent to give it to Balzac, who gave her hand a tentative lick. She fondled his ears as Balzac drank. "We used to have a dog when Jacques was working."

"Is Félix up yet? He's got to get to school."

"I get him up about now, so he comes with me when I go to work."

"Perhaps you could get him up now. Tell him I'm here and want a word with him before school."

When she left, he took a sip from the mixture Félix's mother called coffee and

169

grimaced. Rather than offend her, he poured most if it down the sink. After a couple of minutes Félix appeared, his face washed and his hair wetted down, wearing the same clothes as the previous day.

"Bonjour, Félix. You like horses?" Bruno asked.

"Don't mind them." His mother gave him a bowl of the chicory mixture and the heel of what looked like the previous day's baguette. The boy looked down at Balzac and tore off a piece of the stale bread to give to the dog. He dunked the rest of it in the muddy-brown liquid and began his breakfast. His mother gave him a nudge, and he said a grudging "Thank you for helping yesterday."

"How would you like to learn to ride?"

"What?" His head jerked up, and he swallowed some food the wrong way, choked and coughed his throat clear. He swallowed and then looked up. "Ride a horse, me?"

"You'd have to work hard instead of paying for it, but do a good job and there might even be some pocket money in it for you. But if you do a bad job, or don't turn up for work, it's over."

"How d'you mean? Where are you talking about?"

"The riding school near Meyrals is look-

170

ing for a part-time stableboy. They're willing to give you a trial. You'll spend Saturday mornings and some evenings cleaning out the stables and putting hay in the horses' mangers, and they'll get you started, learning to ride."

"That'd be great." His eyes lit up, but then they dulled again. "How'd I get to Meyrals? It takes two hours to walk there. What time would I have to start?"

"You'd have to be there by eight on the dot."

"I'd have to leave before six." He looked down at his shoes. "I could run part of the way."

"Can you ride a bike?"

"Yes, but I haven't got one."

"Your mother says you like mechanical things. Could you fix up an old bike, repair punctures, keep it oiled and the brakes working?"

"Yeah, Édouard used to let me help him sometimes on his bike at his dad's garage. That's where I learned to ride one."

Bruno nodded. That was interesting; he hadn't known that Félix was friendly with the garage owner's son. Édouard was a good kid and a fine rugby player. He'd flattened Bruno with a hard tackle in the last juniors' match against the old men. Bruno sup-

171

pressed a smile at the memory and led Félix and his mother downstairs, where he pulled the old bike from the back of his van. "Could you fix this one up?"

Félix lifted the front wheel, squeezed a tire with his fingers and then spun it. He tugged at the loose chain, lifted the rear wheel, spun it and tested the brakes. His movements were deft and confident. He put the bike down and used his hand to wipe dust from the seat.

"It's working already, but I could probably clean it up and tighten that chain. It could use a good going-over."

"You fix it up as best you can, and I'll lend it to you," Bruno said. "Then after school today, we'll go to the riding school in my car, and if they like the look of you, they'll give you a chance. You'd better shower and get into some clean clothes before you go. I'll pick you up here at five, and you'd better be ready because there's a catch. If you aren't ready and looking presentable, the deal's off. If the school decides after they try you out that they don't want you or if you don't turn up on time, I take the bike back. So rather than leave it out here at night, you might want to keep it in your room."

"Can I take it up now?"

Bruno nodded and held the door open as the boy shouldered the heavy old bike and staggered up the stairs. When Félix had gone, he looked at the boy's mother. "I'll need you and Jacques to make sure the boy gets up on time every Saturday and that he takes care of that bike."

"I understand," she said, squaring her shoulders before she went on. "He was always little for his age; that's why he gets bullied a bit. It was fine while Édouard was in the same class, they got on well together, but Félix failed his exams and was kept behind for a year."

Félix trotted out through the door of the apartment house, shaking his hands as if he'd just washed them and grinning at Bruno and giving Balzac a pat before he set off beside his mother to the *collège.* Bruno watched them go and then led Balzac into his Land Rover and set off for Fauquet's café for a real cup of coffee and a croissant before he started work.

From his office in the *mairie,* Bruno called Annette to tell her that Pamela was prepared to give Félix a chance at the stables and then asked if her English boyfriend had been serenading her with his troubadour songs. His name is George, she said, chiding him. She reported he'd been in good form the previous evening when they'd gone for dinner in Sarlat. She sounded happy about it, so Bruno didn't mention that George had been seen driving his E-type when he was supposed to be too sick to be in the rally.

He also briefed her on Fabiola's decision to call for an autopsy on Hugon. She might want to warn the *procureur* that there could be a murder investigation to organize, and certainly an inquest into Hugon's death. He promised to send her a report later that morning. Then he began to check his e-mails and found one from the mayor, attaching a copy of a memo from Alphonse suggesting that the *mairie* look into the possible benefits of organizing a rally for electric cars. The mayor asked for Bruno's views.

He raced through the rest of the e-mails, at least half of them from garages trying to sell him a rally car. He supposed they'd seen Philippe Delaron's race report. Another one came from the Périgord rally club saying that he'd omitted to sign up for membership before competing, which meant they could annul the result unless he paid them a retroactive registration fee of fifty euros. He forwarded that one to Annette. He was just finishing his report on Hugon's death when the mayor's secretary, Claire, slinked into the room in a new dress that was too tight for her generous frame.

"A Mademoiselle Oudinot to see you," she said, batting her eyelashes and somehow putting salacious meaning into the words. That would be Fernand's daughter, Martine, obviously reverting to her maiden name since her divorce. He asked Claire to show her in and to make two coffees from the mayor's own blend, not the usual sludge from the communal pot.

"This is business, Claire," he said briskly, hitting the save key on his report. "The mayor has become a rally enthusiast after the weekend, and we're counting on my visitor to help."

Martine was dressed for business in a dark skirt and blue pinstriped blazer over a white blouse. Her hair was severely pulled back into a tight bun in a way that did little for her looks, but Bruno still found her remarkably attractive. She was wearing lipstick and a little more eye makeup than the previous day and was carrying a slim briefcase in black leather. He stood up to receive her, shook hands across his desk and sat down gingerly, trying to avert the usual squeak from his elderly chair. As always he failed.

"I've put some thoughts down on paper about this electric-car rally we mentioned yesterday," she said, pulling some papers from her briefcase.

"Obviously we will need sponsors to finance this, and I've listed those I think most likely to be receptive to the idea. We'll need the mayor's influence to get the other communes up and down the Vézère Valley to cooperate, along with the regional council. I propose we call it the Lascaux Green Grand Prix, since that combines the most famous name in the region with an emphasis on the environmental aspect of electric cars. That should also guarantee support from the tourist board, and it gives media a second reason to cover the race. The combination of the most modern form of transportation with the prehistoric art of Lascaux makes a neat juxtaposition, too."

Bruno sat forward, resting his arms on the desk, trying not to show that he was impressed.

"This is my list of what needs to be done by the mayor, by the Périgord rally club whose backing we will also need and by the gendarmes, who will have to submit a report on the feasibility of the race route I have proposed. It will be my job to recruit the sponsors. I know several of the key figures in the various firms I've listed, and it's an area where I have a lot of experience. Here's my CV with a list of references from companies I've worked with."

Martine then handed him a map that showed the route she suggested for the race, starting at the parking lot by the Lascaux exhibition center, going through the heart of Montignac and across the narrow stone bridge leading out of the village. The route then turned off through the picturesque village of St. Léon-sur-Vézère, past the Château de Losse and up around the prehistoric park of Le Thot. It took the curving hill road after Tursac and turned off to swing around the Château de Marzac and then returned to the main road through a long, narrow street in Les Eyzies. From there it took the long straightaway to the turn that led to the Grotte du Sorcier and through the woods to come down through St. Denis with the finishing line at the far side of the bridge.

"You'll see that I've tried to include as many tourist sites as I could," she said. "But I'm sure we can adapt the route if there are any I have left out or any that we need to add for political reasons." She smiled at him, a sudden hint of playfulness in her eyes. "We certainly don't want any of the mayors to feel left out.

"I'm proposing three different kinds of sponsor, starting with the various car companies themselves along with Électricité de France and all the renewable energy companies we can recruit," she went on. "The second tier would be governmental, the European Union's energy commission, its environmental commission, its commission for tourism and equivalent bodies from France. The advantage of that is that the EU commissions only provide matching funds, so if they offer money the French authorities are under real pressure to provide funds of their own. The third tier would be the international public, starting of course with every school in the Périgord, since we will promote this race as being about their future. We challenge every schoolchild to donate five cents toward the cash prize we offer to the winner of the race — the publicity value will far outweigh the money we raise that way."

She handed over another sheet of paper. "Here's my marketing plan for targeting these different tiers. You can see that my preliminary calculations suggest that with my estimated income target of three million euros the race should cover its costs and make a reasonable profit, which will naturally go to financing green energy at all the other tourist sites in the region, starting with the Lascaux Cave itself."

He sat back, blinking partly in admiration, partly in surprise, at the figures in her proposal. "This is admirable, Martine. You must have put a lot of work into this, and you didn't have much time. I'm really impressed."

"Good," she said coolly. "Here's a note on my proposed terms. We will need to establish a nonprofit foundation to administer and run the overall project as well as the race itself. The foundation will contract with my company for the exclusive marketing rights, from which I will take an agreed percentage of all the outside funds that we raise under my plan. Fifteen percent is the usual rate in the public relations industry. I will also organize and commission all the advertising, to include press, broadcasting and electronic media, and take the standard ad agency rates."

Bruno scribbled down notes as she talked and did the math. He looked up. "Your fifteen percent of three million euros would net you four hundred and fifty thousand. We could never sell that to the council. Once the press got hold of that they'd all be thrown out at the next election. The average income per head in this commune is less than twenty thousand a year. The mayor would reject the whole idea. I wouldn't even take it to him."

"But I don't get a penny unless I make this work by raising the money," Martine snapped. She sat back, her eyes blazing at him. For a moment he thought she was going to walk out. Instead, she sipped at her coffee and then gave him a crisp smile.

"You said you were impressed by my proposals. These aren't just ideas, Bruno, it's a serious marketing plan. I'm experienced at this. What's more, I'm a woman from a local family, and I want this to work."

"Yes, I said I was impressed and I am." He knew he was dealing with an experienced businesswoman who must have gone through many negotiations such as this. She would have presented and sold many marketing plans and met similar hesitation when prospective clients saw the bill. Bruno was out of his depth, but he knew his local politicians.

"I was impressed first of all by your understanding that we'd need to get the enthusiastic support of all the local communes, which means their mayors and councils," he said. "I know you were born and raised here, but you don't live here. I

180

do and I know these people, their concerns and the kinds of budgets and payrolls they are accustomed to dealing with. They simply won't understand these fees you're proposing. They'll be shocked. They'll dig their heels in, which means this goes nowhere."

She was looking at him thoughtfully.

"I'm sure you have a plan B," he said. "And you probably have it in your briefcase ready to show me because the one thing I'm missing here is what happens after the race. This can't be just a one-off event, because if it works half the regions in France will be fighting to stage their own race. We need a long-term plan for another race next year and every year after that. If this is going to work, it will be because the Vézère Valley becomes a household word for racing, like Le Mans or Silverstone or the Nürburgring."

"Of course I envisage that," she said. "There's a note on the list of prospective sponsors that says we're looking for a five-year commitment. That means it will be the biggest boost to the tourism industry this region has ever had," she said firmly. She was still full of self-confidence and showed no sign of backing down from her fees. After a moment, she smiled at him. "Your mayors and council members will all see that, or they will when we explain it to them. You can sell this project, Bruno. They trust you."

Bruno smiled inwardly. She was changing her approach from combative one moment to appeasing the next. Didn't she know that every policeman in France had learned to play good cop/bad cop within months of starting the job? Bruno might not know much about business negotiations, but he knew how to get what he wanted from interrogations, and this meeting wasn't so different. He returned her smile and sat forward. His hands were relaxed on the desk, and he opened them, spreading his arms so that his body language suggested agreement and understanding.

"Yes, Martine, you may be right about that. And I recognize that you're an expert in your field and you're probably worth every centime. But you don't want these people whose support we need to think you're being greedy. You have to make this about them and their valley and their local businesses. Right now, I'm worried that they'll take one look at your proposed terms, and they'll think it's all about you."

She raised her eyebrows and leaned forward, resting her chin on her hands and gazing at him with interest. "So, as the local expert, what do you suggest?"

"Don't try to take all the money up front. Delay the payments. Cut your fee to three percent the first year, and raise it in stages for subsequent years. That gives you a stake in the project's long-term success."

"I'll then have skin in the game," she said. "That's the current business school jargon for sharing the risk."

"I wouldn't know," he said. "Around here we'd say bread today, jam tomorrow."

"Okay," she said, stretching out her hand. "Three percent the first year, five percent the second year, seven percent the third and then ten percent thereafter."

He held up a hand. "You mentioned you would expect the standard agency rate for all advertising. I don't know what that is, but we'd better have it on the same sliding scale."

She withdrew her hand a little and eyed him, considering. Ah, he thought, she's playing the silence trick, putting pressure on me to fill it. But he knew how to do that.

"Of course, all of this is speculative until I take you in to convince the mayor and then introduce you to all the councils in the valley to make your presentation. But on that basis, a sliding scale for both fees and advertising commissions, you'll have my full support."

He held out his own hand. "Do we have a deal?"

She remained still, but she did something with her eyes that made them unreadable. "What about you?"

Bruno raised his eyebrows. Could she possibly be thinking he would take a bribe? He stared at her levelly and said nothing.

"What's in this for you?" she said, cocking her head as though simply curious. "Would you want to be hired as security consultant?"

"I'm the chief of police for St. Denis, so I'll do that anyway as part of my normal work," he said. "I believe we can make this work for the good of my town and the whole valley. That's enough for me." He paused. "There is just one more thing."

She arched her eyebrows. "And what is that?"

"If we shake hands on this, I'll take you to lunch, then we go to see the mayor."

Without a smile or any other visible expression on her face, she reached forward, took his hand and shook it once. "Agreed."

Then she smiled, and suddenly she looked like a different woman, still entirely professional and businesslike but very much more human.

12

Even though Martine had relaxed sufficiently to loosen her hair from its bun so it floated free, the lunch had been a mistake. Bruno was too well known to be permitted an undisturbed meal with an attractive stranger. Ivan himself came from the kitchen to hover and to be introduced. He was followed by Bruno's hunting partner, Stéphane, a local cheese maker; Julien, from the town vineyard, and Rollo, the headmaster at the local *collège*. Then Dr. Gelletreau arrived, declaring proudly that Martine had been one of the first babies he had brought into the world after opening his practice in St. Denis. He promptly sat down at their table.

Once they had finished Ivan's plat du jour of steak-*frites* and returned to Bruno's office, Martine took from her briefcase the thinnest laptop he'd ever seen to amend the papers outlining her terms and printed them out at Bruno's desk. After a brisk and businesslike hour of discussion with the mayor, Bruno excused himself when his mobile rang with the special tone that signaled someone from the brigadier's secure network was trying to reach him. With the sense of foreboding that always came when he heard from this powerful official from the interior ministry, Bruno took the call in his office.

"Bonjour, Bruno," came the brigadier's crisp voice, sounding suspiciously affable. "I'm calling to let you know this is official, and we're giving full support to a multinational operation that's being led by Eurojust. It has to do with money laundering, possibly with a terrorist connection, and it's being led by an old friend of yours, Commissaire Perrault. It seems you parted on difficult terms, so she asked me to smooth the way."

"Would this be the operation in Luxembourg that went wrong?" Bruno asked.

"Where did you hear about that?"

"Just a rumor among cops. Commissaire Perrault used to serve down here, you'll recall. She has a lot of friends in the region."

"Sounds like our friend Jean-Jacques has been indiscreet again. It wasn't serious, just a bureaucratic dispute. It just delayed things a bit, but it's all being straightened out now." The brigadier's tone changed, becoming brisk again. "I'm sure you'll be entirely professional and give her your complete co-operation. I'll fax the usual letter to your mayor. And remember, Perrault is in charge, and she'll call you shortly."

It had been a long time since Bruno had thought of Isabelle as Commissaire Perrault. Even after the passing of time and the pain she had caused him, his heart still skipped a beat at the thought of her. The brigadier's "usual letter" attached Bruno temporarily to the minister's staff. The letter to the mayor, Bruno's nominal boss, was simply a formality. If the brigadier chose, he could activate Bruno's reserve status in the French army and place him under military discipline. That would be disagreeable, but coming under Isabelle's command would be disagreeable in a different and deeply personal way.

During the passionate summer months of their affair he would have called her the love of his life, and the intensity of the attraction and the physical passion remained. But for Isabelle, her career in Paris and now at Eurojust in The Hague took a higher priority than the love of a simple country policeman in the Périgord. If she had stayed as a detective in the Police Nationale in Périgueux, she would by now be the heir apparent to Bruno's friend Jean-Jacques, and they might have stayed together and fulfilled Bruno's dream of a family of his own. He had resigned himself to losing her. But during one of those occasional reunions when they had not been able to resist each other, she had become pregnant and had chosen to abort the child without telling him until the deed was done.

Biting his lip, Bruno went down the old stone steps of the *mairie* into the fresh air and walked to the center of the bridge to stare at the river and tell himself he was no longer in Isabelle's thrall. He had just enjoyed a delightful lunch with an attractive woman, although there had been no time or privacy to navigate that deliciously treacherous terrain that two unattached strangers could explore as they got to know each other. And now Isabelle was coming back into his life. He let out a long sigh and headed across the bridge to the open parkland behind the medical center, waiting for her call and wishing Balzac were with him. Balzac, who had been Isabelle's gift to him after the death of Bruno's first dog, was just as attached to her as his master. His phone vibrated, and he braced himself before answering.

"Bonjour, Bruno, I hope you're well," came the familiar voice, dear but disturbing. "Are we secure?"

"The button on my phone is green. We're secure. The brigadier said you're running a multinational operation. What's up?"

"Money laundering with some Arab connections and links to terrorist financial networks. The Brits, Germans and Belgians are involved, and the Americans are in the loop. There's now a Périgord connection, so I'll be coming down to maintain the surveillance. We've been monitoring two principals, and their cell phones show them moving around St. Denis."

Bruno felt he knew what was coming. There were not many people newly arrived in St. Denis with international financial connections. Was it Sylvestre and Freddy?

"The names are Sylvestre Wémy, a French citizen, and Farid Iqbal, born in India but traveling on a Portuguese passport after buying his citizenship with a million-euro investment. Do you know anything about them?"

"I was sitting by their pool yesterday, and I was racing against them in a rally the day before that," he replied, enjoying the gasp of surprise he heard down the phone. "Sylvestre owns property here, and Farid, who calls himself Freddy, won the rally. Apparently he also won some big race in the Middle East. Sylvestre is from a rich Alsace family and owns a showroom in Abu Dhabi selling classic cars. He had a grandmother who was born in St. Denis. How can I help?"

"You already have. We didn't know Farid was a racing driver. The car business is how they manipulate the money. I'll be arriving tomorrow or the day after with a surveillance team — if the brigadier and I can clear the paperwork in time. Plotting their phone locations on a map, we think they're in a large three-sided building with a farm nearby but no real access road and no other neighbors."

"That's the house Sylvestre inherited from his grandmother. The nearby farm belongs to another wing of the family, and they're at loggerheads over the inheritance. Audio surveillance won't be easy because the farmer is trying to drive them out with hundreds of cackling geese."

She laughed, a sound that touched his heart. "We usually use bailiffs; driving people out with geese sounds very Périgord. Do they have any other visitors?"

"Not at the moment, except for another

family member who's trying to settle the feud. Martine Oudinot is her maiden name. She's in her thirties, married and divorced, so she might have a different name. She runs a PR company in London. I can e-mail you her cell-phone number. She was there at the house when I called on them yesterday."

"Thanks. It's good to be working with you again. I'll call to say when I'm arriving. And be careful not to do anything that might alert them. So far we're just monitoring them." She paused, as if about to hang up, and then in a different tone of voice, she asked, "How's Balzac?"

Bruno smiled at the question; they would always have Balzac. "He's in great form. He runs after me when I'm riding, and he's learning to hunt. But there's a lot of puppy left in him — he still rolls onto his back for a tummy scratch whenever you stroke his ears."

"I'll look forward to that — and remember that some of the truffles he finds will be mine," she replied, chuckling, and he thought he could imagine the grin on her face. "Take care." She closed the connection.

He smiled as he closed his phone, and there was a spring in his step as he returned across the bridge to pick up his van. He had time to stop at Lespinasse's garage before picking up Félix for his interview at the riding school. Jean-Louis's son, Édouard, who had protected the boy from the bullies, was probably the nearest thing Félix had to a friend. That made him a potential ally to steer Félix into a better life.

The garage was, for Bruno, one of the symbols of the way St. Denis was being forced to change. Just like Delaron's photography shop, which had been rendered obsolete by the ubiquitous camera phone and gone out of business, Lespinasse's garage had closed its gas pumps, unable to compete with the cheaper prices at the supermarket. Even the *mairie,* which had long used the garage to refill its various vehicles, including Bruno's police van, had worked out it could save nearly a thousand euros a year by using the discount pumps. And the traditional work of local mechanics had been eroded by the new generations of cars that needed less servicing and more the skills of a computer technician. So Lespinasse had reinvented his business as a place to restore old cars, and Édouard had developed a useful sideline in tuning motor-cross racing bikes and restoring old motorbikes. Spending two days a week at the technical school in Périgueux and four days a week at the garage, Édouard was becoming as good a mechanic as his father and would get formal qualifications when he completed his technical course. But Bruno still felt a pang as he pulled into the garage and saw the gaps where the pumps used to be.

"*Salut,* Bruno," said Jean-Louis, emerging from beneath the hood of the Jaguar E-type that Annette's boyfriend had been driving. He extended his forearm to be shaken, sparing Bruno his oily hand. "You did well at the rally. If you want to take up the sport, I've got a useful little Peugeot for you."

"One rally with Annette was enough for me," he replied. "What's wrong with the E-type?"

"Nothing, but I offered to give it a tune-up just for the pleasure of working on the car. It's a bit different from Jack Crimson's old model. The owner is coming back to pick it up tonight at about seven. I'll have it purring by then."

"Is Édouard around?" Bruno asked. Jean-Louis gestured to the rear garage where the motorbikes were kept, and Bruno found Édouard and Félix working together on the old bicycle rescued from the dump. The bike had been transformed, cleaned and polished, the chrome on the handlebars sparkling and the chain tautened.

"I'm impressed," said Bruno after greeting them. "You guys have done a good job."

"Félix did most of it," said Édouard. "He just needed to borrow some of my tools."

Bruno checked his watch and looked at Félix. "If you leave now, you'll be at the stables in half an hour or so. I'll see you there. I need to talk with Édouard about something first."

Félix set off, pedaling hard, and as they looked after him, Édouard said, "He told me what you did at the supermarket."

"I remember doing something of the kind for you a few years back, when the head teacher caught you pinching his prize tulips."

"I remember," Édouard said, grinning. "It was Mother's Day."

"It turned into father's day pretty fast when I took you back to your dad," said Bruno. "I could hear your howls as I drove off."

Édouard laughed. "Dad always had a strong arm. The spanking probably did me good. Listen, Félix is a good kid at heart, but he's always been too scrawny to play any sports, and he never really fit in. That's why he always got bullied."

"I gather you helped protect him from the

worst of it."

"There was not much I could do, being in different classes. And you know how kids can be. His mother being a cleaning woman at the school made it worse. Even the girls would ask him when he'd be washing the windows, teasing him. I tried telling him to make a joke of it, but he didn't really know how to handle it."

"Has he got the makings of a mechanic?"

"He knows his way around an engine, and he's helped me strip a gearbox. But he's not what I'd call a natural, you know, like some people can just listen to an engine and know what's wrong."

"Like you and your dad," said Bruno. "It must be in the blood."

"He'll do well with the horses," said Édouard. "He always got on well with animals, and I know he likes being at that little farm the new teacher started at the *collège.*"

"We'll see," said Bruno. "I'm glad he's got a friend in you, even though I know you're busy with tech school. Are you enjoying it?"

Édouard nodded. "There are a couple of teachers there who really know what they're doing. One of them was a merchant seaman, working on engines on the Corsica ferries. He's great on diesels and technical drawing, and the electrics guy is brilliant.

We do a lot on car computers because he says that's the future."

He paused, evidently with something else to say but choosing his words with care. "I'll keep an eye out for Félix, but it's not like there's any work for him here. So far my dad is just making ends meet. Maybe if this classic-car business picks up after this week-end . . ."

"I understand," said Bruno. He'd never assumed that the small garage could afford another employee. "I'd better get along and see how Félix does with the horses."

At the riding school, Pamela told Bruno that Félix was doing well enough to be invited back to work on Saturday. They left Félix loading hay into the stable mangers with a pitchfork, and Pamela took Bruno for a stroll around the paddock where Miranda was teaching three little girls to trot on their plump ponies.

"The boy's not frightened of the horses, they seem to know he's comfortable around them, and he's a willing worker. That new Andalusian that Fabiola is interested in can get a bit lively, and he did well to calm her. What do you think I should pay him? I can't afford minimum wage."

"Pay him in riding lessons, and maybe after a while you might want to give him some pocket money. But don't give him too much. I'd say ten euros for a Saturday should do it."

"You'll have me arrested for exploiting child labor," she said with a laugh. "The occasional ten euros won't break me. And what if I paid him in kit? I've got an old pair of riding boots that should fit him, and the last owners left an assortment of riding caps and jodhpurs in the tack room."

"I think he'd be delighted. But don't give it all at once. Dole it out, make him know he's got to work for his rewards."

"Like I did with you, you mean?" she said, turning to him and smiling as she took his arm. "You were very patient with me. It's one of the reasons I always knew you'd be good with horses."

"You said once that I was the first man you'd been with since your marriage broke up."

"It's true, and I'm glad it was you, Bruno. I just hope Miranda finds someone as kind. She's the kind of woman who really needs a man in her life, and it's been hard on her, being left with the children."

Bruno looked at her, startled. Surely she couldn't be hinting that he should take the role. Pamela knew him well enough to read his thoughts.

"*Mon Dieu,* not you, Bruno!" she said, laughing. "Miranda would be quite wrong for you, although I can see many a man would find that plump, pink innocence rather enticing. She'd try to domesticate you and bring you carpet slippers. You'd be driven to drink within weeks."

Bruno paused, wondering what to say in response, and finally came out with something that sounded lame, even to him. "She has a new life now, new friends, the riding school to run."

"That's the problem. The riding school takes all her time in the days, and the children fill the evenings and weekends. It doesn't leave much time to be out and about and meeting new people. Maybe you could talk to her father, tell him to start throwing some more of his parties."

"I have enough on my plate without getting involved in matchmaking," said Bruno, although mentally he was running through the list of the unattached men in the district. There was a new vet in St. Cyprien whom he'd played rugby with and a new teacher at the lycée in Sarlat whom he'd met at one of the junior tennis matches in the summer.

They turned back to the stables, where Félix was whistling as he hosed down the yard in a pair of rubber boots that looked much too big for him. He looked up as they approached, and his face turned solemn as he addressed Pamela.

"I've given them all hay and water, but I thought I'd stay to help the girls unsaddle the ponies," he said. "Is that okay?"

Pamela nodded. "That would be fine, Félix. I'm pleased to see you making yourself useful. Will we see you on Saturday morning? We start at eight to get ready for the first lessons at nine."

"Oh, yes, I'll be here, but could I also come back tomorrow after school?"

13

Bruno pulled in at Lespinasse's garage just after seven and heard the deep and potent roar of a perfectly tuned engine. Young was in the driver's seat, and Jean-Louis stood proudly alongside as Young smiled his appreciation at the work that had been done.

"Would you like to come for a spin?" Young asked Bruno.

"Very much." He climbed inside, surprised at the size of the steering wheel and the old-fashioned knobs and switches on the dashboard. He enjoyed the deep leather seats and the wood trim. He felt very low to the road.

"The only new element is the safety belts," said Young. "They weren't required when this was built. Where shall we take her?"

Bruno took him up the long and winding hill road that led to Boutenègre and then through the woods to the long, straight stretch of road between St. Cirq and Les

Eyzies. As soon as they reached the straight-away, Young dropped into second gear, and the acceleration hit Bruno like a punch in the back. He glanced at the speedometer, and it seemed to indicate a much-slower speed than he would have imagined, and he suddenly realized it must be marked in miles per hour. By the time he had calculated they were doing a hundred and eighty, Young was slowing for the tight bends that led to the bridge over the river and the narrow main street of Les Eyzies.

"I was glad to hear your migraine cleared up so fast," Bruno said as the sound of the engine diminished to a throaty murmur. "I had to stand in for you at the rally, and Annette scared the wits out of me. And now it seems I'll have to do it all over again."

Young apologized, saying some vital business had come up.

"To do with Sylvestre?" Bruno asked, thinking of Isabelle's call.

"In a way," Young replied, glancing at him sideways. "How did you know?"

"Pull in here on the right," Bruno said. "We'll never hear each other once we're on the road. You and Sylvestre both seem to be interested in the same car, the one whose picture you showed me from your phone."

"Did he tell you about the Bugatti?" Young

asked. "Damn him, he may have all the money, but it's my family."

"I don't understand. How do you mean, your family? Did they own it? I thought you said it was lost in the war."

"It wasn't lost. It disappeared," Young replied. "Anyone who finds it will make a fortune, and my family was very much involved in that car."

Young explained that his great-grandmother's brother had been William Grover-Williams, a British racing driver who lived in France, married a Frenchwoman and worked and raced for Bugatti in the 1930s. He'd been born in France in 1903, where his father had been a horse breeder. At the age of sixteen, he talked his way into a job as chauffeur of a Rolls-Royce that belonged to William Orpen, a British artist who had been commissioned to come to Paris at the end of the First World War to do portraits of the participants at the Versailles peace conference. Grover-Williams fell in love with Orpen's mistress, a Frenchwoman named Yvonne Aupicq, and later married her. In 1928, he won the French Grand Prix and the following year, in a Bugatti 35B like the one owned by Sylvestre, Grover-Williams won the first Monaco Grand Prix. Bugatti hired him as a regular driver, along with his friend Robert Benoist, who went on to win the first twenty-four-hour race at Le Mans. Grover-Williams also acted as a salesman for Bugatti among his fashionable friends and was allowed to drive the now-missing Atlantic model around Paris.

"One of the few remaining photos of the car from the period shows Yvonne standing by the car with her dogs, Scottish terriers," Young said.

"So driving is in your blood," said Bruno. "Is that why you're so passionate about cars and about this one?"

"Grover-Williams was a hero in our household. My mother was his great-niece, although she was born after the war and never met him. And he was a real hero in the Resistance with Benoist."

During the war, Grover-Williams had volunteered to join the SOE, Britain's Special Operations Executive, an underground organization that sought to build, arm and train Resistance fighters in occupied Europe. He and Benoist built the Chestnut network in and around Paris, using their racing connections to arrange parachute drops of arms.

"That's where things become murky," Young said. "The official record says

Grover-Williams wasn't parachuted in from England until early 1942, by which time the famous Bugatti had disappeared."

As Hitler planned the German invasion of Russia in June 1941, a crash program to build more weapons took over the Bugatti factory in Alsace, Young explained. The cars and some of the machine tools the Nazis did not need were evacuated to Bordeaux. In February 1941, the factory records show that the famous Bugatti Atlantic left for Bordeaux. But it never got there.

"Was Grover-Williams driving it?" Bruno asked.

"It's not clear. The official records suggest that he was undergoing training in England until early 1942, but we have family letters that say he went to France in early 1941 on some secret mission, and some of his French friends remember seeing him in Paris with Benoist around that time."

Somewhere between Alsace and Bordeaux, the car had disappeared. Both Grover-Williams and Benoist were later arrested by the Gestapo and died in concentration camps. Nobody ever knew what happened to the car nor whether either of the two racing drivers was at the wheel.

"So you are here looking for the car?" Bruno asked. "I imagine you're not the first to try to track it down, if it still exists."

"I found something interesting in the family papers, a reference to friends Grover-Williams trusted, a British family living in a château in the Périgord, at Rastignac. I've managed to track down an old woman who worked at the château as a maid during the war, and I've been trying to see her for weeks. I finally got the call that she would see me on the morning of the rally. That's why I had to let Annette down and leave you in the hot seat. I'm sorry."

Bruno wondered why he hadn't told Annette the truth, but instead he asked, "And did the maid know anything about the car?"

"Not a thing. She seemed baffled by my question. She said everybody else who had wanted to talk to her asked only about the valuable paintings that had been in the château. Apparently the Nazis took them during the war and burned the place down. It looks pretty good now, though."

"Did the château seem familiar?"

"Yes, but I couldn't place it."

"We call it the French White House. The design was copied by the architect who did the one in Washington. Ours is the original, although I wonder if the Americans believe that."

"Well, it was a wasted day. And I'm sure Sylvestre will be miles ahead of me. He's got the money to hire professional researchers."

"So you're competing?" Bruno asked, noting that reference to professional researchers. There were not many of them in the region, other than the late Monsieur Hugon. Could Sylvestre be his mysterious client?

"Absolutely, we're competing," said Young. "I had suggested we join forces, but Sylvestre just shook his head and smiled in that infuriatingly superior way of his. I thought my bit of family knowledge might give me an edge."

"What do you know about Sylvestre and his friend Freddy?"

"That he's rich, does well in his classic-car business, particularly since he and Freddy launched the new showroom in Abu Dhabi. And Freddy is a hell of a driver. I don't know Sylvestre that well. When we meet, usually for a meal or a drink when he comes to London, we talk about cars. But he's never asked about my personal life."

"Does he know of your link to Grover-Williams?"

"Not from me. It's about the only advantage I have, so I've kept it to myself. But that Rastignac connection doesn't seem to be getting me very far."

"There's somebody else in on the hunt now," said Bruno. "A journalist friend of mine who sometimes works for *Paris Match*. His interest is the story rather than the car, but he picked up something that seemed to interest Sylvestre."

Bruno told Young of the downed bomber pilot's memoir, how he was picked up and helped to escape in the Bugatti by someone who sounded like Benoist, though it may have been Grover-Williams.

"Does Sylvestre know what's in this memoir?" Young asked excitedly.

"Yes, and he seemed excited by it, which makes me think he hasn't found any sign of the car itself. He's still looking for clues."

"Just like me," said Young, looking wan. "But from his manner when he last spoke, he seemed a lot closer to it than me."

"There's one thing that intrigues me," said Bruno. "This all happened some seventy years ago. Even if you find the car hidden in some abandoned barn, it will probably be rusted away by now."

"That depends on how carefully it was stored. It was made of a special alloy, part magnesium, so rust wouldn't have been a problem. Magnesium has a low ignition point, which explains why they couldn't weld the car and had to use rivets instead. There's a long ridge running along the roof where the rivets held the bodywork together."

"Still, the chances of finding it must be pretty slim," said Bruno. "And it's even less likely that it would be in a fit state to restore to a point where you might be able to sell it for the kind of money you were talking about."

"There are five key parts," said Young, ticking them off on his fingers as he spoke. "The engine, the chassis, the transmission and the front and rear axles. If someone finds three of those, it counts as a restoration. And with that car's legend, it's worth thirty or forty million, maybe more."

"Maybe you should talk to my reporter friend," said Bruno. "I don't think you're going to get very far on your own."

Bruno drove in front of Young toward Gilles's home. Careful of his car's suspension, Young went slowly up the long approach on the dirt road. As they topped a gentle rise, they could see the old farmhouse in the gentle hollow below. It was flanked by two barns that Pamela had converted into self-contained *gîtes,* the stables and the pigeon tower. The buildings formed a natural courtyard, dominated by an old ash tree in the center, and a vine-covered terrace made a charming spot for dining in summer. Two embracing wings of poplars were set back from the house, and something about the way the farm blended into the landscape made it seem both peaceful and welcoming.

They found Gilles at work in the spare bedroom of the main house, which he had turned into his study, lining the walls with bookcases and filing cabinets and with a big old dining table as a desk. It stood by the window with a fine view over the grass tennis court and swimming pool at the rear of the house. To Young's surprise, on a bulletin board where Gilles had pinned notes, photos of Fabiola and various business cards and reminders to himself was attached a printout of the car Bruno had first seen on Young's mobile phone.

Bruno introduced the two men and, over a glass of wine, Young explained what he knew of the lost Bugatti and his family connection. Gilles had already been researching on the Internet and had downloaded from the Imperial War Museum in London a copy of the memoir by the downed RAF pilot. Young scanned it quickly, asked for an atlas and asked if the Michelin factory at Clermont-Ferrand was inside the border of the territory administered by the Vichy regime. Bruno confirmed that it was.

"So if the car picked him up near Clermont-Ferrand, the direct route to Bordeaux would come through the Périgord," said Young.

"The best road would go through Terrasson and Périgueux," said Bruno. "That would take him right past the Château de Rastignac." Young explained his fruitless visit to interview the former maid.

"Let's be frank about this: my interest is the story, which is a pretty good yarn even if we don't find the car. People always like reading about mysteries," Gilles said, looking at Young. "But what about you? Is your real interest the car or the money it might make?"

"The money would be fine, but I probably wouldn't get much more than a finder's fee," Young replied. "Ownership will be a legal mess. I imagine Bugatti would have a claim, but it was wound up decades ago, and I don't know who would have the rights to the old assets. The heirs of the driver might have some claim, depending on the contract he had with Bugatti to deliver it. The owner of whatever place it might be hidden would have some claim, if only for decades of storage fees. And even if it is found and can be restored, full restoration costs would run into the millions."

"In that case, why not broaden the search by publicizing it?" Bruno asked. "We could bring in Jack Crimson, whose contacts might find something in the SOE archives — the Special Operations Executive did all kinds of espionage during the war. You might consider asking Florence and her computer club to trawl the Internet for any links to any of the people or places linked to Grover-Williams. And why not get *Sud Ouest* to run a story and see if any new information turns up? It might mean you'll have to share any finder's fee."

"Let's not bring *Sud Ouest* into this; they're competition," said Gilles. "At least wait until I run the story of the search for the lost Bugatti in *Paris Match.*"

Young looked uncertainly from Bruno to Gilles, obviously unsure how much to trust them and wondering whether he'd have any chance of success on his own. Bruno and Gilles exchanged glances. They didn't know much about Young, but if Annette liked him, Bruno was prepared to give him the benefit of the doubt. What Bruno couldn't say was that most of his interest in this affair was professional. Sylvestre and Freddy were the targets of Isabelle's operation, which made them serious suspects. And if Sylvestre had indeed been in the market for a professional researcher, there was even a possibility that they might be linked to Hugon's death.

"If we go this route, making the search public through the press, how might the money be shared out?" Young asked. "Please bear in mind that I've lived with this story since I was a boy. I can't tell you how many times I sat at my mother's knee, hearing about this amazing ancestor of ours, one of the great racing drivers as well as a Resistance hero. What I'm trying to say is that this is very personal for me, and I've put a lot of time and effort into it. So however the money gets shared out, I think I should get half."

"That's not just greedy; it's premature," said Gilles. "We don't know what else we'll find out or who might contribute crucial new information."

"I'll be frank," Young said. "The money is quite important to me, but it's not the only thing. If I get credit as the man who played a key role in finding the lost Bugatti, that would be wonderful for my business. It would really make my name and also allow me to give old Grover-Williams his due. It's tragic that a man like that could be almost forgotten."

"I can see that," said Gilles. "He and Benoist both deserve to be better known, and that's one thing I can contribute."

"Yes, but as you said, it doesn't matter to you whether the car is found or not. You still have your story." Young was looking grimly at Gilles as he said it.

"It's a much-better story if it is found," said Bruno, trying to still the sudden note of hostility that was developing between the two men. "Why don't we simply ask Annette to adjudicate anything to do with money? We each know her and trust her."

Young grimaced and gave a long sigh. "Okay, but I have real doubts about doing anything that might bring Sylvestre into this. I don't trust him, and I'm sure he'll have thought through all these questions about ownership, and he can afford the best legal advice. He might even have found some way of buying the rights to any Bugatti lost in transit during the war."

"I understand that," said Bruno. "But once this search goes public, you and he are on an equal footing. And you say your company will benefit from the credit you'll get in *Paris Match* as the man who launched this search. You're also the relative of Grover-Williams. It will be your story, not his."

Young sipped at his wine, looking solemnly at each of them in turn. Then he put out his hand toward Gilles and said, "In that case, I think we have a deal."

14

Bruno drove home to change, check his ducks and chickens and take Balzac for a brisk walk through the woods. It was in the stillness of the trees that Bruno did his best thinking. He liked this time of year when the first leaves had begun to fall, but the canopy above him was still golden brown, tinged with red where it caught the last rays of the setting sun. The birdsong was changing as the summer migrants moved south. The hunting season had opened, but he had not been out yet, preferring to wait until the weather grew colder and Balzac's training had progressed. Bruno whistled, and the dog came to heel at once, but he was still learning the whistled notes that sent him skirting right or left before driving Bruno's much-desired *bécasses* back to his master. Young as he was, Balzac seemed fearless, ready to chase away even a big fox. Feeling a sudden burst of affection, Bruno knelt down to stroke him and tell him what a fine hunting dog he would be.

As he walked back, he thought of his next steps. He would need to ask Sylvestre about Hugon. Even if he denied knowing the man, Sylvestre's face might show some reaction. He should ask Madame Hugon if she'd ever heard the name and whether any new mail had arrived for her husband since his death. He needed to ask other members of the history society whether Hugon had talked about his latest research job. The euro notes in Hugon's wallet were new; the numbers might be traced back to the bank where they were first issued.

As for Isabelle, her investigation into terrorist finance was beyond his skills, though he could help with some modest surveillance. When he reached his home, he went to a locked cupboard in his barn and took out two battery-operated surveillance cameras that he'd salvaged from one of the brigadier's earlier surveillance operations at a local château. He thought they might come in handy someday. Then he called Isabelle.

"Where are our two suspects now?" he asked.

"Their phones show Sylvestre in Trémolat and Farid in central Sarlat, each in a fixed location, so I assume they're having dinner. It might be another day or two before I can get down. This is turning into a real mess," she replied. "Since we've been using the Americans' TFTP, we have to go through all kinds of hoops to abide by European rules on data sharing with the U.S."

"What's the TFTP?" Bruno asked.

"Terrorist Finance Tracking Program. They've got the best data. But in order to use it Europol is required to verify each individual case and ensure every request we make is necessary and tailored as narrowly as possible to minimize the amount of data collected. It's crazy — we're all fighting the same people — but we have to live with it. In the meantime, whatever surveillance we can mount depends on you and Jean-Jacques."

"Leave it with me and let me know when you can get here," he said. "But if you can monitor their movements by their phones, what else do you need?"

"We need to know about any visitors or meetings they have, that's the priority, along with the license plates and registration numbers of whatever vehicles they're using. We want to know if they're visiting Internet cafés to use an e-mail address we don't know about."

"Okay. I might be able to help with the vehicle numbers. I took some photos of the place where they're staying on my phone and their rental cars were parked there. Your technicians should be able to blow up the images. I'll e-mail them to you right away. Is Jean-Jacques providing any support?"

"He's trying but he's short staffed. I know you'll do your best, and thanks, Bruno. Give Balzac a hug for me."

She hung up, and before setting off Bruno mentally reviewed the map of the region that he carried in his head. He couldn't use the direct road that led to Sylvestre's place in case he or Freddy returned early and saw his car. Nor did he want to alert Fernand by using the access through the Oudinot farm. There was a hunting trail he knew that went close enough, so Bruno loaded Balzac into the passenger seat of his Land Rover and headed down the lane, through St. Denis and out on the road to Le Buisson. When he got to the distinctive bend in the hunting path, he pulled out his map and a compass to check the bearing to Sylvestre's house. Ten minutes later, Balzac snuffling at his heels, he reached the road and saw the loom of the *chartreuse*, helped by a porch light that had been left on.

He took one of the cameras from his

rucksack, checked the new batteries and the data stick he'd installed to record the images and used black masking tape to fix it in the fork of a tree where it had a clear view of the muddied track that led to the lodge and courtyard. He put the second camera in a spot where it had a view of both the pool area and the path that Oudinot had sealed off. That would have to do. He checked that neither camera was visible from the road or the house, led Balzac back to the Land Rover and returned to St. Denis. Back in town, his phone was showing four bars of reception so he sent the photos of Sylvestre's place to Isabelle.

There were only two customers left in Ivan's bistro, strangers who seemed to be speaking English. Ivan looked at his watch when Bruno came in with Balzac, gestured him to a seat at the bar and poured out a generous glass of scotch. "I've got some tuna salad left and some apple pie, and you can share the *nasi goreng* that Mandy's making for our dinner. That suit you? And what about your dog?"

"*Santé,*" said Bruno, taking a sip of the scotch. "That all sounds good, and just a bowl of water for Balzac, please. I fed him before I left home, and it's been a long day. How's Mandy?"

Ivan invariably returned from vacation with a girl he'd met, usually one whose cooking skills could enlarge his own repertoire. There had been a Belgian girl who broke his heart but left him with half-a-dozen ways of preparing mussels and the recipe for a thick chicken stew called *waterzooi*. A Spanish girl had introduced St. Denis to gazpacho and paella, and the departure of the German girl with her Wiener schnitzel was sincerely mourned by Ivan's customers. He could never get the breadcrumb coating quite right without her expert assistance. His last vacation to Southeast Asia had raised hopes among the townsfolk that he'd return with a Thai woman who would broaden his menu yet further. Instead, he'd fallen for a breezy Australian who could wipe the floor with Bruno at tennis and was working with Ivan while waiting for her application to study at the wine school in Bordeaux to be approved. Having spent a year in Indonesia before meeting Ivan on the beach at Kota Bharu in Malaysia, she knew how to prepare a range of Asian foods.

One memorable evening she had produced for Ivan's regulars a *rijsttafel* of a dozen different dishes: chicken in peanut sauce, caramelized beef *rendang* braised in coconut milk and chilies, duck roasted in banana leaves and pork braised in sweet soy sauce. There had been different kinds of noodles, rice and spring rolls, and while the names of the various dishes escaped Bruno, the meal had lasted for hours, and he had never forgotten it. Tonight's *nasi goreng,* which Mandy translated as "fried rice," was rice with salted dried fish, prawns, hard-boiled eggs and shallots, all generously flavored with garlic and tamarind. Bruno had enjoyed it before.

"Mandy's fine, but what about you? Tell me about this stylish new girlfriend of yours, Martine."

"Not a girlfriend, just a local woman back for a brief visit to her folks," Bruno replied. "She's going to be helping us set up a new rally for next year, so it was a business lunch, at least until Gelletreau decided he wanted to join us and tell stories about her childhood measles and whooping cough."

Balzac padded across to greet the middle-aged couple who had finished their meal. They made much of him before calling across to Ivan for the bill in broken French, and Mandy came out from the kitchen to say good-bye to them. But first she introduced them to Bruno, saying they were Americans from California on vacation.

Bruno's English had been improved by his time with Pamela, and it was fluent enough if full of mistakes. He was able to ask where they had been so far, and they enthused about their visit to the Lascaux Cave earlier that day. Like most local restaurateurs, Ivan kept a stand by the door filled with tourist brochures, and Bruno pulled out one for them that listed the main attractions. They left, promising to return for another of Ivan's meals, and Ivan steered Bruno to a table set for four and went into the kitchen to fetch the tuna salad.

The *nasi goreng* was delicious, and the apple pie came with a generous scoop of vanilla ice cream. The three of them were chatting over coffee when the door opened and a very late customer came in. Bruno turned to see it was Martine, looking dressed to kill in a little black dress beneath her stylish raincoat, and her eyes blazing.

"I'm glad to see you here because it's you I'm looking for, Bruno," she began. "You only gave me your office phone number or I'd have called your mobile. I came here because I thought after lunch the people here would know where to find you. Sorry if I'm interrupting, but I need to talk about Sylvestre."

"Sit down, join us," he said, pouring her a

glass of wine and then helping her take off her coat. "This is Ivan and Mandy, and my dog is called Balzac. Have you eaten?"

"Yes, thanks," she said, leaning down to fondle Balzac, who always had a soft spot for women. Maybe it was something about their scent, Bruno thought, as he caught a hint of Martine's vaguely familiar perfume.

"A dog like this is just what I need to calm me down," she said as Balzac licked enthusiastically at her hand. "Sylvestre took me to the Vieux Logis in Trémolat, but other than the food it was a wretched evening. That bastard said he wanted a settlement, but what he wants is just outrageous. And now I know why my dad can't stand the man. He had the nerve to tell me that if he doesn't get his way he'll bankrupt my parents with lawsuits. He said he's already filed a complaint that my father's ill treating his geese."

"He won't get far with that," said Bruno. "Your dad runs a model farm, and he's well respected. But if this gets serious, I can recommend a good local lawyer, a retired magistrate who probably knows your father and would certainly know his reputation. His fee would be very modest."

Briefly he explained the family dispute to Ivan and Mandy, who wanted to know what

Martine had eaten at the Vieux Logis, a famed local hotel whose restaurant was said to be on the verge of winning a second Michelin star.

"The food was great — foie gras, *coquilles St. Jacques,* roast veal with truffles — but it nearly turned to ashes in my mouth," Martine said. "He even tried to buy me. Would you believe that he promised me fifty thousand euros in cash if I could persuade my parents to sell the surrounding land to him at ten percent above market price? We were waiting for the dessert, but at that I threw my napkin in his face and walked out. I would have thrown my wine after it, but the glass was empty."

"I wish I'd seen that," said Mandy, laughing. "I always enjoy a good scene in a restaurant."

Martine turned to Bruno. "Remember that Indian friend of his at the *chartreuse,* Freddy? Do you think they're gay?"

"I have no idea, but it seems the more I hear about Sylvestre the less I like him," Bruno replied. "If he's being aggressive with you, it's time to counterattack. We can check in the morning, but I'm pretty sure the land around his *chartreuse* will be zoned for residential use, since there are already buildings there. Your dad can apply for a construction permit to build half-a-dozen very cheap bungalows for social housing all around the *chartreuse.* He doesn't have to build them, just get the permit. It's his land. He could use it as a threat. The cottages would destroy Sylvestre's views and his setting, and when he hears the term 'social housing,' he'll fear the worst."

"You mean he'll imagine being surrounded by unemployed families and immigrants with lots of noisy children who'd sneak into his swimming pool and puncture the tires on his car?" asked Martine, her face lighting up with a mischievous grin that Bruno enjoyed as much as it surprised him. She might sound like a Parisian businesswoman, but he was beginning to recognize the depth of her Périgord roots.

"Yes, that's the idea," Bruno replied. "You said he gave you his proposal. Did you have an alternative plan to make to him?"

"Yes, I spent a lot of time talking my dad into it, as a deal that could work for both sides of the family. But it would mean we'd all have to cooperate, and Dad is reluctant to have any dealings with Sylvestre. I put the plan to Sylvestre over dinner. I suggested that we all cooperate to develop the *chartreuse* and our farm for ecotourism as a unit. Sylvestre would contribute the house,

225

and we'd contribute the farm. We'd create a new company in which we held equal shares, and the company would pay my parents a salary for running the farm. There wouldn't be a cost because the farm makes a good income as it is, but my parents aren't getting any younger, and this way we could run the whole thing as a commercial enterprise."

"It sounds very reasonable, and when your parents retire you could hire a young couple to take over the farm," Bruno said.

"Exactly, and the deal would give them the prospect of getting some equity in the company or the right to buy one of the houses. I thought it was a decent compromise, but Sylvestre turned me down flat and said the only deal he'd accept was one that let him buy the land around the *chartreuse*. That was when he tried to bribe me, with a nasty smile that said he thought anybody could be bought, including me. Frankly, I don't think I could bear to work with him at all."

She turned to Mandy and Ivan, who had been following the exchange with interest. "Sorry to inflict my family feud on all of you. I must be spoiling your dinner, but thanks for letting me get it off my chest."

"Not at all, it's been interesting," said

Ivan. "We'd better think about closing up for the night, and we'll look forward to seeing you again and hearing the next episode in the family saga."

"Maybe the best plan is to bring your cousin to eat here, and I'll put some ground glass or something in his food," said Mandy. They all erupted in laughter.

"If Bruno hadn't heard that, I might have taken you up on it," said Martine before rising to her feet. "Maybe it would be better to sprinkle a heavy dose of laxatives over it, preferably just before he goes off to race one of those fancy cars of his."

Ivan waved aside Bruno's attempt to pay for his meal. Bruno thanked him and left a ten-euro note as a tip. He helped Martine back into her coat as they said good night to Mandy. Escorting them to the door, Ivan noticed that a light rain was falling and handed Bruno an umbrella.

"Where's your car parked?" Bruno asked her, opening the umbrella and holding it over their heads. Balzac was looking up at them, wondering what these humans planned to do. Bruno was asking himself the same question.

Martine gestured down the street. Then she looked at him, flashing that mischievous grin again. "Good thing I rented a car —

otherwise I wouldn't have been able to walk out on Sylvestre."

Bruno laughed, took her in the arm that wasn't holding the umbrella and leaned forward to kiss her good night on both cheeks. To his surprise, as he drew back she leaned forward and kissed him firmly on the mouth, her lips surprisingly soft and a sound like a purr coming from deep in her throat. It lasted only a moment, but it touched him.

"That was a lovely surprise," he said. "Just as lovely as the sight of you when you walked into the bistro. You took my breath away."

"Play your cards right, and it might not be the last of my surprises," she said, taking his hand. "Come on, you and Balzac can walk me to my car. Unless, that is, you want your friend Ivan to keep on watching."

Bruno turned to see Ivan locking up while giving Bruno a wink, Mandy standing beside him grinning widely as she made the thumbs-up sign.

"Our shameless behavior will be all over St. Denis by lunchtime tomorrow," said Martine.

"Sooner than that," said Bruno, smiling as they walked on, huddling together beneath the umbrella. "They'll talk about your loose

Parisian ways, taking time off from Michelin-starred restaurants to lead the innocent town policeman astray."

"Innocent, hah! You forget I was born here. They're more likely to talk about the wicked policeman and the helpless maiden." She stopped as they reached her car.

"If this rally project goes ahead, you'll be spending quite a lot of time here," he said, not letting go of her hand. "There'll be plenty of time to get to know you. I'd like that."

"And I'd like to get to know you," she replied, turning into his arm. In her high heels, she was as tall as Bruno, but somehow she found a way to nestle into his chest. She raised her face to be kissed before sliding from his grip and opening the door of her car. Once installed, she gave Balzac a last pat and blew a kiss to Bruno as he closed the car door, and he and his basset hound watched her drive off into the wet night. As he walked back to his own vehicle, he remembered that he'd again forgotten to give her his mobile number.

15

The next morning Bruno took Hector on
an unusual route, a bridle trail that ran past
the village of Audrix and then through the
woods that led to St. Chamassy. From there
it was an easy canter to the ridge above the
Oudinot farm. He dismounted to go
through an old-fashioned wooden gate
whose catch was too low to reach from the
saddle and walked Hector the rest of the
way. He put Balzac on a leash, knowing that
otherwise the ducks and geese would be too
great a temptation. He hitched Hector to
the fence around the sheltered vegetable
garden and loosened his saddle, casting an
envious eye on Odette's still-healthy crop
of lettuces and tomatoes, and knocked on
the kitchen door. Martine opened it, and
her face lit up with pleasure before she
glanced down at her dressing gown and
carpet slippers, put her hands to her hair
and said, "Oh no, Bruno, you could have

given a girl notice."

"You look wonderful to me," he said, but she was already bending down to welcome Balzac, who was clearly delighted to renew the acquaintance.

"Come in, Bruno, come in, we're just having breakfast, and there are lots of brioches left for you," called Fernand as Martine darted through the archway to the living room and up the stairs to the guest rooms. Bruno took a seat, and Odette poured him coffee and pushed toward him a plate of brioches, still warm from the oven.

"I always make them for Martine," she said. "They're her favorite, ever since she was a little girl." Alongside the brioches was a bowl of fresh butter, probably churned by Odette, and pots of homemade jams.

"She never eats all the ones I make, so maybe your dog would like one." Without waiting for his reply, she handed Balzac a brioche, probably the first he'd ever tasted, and he took to it gladly, wolfing it down in two bites and looking up hopefully for more.

"Sorry to call so early, but I heard that your compromise offer to Sylvestre went nowhere, and I thought I'd better ask what you plan on doing next," Bruno said. "I have to report back to the mayor — you know he's taking an interest."

On the ride over, Bruno had wondered how to advise the Oudinots, now that Sylvestre was heading into such serious legal trouble. But that was not something he could reveal to them.

"Martine talked me into making that compromise offer, but it doesn't surprise me that Sylvestre turned it down flat," said Fernand as Odette brought a pot of fresh coffee. "And would you believe he tried to offer Martine a bribe of fifty thousand euros to reach a deal she could get me to swallow? It's shameful, trying to turn her against her own parents."

"I gather he's trying to buy some of the land from you, which would at least mean you need have nothing more to do with him," said Bruno. "How much is he after?"

"He wants all the land up to the ridge, about three hectares in all, which would give him that land where I've put the geese, the woodland all the way down to the road and about a hectare on each side of his buildings."

"Construction land is going for about eight euros a square meter these days," said Bruno. "But most of the land you'd be selling is too hilly to build on. And forest land is barely a thousand a hectare. You could squeeze three or four units of social housing onto the flatter bits but that's all. So the market price for your three hectares would be around twenty-five thousand. And if he's prepared to pay another fifty thousand on top, that would add up to a decent offer."

"That's just what I was saying when you arrived," said Odette, looking crossly at her husband. "But he won't have it. And it's not as though you were using that land for anything. It's just patchy woodland."

"I grant you that a direct sale would mean we never have to deal with him again but it leaves out all the other matters I was telling you about," said Fernand stubbornly. "There's the loan to his grandmother, the interest they never paid, the family furniture they took. And since he really needs that land I won't sell it for market price. He'll make money from the timber alone. No, I'd want a fifty percent share of the timber sale."

"Say you ask him for forty thousand euros for the land plus the fifty he offered Martine," said Bruno. "Add it up, throw in ten thousand for the timber and you're getting to a nice, round number, a hundred thousand."

"That's exactly what I told him this morning," said Martine, making an entrance in jeans and a black turtleneck sweater, her hair brushed. Bruno's glance lingered on her, remembering how soft her lips had been the previous evening.

"I'll have to talk to him, but I'm pretty sure the mayor would support that," Bruno said. "It's a very good price and would settle the feud. What's more it would spare you those lawsuits he's been threatening. That's an aggravation and an expense you don't need. Shall I tell the mayor you're thinking about it?"

Fernand looked unhappily at his wife and daughter and then back at Bruno. "You can say I'm thinking about it, but I'm not making any promises. And this is my decision to make, not for the womenfolk." He rose and headed for the door, taking a jacket from a row of coat hooks. "I'd better go and see about the geese."

Bruno rose as well, but as the door closed, Odette said, "He'll come around. I know him, he just said that to save face."

Bruno nodded and said to Martine, "You've met my dog. Do you want to say hello to my horse before I head back?"

"Love to," Martine said and plucked a carrot from the vegetable basket as Bruno kissed her mother good-bye and thanked her for the delicious brioches. "I've never met a horse yet that didn't like carrots."

"Do you ride?" he asked, as they left the house.

"Not for years, but if I'm coming back here more often I'd like to take it up again," she said, and then stopped in her tracks as they turned the corner and saw Hector gazing calmly as they approached. "He looks magnificent. What's his name?"

"He's called Hector, and he's got his eyes on that carrot."

Without a trace of hesitation Martine advanced on the horse and began stroking his neck as she fed him the carrot. He joined her, patting his horse's neck but keeping his eyes on Martine's profile. She might have changed out of her dressing gown, he thought, but she hadn't bothered with any makeup. Her complexion didn't need it. Hector had finished his carrot and was enjoying Martine's gentle scratching of the soft flesh under his jaw.

"Would you be free to join me for dinner this evening?" he asked.

"Yes, so long as it's not a fancy restaurant. I had enough of that last night." She turned from Hector to look at him, that cheerful mischief in her eyes again. "And if we go back to Ivan's the gossips will never stop. I'm surprised some busybody hasn't already called my mother."

"I thought I'd cook for you, and you could see my place," he said, and held his breath as he waited for her reply.

"I'd like that," she said, serious now. "But I'd better be back early, otherwise my mother would probably start planning a wedding and naming her first grandchild. And you should know that's definitely not in my plans. I love my mom and dad, but they drive me crazy sometimes. You heard that stubborn father of mine — not a decision for 'womenfolk.' "

Another independent woman intent on her own career, Bruno thought. Why is it they're always the ones to whom I'm most attracted?

"In that case we should start early, about seven, so you can be home by ten or so. Do you know where I live, or should I pick you up?"

"It's out on the Rouffignac road, one of the turnoffs after that prehistoric burial site at La Ferrassie, isn't it?"

"That's right," he said, wondering how she knew that. She must have been making inquiries. "There's a stone tower for electricity just opposite the turnoff. Drive up the road and turn left, and you'll see my home."

"That will be something to look forward to," she said. "I'm spending the day calling

236

on all the mayors from here to Montignac to try to persuade them to back the electric-car rally. Your mayor set it up. I'll tell you how it went when I see you at seven." She leaned forward to give him a quick kiss on the lips and then bent to stroke Balzac as Bruno tightened the saddle and swung himself onto Hector.

"You look very dashing on horseback," she said and waved good-bye. He resisted the temptation to rear Hector up onto his hind legs and leap into a gallop and trotted sedately off with Balzac jogging along behind.

When Bruno got to the *mairie,* the mayor called him in to show him the fax from the brigadier requesting Bruno be given a temporary assignment to his staff. He signed it with his fountain pen and handed the fax to Bruno, telling him to file it with the earlier ones.

"What can you tell me about this operation he wants you for, Bruno?"

Bruno explained briefly and then described the failure of his efforts to help Sylvestre and Oudinot reach a settlement over the *chartreuse.*

"That wouldn't be because you seem to have developed a friendship with Martine, would it?" the mayor said, a twinkle in his eye.

"News travels fast," said Bruno.

"Madame Lespinasse was putting the cat out last night and saw your fond farewells. She told Fauquet at the café, and now it's all over town."

"Between you and me, Sylvestre is one of the targets of this money-laundering operation I've been hauled into. Not that I'll be doing much, just helping with the surveillance. I think we're still a long way from making any arrests. Knowing the brigadier, he'd rather monitor them and track down all their contacts as opposed to locking them up right away."

"Is he coming down himself to run this show?"

"No, it's a Eurojust operation, so Inspector Perrault will be taking charge."

"You mean Isabelle? I hope that doesn't cramp your style with Martine, whom I very much liked when she explained her plans for this electric-car rally. She's a smart woman, probably another highflier like Isabelle. You do like to live dangerously, Bruno, when we've got all these fine young farmers' daughters yearning to settle down with a solid man with a good job like you."

"That's why you are now happily settled

down with a Franco-American historian with a professorship at the Sorbonne," Bruno replied. "Jacqueline is hardly a farmer's daughter."

"Touché." The mayor smiled. "But unlike you, I'm too old to interest them. What about Hugon? Any progress there?"

"An autopsy is being done with an eye on possible cyanide poisoning," Bruno said. "We haven't had the results yet, but Jean-Jacques is now involved. I've made the usual inquiries, but I'm having trouble identifying Hugon's last big research job. Jean-Jacques is getting one of his experts to crack Hugon's password and get into his computer."

"Have you asked any of his friends at SHAP? You remember Doumergues, the retired history teacher from Sarlat, the one who gave us that monograph about the lost artworks of Rastignac? It might have been before your time. He was probably Hugon's closest friend, and he called me the other day asking about the funeral. I suppose the autopsy will delay that. But you might want to give him a call and see if he knows what Hugon was up to. I must say Hugon being poisoned sounds very unlikely, unless it was his wife, of course."

He gave Bruno the telephone number, and

Bruno went back to his office to make the call. He explained that the police were still investigating whether Hugon's death had been suspicious.

"Goodness, that doesn't sound like Henri. And he was in fine form when I last saw him, like a dog on the trail of a good scent. He wouldn't say much about the job he was doing, but he certainly picked my brains clean about Rastignac."

"What did he want to know?" Bruno asked, aware that Young's research about Rastignac had drawn a blank.

"You know about the paintings that disappeared: seven Cézannes, five Renoirs, four Manets, three Toulouse-Lautrecs, a Matisse and one of Van Gogh's Arles paintings?"

"I thought they were destroyed when the Nazis burned the place?"

"Not according to the maid, who says she saw German soldiers loading tubes wrapped in tapestries into some trucks. She thought they were wrapping the paintings, the entire collection of the Bernheim family, who had a famous art gallery in Paris. The Bernheims thought the paintings would be safe with their friends the Lauwicks, the Anglo-American family who owned the château. But it wasn't the paintings that Henri was interested in; it was their friends, particularly any English friends. The widow Lauwick's daughter had married an Englishman named Fairweather, and they had lots of English friends, one of them a famous racing driver."

"Would that have been Grover-Williams?" Bruno asked, sitting up in his chair in excitement.

"Yes, how on earth did you know that? And Henri asked me the same question. Young Jacques Lauwick, the son, worked at *Vogue* magazine and knew all the fashionable people of Paris, and Grover-Williams was part of that beau monde. He and his wife stayed at Rastignac before the war."

"Did the Lauwicks have any connection to the Resistance or to any escape networks to help Allied pilots who'd been shot down?"

"Not that I know of, but if you have any names I can look up the copy I made of the château's guest book."

"A British naval officer named Pat O'Leary," said Bruno, looking in his notebook. He heard a jolt as the phone on the other end of the line was placed on a desk or table, and he heard the squeak of a filing cabinet drawer and then the rustling of paper.

"No, nobody of that name," Doumergues said when he returned to the phone.

"What about Robert Benoist?"

"The racing driver? Yes, he was there before the war with Grover-Williams."

"Did you ever hear anything about a car being hidden at or near the château?"

"That's what Henri asked me. No, I heard nothing about that, and I interviewed all the surviving people who had worked there during the war, before the Nazis burned the place down. They used phosphorus, you know, and the fire burned for five days. A terrible thing."

Bruno carried on with his questions, but Doumergues knew no more. Bruno thanked him, promised to let him know when the date for Henri's funeral was set and called the curator at the Centre Jean Moulin, the Resistance archives in Bordeaux, an expert whom he had consulted before. He asked what was known about an escape route known as PAT.

"It was named after Lieutenant Commander Pat O'Leary of the Royal Navy, but that was a ruse to disguise the founder's real name," the curator replied. "He was a Belgian army doctor named Albert Guérisse, and he got more than six hundred out across the Pyrenees before being arrested by the Gestapo. He was sent to the Natzweiler concentration camp in Alsace, but he survived the war. It was a dreadful place, where they gassed over eighty Jews just so they could obtain their skeletons for some awful anthropological museum that Himmler set up in Strasbourg to demonstrate the alleged inferiority of the Jewish race."

Bruno shuddered but pressed on with his inquiry. "Do you know of any connection the Belgian doctor might have had to the château of Rastignac?"

"Not offhand, but if I look it up will you tell me the whole story next time you're in Bordeaux?"

"Yes, and I'll buy you lunch while I relate it," Bruno replied. He put the phone down and called Jean-Jacques.

"I'm on my way to Hugon's place now with my forensics team," came the familiar cheery tones. "The widow is driving from Sarlat and will meet us there. If you join us, we could have a walk in the garden and talk about this surveillance job."

"There's more than that to discuss," said Bruno. "We may have a suspect, or at least someone we need to question. I've worked out who was Hugon's mysterious last client, and he also happens to be the subject

243

of our surveillance job."

"I should be there in about half an hour," said J-J and closed his phone.

Bruno had a few minutes before he would have to leave. As he was about to call his police friend Thomas in Alsace, he remembered something. He called up the photo of the famous Bugatti that Young had sent him and printed out two copies. One was for him, the other for the collection on Félix's wall. Then he called Thomas, who started to thank him for a pleasant stay in St. Denis. Bruno interrupted him.

"Hang on, Thomas. This is urgent. We're on a murder investigation, involving that researcher whose death took me away from the vintage-car show after the parade. You remember? It seems his last mystery client for a big research job was Sylvestre, which makes him our top suspect. We'll be bringing him in for questioning. I need to know everything you can tell me about him — the gossip, the rumors, everything."

"*Mon Dieu,* are you sure about this, Bruno? Sylvestre's a big man around here, wealthiest family in town, a big employer at that garage of his."

"If you want confirmation, I can get the head of detectives for our *département* to

call you if you like. He's leading the inquiry."

"*Merde,* where do I begin? Well, I told you
about the airfield, so you know where his
family money came from. It must be twelve,
thirteen years ago as a young man straight
out of business school that he started this
classic-car business. I think it began as a
hobby, but he saw the possibilities and then
opened his garage and began hiring top
mechanics and buying up old cars to restore
them."

The boom in old cars hadn't really taken
off then, Thomas explained. Sylvestre's big
breakthrough came with two Mercedes
from the 1930s that he found at an estate
sale of some French general who had died.
The cars were probably loot from the war.
He got them cheap, fixed them up and the
local paper reported that he got over a million for the pair of them at an auction in
Germany. He went on from there, specializing in old Mercedes. He went all over
Europe looking for them in Italy, Spain,
Scandinavia and then eastern Europe —
places where the classic-car business was in
its infancy. Then he opened his showroom
in Abu Dhabi.

That had been in 2007, just before the
financial crash. The next year, the rumor

was that Sylvestre was in real trouble, all his money tied up in stock he couldn't sell. He had to lay off some of his mechanics. The banks wouldn't lend him any cash to tide him over. He tried to sell some of the family's property holdings, but there were no buyers. Then Sylvestre suddenly obtained some financing, waited out the recession and when the oil price went up his Abu Dhabi business turned into a gold mine.

"He's the last of his line, which makes him the most eligible bachelor in Alsace," Thomas went on. "He lost his parents when he was in university. They were both on board that Concorde that crashed at Charles de Gaulle Airport. So now he owns all the land and property and the car business. He's got thirty mechanics working for him, and his collection of old cars is said to be worth more than the shopping malls."

"Any idea where he found the money when he needed it?" Bruno asked.

"Not for sure, but there were rumors about some big Arab investors he'd gotten to know in Abu Dhabi. I don't know if it's true or if he found a bank to bail him out. Sylvestre had a lot of contacts in the financial world from his time at business school, INSEAD, outside Paris."

"What do you know about that Indian

friend of his, Freddy? How long has he been around?"

"I think he was involved in the Abu Dhabi venture from the beginning. He's here in Alsace from time to time, and some people think that he and Sylvestre are a couple, but Sylvestre's always been a man for the ladies. A couple of years ago there was a story that he was getting married to one of those titled German girls, a *gräfin* or something with a 'von' in her name. One of those glossy celebrity magazines had some paparazzi photos of them together on a yacht in Monaco during the Grand Prix. I don't know if anything came of it. I'll ask Ingrid, she knows more about those things."

"Thanks, Thomas. That's very helpful, and I'll be sure to keep you informed of where we're going with this."

"Please do; the mayor will need to know if it looks like our town's leading citizen is about to get arrested. Meanwhile I'll keep this under my hat. And I'll call you after I talk to Ingrid."

"Right, give her my best."

Madame Hugon was standing in the front garden when Bruno pulled up in his car. J-J had not yet arrived. He got out to greet her, and she said, "I'll miss this garden. I planted those roses and laid out the flower beds.

But I can't stay here after this. Suspicious circumstances! It's the last thing I ever expected to hear about Henri, such a gentle man. We had our differences, but we were married a long time and got very used to one another."

"I know, I'm sorry to cause you this extra trouble," he said. "There may be nothing to it. You know how the police like to be sure."

She nodded solemnly, and then J-J's car arrived, the forensic van close behind, and J-J clambered out shouting, "We've driven past this damn place twice already, and if I hadn't seen your police van we'd have gone past again."

"Commissaire Jalipeau, this is Madame Hugon," said Bruno.

"My apologies, madame, and my condolences. Forgive my little burst of temper. May we come in? We'd better dress up first."

He handed Bruno a snowman, police slang for the white paper overalls that forensics rules required, and pulled one from the back of his car to squeeze into it, grumbling about its inadequate size. Bruno and the rest of the team put them on and donned hairnets.

"Do I have to wear one of those ridiculous things?" Madame Hugon asked. J-J replied that so long as she wasn't going into the room they were interested in, she needn't bother. Her own traces would be all over the house, anyway. Yves, the head of the forensics unit, led her to his van to get an oral swipe for DNA and to take her fingerprints.

She finally led them in, and Bruno noticed at once that the place had been cleaned, or at least the dirty crockery in the kitchen had been washed and put away, and there was a smell of cleaning fluid in the sitting room.

"Have you cleaned the study as well?" he asked.

"No, I couldn't bring myself to go in there again," she said. "It's as he left it, or, rather, as you left it. I cleaned the rest of the place the other day after you were here."

"Did you touch his clothes?"

"Yes, I bundled them all up into a couple of suitcases and took them to Action Catholique. I checked there was nothing in the pockets, of course. There were just some papers, a supermarket bill and some receipt from the post office."

"What kind of receipt? Do you remember? It could be important," J-J asked sharply.

"I'm not sure, but it looked like the kind of thing you get when you send something by registered post. Henri was always careful to do that when sending reports or papers to his clients."

"What did you do with it?"

"I must have thrown it away, maybe threw it into the fireplace or the bin. I really don't know. Do you need me anymore, or may I go back to the garden? It's painful for me to be here."

"Of course, madame," J-J said. "Could you let us have your birth and wedding dates, please? We'll try those for the computer password, otherwise we'll have to resort to special measures."

She wrote them down for him on a pad, added her husband's army number from his military service and went back to the garden to sit on a wooden bench, a balled-up handkerchief in her hand.

"Poor woman," said J-J. He stood in the doorway after Yves opened the study, put the laptop into a plastic bag and handed it to one of his colleagues, who returned with it to the van. Bruno leafed through the mail that Madame Hugon had piled onto a hall table. There was an electricity bill, a couple of catalogs and a history magazine wrapped in clear plastic with Monsieur Hugon's name in the address box.

"I'll check the fireplace, you check the garbage," J-J ordered, and Bruno took a large plastic sheet from the pile of evidence bags that Yves had put by the door and emptied the contents of the kitchen bin onto it. Mercifully, there was little but orange peel and a banana skin, coffee grounds and some screwed-up papers: a supermarket bill; a bill from a coffee shop in Sarlat; and a post office receipt for registered mail, sent by Monsieur Hugon to a Monsieur F. Iqbal, *poste restante,* Strasbourg central post office.

"Bingo," Bruno called to Jean-Jacques, and the chief detective hurried into the kitchen at a speed that belied his bulk.

"What have you found?"

"Sylvestre's business partner, Freddy, the Indian racing driver, was Hugon's client, sure enough," said Bruno, showing him the postal receipt. "I'm sure he and Sylvestre are in this together, and they hired Hugon to find out about the lost Bugatti. Who but Hugon's client would take away all the research notes and notebooks about the job? And who but the killer would have come here to Hugon's house to take them?"

"I thought you were supposed to have searched this place when you first came here," said J-J.

"I just had suspicions at the time," Bruno said defensively. But the suspicions had

251

been his, so it was Bruno's responsibility to make sure all the evidence was gathered. "You're right, I'm sorry. I should have looked more carefully at the time. No excuses."

"So now you want to arrest them?" J-J asked.

"We have to question them. This makes them our prime suspects."

"Okay, I accept that. But we're not sure it's a murder yet, not until the Bordeaux lab confirms Fabiola's theory about cyanide poisoning. I'm hoping to get something from them by the end of the day, but I'm told it's a complex process, so it might be tomorrow."

"So then do we bring them in?"

"Maybe so, but let's think this through," said J-J. "Consider the relative importance of a case of local murder here in your little commune against a case of international terrorist finance. What is the brigadier going to say if you derail the whole investigation by arresting Sylvestre tonight? What's Isabelle going to say when you torpedo the first big investigation she has led?"

Bruno bit his lip in frustration, understanding that again J-J was right, even though holding back went against all his instincts.

"And if you are convinced this is a murder, what do we do then?"

"Then we tell Isabelle and the brigadier, and you know as well as I do what they'll say. They'll tell us that we can always bring the murder charge once their operation is complete, but, for now, terrorism trumps murder. And both the minister of justice and the minister of the interior will agree with them, and so will ninety-nine French citizens out of every hundred, me included."

16

He might not be able to arrest Sylvestre, Bruno reflected, but the fact that Oudinot was now considering a sale of some land to his estranged relative gave him the perfect excuse to call at the *chartreuse.* But first he went home to clean and tidy the place for Martine's visit, to put some more wood into his stove and to set the table for dinner. Most important, he had to decide on the meal he would prepare.

Martine was born and raised in the region, so truffles and foie gras would be too routine. Her mother would certainly have prepared a classic series of dishes to welcome Martine's return, and the farm produced ducks and geese and raised some of the best calves in France. Fernand had been the man who had taught him how to recognize a classic veal calf, raised only on its mother's milk. First, he said, peel back the calf's eyelid, and if you see any red veins in the eyeball, it is no longer being raised *sous la mère.* To be sure, Fernand had continued, he steered Bruno to the back of the calf and asked him to raise its tail. Fernand had then leaned forward and used his thumbs to prize open the calf's bottom. "Look at that," he said. "Not a single red vein to be seen. That's the kind of calf you want."

He didn't want to serve a heavy meal, so that excluded beef and lamb. That left fish. Bruno called the baron, a devoted fisherman who was an infallible source of fresh trout, and asked if he planned to fish that day.

"I was in the boat with Antoine this morning, and we got some lovely young trout," came the reply. "Better than that, we went afterward to that little stream that comes down near St. Cirq and got enough *écrevisses* to feed half a dozen. Do you want to join us for dinner?"

Bruno savored the idea of cooking the wonderful local crayfish. "I can't, Baron. I've got a big date tonight, but I'd love to buy enough for two from you."

"Who's the lucky girl? I heard you'd been seeing Oudinot's daughter, the one who went to Paris."

Bruno laughed, shaking his head. "There's no way to keep secrets in St. Denis. Yes, that's the one. I was going to grill some trout, but now I'm thinking of *écrevisses à la nage*. When can I drop by and pick them up?"

"Anytime this afternoon. I'll be working in the garden. I'll save you a dozen. What do you plan to drink with them?"

"I was thinking of a bottle of Pierre Desmartis's cuvée Quercus."

"A fine choice, but what do you plan for the rest of the meal?"

"A zabaglione for dessert, with my own goose eggs. And to begin, you remember that Dordogne food fair we went to in Périgueux, when Pascal, that friend of mine from Neuvic, gave us each a can of the caviar they're making there? I haven't used it yet, so I thought I'd make some blinis and serve that as a first course."

"Don't forget a glass of ice-cold vodka to go with the caviar. That should do the trick. And you might try using Monbazillac instead of Marsala for the zabaglione; it works very well. Are you going to serve it on its own?"

"No, I was going to poach a couple of pears and throw in some fresh blackberries. There're still lots of them in the hedge."

"Excellent. Well, you certainly can't buy the *écrevisses* from me, but next time I catch some you can make that meal for the two of us, or a few more of us if I catch enough."

"Done, even if I have to save up to buy the caviar."

"Wait for when your truffles are ripe this winter, and you can exchange some of them for more caviar from Pascal."

Bruno put a bottle of vodka in his freezer and sat down at his laptop to search for something on the web about Freddy. He knew a fair amount about Sylvestre but nothing about Freddy. Isabelle had given his real name as Farid Iqbal so he entered that name, along with "Abu Dhabi" and "car race." Most of the sites that came up were in Arabic, but there were a couple from an English-language paper, *Gulf News.* He clicked on the first and found a photo of a beaming Freddy on the winner's podium at a racetrack in Dubai that described him as a well-known sports enthusiast and businessman, running the classic-car auctions in the region.

The second article was an interview with Iqbal when he and Sylvestre had opened their showroom in Abu Dhabi and staged the first of their auctions. Freddy described being born and brought up in Ahmedabad, in Gujarat state in India, the son of a successful businessman who had sent him to school in Switzerland, where he had been introduced to go-kart racing. He began to win races and placed third in a European championship race when he was just fifteen. But then his parents were killed in a Hindu-Muslim riot that lasted three days and resulted in over a thousand deaths in Gujarat in 2002.

"My parents were martyred in a Hindu pogrom, and it was then I understood the great responsibility of being a Muslim," Freddy said in the interview. "That is why I am so at home here in Abu Dhabi among the faithful."

Bruno sat back, thinking that Isabelle's connection of the car auctions to terrorist financing suddenly made sense. He could see how it might work. Sylvestre sold cars to wealthy Arabs who then registered the cars in the Emirates. They could transfer legal ownership of a valuable car to someone with terrorist connections who then exported the cars back to Europe to be sold at another of Freddy's auctions. The proceeds would be legal, and the money whitewashed. Bruno scrolled down through more websites but learned only that the total sales at Freddy's most recent car auction had topped ten million dollars.

He put Balzac in the van before setting off for Sylvestre's *chartreuse.* He'd found that people tended to be more friendly and talkative when his dog was present and pondered how far he should go with his questioning. Should he ask Freddy what was in the envelope Hugon had sent to him and whether he knew of Hugon's death? Should he ask Sylvestre if he and Freddy had been the clients for Hugon's search for clues about the lost Bugatti, or would that alert them too soon? He decided to play it by ear.

There was nobody in sight when he arrived, but one Range Rover was parked in the courtyard and another by the gatehouse. He knocked there first, and after a moment heard an answering shout. A few seconds later Freddy opened the door, wearing shorts and a sweat-drenched T-shirt.

"Sorry, I was working out on the rowing machine," he said, and glanced briefly down at Balzac, who was wagging his tail in that friendly way that he greeted strangers. Freddy didn't react to Balzac's overtures and looked back at Bruno. "You need to be fit to be a racing driver. What can I do for you?"

"Is Sylvestre around?"

"He's in the main house, but he's on the

259

phone to China. It's about opening the Shanghai showroom next month." He was standing in the doorway, one hand on the door as if impatient to get back inside and close it.

"Will you be going, too?"

"No, I have business in the Gulf to get back to."

"I can wait until Sylvestre is free," Bruno said. "Is he likely to be long?"

Freddy shrugged. "Who knows? He's been on that call half an hour already."

Trying to find a way to prolong the conversation, Bruno said, "You told me the other day you liked the castles that you'd seen here in the Périgord. Which ones have you visited?"

"I haven't really visited them, just seen them while driving around. There was one on the cliff overlooking the big river; I think it's the Dordogne. I remember Sylvestre saying the English had it, and the French built another castle on the other side of the river. And I saw one by the road on the way to Sarlat and another one from the autoroute on the way down here."

"Do you have castles like that in India? I remember Sylvestre saying that was where you were from."

"Yes, of course."

"I wanted to ask you about that Tesla you were driving," Bruno said, trying a new line of conversation. "What sort of range do you get from it?"

"It's got different settings for whether you want to race or cruise or drive in town, but for normal driving about two hundred kilometers."

"And is it fast?"

"Very."

"How do you find the Range Rover?"

"It's okay around here. I prefer the Porsche Cayenne; it gets better traction in the desert."

"Is that what you were driving in that race you won? I remember Sylvestre telling us about it."

"I've won several, but the one he was talking about was a rally through the desert when I came in second. If there's nothing else . . ." His voice trailed off, and he looked across the courtyard where Sylvestre was coming out of the main house.

"There he is, and now excuse me," said Freddy as he stepped back inside and closed the door.

That didn't go well, Bruno said to himself as he strolled through the courtyard to greet Sylvestre. This time Balzac got a better welcome as Sylvestre bent down to pat him.

"Do you have a moment?" Bruno asked. "It's about the problem you have with Ou-dinot. I notice that I can't hear the geese today."

"They were there at dawn, but he rang the bell about an hour ago for feeding time. He'll probably have them back here later. Can I offer you a coffee?"

"Thanks, that would be good, and maybe some water for the dog."

Sylvestre led the way back to the main house, saying, "I made the family what I thought was a very decent offer. I just want to buy three hectares that would give me the land up to the top of the ridge. Then Oudinot and I need never have anything to do with one another again."

"There's a saying that good fences make for good neighbors," said Bruno. He paused in admiration as he entered the main hall, paved in checkered-black-and-white stone with a handsome wooden staircase curving up to the next floor. A door to the left led to a sitting room and Bruno saw a couple of chrome and leather armchairs. Sylvestre turned right, through a dining room with a long and heavy table that looked antique and into a very modern kitchen, where an iPad mounted on a speaker system was quietly playing classical music. Bruno sat on a high-backed stool at the raised counter overlooking the cooking area where Sylvestre filled an electric kettle and began loading coffee into a *cafetière.* He put a jug of milk and some sugar on a tray with two cups and filled a stainless-steel bowl with water for Balzac, who lapped at it eagerly.

Bruno turned to look out of the French windows to the courtyard. Between him and the windows was a sofa facing a giant TV screen and flanked by two armchairs. There was a second dining table in bleached pine on which stood an open laptop and notebook and a mobile phone that had a headset attached. The table was large enough for eight chairs and for a very futuristic chair in black mesh and chrome that faced the open laptop.

"That looks like a very pleasant place to work. You've done a great job with the remodeling," Bruno said. "I can see how frustrating the situation with your cousins must be for you."

"I'll win in the end," said Sylvestre casually, pouring the hot water into the coffee. "I can afford lawsuits, and he can't."

"Oudinot is aware of that, and I understand he's considering the offer you made to Martine, but he's worried about losing out on the sale of the timber."

"That's a new one. I hadn't heard of any concern about timber, and anyway, I've got no plans to cut these woods down." He poured Bruno some coffee. "In fact I'd rather keep them. They add to the rural atmosphere."

"He's also got some good cards to play," Bruno said. "You may know that all the communes are supposed to provide a certain proportion of social housing for low-income people, the disabled, and so on. We're desperately short of such places, and if Oudinot applies to build some very cheap social housing all around your buildings, he'll get instant approval. The mayor would have no choice. It's Fernand's land, and it's already zoned for residential use. You'd find that just as much of a problem as the geese, maybe more so."

"I see." Sylvestre stared at Bruno for a long moment. "I presume you have a solution to put to me."

"He'll want a high price per hectare, plus the fifty thousand you suggested to Martine and a half share of any eventual timber sale, for a total sum of a hundred thousand euros. You get your peace and quiet, no geese and a good access road. And I'll propose to the mayor that he put the road leading here on the list for upgrading. I think he'll do it because he wants this business settled and your tourists to start coming here and spending money. Of course, he would also like to have the social housing."

"A hundred thousand is a lot more than the land is worth."

"I know that, but it buys you the certainty of the access and the calm you need to make this place a profitable business. Otherwise all the money you put into it could be wasted."

"A hundred thousand also buys a lot of lawyers," said Sylvestre.

"And not one of them would be able to stop Oudinot surrounding you with social housing."

Sylvestre nodded, looking beyond Bruno to the French windows and the garden. He seemed to reach a decision and looked back at Bruno.

"Fine, you can tell him I'll go with that." He stretched out his hand, and Bruno shook it, saying, "You won't regret this."

"And I want the transfer done fast, with a contract of sale signed before I have to leave for China in two weeks. More coffee?"

"Just a quick cup, I've got to get back for a meeting with the Police Nationale," Bruno said, wondering how far to push Sylvestre. "They're investigating what looks like a suspicious death, maybe a murder."

Sylvestre raised his eyebrows. "Really? You don't expect a murder here in the sleepy Périgord?"

"It was the day of the vintage-car parade, the day before the rally," Bruno said. "You might remember I had to leave to go and register the death of a man named Hugon. He was a retired archivist who still did some freelance researching on the side, mainly for local lawyers. It looked like natural causes to me, and the local doctor said it was a heart attack. But one of Hugon's lawyer clients was trying to find some research Hugon was supposed to have finished and found his recent files had all disappeared. So he called the *préfecture,* and they sent detectives. Hugon should have been buried today, but it looks like they're doing an autopsy. His wife is very upset. She was the one who found his body."

"That's understandable." Sylvestre had shown no reaction that Bruno could discern.

"As soon as I've seen the Police Nationale, I'll talk to the mayor and get him to talk to Oudinot and recommend the deal," Bruno said. "We'll try to get this wrapped up quickly. What number can I call you on?"

Sylvestre pulled out his wallet and gave

Bruno a business card with his e-mail address and various phone numbers.

"By the way," Bruno said as he turned to leave. "How's your search for that Bugatti going, the one you and Martine were talking about?"

Sylvestre shrugged. "Nothing new to report, but thanks for coming by and for bringing your basset hound. He's the kind of dog that makes me smile."

17

Bruno checked his watch and headed for Pamela's riding stables. He'd have to take Hector out early if he were to be back in time to prepare dinner. But he also wanted to have a word with Félix. After he pulled in, Balzac went off to paw at Hector's stable door while Bruno went in search of Pamela. She was in the office, looking tired but going through her accounts.

"The good news is that we're no longer operating at a loss," she said, looking up at him cheerfully. "The bad news is that it's only because Miranda and I aren't taking any wages out of the school yet. But in terms of utility bills, taxes, fodder and running costs, our heads are above water. One bad vet's bill, however, and we drown."

"You've only just started, and you haven't started renting the *gîtes* yet," Bruno replied. "They'll provide a good income next summer."

"Yes, but in the meantime we have to pay money to get them repainted, repaired and have the plumbing fixed. Sometimes I wonder why I ever let myself in for this."

"You enjoy the challenge and you're good at it," Bruno said. "How's Félix doing? Is he still turning up on time?"

"Every day, and he's doing well. He's out with Miranda now, helping her escort the pony trekkers. I thought it was time to put him on horseback, and they're only walking along. He's on the Andalusian; she seems to like him. She also seems to like Hector; it's a pity he's a gelding. That might have saved me the stud fees we'll have to pay to get her with foal."

"If Félix is not back soon, can I ask you to give him this with my compliments?" He handed her the printout he'd made of the photo of the lost Bugatti that Young had sent him. "Tell him it's a gift for his wall collection."

"You might find it fighting for space. He found a set of very out-of-date *Cheval Magazines* in a stable loft and asked if he could take some home to put the pictures up in his room. I got the impression that the cars were now taking second place. It's a bit like you, Bruno. Once you got close to horses and began to enjoy them, you wondered where they'd been all your life."

"Thanks to you," he said. "I hope the boy gets as much pleasure from horses as they've given me."

"I know he's been in trouble, but he's a sweet boy, Bruno. The horses like having him around, and so do Miranda and I. He's even started having an afternoon cup of tea with us when he gets here from school."

Ah, the British, thought Bruno, smiling to himself. It's just as we were taught in school: they believe everything can be resolved with a nice, hot cup of tea.

"I'm happy to hear that he's doing well, and I'm grateful you've taken him on," he said. "I understand you can't pay him yet, but could he be useful in the long term? I mean, maybe you could get him to paint the *gîtes* and do some maintenance? I think his dad might be ready to do some odd jobs like that, and it would be good for them to work together."

"Let's wait and see. In the meantime, I've had a couple of phone calls about your new romantic interest. I'm told she's called Martine, is that right? Daughter of a local family who's briefly back from a high-powered career in the big city?"

"I only had an after-dinner drink with her at Ivan's last night," he said. "You know how people talk."

"Passionate embraces in the rain is what I heard," she said, arching an eyebrow and giving him one of those ominously cool smiles that she did so well. "That sounds rather serious. And now you're blushing."

"A good-night kiss in the rain is hardly a passionate embrace," he said, irritated with himself as so often before that he could never control his blushes. "I'm a bit pressed for time, so I'd better take Hector out before I have to go and see J-J about a case he's on. Fabiola probably told you there's an investigation into Hugon's death."

"She said there would be an autopsy, but you know how discreet she is about her work. But if you're pressed for time, I'll take Hector out with the others when Miranda gets back. I always enjoy riding him."

"Thanks so much for that. See you tomorrow." He blew her a kiss and was about to drive back toward town when her mobile rang. Her face went grave as she listened, and she put out a hand to keep him close.

"Bruno's standing right here beside me," she said, after a while in English. "Hold on while I brief him."

"It's Miranda," she said, reverting to French for Bruno's sake. "One of the girls has fallen off her horse and been injured. It could be serious. Some boy was throwing stones at the horses, and one of them hit Denise in the eye. There's a lot of blood, and the other girls are panicking. Miranda fears the girl could lose her eye."

"Find out where Miranda is exactly and tell her I'll get there as soon as I can," he replied. "In the meantime I'll call the *urgences.*" He pulled out his phone and punched in his speed-dial number for the *pompiers.*

When Pamela gave Miranda's location, Bruno knew the *pompiers* could never get there in a vehicle. It was at a ford across a small stream, deep in the woods behind Audrix. He told Albert, the chief fireman, to get to a hunter's cabin known as La Mique, after a local specialty, a dumpling that one of the hunters always made there. From there the *pompiers* would have to proceed on foot with a stretcher, following the trail to St. Chamassy.

"I'll take a horse, it will be faster," he told Pamela. "Is Hector saddled?"

"No, but my Primrose is, I was about to take her out. I can exercise Hector for you later."

"You stay here and start phoning," he said as they strode toward Primrose's stall. "Alert Fabiola and then call the injured

272

girl's parents and tell them to meet us at the clinic. Then you'd better call the other girls' parents and reassure them. Does Miranda know who this boy was?"

"I didn't ask."

"No matter," he said, swinging himself into the saddle. "I'll find out. I'll leave Balzac with you."

Bruno set off at a trot and then into a canter. Both he and the horse knew these trails, and they were mostly too narrow and tangled for any faster pace. He picked up his pace when they came to a firebreak in the woods, Primrose seeming to understand the need for urgency, but then they had to slow again as he descended the narrow trail that led to the stream and then walked the horse upstream to the ford where he found the girls. La Mique was another three or four hundred meters down the path.

"Thank God you're here," said Miranda. She was sitting on the bank, the injured girl on her lap. Someone had tied a rough and bloodstained bandage around the girl's head, but the rest of her face was as white as snow and she was shivering.

The other girls were huddled together on the bank, watching and silent. One of them was crying, and Félix was trying to comfort her. He was wearing an old shirt from which the sleeve was missing. That had probably been the source of the makeshift bandage, Bruno thought. Someone, probably the boy, had sensibly looped the horses' reins together and tied them to a branch.

"Bruno's here," one of the girls shouted, and the injured one moved her head when she heard it. Bruno went across and knelt beside her, recognizing her from his tennis classes. She was ten years old, the daughter of one of the bank managers in St. Denis.

"Hello, Denise, everything is going to be fine," he said, taking her hand and leaning down to kiss the part of her brow that wasn't covered by the bandage. Her clothes were soaked from the stream and from her own blood. Head wounds always bled badly, he remembered. He took off his jacket to cover her and give her some warmth, noting that Félix's old denim jacket was already covering her chest. "And you're being very brave, Denise. The *pompiers* are on their way, and Dr. Stern is waiting at the clinic to fix you up, and your parents will be there, too. Just lie still in Miranda's arms, and you'll be fine. I need to learn what happened, but if you want me, just call, okay?" He felt her hand squeeze his by way of answer.

"It was a big boy, a young man, waiting in

the trees until we were mostly across the stream, and then he came out and started throwing stones," Miranda said. "Denise was last in line, just ahead of Félix. He's been great, taking care of the horses and calming the other girls down and then tearing his shirt for the bandage. And he tied up the horses without being told. I don't know what we'd have done without him."

"Will you know the young man again?" Bruno asked.

"Certainly, I'd know him anywhere."

"How many stones did he throw?"

"Three," came Félix's voice. "The first one missed, the second one hit me, and the third one hit Denise. I know who it was, and I think he was aiming at me."

"Tristan?" Bruno asked, and Félix nodded. Some of the other girls confirmed it. Tristan was well known among the schoolchildren.

"Where were you hit?" Bruno asked the boy.

"Here." He pointed to his thigh. "I'm going to have a big bruise. It's lucky, really. If it had hit the horse, she might have shied, and I'd have come off into the stream like Denise did. She screamed as she hit the water. Besides that wound, I think she hurt her shoulder badly when she fell."

"You've done very well, Félix," Bruno said, clapping him on the shoulder. "I'm proud of you, and I'll make sure Pamela and your parents know what a fine job you did here. Do you know the way back to the riding school from here? Pamela is waiting there, and we've asked the parents of these other girls to meet them there."

The boy nodded again, then said, "Yes, Bruno, I know the way."

"And do you think you could lead the rest of the girls back to the riding school while I wait here with Denise for the *pompiers*?"

"If you take over Denise, I can lead them back," said Miranda before Félix could answer. "We really need Félix to bring up the rear just in case any of the girls fall behind. But I need to get the rest of these girls home. Their parents will be waiting and going frantic. I doubt if they'll want their daughters to come out riding again and we've got that damn mortgage to pay. Oh, God, why did this have to happen?"

Bruno put his hand on her shoulder to calm her. "Denise is what's important now." He knelt down to talk to the girl.

"Will you be okay waiting here with me while Miranda takes the other girls home?" he asked, and heard a faint "Yes." Gently he took her from Miranda, and as he enfolded

276

her in his arms he saw that one shoulder was hanging low. It looked like she'd broken her collarbone in the fall. Bruno's face set hard as he thought of what this meant. Tristan was sixteen, old enough to be judged as an adult.

When Miranda had the remaining girls in their saddles, Bruno asked her to take Primrose back on a leading rein. He'd travel with Denise to the clinic. Shortly after the others had gone, Félix turning in the saddle from his post at the rear to wave a good-bye, Bruno heard noises from the under-growth at the far side of the stream, and Ahmed and Alain appeared carrying a folded stretcher. Ahmed had done the paramedic course required for the *urgences* service, and after splashing and stumbling through the ford he quickly examined Denise.

"The bleeding's stopped," he said. "Who-ever applied that bandage did a good job. But her collarbone is broken." He took off his shoulder bag and found a sling and long bandage that he used to strap Denise's arm in place. They strapped Denise into the stretcher for the hike back to the ambulance and the fast drive to the clinic. Bruno was able to put his jacket back on, still slightly damp and with some smears of blood on the collar. From inside the vehicle, Bruno could hear the siren howling, and he had to brace himself as Alain made fast turns. It reminded him of driving with Annette. Then they were at the clinic, Alain pushing his way through a small crowd gathered on the steps so Bruno and Ahmed could get the girl inside and into Fabiola's examining room. She was waiting there with Denise's parents. She had changed from her usual white coat into scrubs and operating gloves, her hair tucked into a skullcap and a surgical mask hanging around her neck. Bruno had been aware of a camera flashing as they carried Denise in. That meant Philippe was taking pictures for the paper. This was getting more and more serious for Tristan.

"Don't go yet," Fabiola said to Ahmed as they put Denise down. "You may have to drive her to the hospital in Périgueux. But let's get her out of those wet clothes and take a look."

Denise's mother fought back tears as she bent down to kiss her child and take her hand. Her father wrung Ahmed and Bruno by the hand with a muttered "Thanks," and Bruno told him the one to thank would be young Félix.

Fabiola cut the girl's clothes off with scissors, strapped her arm back into place and wrapped her in blankets. Then she removed the bandage and wiped Denise's face and neck and shoulder clean of blood, though more of it had clotted in Denise's hair. "I don't think it's as bad as it looks," Fabiola said, for the parents' benefit as much as for Denise. "The main cut seems to be in the eyebrow, and there's a tough bone there that took some of the force. The cheekbone is also cut but not as deeply. It's strange that there is no mark on the brow."

"She was wearing a riding helmet," said Bruno, remembering seeing it on the bank beside Miranda. "They must have taken it off to apply the bandage."

Fabiola took a small flashlight from the cabinet at her side, gently opened the swollen eye and shone the light inside.

"The flesh around the eye is bruised and scratched, but the cuts aren't too deep," she said after a careful examination. "The pupil is reacting to the light but not as normally as I would like, and I think she's got a concussion. Do you know if she lost consciousness?"

"No, but we can ask Miranda or Félix," Bruno said.

"Do you remember everything that happened, Denise?" Fabiola asked.

"I remember a pain and falling and being

in Miranda's arms and then Bruno came," the girl said, sounding sleepy.

"Good girl," Fabiola said and continued her examination. Finally she looked up at Denise's parents. "I can't be sure and I'm hoping there's no damage to the eyeball, but I'm worried about a possible detached retina. I don't think her sight will be affected, but I'd like to be sure, so the ambulance will take her to Périgueux, and I'll arrange for an eye specialist to be waiting. Depending on what he says, we may have to send her on to Bordeaux. In the meantime I'd better give Denise a local anesthetic and stitch that cut on the eyebrow and then make sure the collarbone is properly set."

Bruno excused himself, and seeing that the hall outside was full, he let himself into Fabiola's surgery to make some calls. The first was to Yveline, to brief her and ask her to meet him at the supermarket where Tristan's father worked before heading to Tristan's home. Then he alerted Annette, as the magistrate in charge of prosecuting juveniles. Bruno was determined to leave nothing to chance. He rang social services in Périgueux, but as soon as they heard Tristan was over sixteen, they said it was no longer a matter for them. Then he went outside to find Philippe, who was on the phone to one of the other girls' parents who was at Pamela's riding school, just having been reunited with his daughter.

"You're sure the youngster throwing the stones was Tristan, the son of the guy at the supermarket?" Philippe was saying into the phone, his eyes on Bruno. "Your daughter is certain of it, and the other girls say the same? Can I quote you on that?" He listened for a moment, nodded and then closed the phone and asked Bruno, "You going to arrest the little bastard?"

Bruno nodded and said, "But there's something else, a good part to this nasty story. The hero of the hour was Félix. Apparently the stones were aimed at him, and one of them hit him. Tristan has been bullying him for years. But when Denise was hit and fell into the stream, Félix took charge." He described what Félix had done and told Philippe he could find the boy at the riding school. "St. Denis should be proud of a youngster like that, who kept his head, bandaged Denise and did all the right things. You can quote me on it."

"I can't use Tristan's name; he's a juvenile."

"Not anymore, he isn't," said Bruno, walking away. "He's turned sixteen."

By the time Bruno reached the supermarket, Yveline was just pulling into the parking lot in a gendarmerie van. As they mounted the stairs to Simon's office, Bruno told her Denise was being taken to an eye specialist in Périgueux. He wanted Yveline to make the arrest. Bruno was not under the same pressure as the gendarmes to meet arrest quotas. They strode together into Simon's office without knocking.

"I'm here only as a courtesy to you, Simon, since your son is now officially old enough to be arrested as an adult," Bruno began. "His bullying has gotten out of hand. He was throwing stones at Félix this afternoon, and one of Tristan's stones hit a ten-year-old girl in the eye, and she may lose it."

Startled and rising to his feet, Simon began to interrupt.

"Shut your mouth and just listen," Bruno snapped. "The girl's on her way to an eye specialist in Périgueux right now. And I'm going to your house with the gendarmes to arrest your boy on a charge of aggravated bodily harm. It's aggravated because that's what the law says if a weapon or a missile is used. And I think I should warn you that Tristan very probably faces a custodial sentence in a youth detention center. You may follow us to your home if you want and

282

arrange for a lawyer."

"But don't use your phone to do so while driving or I'll arrest you for that," said Yveline. "And on no account call your home or your son or try borrowing anybody else's phone to do so. I'll be checking your phone records to make sure of that."

They turned and marched out, leaving Simon to scramble from behind his desk to follow them, firing off questions. Were they absolutely certain it was Tristan? Who were the witnesses? Wasn't the boy still a juvenile? Had he not been provoked by Félix? Was it not some form of accident, perhaps a silly prank that had gone wrong?

Bruno and Yveline ignored the questions. As they got to her van, Bruno saw Simon fishing his own car keys from a pocket and heading for his car. Bruno suddenly became angry, thinking that there was one important question Simon had not bothered to ask.

"You haven't asked the name of the little girl who was the victim," he shouted. "She's Denise, the daughter of Paul-Michel, the bank manager. I imagine that as soon as he stops sitting vigil outside the operating room he'll call his lawyer. You might want to prepare for a lawsuit, and also for some questions from the press. Philippe Delaron was at the clinic when I brought Denise in, her face covered in her own blood."

As Yveline drove onto the Limeuil road, where Simon had one of the expensive houses overlooking the valley, Bruno adjusted the rearview mirror to see Simon following behind in his Mercedes, both hands on the wheel but his mouth opening as if he were talking. Of course he'd have a hands-free phone in his car! He should have thought of that. Bruno told Yveline to be sure to check whom Simon had been calling.

Simon lived in a modern house designed to look like a traditional Périgord building, but the tiles and the color of the stone were wrong and the garden contained some unusual decorations, including a fountain disguised as a miniature stone windmill and an old bicycle that had been deliberately overgrown with plants. The shutters were painted a bright blue that might have been more suitable in St. Tropez, and the flower beds looked as if they had been planted by a drill sergeant with an obsession for absolute symmetry. Yveline rolled her eyes at Bruno as they rang the doorbell and heard it chime the opening notes of "The Marseillaise."

"Bonjour, Bruno," said Amandine, Simon's wife, looking startled to see him with

Yveline and holding up her hands in a way that Bruno knew meant she was letting her nail polish dry. Then she saw her husband's car drawing up behind the gendarmes' van. "What's this about?"

"We need to see Tristan. Is he in?" Bruno asked.

"Yes, he's upstairs in his room. Why?"

"We need to question him about an assault on a little girl this afternoon," said Yveline, trying to move past Amandine who had taken a startled step backward, her jaw dropping, but trying to stop Yveline from entering.

"It's Denise, the bank manager's daughter, and she might lose an eye," said Bruno, trying to distract Amandine long enough for Yveline to get past her bulk. "Several witnesses have identified Tristan as the boy who threw the stone that hurt her."

Amandine's mouth opened and closed, but she stayed immobile and then shouted, "Simon, stop them."

"Madame," said Yveline coldly, "either you let me past or, as well as your son, I'll have no choice but to arrest you for obstructing the police in the course of their duty."

"It's not true, Tristan was with me here all afternoon," Amandine said, grudgingly allowing Yveline to pass. "He's not well, he's delicate . . ."

"That's fine, Amandine," said Bruno. "If you say he was with you all afternoon and hasn't left the house, we'll just take your statement to that effect. Why not show me where I can sit down to take your statement?"

"Don't say a word, Amandine," Simon called from over Bruno's shoulder. "I've got a lawyer coming, and he said none of us should say a word until he arrives."

"Don't be a fool, spending good money on lawyers when I can clear this up right now," she told her husband, throwing him a contemptuous look. "Follow me into the kitchen, Bruno."

By the time he heard footsteps coming down the stairs, Bruno had Amandine's brief statement, signed and made official by the stamp Bruno kept in his shoulder case with other forms, evidence bags and gloves, dog biscuits and carrots for the horses, along with keys to the various municipal buildings. Her statement included the key phrase that it had been made "freely and voluntarily and under pain of perjury."

Yveline pushed Tristan into the room, looking stunned as he stared down at his hands handcuffed before him. A pair of earphones that looked familiar to Bruno were still hanging from the mobile phone tucked into the breast pocket of his shirt. Some tinny music was still playing. Bruno donned a pair of evidence gloves, plucked out the phone and put it in an evidence bag with the earphones.

"Madame Vaudon has just given me a statement asserting that her son was with her in the house all afternoon," he told Yveline, keeping a straight face. "Tristan's phone should therefore bear out what she says. If not, she's in trouble for making a false statement."

"He's under arrest anyway, even without the assault charge," said Yveline, holding up an evidence bag with a half-filled plastic bag inside it. "Almost half a kilo of marijuana. Were you aware, madame, that your son used illegal drugs?"

Amandine rose to move to her son, and Yveline said firmly "Stand back" and then "Stand aside, monsieur," as Simon hovered helplessly in the doorway. She pushed the boy out, Bruno following behind, and heard Amandine berating her husband as "an utterly useless apology for a man."

At the front door, Bruno turned and said, "Your son will be at the gendarmerie until the magistrate comes to press charges. Your lawyer is free to join us there, but it would be a good idea to telephone the gendarmerie first and see when the magistrate will be available. Thank you for your cooperation, and, Simon, you might want to make your peace with Denise's parents while you can."

Sitting in the backseat with a white-faced Tristan while Yveline drove, Bruno pulled out his phone to call Pamela. He needed his van and Balzac, and he still had to collect the *écrevisses* from the baron before Martine arrived for dinner.

18

As he left the baron's place with his bag of crayfish, Balzac sitting up beside him, Bruno pulled off the road to answer his phone. He always did that now, ever since being called to a fatal road accident that had been caused by a woman texting as she drove. The screen told him the call was from J-J.

"The forensics guys have everything they need from the house, but Yves is still trying to get into Hugon's computer," J-J said. "And there's no word yet on the autopsy from the lab in Bordeaux, so we're heading home. There's just one thing: one of my detectives who was watching the rally on Sunday and saw Freddy win swears it was Freddy he saw on the station platform in Le Buisson yesterday evening getting on the train for Agen. But you said you'd heard from Isabelle that he was having dinner in Sarlat."

"Not quite," Bruno replied. "She said his phone was at a fixed location in Sarlat."

"Maybe he's playing games with his phones, leaving the one we know about in one place while he goes off to do business elsewhere, probably with a phone we don't know about. I've assigned someone to check the surveillance cameras at the station in Agen, but if he's being careful about surveillance, they aren't difficult to avoid."

"Have you heard anything from Isabelle about when we should expect her?" Bruno asked.

"No, she must still be held up by paperwork. You wouldn't believe the number of forms I've had to fill in, defining the limits of the surveillance we're supposed to mount. I've still got to get a magistrate to countersign them and witness my guarantee to destroy any film or tapes not needed in court."

Bruno felt a twinge of alarm as J-J ended the call. He'd filled out no forms and asked no permission for his own amateurish attempts to keep watch on the two targets. Perhaps he'd better keep that knowledge to himself or even dismantle his cameras. He'd have to change the batteries by the next evening, he told himself, even if he took the risk of leaving them in place. But perhaps

Isabelle and her team would have arrived by then.

He raced home, stopping only to buy bread just before the bakery closed. He had thirty minutes at the most before Martine was supposed to arrive. That left him no time to shower if he was going to pick some fresh lettuce and feed Balzac and his chickens.

He dealt with the animals first, then picked the lettuce and put another log into the wood-burning stove. He checked that he'd put the vodka into the freezer. He always kept a couple of bottles of white wine and champagne in the fridge. He knew that he didn't have the two hours he needed for the dough to rise to make proper blinis to go with the caviar, so he'd have to offer toast instead. But then he remembered how Pascal at the food show had made what he'd called his instant blinis using egg whites. It was not the best time for an experiment with a new dish, he thought, but what the hell? Bruno washed his hands and face, ran his wet fingers through his hair and then gargled quickly with mouthwash to wash away the taste of the day.

In the kitchen, he began making the court bouillon for the crayfish, pouring into a large saucepan half a bottle of Thomas's

291

Riesling with the same amount of water. He peeled four shallots and sliced them thin and did the same with two carrots. He diced three stalks of celery and a thin leek and put all the vegetables into the saucepan with a couple of chopped cloves of garlic, one whole clove and some coriander and fennel seeds. He ground in some salt and pepper and then took a small *piment d'espelette,* the red pepper grown in the Basque country, from the bunch that hung from the beam in his kitchen, and added it to the broth as it heated. He looked at his vegetable basket, where he kept apples mixed with the potatoes to stop them from sprouting. No, potatoes would make the meal too heavy. Perhaps rice? No, he'd serve it just with the vegetables in the bouillon.

He opened the jar of caviar and put it on the table with a tiny silver coffee spoon for each of them. He'd found them in a *vide-greniers,* one of the town's regular jumble sales where people emptied their attics of stuff they no longer needed. Now for the blinis. He measured a hundred grams of buckwheat flour into a bowl, mixed in a little salt and pepper and made a well in the center of the flour. He took an egg from the bowl by the stove and was about to crack it and separate the white from the yolk when he heard the sound of a car coming up the road and turning into his driveway. Balzac was already at the door, bounding out as soon as Bruno opened it to investigate the new arrival.

Balzac liked new people, and he liked women, so he was squeaking with excitement when he reached Martine's car just as she opened the door. Bruno thought for a moment Balzac was going to leap into the car, but instead the dog put his front paws onto the sill of the car door and gave her a happy bark of greeting and an amiable sniff at her black jeans as she swung her long legs from the car and stood up. Bruno came forward to give her the *bise* on each cheek, but she kissed him firmly on the lips and then bent to caress Balzac. She was wearing a T-shirt of black silk beneath a short tweed jacket of dark blue, white and black checks that had been nipped in tightly at the waist. It had been beautifully cut to work as casual clothing or something more formal. It was somehow businesslike and playful at the same time and made Bruno regret that with the pressure of time he had decided against changing.

"Horses, basset hounds, country dinners and a man in uniform — are there no limits to the props you use to seduce a woman,

Bruno?"

He looked down at his uniform, suddenly realizing he had not cleaned Denise's blood from his collar.

"I'm sorry, I just got back. It was one of those days, dramas, injuries, arrests . . ."

"Not that awful attack on the little girl that was on the radio just now?"

"Yes, that was part of it. But when I had to choose between starting the dinner and having a shower and changing my clothes, the dinner won."

"A true Périgourdin in your priorities, and quite right, too," she said. Suddenly her eyes widened in surprise. "Is that blood on the collar of your jacket? You should soak it in cold water right away." She handed him the bottle she had brought.

"I asked Claire what wine you liked, and she checked with Ivan who said your favorite was Château de Tiregand. But that's what my dad usually serves when I come home, so I thought I'd bring you something different that I came across when I was skiing in Gstaad. I was amazed to see a Bergerac wine, this one, Château Monestier La Tour. I loved it."

From the look in her eye and the way she was speaking quickly, Bruno realized that Martine was probably just as nervous as he about the evening ahead and where it might lead. They were in that enticing but dangerous moment when each of them knew that all was possible between them but feared that a single false step could send the edifice of fantasy they were constructing tumbling down into embarrassment and disappointment.

"What a generous and inventive thought," he said. It was a wine he recalled drinking years ago and not being overly impressed. But he'd heard that the vineyard had come under new ownership, and its wines were now spoken of with deep respect by people whose judgment he trusted. "I always think a wine is better when it comes with a little story attached like that. So now I'll always think of you in the Alps, swooping downhill and dancing with the mountain whenever I see this wine."

She took his arm companionably and asked him to show her his garden. He pointed out the white oaks where his truffles were growing underground, introduced her to Napoléon and Joséphine, his two geese, and to Blanco the cockerel.

"Named for the rugby player," she said, rising even higher in his esteem when she recognized the name. She cast the experienced eye of a country girl over his vegetable garden, noting the well and nodding in approval at the three compost heaps, each at a different stage of fermentation.

"Are those woods yours?" she asked.

"All the way up to the ridge. That's where I get my mushrooms, and there are a couple of spots where I can usually count on truffles. The meadow down below is mine as far as that lower hedge. The stream on the right is the boundary."

"Does your well work?"

"Yes, I used to depend on it for water and still use it in summer for the garden. It's good to drink; somehow it tastes better than the stuff from the water tower. We'll be drinking it tonight with our meal."

"Where do you keep your horse? Is there a barn behind the house?"

"Hector stays at a friend's house to keep her horse company, and so she can take him out for exercise when I'm tied up with police work. I do the same for her when she's busy. It's Fabiola, Dr. Stern, at the clinic." After a moment he thought it politic to add, "She and her boyfriend, Gilles, are good friends of mine."

"Now tell me what you're planning for us to eat."

"*Écrevisses à la nage,* the crayfish caught by a friend this morning about three kilometers from here," he said. "So we're drinking white wine."

"Lovely, I haven't had those for ages." Martine squeezed his arm in glee. "Mandy says you're known in St. Denis as a good cook."

"I wish I could cook Asian food like she does," he said. "Before the *écrevisses* there's champagne and then some vodka to go with the caviar and the blinis that I'm making, and as soon as Balzac comes back from his security patrol of the chicken run we'll go into the kitchen and I'll cook. Meanwhile, I hope you appreciate this sunset I've arranged for you."

"It will last another few minutes. Why not go and put your jacket in cold water and come back with some champagne. Meanwhile I'll enjoy your view."

"It's hardly as good as the view from your folks' house, with the valley and the river."

"That's why I like it, all these ridges, one after the other, and not another house in sight," she said, almost dreamily, as Bruno left. He put his jacket in to soak and donned a black leather jacket over his uniform shirt. Fetching the glasses of champagne, he cast an eye on the court bouillon, which was just about to start simmering. He turned down the gas and added another splash of Riesling. Back on the terrace he and Martine toasted each other, and then Balzac returned, perhaps at hearing the familiar sound of glasses being clinked. She took his hand as they strolled back into the house, and he showed her the sitting room with its dining table set for two and the wood crackling warmly in the stove. He took off his jacket and draped it over the back of a chair.

She did the same, looking briefly around and noticing the absence of a TV before glancing at his collection of CDs. She picked out Francis Cabrel's *Hors-Saison* and said, "I remember falling in love to that song when I was twenty. I'm in a mood to hear the album again, but softly."

In the kitchen, she perched on the high stool at the counter, topped up their champagne glasses from the half bottle he'd opened and then poured herself a glass of his water from the well. She sipped at it, considering, and then said she liked it. She watched as he washed his hands again before going back to the blinis. He cracked the egg he'd put aside when she arrived and poured the contents back and forth over the bowl to separate the white from the yolk. He put the yolk into the flour, added a wineglass of milk and began whisking, pausing only to add, little by little, a second wineglass of milk, some chives and then a tablespoon of butter. When the mixture was well mixed, he began to whisk the egg white until it began to stiffen, then folded it into the batter and put the gas on high under a frying pan he greased lightly with butter.

"One of the few times I don't use duck fat," he said. "This isn't the proper way to make blinis, but I didn't have time for the yeast to rise. I hope this works well enough."

He put a tablespoon into the batter, filled it and poured it into the pan. He did this four times. As the batter spread out and began to sizzle, he reached into the fridge, pulled out a bottle of the cuvée Quercus, opened it and put it in an ice bucket. After a couple of minutes, he used a spatula to turn the blinis over and took the vodka from the freezer.

"How hungry are you?" he asked.

"Two blinis will do for me. Are you serving them with crème fraîche, or do you have some other devious recipe?"

He flipped the blinis one more time, took the bowl of crème fraîche from the fridge and showed it to her and then put the blinis onto a warmed plate with a knob of butter. He then poured the *écrevisses* into the simmering bouillon and invited Martine to the dining room. She brought the vodka, so frozen that it poured sluggishly into their small glasses, and then she divided the caviar into two portions. She spread some cream onto her first blini, covered it thickly with caviar, ate, and her eyes widened.

"That's good," she said, and finished the blini before raising her vodka glass and draining half of it. *"Naz dorovya,"* she said, or that was how it sounded to Bruno. "I think that's what Russians say. There were a lot of them in Gstaad this year, and they seemed to say it all the time when they drank. Another blini for you, too?"

"Yes, please. I can make more if you change your mind," he said, thinking a fashionable ski resort like Gstaad was way out of his financial league. Martine's business probably made her a wealthy young woman, he assumed, remembering the amount of money she seemed to assume was customary for the work she did.

"Where did you get the caviar?" she asked. "Is it Russian?"

"No, it's French, from around here. Now that we have sturgeon in the river again, a friend of mine has started a business. We used to get Russian caviar sometimes when I was stationed in Bosnia with the UN, though I can't imagine how the quartermasters got hold of it. Our Dordogne caviar tastes as I remember it."

"This tastes as good to me as any I've eaten. If our electric-car rally comes off, we can proudly serve our homegrown caviar to the winners. *Vive la France!*" She finished her second blini and downed the rest of her vodka. "And now do we go back to the kitchen to watch the master at work again?"

"No, we go back to watch me fumble to peel the *écrevisses* and get the veins out and then we wait for them to cool a little as we enjoy the white wine and toss the salad."

"You don't peel them before you put them in the bouillon?" she asked.

"I find it easier this way, and it helps me get the tails out without tearing the flesh. Getting my fingers a bit burned seems a modest price to pay."

"Somebody once said that laziness is the origin of genius because smart people look for easier ways of doing things."

He smiled. "I don't think I'm that smart to begin with." And then stopped as he heard the opening notes of the title song on that album. "Here's the song you fell in love to."

"I remember the song better than I remember the guy," she said. "I had a lot of growing up to do."

301

"We always do," he said. "Malraux in his *Antimémoires* says he asked an old priest what he'd learned after a lifetime of hearing confessions. And the priest thought for a moment and then said, 'There are no grown-ups.'"

"Thank heavens for that," she said, smiling, taking his hand and giving Bruno that dangerous feeling that their eyes were saying much more than their mouths. "Time for the *écrevisses*?"

He nodded, took the empty plates and returned to the kitchen, opened the white wine and poured each of them a glass before fishing out the crayfish. He filled a bowl with iced water from the fridge and took a set of evidence gloves from his bag and donned them before twisting off the heads and squeezing out the flesh from the tails and taking out the long veins. Between each one, he dipped his fingers into the iced water to cool them.

"The ice water is a clever trick; the laziness of genius again," she said. "This wine is terrific, and this is the best evening I've had for quite a while."

"I'm glad," he said, putting the crayfish back into the bouillon and turning off the gas before turning to look at her. "I feel the same."

"What now?" she asked, her eyes teasing.

"Now we wait until the bouillon cools to the point at which we want to eat," he said, peeling off the gloves and taking a sip from his wine.

"In that case . . ." She eased herself from the stool and came around to stand close to him and began to unbutton his shirt. She dipped a finger into the bowl of iced water and left it there while looking into his eyes. Then she brought up her chilled finger, rested it lightly against his bared nipple and leaned forward to kiss him as he shivered from the sensation. Her tongue teased at his lips, and she murmured, "You haven't yet shown me your bedroom."

Later, in front of the stove in the sitting room, Balzac was dozing with his head on Bruno's thigh as Martine caressed the dog's silky long ears. She was wearing Bruno's white terry-cloth robe, and he had slipped on a rugby shirt and the trousers of a tracksuit. The emptied bowls of crayfish and salad plates were beside them on the floor. She had declined the zabaglione, insisting she'd eaten too much already. Now she put down her wineglass, looked at him fondly and said, "I'd like to stay, but my mother will be wondering where I am."

"I'd like you to stay, too, but I understand. Can we meet again tomorrow?"

"Will you let me do the cooking?"

He laughed. "You mean the meal was as bad as that?"

She gave him a gentle slap on the thigh. "No, don't be silly. It was perfect. But I'd like to cook for you, and you seem to have everything I might need in your kitchen. Can you get away a bit earlier tomorrow to give us some more time together?"

"I'll try. Coffee before you go?"

"That would be great. You can make it while I dress."

Bruno put the kettle on as she went back to his bathroom. He spooned coffee grounds into his *cafetière,* readied the cups and sugar and then glanced at his phone, which was giving the gentle beep that said he had text messages waiting. The first one was from Fabiola, to say that the specialist had diagnosed Denise with a slightly torn retina, relatively easy to repair, and she would stay in the hospital in Périgueux.

The second was from Yveline, telling him that Tristan had been released into the custody of his parents but would be charged with aggravated assault and illegal possession of cannabis tomorrow at the *procureur*'s office in Sarlat.

The third was from Isabelle, and read: "Paperwork fixed. Arrive this evening. Propose to drop by for briefing unless inconvenient."

He typed back "Not tonight. Breakfast at Fauquet's café at 8 tomorrow," and was just clicking send when he heard a car coming up the road and then saw the glare of headlights turning as it headed for his driveway.

The car stopped, its headlights illuminating Martine's vehicle. Then it reversed back down the driveway and turned to head off toward the road. It must have been Isabelle, realizing when she saw the other car that he was not alone. She had no right to expect that he would be, he told himself, but felt embarrassed just the same. She would probably tease him tomorrow about having a new friend, but there would be an edge to it.

The kettle was boiling. He closed the phone and made the coffee, letting it rest before he pushed down the plunger. He went into the living room to clear away the bowls, plates and glasses, and then Martine was back fully dressed and looking terrific, eyes shining, skin glowing.

"Did I hear a car?" she asked.

"Probably someone who took a wrong

turn. But there's good news from the hospital. That little girl, Denise, her sight will be fine, though they'll keep her in for a few more days. I'll try to get to Périgueux to visit her. Maybe you'd like to come, too, and we can have dinner there."

"Sure, but not tomorrow, that's my evening to cook for you." She leaned forward and kissed him. "The cold water has got the blood out of your jacket. I hung it up to dry, but it will still need cleaning."

She looked at her watch, drank her coffee quickly and said, "Do you think I'll pass my mother's inspection, or will she detect that I've been disporting myself with a louche bachelor all evening?"

I don't know, he thought, since I never had a mother. But he said, "You can complain about the boring local official you had to dine with while persuading him to support your plan for the rally."

"The one who told me that his wife didn't understand him just before he made a clumsy pass at me over the dessert," she countered. "Bad breath, overweight and with hairs growing out of his nose."

"That's the one, but don't pile it on too thick."

She came into his arms and kissed him good night, then bent to stroke Balzac. At the door she stopped, turned toward him and said, "I'm glad about that little girl, Bruno, and thank you for a wonderful evening. Your food more than lived up to my expectations, and so did you. I'll look forward to tomorrow, at about six, unless you call me."

"About six should be fine," he said. "We can walk Balzac together before dinner."

He stood at the doorway to watch the tail-lights of her car disappear, knowing himself to be a very lucky man but wondering how long it would last and how much time they might have to deepen the relationship before her work took her away again. Independent and wealthy, she had her own business to run in London; he could see her coming back to the Périgord only for visits even if the rally project worked out. And even then she'd feel obliged to stay with her parents. He sighed, thinking that his love life seemed to run in a predictable but ultimately unsatisfying pattern, driven by his attraction for women who were determined to forge their own lives without the conventional constraints of a family and children. He shook his head and went back indoors to slip on some shoes and a jacket and take Balzac out for the last stroll of the night.

19

Refreshed by his morning ride on Hector, Bruno entered the café a few minutes before eight and glanced at Fauquet's copy of *Sud Ouest* as the owner put a still-warm croissant on his plate and began making his espresso. Bruno shook hands with the regulars and explained that he was meeting someone and took his croissant and the paper to a table by the window. Some new horror in the Middle East took up most of the front page, but there was a small headline saying "Horseback Girl Blinded in St. Denis?" Below it was a passport-sized photo of Denise's bloodstained and bandaged face that steered him to an inside page, where he found a much-bigger photo of Tristan in rugby clothes, probably blown up from a team photo, with the caption "Teen vandal arrested." A smaller photo of Félix had the caption "Young hero saves the day — Police."

"Specialist eye doctors in Périgueux were battling last night to save the sight of a ten-year-old girl from St. Denis as a local schoolboy rugby star was arrested for throwing the stone that may blind her," the story began. It must have been printed before the good news came from the hospital. Farther down the page there was Bruno's official police photo. He was quoted as saying the town should be proud of Félix. Tristan's lawyer was quoted as saying he would appeal to the public prosecutor for his client, just a few weeks beyond his sixteenth birthday, to be treated as a juvenile for "a foolish schoolboy prank that had ended in tragedy."

Fauquet brought Bruno's coffee, muttering, "Terrible business, that poor little girl. You won't catch me using Simon's supermarket anytime soon. You know there's talk of a boycott?"

"It wasn't Simon's fault," Bruno said. "His son's sixteen, old enough to be responsible for his own behavior. A lot of local people work at the supermarket, so I hope that idea goes nowhere." He handed the paper back to Fauquet as he saw Isabelle heading across the town square toward the café with that unmistakable stride of hers, a long black coat floating out behind her.

"Would you bring an extra croissant and some more coffee for my guest?"

Fauquet turned, looked through the window at Isabelle and back at Bruno. "It's her again, is it? The one who broke your heart."

"Just get the croissant," Bruno replied, shaking his head in mock despair. The one disadvantage of the close-knit community of St. Denis was that his love life seemed to be everybody's business.

"I hope you know what you're doing, just when you've started seeing Oudinot's daughter," Fauquet went on.

Bruno rolled his eyes and then stood as Isabelle came into the café, eyed him grimly and presented her cheeks for the usual *bise* in a way that signaled she wished that courtesy did not require such a greeting.

"Bonjour, Bruno, I'm sorry you weren't able to brief me yesterday," she said coolly. "It means we have all the more work to do today. I see you're in the local paper again."

"Never a dull moment in St. Denis," he said.

"That's not quite how I recall it," she shot back, and then flashed a smile at Fauquet as he served her breakfast and said how pleased he was to see her in his café again. She murmured a polite reply about how much she missed his croissants and turned

310

back to Bruno.

"You can't brief me here," she went on. "I've arranged a room at the gendarmerie. We'll go there as soon as we've finished our coffee. So, tell me, how is that poor little girl?"

"Doing better, she won't lose an eye. But it won't do the riding school any good, and it's a tough enough business venture in times like these without clients having stones thrown at them."

"J-J told me the place is now being run by your mad Englishwoman in partnership with that spy's daughter. I can see why you're concerned."

"That's really not worthy of you," he said mildly. "You know perfectly well that her name is Pamela and that she's Scottish and that Crimson is not just retired but a good friend to the brigadier as well as to me. You'll have me thinking you're getting prejudiced against our friends across the Channel."

Isabelle was the only one who still referred to Pamela as "the mad Englishwoman," the nickname she had been given by the locals when she first arrived in St. Denis. Pamela had long since been affectionately absorbed into the community, but it was one of Isabelle's few unpleasant traits that she would

311

never accept any woman she saw as a rival, even though she had long since left Bruno to focus on her career. He'd have to make sure he steered Martine out of Isabelle's way.

"Are you and Pamela still an item?" Isabelle asked casually, sitting back in her chair as if she couldn't care less either way. "J-J wasn't sure. I'd have thought she was a little old for you."

"I hope J-J said it wasn't any business of yours," he said, irritated, and instantly regretted letting Isabelle see how easily she could provoke him. She'd always known how to get under his skin. He took the final bite of his croissant, washed it down with his coffee and then smiled at her, most of his memories still precious and fond.

"Shall we start again, without any point scoring?" he asked, leaning forward. "You're looking great. From the way you strode across the square it seems like your leg has fully recovered, which is also great. And congratulations on your new job. I'm sorry I wasn't available at such short notice yesterday, but as you know from the newspaper it was a difficult day."

"Okay," she said coolly, as if acknowledging a brief truce rather than a peace treaty. Then she smiled, with what seemed like a trace of an old affection. Perhaps she was mollified that he had made the gesture of reconciliation. "I hope I'll get to see Balzac."

"You can come with me to pick him up. He's having a regular checkup at the vet and getting his nails clipped. I'm always worried about hurting him if I clip them myself. He can come with us to the gendarmerie; they know him well."

As Bruno paid for their breakfasts, Fauquet came across and handed him an envelope.

"I almost forgot," he said. "That kid you called a hero in the paper today came in about seven-thirty and asked me to give this to you. He said he didn't have a phone. Then he rode off on a bike."

Bruno quickly scanned the note, neatly written in individual letters that were not joined up. Félix thanked him for the photo of the car and said he'd seen another photo just like it and, if Bruno was interested, could they meet at the seniors' home at 12:30?

Bruno put the note away, wondering what Félix meant. He thanked Fauquet, and he and Isabelle took his van to the vet's office, where Balzac was declared to be in excellent shape. As the vet brought the dog out,

313

Balzac saw Isabelle and galloped toward her, ears flapping like the wings of some mythical creature, half dog and half bird, before he leaped into Isabelle's arms, licking passionately at her throat.

"That's what I call a welcome," said the vet, staring admiringly at Isabelle as much as at the dog. "I wish I got them like that."

At the gendarmerie, Sergeant Jules gave her a welcome just as warm and enfolded Isabelle into an embrace in which she was almost hidden by his vast bulk. She was delighted to see he was still passing his annual fitness tests, she told him.

"Oh, we don't bother about those around here," he said cheerfully. "How long are you with us for?"

"Not sure yet," she said, and went in to pay her courtesy call on Yveline as post commander and to thank her for offering a work space.

"She hasn't changed a bit," said Sergeant Jules, fondly. "You should never have let that one get away, Bruno."

"If only it had been up to me," he replied.

Isabelle came out with Yveline, who greeted Bruno formally and showed them into the room set aside for Isabelle's team.

"We'll need a statement from you on what you found at the scene of Denise's injury,

Bruno," Yveline said. "Can we do that sometime this morning before the *procureur*'s meeting this afternoon?"

"As soon as I've briefed Commissaire Perrault," he said, and followed Isabelle into the modest room with two desks, two chairs, a phone and an empty bookcase.

"I see the facilities here haven't changed, but it's certainly a warmer welcome than we used to get with Capitaine Duroc," Isabelle said, putting her computer case on a desk and handing Bruno her coat as she took a chair. He found a hook on the back of the door. "So what can you tell me?"

He described what he had learned of Sylvestre and Freddy since meeting them at the Concours d'Élégance, from the family row with Oudinot to Sylvestre's hunt for the lost Bugatti.

"I mentioned that the Police Nationale were planning an autopsy of Hugon, but he showed no reaction," Bruno went on. "I also talked to a policeman in Alsace, a friend of mine, who said there was a rumor that Sylvestre came close to bankruptcy in 2008 with the financial crisis and was bailed out by Arab contacts. Certainly his operation in the Gulf seems to be very lucrative, and he's planning a new showroom in Shanghai."

"What's your impression of him?"

"Very smart and determined, probably ruthless when he has to be, but also ready to cut his losses and strike a deal, which is what he's doing with the family feud."

"You mean you think he might be open to working with us if he knew the alternative was a prison term?"

"I think it's very likely, unless he is a lot more frightened of his Arab friends than of going into a French prison." He paused and added, "There's a complication. J-J and I think Sylvestre and Freddy might be involved in a murder. They were working with a local researcher, a retired archivist who died in suspicious circumstances. There's an autopsy under way in Bordeaux as we speak, and we're waiting for the report."

"How was this man killed?"

"We suspect cyanide poisoning. That's what the lab is testing for. The dead man had recently sent off some papers to Freddy at a *poste restante* in Strasbourg."

"Researching what?" she asked. Bruno explained about the lost Bugatti, its history and the fact that one just like it had sold for thirty-seven million dollars.

She shook her head in disbelief. "That much money may well be worth killing for. But let's wait and see if the lab confirms the cyanide before I discuss the implications with J-J. I'm sure he'll agree to wait until my operation is complete. He'd better."

"He and I already talked about it," said Bruno. "I think you'll find him sympathetic, but as soon as the lab confirms it, he'll have to bring in the *procureur*, who might not be so ready to cooperate."

"We'll see. What can you tell me about Farid, the one you call Freddy?" she asked. "Have you met him?"

"He's not at all forthcoming, and I've met him only briefly. I tried to start a conversation but was politely rebuffed. He's a fitness freak and a very good driver. And he seems to be living in a separate house from Sylvestre, so I don't think they're gay. Can you tell me where you're going with this operation?"

"We're trying to draw a map of what we think is a very sophisticated financial network," she said. "Sylvestre and Farid are the middlemen, taking the money at the auctions from the buyers and then distributing it to the supposed sellers. And from what we can see, Farid is the one in charge, the one making the connections. Sylvestre is just the facilitator. Some of the business is legitimate; we're trying to identify the part that isn't. So far we've found five people

317

involved in different European countries, each of them with known terrorist connections. We're also tracking the bank accounts, the routes and companies through which the money is moved. Once we've mapped the whole network, we'll pounce."

"How close are you?"

"Pretty close, but we might not have mapped the whole thing."

"You know Sylvestre is heading for China in a couple of weeks? That's the deadline he's set for the deal with Oudinot to go through."

"Thanks, I didn't know that. It means we might be facing a deadline when he'll be out of our jurisdiction." She made a note to herself on a pad and then looked up. "Anything else."

"Yes. When you asked me to conduct discreet surveillance I installed a couple of cameras left over from a previous case, the one your American friend Nancy was involved in. I'll need to change the batteries tonight, but I imagine you have much-better equipment."

"You know that's illegal." She raised an eyebrow.

"No, it's not. I'm a licensed hunter and known to be a wildlife enthusiast. Monitoring wildlife movements on a friend's land with cameras is perfectly legal. And I'm not responsible if the wildlife has moved them so they unfortunately cover the entrance to a house rather than the undergrowth."

"You might just get away with that here in the Périgord," she said. "What's the recording system? I hope it's not transmitting on Wi-Fi. If their computers are good enough, they might pick that up."

"No Wi-Fi. It's on a small data card, and Sylvestre was working on what looked like a top-end Apple laptop. I don't know what Freddy was using, or rather Farid, as you call him."

"How friendly are you with Oudinot, the man whose land borders Sylvestre's house?"

"Very friendly, and he often asks after you. We met him a couple of times at *marchés nocturnes* that summer when we were together."

"I can't say I recall him, but I suppose I might remember him if I saw him again. Would he let us use his property for proper surveillance?"

"He'd be delighted. He hates Sylvestre, or at least he did, but who knows, now that they're getting close to a deal? The problem is that I don't know how discreet Oudinot would be. But there's a small hut on his land less than ten meters from Sylvestre's house that would be good for surveillance except for the noise of the geese. I told you about them."

"Could you arrange for the geese to be withdrawn once we're installed?"

"Probably. We could say it's a goodwill gesture to help the deal go through. I can do that today. What about Freddy's trip to Agen when his phone was in Sarlat? J-J was worried that he might know his phone's being monitored."

"We're cool on that. We got him on the security camera at Agen station, meeting someone of interest to us from Toulouse. It helped that you sent us the photos with the license plates."

"I'm glad. Other than Oudinot, how else can I help?"

"Get me those data cards from your cameras tonight."

"Do you want me to remove the cameras at the same time?" he asked.

"Why would I want to interfere in the perfectly legal wildlife-monitoring techniques of a law-abiding citizen?" She smiled, a wicked twinkle in her eye that touched Bruno's heart. He'd never really get over her. He rose to go.

"Just one more thing," she said, a little hesitantly. "Would you mind leaving Balzac here with me for the day?"

"Of course," he said. The dog had been her gift to him when his previous hound had been killed in another operation in which they worked together. "Bálzac would like that."

He left, walked back to his van and then stopped at the wine cave of Hubert de Montignac, whose extraordinary collection of vintages of Château Pétrus and of Château Angélus going back fifty years and more had made it one of the great tourist attractions of St. Denis. For the locals, it was also the place to take their *bidons* of glass or plastic to the huge vats at the back of the shop and fill them from the tap with good Bergerac white and red for a couple of euros a liter. Bruno was looking for something between those two extremes of wine for Martine's dinner that evening. He spent a pleasant twenty minutes gossiping with Nathalie, the saleswoman, and tasting a couple of wines he did not know, before leaving with a bottle of Anthologia, a white wine of sauvignon from Château Tour des Gendres that he could seldom afford. Then he set off to see Oudinot at his farm, wondering if he might be fortunate enough to catch Martine before she set off again to woo the local mayors and councillors into supporting her plan.

20

Bruno was waiting on the bench in the pleasant garden of the *maison de retraite,* a grandiose modern building that the *département* architects thought suitable as a seniors' home, texting Isabelle that Oudinot would be delighted to allow her team to use his hut for a police operation. Bruno had been evasive about the purpose when he'd gone to Oudinot's farm to seek permission. Oudinot had at once assumed that it was to investigate Sylvestre for tax evasion. When Bruno had shrugged his shoulders and refused to deny it, Oudinot had rubbed his hands gleefully together and pronounced himself eager to cooperate. He would withdraw his geese that very day and call on Sylvestre to shake hands on the deal and announce that the geese were gone as a gesture of goodwill. With any luck, Oudinot had added, he'd get Sylvestre's signature on a contract and a check before the taxman took all the money away.

"Bonjour, Bruno," said Félix, suddenly appearing, slightly out of breath after running all the way from school, and holding out his hand to be shaken. "The science teacher showed me what you'd said about me in the paper and read it out in class. And then the headmaster called in my mom to show it to her. It made her cry, and she said I had to be sure to thank you."

Of course, Bruno thought, his parents wouldn't get *Sud Ouest* at home. "It was no more than the truth, Félix. We're all proud of you. And did you hear the good news that Denise will be fine?"

"Yes, Madame Pantowsky told me she heard it on the radio."

That was the science teacher Bruno knew as Florence. "Well, what is this mysterious photo that made you write me that note?" he asked.

"I know of a photo of the same car, that's why we're here. It belongs to my grandfather, so I thought I'd take you to see him, and he'll show it to you and tell you the story about my great-uncle."

"Do you visit your grandpa often?"

"Two or three times a week. I like him. They eat early here, so he brings out a sandwich for me from the dining room when he knows I'm coming. He's over eighty, but he's in pretty good shape."

The St. Denis retirement home was close to the town cemetery, which Bruno had considered unfortunate until he'd learned that most of the inhabitants enjoyed the convenience of being able to attend funerals without having to walk too far. Some even claimed to take comfort from being able to gaze out over their eventual resting place. The home was a curious mixture, a few rows of single-story buildings that contained one-room apartments all surrounding an aggressively modern structure that contained the offices, recreation and dining rooms and wards for those too enfeebled to continue living in the single-room dwellings where they could be surrounded by their own furniture and belongings. The gardens were a pleasant mix of ornamental flower beds and small allotments, where the residents were encouraged to grow vegetables for their family or for the communal kitchen.

Félix's grandfather lived in one of the studios, as the single rooms were called. He came to the door and welcomed his visitors, kissing his grandson on both cheeks and shaking Bruno's hand. Bruno recognized him as one of the group of old cronies who sat around a table in the cheapest of the town's cafés, drinking their glasses of *petit blanc* and watching horse racing as they grumbled that St. Denis and the whole country were not what they'd been in their day.

"I didn't expect you so I didn't bring a sandwich," the old man said, then ruffled Félix's hair. "How's my little nut-brown grandson?" He glanced up at Bruno. "That's what I call him because he's the color of a walnut, best-looking man in the family. I was very proud when I saw what you said about Félix in the paper."

"I brought Bruno to look at your photo album, Grandpa," Félix said. "He's interested in the photo you have with this car." He showed him the printout of the Bugatti that Bruno had given him.

"You know that album by heart," the old man said affectionately as he moved slowly to the bedside table, sat down on the neatly made bed and gestured to the others to join him. He began leafing through to a familiar page that displayed four small, square photos in black and white, each one about twice the size of a passport photo. The images of young Resistance fighters with rifles and Sten guns and armbands that carried the letters FFI, for Forces Françaises de l'Intérieur, were instantly recognizable as dating from World War II.

He put a wavering finger on a snapshot of two men standing by a car that looked to be the very image of the Bugatti on the print-out. One was wearing flying gear, the fur-lined jacket open to reveal a uniform. He was hatless, his hair smoothed back glossily. He was standing beside a young man in farming clothes whom Félix's grandfather identified as his older brother, Henri, a member of the Resistance who had been killed later in the war. Beside this photo was another of the same young man in farming clothes carrying a Sten gun with his hand on the shoulder of a young boy who looked to be about twelve.

"That's me with Henri, the family hero," the old man said. "That was in the summer of 'forty-four, just before he went off to fight. He went from the Resistance straight into the French army and was killed that winter in the fighting around Strasbourg. I never saw him again after the photo was taken. It broke my mother's heart. She died not long after the war, and my dad followed soon after, when I was away doing military service."

He asked Félix to pass him the magnifying glass, and the boy darted across to snatch it from the windowsill beside the room's sole easy chair, clearly its usual location.

"You can see the family resemblance — me, my brother and young Félix here," the old man said, his voice quavering and his hand trembling as he held the glass over the little photo.

"What's that ruin in the background?" Bruno asked.

"Rastignac, after the Nazis burned it. It was springtime, and I remember watching it burn for days."

"The one that was supposed to have all those paintings that disappeared?" Bruno asked.

"That's it, just the other side of Thénon. They were nice people, the owners, even the English ones in the family. My dad worked for them in a way, he was a *métayer,* but every Christmas they'd have all of us *métayer* families up to the château for a party and give the children presents. Not all the landlords were like that, I can tell you."

The *métayer* system was a form of sharecropping that had been common in the region until it was finally regulated almost out of existence by President François Mitterrand's Socialist government in 1983. The tenant farmed the land, and in return the landowner took a half share of everything that was produced — crops, livestock and wine, everything except the family's chickens and their eggs. In the reforms after the war, the landlord's share was reduced to a third, but it was still widely blamed for rural poverty, and the system's existence helped explain the remarkable number of Communist Party members among the rural population.

"How near was your farm to the château?" Bruno asked.

"You can see from the photo, which was taken in our farmyard; it's about a kilometer away. The land we farmed stretched out the other way, toward Labouret, all the way down to the River Cern. We had cattle, wheat and tobacco, an apple orchard and a woods full of walnuts. We spent every winter's night around the stove, shelling them."

"Did you ever see the car that's in the photo?" Bruno asked.

"Only from a distance. The driver wanted to hide it, I don't know why. He was supposed to be a famous racing driver, but I forget the name, maybe never knew it. My brother said he'd hidden the car in one of the old tobacco-drying barns that belonged to a friend of his. The government didn't trust us to dry the tobacco ourselves because it was rationed, so a lot of the old barns were disused."

"Was this friend also a *métayer* for the château?" Bruno asked.

"No, I think the barn belonged to the family of a girl he was sweet on. They'd been at school together in La Bachellerie, where I went to school."

"Do you remember the name of the family?"

"No, but her name was Marie-France. She got married to somebody else after my brother was killed, and they moved away. One thing I do know is that they didn't just hide the car; they dismantled it. My brother said he helped take the body off and the seats out, and they put it in with some other old farm equipment, broken plows and the like. I don't know what they did with the bodywork."

"Did you come back home when your father died?"

"Yes, they gave me a week's leave from the army. I was stationed at Montauban, down near Toulouse, so it wasn't too far to come back for the funeral. It was lucky, in a way; the rest of my unit was sent off to Indochina. A lot of Henri's old Resistance pals turned up for the funeral, and one of them said he'd give me a job when I got out. I'd been a driver in the army, and that was what I did when I came out, drove a truck for the logistics firm in Le Buisson. That's why I settled here."

"You never went back to look for the barn or the car?"

The old man shook his head. "Nothing to go back for, not for me. After my dad died, I still had a year to go in the army, so the landlord found a new tenant. I hadn't really thought about that car until today." He picked up the magnifying glass to examine the photo more closely. "Fine-looking vehicle, isn't it? I bet it would go like the wind."

"What about that pilot in the photo, did you ever meet him?"

"No, but Henri told me he was English, from the RAF. Somebody in the château had connections to another Resistance group that organized escape routes across the Pyrenees into Spain. Henri said he often wondered what had happened to that fur-lined flying jacket. He'd have liked to have it for himself."

He moved the magnifying glass to a photo of half-a-dozen young men, all armed and wearing FFI armbands, standing around an old Citroën. "That's my brother and there beside him is Jean-Pierre, the one who gave me the job. He'd dead now, of course." He looked up at Bruno. "Why are you interested in all this?"

"That car, it's famous, and probably pretty valuable if anybody could find it. I know some people who are looking for it, and there may even be a murder involved. That's why I'm investigating. Is there anything else you remember about it?"

"I can't say I do." The old man put down the magnifying glass and stared at Bruno. "Murder? Who was it got killed?"

"Sorry, I'd better not say anything until we get the results from an autopsy. It's still a matter of suspicion at this stage. When the investigation is over, I'll come back and tell you all about it. Can you tell me if anyone else has asked you any questions about this car recently, or has the topic come up in any way?"

"No, the only one who's ever asked me about it is Félix, when we look through the album together. It's mainly his great-uncle Henri who interests him, but he's always liked cars. I'm only sorry the photo is so small."

"If you like, I could get it blown up for you and also the one of you and Henri," Bruno said, thinking that Philippe Delaron could easily do it; he owed Bruno several favors.

"I'd like that. Do I have to take them out?"

"I'll do it, Grandpa." Félix took the album and gently prized the two photos out of the little triangular pouches at each corner and handed them to Bruno. He carefully put them inside his notebook, shook the old man's hand and thanked him. At the door he asked if Félix was going back to school.

"In a few minutes, then I'm going to the riding school again."

"Thanks for this, Félix. Take care."

Félix didn't move but looked up shyly at Bruno. "Could you do me another favor? I'd like to give Grandpa a photo of me on a horse. Could you take one for me, please?"

"No problem, we'll do it next time I see you at the stables."

Bruno went back to his office and texted Philippe, asking him to come to Bruno's office in the *mairie*. Then he called Florence at home, knowing that she'd be there with her children during lunchtime. Rollo, the headmaster, had excused her from the usual roster of supervising the school lunches because her children were still so little.

"I'm calling to thank you for letting Félix know about the story in the paper today," he said when she answered. "I gather his mother was very touched."

"It was good of you to say what you did," she replied. "I've been worried about that boy, and at the way Tristan bullies him, but he usually makes sure to do it in ways and places so we can never catch him at it. And if we do catch him, there's not much we can do beyond telling him off, so despite what happened to poor Denise I'm glad you managed to nail him. What happens to him now?"

"It's up to the magistrate, which in this case is probably Annette, and as you know she always tries to avoid putting anyone into a detention center. It depends on whether the *procureur* decides to intervene. Given the publicity and the prospect of some political pressure, I suspect that he'll probably feel that he should. He may decide to take it out of Annette's hands and give the case to a more experienced magistrate."

Even as he spoke, Bruno realized that he hadn't followed up on this case as he should have. If he hadn't been in such a rush to get back to Martine he'd have gone to the mayor and asked his advice. The mayor would probably have called the subprefect in Sarlat, who in turn would have had a quiet word with the *procureur* about this being the kind of assault that stirred public opinion. But did Bruno think juvenile detention was really the right treatment for Tristan?

"What do you think should happen to Tristan?" Florence asked. "I know the boy deserves to get punished, and he probably needs a real shock. But I'm with Annette; I never like the idea of putting young people in prison, even a special detention center. If the girl had been blinded, I might think differently, but since they saved her eyesight . . ."

"I was so angry with him when it happened," said Bruno. "All I could think of was making Tristan pay for it. He's been a bully for years, spoiled rotten by his parents and so cocksure that he could get away with anything. And now there's the drug charge as well. The *procureur* can't ignore that after all the fuss he's made about drugs in the past."

"You know possessing drugs triggers automatic suspension from the *collège,* so that means Tristan will not be going to the lycée as he expected."

"What sort of student is he?"

"Lazy and arrogant, doing just enough to get by, and he's intelligent enough to get away with it. He's from a good home with educated parents, books in the house, his own laptop at home. I've caught him plagiarizing his homework a couple of times, just copying stuff straight from some website or other, usually Wikipedia. And he's done the same in other classes. His parents have been warned that it could mean holding him back a year, but they said they'd hire a private tutor to make sure he caught up. They want him in a good lycée and then in a good university. Juvenile detention would probably wreck his life."

"He very nearly wrecked Denise's life and did his best to do the same to Félix, so how do we treat a nasty young thug like Tristan?"

"We get you and me and his parents together and we try to hammer out some agreed course of action," Florence said. "I don't see what else we can do. If Tristan doesn't go to prison, what's likely to happen to him?"

"Two years of community service, probably with a hefty fine that his parents can easily afford to pay. Part of the problem is with them. The husband is henpecked by Tristan's mother, who thinks her little darling is perfect. She swore out a false statement saying Tristan was with her when we know from witnesses and from his phone that he was throwing rocks at Denise at the time."

"Can't you use that to make her see some sense?"

"I don't think the *procureur* would want to charge her with perjury, not for a mother trying to protect her child. She'd get no more than a slap on the wrist."

"She doesn't know that."

"They have already hired a good lawyer for Tristan, who will probably tell the mother she's unlikely to face any trouble. But maybe you're right. Let me discuss this with Yveline. We can't let this drop here."

"I've got to get the children back to school before I start teaching again. Meanwhile I'll have a word with Rollo and see what he thinks. And thank you for calling."

"My love to your children," he said. "And I'll consult the mayor."

Bruno called Claire to ask if the mayor was free, to be told he was in a meeting. She would let him know when it ended. He used the time to call the *mairie* at La Bachellerie to ask if they had any school attendance records for the late 1930s and the 1940s. No, he was told, they would all be somewhere in the archives of the *département* in Périgueux. He looked up the number, called and asked for Madame Tronquet, the same helpful person to whom he'd spoken about Hugon's searches. Yes, she said when he was put through, they kept their school registers, organized by commune.

"Could someone look up the records of La Bachellerie for 1935 and 1938? I'm looking for any other details about a girl called Marie-France who was in the same class as a boy named Henri Boulier. It's very urgent and it's important, part of what we think is turning out to be a murder investigation. If you want to check with Commissaire Jalipeau of the Police Nationale . . ."

"No, no, it's all right, Monsieur Bruno. I was reading about you in the paper today, about that poor little girl who got hit in the eye. I'll do it myself and call you back."

Bruno began going through his e-mails, deleting or acknowledging as he went, when his mobile phone rang. It was J-J, saying that the Bordeaux lab had confirmed Fabiola's theory. Hugon had been murdered with cyanide, sprayed into his face. J-J had a meeting scheduled with Isabelle at the St. Denis gendarmerie in an hour's time to discuss the implications of the murder for Isabelle's operation. The *procureur* would send someone and could Bruno attend? He checked his watch and said yes, telling J-J that he'd already briefed Isabelle on the matter.

There came a knock on his door, and the mayor came in, sat down and said, "I presume you want to know about Tristan? I already had Simon calling me last night, asking if I could use my influence with the *procureur* to go easy on his son. As you know, that supermarket is now the biggest taxpayer in the commune."

Bruno said nothing.

"I know you're not a great fan of putting teenage kids in prison. Nor am I. But you understand the politics of this, particularly with the drugs as a second charge. Rollo tells me that Tristan had so much cannabis he suspects the boy may have been dealing it to others in the school. Have you heard anything about that?"

"No, which makes me feel guilty. I had no idea that amount of stuff was available around here, and I ought to have known, or at least kept more of an eye on the *collège*."

The mayor nodded. "Rollo also said Tristan will now be suspended, but I can't see how that will help. Is there anything we can do that would keep the boy out of jail and also get him back on track? Isn't there some early engagement system for the army?"

"There used to be," said Bruno. "That's what I did. But seventeen is the minimum age now, and the army probably wouldn't have him after this. We'll need to find him a useful and preferably tough job for the rest of the school year, then if he stays out of trouble and Rollo agrees, Tristan can retake his final year and go on to the lycée a year late."

"Any ideas? Remember, we can't give him the kind of job that some unemployed person could fill, which rules out most community service work."

"That means an internship, and it would have to be with someone he could look up to, someone to set an example."

"You mean the way you seem to have taken Félix in hand?" the mayor asked, smiling for the first time since he'd come in.

"No, I couldn't give Tristan full-time attention," Bruno said. "I'd been thinking about a farm, but it would take too long to make him useful. You're on the *conseil régional,* and we've got the state forests. Do you know any foresters who might fit the bill? Get him doing something like that, and the *procureur* might give him conditional probation."

"You mean if he doesn't shape up he goes straight to jail?"

"Exactly."

"I'll talk to the chief forester." The mayor rose.

A few minutes after he'd gone, Madame Tronquet called Bruno back and asked for his fax number. She would send him a copy of the school register. Henri Boulier had been a classmate of Marie-France Perdigat, whose address was listed as Perdigat; the coincidence of names suggested a farm that had been in the same family for generations. Bruno thanked Madame Tronquet profusely and hung up just as his fax machine began to whir. Then came a knock on the door, and Philippe Delaron arrived.

"I was doing some shopping at the super-market when I got your text," he said. "What's up?"

Bruno gave Philippe the two photos and asked him to blow them up and give him two copies and suggested Philippe keep copies for himself, since it could well turn into a story.

"You know Gilles, the guy who used to be at *Paris Match*?"

"Yes, Fabiola's boyfriend, the lucky guy."

"He's been working on the background to this, and I'm sure he'll do the usual deal with you — he gets the story nationally, and you break it in *Sud Ouest* at the same time. One look at that photo of the car, and Gilles will know what it's all about. These were taken in wartime. The kid in the second photo is now a sweet old guy called Boulier who's in the *maison de retraite.* The guy with him holding the gun is his big brother, Henri, a Resistance fighter who was killed later in the war, and the man in uniform is a downed RAF pilot whom Henri helped to escape over the Pyrenees."

"That's a pretty nice story as it stands, but what about the car?" Philippe asked. "It's a beauty."

"Gilles can tell you all about it," Bruno said. "I'll call him now if you can start working on those blowups. I've got a meeting at the gendarmerie on a separate matter that will also be a big story, and I'll make sure you get it first."

He called Gilles to brief him and told him to expect a visit from Philippe with photographic evidence that the Bugatti had been in the region at the time of its disappearance. He briefly related what Boulier had said and added that the car had been dismantled and hidden in a barn somewhere on a farm called Perdigat, near La Bachellerie.

"Jesus," said Gilles. "This is starting to get real. As soon as Philippe gets here, we can go over to La Bachellerie and take a look."

"That's exactly what I hoped you'd say," said Bruno. "If you're still at the house at about four, I may see you. I want to pick up Hector for an early ride."

He ended the call, put on his kepi, checked his appearance in the mirror and strolled down the rue de Paris toward the gendarmerie, thinking it was convenient to have a couple of inquisitive and friendly journalists around. They could save him a great deal of legwork.

21

As he passed the office of Brosseil, the *notaire,* the door opened and Oudinot emerged looking extremely pleased with himself.

"Ah, Bruno," Oudinot greeted him. "The deed is done, the land is sold, and the feud is settled. Sylvestre has signed the contract pledging the sale and paid a fat deposit to ensure that the deal goes through as quickly as possible. You must come to dinner at the farm so I can thank you for all your help, and I still want you to meet my daughter, Martine, properly, over dinner."

"Congratulations," Bruno said, startled, but thinking quickly. "You know, I met your daughter when she came to the *mairie* to explain her proposals for the electric-car rally. She's a charming woman and obviously very good at business; you must be very proud of her."

"Very much so, I just wish her business

let us see a little more of her or at least to get started on making me a grandpa. Then again, my wife tells me she suspects there may be some new romantic interest in Martine's life."

Trying to forestall his blushes, Bruno glanced at the door of the notary's office behind Oudinot, which remained closed.

"Wasn't Sylvestre in there with you to sign the deal?"

"Yes, of course, but he's staying. Apparently he has some other property deal he's arranging, so he stayed behind to discuss it with Brosseil. I have to get back to the farm. So you'll come to dinner and get to know Martine a little less formally. Shall we say Sunday evening at seven?"

"I'll be delighted to come, and I'll look forward to it, but now you must excuse me; I have to get to a meeting at the gendarmerie."

"Of course, but I'm so pleased it all worked out with Sylvestre. I really made him pay through the nose for the land." Oudinot looked around with a conspiratorial air and whispered, "When should I expect those colleagues of yours to come about Sylvestre's taxes?"

"As soon as they get here, I'll let you know, and not a word to a soul. I know I can count on you, Fernand."

"Indeed you can. Au revoir, Bruno."

Oudinot headed to his car, parked immediately behind a Range Rover that Bruno recognized as Sylvestre's. With a glance at the still-closed door of the *notaire,* Bruno walked on, wondering if the sale to Sylvestre would still go through if he were arrested before the final contract was signed. If not, he'd forfeit his deposit, so Oudinot would at least have that. As he trotted up the gendarmerie steps, noting J-J's official car parked down the street with Annette's blue Peugeot behind it, Bruno wondered what other deal Sylvestre might be negotiating.

The meeting was being held in Isabelle's temporary office. J-J was in the visitor's chair, beaming paternally at Isabelle, who rose with a smile to let Bruno kiss her cheeks. Balzac jumped out from beneath her desk to greet his master.

"Thank you for letting me have some time with him," she said, bending to stroke the dog. "Maybe you could bring him again tomorrow? I'd like to keep him with me, but I don't think my hotel would welcome his staying in my room tonight."

"Of course," said Bruno, picking up Balzac's leash from her desk. "I'll buy you croissants again at Fauquet's if you like. I'll be there at eight tomorrow morning."

"If you two dog lovers have finished, our real business is all settled," said J-J. "Isabelle and I have agreed that you and I can continue our investigation into Hugon's murder as far as we can without alerting the two suspects, but once Isabelle's operation is complete, we can move in."

"If Isabelle succeeds in turning Sylvestre into an informant, her operation could last for some time," Bruno said, his tone deliberately neutral. J-J looked surprised, and Isabelle gave Bruno a sour look. "Or didn't she explain that?"

"She didn't have to," said J-J. "Prunier got a call from the minister's office saying that this Eurojust operation was to be given my complete cooperation and top priority." Prunier was J-J's boss, the police commissioner for the *département.*

"I understand," said Bruno. "You'd better make sure nobody from the Bordeaux lab says anything about the autopsy. Murder by cyanide spray is unusual enough for people to start talking. If Sylvestre hears about that, he's smart enough to deduce that the game is up."

"I'll make sure nobody talks," J-J said. "I have to go to Bordeaux anyway. One of the two targets is there today, the Indian fellow, and I have a meeting with the Bordeaux detectives who have been handling the surveillance there."

"I'm told you have another meeting in the post commandant's office over the case with the little girl who was almost blinded," Isabelle interrupted, looking at Bruno. "That young magistrate from Sarlat is going to be there, so you mustn't let us keep you. And don't forget those data cards you promised me."

"Just one thing," Bruno said. "If your surveillance picks up anything about a property deal that Sylvestre is arranging, not the one with Oudinot himself, I'd be grateful to know what it might be."

"So long as it doesn't compromise my operation, of course," she said and fell silent, pointedly waiting for him to leave.

In Yveline's office next door, the mood was grim, and even from the corridor he'd heard their raised voices. Yveline sat stony faced, and Annette's cheeks were flushed and she looked flustered. As if grateful for the distraction, Annette looked at her watch when Bruno entered. He apologized to them both for being late, explaining he'd been called in to see J-J about another matter.

"I was expecting him to be at this meeting

as well," Annette said. "The *procureur* said to be sure to get his views on the cannabis aspect of this case."

"I'm sure he'll be here as soon as he can," said Bruno. "Are you both agreed on how to proceed against Tristan?"

"No," said Yveline firmly while at the same moment Annette was saying, "Not exactly."

"The young man has been told he'll be charged with aggravated bodily harm and possession of cannabis in quantities suggesting he's a dealer. It's open and shut," said Yveline. "Annette is trying to get me to recommend a noncustodial sentence, and I won't. Tristan needs locking up. If he just had a couple of joints, maybe, but he had half a kilo, and I don't want that being peddled around to the kids in this town."

"You know as well as I do that juvenile detention centers are like a high school for criminals," said Annette. "They're understaffed, underfunded and probably do more harm than good. This is an intelligent youngster from a stable and comfortable home who made a bad mistake, two bad mistakes. But there's a chance we can set him right. If he goes inside, we're likely to have a very smart criminal on our hands when he gets out."

"I don't think a stable and comfortable

home entitles him to escape the penalties the law requires. It doesn't seem to have done him much good so far," Yveline replied.

The two women, usually good friends, glared at each other, and then they both looked at Bruno, each of them obviously expecting him to agree with her. He could lose two friends here if he couldn't find a way to move them beyond their immediate argument.

"I don't know what to say," Bruno began. "I think you're both right. Tristan is a nasty piece of work who deserves to be punished. At the same time, if he goes into a detention center he's probably going to come out as even more of a menace than when he went in; we all know that."

He paused. "As I understand it, we're not taking a decision here. We're simply expected to come up with a recommendation for the *procureur* and, if we can't agree, we send him separate recommendations, and he makes the choice."

Yveline nodded agreement, and Annette said, "He specifically asked us to come up with an agreed recommendation."

"Well, it looks like he's not going to get one from you two, but he will be getting one from the mayor, and since the mayor has been a senator and sits on the *conseil régional,* I think he'd take that one very seriously."

"Where does the mayor come into this?" Yveline asked, suspiciously.

"Tristan is one of his constituents, and Tristan's father is the very competent manager of the supermarket, which is the biggest employer and leading taxpayer in St. Denis." Bruno opened his arms and gave an exaggerated shrug, as if to say matters were now out of his hands.

"You can't have one law for the rich and another for the poor," Annette began, and this time she looked in appeal to Yveline, who was nodding vigorously.

"That's shameful," Yveline said.

Ah, thought Bruno, it worked. They're agreeing with each other.

"Shameful, probably, but it's the reality, it's politics," he said. "The mayor is planning to find Tristan some tightly supervised physical labor in the woods with the forestry department. But what if we three agree to insist on putting some real teeth into that? Tristan is prosecuted and found guilty, sentenced to two or three years, but then the sentence is suspended on the strict condition that the court get a satisfactory weekly report from the forester. One false move, one day playing truant, and he goes straight to jail."

Yveline and Annette exchanged glances. Yveline shrugged. Annette said, "If that's the best you think we can do . . ."

"I think it's important that we come up with a joint recommendation," he said. "Let me draft something and then leave you two to tidy it up and put it into the right terminology." Bruno, disguising his relief, took a notepad from Yveline's desk and began to write.

Ten minutes later, escorting Annette to her car, he asked, "How's George Young? Still looking for that famous Bugatti?"

"Don't talk to me about that damn Bugatti. I get enough of that from George. I don't think he's making much progress, and it's getting him down," she said in a tone that suggested she no longer felt swept off her feet.

"I went to a lot of trouble to get him something I thought was bound to cheer him up," she went on, sounding aggrieved. "I planned it as a kind of consolation present, and he barely even thanked me before setting off again on this wild-goose chase of his."

"It sounds like he's a bit obsessed by it," said Bruno sympathetically, thinking that

Annette would naturally prefer Young to devote all his attentions to her. "But I think he has been interested for a long time, through the family connection he has with the English racing driver."

"I suppose so. I just wish he'd talk about something else once in a while." They reached her car, and she stopped, looking appealingly at him. "Am I being unreasonable?"

"No, not at all," he said, an image of Martine unbuttoning his shirt the previous evening suddenly entering his mind and making him think it was sad that Young was wasting that unique and precious time that a kindly Providence reserved for new lovers. "But I suppose you could say that in a way it's flattering that he wants to share with you something that's so important to him."

"It's not just the car, it's also this rivalry he has about the Bugatti with Sylvestre. It gets on my nerves, and I went to such a lot of trouble to get him that damn radiator."

"Radiator?" he asked.

"A real Bugatti radiator, they're very distinctive with a kind of horseshoe shape. You remember Marcel, whose car we drove in the rally? He has one on the wall of his garage, along with ones from a Rolls-Royce and I don't know the names of the other cars. But this one had BUGATTI written on it, and I wheedled and fluttered my eyelashes, and finally Marcel let me buy it from him."

"Young must have been delighted."

"He was, for about thirty seconds, then he asked where I'd found it, and when I told him he said he had to run."

"And that surprised you? You hand him a piece of solid evidence that a Bugatti has been right here in the Périgord, and you don't expect him to go hunting to see which car it might have come from?"

She looked down at her feet, a little abashed. "I suppose so. But he didn't have to rush off right away, did he?"

"No, of course not. And I suppose you never have to rush away in the mornings to be on time for work? Perhaps he sees this as his work. By the way, did Marcel say where he got the radiator?"

"Years and years ago, he said, when he first opened the garage. He found it in some local junk shop in Sarlat that closed down years ago."

"So as soon as Young realizes the trail has gone cold, he'll come back to you," said Bruno. "And you are young and lovely and alive and loving, all the things that a Bugatti radiator is not. I suspect he's the kind of man to appreciate that. So cheer up, Annette."

"Thanks, Bruno." She rose on tiptoe to her full height and kissed him on the cheek before getting into her car and giving him a smile and a wave as she drove away.

With Balzac at his heels, Bruno walked back to pick up his van, noting that Sylvestre's Range Rover was still parked outside the *notaire*'s office. And Freddy was in Bordeaux. That meant the coast was clear. He could pick up the data cards from his cameras, put in new ones and change the batteries before taking Hector out. He headed out to the *chartreuse.*

Half an hour later, leaning forward in the saddle as Hector plodded up the slope, Bruno was wondering how difficult it would be to track down all the closed junk shops in Sarlat. He'd have to find out when Marcel had first launched his garage and restrict the search to those that had been open at the time. It would mean looking through old business directories and then trying to track down members of the family who had owned the shop and see if anybody remembered where the Bugatti radiator had come from. The prospect dismayed him, until he remembered that he could ask Gilles to do it. And then he thought, as he

355

topped the rise onto the ridge that looked down on St. Denis, he had the evening with Martine to look forward to. He looked back to see that Balzac was still following along behind, running as fast as his short legs would allow. Bruno leaned forward and loosened the reins to let Hector know it was time to run.

For a time, at least, the ride drove all the other thoughts and concerns from his head. There was nothing but this moment, this speed, this wind in his face and this powerful, galloping creature that seemed almost to be a part of him. More than that, on horseback he felt himself to be much more a part of the physical world around him even as its trees flashed by sensed rather than seen.

As he slowed at the end of the ridge, the thought stayed with him. This sense that he felt of being connected to nature was at its most immediate and dramatic when he was riding, but it was also something he felt with his dog and even with his geese and chickens. Humans were meant to live with animals, he concluded, to know that humankind was not alone on this planet but shared it with other species in a state of mutual interdependence. People who lived in cities might know that intellectually, but could they ever truly feel it in the way he did in the woods with his horse and his dog? He turned in the saddle to watch Balzac catch up, and then unbidden Hector set off at a walk down the familiar bridle path that led to the ridge for the long canter back to the stables.

As Bruno finished rubbing down his horse, Gilles drove into the courtyard in Fabiola's old car, the Twingo that he'd started to use now that she had her new electric vehicle. They shook hands, and Gilles said, "The Perdigat farm is now a housing estate, a filling station and a couple of warehouses for supermarkets. It's right by the extension to the new autoroute. There's no trace of any old barns, and the farm and its contents were auctioned off fifty years ago. The next step is to check the old newspapers and try to find an announcement of the sale, which will give us the name of the auctioneers, and we can see if they have kept any records."

"There might be a shortcut," said Bruno, and pulled out his phone to call his counterpart, the municipal policeman of Terrasson, the nearest town to La Bachellerie. Grégoire was a pillar of the *département*'s tennis federation, and Bruno had met him often;

his father had been the St. Denis policeman before him. They exchanged greetings, and Bruno explained he was trying to find out which company had auctioned the farm of Perdigat.

"Probably the Melvilles from Périgueux, they've always done most of the auctions around here," Grégoire replied. "But I'll ask my father, he might even remember it. The farm's partly built over now, of course. I'll call you back."

Gilles grinned. "You and your local knowledge, Bruno. I should have thought of that."

"I didn't know Grégoire's father was still alive, or I'd have gone straight to him," Bruno said, thinking that Grégoire was nearing sixty, close to retirement, so his father would be close to ninety. He'd certainly have been around at the time of the auction. He might even have known Félix's grandfather. If so, perhaps he could find a way of bringing the two men together.

"I have to go, Gilles, but there could be another clue," he said, and recounted how Annette had found the radiator at Marcel's garage and given it to Young.

"I'm disappointed that Young didn't tell me that himself," said Gilles. "We're supposed to be cooperating."

"Maybe he feels he's getting close to the

car and the money it could bring him."

"We went through all that, remember? I'd better give him a call, and I'll count on you to call me back when you hear from Grégoire. Do you mind if I follow up with Marcel? His place is the big Citroën dealership, is that right?"

Bruno stopped at the gendarmerie to give Isabelle the data cards from his cameras and got home not long after five. He fed his geese and chickens, got the fire going in the wood-burning stove and set the table for two. He was about to climb into the shower when Grégoire called him back to say his father remembered the sale. The auctioneer had indeed been Melville. The farm had been broken up into lots, and all the old farm equipment, mostly out of date, had been bought by a scrap-metal merchant and junk dealer in Sarlat named Bérégevoy.

"I don't think they're still in business, Bruno," Grégoire added.

"Thanks anyway," Bruno said. "You might also ask your dad if he remembers people called Boulier; they were *métayers* at Rastignac. One of them is in our *maison de retraite,* and he told me that he remembers seeing the château of Rastignac burning during the war. Your dad will certainly remember that. He's about your dad's age so they were probably at school together. He had a big brother, Henri, a Resistance fighter who died in the war. If your dad remembers the family, it might be nice to bring the two of them together to reminisce about old times."

"Good idea," said Grégoire. "I'll ask him. My father's always been interested in what happened at Rastignac, spent years talking to everyone in the area to try to establish whether the paintings had been stolen or burned in the fire. I'm sure he'd love to get together with someone who could talk about it with him. Old folks like to reminisce about their young days. Maybe one day someone will do the same for the two of us. Keep well, Bruno."

Bruno called Gilles to tell him about the Bérégevoy scrap-metal merchants and to commiserate. If the old tobacco barn at Perdigat had indeed been the last resting place of the chassis and engine of the legendary Bugatti, it had probably long since been melted down for scrap.

"It's not bad news as far as I'm concerned," Gilles replied. "Quite the opposite — it makes a good, haunting ending to my story. The most valuable car in the world, melted down and recycled, and some of its molecules are probably now speeding around in some of the family cars in France."

Bruno put his phone down and climbed into the shower that he'd built and tiled himself, thinking that someday he might invest in one of those grand multijet showers his friend Horst had installed. He shampooed his hair and was soaping himself down when he was suddenly aware of a shadow against the frosted glass of the sliding door. Then he heard a tap on the door and a woman's voice said, "Bruno?"

Was that Martine, arriving early, or was it another voice? With the shower running, he couldn't tell. Heaven forbid it was Isabelle making an unexpected visit. He slid open the door a crack and with relief saw it was Martine, smiling cheekily at him and swiftly unbuttoning her blouse to reveal a black bra. She began unzipping her jeans.

"I just showered at home before I came," she said. "But I think I'm in the mood for another." She reached behind her back to undo her bra. "I've brought the food, but I'm not hungry yet — at least, not for the food."

She climbed in to join him in the running water and put her arms around his neck. "You're already soapy," she said. "Why don't you soap me?"

22

For Bruno, it began as just another Saturday morning, rendered more piquant by the expectation of breakfast with Isabelle. This was the second, smaller market day of the week, and a few minutes before eight most of the stalls were already erected, and the early customers were moving purposefully from one to the next. Bruno had noticed that most of them shopped in the order in which they ate: first the olives stall and the organic bread, then the fish or the duck, then the fruit and vegetables and finally Stéphane's cheeses. Even those he knew to be apartment dwellers paused at the flower stall, the last one before the bridge, picking up seedlings of herbs for their balconies and window boxes. Bruno moved through the stalls, shaking hands and kissing cheeks, tasting a ripe fig and then a fat black olive.

"Not hot yet, come back later," Madame Vinh called to him from the glass-fronted stand where she kept the samosas and the *lumpia,* the prawn curries and *rendang* beef, for all of which the people of St. Denis had developed a taste. Takeout containers were stacked beside the vast cauldron of pho soup heating on the portable gas stove. It would be empty by noon. In the decade that Bruno had been the town policeman, the usual radishes and cucumbers had been joined by mangoes and papayas, heirloom tomatoes and pomelos. Sausage rolls and Cornish pasties now stood beside the quiche Lorraine. But the cheese and the charcuterie stalls were still the most thronged. The people of St. Denis were prepared to experiment and the stallholders were ready to adapt, but all of them always returned faithfully to the foie gras and smoked duck sausage, to the Brie de Meaux and Vacherin Mont d'Or, emblems of a nation that still liked to define itself by the way it ate.

Fauquet's café was crowded and the windows steamed up, people standing three deep at the bar and all the tables filled. This was no place for his dog. He tied Balzac's leash to a railing and then moved through the crowd, shaking hands until he caught Fauquet's eye and asked for coffee and croissants on the terrace. The café did not usually put the chairs and tables out into the open air until later, but Fauquet nodded and Bruno leaned across the counter to pick up a dishrag and the key that hung by the cash desk. He went outside to open the padlock to a discreet door into the storage area, pulled out two chairs and a small table. He put them at the far corner of the terrace, by the stone balustrade that overlooked the river, where he and Isabelle would be out of earshot of any other arrivals. He wiped the furniture clean with the rag, collected Balzac and took his seat. Once Isabelle arrived, the coffee and croissants had been served, and other regulars had liberated another half-dozen tables and lifted their faces to enjoy the gentle early morning sun.

"In Paris the cafés are installing heaters on the terraces," she said as he rose to greet her.

"It being Paris, they will probably be denouncing the perils of global warming while they cluster beneath the artificial warmth," he said and pointed up to the clear blue sky. "Here in the Périgord, we prefer solar power."

"My team has finally arrived and been issued its warrants from the prefect, so at last we can get started," she said, sitting down to pet Balzac and tell him what a fine dog he was and how much she'd missed him.

"I hope you had a more interesting evening than I did," she said, looking up at Bruno. "I was staring at those images from your data cards until my brain flagged. It was always the same two Range Rovers coming and going, and so the high point was when a new vehicle turned up, until I realized it was you. The postman didn't even get out of his car, just pushed the supermarket flyers and catalogs into the box. And there was one courier delivery."

"Any result from the Bordeaux surveillance?"

"He had lunch with a junior professor of sociology whom we're now checking out, French but a Muslim convert and wearing her head scarf as if it were a veil. The guy from Toulouse whom he met at the station in Agen was interesting, a trade union rep at Airbus, already on the brigadier's watch list. They went to a kebab house to eat."

"These legalistic delays must be very frustrating for you," he said.

"They are, but that's the price Europe pays for human rights," she said wryly. "And since we French invented them, we've only got ourselves to blame. But the surveillance is only part of the operation. Mostly it's about tracking bank accounts and money trails, which is why we need the Americans, and that's going well."

"How much money are they moving through the vintage-car system?" he asked.

"They're being discreet, mostly cars in the very low six-figure range, nothing above two hundred thousand. But we think they're doing three or four at every auction, so the total is already close to five million."

"Do you know where the money is going?"

She shrugged. "Some of it, not all by any means. But we're building the map of local paymasters, giving the brigadier and his counterparts in other countries the names of people to watch. It's slow, but as the brigadier says, this is going to be a very long war."

"Do you want me to take your surveillance guys up to meet the farmer whose hut they'll be using?"

"That's the plan. We meet at the gendarmerie at eight-thirty and you can take them. The sooner they get started the better. Do you need me to come along and show our Eurojust credentials?"

"No, the farmer thinks it's a tax investigation. Eurojust will simply confuse him. His feud with Sylvestre is nominally over — they signed a deal for Oudinot to sell the land.

But he still enjoys the thought of Sylvestre in tax trouble."

They made their way to Isabelle's temporary office in the gendarmerie just as two men in hunters' garb came into the building wearing rucksacks.

"Bruno, this is the team, Hanno and Friedrich. They've just been taking a preliminary look at the target building. And, guys, this is an old friend of mine, *chef de police* Bruno Courrèges, who runs this town. If you're very good and very lucky, you might get him to cook for you some evening."

"Are you the one who warned us about the geese?" Hanno asked, in serviceable French with a heavy Dutch accent. "Christ, I've never heard anything like it."

"There seemed to be two tribes of them, white geese and gray ones," said Friedrich, who was German. "They didn't seem to mix much. Is there any difference?"

"A lot," said Bruno, smiling as he explained. "The white ones get roasted to eat in wintertime, usually at Christmas, and the gray ones have the best livers, so we use them for foie gras."

"In Germany we eat them on the eve of St. Martin's Day, November eleventh," said Friedrich.

"Any excuse will do," Bruno replied, grinning. "How do you stuff them?"

"Pork sausage and apples."

"Guys," Isabelle chided, "if we can get back to business. Did you see a small hut near the target house? Bruno thinks he can get you installed there and the geese removed. Would that help?"

"Perfect, we should be able to get full audio there," said Hanno. "And we may be able to get into his computer."

"How would you do that?" Bruno asked.

"A pinhole camera to get the keystrokes for his password."

Isabelle rapped the table. "Okay, let's get started."

Well before nine, Bruno and the two technicians arrived at Oudinot's farm and declined the offer of coffee, only to learn that they had missed Martine. She had a few minutes earlier walked across to the *chartreuse* to thank Sylvestre for agreeing to the deal that would end the feud.

"Good," said Bruno. "That will provide a distraction while these men install their equipment in your hut."

Hanno and Friedrich, their surveillance gear in their rucksacks, followed in Bruno's footsteps as he crept carefully through the woodland and the undergrowth toward the hut. The area was littered with geese droppings, and the ammoniac stench inside the hut was daunting, even with the door open. The two technicians wrinkled their noses and glared their dismay at Bruno. He left them to it, heading back to Oudinot's farm where his van waited, when the phone at his waist began to vibrate. He pulled it out to look at the screen and smiled when he saw Martine was calling.

"Bonjour, *ma belle*," he said. "I'm missing you already."

"Bruno, stop. This is serious. It's Sylvestre. He's dead. I couldn't find him anywhere although all the doors were open, and then I looked in the pool. He was facedown."

"Merde." He gasped. "I'll be right there. Don't touch anything."

"I already pulled him out and tried to revive him."

"That's fine. I'm at your dad's place and I'm on the way."

He turned and crashed through the woods, skirting Oudinot's fence, and along the road to turn up the dirt path as he had on his first visit. Martine, her clothes drenched, was on her knees by the pool. The sliding glass arches that covered the pool had been partially opened. As he approached, Bruno saw a male body stretched out beside Martine. Nude except for bathing shorts, its eyes were open and glassy. He could detect no sign of injury. Draped on the rim of the pool lay a dark-colored, sodden bathrobe.

Bruno knelt down and put the back of his fingers on Sylvestre's neck. He was cold and had no pulse. The body was white except for the chest, which seemed bruised and red.

"You tried pumping his chest?" he asked.

"I came looking for him, found him in the pool, climbed in to haul him out and began pumping him. I was hopeful at first because a lot of water gushed from his mouth and nose, but that was all. Then I called you and started again."

"He's dead, sure enough." He helped her to her feet and hugged her. "It must have been a shock to find him this way. I'm sorry you had to see it."

"I'm fine, just sorry I came too late to be of any use. He must have drowned. Maybe he was drunk."

"Was the bathrobe there when you arrived?"

"No, he was wearing it or, rather, half wearing it, on one arm and shoulder. It came off when I was trying to get him out of the pool."

"You did well to get him out."

Bruno looked around. On the table were two tall glass vases, each with a burned-out candle inside. Beside them was a book, an ashtray, cigarettes and a lighter, two empty brandy glasses and an empty bottle of Drambuie, a Scottish liqueur that Bruno had drunk after one of Pamela's dinners. He rose to look more closely. A bath towel was draped over one of the chairs. At each end of the table was what looked like a metallic umbrella, an outdoor heater with a gas bottle in its base, designed for the heat to come out at the top and be reflected back down by the metal parasol. Each of the heaters was switched to ON. He slipped on some evidence gloves and rocked the gas cylinders. Each one was empty as if it had burned all night until the gas ran out.

The book was square, glossy and in English, with the photograph of a silver-blue Type 57 Atlantic on the cover, the one that he recalled was now in a California museum. The title was *Bugatti Yesterday and Today.* Beside the cigarettes on the table was a small leather pouch of the kind used for pipe tobacco. Bruno opened it and smelled marijuana. There were several stubbed-out joints in the ashtray alongside the cigarette butts. He put the ashtray, the glasses and bottle, the lighter and cigarette pack into separate evidence bags and called Fabiola to ask her to come up to certify a death. Then he called Isabelle.

"Bad news," he said. "One of your targets, Sylvestre, is dead."

"Putain," she said. "What happened?"

"He drowned in his pool sometime in the night. There are no visible injuries and nothing immediately suspicious. It looks like he was drunk and stoned."

"Maybe it was meant to look that way," she said. "Was it you who found him?"

"No, he was found by a neighbor, his cousin, less than half an hour ago. She got him out of the pool and tried to resuscitate him but no luck. Then she called me, and I got here maybe five minutes ago, no more."

"Is Freddy there?" she asked immediately.

"No immediate sign of him, but I'm about to take a good look around. Shall I bring Hanno and Friedrich here?"

"No, I'll do that when I arrive. I'll leave now."

"I already called a doctor."

"Merde," she said. "I wish you hadn't done that yet."

"No choice," he replied. "It's the law."

"See if you can find his phone or laptop anywhere and secure it, that's the priority now. And if you do find Freddy, hold him."

"What about J-J? Should I call him?"

"Not until I get there and see for myself. I'll probably want a full autopsy and forensic check. I'll ask the gendarmes here to send a team up to secure the grounds."

She sounded as if she were about to hang up, and he said quickly, "Don't forget your own laptop — the data cards, remember."

"Of course, thanks for reminding me," she said. "I remember that one of them covered part of the pool area, so it's a pity they're not infrared." She hung up.

"Sorry," he said to Martine. "Police commissioner."

She looked at him skeptically. "And who are Hanno and Friedrich?"

"Did your dad tell you about the surveillance operation?" She nodded. "They're the ones in the hut, installing the surveillance gear, which now won't be needed. Did you look in the lodge by the gate?"

"Yes, the door is open there, too."

"Do you mind staying here while I look around?"

"I'd rather come with you, and I need to get out of these wet clothes. Sylvestre isn't going anywhere."

"Call your mother and ask her to bring you a towel and some fresh clothes. You can tell her what happened but that she is not to tell anyone else, okay? I'm sorry about this, but there's a lot more involved than I'm able to say."

"All this for a tax inspection?" she said, raising a cynical eyebrow. "I find that hard to believe."

Bruno shrugged. "When I can, I'll tell you the whole story, but it's likely that I don't know all of it."

"That was a woman's voice on the phone," she said. "All the police commissioners around here are men. I know that because I went to see them to talk about the plans for the rally."

"You're right. But she is a police commissioner, a Frenchwoman who used to work for the Police Nationale in Périgueux, but right now she's attached to Eurojust, and the surveillance is her operation. Now, excuse me, but I need to look around."

Martine looked at him, exasperated, then picked up her phone and began dialing. Bruno smiled apologetically and turned to head for the lodge where he had found Freddy on his last visit. Then he remembered something. He called the gendarmerie in St. Denis, and Sergeant Jules answered.

"Something very urgent, Jules," he said. "You know the big truck park in Le Buisson? I need you or someone to go there right away and secure the big van belonging to the guy from Alsace who had that old car at the parade. His name is Sylvestre Wémy, and there should be two cars inside, the one he showed off and a new electric car. Don't let anybody touch it until I get there or some of J-J's forensics people arrive."

"There's only me and Yveline here," Jules replied. "Just as Isabelle ran out the door she asked for the others to head up to Sylvestre's place to meet her there and be prepared to stay guarding it all day, but she didn't say why."

"You can tell Yveline that we found Sylvestre dead, drowned, and that Indian guy who was with him has disappeared. But I really need that truck of theirs to be secured if you have to do it yourself."

At the lodge where Freddy had stayed, the door was open, leading into a sparsely furnished sitting room with an armchair, a TV set and a rowing machine. He called out but heard no reply. Car magazines were scattered around the floor, and a driver's helmet was perched on top of the TV. The kitchen contained a machine to make espresso that looked complicated and expensive. The fridge contained bottles of mineral water, milk, apple juice and some yogurts. In the freezer compartment were ice cubes and two frozen pizzas. Upstairs were two bedrooms and a bathroom, soap and toothpaste on the sink, a towel that was still wet on the floor by the shower. Freddy had not been gone long. One bedroom was empty; the other contained an unmade bed, more car magazines and a handsome antique armoire that was empty. An adapter was still in the plug in the wall beside the bed, but whatever it recharged was gone.

Sylvestre's house was also deserted, but the bed in the main bedroom was made, the wardrobe was full of clothes, and the bathroom contained the usual range of toiletries. On top of the bed was a shirt, a sweater and trousers and on the floor beside it a pair of underpants, socks and shoes, as if he'd undressed in a hurry, perhaps before getting his bathrobe and going out to the pool. Bruno saw a wire snaking from an electric plug in the wall and disappearing beneath the underpants. He pushed the pants aside with his foot to reveal the charger for an iPhone, but the phone had gone. He put an evidence bag on top of it.

The bedside table was piled with books. The top one was titled *Bugatti 57: The Last French Bugatti.* It seemed to have more photos than text. Beneath it was a paperback that looked like a novel or a history book in

English, *The Grand Prix Saboteurs* by Joe Saward. On the cover was a photo of a Bugatti like the one Sylvestre had brought to the vintage-car parade, with a swastika atop it. The long subtitle heralded the unknown story of the Grand Prix drivers who became wartime intelligence agents. At the bottom of the pile was a hardback, also in English, *A Different Danger: Three Champions at War* by Richard Armstrong.

Down in the kitchen everything was as he'd remembered it, except that the laptop was gone, and there was a single glass and an empty bottle of Chablis on the counter. He looked in the other rooms but failed to see the laptop anywhere. In the sitting room with its armchairs of leather and chrome was a large bookcase, almost filled with books on cars and issues of classic-car magazines, auction catalogs and invitations to more Concours d'Élégance. Bruno marveled at the scale of the subculture all this represented. Between the armchairs was a glass-and-chrome coffee table with several magazines on top, all of them from the Club Bugatti of France. The one on top was dated November 1996, and a bookmark had been inserted into its pages.

Bruno looked inside and skimmed an article by a woman named Stella Tayssedre, who had been Ettore Bugatti's secretary in Paris and a member of Benoist and Grover-Williams's Resistance network. She had been arrested by the Gestapo the same day as Benoist, along with her husband, and had been five months pregnant at the time. She was taken to the railway station at Compiègne along with Benoist and the others to board what she called "the train of death" to Germany. At the station, someone from the International Red Cross noticed her pregnancy and took her off the train. The Swedish consul subsequently managed to get her released, but her husband never returned.

Bruno closed the magazine, shaking his head at the thought of those grim times, but struck also by the breadth and depth of Sylvestre's research. Annette might have been irritated by her English boyfriend's fixation on the lost Bugatti, but Sylvestre seemed just as obsessed.

The other two houses, one in each of the wings around the courtyard, were locked and the shutters closed. He walked back to the pool, where Martine and her mother, Odette, were standing by Sylvestre's body, Martine in dry clothes, jeans and a cotton sweater.

"Such a young man, it's so sad," said

Odette. "What a terrible accident and such a shame that Martine had to be the one who found him."

He heard the sound of a car being driven fast, too fast for the road, and it went rushing past the entrance. It braked hard, reversed and then Isabelle climbed out, walking across and leaving the car door open and the engine running.

"Bonjour, mesdames," she said briskly. "I understand you live next door. You may return home. Thank you for your help, and we'll contact you as soon as we're done here. Just one question: did either of you see or hear anything in the course of last night?"

Martine and her mother shook their heads and left for Odette's car, parked in the driveway. Isabelle had to move her own car to let them out. When she got back, Bruno said, "Sylvestre's phone and laptop are both gone."

"What about cars?" she asked.

"That's Sylvestre's rented Range Rover in the courtyard. The one Freddy was using isn't here."

"Right." She pulled out her phone, dialed, introduced herself and said she wanted an emergency watch-and-detain order to go out to all airports, airlines and traffic police.

379

She gave Freddy's name, two aliases that were new to Bruno and the license-plate number of his Range Rover.

"That was the brigadier," she said. "Now I have to try to get Europol to move as fast." She dialed again and then said to him as she waited, "Could you bring Hanno and Friedrich here, please?" Then she turned back to her phone.

Bruno headed for the rear of the *chartreuse,* called out to identify himself, and Hanno poked his head around the door.

"Operation's over," Bruno said. "The target's dead, and Isabelle is here and sent me to get you."

"You're kidding," said Hanno, rolling his eyes. "At least we'll be out of this smell of duck shit."

"They're geese," said Bruno, and the two men started to repack their gear. Bruno pushed down the fence to let the two men come across and told them to follow him when they were ready and join him and Isabelle at the pool.

By the time Bruno got there, Fabiola had already arrived and was examining the body. Isabelle was still on her phone.

"Scratches on the back of his shoulders and some of his hair is pulled out at the back," said Fabiola.

"Could that have happened when Martine got him out of the pool?" he asked. "He's a lot heavier than her so she would have had a hard time."

"I doubt it, looks more like a struggle to me, as though somebody might have been holding his head underwater," she said. "We'll need to examine his fingernails, see if he scratched anybody. Could you bag his hands? And I'll want to know how much of that alcohol he had."

"That might not be all he had. There's an empty bottle of wine in the kitchen as well as that empty bottle of Drambuie out here. It's inside one of those evidence bags," said Bruno. "And he'd been smoking joints."

"Drunk and stoned, it wouldn't have been difficult to drown him." Fabiola turned to look at the surface of the pool. "Is that a bit of hair floating there?"

"There was a second glass with the Drambuie bottle. He may not have been drinking alone."

Isabelle joined them. "Are you saying it looks like murder by drowning?"

"I'm saying it could be, maybe even probably. There are signs of some kind of struggle. But if he was extremely drunk, he might have passed out in the pool and drowned that way."

"We're going to need J-J and the forensics team," Bruno said to Isabelle. "By the way, Sylvestre has a big van in a truck park near here, containing a vintage car and a fancy electric one. It looks like a traveling workshop inside. I've asked Sergeant Jules to secure it."

Isabelle nodded, dully. "Check on that, if you would. And see if there are any keys around here that might open it." She looked across at him, shaking her head. "If it hadn't been for those delays in getting the warrants — ah, there's no point crying over spilled milk. I'll call J-J now."

"I trust this means that J-J can now make public the murder inquiry into Monsieur Hugon," Bruno said.

"I suppose so," said Isabelle, as though it didn't much matter to her.

"In that case, do you mind if I look around for anything that might establish a link that could connect Hugon with Sylvestre and Freddy, perhaps papers or letters?" He wondered if he should tell her to pull herself together and act like the efficient, purposeful Isabelle he knew.

"Be my guest," she said. "You'll wear gloves, of course. Anything to do with finance or Dubai or Abu Dhabi, put it to one side."

She sighed deeply and looked at him. "This was the operation that was going to make my name and really put Eurojust on the map, penetrating the finance network, turning Sylvestre so he worked for me."

"I understand," he said. "I'm sorry it didn't work out as you hoped. But then you never want things to be too easy. And it's not as though you failed. You've mapped the network, traced some of the payment routes in Europe and the paymasters in the Gulf. And you've still got a shot at picking up Freddy."

"Dear Bruno, always looking for the positive in every disaster." She gave him a fond look and then braced herself. "And you're right. Time to gather what we can from the wreckage and start all over again."

23

The whole panoply of a murder investigation began to build around Bruno, forensics teams and photographers, uniformed police searching the grounds and detectives sifting through Sylvestre's Range Rover and all the contents of the houses. Bruno sat by the pool with his notebook out, skimming through it as he tried to work out what motive Freddy might have had to kill his partner and flee. Did he suspect that they were under surveillance and that Sylvestre might agree to work for the authorities to gain immunity from prosecution? Had Freddy learned that Sylvestre was taking money meant for the cause? Had he simply become too much of a risk? Might it have been personal, Freddy trying to take over Sylvestre's business? But in that case, would he not have prepared matters better? From the look of Freddy's place, he'd left in a hurry if not in a panic. And how could he take over Sylvestre's business ventures, unless Freddy was certain he could thumb his nose at a French extradition request?

Bruno could see no explanation that satisfied him. And Freddy had left all the books and journals behind that dealt with the lost Bugatti. Perhaps he had no interest in it, but it had been to Freddy that Hugon had mailed his research report or whatever it was. That reminded Bruno; he should ask J-J if his team had been able to break into Hugon's computer. The research report should be in there. And had Freddy and Sylvestre together killed Hugon or just one of them? There had been three coffee cups, Bruno remembered. And what was Sylvestre's second deal with the *notaire*? At least he could check that. He was about to ring Brosseil's office when he remembered there was someone who would need to know about the death. He called his friend Thomas in Alsace instead.

"I've got unpleasant news. Sylvestre was found dead this morning in his swimming pool."

"*Mon Dieu.* Was it an accident?" asked Thomas.

"We're not sure yet." Bruno explained the circumstances, said that the family feud had been settled and that two of Sylvestre's land deals were almost completed. "There's an autopsy later today, and I'll keep you informed."

"Thanks, I'd better tell the mayor. That's our richest citizen gone and the last of his line."

"Can you let me have the name of his lawyer, and find out if there's a will?" Bruno said, and then stopped. "Last of his line?"

"He was an only child and had no direct heirs. His father and grandfather were only sons."

"So who are the nearest relatives?" Bruno asked.

"None around here. I imagine it will be the ones he was having the feud with. They'll inherit a fortune."

"Mon Dieu," said Bruno, his mind racing. "That's quite a motive. And it was his cousin Oudinot's daughter who found the body."

Martine had left him not long before eleven, he recalled. Fabiola was putting Sylvestre's death at somewhere between midnight and four in the morning; Sylvestre's immersion in the heated pool had made the usual body temperature tests meaningless. But did she and her father know there were no other heirs to Sylvestre's estate?

"I'll call the lawyer and find out about a

will, just as soon as I've seen the mayor. He'll probably want the body brought back here for a big funeral. It's quite an event in a town like this."

"I understand, and thanks, Thomas, and my love to Ingrid."

Rocked by the prospect that the woman he was sleeping with might be a murder suspect, Bruno tried to remember every meeting he'd had with Martine and Sylvestre, including that first time when the two cousins had been together at this very spot by the pool. There was nothing that suggested that Martine was anything but what she said, keen to help resolve the family feud, and a bit embarrassed by her father's hostility. Surely he now knew Martine well enough . . .

No, he didn't, he told himself. There had been only a few meetings, a lunch, some meals, two glorious evenings making love, a sense of mounting excitement that went beyond his attraction to her looks and brains and talent, the enjoyment he took in her presence, the pleasure he felt at the prospect of seeing her again. He liked her a lot, no, he more than liked her, and Bruno knew himself well enough to suspect that he was falling for her more and more deeply. And that would skew his judgment. Duty as well as decency required that he hand this over to J-J to investigate.

In the meantime, he had work to do. He called the *notaire*'s office, and after a short pause Brosseil came on the line.

"Bad news," he began. "Your new client, Sylvestre Wémy, is dead. Drowned in his pool last night. I'm at his place now. Those deals of his won't go through now, and I need to find out what they are. I know about Oudinot; it's the other one."

Brosseil stuttered something, dropped the phone and then said, "Sorry, it's a bit of a shock. At least the deposits are paid. He did bank transfers for each of them from my office, so I'll get my fee, or some of it. The second deal was with Jérôme at the amusement park. Monsieur Wémy was planning to buy it, enlarge it and build it up. He said something about adding a car museum."

"The mayor will be sorry to hear that's fallen through," Bruno replied, recovering quickly from the surprise. "How much of a deposit did he put down? The usual ten percent?"

"No, fifty thousand to Oudinot, half the final price, and two hundred thousand to Jérôme, twenty percent. He paid extra because he wanted the deals wrapped up quickly before he went to China. I'd better get onto Oudinot and Jérôme."

"Oudinot already knows," Bruno said. "His daughter found the body, but don't pass that news around yet."

As he closed his phone, he wondered if someone other than Freddy had been involved in Sylvestre's death. The Oudinot family had a motive to loathe him in the past, but surely not once the land deal was agreed. Oudinot had been very pleased with the sale when Bruno had seen him. But then, he might expect to inherit. And Jérôme was looking at a million-euro payday if the sale of the amusement park had been completed. Could the lost Bugatti have been sufficient motive, perhaps for someone equally obsessed, like George Young? Certainly with all his books and hiring a researcher, Sylvestre had been far better organized in his search than Young's dependence on some old family memoir that hadn't taken him far. But that was hardly a motive for murder. And Young was aware of the legal complications of the vehicle's ownership if it was ever found. However much it might be worth, the finder would get only a fraction of an eventual sale price.

"I wish I could sit around a pool all day while others slave away," came J-J's booming voice.

"I'm thinking," said Bruno. "I'm trying to work out if anyone but Freddy might have had a motive."

"Start by asking yourself who else has fled the scene. That van you mentioned with Sylvestre's cars in it, did you find the key?"

"I found a key case in the kitchen with a lot of keys on it. I left it there in an evidence bag to be fingerprinted."

"That's done. Can you go down to wherever the van is parked with a forensics team, let them in and give them a hand? They've just arrived from Bergerac with Inspector Jofflin. You've worked with him before, and you've at least seen inside the van and know the cars."

"Okay, any interesting papers turned up yet?"

"Isabelle's handling that with her two guys, and she knows to keep a special eye out for anything that might have come from Hugon."

"What about Hugon's computer?"

"Yves can't get into it. We may have to send it to Bordeaux, maybe to Paris; they have machines that can run through millions of possible passwords in a few minutes. Given time, they'll break it."

"There's something you need to know," said Bruno. "The young woman who found the body, his cousin Martine. I'm involved with her, so I can't follow this up myself. But I've just learned from a friend in Alsace that Sylvestre has no other heirs. That means his estate will go to Martine and her parents, and there's been a long-standing and bitter family feud that I thought had been settled. Given Sylvestre's wealth, that's quite a motive, and I think you ought to pursue it, even though I've known the family for years, and I really don't think they are killers, least of all Martine. It would break my heart if I'm wrong."

J-J studied him in silence for a long moment. "Okay, Bruno, I'll look into it myself." His voice was quiet and sympathetic. "And thanks for telling me."

Bruno rose, went to get the keys, joined the team from Bergerac and headed for the truck garage at Le Buisson. Bruno did not know the security man on duty, but at the sight of Bruno's uniform and the police van that carried the forensic specialists, the guard opened the electronic gates to let them in. One of the keys opened the door. They pulled out the ramps, and Inspector Jofflin and Bruno donned their snowman suits and bootees and climbed in. From their van, two members of Jofflin's crew unloaded a portable generator, fired it up and connected two flood lamps to illuminate the two cars, ancient and modern, that dominated the van's interior. But that was not where Jofflin began his search. He looked at the racks of oils, lubricants and chemicals that lined one side of the van, each of them secured for travel with bungee cords. Then he looked at the workbench and the tools above it on their sturdy hooks. Beneath the workbench were several pieces of equipment. One by one, Jofflin pointed to a welding kit, a generator and something else that Bruno did not recognize.

"Three-dimensional printer, industrial size," said Jofflin. "All the race-car teams use them these days. They can design a new component or piece of bodywork over dinner, print it overnight and have it ready to test the next day. This one has DMLS, direct metal laser sintering."

"You mean they can print metal, not just plastics?" Bruno asked, thinking that Jofflin relished showing off his knowledge.

"Absolutely, that's the point. But this system can print both. Whoever designed this van really knew what they were doing. It's better equipped than most garages." He pointed to the van roof, where six curved steel girders, each anchored to the floor, rose up the walls and then curved in to meet at a fixture that held a hook and chain. "That's a heavy-duty engine hoist. They can lift out engines, print new parts and even electroplate them. Let me see . . ."

He looked along the cans of chemicals, muttering something about permits. On a bookshelf above the workbench, Bruno saw a book-sized file marked "Permits" and asked Jofflin, "Is this what you're looking for?"

"That's it," said Jofflin and began leafing through. "Acids, hydroxides, metallic oxides, halogens, diisocyanates, it looks like all the approvals are here, even cyanide. That's for the electroplating."

Bruno's eyes widened. "You know J-J already has a cyanide-poisoning case, another murder. Could a specialist lab tell us whether the cyanide that was used in that killing came from the stuff they have here?"

"I don't know, but if the guys who drove this truck are possible suspects, you'd better tell J-J right away," Jofflin replied. "Meanwhile we'll inventory all this and check for fingerprints."

When Bruno called J-J to inform him of what had been found, J-J suggested that Jofflin call the Bordeaux lab directly to see if the batch of cyanide could be identified.

"In the meantime, Isabelle has come up

with some papers from Sylvestre's house that look as if they're related to Hugon," J-J told Bruno, adding that it seemed to be a research report on the Bugatti. Even more interesting was a handwritten note of a phone conversation with Hugon, attached to it with a paper clip.

"I think Hugon was trying to blackmail Sylvestre," J-J said.

"How do you mean? What could he have on Sylvestre?"

"Information," said J-J. "At least, that's how I interpret the note."

It contained just a handful of words and figures: "Hugon," "Bugatti," "new lead," and then "bonus." Finally came the figure 5 followed by four zeros. After the figures had been scrawled, an exclamation point had been made so hard the pen had ripped the paper.

"Whoever wrote it was angry or maybe just excited," said J-J. "Maybe you should come back here and take a look."

"Sylvestre was rich," said Bruno. "Fifty thousand was like pocket change to him, but I suppose it could be a motive for murder. And we found no trace of fifty grand in Hugon's bank accounts."

"It certainly meant Sylvestre could no longer trust Hugon, and maybe Sylvestre wanted him silenced anyway," J-J replied. "Isabelle has people looking at Sylvestre's bank accounts as we speak. By the way, I went to the farm and talked to the Oudinots, and while they have only each other as alibis, they seemed genuinely stunned by his death. I think they're in the clear. Of course, I may be biased by the brioches Oudinot's wife served with the coffee. And that daughter of theirs is really something; you're a lucky man."

"Let's hope I'm still lucky after she's been grilled by you. I'll leave Jofflin and his guys to go over the truck, and I'll head back."

"One more thing — Isabelle has started to track Freddy. He took an early morning flight to Amsterdam from Bordeaux. It left just after six, so he must have set off from the house by four this morning at the latest. They're trying all the outbound flights from Amsterdam now but suspect he's using other ID."

"How did he buy the ticket?"

"At the airport with a platinum credit card, but he paid for a business-class return so was waved right through. He must have known they do extra checks on one-way tickets bought at the last minute."

When Bruno returned to the *chartreuse,* he found Philippe Delaron in the driveway,

395

trying to take pictures of the house despite the two gendarmes standing stolidly in the way. Bruno brushed aside Philippe's questions and went looking for J-J. He was out of reach, closeted in Sylvestre's kitchen with Isabelle and the *procureur,* who had driven down from Périgueux to take charge of the inquiry. While Bruno had been at the truck garage, the forensic pathologist confirmed Fabiola's suspicion that Sylvestre had been held underwater until he drowned. That meant they were now dealing with two related murders. As he waited for J-J to be free, Bruno called Fabiola to tell her it looked like she'd been right about the cyanide.

She quickly changed the subject. "Gilles texted me to say he'd be back late. He's out at Rastignac again, seeing some local policeman who's a friend of yours," Fabiola told him. "He's gone with George Young in the E-type. They seem to be interested in junkyards all of a sudden."

"Have you told him about Sylvestre's death?" Bruno asked.

"Yes, I texted him back. Why, is it a secret? I assume he told Young, since they seem to be working together."

"Not a secret, it's just that we may need to talk to Young about his whereabouts last night. Since he knew Sylvestre, and they were rivals for the Bugatti, he's on the list of potential suspects."

"Annette won't like that."

"It's just routine; he's not a serious suspect. Anyway, since I assume they're sleeping together, she's his alibi."

"I'm not sure they are. She called me last night to complain about him being so obsessed with that old car he's hunting for," Fabiola said. "I told her I sympathized, since Gilles was also getting caught up in the thrill of the chase." Her voice dripped sarcasm, then became matter-of-fact. "I have a waiting room full of patients, so I may see you later with the horses. Bye, Bruno."

As Bruno put his phone away, Isabelle, J-J and the *procureur* came out of Sylvestre's house, and J-J waved him across to join them.

"It's me who wants to speak with you," said the *procureur*. "It's about this young man who nearly blinded a little girl. I've seen your recommendation, and I spoke to the mayor this morning on the drive down. I'll go along with the plan, but only on the condition that the parents sign a guarantee to enforce it. After all the fuss in the media about the case, I'm going to be criticized for being too soft, so the regimen is going to have to be really strict. And I don't want this kid to think he's getting away with something, so that means no phone for him and no computer. I'll e-mail you the text to print out, and I want it signed by both parents."

The *procureur* left, Isabelle had disappeared, and J-J led him into the kitchen and showed him the research report and the attached note. Bruno glanced at it and agreed; it was hard to put any other interpretation on it. Hugon was demanding more money for his new lead.

"Take a look at that document underneath," J-J said. "You know more about this business than I do. Let me know what you think, and then you'd better take care of whatever the *procureur* asked you to do. We've got more than enough manpower here."

The report was mainly a list of negatives. No Bugatti had been registered in the Dordogne or any neighboring *département* between 1939 and 1946, except for the Gironde, where most of the stock in the Alsace factory at Molsheim, which the German military had requisitioned, had been moved to a replacement factory on rue Alfred Danat in Bordeaux. There was nothing in the Vichy archives that suggested the car had been authorized to enter the Vichy zone. And there was no indication of any insurance policy being taken out on a car with the relevant chassis number after 1940.

Hugon had researched the history of the four Bugatti Atlantics, and Bruno was surprised to learn that until little more than ten years ago it had been assumed there were only three. The two bought by the English customers, Lord Rothschild and R. B. Pope, were silver-blue and sapphire blue. All the known photos of the black Atlantic were assumed to feature the car bought by the Holzschuch family, the car that was wrecked by a train at a level crossing in 1955.

Then a sharp-eyed French historian, Jean-Pierre Cornu, realized that the photos of the black Atlantic were of two different cars with different headlamps and different bumpers. In the spring of 1937, there had been a Concours d'Élégance in Juan-les-Pins on March 31, and another at Nice the next week. Each featured a black Atlantic, but they were different cars. In the first photograph, from Juan-les-Pins, Madame Holzschuch stood next to the car. In the second, at Nice, Yvonne Williams, the wife of William Grover-Williams, was featured, and this was the photo that appeared in the Bugatti catalog for 1938. This was also the car that Williams had taken to 121 miles per hour on the outskirts of London at a road test during the British automobile show in 1937, and it had also become the first car to reach 200 kilometers per hour, 125 miles per hour, at the Montlhéry circuit south of Paris.

Then came the crux of the report. The researcher confirmed that Grover-Williams and his wife had been guests at the Château de Rastignac, the first real connection between the car and the Périgord. He had now found evidence that a black Bugatti Atlantic had been seen at the château in 1941 and had then been dismantled and hidden in a disused tobacco barn just a few miles away. And he was now close to learning what had happened to it.

The researcher had to be Hugon, although no name was listed on the title page. The report, which included copies of the photos described in the text, was dated the day before the date on the post office receipt that had been in Hugon's pocket. That in turn was five days before Hugon's death. Bruno began to scribble down in his notebook the timeline of events.

The report was bound to have excited Sylvestre and Freddy. Presumably it was a day or two later that they had received Hugon's phone call, demanding another fifty thousand euros. At that point they must have decided to take up the invitation to the St. Denis vintage-car show. They could then have visited Hugon and either forced him to tell them what he knew or gave him a check and learned the Atlantic's fate. Then they killed him in a way that looked like a heart attack and tore up the check.

That made sense, but it left two big questions. The first was Freddy's role. Sylvestre was the one obsessed by the car. Why had the report been sent to Freddy? Possibly, Bruno thought, because Sylvestre wanted to cover his own trail, probably because he was so well known in Alsace that collecting a parcel of documents from a *poste restante* would provoke unwelcome curiosity. And why use a *poste restante* rather than Sylvestre's home address, unless Sylvestre had wanted to conceal his interest? The far-bigger question was, if Sylvestre had learned of the car's fate and its hiding place just before killing Hugon, why had he not gone to find it and reap all the fame and fortune that would go with the dramatic discovery?

Perhaps Hugon had not finally established the car's whereabouts. Maybe the car's location was known, but it had been cached somewhere Sylvestre could not obtain physical possession. Or perhaps he could not even see it to confirm its presence; somewhere like a junkyard, mused Bruno, buried under tons of scrap metal.

He went to share his thoughts with J-J and found him with Isabelle, who was looking exhausted and elated at the same time.

"We're onto him, your Freddy," she said, looking at Bruno. "You've got us all calling him that now. It was Sylvestre's iPhone that did it. Freddy forgot to turn it off. We picked it up in the Bordeaux airport, and then in Schiphol in Amsterdam, where he landed not long after seven. We then lost the signal when he took off on another plane at eight-thirty. That gave us five flights to choose from, and we monitored each destination. He arrived in Athens just before noon. He's still there, and we're trying to get the Greek police to pick him up. And we think we have the name and passport number he's now using."

"Unless he spent the flight downloading everything on Sylvestre's iPhone onto his own," said J-J. "Then he could have emptied the memory and tossed the phone into an Athens wastebasket, where it's still transmitting. Meanwhile Freddy's on a new flight to

Abu Dhabi or somewhere."

"Thanks," she said, tiredly. "Just what I needed. But that's not all. Sylvestre's bank accounts have all been emptied. Freddy must have used Sylvestre's laptop to do it, programming it to order the transfers while he was on the phone to Amsterdam. He hit the send button just after eight, but at least we now have all the details of the accounts to which he sent the money, and now we're able to monitor them."

"How much did he get?" J-J asked.

"Just over a million. Sylvestre had loaded up one account to finance the new Shanghai venture."

"So your operation has been a success," said Bruno. "You've mapped their finance network."

She nodded and said, "It's like that old medical joke. You know the one, where the doctor comes out of the operating theater wearing his scrubs and mask and tells the patient's family that the operation was a success, but unfortunately the patient died."

Isabelle walked out with Bruno when he left. At first she said nothing, but once they were out of earshot of the others, she turned to him. "I just did you a favor. I took down your two cameras before the forensics team turned up because I didn't want them found. For both our sakes, I didn't want the *procureur* realizing that we'd started the surveillance before we were legally authorized to do so. I'll get them back to you, but I want to review the data cards first."

"You won't be able to use them as evidence."

"Agreed, but it might help me know what happened. I'll keep you posted."

24

Bruno went first to Oudinot's farm to make sure all was well there and to ask Martine if she might be free that evening. In the house he found only Odette, rolling pastry and listening to a call-in show on Périgord Bleu about gardening. He said he hoped J-J's questions had not been a strain. Odette continued her rolling, cocked her head at the radio and said, "Idiots."

"They're saying it's a good weekend to plant mâche, which shows how little they know," she said, looking at Bruno. "You use the lunar calendar, don't you? Have you seen what it says for today? No gardening of any kind."

Bruno nodded; he had seen it, and it had eased his guilt a little for neglecting his garden with all the extra work involved with Sylvestre and Félix and the time he was spending with Martine.

"And have you seen the horoscope today?

Read what it says about Virgo, that's Martine's sign. Read it out."

Bruno picked up *Sud Ouest,* already turned to the horoscope page. It was something that always reminded him of that happy first summer with Isabelle; she always read out both his and hers. He read aloud: "This is not a good time for romance. Avoid any new amorous entanglements; they are doomed to fail and make you miserable. Stick with old friends and family and take lots of exercise."

He put the paper down, and Odette looked him in the eye. "I'm not a fool, Bruno. I know Martine is seeing you, and she seems very happy about it, but it's not going to last. She's never going to settle down here, whatever fantasies Fernand may have about his daughter coming home to breed grandchildren. She never will. She's a big-city girl now, able and ambitious, and that's fine by me. If you two go on with this affair, you'll both be unhappy. What's more, she's a Virgo, you're a Libra; it can never work."

"I think you're reading a lot into a newspaper horoscope, Odette," he replied, embarrassed.

"I know my daughter. Anyway, you're coming to dinner tomorrow night, and then she's off, back to London next week, which is for the best."

"Isn't she staying for the funeral? Do you know if it's going to be here or in Alsace?"

"I don't know. It would be a bit hypocritical of us to put on a great show of mourning. Still, family is family when all's said and done."

"I'll see you tomorrow evening, and thank you for the invitation. I'll just go and have a word with Fernand and Martine."

"You'll find them down with the newborn calf, but they'll probably be talking about Sylvestre's will and who's going to inherit. I hope it's not us. Fernand and I aren't the kind of people who know what to do with money. Martine's different."

In the barn, the calf was being licked clean by its mother and trying to stand, rear legs first, and tottering. Martine squeezed his hand as he greeted her with the *bise* on both cheeks, and then he shook hands with Fernand.

"So the *commissaire*'s interrogation wasn't too difficult for you?" Bruno asked.

"No, he was very polite, just wanted to know if we'd seen or heard anything and if we'd all been together in the house all night," Fernand said. "Do you know anything about Sylvestre's will?"

"I spoke to the police in Alsace, and they are contacting Sylvestre's family lawyer. We should know on Monday. And the mayor of his village in Alsace may want to have the funeral there."

"It's quite a shock," said Martine. "We're all a little bit stunned by what's happened, so I think the three of us will just have a quiet evening together here."

Bruno understood her message: no love-making tonight. "Well, I'll look forward to seeing you at dinner tomorrow."

The calf had made it to its feet, and the mother stood and nudged it with her head to get under her belly and toward her teats. The calf licked around her udder but seemed unsure what to do next. Martine reached down and put a teat firmly into the calf's mouth and then began stroking its throat to start the sucking and swallowing reflex. Her father watched her proudly and said, "Still a country girl at heart, our Martine."

Bruno went back to pick up his van and drove to the supermarket. Simon was in his office, leafing through what looked like sales figures, when Bruno came in, closing the door behind him. He sat down and handed across the printout of the *procureur*'s draft. Bruno had used his own official notepaper, with the seal of St. Denis and the heading of the Police Municipale.

"If you want to keep your son out of jail, you and your wife need to sign this. Where is she?"

"She's taken Tristan to our cottage near Arcachon," Simon replied. "She thought he needed a break after the shock of the arrest and being handcuffed."

Bruno shook his head. "You never learn, do you? Here I am trying to save that son of yours from a juvenile detention center, and you send him off for a vacation at the beach. You're thinking of him as some kind of victim in all this when in reality he's the perpetrator."

"It wasn't my idea. In fact I was against it —"

"But you never argue with your wife," Bruno interrupted. "That's half the trouble. She spoils him, she lies for him, perjures herself for his sake. And you put up with it, Simon. I think you're rotten parents. You've certainly done a lousy job of raising your son."

"One mistake . . . ," Simon began.

"More than one. Let's not forget he also faces a charge of possessing illegal drugs in commercial quantities. I doubt it will take me more than twenty minutes to get a few affidavits from his classmates saying he's been dealing drugs in the *collège.*"

"You say you can keep him out of detention?" Simon began to scan the document, frowning as he read it. "You're going to make us responsible for his behavior?"

"It's called being a parent."

"And what's this forestry business?"

"It's part of the tough regimen the *procureur* requires as the price for keeping Tristan out of jail. You can guess what's likely to become of him in there and what kind of life lies ahead of him when he gets out. This way, he has a chance of finishing his education and maybe even going on to university. It's his last chance, and you and your wife have to sign up for it or it won't happen."

"He won't like this — no phone, no computer, not to be out of our custody at any time when he's not working. It sounds like house arrest."

"It's punishment; Tristan is not supposed to like it. Maybe if you'd been enough of a father to punish him earlier he wouldn't be in this mess now."

"They won't be back from Arcachon until next week."

Bruno sighed heavily. "You just don't get it, do you, Simon? If they're not back here tonight with that signed document on the *procureur*'s desk by Monday morning, the Arcachon police will go to your beach house and arrest your son. They will then hold him in a police cell until we get around to sending a prison van to take Tristan directly to the detention center to await trial."

"Will it be enough if I sign?"

"No, I've told the *procureur* that your wife is more than half the trouble. And if she doesn't sign, then we still have the perjury charge hanging over her."

"Our lawyer says —"

"Bullshit. Call your lawyer if you want, and he'll tell you that charging her with perjury is a matter for the *procureur*'s discretion. I just spoke to him, and he's decided to go with my recommendation to keep Tristan out of jail even though he knows he's going to get a lot of flak for going soft on your son. If you spurn his offer, he'll throw the book at all of you, starting with your wife."

"You say this plan for Tristan is your suggestion?"

"It's a joint recommendation to the *procureur* from me, the head of the gendarmes and the magistrate in charge of juvenile justice. It's been endorsed by the mayor, who personally arranged this forestry work."

Simon signed the document in small neat handwriting and printed *"Lu et approuvé"* above it — "read and approved" — the legal requirement in France.

"I'll get them back tonight and somehow I'll get her to sign it."

"And you will hand deliver that document first thing Monday morning to the *procureur's* office in Périgueux. And you'd better get a receipt from his office because the mayor and I will need to see it."

Bruno rose and left without another word. He headed to the *mairie,* still fuming at the thought of Tristan being rewarded with a trip to the beach, to report to the mayor on Sylvestre's death. It might be a Saturday afternoon, but the mayor would be at work on his endless project of writing the history of St. Denis if there were no official duties to be performed. Bruno also wanted to check his e-mails. As he scrolled through, his phone pinged with an incoming text. It was Gilles, asking for a meeting at the *maison de retraite* in twenty minutes. He texted back confirmation and went back to the e-mails. One was from Tristan's mother.

"I will never forgive you for that dirty trick you played on me nor for what you have done to my boy. I'm one of the people who pays your salary and I begrudge every penny of it. You're a disgrace to your uniform," he read. He sighed, and forwarded copies to the *procureur* and to Annette. Then he printed it out twice, added one to his file on Tristan and took the other to the mayor, who was at his desk, fountain pen in hand, his manuscript before him and several old books open around him. He looked up as Bruno entered and gave him a copy of the denunciation.

"One of your voters doesn't like me," he said.

"What was the dirty trick?"

"She swore that Tristan was at home with her when he threw the stone that hit the little girl. I got her to sign a formal statement to that effect. Yveline was present when it all happened."

"I don't think the *procureur* would bring a perjury charge against a mother lying to protect her son."

"I think he will if she tries to block the forestry job you arranged as too tough on her precious son. She's taken him off to their weekend cottage in Arcachon so the poor boy can recover from his ordeal. She's the problem, and her false statement is our leverage."

The mayor put down his pen, removed his spectacles and rubbed his eyes. "What a

413

foolish woman. Human folly never changes," he said, sighing. "I'm just working on the saddest moment in the history of our town. Do you know that St. Denis and its convent were sacked and burned in 1577, during what we call the Wars of Religion? The troops were Protestant, but they were having a private war among themselves, between Galliot de La Tour, the lord of Limeuil, and his brother Jacques. We have a square called la place du Temple because they built a Protestant chapel after the town was burned. The chapel was itself demolished a hundred years later when Louis XIV revoked the rights given to Protestants under the Edict of Nantes."

"I sometimes wondered why the square was so named when there was no temple."

"Now you know. What do you want me to do with this?" he waved a copy of the e-mail from Tristan's mother.

"Nothing really. I just wanted you to know about it. I've told Simon to be sure that Tristan and his mother return from the beach today. I also wanted to tell you that we have the results of one autopsy that confirms Hugon was murdered with cyanide and another that says Sylvestre was deliberately drowned in his pool."

When Bruno left the mayor's office, he

went to the retirement home and was there to greet Gilles when he arrived in Fabiola's old Twingo with an elderly man in the passenger seat.

"Bonjour, Bruno," said the passenger, grinning at him. "Grégoire sends his regards."

Bruno realized this must be Grégoire's father, Étienne, come to visit Félix's grandfather. He had white hair and a white mustache and was wearing dark glasses, a suit and a tie. Bruno had always been struck by the formal way so many elderly people chose to dress.

"Am I right to think you're coming to visit an old schoolmate?" he asked, shaking the elderly hand through the open car window.

"That's right. Gilles called the *maison de retraite* and got him on the phone. I've brought an old school photo to see if he can pick me out. I'm pretty sure I recognized him, but it's a lifetime since we were last together."

Gilles let Étienne out and went off to park. Bruno matched his pace to the elderly shuffle and steered Étienne to the right door, already open, with their host rising to greet them. His photo album was under his arm. It was crowded in the small room, but Bruno perched on the windowsill, and

415

Gilles was offered the easy chair when he arrived but remained standing. The two old men sat side by side on the bed to look at the photos and reminisce.

"Can I bring you gentlemen some coffee or some tea, maybe a glass of wine?" Gilles asked.

They agreed that they would each like a *petit blanc.* Gesturing with his head for Bruno to follow, Gilles led the way out and across the road to pick up a bottle of chilled Bergerac Sec from the corner shop. They then borrowed some glasses from the kitchen of the *maison de retraite.*

"I'm sure that Étienne knows something about this junk shop, but he's not talking," Gilles confided as they went. "He just said he wanted to see his old friend and talk to him. He thought it might trigger some memories."

"How much have you told him?" Bruno asked.

"Everything about the car, nothing about Sylvestre."

"You know Sylvestre was found dead in his pool this morning."

"Yes, Fabiola sent me a text. Naturally, I told Young. He made some joke about giving a medal to whoever did it. What was it, heart attack or something?"

"We won't be sure until the autopsy," Bruno said quickly. If Fabiola had not told Gilles of her suspicions, that meant Young would also not know. "I thought you and Young were going together to see Étienne in the E-type."

"He called to ask if we could go separately. He wanted to get back to Annette, feeling guilty about neglecting her on a Saturday, one of her days off."

They took in the wine and glasses, the two old men pausing in what had been animated conversation over the photo album. Bruno had the feeling they were up to something.

"Funny how the old photos bring it all back," said Gilles as Bruno opened the wine and poured out four glasses.

"Maybe with young memories like yours," said Étienne, raising his glass. *"Santé."*

"So were you two in the same class?"

"Same school, different class. Étienne's older, but we were on the same soccer team. And his big brother is in the photo with Henri." Félix's grandfather pointed to another of the young men with an armband and Sten gun. "They'd been at school together, too, chased the same girls."

"So what happened to the scrap merchant Bérégevoy?" Bruno asked.

"He died sometime in the early seventies,

417

but he'd run down his stock by then," Étienne replied. "He had a place near the viaduct in Sarlat, and when they started cleaning the town up they changed the zoning and he was told to move. I don't remember where he went, if I ever knew. He had a daughter, but she moved away when she got married."

"Her name was Célestine," said Gilles. "I checked her out in Sarlat, where she worked at the *mairie* before getting married in 1961. I'm trying to trace her now. She might know what happened to the remaining stock."

"Sounds like a dead end to me," said Étienne, with a quick, sideways glance at his old schoolmate.

Bruno's phone vibrated, and he saw it was Thomas calling from Alsace. He went outside to answer it, to learn that Thomas had tracked down Sylvestre's lawyer, passed on the news of his death and asked about a will.

"He hadn't drawn one up, although the lawyer had advised Sylvestre to do so," Thomas went on. "He said he might have used another lawyer, maybe in Paris because of the scale of the family holdings, but he'd check in the registry of wills and get back to me on Monday. Any more news?"

"The autopsy has been done, and it was

murder, but we're not releasing that news yet. Somebody held his head underwater, but he was very drunk and also stoned."

"*Putain,* that's going to cause a stir. Any suspects?"

"That Indian partner of his took the first early morning flight from Bordeaux and cleared out Sylvestre's bank accounts. He's the obvious suspect and Europol is trying to track his movements after he landed in Amsterdam. If they lose his trail, the *procureur* will announce that it's a murder inquiry, but that probably won't be until Monday morning. I'll let you know. Keep this to yourself, or it's bound to leak."

They hung up, and Bruno turned on the record function on his phone, held it up to his ear as if still talking and went back to join the others. He said some words of farewell as if to end a conversation and then asked if anyone wanted more wine. Étienne held up his glass, so Bruno poured out some more, in the process leaving his phone discreetly behind a potted plant on the windowsill.

"We'll leave the wine with you. Gilles and I have a couple of errands to take care of," he said and turned to Gilles. "Will you drive Étienne back?"

Gilles nodded, saying he'd be back in an

hour or so. Bruno and Gilles left the two old men together. Once outside, Bruno asked his friend to collect the phone when he picked up Étienne, saying Bruno had forgotten it.

"My phone is recording because, now that they're alone, I think we might learn something," he said. "What are your plans for this evening?"

"Nothing particular. Fabiola wants to exercise Victoria, which reminds me: you know Pamela and Fabiola are going fifty-fifty on the Andalusian horse? They also want to move all the horses, your Hector included, to the riding school. Pamela reckons that Victoria will be placid enough for the children when they move on from ponies. That would mean leaving Hector alone in our stables, which doesn't seem like a good idea. And having Hector there would mean an extra adult horse for her customers."

Bruno raised his eyebrows. He had once thought of stabling Hector on his own property, but he didn't like the thought of leaving him alone. And police work meant he could not always be back in time to exercise the horse. Until now, he could count on Fabiola to take Hector out behind her on a long rein. It made sense to leave all the horses at Pamela's stables, but would it change his relationship with his horse if others were to ride Hector from time to time? He wouldn't even have owned a horse if Pamela had not organized all his friends to band together and buy Hector for his birthday. He owed her too much to refuse.

"It makes sense," Bruno said. "Fabiola and I could ride Victoria and Hector over to Pamela's place this evening while you drive Étienne back."

"Pamela is coming back here for dinner afterward," Gilles added. "Why not join us? I bought oysters in the market this morning, and Fabiola is making her fondue. We all know how much you like it."

"That sounds good, and I'll bring some wine," said Bruno. "Just don't forget to pick up my phone when you collect Étienne."

25

That Sunday morning in St. Denis, the church bell was summoning the faithful to mass, Father Sentout was donning his vestments, and the less religious citizens were thronging to Fauquet's to buy the special *gâteaux,* fit to grace a Sunday lunch en famille. Bruno, wearing civilian clothes, was sitting on the café terrace and feeding the heel of his croissant to Balzac. After checking on the chickens, they had taken Bruno's morning run through the woods together and then, feeling the need for some more exercise, Bruno had cleaned out the ashes from his wood-burning stove while Balzac sat patiently watching. The dog had followed to observe Bruno empty the ashes onto that part of his vegetable garden that still lay fallow. Then he had turned over the soil to dig the ashes in, thinking that did not count as the kind of gardening forbidden by the lunar calendar. He had changed his sheets and towels, filled his washing machine, showered, shaved and headed into town, singing along to Piaf's "La Vie en Rose" on the radio.

Once in town and alone on the terrace with his dog, Bruno turned on the playback feature of his phone and tried once again to make out the indistinct and mumbled words it had recorded between the two men in the retirement home once he and Gilles had left them. The previous evening, over Fabiola's fondue, he and Gilles along with Fabiola and Pamela had tried with only occasional success to follow the conversation. But some words had come over clearly. One of them had been "Bugatti," a second had been "millions," a third had been "park," and the fourth had been "Bérégevoy," the name of the junkyard owner who had bought the contents of the barn at Perdigat.

Bruno was almost sure of a few more phrases, but there were some loose ends to tie up first. He called Marcel, the owner of the garage where Annette had bought the Bugatti radiator. Marcel remembered the name of the junk shop where he had bought the radiator. It had been the closing-down sale of Bérégevoy's place when the owner died. Had anyone else asked about that recently? Bruno asked. Yes, Marcel replied, two people: the Englishman who was supposed to be driving with Annette and then, in a separate visit, a reporter from *Paris Match.*

Another of the recorded words that Bruno was sure of was "Félix." The previous evening when they had been listening, Pamela had said that there had been a phone call for Félix at the stables that afternoon. The boy had then asked to use the computer in her office when he'd finished work.

"I was checking e-mails before coming over here, and there was a window that he must have left open on the computer. I remember it had a photo of an old car, which didn't interest me so I closed it," Pamela had said. She said she would look up the history function on her browser; Gilles had written down the steps she should take.

Bruno ordered a second cup of coffee and called her. Pamela reported that Félix had looked up websites about Bugatti, the Type 57 Atlantic, and the latest Concours d'Élégance at Villa d'Este in Italy, which had been won by Ralph Lauren's car. Félix had then looked at a YouTube video of that same *concours,* which carried the headline in English "Ralph Lauren's $40 million

Bugatti Atlantic."

One did not need fluency in English to understand that, thought Bruno, thanking Pamela and then listening once again to the voices of the two men talking. But he heard only odd words or snatches of phrases. At one point Étienne had said "Rome," which baffled Bruno. He listened to that section again, and shortly before the reference to the Italian capital he was almost sure he heard the words *Naud qui l'a acheté.* Who or what was *"Naud"* and what had he bought? Bruno gave up and put the phone down. Perhaps if he gave it to J-J's forensics experts they could find a way to enhance the recording.

"Bonjour, Bruno," came a voice, and Bruno looked up, surprised to see his colleague Grégoire, Étienne's son. He invited him to sit down, share a coffee and recommended the quality of the croissants. Then as Grégoire made friends with Balzac, Bruno asked what brought him to St. Denis.

"My dad," came the reply. "He's always been religious and he said this morning he wanted to hear mass with his old school friend. He asked me to drive him over so here I am."

"Not religious yourself?" Bruno asked.

"Not really, just marriages and funerals, but it's a nice day for a drive, and it's not a day for gardening, so I was happy to agree. My wife's with them in the church now."

"Lunar calendar," said Bruno, smiling. "We're gardening by the same rules."

"They always worked for my dad, and his garden's still a sight to behold," Grégoire said. "Dad told me he'd often wanted to visit the amusement park here in St. Denis, so we'll go there after church. Then I thought we might make a day of it, go out for lunch and then drive home the long way up the Dordogne Valley and back through Sarlat."

Grégoire's coffee came, and then Balzac jumped to his feet and looked across the square giving a little yelp of welcome before trotting across to welcome Isabelle. She dropped to one knee to greet the basset hound, struggling to manage her shoulder bag, a plastic bag and a large manila envelope as Balzac tried to clamber onto her lap. Bruno called to Fauquet, standing in the door to enjoy the sun on his face, for another croissant and coffee.

"Bonjour, Bruno," said Isabelle, offering each cheek for his *bise.* He introduced Grégoire, told her that he was also a cop and

426

that the coffee and croissant were on their way.

"I remember you," said Grégoire. "You used to work for J-J in Périgueux. I think you were Inspector Perrault back then."

"And you were the municipal cop in Terrasson," she declared. "I remember you as well, that bank robbery that turned out to be an inside job. The guy went down for five years."

"A good case," said Grégoire. "I haven't seen you for ages, but J-J always said you'd be the one to succeed him."

Isabelle shook her head. "I transferred out. I'm with Eurojust these days, up in The Hague."

"So you're here on holiday, visiting old haunts?"

Bruno was sure Grégoire was simply making conversation, but Isabelle clammed up, saying simply, "Old haunts, old friends." She fell silent and devoted her attention to her croissant. Grégoire took the hint and rose to his feet, muttering something about the sermon being over by now.

"Mission complete?" Bruno asked Isabelle once Grégoire had gone.

"Pretty much, but we have a lot of follow-up to do on the banks they used," she said. "And there's going to be a legal

427

row over whether we can confiscate his cars and garage as proceeds of a criminal enterprise. That's pretty much all that's left. Sylvestre was running out of money. Most of his Alsace properties were mortgaged up to the hilt."

"What about Freddy?"

"They lost him in Athens, found his phone dumped in a trash bin at the airport. The police showed his photo at all the check-in desks, and one of the attendants thought she checked him into a flight for Beirut, but she wasn't sure. We've got the numbers of the credit cards he used to buy tickets, so we're monitoring them, and we're asking the Emirates police to seal off the Abu Dhabi showroom.

"We've sworn out a murder warrant for him, but I'm not altogether sure Freddy was Sylvestre's killer," she went on. She finished the remainder of her coffee and handed Bruno the manila envelope and the plastic bag. "Your two cameras are in there, and I printed out some of the better stills from the data card."

She led Bruno through the photos. There was no sign of Freddy until he drove off in the middle of the night in his Range Rover. The timer on the print said he left at ten to four. But another car had come to the *char-*

treuse after midnight. The image was too vague for the driver to be identifiable, but then the next print showed two people sitting by the pool. One of them was Sylvestre in a dark dressing gown. The other one had his back to the cameras. The image wasn't helped by the flaring on the film from the open-air heaters that Bruno remembered. It could be Freddy, it could even be a woman with short hair and wearing slacks, or it could be someone else altogether.

"It's clear that this other person and Sylvestre were drinking and smoking for over two hours," Isabelle said. She turned over the next still, which showed Sylvestre standing by the pool and the other person rising from a chair. The person was wearing what looked like jeans and a sweater. The next image showed Sylvestre being pushed into the pool, his unidentified companion following right behind.

"I've never watched a murder in process before this," said Bruno, shaken by what he was seeing but fascinated. "Could we enhance some of the images?"

"I tried, and I've got very good enhancement software on my computer. This is as good as you'll get."

The cameras couldn't see into the pool, and the next movement that was triggered was of the second person climbing out, still fully dressed, still with his or her back to the cameras.

"Here's your killer, standing right beneath one of the heaters and drying himself with a towel from the chair," she said. "Because of the flare we can't see the face, and then he covers his head with the towel and disappears. I say 'he' because his clothes are wet, and there's no sign of female breasts. The next thing we see is Freddy leaving in his car and that's all."

"I couldn't identify anyone from that," said Bruno.

"You may not need to. And if you take my advice, you won't use the prints in interrogation or when it comes to trial. Any decent lawyer would see through your little story about wildlife photography and argue the evidence was illegally obtained. If you have a suspect, don't let him know that you have the prints but use what the images tell you. You know when the killer arrived, what he did, when he left, and you have a car. It's a Peugeot, but it wasn't driven far enough onto the property for us to pick up a license number. If you can't leverage all that into a confession, you're in the wrong business. Above all you have the towel. I made sure it was bagged, and the forensics guys should be able to get some of the murderer's DNA from it."

She leaned forward and kissed him on the lips. "Good-bye, Bruno. Good luck," she said, giving Balzac a final caress. She headed back across the square to her rental car.

Bruno watched her go, called for the bill and began looking again through the prints, hoping against hope that something in the stance or dress of the killer might trigger something. Bruno was almost certain it was a man, but could it be Martine? She was tall enough, but there was no way she could ever have concealed her lovely breasts. It could be Freddy, but the skin of the arms seemed too pale. Who else might it be? Bruno looked again at the photos, pondering.

After a moment wrestling with his conscience, he called Fabiola and said, "I need you to do me a very big favor, but if you feel you can't do it, just tell me. I wouldn't ask if it wasn't really important."

"Tell me what it is," she said, and he explained. He could hear the reluctance in her voice when she replied that she'd think about it and call him back. Bruno put the photos back in their envelope and the envelope into the bag with the cameras and then glanced across the square where people were coming up the rue de Paris from the church.

As the crowd reached the crossroads, the numbers thinned, and Bruno saw the two old men. Félix was beside them and an elderly woman followed, whom Bruno did not know. Grégoire appeared in his car and greeted them all. The old men and the woman, presumably Grégoire's wife, climbed into the car, and Félix went to his bicycle, parked in the rack outside the *mairie,* and unlocked a chain from around the rear wheel. He cycled off, following the car.

Then Bruno recognized three more people, dressed for church, coming across the square toward him. It was Simon, his wife and Tristan. They came onto the terrace of the café and stood awkwardly before him. He rose saying "Bonjour, *monsieur-dame.*"

"As you can see, I got them back from the beach," said Simon. "And I heard from the mayor, so my wife has something to say to you."

She squared her shoulders, fixed her eyes at some point a little above Bruno's head and said quickly, without drawing breath, "I want to apologize for writing you that e-mail. I was very upset and not myself. And now that I know you are doing everything you can to prevent Tristan from being sent to prison, I want to thank you."

She stopped, dropped her eyes to look him in the face and nodded. Then she nudged her son, who kept his eyes on the ground. She nudged him again, and in a strained voice Tristan said, "Thank you, Bruno, for giving me this chance. I'll try not to let you down."

Mother and son then both turned to look challengingly at Simon, as if they had been given some grueling but unwelcome test and had managed, despite themselves, to pass it. Simon ignored them and stepped forward to hold out his hand. Bruno shook it.

"Thanks, Bruno. That document will be in the *procureur*'s hands tomorrow morning."

He led his family back to his Mercedes, opening the passenger door for his wife. Bruno watched them leave, wondering what art of persuasion or force of character Simon had deployed for the apologies to be delivered. Or perhaps it was something the mayor might have said to Simon.

"It's a good job that family didn't try coming in my café," said Fauquet, coming out to clear away the coffee cups. "I wouldn't have served them, not after what that boy did. I never liked his mother anyway, stuck-up old bitch. Thinks she's the lady of the manor just because her old man manages a supermarket. It's just a big shop, when all's said and done."

"You've never liked him since he opened the bakery department in the supermarket and took some of your business away," said Bruno.

"You'd have to be pretty hard up to eat that frozen muck they reheat and sell as fresh bread, and don't even get me started about those mass-produced things they call cakes.

"They say it's not even his son," Fauquet went on. "Simon had just arrived in town as one of the undermanagers, and Amandine was working as a cashier. She'd been going out with a man from the butchery department who looked a lot like Tristan. He left town, and before you could turn around she was going out with Simon and married him a couple of months later. It was all before your time, Bruno. And then Simon was promoted to manager, and she started putting on airs. But some of us have long memories. Arnaud, his name was, Arnaud Messager. I wonder what happened to him?"

Something clicked in Bruno's mind. That phrase on the recording that had eluded him, the "Naud" who had bought something. It could have been Arnaud.

He reached for his wallet to pay Fauquet, who looked at him in surprise and said, "Losing your head? You already paid me once." Then he handed Bruno a large brown paper bag, big enough to hold a dozen baguettes. "Stale bread for your chickens," he said. "No charge, just give me a few eggs if you get any extra this week."

"Thanks, Fauquet," said Bruno. "Do you know of anyone else around here called Arnaud, apart from the guy you were just talking about?"

"Nobody who's still alive," said Fauquet. "There was a man who used to sell cheese in the market before Stéphane, but he wasn't from St. Denis. I think he was from Belvès. And there was Jérôme's dad, who started the amusement park, but he's been dead for over thirty years."

"Park," thought Bruno. And "Rome," that could be for "Jérôme." And Grégoire had said the two old men wanted to visit the amusement park. Bruno slapped a fist into his other hand and turned to kiss an astonished Fauquet on both cheeks.

"If I'm right, my friend, I'll get you a lot more than half-a-dozen eggs. You might just have solved a murder case!"

435

He used his key to get into the *mairie,* closed on Sundays, and went to his office to drop off the plastic bag. He then went into the registry to check the cadastre, the giant map that listed each house and property lot in the commune. He looked up the section that included the amusement park and then compared that with the tax records. He called the mayor and then Gilles.

"I think we're getting to the endgame for your story on the Bugatti," he told Gilles. "Can you meet me at the amusement park just as soon as you can? Call Young and see if he wants to join you. I finally worked out what the old boys were saying on my phone."

"On my way," Gilles replied, and with Balzac at his heels, Bruno walked over the bridge and turned right at the bank to go down the rue de la Paix toward the amusement park.

26

Bruno recognized Félix's bike, chained to the cycle rack outside the entrance to the park. He pulled out his wallet to buy a ticket, handed over a ten-euro note and asked the cashier if Jérôme was available.

"He's in the back," said the cashier, handing back a two-euro coin and calling for his boss. "But no dogs allowed."

"Bruno's an exception," said Jérôme, coming out to shake Bruno's hand. "What can I do for you?"

"You know your sale has fallen through?" Bruno began. "Sylvestre was found dead in his pool yesterday."

"I know, it was on the radio. Still, I get to keep the deposit, the *notaire* says, even if his heirs don't want to conclude the sale. That will give me enough to go ahead with the expansion."

"Remember you told me about your father's idea to expand the park with a museum of local life here in the nineteenth century? You said something about re-creating an old village and farm. How far did your dad get with the project?"

"I was still a boy at the time, but I have the plans he drew up and, with just a few modifications, that's what I'll be using."

"Did he buy anything that he planned to use, like old school desks, blackboards, farm equipment?"

"He bought a classroom full of those old double desks where two kids sat side by side. And he got some old farm gear, plows and reapers, all horse drawn, a threshing drum, stuff like that. He bought a job lot from some junkyard that was going out of business. If the mayor gives me the go-ahead I'll look through it and see what can be salvaged."

"Where do you keep it?"

"In the old barn just beyond the windmill. Nothing's been moved since my dad put it there."

"Do you mind if I take a look around with my dog? I paid the entrance fee."

"You didn't have to do that, Bruno. And sure, take your dog. It's too late in the season for me to be busy."

"When the mayor turns up, tell him to look for me near the windmill."

Bruno strolled past the carousel and skirted around the line of parents and children waiting to buy *barbe à papa,* the tendrils of spun sugar on a stick that would turn their faces pink and ruin their teeth. He could hear the pop of air rifles at the shooting range and glanced across to see Grégoire taking aim, his wife at his side. Bruno could smell the aroma of frying sausages. He nodded and waved regretfully in return to a greeting and an invitation to join a group at the beer tent. Nobody was dancing on the stretch of bare ground, but three musicians were dutifully playing bal musette songs from the years before the war, or maybe even before the Great War.

He strolled on, through the water garden with its copy of a Japanese bridge and the benches in discreet corners beneath the fronds of the willow trees where courting couples could go after a successful navigation of the Tunnel of Love, or when the young lady had been suitably terrified by the Ghost Train.

Ahead of him stood the windmill on its slight mound and beside it stood the two old men, looking across the fence to the old barn where Jérôme's father had stored his junk. Bruno ducked back into the willows and knelt down to stroke Balzac into silence until he heard footsteps and a quiet, familiar voice saying his name. He beckoned the mayor to join him and put his finger to his lips.

"Did you check the cadastre and the tax files?" Bruno whispered.

"It's definitely town land, and no taxes have been paid for more than thirty years. I wasn't even mayor then. It must have been forgotten."

After a moment, a small figure emerged from the old barn and began running across the open ground toward the windmill. As he neared the fence, Bruno saw it was Félix and heard him call out, "Grandpa, I think we found it." He waved a flashlight in one hand and a small notebook in the other and then ducked beneath the fence and hugged his grandfather.

"I found the plate on the chassis and cleaned it. It's Bugatti, serial number 57453SC," Félix said. "But that's all there is, the chassis, the engine and the axles."

Bruno pushed through the willow fronds, the mayor behind him, watching the stunned faces of the two old men and returning a cheerful greeting from Félix.

"That's all you need," Bruno said. "That's enough for it to count as a restoration. Only the transmission is missing, and we might even find it with the rest of the junk. Bonjour, messieurs, and my congratulations."

"On behalf of St. Denis, my friends, let me thank you for your efforts," said the mayor. "But since this land and barn belong to the town, and we are claiming the contents in lieu of thirty years of unpaid rent and taxes, I'll have to ask you not to trespass again, young man. This time, of course, we'll let it go."

"Merde," said Étienne and then looked over Bruno's shoulder to where Gilles was pushing through the willows.

"Success, sort of," said Bruno. "What's left of the Bugatti is in the barn over there. Shall we go and see? And don't look too crestfallen, messieurs. St. Denis is a generous town, and I'm sure there'll be some suitable finder's fee for you to share."

They set off across the field, Bruno and Félix holding up the wire fence and helping the old men to get through before helping them across the uneven ground. The wooden doors of the barn were closed with a rusted chain and padlock that hadn't seen a key for decades.

"Come around here," said Félix and led them to the far side of the barn where a plank had been pulled away and then clumsily replaced. He pushed the plank aside and squeezed inside.

"I'll never get through there, pull another plank away," said the mayor and Bruno heaved the rotten wood aside.

"Careful," said Félix, shining the flashlight at Bruno's feet, illuminating a tangled maze of rusted machinery, plows, desks and rotted wooden shafts of farm carts. "I had to pick my way through, and some of it's still pretty sharp."

The mayor and the two old men stood at the gap, peering inside as Bruno and Gilles carefully picked their way through. Each of them pulled out his phone and started taking photos of the tangle and finally of the plate on the long chassis with that magic name BUGATTI.

"Lost for seventy years," said Gilles. "I never believed we could find it." And at that point, two phones began to ring, one immediately after the other. The mayor pulled out his phone and Gilles followed suit.

Bruno heard the mayor say, "Yveline, yes, we'll need gendarmes right away," while Gilles had a finger in one ear to cut the background noise and was loudly telling someone, probably George Young, where to find the barn.

Bruno picked his way out to the open air, and his phone began to vibrate at his waist.

He saw that Fabiola was calling him back and hit the button to accept the call.

"I did as you asked, but it wasn't easy, and I feel bad about it. I don't even know if we'll still be talking after this, so I hope it's worth it," she said, her voice colder than ice. "And the answer is no, not last night and not for the last three nights." The phone cut off at her end.

The mayor came up and suggested that Bruno try to break the padlock, saying, "It's town property and I authorize you to open it."

"Shall we call in Delaron to take some photos?" Bruno asked. "We can tell him to hold the story until we have the car secured, and it would be good to have everything properly recorded."

The mayor nodded and pulled out his phone. Bruno sent Félix trotting back to ask Jérôme for a crowbar or a heavy screwdriver and invite him to join them.

"But don't tell him what you found," he called after the boy's disappearing back. Félix crossed another figure on the way, ducking though the fence and approaching them.

"So you finally found it, here in this barn," said Young, once he arrived. He shook hands with Gilles and Bruno and then looked curiously at the two old men. "Congratulations," he added, his tone sounding forced. "Was it kept here all along?"

"For about thirty years," said Gilles. "It was the former owner of the amusement park who bought Bérégevoy's junk and brought it here, planning to open some kind of old farm museum. He died before he could look through it, and the plan fell through. So here it all stayed."

"So in the end Sylvestre never knew where it was?" Young asked.

"I think he did," said Bruno. "He'd signed a contract with Jérôme, the current owner, to buy the whole park. Sylvestre assumed that would include this field and barn and all the contents. He was wrong. It belongs to the town. Jérôme's father was apparently a good friend of a former mayor, who said he could use the barn for a nominal rent and taxes. They signed an agreement to that effect, which is still in the town files, but neither rent nor taxes were ever paid."

Félix returned with Jérôme, carrying a crowbar. The mayor explained everything all over again as Jérôme's face first lit up with hope and excitement and then fell into gloom.

"Cheer up, Jérôme," the mayor went on. "I'm going to support your plan to enlarge the park and build the nineteenth-century village you told Bruno about. I think it will be a splendid addition to the town and bring in lots more tourists than your falling guillotine ever did. We'll even let you have this land and the barn and almost all the contents, once we've removed the Bugatti."

The siren of a gendarme van could be heard coming closer, and then they saw it at the far side of the field, on an unpaved road that skirted a campground. The van stopped, disgorged four gendarmes, and then Yveline climbed down from the driver's seat. They all ducked through the fence and headed toward the barn.

"Good," said the mayor. "They can help us move some of this junk so we can see the Bugatti properly, and then they can secure the barn. Bruno, break that padlock."

Bruno took the crowbar and levered free one of the clasps holding the chain, and Gilles helped him swing open the tall wooden doors, the rusted hinges groaning in protest after decades of disuse. With daylight streaming in, the contents of the barn seemed less of a jumble, even though the haze of ancient dust their entry had stirred up still hung in the stifling air. Most of the school desks were piled, quite neatly, by the entrance. Behind them were three antique farm carts.

Bruno left the mayor to deal with the gendarmes, and he and Jérôme squeezed past the desks and clambered onto a cart. Reapers were stacked against the rear wall, and plows had been piled against the side of the barn through which Félix had first made his entry.

"Is that an oil drum?" Bruno asked, pointing to a large cylindrical object that was resting on the Bugatti's chassis.

"No, it's an old threshing drum," Jérôme replied. "And I think that's a twine baler beside it. They stopped using wire to hold the bales when they found animals swallowing little strips of it with the hay."

Gilles and Young clambered up onto the next cart to look down in silence at the object of their search. Young moved gingerly forward, lowered himself down and picked his way to the chassis, bending down to examine the vital plate.

"Five, seven, four, five, three followed by an *S* for *Surbaissée,* the lowered chassis, and a *C* for the supercharger," he said very quietly, as though to himself. "The most beautiful car in the world."

A gendarme's face appeared in the gap in the side of the barn, and Yveline was clambering up onto the third cart.

"I'm glad you're here," said Bruno, and

then turned to look down at Young, still kneeling in reverence beside the chassis.

"While you're down there, would you mind telling me where you were the night before last, Friday night?"

Young looked up at him, startled. "What? Friday night, I was having dinner with Annette?"

"And after dinner?"

"None of your business."

"I'm afraid it is. This is important. Where were you from midnight until four in the morning?"

"I was with Annette."

"That's not true. You haven't slept with her for the past three nights."

Young's eyes flickered toward Yveline, and he swallowed. "It's true that we weren't together last night; we had a bit of a row over dinner."

"I'm not asking about last night. It's the night before that interests me, the night Sylvestre was murdered."

"Murdered? The radio said he drowned in his pool."

"He did. You pushed him in when he was drunk, jumped in after him and drowned him, and then you woke Freddy, told him the police were already after him and they'd be sure to blame him for Sylvestre's death."

Young gave a mocking laugh. "This is all a fantasy. You're making it up."

"No, I'm not," said Bruno. "You got to the *chartreuse* around midnight, and you sat beside the pool with Sylvestre, under those outdoor heaters. You were drinking Drambuie, him a lot more than you. And he was smoking joints. He was celebrating because he'd beaten you. He knew where the Bugatti was, and he'd just signed a contract with the owner of this amusement park to buy the place along with all its contents.

"He had one of his Bugatti books there on the table with him and, knowing Sylvestre, he probably started to gloat about how smart and rich he was and to mock you for having failed. You sat there, taking his taunts, getting angrier and angrier, trying to hold it in. When he went to the pool something inside of you snapped. You pushed him, jumped in after him and held his head underwater until he drowned."

"You have no evidence for this outlandish story," Young said.

"Yes, we do. And now we'll take you to the gendarmerie to test your DNA, and I'm pretty sure we'll match it to the traces on the Drambuie glass."

"Not so," Young shouted, triumphantly,

shaking his head.

"You were about to admit everything by saying that you cleaned it before you left. I know. And I doubt whether we'll find any traces of you on the joints. That was Sylvestre's little vice, not yours. You don't even smoke. But you forgot one important thing."

"What do you mean? I admit nothing."

"You forgot the towel on which you dried your hair when you came out of the pool after killing him. That's what will convict you. Too bad, while you're in prison the Bugatti will be restored and looking magnificent."

EPILOGUE

For dinner with the Oudinots, Bruno had thought of taking a bottle of champagne to celebrate the finding of the Bugatti and the closing of the two murder cases. But since the family had been shaken up by events, he decided against it and instead took a bottle of Château de Tiregand from his cellar. It went perfectly with the veal escalopes that Odette had prepared with *morilles* mushrooms that she and her daughter had picked in the woods that day. The first course had been *oeufs mimosa* from goose eggs, for which Martine had made the mayonnaise. And when Bruno had arrived, she had insisted on champagne anyway to toast the end of the family feud.

"You didn't garden today, did you?" Odette had asked by way of greeting. He confessed to digging in some ashes, which she said might bend the lunar rules but probably wouldn't break them.

"I wouldn't get your hopes up," he had replied when Fernand had asked if there was any news yet about Sylvestre's will. He told them about the mortgaged properties in Alsace and the state's determination to seize what was left as criminal proceeds. "Hard to say what's going to happen to the *chartreuse*, but you'll keep your deposit money."

Young was in a police cell in Périgueux, and the British consul in Bordeaux was arranging a lawyer. Annette had arrived at Fabiola's house in tears. Gilles was writing up his story for the *Paris Match* website, with a longer story with photos for the next printed issue. Delaron was preparing his version for tomorrow's *Sud Ouest*. The chassis was now stored securely in the gendarmerie car park, along with the missing transmission, which had been found beneath an old plow.

"So what happens to the Bugatti now?" Martine asked.

"That's up to the mayor and the council," Bruno said. Possession might be nine-tenths of the law, but the commune could not afford a long legal battle with the Bugatti heirs and other potential claimants, he explained. And St. Denis certainly could not afford to pay for the restoration, which was certain to cost millions. Full restoration would mean re-creating the special bodywork, which of course could not be welded because the special alloy Bugatti used contained magnesium. It might not even be legal to re-create it because of the fire risk.

"The mayor is thinking of making a deal with the state, donating the car in return for a very handsome finder's fee and then putting it on display at the national auto museum as one of the greatest cars ever made, and made in France," Bruno said.

There would be a lot of people hoping for a share in that finder's fee, he thought: Étienne, Félix, Jérôme, Gilles and perhaps even Madame Hugon.

"But I don't know whether that idea will last," Bruno went on. "Not after the voters open their copies of *Sud Ouest* tomorrow and learn that it's worth forty million."

"Mon Dieu," said Fernand. "I had no idea any car could be so valuable. Why, for that amount of money we could scrap all the taxes in St. Denis for years and years to come."

Bruno exchanged a glance with Martine and said, "See what I mean about the reaction of the voters?"

He let his eyes linger on her. She was wearing a simple dress of dark blue, her arms bare, and a thin gold chain around her throat that carried a St. Christopher medal. He smiled to himself at the memory of how closely he'd been able to examine it and wondered whether he'd ever be fortunate enough to get so close again. Something of his thoughts must have been clear in his eyes, since she gave him a brilliant smile.

"Sadly, I've got to fly back to London tomorrow for at least a few weeks to find more sponsors for the electric-car rally," she said. "But then I'll be back to find out what happens to the *chartreuse* and Sylvestre's estate."

"So it's au revoir rather than farewell," Bruno said, raising his glass. Ah well, he thought, life would go on. He'd be dining with his friends at Pamela's house the following evening, the now-ritual Monday dinner, and hoping that Fabiola had forgiven him for getting her to ask Annette that crucial question about sleeping with Young.

"If the *chartreuse* somehow comes back to us, I told Dad I'd like to take over the small lodge house since I'll be back here a lot organizing the rally, and it would be good to have a permanent place here of my own." She raised an eyebrow at him as if expecting some reaction.

"In that case, you had better set two conditions," said Bruno. "Your dad will have to let you fix the driveway —"

"And he'll keep the geese back on this side of the hill," Odette interrupted. "You can leave that to me."

ACKNOWLEDGMENTS

This tale began with my elder daughter, Kate, a motor-sports journalist who specializes in Formula 1 races and their history. Knowing my interest in the French Resistance during World War II, she asked if I knew the story of William Grover-Williams and Robert Benoist. They were two legendary drivers of the prewar years and close friends. During World War II they together ran a Resistance network in occupied France, arranging arms drops from Britain and carrying out a number of sabotage operations, principally against the Citroën factories. They were betrayed, arrested and killed, Benoist in Buchenwald and Grover-Williams in Sachsenhausen. My daughter then told me of the lost Bugatti, a Type 57 Atlantic, one of four ever built and the only one whose fate remains unknown. She then showed me a photograph of Yvonne Grover-Williams standing beside it in 1937, and another photo of Ralph Lauren's Atlantic. These images of this sensationally elegant automobile took my breath away and, at that moment, this novel came into my head and refused to leave.

I have taken a few liberties with the facts as they are known, suggesting that Grover-Williams was in France in 1941. He was parachuted in the following year. The incident of the downed RAF pilot is invented, but the PAT escape network was real and steered some six hundred airmen and other escapees over the mountains into Spain. Save for the presence of the Bugatti, the burning of Château de Rastignac in March 1944 is as described here. It has happily been rebuilt, to display once again its uncanny resemblance to the White House in Washington. Other than the sad fact that the fate of the lost Bugatti remains unknown (like the fate of the paintings stored at Rastignac), everything else is as faithful to the history of that glorious car as I could make it. I was greatly helped by a genial New York–based Bugatti enthusiast and historian, Walter Jamieson, who was extremely generous with his time and his library, and I am very grateful to him.

The amusement park is my invention, but Jérôme's plan to replace Joan of Arc and

Marie Antoinette with a nineteenth-century French village owes a lot to the charmingly re-created village of Le Bournat in Le Bugue, on the banks of the Vézère River. It has an old schoolroom and parish church, a windmill and bakery, functioning workshops for the blacksmith and the knife maker and much more. On Wednesday evenings in summer it offers feasts, with vast joints of ham suspended and roasted over cinders, which are strongly recommended. Of the *marchés nocturnes,* I cannot speak too highly. They have added a wonderful new dimension to the attractions of the Périgord as a great tourist destination. Our family has been attending them since they began in the village of Audrix on Saturdays, which was when my wife first wrote about the culinary charms of these evening events in *Gourmet* magazine. Beaumont-du-Périgord has another excellent night market on Mondays, and now the big towns are offering their own.

All the Bruno books are indebted to my friends and neighbors in the Périgord and the lovely landscape they nurture. It has fertile soil, wonderful food, excellent wines, a temperate climate and more history packed into its borders than anywhere else on earth. It is a very special place, filled with enchantments. As Henry Miller wrote in *The Colossus of Maroussi:*

I believe that this great peaceful region of France will always be a sacred spot for man and that when the cities have killed off the poets this will be the refuge and the cradle of the poets to come. I repeat, it was most important for me to have seen the Dordogne: it gives me hope for the future of the race, for the future of the earth itself. France may one day exist no more, but the Dordogne will live on just as dreams live on and nourish the souls of men.

My profound thanks go to my family, who were the first to read this book, with special gratitude to Kate for giving me the idea and to our basset hound, Benson, on whom I practice dialogue during our walks. I am also very grateful to Jane and Caroline Wood in Britain, to Jonathan Segal in New York, and Anna von Planta in Zurich for their matchless editing skills.

ABOUT THE AUTHOR

Martin Walker served as foreign correspondent for *The Guardian* in Africa, the Soviet Union, the United States and Europe and was the editor of United Press International. He is a senior scholar of the Woodrow Wilson Center and directed the Global Policy Council, both in Washington, D.C. He now lives mainly in the Périgord region of France, where he writes, chairs the jury of the Prix Ragueneau cooking prize and is a chevalier of the Confrérie du Pâté de Périgueux. This is his ninth novel featuring Bruno, chief of police.

The Book of
OLD SILVER

The Book of
OLD SILVER

English ~ American ~ Foreign

BY SEYMOUR B. WYLER

WITH
ALL AVAILABLE HALLMARKS
INCLUDING
SHEFFIELD PLATE MARKS

PROFUSELY ILLUSTRATED

CROWN PUBLISHERS, INC.
NEW YORK

LIBRARY OF CONGRESS CATALOG CARD NUMBER: 37-24775

Twenty-ninth Printing, March, 1974

PRINTED IN THE UNITED STATES OF AMERICA

To
*MY MOTHER AND
MY FATHER*

AUTHOR'S NOTE

In the preparation of this book I was fortunate in having the counsel and assistance of many friends and the co-operation of many fellow-dealers. I want to thank them all, and especially Mr. Nathan Nathanson of the U. S. Customs; Mr. Ivan Shortt of Ellis & Co. Ltd. of London and New York, from whose great collection of photographs of silver many of the illustrations in this book were made; Mr. Stephen G. C. Ensko and Mr. James Graham, Jr., for permission to incorporate in my tables of American Silversmiths' Marks, their respective compilations of American marks.

SEYMOUR B. WYLER

CONTENTS

LIST OF ILLUSTRATIONS

The Book of
OLD SILVER

I

OLD ENGLISH SILVER

SILVER has always been the most favored of the precious metals for articles of personal or ceremonial ornament and use. Gold, though equal or superior in beauty, malleability, polish and suitability to fine effects, is twice as heavy and therefore much less practical. But the workers in one of these metals almost invariably worked in the other and goldsmithing and silversmithing really constitute one craft. Until recently goldsmith meant a worker in gold and silver.

From the earliest times, and all over the world, this craft of goldsmithing has attracted the best of artists and artisans. The value of the metals compelled a high standard of workmanship and automatically eliminated the inferior producers.

The history of ancient silversmiths is obscured in the fog of time, but since practically none of their silver is available it is not important in the understanding and appreciation of the Old Silver that exists today. It is only when we get to the history of the Art in England, the early customs, regulations and laws, that there is meaning for the amateur or connoisseur of Old Silver.

England produced more fine silver than any other country and the craft had its greatest flowering there. The customs, practices and methods originating in England influenced all other silver producers as English culture and influence spread throughout the world. The "Sterling" standard is an indication of this, though this word owes its origin to a band of immigrant Germans. They called themselves the Easterlings because of the direction in which they lived, and they were first called by King John in approximately 1300 to refine some silver to purity for coinage purposes. In a statute of 1343 the first two letters were dropped from the word "Easterling" and the application of the word "Sterling" to silver commenced.

Silver design, like architecture, followed the great movements and influences of culture and domination. And the periods and styles of silver are on the whole the same as of architecture and furniture.

At the time of the smithing of the first pieces in England, the Church reigned supreme, and the majority of the pieces made were for religious institutions. They were great rarities because of the prohibitive price of the metal in those days. But the shrines, chalices and magnificent altar frontals made for wealthy abbeys were not always the work of monks who worked at goldsmithing. Rather, in many instances, goldsmiths who had reached a high position in their field were admitted to the better abbeys and rapidly promoted because of their artistic skill. The ordinary goldsmith was not a monk vowed to a life relieving him of the normal cares in the struggle for existence, but rather a layman following a highly skilled profession of economic importance and accounted remuneration. Probably at no time during the history of goldsmithing were these men better paid for their labors, and a great number of new craftsmen joined the ranks of this little known industry and apprenticed themselves to the early masters.

The styles of the pieces made then showed a surprising gracefulness of line and proportion, for in those days a silversmith might work on one piece several months in order to complete an object of great beauty. During the Middle Ages goldsmithing was ranked among the highest of the arts, and the work of the various smiths of the time were indeed pieces of great artistic merit. During this period, goldsmiths apprenticed themselves for many years before entering the trade as finished workers. Medieval goldsmiths, however, did not confine themselves only to the production of plate but dabbled as well in many lucrative side-lines. Some were members of the other richer crafts, some often acted as pawnbrokers and they were often especially useful to the Crown. During the twelfth and thirteenth centuries, the machinery of government was becoming steadily more complicated and there were many instances where goldsmiths were called upon to aid in the construction and decoration of royal buildings, as well as the administering of the mints and exchanges.

As time passed and commerce with foreign countries developed, greater quantities of raw silver were brought to England. The English people took largely to the new luxury, and the demand for it increased rapidly. Goldsmiths in the tenancy of the monasteries found they could no longer meet the increased demands for pieces in the precious metals. They wisely took the precaution of forming themselves into guilds or fraternities. The first mention of a goldsmith's company is in the year of 1180, but it appears that this was a voluntary association and carried but little power. As early as the year 1238, many inferior silversmiths immediately took advantage of the trade to make silver of a very much lower standard than was used for government coins, and sold it for the same price as a piece of the correct alloy. With the formation of the first silver guilds in England, a Law of Parliament stated that no silver should be melted unless it had first been assayed by an appointed committee and proved to contain the correct amounts of silver and alloy. In 1335, a second "statutum de Moneta" decreed that each gold- or silversmith must punch on his wares a particular mark of his own, assigned to him by the King. In 1423, an act by Henry VI fixed the price of silver at a definite valuation of twenty-two shillings to the pound. In the succeeding years, this valuation was changed several times. In 1477 a very important law was passed by the London gold-smiths' company, compelling stamping of the leopard's head or crowned leopard's head on every piece of silver of the accepted standard.

In the year 1479, the use of the date letter was first inaugurated. The year of manufacture was to be indicated by stamping a specified letter of the alphabet in a distinctive type of lettering. Thus in the following years we find silver pieces punched with a complete set of hallmarks: the leopard's head, the date letter, the maker's mark.

Although by far the greater portion of silver made during the Gothic period was used and produced for the Church, by no means is it to be thought that plate for use in the private home was over-looked. The birth of secular plate may be said to have been caused by the desires of medieval monarchs to flaunt their power and wealth by displays of magnificent silver and gold objects within their castles. From this arose the inspiration for what is termed domestic silver, as distinguished from that made by the craftsmen of the religious fraternities for use in their ecclesiastical buildings. As we have seen, by the thirteenth century the secular silversmiths had established the foundations of their craft and had developed styles and traditions of distinctly original design. During the thirteenth and fourteenth centuries, silver plate had come into general use in the homes of royalty, and no restrictions were ever placed on the number of articles made for the table. The most popular pieces produced were basins and ewers, ceremonial salts, large dishes, chargers and drink-ing cups of many varieties. A greater number of drinking articles existed than other pieces, for each man reserved the right to his personal cup. This tradition is found not only among the wealthy but even in the peasant classes, but their drinking cups were made of wood.

Gradually foreign influences entered. During the sixteenth cen-tury, domestic plate was greatly influenced in design and style by the influx of foreign silversmiths who came from Italy, France and Germany, in which countries the Italian Renaissance had been fully accepted. The Gothic waned and the Renaissance styles took hold.

Nevertheless there are so few pieces in existence made prior to the sixteenth century that the study of the early goldsmiths can be accurately made only from the libraries of the first silver guilds, and the diaries of prominent persons of the day. The long and bloody Wars of the Roses were undoubtedly responsible for the melting of many magnificent pieces scheduled in ancient inventories. It is for this reason that secular plate from this time is practically unknown. The few remaining examples which unfortunately are not always the representative workings of the better type, are to be found only in private collections and museums. Whenever a piece dating before 1600 is offered at public sale, the price realized is almost fantastic.

This explains the scarcity of secular plate, but what of the pieces carefully stored in the Churches and produced in so much greater profusion? These art treasures carefully protected by the Abbeys were to undergo a fate similar to that of the plate in the homes of royalty and nobility. During the Reformation, the pillage and destruction of practically the whole of the treasures of the Church was effected. However, a further cause for the scarcity of ecclesiastical plate is found in the forced loans which the Tudor and succeeding monarchs commanded from the corporate bodies of the City of London. Many a highly prized specimen was regretfully sacrificed in order to meet the imperious requests of the Sovereign.

During the reign of Elizabeth, internal prosperity resulted in an era of far flung luxury. The stream of art diverted from the Reformation, and from the ecclesiastical channels turned toward domestic and civic comfort and splendor. Wealthy patrons of colleges and universities abundantly endowed their respective Alma Maters with magnificent plate. But the destruction of the majority of this plate was caused by Charles I directly after the Civil War. He borrowed as much money and plate as he could obtain from the leading universities. He promised to repay them for these treasures but did not, and the money was dissipated by this luxury loving monarch. During the Cromwellian era, similar proceedings took place, but during the reign of Charles II the silver business flourished.

Much of the plate had been made from the silver coin of the realm, and in order to prevent the resulting scarcity of coin, the Act of 1696 fixed the standard for plate above that of the silver coinage. The mint had offered a high price for all plate and large quantities were melted down to the ore state.

Laws regulating the silver trade were enacted and especially drastic was the penalty for fraud. In two instances, the penalty for marking inferior silver with the sterling hallmark, was punished by death. It is because of these stringent laws of the English government, upheld today as well as in early times, that practically no forged antique silver is found in Great Britain, for as quickly as the government punished the offender, so it destroyed his wares.

Moreover, the governmental influence on the craft in other ways was so great, that the reasons for many of the features of the craft cannot be understood without a knowledge of the important laws and regulations.

II

LAWS AND REGULATIONS AFFECTING ENGLISH HALLMARKS

A COMPREHENSIVE study of the complete legislation with regard to the ancient art of goldsmithing and silversmithing might well fill several volumes. The laws passed are many, and invariably written in great detail. Here we will attempt merely to give in a very concise form the high-lights or most important acts and laws that influenced the production of old silver.

The year 1180 commemorates the earliest mention of a guild or fraternity with regard to silversmithing. However, little importance is attached to it as the association was purely a voluntary one and had but few laws to govern it. After its inauguration, the founders were fined for being irregularly established without a proper license from the King.

As early as the year 1238, many inferior goldsmiths took advantage of their trade and produced silver of a very much lower standard than was used for government coins. These pieces were marketed for the same price as those of the correct alloy. Because of these numerous frauds, Henry III ordered the Mayor and aldermen of the City of London to choose six of the most discreet goldsmiths to superintend the craft. This order was duly obeyed and in the succeeding years these men were in turn followed by others in the so-called offices of superintendents or wardens.

The wardens were given more and more power as time went on and in 1300 were authorized to assay every silver vessel produced, to ascertain whether or not it contained the correct proportion of silver and alloy. They became known as "gardiens."

In the year 1327 the Guild of London Goldsmiths became regularly incorporated by Royal Charter, under the title of "The Wardens and Commonalty of the Mystery of Goldsmiths of the City of London." The most important legislation enacted by this Congress was that requiring every silversmith to use a particular hallmark of his own.

The second "Statutum de Moneta" in 1335 declared that inasmuch as counterfeit money had been imported by foreigners, plate was not to be exported without official license in order to protect the coin within the realm of the people. It is interesting to note here that the only means of exit from England officially allowed was from

Dover, at which place foreigners were searched and then permitted to depart from England.

A Statute passed in 1363 commanded that no goldsmith should work gold or silver into a wrought article unless it was of the alloy of good sterling. In the succeeding years, numerous by-laws were enacted in regard to the trade, all of varying importance.

The Guild was reincorporated by charter in 1392 with vastly extended powers. In the provinces there is also evidence of the existence of similar guilds. These, however, will be discussed in detail in their proper place.

During the reigns of Henry VIII and Edward VI the silver coinage in England had been scandalously debased to the extent that in 1551, the coin minted consisted of only three ounces of silver to every pound weight of coins. But in 1560, an act of Elizabeth definitely established the Sterling Standard of 11 ounces 2 dwt. This is the equivalent of 92.5 per cent pure silver and this standard has remained until the present time (with the exception of one period from 1697 to 1720). In order to correct the existing evil state of the coinage at this time, all existing base money was recalled by Royal proclamation on February 19, 1560.

In order to stop the melting of coins for use in silverware, a law was passed in 1696 raising the silverware standard above the coin standard to 11 ounces 10 dwt. (95.8%). Pieces made of this standard were to be stamped with a new mark known as Britannia.

But in 1719 the old standard of 11 ounces 2 dwt. was revived since wares of this content were proven to be more durable than the softer Britannia ware and the higher standard did not accomplish its purpose. Silversmiths merely added pure silver to coin silver to increase the standard. The higher or Britannia standard was not abolished but left to the discretion of individual silversmiths. It is interesting to note that the silver standard of 1719 has never changed since. This same act, which was one of the most important recorded in the annals of the Guild, also imposed a tax of sixpence per ounce on all silver made in Great Britain. This is the first known mention of any duty on plate, but because of the ineffectuality of collecting the duty, this act was repealed in 1757. In its place a law was passed which required a license to be purchased by every goldsmith and silversmith, for which a nominal fee was charged.

The duty on plate was reimposed in 1784 and continued until 1890. The head of the reigning sovereign was punched on the piece in order to denote that the full duty had been paid.

In 1890 the duty on silver was repealed, and the use of the sovereign's head was discontinued.

HALLMARKS

Because of the correct and continued use of hallmarks on English silver, the collector and research student of today is enabled to trace the complete ancestry of nearly any piece made subsequent to 1300. However, let it not be thought that hallmarks were ever originally used for any other purpose than to prevent fraud. On all pieces made from the beginning of the fourteenth century, a series of hallmarks was to be impressed denoting the quality of the piece made, and indicative of the individual maker.

The Leopard's Head mark was first established in 1300 and may be said to be the earliest known hallmark on English silver. In 1363 the name was changed and this particular mark was called a King's mark. Through an error in translation from the French, the name leopard was applied to the head as depicted in the hallmark, but actually the figure used was that of the head of a lion. From 1478 to the George II era there was a crown on the leopard's head. After this time, however, the size of the head was diminished and again through an error in reading the original laws of the guild, the crown was omitted.

MAKER'S MARK

This mark is next in chronological order to the leopard's head. The act of 1363 ordained that every Master Goldsmith should have a mark of his own which was to be impressed on each piece after it had been assayed. The first maker's marks were generally flowers, animals, hearts, crosses, or other symbols generally selected in allusion to the maker's name. It is probably because most of the population at this time was illiterate that this form of mark was used. Shops in London of this period were rarely advertised by name since so few people were able to read. Therefore, we may assume that the earliest silversmiths aped the styles of shopkeepers in advertising or hallmarking their own products. This system fell into disuse in the seventeenth century and by the time of Charles II, initials and letters were used. During the years of the Britannia standard many makers used two individual marks, in order to distinguish silver made of one standard from the other. This caused so much confusion that in 1739 a statute decreed that all silversmiths should use the first initials of their Christian name and surname. At this time all previous marks were discontinued.

DATE LETTERS

Although there has been definite proof of the use of the date letter on silver as early as 1500, the first actual mention is in 1629. From this time on, date letters were used with sufficient frequency to enable one to fill in the missing years, and so be able to determine the exact year in which a piece was made. The use of the date letter was arranged in cycles of twenty years using the letters A to U or V, but excluding J. At the end of each twenty years, a different type of letter was used and the cartouche was changed. It must be mentioned here that dates that one often finds engraved on a piece of silver are of but little help in determining the actual year in which a piece was created, as many pieces were given or bequeathed and the date inscribed signified the time of the presentation, not the time of making.

LION PASSANT

This mark was adopted as the official stamp at the Goldsmiths Hall in London in 1544. All London silver made since then must have this mark.

LION'S HEAD ERASED AND "BRITANNIA"

The only importance to be attached to these two marks is that they denoted pieces made of the higher standard and were used for only 23 years, from 1697 to 1720. It is because of the short term of use of these marks that pieces bearing the Britannia are rare and always sought after by collectors.

SOVEREIGN'S HEAD

This mark should be found on all plate assayed in England from 1784 to 1890 as it was required to be used to denote the payment of duty by the silversmith to the Crown. This mark is actually the head in profile of the reigning King or Queen.

Thus the use of these marks enables us to identify the place, year, and maker of old silverware. Complete tables and the method of using them will be found in a separate section of this book.

III

FRAUDS

WE have seen the great and complicated efforts to maintain the regularity and genuineness of silverware. That was because the continued growth of an industry not only produces craftsmen of merit and ability but also individuals who are not content to deal fairly and earn the rewards of honest labor. The establishing of silversmithing as a permanent and lucrative business was the loophole for many dishonest workers to seek unethical methods by which to prosper. The English, being a keen and farsighted people, took precautions as early as 1327 to try and stop any forms of malpractice. In this year, which marks the incorporation of the Goldsmiths Company, the first measures were taken to guard against the counterfeiting of silver. With the passing years, the Goldsmiths Company grew more powerful and for the last five centuries their word has been law in England. Even today, they assay and hallmark all pieces of English origin, and for this reason very little forged silver is to be found there today. Not only did the Company have the right to punish an offender, but they were privileged to confiscate and destroy his wares as well. In early days, the penalties for forging silver were very severe.

There are many ways in which deception may be practiced in the silver trade, and an attempt will be made here to simplify and explain the various means. However, it must be remembered that the actual contact with a fraudulent piece is the most certain way of detecting the deception.

The earliest known fraud was the sale of plated ware, represented to be of the silver standard. The maker hallmarked the pieces himself and thus the payment of duty and all contacts with the Goldsmith Company were avoided. However, legislation and supervision did away with this type of deception. The quality of the silver in a piece may be proved by the application of acid, the resulting reaction on the metal being definite proof of its fineness. This method is used commonly by tradesmen today in dealing with unmarked pieces.

One of the frequently practiced frauds today is that of subtraction which is in effect the removal of a part or parts of an article after it has been hallmarked. For example, let us say that a silver cup of a certain type is wanted, and the nearest thing available is an urn of similar proportion. By removing the spout, the urn becomes a cup and the order is filled. Also, trays are often found which were originally patens. The feet having been removed and the abrasions carefully erased, a more valuable piece has been created. It is safe to say the fraud of subtraction is usually perpetrated only to create a piece of greater saleability.

A similar fraud is that of addition. This is the adding on of a part to an original piece after it has been hallmarked. The law provides that permission must be obtained from the authorities before making an addition, and that if the additional piece increases the weight of the article by more than a third of its original weight, the added silver must be hallmarked. However, it also decreed that an addition could not be performed if it in any way changed the character of the original article. In other words, a foot, a handle or a spout might be put on, but a coffee pot could not be made from a tankard.

Another type of forgery is that of transformation and this is done to turn an original into a piece of greater worth and more character. A tray might be created from a meat platter, as it is far more saleable from the standpoint of the dealer, and definitely more valuable. Although in this type of fraud the hallmark is left untouched, it often becomes twisted and frequently appears upside down or in the wrong place.

More frequent than these frauds is the transposition of the marks from an article that is old into a piece of modern manufacture. As a rule the marks are taken from an old piece of little value and put into an article which if it were old would command a high price. For example, the part of a handle of a teaspoon on which the marks are impressed is removed and transposed on to the side of a coffee pot that is a good reproduction. In this way, new pieces of apparently antique silver are created.

The counterfeiting of marks constitutes the marking of a piece by other than the Goldsmiths Company and the reasons for this deception are easily discerned. Because of the extreme similarity of some new marks to some old ones, this type of fraud is sometimes found. For instance, the fact that the Britannia standard mark is in use today if the piece is of the recognized quality, is reason enough to promote this fraud. As the old standard mark and the new are alike, all the unscrupulous dealer has to do is to have the date letter omitted, and the piece might well be a fine original from the Queen Anne period.

From all the preceding indictment and explanation of fraudulent practices, the innocent bystander might easily remark that with so many varied types of forgery being practiced, it is impossible to purchase a fine original and be completely certain of its authenticity. However, by no means does the author intend to convey the impression that the majority of these frauds cannot be detected. It is a safe practice though, when in doubt to consult an expert, and if necessary pay him for his advice, for in the long run it will be the cheapest investment.

There are many ways in which to detect the forgeries on pieces of silver. Silver can be tested, hallmarks should be properly placed, and the piece must not antedate its introduction. What is meant by the latter is that if tea caddies were introduced during the reign of Queen Anne, one bearing the hallmark of say 1640 must obviously be a spurious piece. It is well also, to consider carefully the period in which the piece was made. More than often it is just such errors as these that lead to the eventual detection of fraudulent pieces. Even the cleverest forger will slip up somewhere, and as a rule it is the lack of knowledge of the history of silver that defeats the counterfeiter.

To an expert, the easiest method of judging the age of a piece is by its color, and although this rule is not infallible, it generally proves true. Silver over a period of years becomes oxidized many times, and this continued action of the elements on the metal gives it a certain softness of texture and color that is known as patina. Frequent cleaning and use in service mellow the piece, and it assumes a certain smoothness that time alone can produce. One often revels in the beauty of old silver, because of its soft bluish color. This is an integral part of the make-up of the patina.

The insertion of an old set of hallmarks in a modern piece, has been said to be the forgery most in use today. This malpractice entails a great deal of labor such as filing, fitting and soldering the marks into place. The heat of the hard soldering discolors the silver, and necessitates the polishing of the piece to hide the defect. After a time, the solder marks will be visible, and it is for this reason that dealers so often blow their breath on the hallmarks. In this way they can sometimes see signs of the transposition. An excellent test is to put the piece in fire and after a few minutes if the marks have been soldered in, the outline will become visible.

Hallmarks on silver are punched in separately and if one finds a set of four salts or a dozen service plates with all the marks perfectly aligned, there is just cause for suspicion.

IV

THE COLLECTION AND CARE
OF OLD SILVER

IN purchasing pieces of silver from those who are not absolutely reliable, it is well to beware of these so-called bargains. It is a fairly safe axiom to remember that good things are never too cheap. The reason for this may be explained if one considers that the market for silver is very steady, and purchasers, whether dealers or private people, are almost always ready to increase their collections.

Pieces that have additions such as later chasing or engraving, or badly eradicated hallmarks, can be purchased for very little. However, their worth is little more than that of modern silver, for old means antique, and that in turn may be translated into meaning original.

It is best to buy your silver from an unquestionably reliable dealer. He is more likely to detect a fraud than you and if it is not genuine he won't sell it to you except for what it is. If, however, you are acquiring silverware in one way or another not from a reputable dealer, be careful. First, determine what the piece is supposed to be. Look for the hallmarks. Are they complete, consistent and genuine? The marks must not be too regular. They must not be upside down and each detachable piece must be hallmarked. Then determine where it was made, when and by whom. Consider whether the style of the piece is consistent with the period and whether it has the proper patina for its alleged age. If you are at all uncertain give it the acid test to determine whether it is really silver. Then look for abrasions, rough edges, etc., to see if there has been any subtraction. Look carefully to determine whether by irregular joining, welds, curves, solderings you can detect transformation or addition. And most important check the hallmarking to see whether genuine antique hallmarks have been soldered into a more recent article. The extent of your testing and verification will naturally vary with the price and the importance of the ware.

If the hallmarks are not genuine or not genuinely of the piece, then the ware will not have value as an antique. If the fault is in subtraction or transformation, the piece will have value as an antique, but much less than its apparent value. If the fault is in addition, its value as an antique will be that of a piece without the addition.

The absence or incompleteness of hallmarks does not in itself mean that a piece is worthless as an antique. It merely raises that presumption and makes identification and proof very difficult. In the case of incomplete marks, first be sure that the reading is accurate. The absence of the leopard's head or date letter may mean merely that the piece is not London silver but American or French or the ware of some other country. If the marks that are on the silver do however indicate its origin there may be good and interesting reasons for the omission of the other marks. And the least likely of these reasons would be fraud, because a forger taking the trouble to fake an antique would probably be sure to have his hallmarks complete.

If a piece can be positively identified and proven of standard it will have the same value whether or not the hallmarks are complete because the entire purpose of hallmarks is merely to certify when and by whom a piece of standard silver was made.

Worn, badly erased or eradicated hallmarks are a definite fault. Old silverware, to be worth its true value, must be in good condition and a worn mark besides being an indication of a worn piece makes exact identification impossible.

The relative importance of the imperfection can best be gauged by understanding the factors that determine the value of old silver. First and by far the most important is age or scarcity value. Second is size. As a general principle all other things being equal the bigger the piece the more its worth. But this is not absolutely true. The third factor might be considered to be supply and demand, which is another facet of the scarcity factor. For example, there is very little eighteenth century silver available. Therefore, whatever there is, is very valuable. Of course, a large tray will be worth more than a small tray. But a small coffee pot might be worth more if it happened to be a rare example, or if someone needed it to complete a set. Style, workmanship, the intrinsic beauty of the piece, the maker are other factors that have effect upon the value of the silver.

Nevertheless silver other than antique pieces may have considerable value and may be worthy of collection. Careful selection of low and moderate priced pieces today will probably also bring dividends, in time, to the collector.

Authentic reproductions, any hand wrought ware that is genuine will have in the ordinary course of events important and increasing value. The craft now, as a handcraft is almost non-existent. With the passage of time the absorption into private hands of more and more of this later silverware and the inevitable loss and destruction of pieces, the scarcity and therefore the value will increase. The demand also will increase as the custom and fancy of collecting increases and the standards of living improve.

Silverware has always been a premier investment with ever increasing values and it will continue to be so because the supply of it cannot increase, it must decrease.

Machine made silverware may have a collector's value in time, but only in a limited degree. After all, the chief determining factor is scarcity and machines are used to produce quantities.

However, Jubilee Silver made during 1934-1935 and impressed with the mark of the double sovereigns-head (King George V and Queen Mary) has already risen in value.

THE CARE AND CLEANING OF SILVER

The possession of old silver carries with it a responsibility, as pieces of such rarity must be given great care. Old silver should be cleaned regularly with an accepted standard polish or paste, which will in no way be harmful to the texture of the metal. Inasmuch as the great beauty of antique silver lies in its soft color, it is heartily recommended that all cleaning be done by hand rather than by machine. At no time should silver be left to tarnish to such a degree that it makes it necessary to have it buffed, as in doing this, the hallmarks may be eradicated.

With regard to storage of fine pieces, it is suggested that they be wrapped individually in anti-tarnish flannel bags, which will serve as a means of protection. The author has found from practical experience that many people attempt to have their silver lacquered so as to save work in the house. This is definitely not approved of as the lacquer imparts to the old patina a glaring finish which detracts from the beauty of the piece.

V

FAMOUS ENGLISH GOLDSMITHS

THROUGHOUT the history of silversmithing in England, a few smiths are outstanding for the quality of the work they produced. An attempt is made only to give the highlights in the careers of the most brilliant of these craftsmen.

PAUL LAMERIE

Paul Lamerie was born in Holland April 14, 1688. His family had settled there after escaping from religious persecution in France, one of many of the Huguenots who fled to foreign lands. Because of these family ties of Lamerie which were distinctly French, he is often erroneously thought to have been a French silversmith.

In 1691 Lamerie's father arrived in England and having been of the French aristocracy, would not permit himself to work in a trade. The only profession which embraced manual labor that was acceptable was that of the goldsmith.

At the age of fifteen the young Paul was apprenticed to Peter Platel and it is to this celebrated craftsman that he owes all of his early knowledge of the trade. Very few students were given better opportunity, as Platel's works had been accepted as having reached the zenith of the goldsmith's art. Seven years after his apprenticeship, Lamerie was admitted as a freeman and opened up his first shop. Within a short time his instant success was evidenced by the establishing of a second place of business. In 1717, he was admitted to the livery of the Goldsmiths' Company, and eventually was within reach of the Prime Wardenship of the Guild. During his lifetime he connected himself with the army, and in 1743 attained the rank of Major.

He died in 1751 after a very colorful career. No silversmith throughout English history attained such world-wide fame as did Lamerie, for the quality of his work was distinctly superior to any previously known. As a craftsman, he had a distinct genius for creation and brought many new forms of decoration to the public eye for the first time. It is indeed strange, however, considering his great popularity and success, that he was never appointed as a goldsmith to the crown. Not one article made by Lamerie is to be found in the collection of Royal Plate at Buckingham Palace or Windsor Castle.

Throughout the study of the life of Lamerie, one is apt to be confused by the various spellings of his name. No serious notice need be taken of this if one realizes that that age in which he lived was an illiterate one and people spelled mainly phonetically.

MATTHEW BOULTON

The city of Birmingham is justly proud of Matthew Boulton. Throughout his entire life he was associated with his home city and was one of the earliest of the provincial silversmiths to achieve more than a local reputation. His talents were not confined to silversmithing. During his lifetime he was connected with several other industries, in each of which he left a name well to be remembered. In his younger days, he engaged in the manufacture of hardware and then went into the trade of artistic productions which included articles of Sheffield plate, silver, ormolu and paintings.

Later on he devoted his entire time to the development of Watt's steam engine and made great strides in the field of engineering. In the final stages of his life he brought about numerous improvements in the coining of money, several of which were accepted by the Treasury of England for practical use.

The Boulton family was typical of many known in the seventeenth century, the landed gentry engaged in the manufacturing pursuits. Matthew was born in 1728 and attended school in a suburb of Birmingham. At the age of fourteen he was apprenticed to a trade which he left a short time later to enter business with his father, who was a toy manufacturer. The toy business, as it was then known, was not one in which children's playthings were made, but rather a shop wherein all sorts of trinkets, buckles, seals, boxes and articles of hardware for household purposes were sold. The young Matthew applied himself diligently to this business and before long was entrusted with the entire management of his father's interests. Boulton was married at an early age, but was widowed a short time after. Scarcely a year had elapsed, when his father died and it was this occurrence that brought him into greater prominence than ever before. As his business grew, he became a combined manufacturer and retailer, and was compelled to take in a partner, John Fothergill. Unfortunately, he turned out to be more of a detriment than a help.

Shortly after the discovery of the process known as Sheffield plating, Boulton went to the city of Sheffield better to acquaint himself with this new technique. He realized the tremendous future in store for this new industry and spent several weeks in the work shops of Richard Morton, one of the ablest of the early makers. The earliest mention of a piece of plate by Boulton is in 1762, and he carried the distinction of having the only foundry outside of Sheffield where plate was made. He was one of the first craftsmen to adopt the sterling silver thread edge in place of the plated wire, as he was convinced that this newer process would protect the pieces at the points of hardest wear. Many of the Boulton pieces are stamped with the words: "Silver Borders," in conjunction with his own mark of a sun which he registered in 1784.

After his success in the production of Sheffield plate his thoughts naturally turned to the industry of solid silver making. However, he was faced here with a very serious obstacle, as the silver had to be hallmarked and the nearest assay office was at Chester, seventy-two miles away. The only alternative was to send the pieces to the London assay office, but as this was even further distant, the cost was too great and the likelihood of damage was ever-present. Boulton gave a great deal of thought to this difficulty and soon became determined to appeal to Parliament for the establishment of an assay office at Birmingham. He voiced his opinions on this subject most intelligently and was given a great deal of publicity. Before long, his fellow workmen in the city of Sheffield gave him their whole-hearted support and the two towns requested individual assay offices at the same time. After a great deal of argument, on the part of the Goldsmiths of London, against this measure, permission was granted in 1773, and offices were opened at Birmingham and Sheffield.

Matthew Boulton died in 1809, and conclusive proof of the tremendous success he enjoyed may be gleaned from his will. This provided for the disposition of close to three quarters of a million dollars which in those days was considered a huge fortune. Truly, it may be said that he was successful in every enterprise he undertook, but that in the production of Sheffield plate he achieved a prominence never since equalled by any other craftsman. He produced plate of rare quality, and his works are eagerly sought after today as they are considered among the best specimens of the period in which he lived.

PAUL STORR

Paul Storr was the most celebrated of the late George III silver-smiths, and his works showed a degree of skill equalled previously only by Paul Lamerie. Throughout his career he enjoyed the distinction of royal and artistic patronage and executed many important dinner services to special order. He was a great artist and developed many new modes of decoration in his work. During the last ten years his skill has become more appreciated than ever—and today many collectors are specializing in the acquisition of pieces by him.

Paul Storr first entered his name at Goldsmiths Hall in 1792, at which time he was a partner in the firm of Rundell and Bridge. In 1821, in conjunction with John Mortimer, he opened the shop of Storr and Mortimer, which has been carried on to the present time in London under the name of Hunt and Roskell.

ANTHONY NELME

Nelme was one of the earliest smiths to achieve prominence and was extensively patronized throughout his career. He entered his mark in the Hall in 1697. Upon his death in 1722, he was succeeded by Francis Nelme, who adopted Anthony's mark and continued his work in the same style.

PETER PLATEL

Platel was one of the Huguenots who escaped to England where he enjoyed a large and extensive patronage. He produced many magnificent pieces for royalty, but he is probably better known as the tutor of Paul Lamerie.

BATEMAN

The members of the Bateman family, which included Anne, Hester, Jonathan, Peter, and William, were all prominent as silversmiths in the George III era. They were among the most popular smiths of their time and their work portrays clearly the exacting apprenticeship to which each was subjected. The name of Hester Bateman is by far the best known of the five, and the work by this celebrated lady smith is greatly in demand. The delicate craftsmanship which was characteristic of her has influenced greatly present popularity. As only a few pieces bearing her hallmark are available, higher prices are paid than ever before.

Among many other craftsmen who achieved fame were: Simon Pantin, Peter Archambo, David Willaume, Richard Gurney, John Cafe, Henry Chawner, and John Emes.

VI

TEA SERVICES

THE spirit of the tea hour seems to be indelibly associated with England, for in no other corner of the world is this simple function still preserved with such dignity and care.

Tea was originally introduced to the English people through an advertisement that appeared in a London newspaper in 1658. "That excellent and by all Physicians approved China Drink called by the Chinese Tcha, by other nations Tay, alias Tee, is sold at the Sultaness Head, a coffee-house in Sweeting's Rents, by the Royal Exchange, London." It was mentioned again in the diary of Samuel Pepys, who in 1660 wrote of having tasted a new beverage from the East and having found it to his liking. However, it was not until 1664 that tea came to be better known. In that year, the East India Company, one of the largest trading establishments of its day, presented two pounds of this new luxury to His Majesty Charles II. Tea cost over one hundred shillings a pound at that time so that the mention of a gift of two pounds of tea to the reigning king of England, need not seem strange.

Although tea was first considered to be expressly for medicinal purposes, it soon grew to be better known as a refreshment. It is recorded that tea found instant favor with the ladies and gentlemen of the court, and it was not long before it was imported in larger quantity. As the importation increased, so the price was lessened and in about 1720, tea had reached a price level where it could be enjoyed by others than just the select and wealthier classes. Leading figures of the day with sufficient funds to indulge themselves, consumed as many as twenty to twenty-five cups daily.

The introduction of tea into England is responsible for the production of many beautiful silver vessels for use in service, and were it not for the instant popularity which greeted its importation into England, the world might well have lost these splendid examples of superb craftsmanship displayed by the silversmiths in the making of silver tea ware.

TEA POTS

The earliest known silver tea pot was made in 1670, this priceless treasure now being in the possession of the Victoria and Albert Museum in London. The pot bears the arms of the East India Company, and is engraved with an inscription of presentation as follows: "This Silver Tea-Pott was presented to ye Comtte of ye East India Cumpany be Ye Honoue George Lord Berkeley Castle A member of that Honourable and Worthy Society and a True Hearty Lover of Them 1670." Were it not for this inscription it might well have been thought to have been a coffee pot, for its shape and size were very similar to the accepted style of coffee pot produced since about 1700. Very few silver tea pots of contemporary date are known. During the reign of Queen Anne many fine specimens of pots were executed to special order of the nobility, but in small sizes only for tea was still very expensive. Not until the reign of George II, 1727-1759, were tea pots made of larger size or in greater profusion.

The early tea pots were severely simple in style, but as the demand brought more and more activity to the silversmiths of the day, many of the early masters indulged in fine chasing and gave full expression to their creative ability. Many of the silver pots made were copied from the exquisite Chinese masterpieces fashioned in porcelain by the potters from the East.

Since the time of George I, tea pots have constantly changed in shape and decoration, as silversmiths all over Europe tried to create pieces expressing the individual tastes of their clients.

Tea pots with characteristic spouts first began to appear in the last quarter of the seventeenth century. The Chinese custom of preparing tea differed from that of the English, and this greatly influenced the change in the shape of the pots. The Chinese poured hot water out of the pot on the leaves, while the English infused the tea in the pot. Tea pots of the Queen Anne and George Ist period were very beautiful, as a rule being of a pear shaped body with a domed lid, the outline being either rounded or polygonal. The popular type with the inverted pear shaped body was introduced about 1730. As the demand for silver tea pots increased to the point where practically every home of good standing owned one, styles repeatedly changed. The Adam period was extremely prolific in designs for tea pots. Typical specimens of the time were made with a circular, oval or octagonal drum shape body, usually with a straight spout. Many in this period had stands to match, as the bottoms were constantly burning and scratching the highly polished wood surfaces of the tea table. It is not unusual, however, to find a tea pot by one maker, and a stand to match by a different smith of a few years later date. This was because people did not realize at first how essential the stands were if their fine tables were to be preserved. The tea pot so popular in Scotland for many years, of a globular shape on a tall foot, remained purely local, and never found much favor south of the Tweed.

TEA CUPS AND SAUCERS

Silver tea cups and saucers are among the rarest known objects in silver, but a few specimens dating from 1684 to 1700 have survived. These, it may be added, are nearly entirely in private collections or on display in leading museums. Both cups and saucers were of the convex fluted style, later copied by leading porcelain factories. All were made without handles, proving beyond doubt that the earliest vessels connected with this beverage were influenced by the Chinese forms.

COFFEE POTS

Coffee first found its way into England during the Commonwealth, 1649 to 1660, so as a beverage, it antedates tea in England. However, it was greatly frowned upon at first, as many thought it to be a drug, and that its constant use would cause the men of the nation to "dwindle into a succession of apes and pygmies." So radical was the feeling against coffee that many bills were introduced into Parliament to prohibit its sale.

The earliest known uses of coffee are traced to Abyssinia, where it was consumed as early as the fifteenth century. Coffee was also used in early Mohammedan religious ceremonies as an antisoporific. However, it was later excluded from these services, as many thought it to be intoxicating, and contrary to the teachings of the Koran.

Eventually, coffee became popular in England and in 1651 the earliest known coffee house was opened by a Syrian, Cirques Jobson, Oxford. However, these places did not meet with the favor of the King, as he considered them a meeting place for political agitators. Years later, after much legislation concerning them, coffee houses were firmly established throughout England. Even today one may find some that are a few centuries old.

The first silver coffee pot is dated 1681, and was less than 10 inches high, being considerably shorter in height than the "tea-pott" of 1670. However, the general shape resembled that of the tea pot, the main difference being that the handle was opposite the spout. The next examples known had the handles placed at right angles to the spout, and this style remained unchanged until the beginning of the George II period. Shortly before 1700, the spout was curved, and as the Queen Anne period progressed a style of coffee pot of octagonal shape was very popular. This was merely an alternative to the regular tapering cylinder. During the George Ist period, the silversmiths created an object of more beauty, by modifying the tapering cylindrical shape, and curving the base into the spout. The lid became flatter and more deeply moulded, and gradually as the years passed, the accepted style of pot was decidedly dissimilar to the first creations of the earliest craftsmen.

SUGAR BOWLS

Little sugar was imported into England before its use in tea, and consequently the first silver sugar basins were not introduced until the reign of William III, 1695 to 1702. These were originally made with a rounded base, with a saucerlike cover, so very similar to the Chinese tea cup. However, the style was later discarded for a type set on three feet, and many years later were made to match tea pots. Sugar baskets were first made at the time of Queen Anne and reappeared again at the end of the eighteenth century with colored glass linings. About this time, the flair for pierced work found great favor with the silversmiths of the day, and it is for this reason that so many pierced as well as richly embossed sugar bowls are known.

At the time of the production of the first tea services, sugar bowls were decidedly out of proportion in size to the balance of the service. Frequently, they were fully as large as the tea pot. This was because at that time only unrefined sugar was known, the pieces were large and bulky and it was necessary to have a vessel of ample size to contain them.

CREAMERS

The Chinese did not use cream in their tea so that no cream pitchers in silver are known earlier than the time of Queen Anne, when the English adopted their own method of tea drinking, which involved cream and sugar.

The earliest specimens of creamers were made with simple round feet, but this style changed as the shapes of tea pots varied. In later years, as a rule, creamers resembled the general style of the tea pot. The popular type of helmet-shaped creamer was introduced during the George III era and the oval forms of the nineteenth century that followed were called squat creamers.

Various curious shapes were adapted to small creamers. Many eccentric forms are known today, the best known of which is in the shape of a cow. (Such specimens are exceedingly rare and may be confused with the modern Dutch ones that have flooded the market for years.) This was originally a creation of Nicholas Sprimont, a silversmith connected with the Chelsea porcelain factory.

TEA CADDIES

Tea caddies were introduced during the reign of Queen Anne, and specimens from this era are very rare. They were made in greater numbers during the George Ist period. The word caddy is derived from the Malay "kate," which means a weight equivalent to 1 1/15th of a pound. As tea was always sold by the "kate," the name became by transference applied to the case in which it was contained. The word canister, sometimes used instead of caddy, antedated the English adoption of caddy. Its use has been found in an advertisement of 1711.

Caddies were originally made in sets of three and later two, as different blends of tea were used, according to taste preference. It has been suggested that many times the center caddy of a set of three was originally made to be used as a sugar bowl, but this can only be surmised. The earliest known caddies were small, because of the prohibitive prices of tea, but as the beverage became more generally consumed and the price lessened, they were made of a more substantial size. The first caddies were made with a sliding panel and a domed top. The object of the panel was to prevent waste in transferring the tea from the original package, since it was much simpler to insert the tea through the larger opening at the base. Later, caddies were almost invariably made with hinge covers like regular boxes. It is perhaps because of this that so many have been adapted to present day use for cigarette containers.

As a general rule, caddies were placed in an outer case of beautifully decorated wood or shagreen and fitted with a lock and key. However, it is rare to find an original case in use today, as through hard wear and constant usage they were discarded or replaced. Not only were the cases of the caddies supplied with locks and keys but the pieces were, also. Tea was so expensive at that time, that people feared unless it were fully protected, servants might be tempted to steal some of it.

Some of the finest works of celebrated silversmiths are represented in caddies, as specimens of Lamerie and other famous smiths prove. However, the demand for elaborate decoration that came many years later was also transferred to tea caddies. Some of the fantastic and ornate creations applied to caddies are almost unimaginable.

TEA KETTLES

The tea kettle was the natural outcome of the tea pot, for in style it is little more than a tea pot mounted on a base with a spirit lamp for purposes of heating. However, it was not until twenty years after the introduction of tea pots that kettles were made in silver. The earliest known mention of one is in a Royal Warrant of 1687, but no example from that date is known to exist. The earliest one known today is the work of David Willaume executed in 1706, and the next in order, 1709, is the work of the celebrated Anthony Nelme, now owned by the Duke of Portland.

Tea kettles of the first quarter of the eighteenth century follow the lines of the early pear-shaped tea pots, and are circular or polygonal in plan. Later, a globular form was introduced and finally the popular inverted pear shaped type. As a general rule the stands were of delicately pierced work and contained in the center a lamp used for purposes of heating. During the George II era, many richly embossed pieces were created to harmonize with the changing trend towards decorative silver. Kettles of this period were often made with a small triangular stand, which prevented the tea table from being scorched by the heat of the flame of the lamp. In the latter part of the Queen Anne period, occasional mention is made of a huge stand sometimes three feet high on which conveniently to place the kettle next to the table, but only one or two such specimens are extant.

Because of the high cost of tea, the beverage was infused right at the table to prevent waste, and this readily explains the introduction of the tea pot with the lamp. It is very important in purchasing antique silver kettles to note that the hall marks on the bodies and stands match, for over a period of years stands were lost, and replaced by ones of later date. Also, many of the first owners of tea pots had stands made to fit them, to avoid the cost of an extra new piece. These, naturally, are not so desirable nor of value equal to those that are completely hallmarked in stand, body and lamp, and of uniform design as originally made.

URNS

The demand for a larger vessel to be used at social functions caused the silver tea urn to be made. It was usually of immense size and used to contain hot water. Many people actually tried to brew the tea inside these urns, but found upon experiment that the resulting beverage was far from palatable.

Tea urns were introduced about 1760, and at first were made similar to a kettle with a spirit lamp. This was soon altered, and urns were made with a compartment on the inside to hold a heated iron. This was heated in the kitchen and dropped in the compartment. It actually kept the beverage hot for hours. The iron heaters were connected on the inside to the handles.

The styles and shapes were influenced along with other pieces of the day by the contemporary styles. Rarely were they made to match tea services, though, as were kettles.

CHOCOLATE POTS

Although the chocolate pot is not actually a part of the tea service, its history in silversmithing is so closely allied to the coffee pot, it must be mentioned.

Chocolate originated from the West Indies, and was first heard of in England in 1657. As a beverage it grew rapidly in popularity, but being too rich for constant use, vessels for its service were not created in great numbers.

The main difference between a chocolate pot and a coffee pot, is that in the top of the former there is an opening covered by a small hinged lid, rather than a spout. Through this lid, a circular wooden stick was placed to aid in crushing and mixing the chocolate. This was known as a swizzle stick.

As for the changing style and decoration of the chocolate pot, it can only be said that it followed the coffee pot very closely, and was only distinguished by its lack of spout. In later years, as even today, chocolate pots were made with the handle at right angles to the spout.

COFFEE BIGGINS

A biggin, or coffee biggin, is a particular type of coffee pot, conceived by a man of that name. It was in reality a percolator. The coffee was first placed in a separate compartment fitted into a larger vessel, and this larger vessel contained water which was heated from below by an alcohol lamp as used in the kettle.

TEA SERVICES

The first complete tea service incorporated a tea pot, a sugar and a creamer. These three-piece services were made about 1790. A few specimens of prior date are known but are very rare. During the latter part of the George III era, coffee pots to match were added. However, it was not until years later that the complete tea service of six pieces with a kettle and a waste bowl of uniform design was introduced. It may be noted that the waste bowl is comparatively a new note in silversmithing. Judging from the varying styles and profusion of tea services dating later than 1850, it may be safely assumed that afternoon tea was at the height of its popularity during the reign of Queen Victoria. Many of the styles, so popular during the latter part of the Georgian era were reproduced, and are greatly in demand today. It is unfortunate, though, that so many of the earlier models were richly chased and embossed to suit the taste of the hour, for more than often the application of too much ornamentation detracted from the original shapes. It is difficult to realize the tremendous quantity of tea services produced during this era, unless one has viewed the countless different styles copied from the art motifs of foreign countries.

The collection of an antique silver tea service may entail much searching and a great difficulty in matching pieces. However, since no complete services were ever executed, it is within the full right of any collector to own a service of assembled pieces. Many times, makers are asked to make modern matching pieces to an original service of three units. However, a true lover of antique silver will never object to a service that does not match exactly. Rather, it is much more interesting to spend months searching for just that particular coffee or kettle to use with your own service, and finally realize that if you have been fortunate, you have succeeded in accomplishing what every silver dealer is continually trying to do.

VII

MAZER BOWLS

MAZER bowls are among the earliest examples of English domestic silver. They were turned from bird's eye maple wood, which being of a fibrous texture, permitted the bowl to contain liquid without cracking or warping. Frequently the rims were ornamented with precious metals, although many mazers were executed for the poorer classes and were without silver embellishments. Mazer bowls were commonly in use during the thirteenth, fourteenth, and fifteenth centuries. During the reign of Queen Elizabeth they ceased to be made, as other creations of the silversmiths were found to be more useful.

The name "mazer" was probably derived from the German word "mazo," which means a spot. This referred to the speckled nature of the wood; however, the word may have derived from the Dutch "maeser" which means "knot of wood."

Some examples have a silver collar around the rim, which was probably used to conceal the marks of the turning lathe. They may have been copied from the early Roman pottery pieces which had a similar design. Occasionally a mazer was raised on a silver trumpet-shaped stem with a deep foot, ornamented with an open crest for use as a standing cup. In this way, the importance of the piece was often increased.

The usual silver mounts of a mazer were a band around the lip and a circular medallion in the bottom of the inside of the bowl, which was referred to as a "print" or "boss." The early examples are usually deep with narrow lip bands, while the later specimens are shallower with wider bands and an increased capacity. The band was generally used for the purpose of bearing an inscription of presentation or ownership.

Prints on the inside of a mazer were decorated in many varied fashions, although for the most part they consisted of a medallion depicting a religious device, a coat of arms, or a floral motif. Another name occasionally used to describe this medallion is "frounce." Covers for mazer bowls were not unusual although of the sixty examples which have survived to the present day, none is known with its original cover. Although so few mazers have survived the years, at the time of their introduction to English society they were very popular and were made in great profusion. However, by far the greatest number were made of solid wood as each man reserved the right to his personal drinking cup and only a few could afford the luxury of the increased cost of the addition of silver mounts.

The popularity of the mazer may be gathered from the fact that in 1328 there were 182 in the refectory of Christ Church in Canterbury. But eventually silver mounted mazers lost their popularity as pure silver gained in favor.

Mazers were used as early as the twelfth century by the rollicking monks to drink what they called "celestial nectar." One of the most famous is the masterpiece of 1398 in Yorkminster. A most unusual type is John Northwode's mazer of the late fourteenth century at Corpus Christi College, Cambridge. Fixed inside the center of the bowl is a hexagonal pillar with a battlemented top, upon which rests a swan. On the inside of this pillar is a hollow tube, open at both ends and so adapted that the bowl cannot be filled with wine above the top of the tube. Upon reaching that height, the wine begins to flow out, escaping through the end in the bottom of the bowl until empty. A few important mazers are owned by the Harbledown Hospital, one dating from the reign of Edward II.

An interesting allusion is made by Samuel Pepys, in his diary, wherein he describes drinking "In a brown bowl, tip't with silver which I drank off and at the bottom was a picture of the Virgin with the Child in her arms." He refers to the medallion of the sacred subjects found at the bottom of so many mazers.

Mazers were frequently engraved on the silver rims with appropriate inscriptions in Latin and occasionally in English. Many of the early specimens were converted into standing cups by ingenious silversmiths who followed the demand by the wealthy classes for pieces of more importance.

The value of a mazer cannot be measured except by its rarity, and the fact that it is probably the first piece of English domestic plate. The work on them is certainly not representative of first class silversmithing.

DRINKING HORNS

The use of horns for drinking vessels has been recognized from early times, and the medieval silversmiths were quick in adding to their beauty by the addition of fine mountings of silver gilt. Although very few of these early specimens have survived, much curious data has been handed down regarding their use. From remote antiquity comes the superstition and belief in horns as an antidote for poison.

The horn was supposed to vibrate as it came into contact with a substance containing poison. This superstition prevailed as late as the sixteenth century. The medieval member of royalty who possessed a small piece of this horn would attach it to a chain and dip it into the wine before partaking of it, thus reassuring himself. The most prized and theoretically most effective horns were those of the unicorn, an animal which never existed. But the horns of other animals such as the "narwhal" and the rhinoceros were sold by unscrupulous people as genuine unicorn. The form of this fabulous animal of India is well-known as the sinister supporter of the Royal Arms of England.

The influence of the early horn never quite disappeared as many tankards of later years and even of the present day retain the original horn shape. The use of horns, which was widespread in Anglo-Saxon times, steadily decreased and reference to them in later medieval documents is relatively uncommon. The later types of horns were equipped with feet so that they could be set down on the table. Another use of horns was for the purpose of serving as a charter for lands during the middle ages. Accurate proof of this is found in the horn presented to Pusey by King Knute with an inscription confirming the grant of property.

Medieval drinking horns are so rare as to be of little interest to collectors. Actually only five specimens are known. Among these, three important examples are herewith described. The first, now in the possession of Queen's College, Oxford, is engraved with Latin letters on each of three silver gilt bands mounted on the buffalo horn. The second, dating from the first half of the fourteenth century is less ornate, and became the property of Corpus Christi College, Cambridge, in 1352. Another treasure of its type dates from the reign of Henry VII, and is in possession of Christ's Hospital, Horsham.

STEEPLE CUPS, STANDING CUPS AND COVERS

These articles are sequels to the mazer bowl, and they carry certain rites and ceremonies that have been retained to the present time by corporations and fraternities that have rituals dating from the past. Among them is the age-old observance of the taking of wine from a loving cup as a token of friendship. Inasmuch as there were innumerable instances when a foe stabbed an enemy while in the act of drinking, it was not unusual for a guest in a strange house to have a comrade standing by his side while he drank. With dagger drawn, his ally stood ready to defend him in case an attack were made on the drinker. From this sequence we have inherited our present day manner of toasting with regard to loving cups. There are always three people standing; two facing each other and the third behind the person drinking as a safeguard against perfidy.

The standing cup was usually tumbler shaped, resting on a baluster or vase-shaped stem. The cover was slightly domed and surmounted in the usual way by a human figure. Some examples were plain, while others were repoussée with fruits and masks. Sometimes, cups of the early part of the seventeenth century assumed the conical shape with a dome-like cover, surmounted by a high finial, obviously copied from the spires of a church. These so-called steeple cups are generally found in sets of three, one being slightly taller than the other two. They are distinctly peculiar to the reign of James I. Among the many magnificent examples of standing cups and covers that have been handed down to the present time is the "Anathema cup" dating from 1481, and now in the possession of Pembroke College, Cambridge. This is the earliest known hallmarked cup. The second earliest surviving cup is the magnificent Leigh standing cup and cover, dated 1499.

The majority of cups of this type were highly chased with figures in relief and delicate piercings, such as demonstrated in the "Foundress" cup of Christ College, Cambridge. One of the few plain examples is the previously mentioned "Anathema cup." Although simple in form and practically void of decoration, it is by no means lacking in beauty.

Probably more fine specimens of standing cups and covers were executed in Germany than in any other part of the continent. The surviving examples clearly illustrate the importance of the German silversmith of the day. It may be assumed that many of the English cups were the work of German silversmiths who migrated to London.

Two of the finest known cups were sold at the disbursement of the Swaythling collection; one being the Rodney cup and cover of the late fifteenth century which fetched the sum of $38,000, and the other, the Tudor cup bearing the London hallmark of 1500, which was sold for $15,000. These prices readily indicate the appreciation and rarity of these masterpieces of early silversmithing.

COCOANUT CUPS AND OSTRICH CUPS

Many standing cups of the fifteenth and sixteenth centuries were formed of a cocoanut or an ostrich egg mounted in silver and raised on a tall stem. Few early specimens have survived, as the brittle texture of these pieces caused many to be damaged and discarded throughout the years of service. In effect, they were a variation of the standing cup and cover and may be definitely assumed to have been copied from workings of European silversmiths. As a general rule the work was very elaborate and covered a section of the top of the shelf and a part of the base.

Probably the main reason for the use of the cocoanut cup was its great rarity. By owning a specimen of this type, a definite display of wealth could be shown. However, some thought was given to the idea that wine imbibed from these shells contained medicinal properties. In a volume of 1640 they were accredited with having protective powers against colic, rheumatism, and epilepsy.

As early as 1259 a cocoanut cup was mentioned in a will, but no surviving example antedates the middle of the fifteenth century. Evidence of their popularity at the time of their inception may be judged by the inventory plate of Winchester College, in which eleven specimens occurred.

London silversmiths ceased to regard cocoanut shells as curiosities worthy of their skill after the reign of James I. However, for some unexplained reason the fashion was revived about 1770 when large numbers of shells were mounted as cups and goblets with silver lips, linings, and feet. This fashion continued until the early years of the nineteenth century.

Far rarer than the cocoanut cup in England is the ostrich egg cup. A notable example is dated 1592 and is in the possession of Corpus Christi College, Canterbury. The silver garnishings comprise a stem fashioned like the twisted trunk of a tree in the manner of many German cups. The egg of the Ostrich was definitely regarded as worthy of the skill of the greatest silversmiths, as evidenced by the large number of articles such as tankards, cups, ewers and pots fashioned from silver and the egg. Ostrich egg cups appear frequently, although they were usually described as being griffins' egg cups.

The nautilus shell cup, so popular with the silversmiths in Germany in the sixteenth and seventeenth centuries, found little favor in England. Only one specimen has survived, although the delicate character of the shell may account for the destruction of the other examples. This cup is in the form of a melon shell, mounted as a monster of the sea. It was the work of a London silversmith in 1577.

One finds during the medieval times and the Renaissance, numerous objects of little intrinsic value mounted as cups by English silversmiths. It may be, that coming from parts of the earth then little known, these shells were invested with much mystery which enhanced their value and importance. Probably the only reason that any of the early specimens has survived is, that having a small quantity of silver in the mountings, they were hardly of sufficient importance to melt down.

FONT SHAPED CUPS

Another type of cup originating at the beginning of the sixteenth century had a shallow bowl with straight, vertical sides, resting on a wider splayed circular foot, the diameter of the bowl being approximately equal to the height of the cup. These are known as font-shaped cups. The earliest known examples are in the Victoria and Albert Museum and were executed in 1500. Probably the best type known of the few that have survived, is the one owned by the Goldsmiths' Company, which bears the London hallmark of 1503.

As a general rule, font cups are thick and heavy and void of decoration. However, some specimens were embossed as evidenced by the cup of 1515 now in the possession of Corpus Christi College, Oxford. Occasionally these pieces had covers which were almost flat with a knob, and a top suitable for a coat of arms.

BEAKERS

The form of most drinking vessels in use during the middle ages may be classed roughly into two stages: those derived from the beaker and those from the bowl. In all probability the beaker originated from the use of a straight section of ox-horn with one end stopped up. However, it has been impossible to trace either the name or the shape further back than the fourteenth century. It has been suggested that the introduction of the beaker was probably due to traders between England and the Low Country, or to the Protestant refugees, who sought escape from England in the seventeenth century.

Silver beakers were popular as long ago as the Elizabethan era and continued to be made and developed. During the reign of Charles II they were sometimes embossed or ornamented with a band of Acanthus chasing. Otherwise, the majority of these examples differ very little from the early Elizabethan types. They are usually about six inches in height, spread toward the top and made with a molded base. Very few beakers were made in the eighteenth century. A type more popular and differing distinctly from the early examples was that shaped and engraved as a beer barrel. It is curious that so few examples of standing beakers are known with English hallmarks, for on the continent they were by far the most popular type.

By the seventeenth century the original straight table beakers developed a flare in form, and although they remained in use, there is little doubt that they were for the most part replaced by individual cups for drinking. Beakers of the Elizabethan and James I periods were usually embossed in low relief and engraved with foliage. The earliest types were originally made of horn and date back to the middle ages. These shapes were later reproduced by the silversmiths.

Although beakers were reserved for personal use, specimens in silver were indulged in only by the wealthy, and it is for this reason that early examples are very rare and command huge prices. However, as the specimens of the eighteenth and nineteenth centuries were produced in far-flung profusion, they have not yet come to be known as rarities among pieces of Old English silver.

TANKARDS AND MUGS

Certain names applied to silver objects have more or less romantic origins, and such a survival occurs in the word "tankard." Although long since forgotten, the word originally indicated the clumsy hollowed logs bound with iron and used to carry water from city conduits. In later years the name was applied to great wooden mugs bound with metal.

No English silver tankards are known prior to the sixteenth century and generally speaking, many of the earliest specimens displayed some tendency to the natural taper of the early ox-horn. Although made in a vast variety of sizes and shapes, they were all generally of the same tapered type. The exceptions were the few straight cylindrical bodied ones, reproduced from continental models. Many of the earliest tankards were made with bodies of horn or bone which were then mounted with silver covers, neck bands and feet. It was believed that with the bone or horn substance contained therein, the presence of any poisonous substance in the beverage could be immediately detected. Some tankards are found with a body of crystal, for it was generally believed that if the liquid contained any poison it would cloud the crystal on coming in contact with it.

During the James I period the in-curving taper of the horn disappeared in the shape of the tankard, and was replaced by straight sides. During the reign of Charles II, many tankards were produced and while the ornamentation was retained for a short time, molded lips disappeared, covers were made of much simpler style; and the finials of the early types were discarded. Later on in the century, a shorter type of a plain cylindrical body with a flat projecting rim became fashionable. Although tankards were originally made in pint sizes in the beginning of the seventeenth century, they were later made of much larger proportion. Tankards were generally of a uniform shape with an "S" shaped handle. Many are found with encircling bands of silver and these may be said to have survived from the early metal bands on the original wooden receptacles.

Among the types of tankard most sought after by collectors, is "peg" tankard. This type contained a vertical row of pegs fitted on the inside of the body at equivalent distances, and was used to mark the quantity of wine or beer permitted to each man at the passing of the cup. An interesting feature of many of the early tankards was a slot on the under side of the handle. The idea has been suggested that this was used to summon an attendant when a vessel was empty, but whether it was designed for that purpose or rather as a vent to allow the hot air to escape, can only be surmised.

Tankards were made in great profusion throughout England as well as Europe, and the continental influence is easily detected, particularly in those mounted on feet.

During the late 17th century, an offspring of the tankard known as the mug, was introduced. This, in effect, was actually a tankard on a smaller scale, but lacking the cover. These mugs were tremendously popular as beer drinking vessels at the leading universities throughout England.

GOBLETS

Although there is a slight difference between a goblet and a wine cup, they may be classified together as they grew in popularity in the late Tudor period, at which time they replaced the earlier beakers. These were actually vessels made for individual service and numerous examples from the 17th century are available. Goblets date back to very early times and have practically never ceased to be made. After the general adoption of silver wine goblets, the silversmiths lost many of their opportunities for producing varied pieces, as these replaced practically all of the earlier types of drinking equipments. However, with the general importation and use of crystal at the dinner table, wine cups and goblets fell into disuse. It is interesting to note though, that the modern adaptation in crystal for individual service carries out almost perfectly the original design of the goblet or wine cup. Goblets were used for other purposes besides drinking as frequently specimens are found that were made as presentation cups.

TUMBLER CUPS

Originally known as a "bolle," the tumbler cup was introduced during the middle ages for use as a wine vessel. However, no surviving specimen earlier than the end of the 17th century is available. A tumbler cup is quite different from all other drinking vessels in the manner of its construction. It was usually of very heavy silver, the lower part of the bowl being hemispherical and hammered in such a way as to leave a thick bottom. When filled with wine, the round bottom caused the bowl to tumble from side to side, but it was prevented from toppling over by the extra weight of the metal on the under side. Sets of these tumbler cups are found complete rather often because they were usually nested one inside the other. They were quite small in size, being designed, as a rule, to contain only a single drink.

POSSET CUPS, CAUDLE CUPS AND PORRINGERS

The little two-handled cups with covers which came into general use during the second half of the seventeenth century were intended to hold caudle and posset. The squat pear shaped vessels were doubtlessly inspired by objects imported from the Orient. Caudle was made largely of wine, or some alcoholic liquor, to which sugar, spice, and crumbled bread were added. Posset, on the other hand, was somewhat similar to what is known today as porridge, and was composed of bread or oat cakes mixed with curdled milk, combined with wine or beer, and flavored with spice.

These little cups and those referred to as porringers were used for wine and hot drinks. However, from the name porringer which is doubtless a corruption of the word "porridger," it is safe to assume that they were used to serve stews and similar refreshment as well. Porridge, at the time of the making of the little silver containers, was actually a thick soup, while the now obsolete word "pottenger" indicated a maker of pottage, which was a stew of vegetables and meat.

Porringers, as a rule, were made without covers, the bowl usually being less than four inches deep, while caudle and posset cups invariably had lids and were both larger and deeper. Caudle and posset cups, as well as porringers, all appear as early as in sixteenth century inventories, but no examples have survived from this date. Caudle cups were generally decorated in relief with the large animals and fruits characteristic of this period, and sometimes the wide rim of the saucer-like stand in which they were placed, was ornamented, too. Porringers were introduced about 1680 and were popular until about 1715. It is indeed curious that these little vessels have become the most popular of all christening presents as their long association with intoxicating foods and drinks scarcely seems to be congruous with the partaking of nourishment by a child.

BEER JUGS AND CLARET JUGS

Silver beer jugs were made as early as the time of George I, but did not come into general use until the period of about 1770. It is very rare to find original beer jugs as many of the ones sold today have been fashioned from chocolate pots and tankards. Beer jugs resembled in style the water pitcher as known today, while claret jugs were similar to hot water jugs introduced during the early Georgian period.

PILGRIM BOTTLES

Huge pilgrim bottles appeared late in the seventeenth century and continued until the early years of the eighteenth century. As a rule, they were beautifully ornamented, although on many, an over-profusion of decoration is found. The original use of pilgrim bottles was to hold wine for use at large dinners, although they were also made as ornaments for sideboards. There is little doubt but that these massive silver bottles were designed after the outlines of the ancient pilgrim bottles. Earl Spencer owns one of the earliest known pairs, made in 1701, and probably the work of John Goode.

FLAGONS, STONEWARE JUGS AND BLACKJACKS

The word Flagon was definitely derived from the early French "flacon," which denoted a bottle-shaped vessel of leather, having a narrow neck and a plain ovoid body. Closely allied to these flagons were stoneware jugs and blackjacks, which were in use about the middle of the 17th century. Stoneware jugs were popular during the latter half of the sixteenth century, at which time they were imported from Germany and fitted with silver or gold neck bands, feet, and covers, by the English silversmiths. Stoneware is exceptionally hard and non-porous, the surface being glazed by throwing salt into the furnaces while the clay vessels are being baked. The jugs followed the form of the early flagons with the bulbous bodies and narrow necks. The color of the ware varied from a dull gray to a common spotted surface from which was derived the name "tiger Ware." Other rare examples of this type of jug were made of blue glazed earthenware, in the old Lambeth potteries, while occasionally specimens of Rhodian faience come into the market. Examples of these pieces with Elizabethan mounts are extremely rare and fetch high prices at auction.

Blackjacks were vessels of waxed leather used for centuries for carrying and storing liquors. The larger ones became known as bombards, the name being derived from their resemblance to the old cannons of that name. This type was used exclusively for the purpose of storing fine liquors. A smaller type intended for use as a drinking vessel was sometimes mounted with silver and engraved with a coat of arms. The dates of these articles can only be estimated as the silver mounts rarely, if ever, bear any hallmarks.

During the first half of the 17th century, flagons retained the style of decoration which characterized the work of silversmiths of the previous century. The pieces were tall and cylindrical, with feet splayed out into a handle formed by an "S" scroll. Fruits and fishes were commonly the motifs of the design, alternating with other delicately engraved ornamentation. Flagons and stoneware jugs were commonly in use by the churches of England as early as Elizabethan times. They were employed when it was necessary to bring wine to the communion table. Before the middle of the seventeenth century, flagons had developed into vessels of great size and capacity and were frequently made in pairs. As a rule, they were plain and without gilding. The churches of London were particularly rich in such vessels, and a group covering nearly every successive year from 1605 to 1660 is available.

COASTERS AND DECANTER STANDS

The wide use of crystal decanters led to the making of coasters, the commonest type having a wood turned bottom and a solid or pierced silver side. They were introduced during the Adam period while decanter stands were first made during the George I era. However, they were not produced in quantities until nearly forty years later.

Many decanter stands were doubled or tripled, and joined together by a bar and mounted on wheels. These pieces had a small silver handle and resembled the general shape of a cart on wheels, hence the applied name of wine wagon.

A coaster or decanter stand is a clear illustration of the outcome of changing social customs which caused the introduction of many new pieces in silver. As the fashion prevailed to remove the cloth from the dining table for dessert, someone probably conceived the idea of placing the bottle in a stand and coasting it along the table. This explains why the base is covered with baize on the bottom, to prevent any markings on the polished mahogany tables. It is also probable that after the bottles had been refilled several times and the guests had become slightly inebriated, the decanters did not always reach their intended destinations while being passed.

Coasters were made in a wide variety of designs and included examples of delicately pierced work as well as richly embossed specimens. Many were ornamented with a band of grapes and leaves which was appropriate to the wine decanter which it contained. As a rule, coasters were made in pairs or sets of four, six or eight.

EWERS

Many articles in use today were made for entirely different purposes at the time of their conception. These changes are to a large extent due to the refinements which gradually appeared in the social observances connected with the dining table. The common instance, is our practice of washing the hands before sitting down to dinner, which, in effect, is actually a perpetuation of washing the hands at the table. This custom instituted many centuries ago, was symbolized by the use of basins and ewers among the noble families, from the middle ages to the seventeenth century.

Ewers were introduced originally from Italy and quickly rendered the medieval finger bowl obsolete. As a rule they were gilded, and many displayed the graceful forms of the Italian Renaissance. Probably the outstanding creation of the Tudor silversmiths with regard to splendor and magnificence, were their rosewater ewers.

Until the introduction of the fork, the washing ceremony was an essential part of dining, as in those days it was the custom to hold the food in one hand, cut it with the knife, and then lift it to the mouth with the fingers. It was customary for a servant to hold a silver basin in front of each guest. The water was then supplied from a ewer carried by another servant who poured it over the hands of the guest into the basin. At the conclusion of this ceremony, the servant produced a towel with which he dried the hands of the diner. This was recognized as a part of the general etiquette of the dining table, and guests received attention in accordance with their rank.

The custom of using a ewer and basin at the table was not restricted to the wealthy classes as those in more moderate circumstances used specimens made of brass. Although silver ewers and basins were mentioned frequently in wills and inventories, very few have survived to the present day. The amount of precious metal expended on their manufacture rendered them extremely liable to be consigned to the melting pot in time of financial difficulties.

There were three distinct types of ewers made and they are clearly demonstrated by the following examples. An early specimen is that presented to Corpus Christi College, Cambridge, in 1570. This piece has a rounded foot and a swelling octagonal body, the sides of which were alternately engraved with arabesques. Two of the remaining sides were plain and occupied by the angular handle and spout which was attached to the whole of the length of the body.

The second known variety had a vase shaped body and a narrow neck with a spout and scroll handle. It was richly chased and the handle was in the form of a demi-lion. This type is exemplified by one made by Robert Signall, in 1583, which may now be seen in the Victoria and Albert Museum. The third, which appeared during the reign of James I, was, as a rule, undecorated except for heraldic achievements.

The ewers resembled a straight sided goblet with scroll handle and curved spout. The introduction of a vessel so conspicuously lacking in aesthetic charm is typical of a period when silversmiths were seeking originality at all costs. Just previous to 1700 appeared the last standard pattern of ewer. This was known as the helmet shape and was a magnificent example of the proper combination of a good shape with restrained ornamentation. About the middle of the George I period, ewers and basins were discarded and used only as ornaments.

Ewers are very rare and fine specimens fetch fantastic prices. Some are known to have reached a figure at auction of $100,000.

MONTEITH BOWLS, PUNCH BOWLS, AND ACCESSORIES

The magnificence which prevailed in the production of so many silver vessels connected with the ceremony of drinking, is often present in punch bowls. Punch, which was of Oriental origin, consisted of five ingredients: spirits, water, lemon juice, sugar and spice. Thus the assumption is made that the word punch was probably derived from the Hindustani "panch" which meant five. Although the brewing of punch was introduced into England during the reign of Charles I, silver bowls for service do not seem to have been made until after the Restoration.

The earliest known punch bowls were small and of simple design, while those wrought in the later Georgian era were of far greater capacity and generally with a wealth of ornamentation. As early as the Stuart period examples are found with notched rims. However, the type with the removable rim known as the monteith bowl was not introduced until nearly the end of the seventeenth century. The introduction of this type of bowl was attributed to a Scotchman named Monteith, who gained considerable reputation from his ability to brew punch of excellent character. Because of the fact that he wore a cloth coat scalloped in the bottom, much in the same style as were the punch bowls of this time, his name was applied to them. From this time on, all bowls with removable rims were known as monteiths. Many explanations have been advanced regarding the addition of the removable rim, and the most probable of these is that the glasses were placed in the notches to prevent their breakage, when being brought into the dining room by the footman. Another theory advanced was that the bowl was filled with water and the glasses hung from the notches to keep cool.

There seems to be no limit to the sizes of punch bowls, and many were used at important functions. The majority of them have fluted bodies with lion's head ring handles. Monteiths were very popular and a great number were made until the end of the eighteenth century, and may be found today among the plate of most of the corporate bodies who would quite naturally have had frequent opportunities to use them.

Several small accessories necessary to the brewing of punch were introduced by the silversmiths of this time. However, the only one that has survived in any degree is the long handled ladle used for transporting the liquid to the jugs. Occasionally one finds a circular strainer with two wrought handles, which was placed across the jug to strain the punch. Punch ladles were made in a variety of designs and were hammered out of Spanish silver dollars or crown pieces in such a way that the marginal description still appeared on the lip of the ladle. The placing of a coin at the bottom of the bowl was also a common trick.

With the return of entertainment on a larger scale, Georgian drinking accessories have once again come into demand. Because of their low price, punch ladles make ideal items for those interested in old silver.

WINE FOUNTAINS, WINE CISTERNS

These two articles reflect beyond a doubt the indulgence used to achieve the sumptuous display of magnificence in silver but very few examples of wine fountains or cisterns exist now. Wine fountains were actually massive upright vase-shaped covered vessels, fitted with an ice chamber and a small tap from which the wine was drawn into the glasses. Cisterns, on the other hand, were enormous oval bowls, intended to hold water and ice, in which the bottles of wine were placed to cool. Although these pieces were of huge proportions and more than extravagantly covered with ornamentation, they still retained the basic form suggestive of the work of the early silversmiths. The detail of the embossing, usually suggested mermaids, dolphins, or figures of Neptune, and was of the highest quality. Wine fountains are known to have weighed more than 1000 ounces and measured close to four feet in height, while wine cisterns were usually about four feet long and weighed close to 2000 ounces.

The largest piece of English plate known, is an enormous wine cistern made in 1734 by Charles Kandler for the Czar of Russia. The immense proportions will be immediately realized if one notes the excessive weight of nearly 8000 ounces contained in the piece. The actual dimensions of it are five and one half feet long, three and one half feet deep, and three and one half feet wide. In 1672 Charles II presented his mistress with a massive creation weighing over 1000 ounces, but this unfortunately has not survived. The earliest example known today was made two years later, and is now in the collection of the Earl of Rosebery. Although wine cisterns in silver were not made until after the Restoration, specimens of base metal were definitely used during the early part of the seventeenth century.

The wine fountains made during the early part of the eighteenth century were greatly reduced in size and were much more usable. As a general rule they were urn-shaped with a tap at the front and had two or four handles. Shortly after the introduction of silver wine cisterns, practically every home of importance owned one. Further proof of their constant use and even earlier introduction than is originally credited, may be found in many of the early pictures painted by Dutch artists.

WINE COOLERS AND ICE PAILS

The eventual outcome of the early wine cisterns was the smaller and more graceful wine cooler made to contain but a single bottle of wine. The interior was fitted with a removable jacket which held the wine, while the space between the jacket and the wall of the vase formed the ice chamber. These were generally of a vase shape in a single foot and invariably made with two handles. At first wine coolers were very simple in design, but the increasing flair for vessels of excessive ornamentation and richness of design caused the smiths to yield to popular demand. Although most wine coolers were not over twelve inches in height, a few enormous specimens are known. However, as the demand for huge pieces waned, the purchase price was lowered and wine coolers became more and more popular. By the beginning of the nineteenth century, literally thousands of pairs of silver and Sheffield plate had been produced. Also occasionally wine coolers were made with linings of base metal.

The wine cooler was probably an importation from France, as vessels of similar style and shape made in other metals than silver were known there.

Ice pails which were similar in shape to the coolers are known during the eighteenth and nineteenth centuries, and the ornamentation on them was similar to that found on the wine cistern and fountain of a century previous. The main distinction between an ice pail and a wine cooler is that the former was made without an inner jacket and the bottle was not placed in it to cool.

WINE LABELS, WINE FUNNELS, WINE TASTERS

During the reign of George III, the use of small silver labels pierced or engraved with the name of a particular wine, became increasingly popular. These labels were attached to a hanging chain and fitted around the neck of the bottle. It is not unusual to find a complete set of these little gadgets with as many as forty varieties of liquid refreshment included. It is actually necessary to study in detail the various types of wine consumed throughout England, to comprehend the vast number of labels produced. It is rather interesting that only of recent date have labels attracted the attention of the collector. Inasmuch as they require but a small investment, and since many are examples of exquisite workmanship, it is difficult to understand why they have never been appreciated heretofore.

The earliest known funnel for decanting wine is the example of 1661 in the Victoria and Albert Museum. Although these little silver articles were made extensively during the Georgian periods, early examples are scarce. But little attention has been given them, since from the artistic standpoint they are of no great interest. No home in England was considered fully equipped for the service of wine unless it had a funnel and strainer, and for this reason hundreds of later specimens are known today. Inasmuch as funnels are fitted at the base with a detachable strainer many collectors, unable to find suitable tea strainers, have purchased these funnels and retained only the strainer part for use.

The original purpose of the wine taster may be traced back to the time of the middle ages, where it was used on ceremonial occasions by deputised tasters, to see if the beverage contained any poison. In this way the important people who were at the dinner were protected from evil intent. Another use of the wine taster was to aid the vintner in sampling the wine which he was proposing to purchase. For this purpose it was necessary to have a small shallow bowl which would show the clear color of the wine. The vintner's silver taster was a well-known feature in late medieval times, and an example of 1383 appears in the inventory of the owner of a Norwich tavern. The earliest wine tasters were mostly plain saucer shaped articles with a raised dome in the center, the purpose of which was to prove that if the liquid was clear, it could be determined as it passed over the plain surface of the silver. The sides of these tasters were usually embossed with various floral designs or punched with flutes. In the latter half of the sixteenth century, a new type of wine taster was introduced. This was in the shape of a small bowl with a sloping side and a dome bottom, which showed the wine to great advantage. One of the earliest known examples of this type bears the Norwich hall mark of 1573. The next earliest known tasters were the shallow two-handled bowls, about three inches in diameter with wire handles. The early cups used for sipping were generally straight sided on short trumpet shaped feet. There is little doubt that many other vessels of similar type were employed in the tasting of wine, and among these may be mentioned the porringer, or, as it was sometimes called in England, the bleeding bowl. Their use as wine tasters can only be assumed from the few known examples which bear engraving suggestive of that particular service.

Although wine tasters have long since lost their original use, they are popular today for use as ash trays. However, it is most rare to find originals.

VIII

CONDIMENT SETS

THE standing salt was introduced during the middle ages. At the time of its use it was a symbol of social distinction because only a family of great wealth could afford it.

In medieval times, salt was very expensive, it was among the rarest of all table condiments, and for this reason important silver holders were used for it.

Salt has always been regarded with superstition as is evidenced by its uses at rituals among the ancient peoples to whom the "eating of salt" and the "breaking of bread" signified brotherhood. It was the belief that salt was a protection against the evils of witches and today many of us still adhere to the legend that the spilling of salt brings misfortune unless a pinch is thrown over the shoulder. The name saltceller is actually a corruption of the old French "saliere," meaning salt holder.

Originally the master saltcellar was placed in the center of the table at which the master of the house was seated. This particular table was denoted as the high table and distinguished from the others in that it was raised on a dais above the floor level. The position of each person in relation to the master salt was dictated by his social rank and until the seventeenth century, the entire household, from master to servant, ate together in a commonhall. The normal use of salts in the fifteenth and sixteenth centuries may be gathered from the books of "Curtesy" and "Nurture," published in 1508, wherein the passage is quoted: "set your salts on the ryght side where your soverayne shall sytte . . . and at every ende of ye table set a salte sellar . . . and when your soverayne's table, thus arrayed, cover all other bordes with salts, trenchours, and cuppes."

Those sitting at other than the high table were designated as being "below the salt," often causing much ill feeling because of the distinction. In addition to the ceremonial salt were smaller holders known as trencher salts to be placed at varied intervals around the table. The name was derived from the custom of lifting salt from the holder to a wooden trencher with the end of the knife. From descriptions in inventories we note that some of the early salts were often cast of solid gold, beset with jewels. An example of this is known from the diary of Charles I, wherein it is recorded that when he came to the throne in 1625, he sold a gold salt weighing one hundred and fifty ounces that was studded with sapphires, rubies, pearls and emeralds. One of the earliest English standing salts is the Huntsman salt which definitely portrays the Gothic influence in its ornamentation. Although the earliest salts were pieces of great importance in meaning, they were but slight in stature in comparison to the later types, as those known as early as 1313 weighed between six and eleven ounces.

The coming of the Renaissance styles influenced the shapes of standing salts for then they began to assume greater splendor. The early Gothic forms in the sixteenth century were replaced by those known as pedestal salts. In the Tudor period the bodies were rectangular or cylindrical, richly chased or embossed with foliage, fruit and figures. The cover was generally surmounted by a vase which supported a modeled figure. Such ceremonial salts frequently measured sixteen inches in height. Although popular for a considerable time, they were later replaced by the far simpler bell-shaped salt which appeared about 1590. These were made in three sections comprising two salt cellars and a pepper caster, and could be either joined together on ceremonial occasions or used separately. This type which was about eleven inches high was finally superseded by the steeple salts which assumed a greater proportion than ever previously known. Not infrequently steeple salts were made with two bowls.

During the latter part of the seventeenth century the custom of fitting a removable cover to the great salts was discontinued and in its place a bracket was fitted to the rim to support a napkin or plate which protected the salt from dust. These brackets are often mistaken for handles although only rarely does one find examples made with them. During the latter part of the fifteenth century and the first quarter of the sixteenth century standing salts were made in the shape of an hour-glass; ten examples of this type are extant. The finest of this collection is the one given by Walter Hill to New College, Oxford, of which he was Warden from 1475 to 1494. It is one of the unusual types combining beauty in silver work with richly engraved crystal. The use of salts in fancy shapes was very popular during the latter part of the 16th century, and much knowledge of them has been gleaned from the inventories of the royal plate wherein several are mentioned.

One was in the form of a dragon issuing from a shell; another had the shape of a crown falcon, and others were made in the form of men and women holding the receptacles for salt in their hands. These quaint forms of decoration although no longer familiar to us, suggest the fertility of the imagination of the early silversmith. In the will of Edmund, Earl of March, two unique specimens in the shape of dogs are listed. Another interesting example which has survived is known as the Monkey salt and is now in the New College, Oxford.

An early piece which shows the Renaissance influence is an hour glass salt made in 1522, belonging to the Goldsmiths' Company. It is of extreme interest because it is considerably ahead of most of the work of the first fifteen years of the English Renaissance with regard to form. Although the silversmiths in Germany and France greatly influenced the workers in England on much of the domestic plate, the designs for standing salts were original.

During the reign of Queen Elizabeth there was a definite increase in the production of small salts, although some of these are merely reproductions in miniature of the contemporary standing salts. Others which were of circular or triangular shapes were the forerunners of the great variety made in the later periods. The disappearance of the large standing salt is a direct result of the increasing popularity of the individual type. During the Charles II and Queen Anne periods a considerable number were produced which were either faceted or moulded, while those of a few years later assumed more elaborate decoration. From about 1720 to 1740 a salt with a circular bowl and a round foot was much in evidence, many examples of these being attractively decorated with applied leaf work. Towards the middle of the century the prevailing type consisted of a small bowl on three or four feet. Many of these were embossed with floral swage and lion masks above the feet, while others were pierced with rococo designs and fitted with glass liners.

During the Adam period the continued use of pierced work was much in evidence and the use of a blue crystal liner was seen much more frequently. These later salts were made in a wide variety of forms, all of which can be traced back directly in shape and feeling to the trenchers.

Sets of four early Georgian salts are very rare although greatly in demand. However, those of the later period can usually be purchased in their entirety as originally produced.

SALT AND MUSTARD SPOONS

Salt spoons are unknown before the end of the seventeenth century, at which time those made resembled miniature table spoons. The familiar ladle shape appeared at a slightly later date, while those varieties with a shovel shape bowl in use during the George III period as well as a number of eccentric types do not require much description. Mustard spoons, formed like small sauce ladles, date well into the eighteenth century. However, one is mentioned in an advertisement as early as 1678.

CASTERS AND MUFFINEERS

Although white pepper was known for use in England as early as the twelfth century, no form of caster appears among English silver previous to the reign of Elizabeth.

At this time they consisted of a small perforated section attached to bell shaped salts, but as individual articles they were not found earlier than the late Stuart period. The name muffineer was derived from the use of sprinkling salt on buttered muffins and, although, similar in form to casters they were somewhat smaller in size. Those known in the time of Charles II are cylindrical, the top being attached to the body by an elbow joint which consisted of two projection lugs soldered to the lower part of the top. The ears passed two notches in the grooved moulding around the rim of the body, which after being turned slightly, engaged firmly with the top.

Muffineers were made as a rule, in sets of three, one being considerably larger than the other two. The smaller pair were used for pepper, one being for Jamaica and the other for cayenne; while the large one was used for sugar. Casters were made in a variety of shapes and it is not difficult to estimate their approximate date from the form and style of ornamentation. During the Queen Anne period the pear shape, or pyriform, copied from Oriental vases, replaced the cylindrical bodies. This evidently was superseded by an undulating pyriform, with a tapering cover. As a rule, the ornamentation was restricted to bands or engraving around the edge of the cover, the bulging part of the body and the foot. The high domed covers of casters afforded the early silversmiths an opportunity to exercise a branch of their skill soon to become a feature of great importance. This intricate piercing found on so many Georgian casters plus the simplicity of the bodies made them objects of great beauty.

During the first half of the eighteenth century, a small type of caster with a handle, generally known as a kitchen pepper, was introduced. Later in the Georgian era smaller casters in sets of four or six were used to contain pepper and salt for individual service.

CRUET STANDS

Although cruet stands may have existed prior to 1700, the series of surviving pieces seems to begin with the latter part of the reign of Queen Anne. Undoubtedly owing to the difficulty of replacing the fragile contents large numbers were allowed to perish. Cruet stands are important examples of silver work because the finest smiths devoted their full talents to their production. During the medieval times they consisted of glass bottles which were used for vinegar and other flavors, while in the first quarter of the eighteenth century, a combination of bottles and casters fitting into a silver frame was introduced. This type was used on the table and known as a Warwick cruet. Good examples fetch high prices as the rare casters in them increased their value many times. The glass bottles were invariably made with small silver caps which could be placed in the small holes fastened on the sides of the stand. During the eighteenth and nineteenth centuries many varied styles were made among which one of the most popular consisted of a boat shaped stand with handles. In the early part of the nineteenth century, a circular type was introduced and at the same time individual bottles were supplied with the little labels similar to those used on decanters to identify the casters.

MUSTARD POTS

Although mustard was used in England much earlier, there is no evidence of silver containers for it prior to the reign of George I. Specimens from this time are very, very rare and most types obtainable now date from the latter part of the eighteenth century. These were generally made with a cylindrical body and a hinged flat lid, or oval body with domical lid, the sides often pierced and the body fitted with blue glass liners. The earliest known reference to a silver mustard pot appears to be in 1670 in a bill for plate made by Alderman Backwell for Prince Rupert, while the next earliest mention is four years later. One of the most beautiful known examples was executed in 1724 by Paul Lamerie in the shape of a barrel with a scroll handle and domed lid.

IX

FLAT SILVER

FLATWARE SERVICES

GENERALLY speaking, the service of flat silver occupies the throne of honor in the home today, for what bride does not thrill to the thought of possessing her own table silver. In most cases, it is the first purchase in the assembling of the trousseau, and usually the most cherished.

The demand for services in antique silver far exceeds the supply, for flat silver in complete services is distinctly a modern note. However, fine matching services can be collected over a period of time, and for the amateur collector this presents the ideal field of endeavor. A large initial investment is unnecessary, as the chances are that after one has selected a pattern, only a few pieces at a time will be available to purchase. Dealers in old silver are continually buying as much flat silver as possible, for it can be purchased most reasonably in oddments, and yet commands a high price when assembled in a complete service. A few years ago an important collector, well able to indulge herself in the luxuries she wished, wanted to assemble a matched service, all dated prior to the reign of George III. The forks were to be three pronged, the spoons "rattail," and the knives pistol handled. Although she allowed "carte blanche" as regards price, it took over four years of diligent searching all over the world in order to complete the set.

For those who are as well pleased by authentic reproductions, the finest patterns have been copied by contemporary silversmiths with great skill.

SPOONS

The spoon was probably suggested by the shells used in prehistoric times for eating liquid foods. In the Middle Ages spoons were made of bone, horn, crystal, and wood. There is also indication that some were fashioned from metals such as pewter and brass, but the earliest silver spoons in England date no further back than the end of the fourteenth century. The first known mention of a spoon made of a precious metal is in the Bible, wherein the Lord instructed Moses to make golden spoons for the Tabernacle. The age old custom of using a spoon for anointing a sovereign at a coronation is also noted in the Bible. It records how Nathan the Prophet anointed Solomon as King of Israel.

The first known English spoons are really only reproductions of the original ones made in bronze by the Romans and Greeks. However, the word spoon was doubtlessly derived from the fact that in early English times spoons were made of wood and the old English word for a splinter of wood is "spon."

The characteristics of these medieval spoons are a long slender polygonal stem tapering towards the head, and an elongated pear-shape shallow bowl. This definitely suggests that they were not used for thin liquids, but for thicker foods such as cream, custard or posset.

During the 250 years that followed the making of the first silver specimens, the basic form of the spoon remained the same, only the ornamentation or shaping being changed or modified. Such variations as occur are restricted to the ornamental knops at the end of the stems, but the oval or fig shape of the bowl was constant until the reign of Charles I.

A further development is noticed in the style of the stem which was changed from a thin round taper to the more robust hexagonal. The flat stem was not introduced until the Commonwealth.

From the latter part of the fourteenth century until the arrival of the flattened stem, different types of knops distinguished more or less definitely the individual periods. The earliest known was the acorn top, while during the fifteenth and sixteenth centuries, the diamond point and maidenhead predominated. With regard to the last mentioned type, it is interesting to note the variation in the style of headdress in the figure depicted, according to the prevailing fashion of coiffure at the time of the making. During the Tudor period, the knop resembled an inverted bunch of grapes, and sometimes was in the shape of a bird. Seal tops and those with the lion sejant are also known and the influence of the continental silversmiths is noticeable in the series of figures at the end of the stems.

A spoon that became common in the seventeenth century, was an absolutely plain type with a flat handle. It became very popular with the Roundheads, and hence was given the name Puritan spoon.

Apostle spoons are interesting. These were originally made in sets of thirteen, comprising a figure of the Lord and twelve disciples. Complete units of Apostle spoons are perhaps among the rarest known articles in silver, as evidenced by the fact that only a few years ago, a set of thirteen dated 1536 was purchased at auction for a sum in excess of $25,000. Other religious types of spoons depicted the figures of saints, cherubs and angels. Apostle spoons are more plentiful today than these other types, due to the custom of presenting one to each child on the occasion of his baptism.

At the time of Charles I, the bowls of spoons became egg shaped, and the stems took on a flat broad rectangular form, the ornamental knops being discarded. After the Restoration in 1660, the stem was flattened with the top cleft in two places to suggest a trifid. Also, at this time, the triangular tongue at the back that covered part of the bowl, appeared. This style was known as the "rat-tail," and enjoyed much popularity.

By the end of the seventeenth century, the spoon began to assume the shape that is commonly accepted and used today. The clefts disappeared from the handle, and were replaced by a rounded end that widened in a concave curve to form the handle. At this time, the bowl was broad and elliptical, although later it took on a more pointed shape. In the following years, the handle was turned upwards towards the face of the bowl and formed a distinct hook. About the middle of the eighteenth century, the more convenient down turn superseded the earlier type, and is the accepted style of handle today.

All manner of engraving and chasing was incised on spoons during various periods, and in some instances the bowls were ornamented with scrolls, foliations and shells. These were often symbolic of either the use of the spoon or else the person for whom it was intended. During the last hundred years or so, other styles have evolved, the most popular being the fiddle-back. This in turn was changed into the fiddle and thread, sometimes surmounted by a shell.

Teaspoons were introduced in the late seventeenth century, and were so small they resembled our present day after dinner coffee spoons. By the time of George I, the proportions had grown though, until they were of similar style to those used now.

The dessert spoon was not popular until after the Restoration, and from then on closely followed the style and shape of the table spoon.

FORKS

Comparatively speaking, forks are very recent to civilization, for although knives and spoons are known to have existed in crude forms, since ancient times, the general use of forks is not found until the end of the fifteenth century. At this period in history, forks were known only in Italy, although a few scattered continental

DINNER SERVICE

SHEFFIELD TEA MACHINE

Daniel Holy-Wilkinson and Co., London, 1798

ROSEWATER
DISH
London, 1569

ROSEWATER DISH

London, 1680

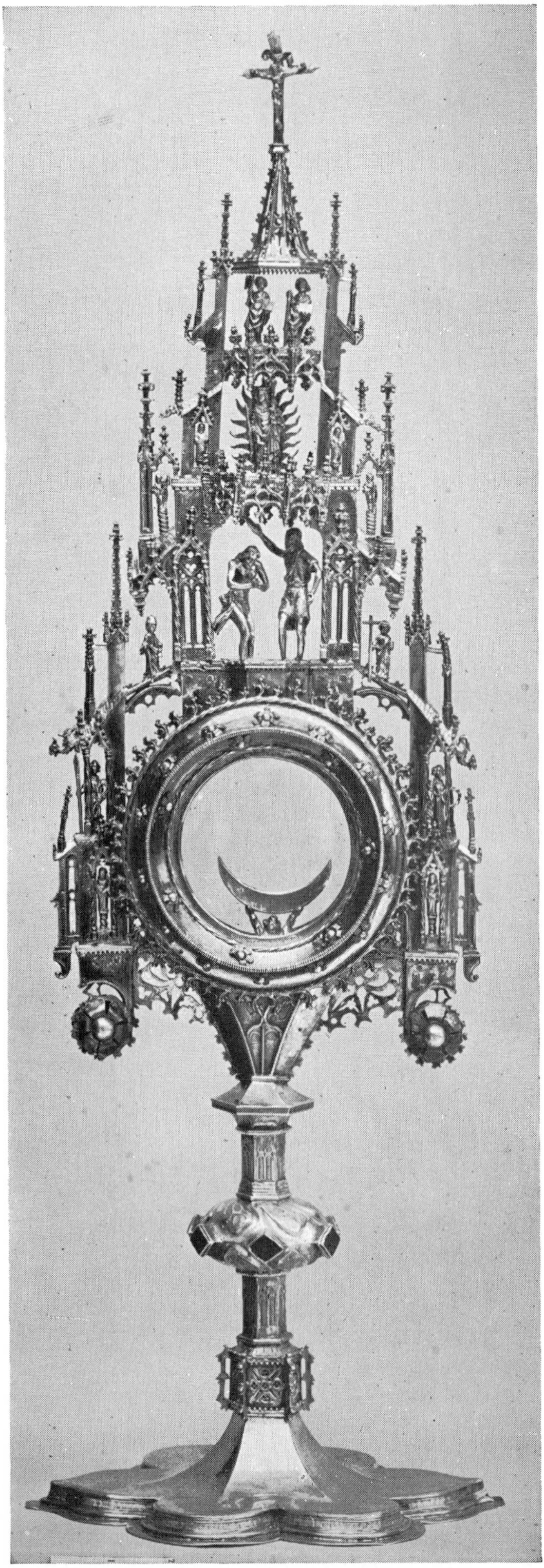

Courtesy Metropolitan Museum of Art

Silvergilt Monstrance German, 16th Century

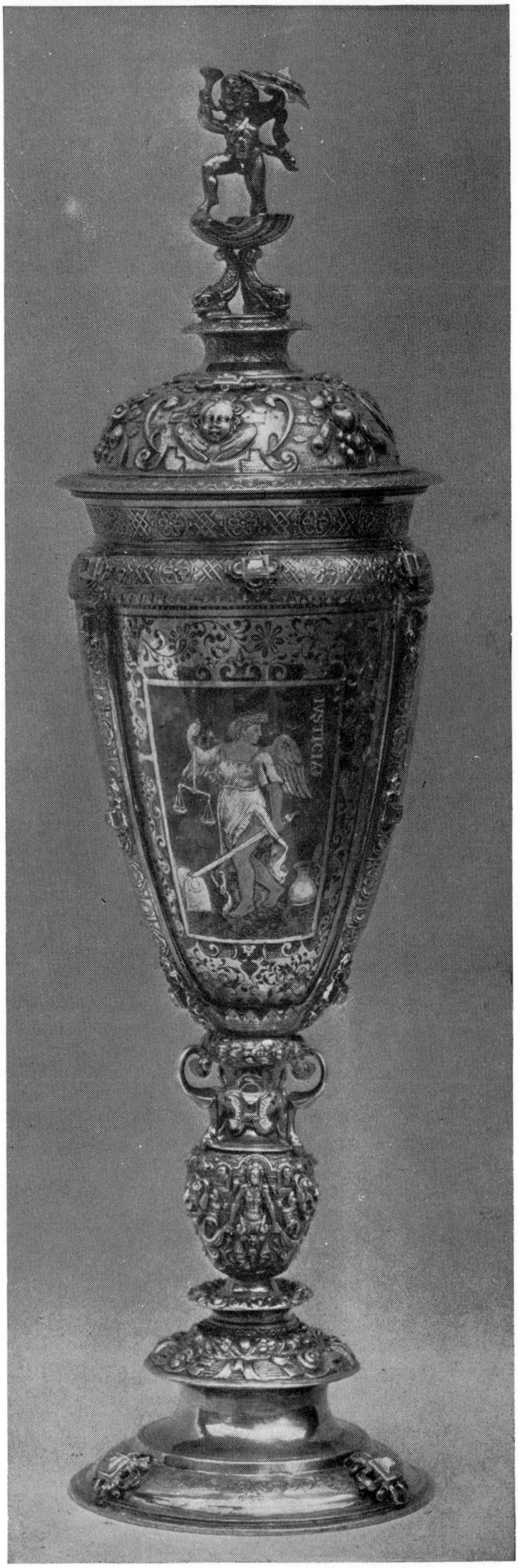

Courtesy Metropolitan Museum of Art

Covered Cup Salzburg, 16th Century

BRANDY SAUCE PAN   John Boddington, London, 1708

Courtesy J. E. Caldwell & Co.

PORRINGER   London, 1683

Courtesy J. E. Caldwell & Co.

GOBLET   London, 1654

CANDLESTICKS   Wm. Denny and John Barnard, London, 1697-1703

KETTLE AND STAND

Francis Garthorne, London, 1716

CENTERPIECE

Courtesy Marshall Field & Co.

Paul Storr, London, 1820

CANDLESTICKS

Anthony Nelme, London, 1723

CHOCOLATE POT

COFFEE POT

Tazza   Paul Lamerie, London, 1722   *Courtesy Tiffany & Co.*

COVERED CUP

Paul Storr, London, 1813

William Kingdon, London, 1821

BACHELOR TEA SET

London, 1784-1795

TEA AND COFFEE SET

Courtesy J. E. Caldwell & Co.

Gabriel Sleath, London, 1714

CHOCOLATE POT ON STAND

TEA CADDY
London,
1752

Courtesy J. E. Caldwell & Co.

E. J. Welsh, London, 1722

Courtesy J. E. Caldwell & Co.

Hester Bateman, London, 1787

COFFEE POT

Courtesy Marshall Field & Co.

Peter and Anne Bateman, London, 1791

COFFEE POT

KETTLE
Ed. Fennell, London, 1767

KETTLE AND STAND

Thomas Whipman and Charles Wright, London, 176

TANKARD   London, 1677   PAIR OF TUMBLER CUPS   London, 1686   WINE TASTER   London, 1649

CAUDLE CUP AND COVER
Gerrit Onkelbag, New York, 1670-1733

Courtesy James Graham, Jr.

Mabel Brady Garvan Collection, Yale Museum

John Coney, Boston   Samuel Vernon, Newport   Adrian Bancker, New York   *Courtesy James Graham, J*

pieces have survived. They were eventually introduced into England about two centuries later, after having been noticed by English travelers in Italy.

An interesting reference to forks was published in a book called "Crudities," written at the beginning of the seventeenth century. The allusion is the expression of the author, Thomas Coryate, an Englishman traveling in Italy in 1620. "I observed a custom in all those Italian cities and towns through which I passed that is not used in any other country that I saw in my travels, neither do I think that any other nation of Christendom doth use it, but only Italy. The Italian, and also most strangers that are commorant in Italy, do always at their meals use a little fork when they cut their meat . . . their forks being for the most part made on iron or steel, and some of silver, but these are used only by gentlemen. The reason of this their curiosity is because the Italian cannot endure by any means to have his dish touched by fingers, seeing that all men's fingers are not alike clean. Hereupon I myself thought to imitate the Italian fashion by this fork cutting of meat, not only while I was in Italy, but also in Germany, and often-times in England since I came home."

It seems incredible that in a period of English history so famed for its extravagance and luxury, that forks were rarely used. This new display of refinement was indeed slow in being generally accepted, as evidenced by the few specimens made. However, their use may have been retarded somewhat, because ministers contended it was an insult to God not to touch meat with one's fingers. As more and more travelers noted their use and general advantages in the consumption of food, silversmiths produced forks in greater quantities. It was not until late in the eighteenth century, however, that they were in common use.

The earliest forks made were probably used only for serving pieces, as one in the inventory of the Royal Plate of 1399 weighed fifteen and one-half ounces. Another in a will of 1463, was listed as being used for "grene Gynger." Early in the Tudor period, a type of fork which was really a rudely wrought piece of silver with two prongs at one end, and a small spoon bowl at the other, was known. This was used for lifting "suckets" such as plums or other fruits preserved in syrup.

Even after the introduction of forks, it remained customary for dinner guests to provide their own utensils for eating. This undoubtedly explains the ingenious one-piece combinations which were made to serve the purpose of a spoon and fork. The three pronged fork would serve as the handle for a spoon bowl, by fitting the prongs in two loops and fastening it to the back. The handle hinged back to permit folding for convenience when carrying in the pouch. Surviving examples of these of English origin are very rare, and the few known today are all of continental make.

The earliest forks made were for the most part of iron and steel, with a few in silver owned by families of great wealth. Until the early part of the eighteenth century, a gentleman who traveled carried a knife and fork of his own, as the inns were not likely to have them. Visitors to England were continually criticizing the lack of forks, as they thought the English custom most unsanitary. Even after forks attained a fair amount of popularity, rich people did not possess many of them. Hence it has been suggested that the custom of serving a sherbet in the middle of the meal was introduced in order to permit the servants time to wash the forks for the next course.

The introduction of forks caused silver ewers and basins to fall into disuse completely. The earliest known fully hallmarked English fork is dated 1632. It is 7 inches long, two pronged, and bears the interesting crest of the Earl of Rutland. It remains today on exhibition at the Victoria and Albert Museum in London.

There was very little change in the style of the forks made from the beginning, until nearly the middle of the seventeenth century. At this time, a three pronged type with a flat rectangular handle appeared that closely resembled the Puritan spoon. This was probably copied from a contemporary French specimen, as forks are known to have existed in France as early as 1300. Until about 1730, English forks are found having two, three or four prongs. Thus the number of prongs cannot indicate any particular period. While during the Commonwealth, three prongs are common, after the Restoration three or four prongs were in use and dating from the reigns of William III and Queen Anne, many have only two tines.

With the passing of the Puritan austerity, more refined stems began to appear following the design of contemporary spoons. At first, the flat stem had the wide trifid end, but this soon developed into the more graceful trifid shape, although for some time it retained the notches. From then on, the fork was made similar to the spoon, until the introduction of the plain Old English type with the curved back, which has been generally accepted today, as the most useable and graceful. During the Georgian period stems of forks were ornamented with bright cut engraving or feather edging, although retaining the Old English pattern.

Mention must be made of the pistol handled forks, which were made to match the knives of the period. And there was also a type with a steel prong and a handle of thinly stamped silver filled with a resinous substance.

KNIVES

Knives are known in history a great deal earlier than forks, although ones with silver handles were not made prior to the eighteenth century. The origin of the knife may be traced to prehistoric times, at which time those executed were hardly more than pieces of flint. However, as time progressed, they were made of stone, and later of bronze, iron and steel.

The original use of the knife was of course in hunting and as a means of protection, but evidence exists to prove that the early Greeks used knives in the service of food. This was actually only a large serving knife, employed to cut the meat into smaller pieces, but it definitely laid the foundation for the making of individual table knives in later years.

There is no actual date which can be recorded for the introduction of the knife into England. However, Chaucer who died in 1400, speaks of a Sheffield whittle, the English term for knife. Thus, we may assume that they were used from this time on. Before the introduction of the fork, the diner held his food with one hand on the trencher, and cut it with his knife. In early English times, men carried a knife in a sheath. This type often had an ornamented silver handle, and we know it was used both at meal times and for defense. The custom of carrying a sheathed knife continued until the seventeenth century, and by the end of that age, a knife and a fork were encased in a single sheath. These coverings were exemplary of the beautiful silver work of the period, and many were studded with precious stones. By the beginning of the eighteenth century, the use of the sheathed knife at meal times fell into disuse, and the rich man's table at that time was set with silver handled knives.

One of the most popular types of knife was the pistol handled shape, many of which are reproduced today in modern silver. Other types are the "pied-de-biche," and later on the reeded and plain forms with the shell. While Georgian silver table knives are very rare and sought after by collectors, they are not too desirable for present day service, as they are somewhat too heavy and cumbersome.

Much interest is found in the shapes of the blades fitted to various silver handles during the eighteenth century. Many retain influences of former centuries, and these in turn can be traced back to flint instruments of prehistoric times. As silver blades were only introduced at a much later date, all early knives are hallmarked on the handles. However, many times, only a few out of a set were marked, so the collector need not feel discouraged if he cannot obtain a completely marked lot.

In the early part of the George III era, 1760-1820, dessert knives were introduced, usually with a silver blade and an ivory handle. Often the ivory was colored, purely for decorative purposes, and complete sets in good condition are practically unknown.

SKEWERS

Among the late Georgian table plate is the long pointed skewer used to hold joints of meat in shape. Apart from those having ornamental rings or tops, they vary little in style, and are not attractive as examples of the silversmith's art. In present times, they have been adapted for use as letter openers, in which capacity they are more presentable.

MARROW SCOOPS

The marrow scoop was originally a variation of the bowl of a spoon moulded into a long narrow gulley, which would enable one to dig into the inside of a bone in order to remove the marrow. Marrow now being extinct as a delicacy, their use has been given a distinctly modern note, and they are now employed as highball mixers, and drink stirrers. They were introduced at the time of Queen Anne and made in great profusion, because marrow was the epitome of the fastidious diner's art.

SERVING PIECES, LADLES AND SPOONS

A great variety of spoons suitable for serving and stuffing were made during the Georgian eras. Some, such as sauce ladles are rarely found earlier than the George II period, while long handled tasting spoons are known as early as the time of Queen Anne. Fish slicers, introduced about 1735 were very popular and a great variety with delicately pierced bowls were executed.

X

TABLEWARE

EPERGNES AND CENTERPIECES

EPERGNES and centerpieces were introduced during the latter part of the George I era, replacing to a large extent the standing salts which had gone out of use. The word epergne was doubtlessly derived from the French "epaigner," meaning to be thrifty. Inasmuch as the small baskets on the epergnes were used to contain condiments, fruits, nuts and similar luxuries from the Far East, the use of these large objects in the center of the table avoided waste. Each person helped himself from the one main epergne, and in this way, those delicacies not used were left on the table and not extravagantly thrown away with the leavings on the plate.

The first epergne fashioned was long and low with a bowl in the center and sweetmeat dishes on either end. In some instances they contained candle holders as well as casters, although such examples are rare. However, the later models were pieces of great height, elaborately decorated and generally consisted of a fruit or flower dish in the center surrounded by any number of small hanging baskets. Later in the century delicate piercing was introduced, and no article of domestic plate illustrated more clearly the height to which that phase of ability had risen. The hanging baskets were often replaced by small dishes on flat stands which could be adapted to individual use. One of the most popular types during the eighteenth century was made in the shape of a pagoda, the Chinese influence also being discernible in the styles of the pierced lattice work and series of semicircular shapes. In the latter part of the century boat shaped center pieces with smaller ones to match were greatly in demand. Epergnes are also found without the side embellishments and resemble huge flower vases with heavy crystal liners.

The extreme popularity of epergnes is readily understood when one realizes that the leading smiths of the period exerted their full efforts to produce masterful creations in silver. Paul Lamerie produced several of great beauty. They afforded him the opportunity for the lavish display and magnificent ornamentation in which he took so much delight. There was an extraordinary one made by him in 1734 for Count Bobrinsky of Russia, and the electroplated reproduction now in the Victoria and Albert Museum affords ample opportunity for inspection. It was a large piece, fitted with casters, candle brackets and cruet frames surrounding the center body. Because it was impossible to use the entire equipment at one time, the pieces were all removable and could be replaced by ornamental knobs. Another important epergne by the same maker is the specimen executed for the Newdegate family.

The epergne was probably copied from pieces of similar plate made in France at an earlier date. In the nineteenth century crystal dishes were used in place of the silver bowls because of the lower cost. For this same reason many more examples were produced in Sheffield plate than in solid silver. Epergnes, unfortunately are not in great demand today, as the massive proportions hardly blend with the present small dining rooms. It was not unusual for some to weigh as much as one thousand ounces, and specimens of that character are recorded in the inventory of royal plate as early as 1725.

Before the middle of the eighteenth century actual silver centerpieces were introduced in place of epergnes. Many of these large covered fruit bowls were made, but very few escaped the melting pot.

DINNER PLATES AND PLATTERS

Although silver dishes and plates were used as early as the middle ages by royal families but few examples have survived. The predecessors of the modern platter, known as chargers, were used previous to the Tudor period for carrying the joint of meat to the table. Another piece of similar design known as a Voyder was used for collecting the broken food that remained on the trenchers so that it might be distributed for charitable purposes. But enormous quantities of this plate were melted down during the Civil Wars in England and very few examples antedate the Restoration in 1660. However, a magnificent set of twelve bearing the London hallmark of 1567 has survived. The plates were parcel gilt and finely engraved with scenes depicting Hercules performing feats of strength. They were eight inches in diameter with a side rim, and although the center depression was somewhat smaller than in the later plates, they clearly show the evolution from wooden trenchers. The continuation of this shape has remained with silver plates. After the Restoration, plates were produced in great quantity and the former types which had been quite plain with simple moulded edges assumed ornamental mounts for the first time.

The French craftsmen who migrated to England were directly responsible for this new style and for many years rococo shells and elaborate scrolls were applied to the borders. However, with the gradual return to pieces of simpler design, the gadroon or bead edge replaced the more elaborate borders. Some of the early dishes of the latter half of the seventeenth century clearly illustrate again the definite influence of the Orient on English crafts. With the importation and continued popularity of Chinese porcelain in England, the silversmiths were soon reproducing the band of decorations by engraving quaint Oriental scenes and figures on the plain surfaces. Early plates command huge prices today as it is indeed rare to assemble a set of twelve or eighteen with the same date letter and by the same maker. For a time plates were so common that they fetched but little above the silver value, but today they have grown exceedingly scarce and are in constant demand.

With the introduction of the large silver dinner service, oval meat dishes of varied sizes appeared. They measured from the small types of ten inches to the venison dishes often as long as twenty-six inches. Those pieces used to hold the meat were equipped with what is now known as the "well and tree" which was, in effect, a series of small channels which allowed the gravy to run through into a large depression at one end of the dish. In the latter half of the nineteenth century porcelain services for dinner plates had come into general use and silver services of this type were no longer made except upon special occasions.

Soup plates as well as dessert plates closely followed the designs of dinner plates although they generally appear at a slightly later date.

SOUP TUREENS

The name tureen as applied to the containers for soup is said to be derived from the fact that Marshal Turenne of France, on one occasion, used his helmet to hold soup.

The tureen was introduced from France, from whence so much English domestic silver has been taken. During the time that Charles II lived in exile he learned many new customs from the French, among which was the custom of serving soup from a large bowl placed on the dining table or sideboard.

Soup tureens are pieces of large proportion, frequently being 22 inches in height including the cover and that they were considered pieces of notable importance is evidenced from the fine display of ornamentation so perfectly executed by the smiths of the period. Those made in the early Georgian period were large oval bowls generally ornamented in the rococo style and set on massive feet, while those produced a short time later displayed the more dignified forms of the Neo-classic era. Tureens were sometimes accompanied by a standing plateau which was placed directly underneath with the intention of protecting the table from the heat of the tureen containing the hot soup.

The earliest known specimen was made in 1703 by the celebrated Anthony Nelme, and formerly was in the possession of Lord Bateman. Further evidence of the popularity of the silver soup tureen or "soupiere," as it was known, is seen at Windsor Castle where numerous examples include thirteen pairs. Many of these were executed by Paul Storr who probably produced more fine specimens than any other maker. During the George III and George IV periods, soup tureens were considered inseparable adjuncts to the dining table, and during the last few years the old custom of serving soup at the table has been revived.

SAUCE BOATS, SAUCE TUREENS AND ARGYLES

The earliest known sauce boat was made in 1698 by William Scarlett. It was of a type directly copied from the French goldsmiths with a low, plain, oval body with double spouts and handles set on a low molded foot. In the second part of the eighteenth century, these types were discarded for boats on three feet with a single spout directly opposite to the handle. In general they followed the prevailing fashions in decoration and were produced in great quantities until the introduction of sauce tureens which were executed as exact replicas in small size, of the soup tureens. The sauce boat is a natural accompaniment to the dinner table and large services often have as many as four pairs with them.

An unusual type of small vessel used for gravy was introduced about 1750 and was called "argyle." These vessels are supposed to have been named after John, the fifth Duke of Argyll. Actually they were gravy tureens with spouts fitted on either side to hold a piece of hot iron which maintained the heat of the gravy. This style was greatly improved a short time later when a jacket was introduced which contained boiling water. Argyles are very rare and only a limited number were produced.

A curious form was made with a bulbous body and a small foot that served as a special compartment for the hot water, in this way offering a greater capacity for the gravy. Many of the early argyles were later converted into coffee and tea pots for which purpose they were admirably suited.

ENTRÉE DISHES, BACON DISHES, CHAFING DISHES, REVOLVING
DISHES, DISH COVERS AND HEATERS

Entree dishes were introduced from France and originally called
cover dishes or second course dishes. Similar articles generally
referred to as sweetmeat dishes, although they were used to hold hot
foods, were in use as early as the reign of Charles II. The custom
of using the cover as a second dish was introduced during the
Georgian era when the dishes were supplied with a removable
handle. The dishes made in the Stuart period were restricted to oval
shapes and circular domes with molded borders, while those of the
later period were oval, circular, or oblong and generally ornamented
with a gadroon, thread or bead or similar mount. Many entree
dishes which are found in sets of four, six or eight were furnished
with so-called heaters in which hot charcoal or boiling water was
placed. Some were made with a heater as a combined part and these
generally had a small opening with a screw cap at one end into
which the water could be poured.

Another type of dish which was originally used for the serving
of marrow was known as a second course dish and these are rarely
found with covers. An article known as a bacon dish was furnished
with a hot water base directly under the dish. It was generally fashioned with a long wooden handle which screwed into a socket at
the back of the dish, the socket serving as the opening through which
the hot water could be poured into the base. These were used in
the service of eggs and bacon and other breakfast foods and during
the past few years have become most popular at cocktail parties to
hold hors d'oeuvres. Of little interest are the massive domical shaped,
deep covers which have now fallen into complete disuse.

Inasmuch as the kitchens of all large houses were quite a distance from the dining rooms, it was necessary to use these covers to
keep the food hot while being carried. The problem of heating food
at the table was eventually solved by the introduction of the chafing
dish which was, in effect, an entree dish fitted into a stand which
contained an alcohol lamp in the center. The earliest known types
of these were called braziers and were originally introduced by the
colonial silversmiths of America. The bodies were pierced with
scrollings and ornamental designs and appear to follow the style of
a similar object more commonly used in France than in England.

During the Victorian era, another article known as the revolving
tureen was first made. It was in the nature of a vegetable dish with a
strainer fitted into a large deep oval stand which contained hot

water, and also fitted with a corresponding cover which could be rolled back when the food was ready to be served or else left closed in order to retain the heat and keep the food clean.

As prosperity increased in the second half of the eighteenth century, plate was made heavier and heavier and large dinner services were produced for the first time. Soup tureens, sauce tureens, entree dishes, plates, and platters were incorporated into an enormous set containing hundreds of pieces. Complete services are now very rare as upon the settlement of estates in England, they were usually divided among the heirs. However, now and then a magnificent creation practically in its entirety is seen. Unfortunately many of the large pieces in them are too large, useless and obsolete. Throughout history these massive pieces have, as a rule, been converted into other articles.

XI

LIGHTING APPLIANCES

CANDLESTICKS

THE Bible mentions candlesticks, but these solid gold articles were actually for lamps and not candles. The Romans used a crude sort of candle which resembled a modern torch, but it was not until the third century that candles as they are known today were in use. At first these were used exclusively in churches, and the institution of Candlemas Day by Pope Gelasius in the fifth century, was probably the legal adoption of the candlestick. The large number of candles used is an important feature of the ceremony, and the need of some receptacle in which to place the candles was the cause of the origin of the candlestick. The earliest candlesticks were probably made of wood, but later on precious metals were used.

In the description of gifts given by Bishop Aethalwald to the monastery of Peterborough, in 963, candlesticks are mentioned. During the eleventh century, the Abbot Robert sent as a gift to his fellow countryman, Pope Adrian IV, two wonderful candlesticks of gold and silver, which the Pope admired so much that he had them placed in St. Peter's. During the Tudor period mention is made of a banquet given by Cardinal Wolsey to the French embassy and retinue at Hampton Court. As an example of lavish magnificence and splendor by those nearest the throne, the dinner was outstanding. Candlesticks are noted in the following manner: "and upon the nethermost dish garnished all with plate of clear gold, having two great candlesticks of silver and gilt, most curiously wrought, the workmanship thereof, with the silver, cost three hundred marks, and lights of wax as big as torches burning upon the same."

The earliest candlesticks were the type known as prickets. The pricket was actually a sharp point in the top of the shaft to hold the candle, and usually surrounded by a saucer to catch the wax. Although many of the English cathedrals used pricket candlesticks in the Middle Ages, in the sixteenth century they came to be considered monuments of superstition and were destroyed. The pricket was replaced by the socket which held the candle firmly in place.

Although it is accepted as fairly definite that the date of introduction of the socket candlestick was after the sixteenth century, proof of an earlier existence is found in a German picture of 1560, in which a pair is depicted.

63

Mention is found in wills and inventories of candlesticks which must have been of enormous value. One extremely important example is the pair of sticks given by Henry VI to Cardinal Beaufort in 1439 which were wrought of solid gold, and set with pearls, rubies, sapphires and emeralds.

Very few candlesticks from before the Restoration have survived. An unusual example of the Elizabethan period formed of silver and rock crystal is known, as well as a pair made in 1618, formerly in the possession of Lord Swaythling. They were of curious design, being set on a tripod base. An important set of four bearing the London hallmark of 1637 actually represent in the fuller sense candlesticks as we know them today. Each had a cylindrical stem and a base in the form of an inverted wine glass, with a wide circular disk in the middle to serve as a grease pan. These were probably inspired by a continental model. A magnificent pair from the Restoration period bearing the London hallmark of 1663 was formerly in the Treasury of the Kremlin, Moscow. They were richly ornate with large floral and animal decorations characteristic of the Charles II period, and were no less than 17½ inches in height.

Candlesticks of the Charles II and Queen Anne periods are found in considerable numbers and of varying design. An early form was of square plate throughout while a variation doubtless suggested by French work was octagonal in design. Closely akin to this was another type which had a round fluted column with a square plinth and abacus rising from a square plain moulded foot. Variations giving way to octagonal members with either plain or gadrooned borders are known. These sticks were generally of hammered silver and varied in height from seven to twelve inches.

The law compelling the use of a higher standard attracted the attention of the craftsman to cast work, the softer metal not lending itself to the hammer. Consequently from 1700 on, numerous sets of cast candlesticks are known. This new type was shorter in height than its predecessor and the form had much in common with the standing cup of the period, with the foot generally enriched with mouldings of gadrooned ornamentation. The whole surfaces of the candlesticks were at first left very plain, so that the reflecting light from the candle would be most brilliant. However, the demand for pieces of increased ornamentation which dominated the George II period, had its effect on candlesticks. With the introduction of the rococo style, a new and heavier type of candlestick, sadly lacking in the simplicity and beauty of the earlier type was wrought. Towards the middle of the century, a return to simplicity is noted, and many new varieties in style were produced. One of the popular types was in the form of a column, copied from the early Greek architecture. By now decanters of unusual design were applied, among the most popular being ram's heads, rosettes, medallions and festoons.

About the year 1760, a great change took place in the production of candlesticks, the pieces being made of thin stamped metal loaded with pitch to give them strength. Although this style would undoubtedly have been repugnant to goldsmiths of the Renaissance, the increased economy over cast sticks was found to be most practical.

Cast candlesticks are very much in demand, as a feature was the unusual weight which was quite natural in view of the larger quantity of silver used. The general practice of preparing a model of the candlestick in wax, and then pouring the molten metal into the mold, continued for many years. This same method was employed in making the more elaborate rococo styles. Here the work was in relief, and the separate ornamentations were cast in molds and soldered to the candlestick.

Sets of four early candlesticks are rare and for this reason many people who need four to complete a formal dinner table, have to be satisfied with owning two similar pairs. This situation is true throughout the collection of old silver, for complete services as needed today are rarely found.

CANDELABRA

In ancient Roman times candelabra were known, but at that time candelabra meant, in most cases, a support for a lamp. They were wrought in many different materials including the precious metals, but most of those that have been excavated were in bronze. Some fifty or sixty years ago, parts of a Roman silver candelabrum were found near the city of Hanover. The piece was probably made about the first century or earlier. The general form of early metal candelabra was similar throughout, the base being composed of three spreading feet with the lamps suspended from the arms. On top of the shaft there was usually a figurine or statuette, and the height ran anywhere from twelve inches to ten feet. The early churches possessed many examples patterned after the early Roman form, but there are no examples known today.

Silver candelabra dating prior to the reign of George III are rare. As prosperity increased during the second half of the eighteenth century, the silver was made heavier and heavier and massive candelabra were not uncommon in the great houses throughout the land. The nineteenth century produced many magnificent specimens with three or five lights, and occasionally one finds an important pair made for a large dining hall with as many as twelve lights.

Candelabra for the most part followed the designs used in candlesticks during the Queen Anne period. The prevailing patterns had three branches radiating from a center stem which was surmounted by a molded finial. During the rococo period, twisted branches were not uncommon and the finial center was frequently replaced by a socket. No doubt because of the excessive cost of silver candelabra many more pairs were made in Sheffield plate. For this reason the most representative work of the silversmiths who specialized in the production of candelabra is found in the plate examples.

CHANDELIERS

Chandeliers are known to have existed as early as the twelfth century when they reposed in churches, and although very common among the more important English families, practically none have survived to this date.

One of the most famous executed in silver is the specimen at Hampton Court. It is a massive piece with twelve branches richly decorated with laurel leaf bands and bosses. The upper part is ornamented with four cartouches containing a rose, thistle, harp and fleur-de-lis, each surmounted by a crown. It dates from the reign of William III. Earlier types combining the acanthus decoration of the Charles II period are also known as well as an important pair with eight branches now at Knole Park, Kent. Perhaps the most magnificent English silver chandeliers are found in Russia and outstanding among those is the pair, made by Paul Lamerie in 1734, which formerly hung in the Treasury of the Kremlin. They were in the best style of Lamerie, combining a wealth of decoration and strap work surmounted by a Russian imperial crown. Each was wrought with sixteen individual branches, so an idea of the immensity may be surmised. During the invasion of Napoleon's troops important pieces made in 1630 for the Cathedral of the Assumption in Moscow were melted down. Although chandeliers are recorded among the pieces of larger plate belonging to Charles II, none from his reign have survived in the world's collection.

SCONCES

During the exile of Charles II in the Low Country, he became familiar with many silver vessels previously unknown in England. Among these were silver sconces and shortly after the introduction of these sconces into England, they became very popular and fashionable. A large number have survived from the late seventeenth century and also from the eighteenth century, and handsome specimens make their appearance quite frequently. It appears that they were known as early as the time of Henry VIII as there is mention of them in the account given by George Cavendish of the reception given by Cardinal Wolsey to the French ambassador in 1527. Further references to their use are found in the inventories of royal plate during the Tudor period. From 1660 until the time of Queen Anne, wall sconces were extremely popular and the scarcity of the early examples can be blamed on the wholesale destruction of plate in later years. From an artistic point of view, sconces are representative of the better work of the silversmith and clearly illustrate the high degree of excellence attained by workers in the late seventeenth century. They were made in a variety of patterns generally with the back plates richly embossed. Three principal types are known, among them being one made in 1665 with a single socket attached to the oblong back plate with a rounded top. It was engraved and embossed with elaborate floral designs. Another type which is somewhat less common has an enriched truss in place of a back plate, and a scroll branch with a socket. However, the most standardized pattern consisted of a richly embossed back plate with either one or two branches with sockets. Among the many variations executed, is one which has in the center of the back plate a human arm, grasping in its hand the branch. Silver-framed, mirrored sconces were once very popular but they are seldom encountered today.

The fashion of lighting rooms by means of sconces was generally known throughout England after the accession of Queen Anne. Illustrative of the type most in demand at that time are a pair made in 1703, now in the Victoria and Albert Museum, and a magnificent set of six by the celebrated Peter Archambo. A splendid collection of early sconces is owned by the royal family, and includes two lovely sets bearing the monogram of William and Mary, surmounted by a royal crown. These were all in high relief with strongly defined ornamentation, the craftsman's intention being to reflect as much light as possible.

CHAMBERSTICKS

Throughout the eighteenth century many types of portable chamber candlesticks were used for lighting the way to one's bedroom through the long dark halls, and also to illuminate the chamber itself. In the royal plate of 1438 mention is made of a "hond candil-stikke" which may be considered the ancestor of all chamber candlesticks. Although examples prior to 1700 are very rare, an outstanding chamberstick with a circular pan to match, made in 1688, may now be seen at Exeter College. Also, they are rarely found complete, because over a period of years the snuffers have generally been lost.

An ancient custom which descended from medieval times was an auction sale conducted "by inch of candle." A small piece of candle was lighted and allowed to burn itself out and the final bidder before the flame expired was the successful purchaser of whatever was offered for sale. For this purpose special silver holders were made.

TAPER STICKS

A taper stick is actually a reproduction of a candlestick in miniature and was used for melting wax to seal letters, or when impressing a seal to accompany a signature on a document. Tapersticks date back to the time of William and Mary in 1688 and were in use only until the introduction of the gummed envelope. They were intended for use on the writing desk, but later in the century became an actual part of the silver inkstand. Their development followed closely that of the candlestick.

WAX JACKS

Another implement made in silver and used on the writing desk during the eighteenth century was an article called a wax jack. This was actually a wax taper coiled around a spindle. It passed through a socket enclosed in a sort of openwork bird cage. The earliest specimens which date as far back as 1698, were enclosed in a cylindrical box which had a hole in the center of the lid for the wax to protrude. Although often found in completely enclosed silver units the loveliest types were usually pierced.

SNUFFERS

Requisite to early candlesticks were the small snuffers on trays which were evidently in use as early as the sixteenth century. As candles in the early days burned more slowly and the wax ran down the sides of the candlestick, it was frequently necessary to clip the charred pieces of wick. Snuffers were a household essential before the invention of candle wicks which could be entirely consumed by the flame.

Snuffers resemble in shape a pair of scissors, but differ in that one blade is broad, the solid piece set perpendicularly at the end. Those of the post-Restoration period were generally fitted with a box on one blade and a pressing plate on the other which fitted inside. At this time many were equipped with little pans shaped to the form of the snuffers, but later on these gave way to attractive stands made with little handles so that they could be carried about.

The earliest known reference to a snuffer is in the list of plate at All Souls' College at Oxford in 1448. Several examples are known from the sixteenth century, including the specimen in the British Museum which bears the arms of Henry the Eighth.

XII

BOXES

UNFORTUNATELY silver boxes are not representative, as a whole, of the better workmanship of the English and Irish silversmiths. The finest specimens were executed in European countries. Although hallmarked silver boxes are known to exist from as early a time as the reign of James I, 1603 to 1625, they are far from plentiful, few having survived throughout the years. They were rarely made in great profusion, being almost exclusively for royalty and those in court circles.

They were very small in size and consequently many were lost or buried. But it is just because of this scarcity that early silver boxes are so much in demand. Well-marked specimens of authentic date fetch fantastic prices in sale rooms, and collectors and dealers all over the world are always in the market for the better types.

Nearly all small boxes were originally parts of elaborate toilet services, although a few spice and sweetmeat boxes are known to have existed prior to the making of these handsome toilet sets. It may be said, without a doubt, that silver boxes were considered a luxury, and as a rule, were only made to special order for a chosen few.

FREEDOM BOXES

Among the many styles of silver boxes known in England, were small shallow receptacles known as freedom boxes. In shape they were similar to tobacco boxes. They were originally made to hold the vellum certificate used at the presentation of the freedom of a borough to some important personage. As a general rule, the lid was engraved or embossed with the arms of the borough to which the freeman had been admitted.

Freedom boxes are very rare. However, they are not greatly in demand as they are a poor representation of the work of the English silversmiths. Outstanding among freedom boxes were the two executed in solid gold and given with the freedom of certain Irish towns to the fourth Duke of Devonshire and the fourth Duke of Rutland, both holding the same office of Lord Lieutenant of Ireland. Both examples being unmarked, one can only surmise as to their origin, but data that have been handed down concerning the lives of these two prominent men prove fairly conclusively that they were the work of Dublin goldsmiths. Unfortunately, these two fine examples are no longer in their original state, having been melted down. In 1801 and 1813 the gold in them was made into a salver and a platter by the celebrated Paul Storr.

Cork silversmiths in the eighteenth century were busily engaged in making gold and silver freedom boxes. Outstanding among the fine examples extant today, are the ones originally belonging to the Earl of Shelbourne and Admiral Lord Redding, both the work of the famed Irish silversmith, William Reynolds. An earlier example was made in Cork in 1737, and carried with it the freedom of that city. This box is now in the collection of Dean Swift.

POMANDERS

Pomanders were in general use among the wealthier classes as early as the fourteenth century, but examples from this period are no longer obtainable. Such few as have survived from the sixteenth and seventeenth centuries are now in museums and private collections only.

The pomander is a curious corruption of the French word "pomme d'ambre," which means apple of amber. The amber referred to the ambergris, which, when worn, diffused a pleasant odor. A small bar of ambergris, or musk, was enclosed in a silver container and worn around the neck or hung from a girdle. The original "pomme d'ambre" eventually came to be spelled "pomander" and, as such these little boxes are known today.

Pomanders were originally carried to counteract fever and to protect the olfactory nerves from offensive smells prevalent in the Middle Ages. These small boxes which were originally relics of old silver toilet services were practically a necessity for those who wished, and could afford the luxury of protecting themselves against the existing unsanitary conditions. It is said that the pomander owes its general use to Cardinal Wolsey, who filled an orange with a sponge soaked in vinegar, worm wood, rosemary and spices, and carried it with him everywhere. The silversmiths of the day quickly perceived the need for such an article and produced them profusely.

TOILET SETS

In the study of the history of silver, mention is made of small silver boxes, perfume flasks, and other toilet accessories that were used by Queen Elizabeth, but no complete English toilet service dated prior to the seventeenth century is known. However, it is probable that they were in use many years before that as they are noted in the luxurious domestic appointments which appeared in Spain after she began to obtain quantities of silver from her American colonies.

Full credit, however, must be given to France for the general popularity of the toilet set. They were widely used by the court of Louis XIV, and from there the use spread to England; for the court of Charles II used only typically French ornaments in the gold and silver appointments. The only complete English toilet sets which have survived are all dated after the Restoration, 1660.

These services often comprised as many as from 20 to 35 pieces, including all the toilet implements, table mirrors, silver candlesticks, powder and page boxes, precious salvers, pin-cushions, flasks, and innumerable other small articles which help to complete the lady's toilet.

Probably the finest known toilet service in the world today is the one presented by Charles II to Frances Stuart, Duchess of Richmond, and hallmarked Paris, 1672 and 1680. The King himself paid close to ten thousand pounds for this service when it was made, so one can readily imagine the fantastic value placed on it today by collectors.

Although Irish silver toilet sets are very rare, one made by a Dublin silversmith in 1791 is known. Several noted English silversmiths are regarded as the makers of beautiful and elaborate toilet sets. Among these are: David Willaume, Anthony Nelme, and Paul Lamerie.

Toilet sets are very rare. Recently a partially complete set by Paul Lamerie reached a price close to thirty thousand dollars.

TOBACCO BOXES

Tobacco was originally introduced into England by Ralph Lane, the first governor of Virginia, during the reign of Queen Elizabeth. It was carried in small boxes of either base metal or silver, although the latter were not in general use until the following century. No tobacco box antedating the Restoration is known, and the few remaining examples of the period are merely plain, shallow containers of little beauty and no great importance as examples of the silversmith's art in England.

MULLS

Scotch mulls were large or small horns frequently mounted in silver and used for snuff boxes. They are generally found bearing presentation inscriptions and are in demand today, as Scotch silver of early date is always desirable. One of great historic interest is a five-compartment box which was given to the Perthshire Regiment of Gentlemen and Yeomenry Cavalry by James Hay, Esq., captain of the Cassé troup in 1804.

NUTMEG GRATERS

Small boxes suitable for carrying in the pocket, and used to contain nutmeg were particularly popular during the eighteenth century. At this time nutmeg and other flavors had been introduced from the East and were in great favor throughout England. A nutmeg grater was actually a small silver container fitted with an inner grate attached to the cover on the inside. This permitted the dust to fall through into the box. The graters were made in a great variety of styles and shapes, but the general purpose of all was alike. It is interesting to note that they were in use throughout the first half of the Victorian era.

SPICE AND SNUFF BOXES

Spice and sweetmeat boxes appear to have been fashionable during the sixteenth century, and there is direct evidence of their popularity in court circles in the latter half of the following century. However, few English snuff boxes can compare in detail and workmanship with the masterpieces executed by the French craftsmen. One of the earliest known spice boxes dated 1598, survived from the Elizabethan era. It was recently sold at Christie's for upwards of six thousand dollars. It was in the form of a cockle-shell on four feet, the sides ornamented with arabesque on a matted ground and the handles molded with an egg and tongue border.

Another specimen, an oval box made in 1677, was sold at auction for nearly three thousand dollars. These prices are mentioned merely to indicate the great rarity of such articles.

Probably the best known of all snuff boxes are those associated with the Russian silversmiths. In very few countries in Europe were these superb creations so fully appreciated or expertly conceived as there. Many magnificent specimens in gold and enamel date from the nineteenth century and their popularity today for use as table cigarette boxes is wide. These Russian boxes were covered with niello which was a metallic alloy of sulphur and silver having a deep black color. Pieces were decorated with inside designs filled with niello.

It is interesting to note here the collaboration between makers and decorators of English silver pieces. Conclusive proof that articles were often executed by more than one maker is found in the historic gold tobacco box of 1741, made by Humphrey Payne in London. The piece bears his makers' mark as well as the signature on the inside cover of the engraver, John Ellis. Therefore, it is not unusual to find that, although pieces were often completed by one maker, heraldic devices and other ornamentations were often added by contemporary or later craftsmen.

In the past decade, prices of antique silver snuff boxes have risen tremendously, chiefly because many of these early snuff boxes were of a sufficient size to fit cigarettes used today. In this way a person wishing to assemble a well-appointed table of completely original silver might find the necessary containers for a modern note.

VINAIGRETTES

Silver vinaigrettes were regarded as indispensable until the middle of the nineteenth century, and were carried by as great a number of ladies as might outfit themselves today with compacts. These little silver boxes varied greatly in size and style, but being made exclusively for the feminine interest were all of a pretty and pleasing design. The general construction of all vinaigrettes was generally the same. A perforated inner lid permitted the choice aromatic scents to escape, and diffuse a very pleasant scent. Actually, they are a modern adaptation of the sixteenth century pomander, as their original use was much the same.

Vinaigrettes, as a rule were hallmarked under the lid, and the majority of them are of Birmingham origin. In glancing over a collection of possibly a hundred varied types, one would probably find that over 75 per cent were made there, and that in all probability, not more than seven or eight different makers would be represented in the entire lot.

Vinaigrettes are often found with a ring attachment through which a chain was passed, as very often they were worn as lockets.

Vinaigrettes in general exhibited a finer type of workmanship in the fine piercing of the inner lids and delicate repoussée work, than any other of the small silver boxes. Today they are greatly in demand by collectors the world over and in the past ten years their value has increased many fold. One of the most recent adaptations of the vinaigrette is for use as a pill-box or else as a container for saccharine tablets.

XIII

MISCELLANEOUS PIECES

TRAYS, SALVERS AND PATENS

IN the last half of the seventeenth century, small circular trays were used as stands for large silver tankards, but specimens of these are far from plentiful. The earliest known mention of such a piece is in 1661, wherein it is described as follows: "salver . . . is a new fashioned piece of wrought plate, broad and flat, with a foot under neath, and is used in giving beer, or other liquid thing to save the Carpit or Cloathes from drops."

As a general rule the earliest salvers, now referred to as card trays, were simple in design and void of decoration, as opposed to the later types which combined molded or cast borders with engraving, or heraldic insignia in the center. Occasionally small engraved trays of early date are found, and they are by far the most valuable because of their extreme rarity. The introduction and continued use of the circular salver, many of which assumed massive proportions, was undoubtedly influenced by the early rose water dishes. Although many of the larger salvers weighed as much as 200 ounces, largely because of the heavy rococo mounts, examples displaying the full ability of the silversmith's skill may be seen. These excelled particularly in the manner of the engraved and flat shaped work. Perhaps no other article of domestic plate retained the quiet dignity of Queen Anne's time as fully as the salver. During the George II period when the flair for over-ornamentation was prevalent everywhere, a simple style of tray was introduced known as the "Chippendale." The name was applied to them because the borders were reproduced from the rims of tables designed by that great furniture designer. "Chippendale" as well as other salvers were made in a great variety of styles and shapes, including square, circular, oblong and shaped specimens.

Dating from the beginning, the tea service was placed on what is now known as a tea tray. They were almost indispensable to the serving of tea, and increased in size as more pieces were added to form a service. Although made in a wide variety of sizes and shapes, generally supported on four feet, their beauty was not confined to the work on the borders, for the finest decorative engraving was lavished on the plain surfaces. The ordinary tea tray as we know it measured anywhere in length from eighteen inches to twenty-four inches, and was placed on a large table at tea time. However, in the middle of the eighteenth century, a wooden stand was devised with a top of the same size as the silver tray with sockets to hold the feet. These never attained great popularity though, for the regulation tray with its two easily grasped handles was found to be more convenient.

At the time of the neo-classic vogue, a complete change in ornamentation is noted. The craftsmen used flat chased motifs, generally in a wide band around the edge, with the center left plain for an engraved coat of arms. Other variations noted at this time were the introduction of large oval and oblong waiters with high pierced gallery borders, as well as some with wooden or papier mache bases. Waiters for use in large houses were often made in pairs or sets of three, but are rarely found today.

During the Queen Anne and George I periods the paten was introduced. This was in the nature of a circular waiter standing on a low trumpet mouth foot, the joint of which was frequently masked by a circle of cut-card work. Although generally used by the church for sacred purposes, patens were employed in ordinary life to serve as containers for fruit.

INKSTANDS AND STANDISHES

Inkstands or standishes, as they were called at first, were introduced in the first half of the seventeenth century. As a matter of record, the earliest known hallmarked specimen was made in London in 1630.

Within a short time, silversmiths were producing inkstands of great beauty, and also at all times during the history of their production, simplicity was the keynote. Hardly ever did they assume the fantastic forms and over-ornamentation that influenced the other domestic plate during the rococo period. In time they became essentials of the well-appointed writing table and their popularity never waned during the history of silversmithing in England.

The inkstands or standishes made during the reign of Charles II were fashioned like large plain rectangular boxes with two flat covers and a handle in the middle. A specimen of this rare type dated 1685 is now in the Treasury. As time progressed, inkstands were greatly altered in style, and by the eighteenth century the casket type was introduced. Occasionally, these were fitted with a slide drawer below, to hold the sealing wax. This general style of a rectangular tray with receptacles for ink, sand and wafers prevailed during the century. Slight variations occur in some specimens wherein the wafer box in the center was covered by a hand bell which was used to summon the servant when the letter was ready to be sent. In later years, the bell was replaced by a taperstick which previously had been a separate unit. During the George III era, the silver fitments were replaced by glass receptacles with silver tops fitted on to the tray base. One top was pierced with holes in which to place the quills when not in use, another had finer perforations for use as a sandcaster, while the third well contained the ink. The trays were somewhat larger than the earlier examples, the border being ornamented with a concave depression on either side to hold the wax. Steel pens were introduced in 1805, but were not generally used until many years later. For this reason it is not unusual to find inkstands fitted with sandboxes and quill holders, dating well into the nineteenth century.

There was an early mention of an inkstand in the inventory of the plate of Henry VIII, where two are recorded in 1520. One was of Spanish origin, while the other was probably of English make. The specimen of 1630 belonging to Sir John Noble appears to be the only surviving inkstand of those made before the Civil War. One of the most magnificent and largest inkstands ever made, is the one executed by Paul Lamerie for the Duke of Cumberland. One famous inkstand was used by Sir Joshua Reynolds in many of his portraits.

In the collection and purchase of old inkstands, it is essential to make sure that each individual piece is marked, for over a period of years parts may have been lost and replaced. Also many of the early snuffer stands have been converted into inkstands by the addition of wells. It is well to remember that when parts have been added or alterations made, the value of the piece has been greatly lessened.

BREAD, CAKE, AND SWEETMEAT BASKETS

Oval pierced baskets with handles were introduced during the reign of George II at which time they were used for bread, thereby accounting for the decorative wheat sheaves often noted. The earliest examples were low and very heavy, while the later types were generally pierced and much lighter in feeling. However, towards the end of the eighteenth century the piercing was abandoned and baskets were again made with stands that followed the circular or oblong shapes then in vogue.

Baskets were made in a wide variety of shapes which changed with each successive period. Originally the basket was made with a small handle at either end, but this was replaced later by the large swinging handle. Among the interesting examples known of unusual baskets is a George III specimen with a pierced separation in the center, one side of which was marked "fresh" and the other "stale" to indicate the place for each kind of bread. A very rare type, beautifully pierced with an original wicker work pattern typified the unusual designs created by Paul Lamerie. It was made in 1733 and formed part of the collection of Lord Swaythling. In the George II reign, baskets were often made in the form of a large shell on dolphin feet, an example of 1751 being in the collection of Royal plate at Windsor Castle.

The middle of the eighteenth century showed the popularity of delicately pierced sweetmeat baskets. They were actually reproductions in miniature of the larger cake baskets and carried out to the minutest detail the same character of workmanship found in the larger pieces. A variation of the candy dish was in the shape of an escalloped shell, examples of which are very rare. A magnificent pair, formerly in the possession of Sir Montague, were made by Paul Lamerie in 1732, which date is the earliest known reference to a shell. Shells are among the most desirable pieces of old silver as they fit in perfectly with the table appointments of today.

DISH RINGS

Dish rings are peculiar to the work of Irish silversmiths, in whose country they seem to have first come into use about 1750. From this time on they remained as one of the principal articles of table plate until the latter part of the nineteenth century. The dish ring, as made in Ireland, was always circular and resembled in shape an enlarged napkin ring, while English examples of oval body are known. The dish ring was probably introduced in the attempt to avoid the damaging results of standing hot dishes directly on the table. The ring remained on the table throughout the meal to support in turn the soup bowl, the potato bowl, the dessert bowl, and occasionally the punch bowl. Inasmuch as the fashion in Ireland was to serve potatoes in a large wooden bowl which was placed on top of the silver stand, it is not strange that for years these silver articles have been erroneously termed potato rings.

The earliest type of dish ring made is very shallow, the sides of some being less than three inches deep, and the diameter at the rim being generally identical with that of the base. As a rule, the sides were ornamented with shaped and pierced scrolls and flowers, with chased cartouches framed by scrolls for the armorial insignia. Dish rings often portrayed pastoral and farm scenes. Many rings bore the Oriental influence in the Chinese architecture and native figures, these subjects often being combined with European hunting scenes. Dish rings of this character are greatly in demand as specimens of unusual creation by silversmiths in piercing. The later type of dish ring does not have the same amount of appeal since it lacks the charming decoration of the preceding style.

The earliest known reference to a dish ring is in an anonymous inventory of plate dating from 1697, wherein two are mentioned. An advertisement of the same year refers to two rings for the table, although it can only be assumed that dish rings were meant. However, an example as early as 1704 has survived and it is thought most probable that some specimens may have existed a few years earlier. It is interesting to note that the Irish dish rings retained the elaborate ornamentation of the rococo period long after that style had gone out of fashion in England. Reproductions of these rings are made today and have been improved upon by the addition of a blue glass liner which enables them to serve as attractive flower bowls and centerpieces.

DISH CROSSES

As dish rings fell into disuse, dish crosses were introduced to serve the same purpose. They were a great deal more practical than their predecessors because the supports and the feet were made to slide along the rods of the cross in order to contain various dishes. They were introduced during the time of George II and used extensively throughout England. However, they never grew in popularity in Ireland and the dish ring remained there for many years. Dish crosses were sometimes fitted with spirit lamps which helped to keep the food hot.

SILVER FURNITURE

Previous to the Restoration, nearly all plate made was for domestic use, but with the accession to the throne of Charles II many fantastic objects such as silver furniture were introduced. All of these silver pieces are symbolic of the waste of money fostered by the Merry Monarch, who sought to emulate the costly furnishings he had known at the French court. The prevailing extravagance is noted as early as 1674 when a silver bed was made for Nell Gwyn. Although the bed was the work of a foreigner, John Cooqus, it started a vogue among English smiths. A true picture of the lavish splendor of the period is best recorded by the Duchess of Portsmouth, in 1683, on her return from a visit to the apartment of the king's mistress—"great vases of wrought plate, tables, stands, chimney furniture, sconces, branches, braseras, etc.; all of massive silver and out of number."

However, previous references to silver furniture are noted as early as 1508, when a silver weaving stool appeared in the list of Princess Mary's trousseau and again in 1520 at which time Henry VIII possessed a silver mounting block.

In the Royal collection at Windsor Castle, the remains of three magnificent sets of silver furniture are found. Two of them were presents to Charles II and William III from the city of London, and from descriptions, one table alone weighed over eight thousand ounces. In this furniture, as well as in similarly made pieces, only a minimum of wood and iron were used in the construction. Among the numerous other pieces which reflected the wild orgy of spending, are silver mirrors, andirons, and candlestick stands. Mention must also be made of the existence of silver clocks which are known since the latter half of the sixteenth century. Huge silver vases, specimens of which are very, very rare, were made in these times. As a rule they consisted of a garniture of three pieces which included a vase flanked by two enormous flasks.

There is little likelihood that any of the silver mounted furniture will ever come into the market as most of it is preserved at Windsor Castle, Knole House, Seven Oakes, and Ham House.

BUTTER DISHES

Made in great number chiefly in Ireland butter dishes typified the Celtic love of figures and pastoral scenes. They were usually in the shape of a deep oval box, about seven inches long with a high cover surmounted by the figure of a cow which formed the handle. Butter dishes and dish rings show a decided resemblance in treatment, although the former are by no means as fine.

TABLE BELLS

Silver bells were introduced about the time of Queen Anne, and later accompanied inkstands as the center ornament. They are rarities.

SERVING PIECES

Grape shears and asparagus tongs were introduced during the reign of George II. The former were generally made with a wealth of ornamentation while the latter were, as a rule, very simple in design. Cheese scoops were not made in profusion until the late Georgian periods although a few examples of earlier date have survived. They were often combined with ivory and agate handles and are attractive as well as useful.

THE ENGLISH PROVINCES

SILVERSMITHING IN YORK

YORK was by far the most important provincial city in England in the Middle Ages and was the first town to receive a touch mark by the Act of 1423. However, it was not until twelve years later that statutory recognition was given to it, according to the ordinance of its Mayor. The law provided that no goldsmith anywhere in England should make silver of lower alloy than sterling, nor offer any article for sale without first impressing it with his own mark. In the following years of the fifteenth century, many references to York goldsmiths are found in wills and inventories. In 1560 it was ordained that all work should be "towched with the pownce of the citie, called the halfe leopard head and halfe flowre-de-luyce," that no silver should be worked of "worse alaye than sterlyng" and anyone working gold or silver below these standards should forfeit double the value of the article.

At the time that the city mark and maker's mark were compulsory, a date letter was introduced, so that all York plate made from about 1560 to 1698 should bear three hallmarks. Upon the reestablishment of the York Assay Office in 1700, the town mark was changed and the arms of the city, a cross charged with five lions passant, were thenceforward used in addition. Pursuant to the terms of the Act of 1700, the lion's head was erased, and the figure of Britannia was struck, thereby increasing the number of compulsory marks to five. It was also decreed at this time that the maker's mark should be formed from the first two letters of the surname, as in the case of London. In 1717 the assaying of plate at York was discontinued, as the two principal goldsmiths of the town entered into an agreement with the Newcastle Goldsmiths Company to have plate assayed there upon payment of an annual fee. For this reason no York-marked plate is known between the years of 1714 and 1779. Many variations occur in date letters as shown in the table of marks. In 1858 the office was finally closed and it is likely that it will never be reopened.

SILVERSMITHING IN NORWICH

It is probable that Norwich plate approaches more closely the date of York work than that found in other provinces. The work of the sixteenth century goldsmiths of Norwich is entitled to the highest rank in all of the English provinces, and many of their Elizabethan pieces are fully equal to those produced in London at that time.

Norwich records show a great many goldsmiths working from the end of the thirteenth century and with few intervals names of prominent makers are known down to the end of the seventeenth century. Norwich was one of the seven cities appointed in 1423 to have a "touch." The town mark consisted of a castle and lion and was practically unchanged from 1565 to 1575. No plate was officially marked before 1565, but from that date on, the compulsory assaying and marking with the arms of the city took effect. Although no mention is made of a date letter, it seems clear from the earliest examples that this practice was also begun in 1565, but no date letter mark between the years 1585 and 1624 has appeared, and in all probability, none was used.

The use of the date letter was again resumed in 1624 but discontinued between 1643 and 1688. Finally in this last year, an effort was made to institute a regular system of hallmarking and, with but few variations, marks show a consistency not previously found. The Act of 1697 prevented the Norwich goldsmiths from continuing to work under the old regime, and it appears that only a few survived to take advantage of the legislation in 1701 which permitted them to reestablish an assay office.

Peter Peterson was the one outstanding Norwich silversmith but towards the end of the seventeenth century the craft of Norwich goldsmiths dwindled and disappeared.

SILVERSMITHING IN EXETER

Judging from the examples of plate which have survived to the present time, the goldsmiths of Exeter were probably next to those of Norwich in order of antiquity. But apparently Exeter did not have an official "touch." No assay office was established until 1701, and consequently no records are available prior to this time. Exeter was too far removed from London, it was not convenient for its goldsmiths to send their plate there to have it assayed, and therefore, we may infer that the goldsmiths of Exeter worked under the privileges of a royal charter, although its existence has never been discovered.

During the sixteenth and seventeenth centuries the Exeter town mark was the Roman letter "X." In some early Elizabethan pieces, the mark varied from that of an "x" with a crown over the letter and a pellet on either side, to an "x" in a circular stamp without surrounding dots. In 1701 the Exeter town mark officially used was composed of the arms of the city which consisted of a triple towered castle.

Although only an inference can be drawn due to the lack of records, it seems most probable that the small letters found on early pieces of about the year 1600, were date letters. With the passing of the Act of 1700, date letters were uniformly incorporated into the marking of silver, and thenceforward were changed annually. Their use continued until 1883, at which time the office was closed.

In the absence of records it is impossible to say what plan was used in testing and assaying Exeter plate prior to 1701. However, as it is likely that masters and wardens were used, each was probably entrusted with the punch for striking the town mark. In those instances where a mark occurs which is neither the town mark nor the maker's mark, it may be safely assumed that it was struck by the master or the warden.

SILVERSMITHING IN NEWCASTLE

The earliest known reference to a Newcastle goldsmith occurs in an ordinance of 1248, wherein two goldsmiths were appointed to be in complete charge of assaying the money coined. In 1423, Newcastle was given a touch mark of its own. No further reference to these smiths appears until 1536 when they were incorporated in a common company with freemen of many other trades. Although no Newcastle plate of earlier date than the middle of the seventeenth century has survived, it is known that the art of the goldsmith flourished during the sixteenth century, and in all probability those pieces made were melted down in the troublous times of Charles I.

The Act of William III, which conferred on the Goldsmiths Company of England the sole rights of assaying, reflected great hardship and inconvenience on the goldsmiths of Newcastle, who were put to great expense, risk and delay in sending their plate to London. This hardship was remedied in 1700, when assay offices were established at Exeter, York, Chester, Norwich and Bristol, but Newcastle was not one of the places where mints had been established to recoin money and it was not included. However, there is little doubt that although it was illegal, much plate was made during this time. After many petitions and entreaties set forth by the goldsmiths of Newcastle, royal assent to reestablish the assay office of Newcastle was granted in 1702. This same act provided that all smiths who were freemen of Newcastle should be incorporated and known as the Company of Goldsmiths of New-castle-upon-Tyne. At this time it was compulsory for all plate of the required standard to be struck with the maker's mark, which consisted of the first two letters of his surname, the lion's head erased, the Britannia mark, the town mark, and a variable date letter.

Although the goldsmiths of Newcastle had been constituted as an independent corporation, they continued in association with other tradesmen until 1716. In 1844 the Goldsmiths Company of London endeavored to obtain jurisdiction over all the provincial offices, claiming that great illegalities existed in these places with regard to the correct assaying of plate. Through dint of pressure brought to bear by the London Company, silversmithing at Newcastle finally simmered to nothing, and in 1884 it was finally resolved to discontinue the assay office there.

The town mark of Newcastle, which was probably derived from the original arms of the borough, consisted of a single castle, and was used until about the middle of the seventeenth century. In 1670 the mark was changed and the entire coat of arms of Newcastle, which consisted of three castles in a plain heraldic shield, was struck. About ten years later the shape of the shield was altered and it assumed a more elaborate form. However, the only distinguishing mark is the often repeated use there of the lion passant, "to sinister."

SILVERSMITHING IN CHESTER

The silversmiths of Chester are really entitled to a preference over those of the other provincial guilds, as they are the only ones who still maintain an assay office today. It is fully alive and in constant competition with those of the other large cities in England. It is known that the goldsmiths and money coiners of Chester are recorded as early as 925, which gives them further distinction. From the twelfth to the fifteenth century there is occasional mention of prominent goldsmiths in Chester, but it is not until 1540 that any amount of data is available. From this time on Chester goldsmiths are recorded in a fairly continuous line down to the present day.

Chester was not appointed along with the other provinces in 1423 to have a touch, the reason for it being, that the smiths already had this privilege and had been enjoying it for almost 200 years. Coins were minted in this city as early as the time of Athelstan. Prior to 1573 a maker's mark was not struck, nor was the mark of the assayer used. From this time on, however, all goldsmiths were re-

Bowl (Pair)   W. Fountain. London, 1802

Pair of Mugs   Henry Cowper, London, 1774

Bowl   Fuller White, London, 1765

Tobacco Box   Henry Cowper, London, 1792

SHEFFIELD PLATE BOWL c. 1800 *Courtesy Black, Starr & Frost-Gorham, Inc.*

ONE OF PAIR OF SHEFFIELD SOUP TUREENS   *Courtesy Black, Starr & Frost-Gorham, Inc.*   T. & J. Creswick, c. 1800

TRAY WITH ARMS OF LORD MACKENZIE

Jno. Crouch, London, 1810

CRUET   J. Delmester, London, 1758

CRUET   Andrew Fogelberg, London, 1772

TEA SERVICE   Peter de Riemer, New York, 1769   *Courtesy Robert Ensko, Inc.*

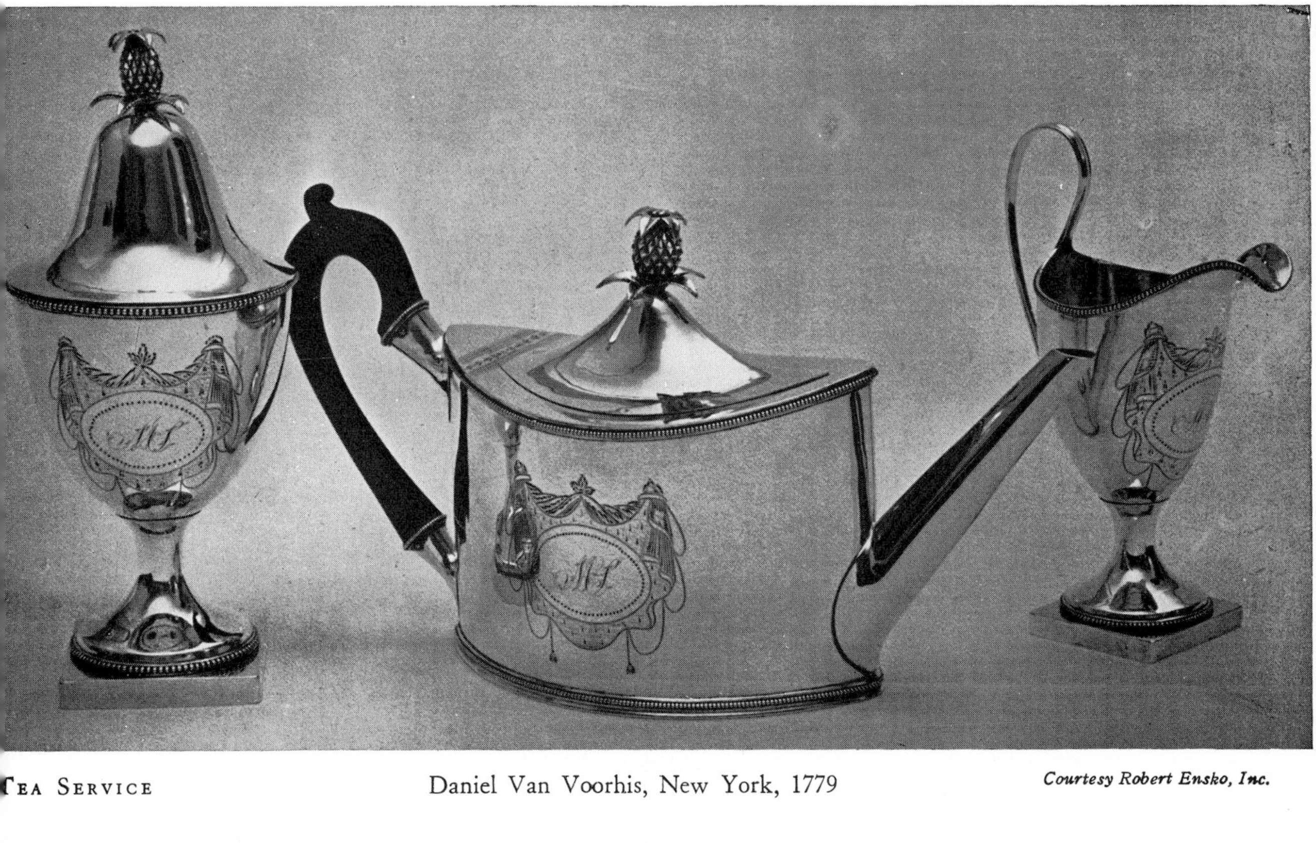

TEA SERVICE   Daniel Van Voorhis, New York, 1779   *Courtesy Robert Ensko, Inc.*

Courtesy Metropolitan Museum of Art
John Coney, Boston

TEAPOT

Courtesy S. Wyler, Inc.
John Jackson New York 1736

TEAPOT

Courtesy James Graham, Jr.
Robert Evans, Boston, 1770

PITCHER

RATTAIL SPOONS

John Ladyman, London, 1715

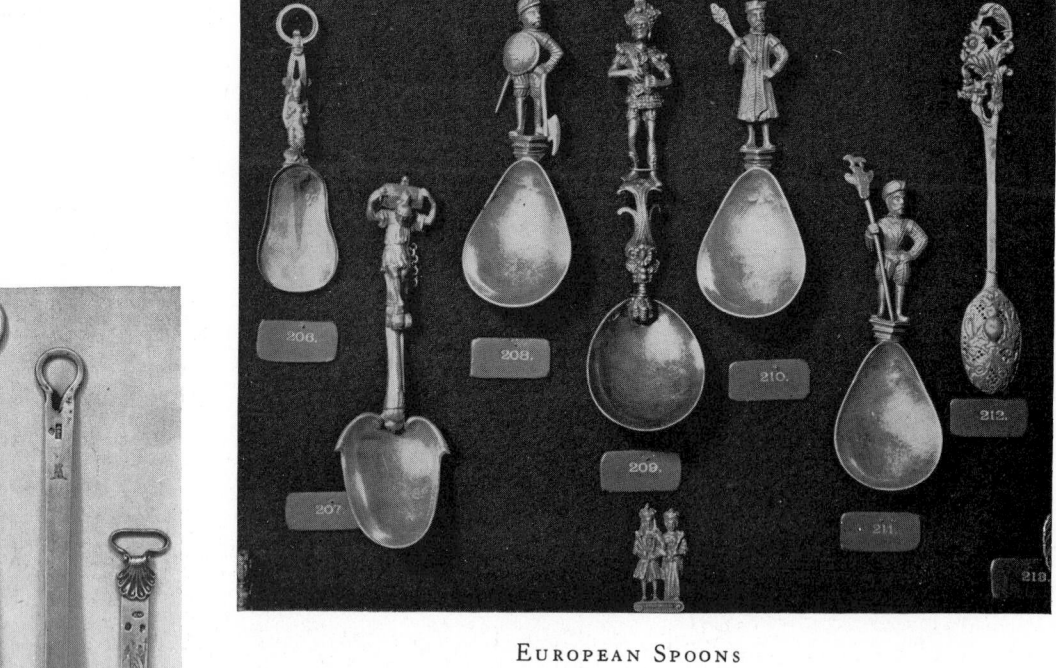

EUROPEAN SPOONS

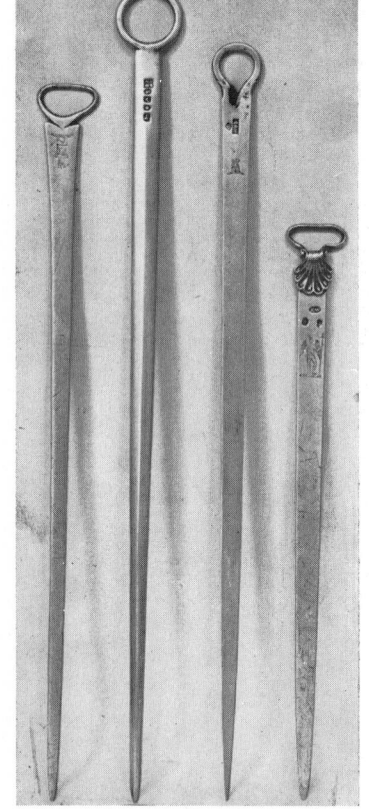

Courtesy J. E. Caldwell & Co.

SKEWERS   1770-1792

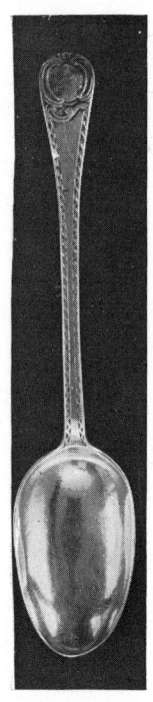

Paul Revere

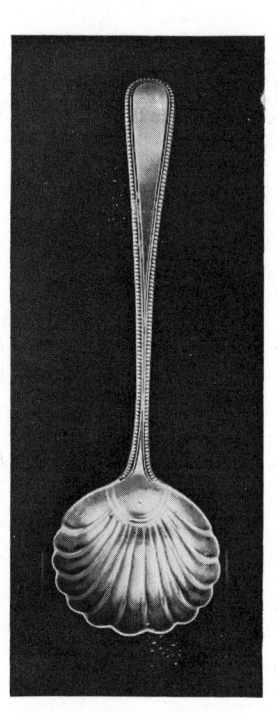

Hester Bateman

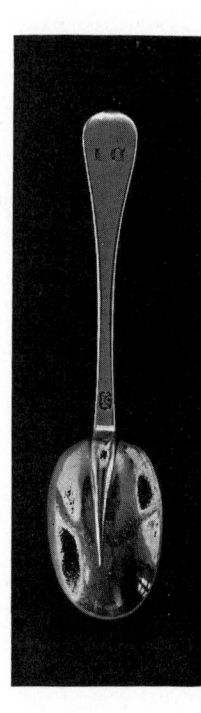

John Coney

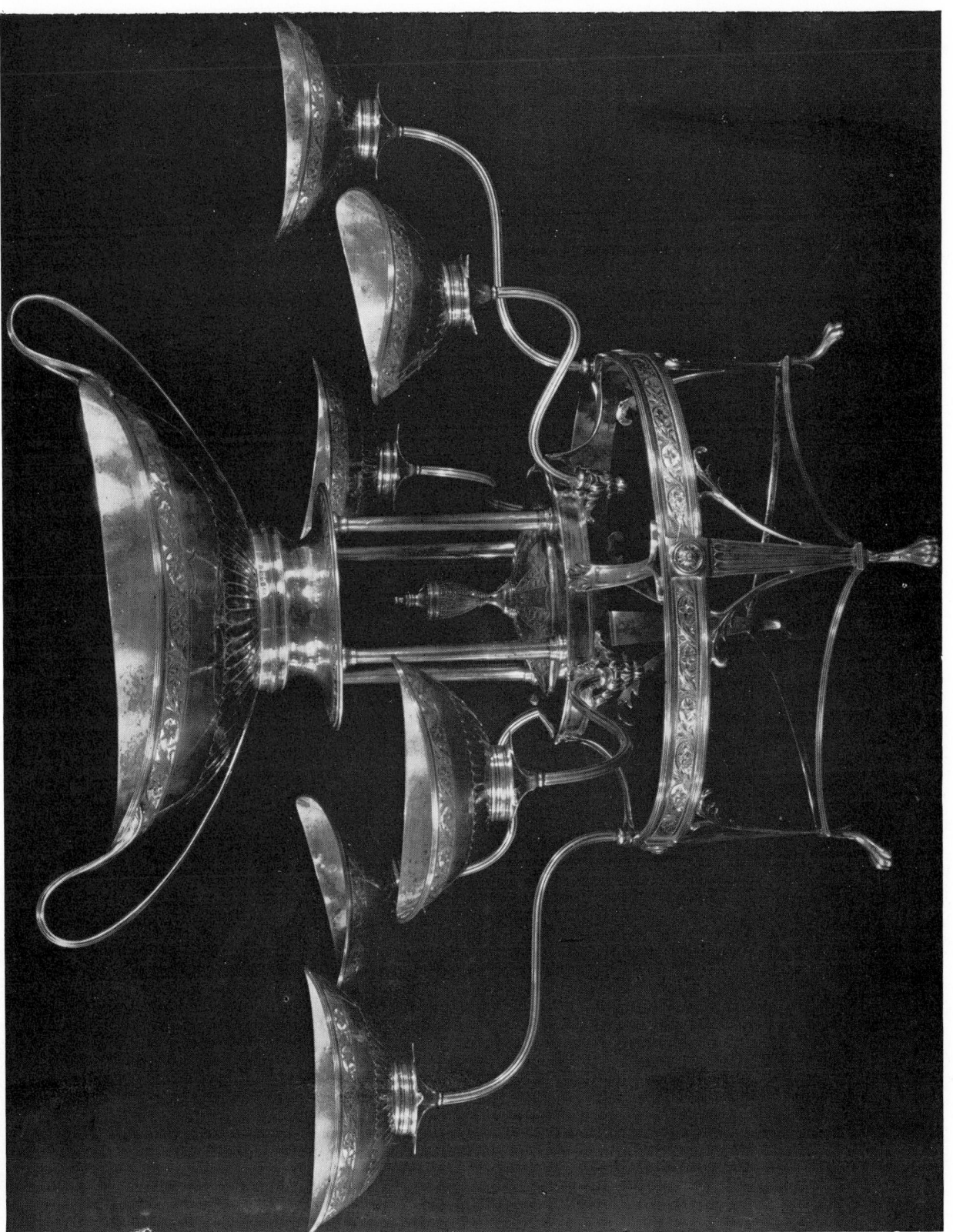

EPERGNE

James Young, London, 1792

SOUP TUREEN   Wm. Fountain, London, 1806

ENTREE DISHES   Wm. Bateman, London, 1818

CANDELABRA   W. Pitts, London, 1808

CHAMBER CANDLESTICKS   Matthew Boulton

Top: Nathaniel Smith & Co., Sheffield, 1799-1801
Bottom: J. Parsons, Sheffield, 1783

BOULTON AND FOTHERGILL   Birmingham, 1773

OLD SHEFFIELD TEA TRAY   Circa, 1810

D SHEFFIELD INKSTAND   *Courtesy S. Wyler, Inc.*   Watson and Bradbury, London, 1812

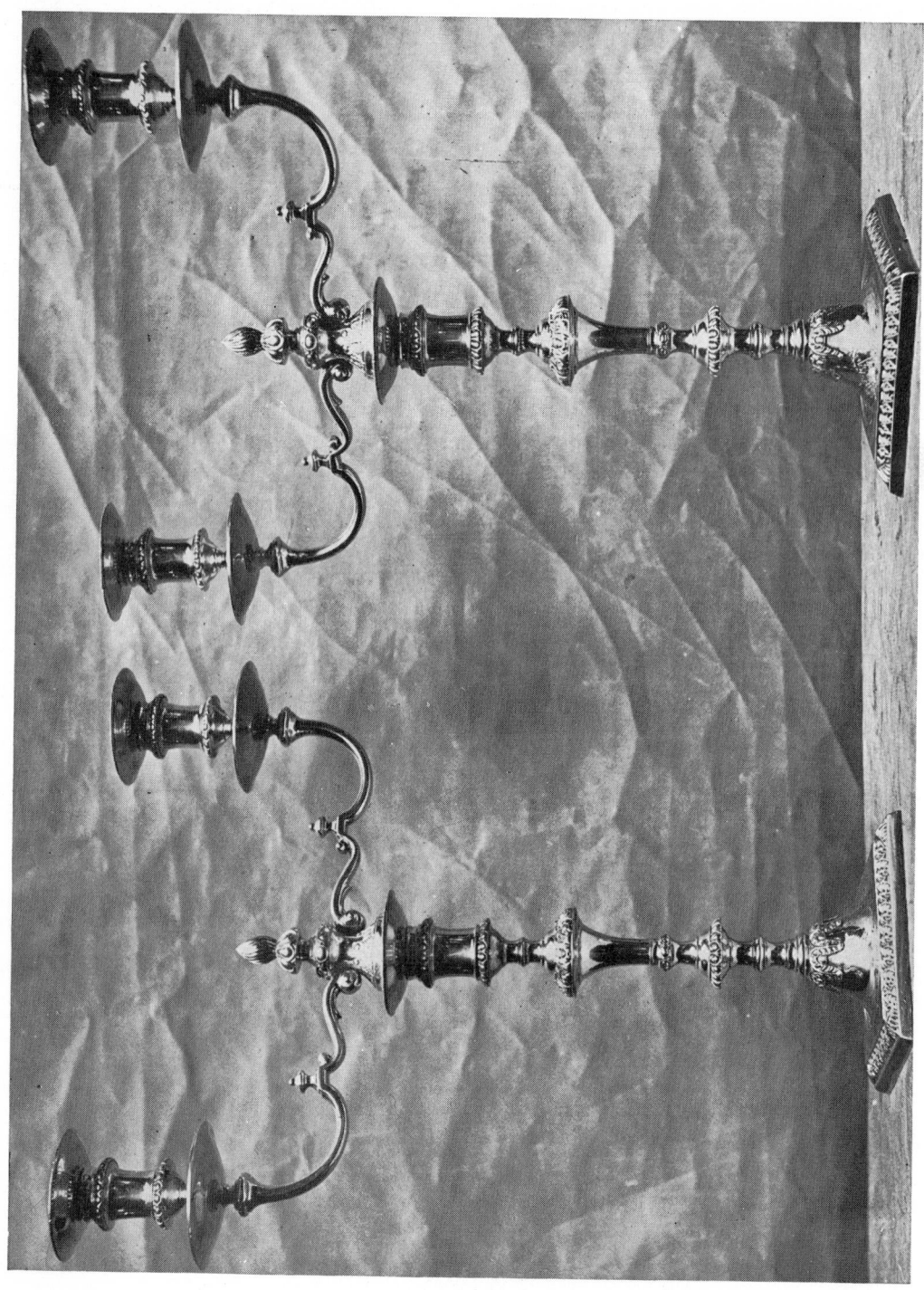

CANDELABRA

E. Capper, London, 1767

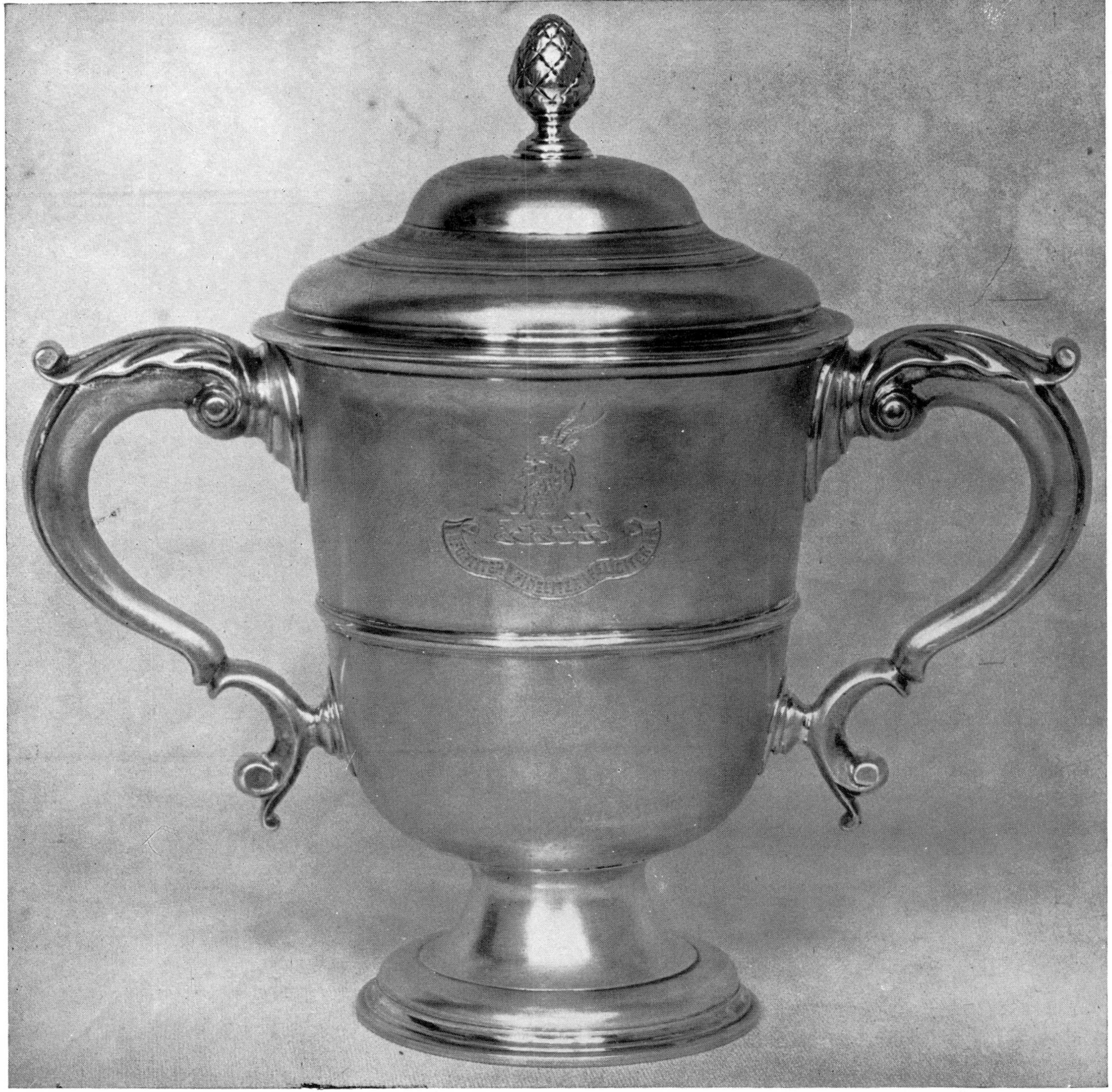

Covered Cup — Sam. James, Newcastle, 1759 — *Courtesy J. E. Caldwell & Co.*

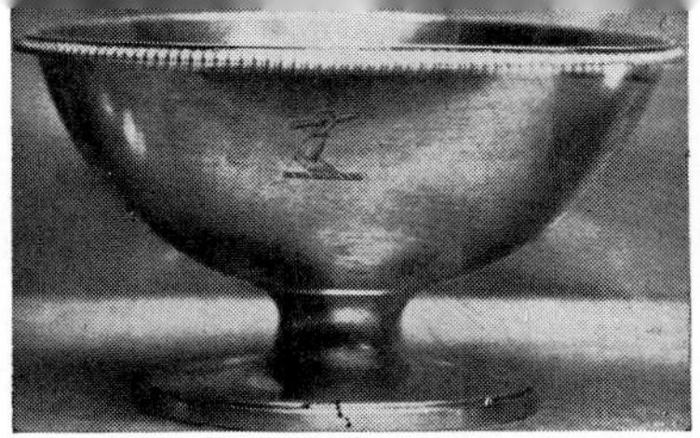

Newcastle, 1800

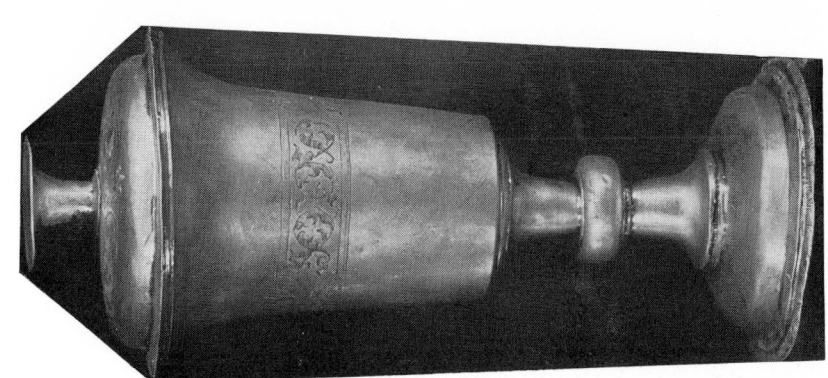

Cup — Shrewsbury, 1560

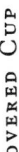

quired to punch their wares and guarantee them to be of the required standard.

In 1685 the city of Chester was granted a charter by James II, and although a diligent search has been made, no evidence has been found to indicate that a town mark or date letter was used before this time. Although much plate disappeared from Chester during the reign of Charles I, it must not be imagined that none remains. It is far more probable that much of it is in private collections today and, unfortunately, cannot be accurately identified, as only a maker's mark was used. The operation of the charter granted by James II was suspended by the Act of 1695. However, in 1701, Chester, being one of the principal cities where mints had been erected, was reestablished as an assay office. Until the present time it has continued to flourish, the work executed there in recent years being greatly in excess of that done in past history.

The word, "sterling," found quite frequently on pieces of Chester plate, was probably used as the maker's guarantee that the piece was of a legal alloy. Date letters are known as early as 1688, but one date letter was often used for two to three years. When, in 1701, the assay office was reestablished, the marks followed those used in all the other English provincial towns—the lion's head erased and Britannia. In addition a new form of the town mark, composed of three lions of England dimidiating the three garbs of the Earldom of Chester in a plain shield, plus the date letter and the maker's mark was used. In 1779, an entirely new set of punches was instituted and the town mark was changed accurately to represent the arms of the city, as formerly used from 1687 to 1692. At this time, two new stamps were obtained for the leopard's head and lion passant, and these continued in use until 1784 when the King's head was impressed. In 1823 the leopard's head first appears uncrowned and a new set of date letters was inaugurated.

SILVERSMITHING IN BIRMINGHAM

The establishment of an assay office at Birmingham in 1773 was mainly due to the efforts of one of the great silversmiths. Matthew Boulton, who was by far the outstanding Birmingham smith of all time, personally prepared, on behalf of himself and the other goldsmiths, a petition which was submitted to the London Goldsmiths Company. In the petition was stated the extreme difficulties suffered by the plate workers in the exercise of their trade because no assay offices were conveniently located. The result was the granting of a charter to both Birmingham and Sheffield, and both offices are now in existence. The Act of 1773 provided that all plate should bear the town mark of an anchor, a distinct variable date letter to be changed annually, the lion passant, the figure of Britannia for plate of the standard of eleven ounces, ten dwt., and the mark of the maker, which should be the first letters of his Christian and surname. Very small wares, incapable of being fully marked without injury being done to them, were excepted. For this reason, one often finds vinaigrettes and the like, struck with only a maker's mark and the anchor. There is no particular reason why the anchor should have been chosen as the town mark for Birmingham except that a great deal of overseas commerce was transacted there.

SILVERSMITHING IN SHEFFIELD

As previously mentioned, the assay office in Sheffield was established in 1773, when this right was conferred on Birmingham. The silversmiths of Sheffield lost no time after the Act was passed to proceed in business, and production flourished on a great scale. The marks required to be stamped on all wrought silver assayed at Sheffield, are the town mark of a crown, a date letter, the standard mark which is either a lion passant or Britannia, according to the alloy, and the maker's mark.

From 1784 to 1890 the duty mark was added, as on London plate. In the marking of many pieces the date letter and town mark were combined in one stamp to save space, but this was discontinued many years ago and never again resumed. From 1815 to 1819 the town mark of the crown was struck upside down and the only reason for this can be to differentiate between similar marks of a few years earlier date. It is curious that Sheffield was one of the few places where gold was never assayed until 1904, though in the other provinces both silver and gold objects were wrought.

SILVERSMITHING IN HULL

The goldsmiths of Hull are mentioned as early as the fifteenth century, but they were never incorporated by statute or charter.

Several examples of the plate have been found in and around Hull, stamped with the letter "h" to indicate the town of manufacture. During the seventeenth century the arms of the borough, "three ducal coronets in pale," were adopted as the town mark. Although there is no evidence of any regular assay office having been established, several attempts were made to introduce a system of marking with date letters. Those examples which have survived, however, clearly indicate that this practice was never continued. Although goldsmiths' names are recorded in the archives of the borough as late as 1774, not more than one example of Hull plate of the Queen Anne period is known. It is most probable that those names listed were of dealers in goldsmiths' work, and not manufacturers.

SILVERSMITHING IN LINCOLN

Practically no information regarding the workings of the goldsmiths in Lincoln has ever been found, outside of the fact that it was one of the seven towns appointed by the Act of 1423 to have a touch. However, records and inventories allude to goldsmiths from the twelfth century onwards, and these references appear down to the year 1708. The arms of the city were used as the distinguishing town mark, and were adopted from the coat of arms of the city which consisted of "argent, on a cross gules, a fleur-de-lys or." Pieces bearing the Lincoln mark are very rare and consist mostly of church plate, or an occasional drinking vessel.

SILVERSMITHING IN SHREWSBURY

Although Shrewsbury was not one of the appointed towns in 1423, goldsmithing is known to have been in practice there during the Middle Ages. The provisions of the Statute of 1300, decreeing that "no manner of vessel or other work of silver should be set to sale without having the mark of a leopard's head upon it," were an aid rather than a hindrance to the Shrewsbury silversmiths because the arms of the town were "azure, three leopards' heads, or." One of these heads would naturally be the mark adopted by the Shrewsbury goldsmiths. Many examples of plate marked solely with an uncrowned leopard's head are wrongly ascribed to London. Some of these pieces are undoubtedly the work of Shrewsbury silversmiths.

SILVERSMITHING IN LEWES

The only information relative to this town is the mark adopted by the goldsmiths in the late fourteenth century. It consisted of "Checky (or and azure) on a conton sinister gules a lion rampant or," and pieces of plate bearing this mark are only rarely found.

SILVERSMITHING IN BARNSTAPLE

The most celebrated of all goldsmiths known to have worked in Barnstaple is Thomas Mathew, examples of whose work have been found in many parishes. Much of the plate wrought by him bears, in addition to his name stamp, the mark of a flower or fruit on a slipped and leaved stalk, which is intended to be a representation of a pomegranate. This device is portrayed in the Tregoney arms and it has been suggested that Mathew used this to denote that he was a native of that place. The town mark of Barnstaple was taken from the borough shield and used until 1624. The shield consisted of a bird in a circular stamp, but in 1625 the mark of a triple-turreted tower was granted to Barnstaple as its arms, and this was used until the end of the seventeenth century.

SILVERSMITHING IN PLYMOUTH

A few pieces of plate impressed with a representation of the arms of the borough of Plymouth are known as early as the beginning of the seventeenth century. The arms are composed of "a saltire between four castles." Certain examples bear the sterling mark indicating the legal standard. A curious form of the Britannia standard mark is known on a lighthouse salt made in 1698, on which the standard is described by the technical term "Britan." This mark suggests, therefore, that the piece was probably made about 1698 immediately after the introduction of the new standard, and it became technically represented by the Britannia mark.

SILVERSMITHING OF BRISTOL

It seems most unusual that no record of any assay office has ever been found in Bristol, nor any allusion to a guild of goldsmiths in a town of such importance. Although mentioned in the Act of 1423 as one of the seven towns appointed to have a touch mark, and again in the Act of 1701 as a place where an assay office could be legally established, no trace of any reference to goldsmithing has appeared. A few pieces of Bristol plate are struck with an oblong punch mark bearing the arms of the city, which consist of a ship issuing from a castle.

SILVERSMITHING IN OTHER PROVINCIAL TOWNS

Examples of the work of medieval goldsmiths are known in many outlying communities. As a general rule only a town mark was impressed and but little data of the history of goldsmiths in these provinces is available.

Dorchester	Salisbury	Coventry	King's Lynn
Sherborne	Colchester	Poole	Taunton
Rochester	Channel Islands	Carlisle	Gateshead
Sandwich	Leicester	Leeds	

CALCUTTA

Gold and silver wares have been wrought in India for centuries, but it was not until the eighteenth century that articles made by workers of British origin are noted. In 1808 the firm of Hamilton and Company was established in Calcutta and numerous fine examples of their work are known. The mark used was that of an elephant.

XV

IRELAND

SILVERSMITHING IN IRELAND

SILVERSMITHING was practically the only art developed to any high degree in Ireland. There were skilled goldsmiths there prior to the date of the Norman Conquest. The Ardagh Chalice found by a peasant while digging near Limerick indicates the high merit of the craftsmanship of this time. Although several other examples of plate have survived to the present time, by far the majority are lost forever to posterity. Ireland then as now was turbulent, constant political upheavals took heavy toll of family silver, and the enthusiastic champions of the various causes cheerfully surrendered their plate in order to finance their parties.

The similarity of basic forms as compared with English silver is always to be noted, but the decorative scheme was for the most part original, rather than copied from the arts of continental Europe. The silversmiths in Ireland were greatly influenced by their environment, and their native whimsicality is reflected in the original designs found in so many pieces of Irish plate. Of particular notice are the pastoral scenes taken from the every-day farm life and its environs so dear to the hearts of the Celtic race. The chasing on pieces of Irish plate is always to be recognized, because the silversmiths apparently did not care to risk the process of flat hammering on the chased articles. Pieces of this particular style are to be found nowhere but in Ireland.

By the middle of the eighteenth century the prevailing rococo styles waned, and the classic influence introduced by the Adam brothers grew in favor. For many years, however, the delicate embossing enclosing escutcheons for crests and coats of arms, was distinctly reminiscent of the earlier elaborate designs.

The craft of the great Irish silversmith was not confined to Dublin. The city of Cork, with its natural silver mines, became a large center for silversmithing, and examples from the seventeenth century are known. Among other provincial towns producing silver in Ireland may be mentioned Limerick, Galway and Youghal. The curious practice of impressing the word, "dollar" on many provincial pieces is noted, thus bearing witness to the custom, prevalent also in America, of melting Spanish dollars for use in the silver craft. Another variation of hallmark often found on pieces of Cork manufacture is the word, "Sterling." In 1710 this mark was often inscribed to indicate that the pieces were equal in quality to that of the English silversmiths. The story of silversmithing in the provinces may be said to end with the year 1848. Very little silver was made from then on, and today practically all Irish plate is Dublin-made.

Irish silver is regarded by collectors throughout the world as most desirable. Because of the loss of so much of the early plate, very few pieces dating from the seventeenth century are encountered, nor are examples prior to the reign of George III plentiful. Many famous silversmiths are known who worked in the leading cities of Ireland, and examples by them fetch tremendous prices today. However, with the steadily decreasing supply of pieces of Celtic origin, it is safe to assume that within a few years all fine specimens will be in private collections or museums.

SILVERSMITHS OF DUBLIN

The earliest known reference to a guild of goldsmiths in Ireland is recorded in the archives of the Dublin Corporation. The guild is mentioned in the reference to the festival of Corpus Christi in 1498, wherein the town goldsmiths were represented. In 1555 the Dublin Goldsmiths presented a petition to the City Corporation stating that the charter which had been previously given to them had been accidentally burned. They wished to enjoy the privileges to which they were entitled, so they applied to the City Assembly for leave to enter a copy of their charter. In 1557 the application was granted.

Throughout the next fifty years, there appears to have been no entry in the records with reference to any marks to be impressed on gold or silver articles. Because of the continued fraudulent practices and abuses, it was resolved in 1605 by the Dublin City Council that henceforth certain marks should be stamped on all wrought plate, which, in quality, had to be equal to the silver standard coin then current. The above legislation, which is the earliest known reference to the marking of Dublin plate, required the use of the figure of a lion, a harp, and a castle, in addition to the goldsmith's own punch. However, not a single example appears to be known bearing these marks, which were supposed to have been used until 1637. At this time the Dublin goldsmiths became dissatisfied with their status under the domination of the City Corporation. They probably felt their inferiority to the London goldsmiths who had full control of all matters pertaining to the assaying and marking of pieces, without interference by civil authorities. A petition to the King was presented, in which they asked to be incorporated by Royal charter. Their petition was favorably received and in 1637 Charles I granted it.

The archives of the Dublin Goldsmiths Company refer to various articles which were brought in to be assayed. These included ewers and basins, caudle cups, sugar boxes, porringers, trencher salts, spoons and candlesticks. The entries of plate continued until 1649 when a break occurs owing to the loss of records and no further entry appears until 1694. Mention must be made of the strict vigilance shown by the Company in the detection of fraudulent pieces. The punishment for these offenses was severe, and Irish goldsmithing was raised to a high plane. Although we know of the use of hallmarks prior to 1637, no example is known bearing them. The charter of 1637 described the use of the crown harp, which was the king's stamp, as well as the standard mark, plus the makers' marks. The first article made under the new law was dated April 6, 1683, and from that time to the present day no article in silver or gold of Dublin make can be legally sold without being so distinguished. The use of the date letter was adopted at this time, in addition to the crown harp and the maker's mark. A fourth mark, the figure of Hibernia was incorporated in 1730 and was used to denote the payment of duty as ordered by the Commissioner of Excise. From 1807 to 1890, a fifth mark, consisting of a representation of the head of the Sovereign was impressed. This superseded the Hibernia stamp, and was applied to all plate wrought in Ireland, as in every other assay office then open in the United Kingdom.

SILVERSMITHS OF CORK

There is good reason to believe that goldsmithing of high merit was practiced in Cork as early as the Middle Ages. Some of the exquisite chalices, patens, and other church pieces are confidently ascribed to this city, although very little is known of the early history, and the records of the guild date no further back than 1656. In 1631, by a charter of Charles II, the Corporation of Cork was granted privileges which included the power to appoint a Clerk of Assay. His duties combined the testing of weights and measures, rather than the assaying of precious metals.

There being no regular assay at Cork, it seems probable that the only test used was that of the touchstone, except when an assay by cupel was required, which necessitated sending the plate to Dublin.

Cork was situated in a direct line with the Spanish peninsula

and the west of France. This afforded increased advantages of inter-
course with these countries, whence the city received not only its
supply of silver, but innumerable emigrant craftsmen who brought
with them knowledge of designs applied by European smiths. This
accounts for the frequent examples known which resembled the
contemporary styles that prevailed on the continent.

The earliest known example of the Cork town mark consists of
a ship duplicated, or a ship between two castles; adopted from the
arms of the city. There were many variations of this mark and it
would appear that each goldsmith adopted his own peculiar town-
mark stamp. Early in the eighteenth century the use of this mark
was discontinued, and between 1710 and 1719 the word "STER-
LING" was introduced as a mark for Cork plate. This mark is also
found in various forms including abbreviations to STER and
STERG. The spelling also varied and specimens are known with
impressions as follows: STARLING, STIRLING, STARLIN,
and STERLIN. As previously mentioned, indication of the plate
having been wrought from Spanish dollars is found in the use of
the word, "dollar," just as the sterling stamp indicated the fineness
of eleven ounces, two dwt.

Makers' marks in Cork, used in the seventeenth and early part
of the eighteenth century, were generally composed of the initials
of the maker combined with a heraldic device. These combinations
disappeared shortly after 1731 when the Dublin Goldsmiths Company prohibited the use of such ornaments. Here may be seen the
complete power of the Dublin Goldsmiths Company to regulate the
production of plate throughout all of Ireland. No date letter was
ever used on pieces of Cork plate, except those assayed at Dublin,
and it is difficult to ascertain the exact year in which a piece was
produced. However, a study of the makers' marks plus the style in
vogue at the time, helps to approximate the date within a score of
years.

SILVERSMITHS OF YOUGHAL

By virtue of a charter granted in 1608 by James I, the Corporation of Youghal was empowered to arrange the various craftsmen
into appropriate guilds. But probably never more than a dozen
goldsmiths were working in the town at any one time. The mark of
a small single masted sail boat by common adoption of the goldsmiths is approximated at about 1620. The boat was commonly
known as a yawl, but heraldically speaking, as a lymphad. Several

names of prominent goldsmiths have been gleaned from the records and the few marks are reproduced.

SILVERSMITHS OF GALWAY

The goldsmiths of Galway adopted the mark of an anchor, generally found in a shaped cartouche. Only rarely is the name of a Galway silversmith apparent as no plate earlier than 1648 or later than 1730 is known. In the George III era, the names of nine goldsmiths are recorded in the books of the Dublin Goldsmiths Company as required by the Act of 1783.

SILVERSMITHS OF LIMERICK

As in the case of the silversmiths of Galway, many Limerick craftsmen are registered with the Company of Goldsmiths in Dublin. The Limerick marks closely resemble those used in Cork, being a triple towered castle plus the maker's initials. For many years these marks remained unidentified, until the discovery of an old Limerick toll-stamp, bearing a castle of similar form.

The word, Sterling, is often found on pieces made in and around Limerick, and these are frequently confused with plate produced in Cork. No records of the existence of a goldsmiths' guild are known in Limerick, but it may be assumed that associations were formed for protective purposes.

SILVERSMITHS OF OTHER PROVINCIAL TOWNS

Pieces have appeared which indicate clearly the production of plate in many smaller communities throughout Ireland. It is commonly supposed that the mark of a hand erect was the town mark for Belfast. Names of goldsmiths are recorded in Dublin which give sufficient evidence that some plate was wrought there.

References to the existence of guilds which included goldsmiths and silversmiths are known in the records of the towns of Kinsale, Derry, Kilkenny, Tipperary, Newry, and Drogheda. Unfortunately no ascribed marks identifying these towns or their goldsmiths are known.

XVI

SCOTLAND

SILVERSMITHING IN SCOTLAND

THE characteristic traits of a people are often reflected in the quality of their art, and so it is with the history of the early Scotch silversmiths. The austerity and simple tastes of the Scotchman are brought to notice by the work of the earliest craftsmen. The majority of silver articles made were definitely for practical use, rather than for purposes of decoration. Most of the early Scotch silver was used in churches, or else in the gentle art of drinking.

Perhaps the most definitely Scotch of all articles made of silver was the quaich, which was originally a small two-handled bowl, made of wood with silver stripings and used for drinking brandy. However, a few of the more affluent Scotchmen had these quaiches especially made to order in solid silver. Only a limited quantity of these are available, hence they have come to be recognized as the most valuable pieces of Scotch silver to be had. Among the other articles definitely attributed to these silversmiths were mulls which were made of large or small horns mounted in silver and used as snuff boxes. Tankards, caudle cups, flagons, jugs, and mazer bowls are all found among the earliest examples, and to a Scotch silversmith named Monteith, we are indebted for the introduction of what is now called a monteith bowl.

Unfortunately, there is very little early Scotch silver available to the collector today, as even the wealthy lairds and chieftains did not indulge in lavish appointments for the home. Also, due to the fact that much plate was melted during the seventeenth century to foster political causes, but little remains today. Since the early smiths could not find sufficient work in any one town, they led a nomadic existence, making small pieces here and there to order. The careful attitude towards spending money, so often characteristic of the Scotch as a people, had its effect on silversmithing. Complete tea services are practically non-existent because families would add but one piece at a time every few years to their sets. Consequently, to find a Scotch tea service of similar date and maker is almost an impossibility. It is interesting to note that in the earliest days of silversmithing in Scotland, it was the general custom for the client to bring his own silver or gold to the craftsman to be wrought at his order. It appears that dishonest workmen diluted and adulterated the metal, and outrageously cheated the customers. Because of this the amount of alloy permissible was regulated by law. Perhaps in no country was stricter adherence to the legislation of the silver craft demanded, and for this reason nearly all Scotch silver found today is of legal standard. The same laws conceived as early as 1483, regulating the quality of the metal, are still in use today.

From the standpoint of the collector or dealer, the original marks used by deacons in Scotland have been invaluable in determining the approximate dates of the earliest pieces, as date letters were not inaugurated until a much later time. Frequently in the provincial towns as well as Edinburgh and Glasgow, just the name of the city was impressed and therefore dates can only be surmised.

Scotch silver presents a field of high endeavor to the collector, not only because of the rarity of pieces, but also because there is a ready market at all times for good specimens regardless of price.

SILVERSMITHING IN EDINBURGH

Previous to the year 1483, silversmiths in Edinburgh were associated with other hammer-wielding trades under the general description of "Hammermen." At this time they presented a petition to the town council asking for certain privileges which would give them more freedom in the furthering of their craft. Before fifty years had elapsed from the time of this grant, they became an independent corporation, as recorded in the records of the oldest minute book, dated 1525.

A statute of the year 1485 decreed a Deacon and searcher were to be appointed to regulate the marking of all pieces of plate. In 1555, a further act of Parliament ordained that each goldsmith was to use his own mark, and that every piece must bear, in addition to this, a deacon's mark and a town mark. It is important to note that the introduction of the deacon's mark was instituted in order to regulate quality of the wrought metal. In 1586 the "Craft," which included the deacon and the masters of the goldsmiths, was empowered to seize any pieces deficient in the required fineness. Finally, in 1687, the first charter was granted to the silversmiths of Edinburgh, and all privileges previously enjoyed were confirmed in addition to more extensive powers.

With the issuance of this charter, notice was given to the smiths of other Scottish towns directing their attention to the necessity of maintaining their gold and silver work up to the required standard.

At the time of the adoption of the Britannia standard in England, all wrought plate was raised to a fineness of eleven ounces, ten dwt., but this was never operative in Scotland. However, with the union of the English and Scotch Parliaments, the Scotch standard for plate was raised in 1720 to conform with that of the English. This same act imposed a duty of sixpence per ounce on all plate manufactured in, or imported into Great Britain. In 1757 the duty on plate was repealed and in its place a license tax was levied which required every person dealing in gold and silver wares to pay a sum each year for the privilege of trading. The former duty was reimposed in 1784 and twenty-three years later the duty on plate was increased from sixpence to one shilling.

It is probable that no marks were used in Scotland before 1457 when the statute of that year provided for the use of a deacon's mark. These requirements with respect to the marking of plate have enabled us to approximate quite clearly the date of their manufacture. A further aid in identifying silver was the adoption of the town mark which was taken from the arms of the burgh which are "Argent, on a rock proper, a castle, triple towered and embattled, sable." In 1681 a variable annual date letter was adopted mainly for the reason that any manufacturer of plate in fraudulent practice might more easily be detected. From 1681 on it is possible to determine the exact year of any marked piece of Edinburgh plate. With the adoption of the date letter the Edinburgh goldsmiths abolished the deacon's mark and in its place substituted the mark of the assay master, which originally consisted of the initials of the assayer. A further alteration in the marking of plate was instituted in 1759 when the use of the assay master's initials was discontinued, and in their place the mark of a thistle was substituted. With the reimposition of the duty on plate in 1784, a fifth mark which consisted of the sovereign's head was struck on all plate to indicate the payment of the duty. As found in England, this mark continued in use until 1890, when all duties on plate were repealed.

SILVERSMITHING IN GLASGOW

The city of Glasgow, although not always as it is now, the largest and most densely populated town in all Scotland, may well lay claim to the premier place among Scottish provinces in importance as the center of the goldsmiths' craft. As found in Edinburgh the goldsmiths were originally incorporated in a large group under the designation of "Hammermen." But the earliest minute books have been mislaid, and little information is available regarding the progress of the guild. However, no Glasgow plate of earlier date than 1681 is known. At this time a date letter was adopted, but its use was discontinued about 1710, and not found again until 1819. For this reason it is necessary to approximate all pieces made during the interval. Between the years 1730 and 1800, a curious punch which consisted of the letter "s" in various shapes, was generally used. Although no definite explanation of this mark has ever been ascertained, it is probable that it was meant to indicate the word "sterling," to guarantee the piece to be of the accepted standard.

The Glasgow town mark adopted from the arms of the burgh is commonly known as the "fish, tree and bell." The actual heraldic description of it being "Argent, on a mount in base an oak tree proper, the trunk surmounted by a salmon proper with a signet ring in its mouth, or, on the top of the tree a red breast, and on the sinister fesse-point a hand-bell both proper."

There appears to be no evidence of the existence of a regular assay office at Glasgow before 1819, proof of which is derived from the variety in the form of the town mark used by the different makers at the same time. The 1819 statute incorporated the Glasgow Goldsmiths Company, empowered it and placed it under similar regulations to those ascribed to Edinburgh.

SILVERSMITHING IN ABERDEEN

It appears that in early times Aberdeen was divided into two distinct towns, known as Old Aberdeen and New Aberdeen. Each maintained its own distinct guilds and trade privileges, the only similarity being the incorporation of the smiths again under the common title of "Hammermen." In neither burgh was the town mark taken from the arms of the city but it was composed of the first two letters; AB or the first two and fifth letters; ABD. It has been suggested that this curious departure in the adoption of a town mark was taken mainly because the arms of the burgh resembled those of Dundee so much.

New Aberdeen, as it was called, until the extension of its boundaries into the adjoining burgh, records at least two goldsmiths as early as the fifteenth century. We have seen that the town mark was varied from AB to ABD and occasionally the Roman capital A was found struck three times instead. Early in the eighteenth century a new stamp composed of three castles in a shaped shell was used by one silversmith who was, in turn, followed by many others in this respect.

SILVERSMITHING IN DUNDEE

A reference in the year 1550 mentioning one David Stevenson as a goldsmith gives credence to the thought that plate was produced as early as this time. The arms of the town were adopted as the mark and consisted of "azure a pot of growing lillies argent." Further variations were adopted by smiths in the seventeenth and eighteenth centuries and in some instances the word Dundee was impressed as well as a thistle mark.

SILVERSMITHING IN ELGIN

The town mark of this burgh was contracted into ELG or ELN, and is sometimes spelled out. A variation is found on some of the earlier pieces which consisted of the representation of a mother and child in an upright, oblong cartouche. Here, again, a supposed town mark is sometimes noted, as well as a thistle as seen on Dundee plate. There does not seem to have been any incorporation of goldsmiths at Elgin, and the earliest record of any smith is 1701.

SILVERSMITHING IN OTHER PROVINCIAL TOWNS

Throughout Scotland many of the smaller provinces are recognized as having produced plate. These include Arbroath, Banff, Greenock, Inverness, Montrose, Perth, St. Andrews, Stirling, Wick and Tain.

XVII

SHEFFIELD PLATE

THE history of the trade known as Sheffield Plating reads like fiction, for its discovery was purely accidental, and its rise as an industry phenomenal.

In the 18th century silver, as an essential part of the well appointed home, was recognized in England as well as abroad, and workmen were busily engaged in creating new ideas. But the price of silver was still too prohibitive to permit any but the noble and wealthy to indulge themselves. It was the discovery of Sheffield Plate that enabled people of moderate means to own exact replicas of the solid silver domestic articles at a fraction of their cost.

The discovery of plating was an accident, but one of sufficient importance to revolutionize the trade life of a city. In time it became a leading industry in England, and the growth of the city of Sheffield from a London suburb, so to speak, to a great manufacturing center, is attributed to it.

It is unfortunate that so little data on the subject of combining metals is available, for there is evidence to show that many centuries earlier, the Jews and Egyptians worked along these lines with a fair amount of success. The Romans as well keenly appreciated the beautiful gold and silver objects which were produced, but so few have survived, that their methods of plating and gilding are practically unknown. There is no doubt though, that none of the early processes resembled plating as discovered and perfected in England.

In 1742, in the garret of a small building known as Tudor House, a mechanic, one Thomas Boulsover, was repairing the blade of a broken knife. He accidentally fused silver and copper during this operation, and discovered that when these two metals were heated to a certain degree they became inseparable. He immediately realized that this strange occurrence might be turned to good purpose, and upon further experimentation found he was able to manufacture small bits such as buttons, boxes and buckles. These are the earliest known specimens of Sheffield Plate.

However, Thomas Boulsover can hardly be called the father of Sheffield Plate, for although he discovered the process and produced a few pieces, he was soon forced to abandon it. The man he employed to travel on the road to introduce his new product, cheated him outrageously, and before long he was left without sufficient funds to continue.

But during the first few months of Boulsover's experimenting, he apprenticed a young man named Josiah Hancock. This young employee was a lad of great vision, and soon realized that the new industry might grow to huge proportions if properly managed. After diligent work he began to progress rapidly, and within a few years Sheffield Plating became a recognized industry largely because of his efforts. New pieces were created, faithful reproductions of sterling pieces were made and there was an increased demand for them, especially because excessive government taxation had forced the price of wrought silver articles to higher levels. The goldsmiths tried to combat the new industry by burdens of taxation and bothersome regulation but it prospered.

Although the city of Sheffield fostered the production of nearly all the Plate made in England for many years, very few pieces can be found in homes or collections there today. Most of the articles made were marketed in the larger cities and in foreign countries.

The first pieces of Sheffield Plate produced were probably purchased by royalty and families of wealth, as evidenced by the number of old pieces found today bearing original crests and coats of arms. It is for this reason that pieces have survived until today in such fine condition, for it was necessary to plate the articles made with an increasing amount of silver, in order that they might not be ruined by the inscriptions and arms being engraved upon them. The better quality pieces were invariably made with a circular, oval or shaped inset of pure silver, designed expressly for the purpose of cresting. As the industry grew and pieces could be produced for lower prices, the so-called middle class families quickly purchased articles for domestic use and the industry enlarged rapidly.

Plate was produced in foreign countries as well, but the English craftsmen so far excelled their neighbors in workmanship and originality, that they received more than 90% of the business. Ireland was one of the largest consumers of Sheffield Plate and today many outstanding collections are to be found in Dublin and other important cities, though there is no evidence of Irish plating.

During the first twenty years of Sheffield Plating, many beautiful articles were produced, which in design and workmanship often equalled the originals in solid silver. The first manufacturers of Plate quickly sensing the opportunities for deception, impressed hallmarks similar to those on silver articles. Examples showing these are extremely rare. The silver manufacturers immediately protested to the Guild, and the hallmarking of Sheffield Plate was forbidden. But in 1773 Sheffield was granted its own assay office and in 1784 smiths were allowed the privilege of using a maker's mark of their own, providing it had been approved by the Guild.

The history of Sheffield Plating may be divided into two periods. During the years from 1750 to 1780, pieces were made of entirely different style from those which followed in the later period. It is not rare to find many embossed objects, for the original manufacturers knew that with a wealth of design and ornamentation they could easily conceal those defects which so often appeared on the earliest pieces of Plate. This was due solely to their inability to turn out a perfect product, for the corresponding pieces produced in solid silver of that period, were of a much simpler style. But as the years progressed, the ability of the platers reached a higher degree, and for ten years or so delicately pierced objects were made. These, while not so graceful as the contemporary pieces in solid silver, met with much favor. During the first period which might be called probationary, Dish Rings, Baskets, Cups and Covers, Water Jugs, Epergnes, Cream Pails, etc., were produced. And it is easy to recognize pieces from this period by their lack of applied borders, and silver rims. It is practically impossible to find pieces from the first period in fine condition, for the process of plating whereby the silver would not wear through to the copper, had not yet been perfected.

From 1780 until 1820 the finest Sheffield Plate was produced in large quantities. By this time, the majority of leading cutlers in Sheffield had begun to manufacture Plate, and the industry was at its height. With the advent of the Adam Brothers in England, the demand for pieces of extreme simplicity was so pronounced it influenced the designs of Sheffield Plate objects. Many important pieces such as Tea Services, Cruets, Candelabra, Trays and various other household appointments were manufactured in quantity for the first time. As the years passed, the influence of the master silversmiths in vogue in England at the time caused the designs and shapes of Sheffield Plate objects to follow in the footsteps of their creations.

During this, the second period, we find the introduction of a white metal known as German silver, first used as a base. This new process was much favored, as the lasting qualities of Sheffield Plate objects were doubled. This new base would not show through when the silver was worn off, as did the copper. However, German silver was not fully accepted until about 1835. It derived its name from a Mr. Guitike of Berlin, who came over to Sheffield with the first examples of this new compound of nickel, copper, and zinc. The metal itself is of Chinese origin, and was used for centuries in the East before its introduction into England from Germany. The first English smith to avail himself of the new base product was Samuel Roberts. In 1830 he applied for a patent to plate silver on a German silver base.

The process of Sheffield Plating was definitely terminated in 1838, in which year electroplating was discovered by Elkington. Actually, the term Sheffield Plate was the name applied to articles made of copper and coated with silver by fusion. It is not to be confused with the modern silver plate as produced today by means of electrolysis.

Sheffield Plate from the collector's viewpoint, presents an admirable field of endeavor, for as yet prices have not risen to the heights commanded by solid silver articles. However, when one considers the limited supply available and the short period in which it was produced, it seems probable that as time goes on, prices will reach those paid for solid silver articles of similar date. In the past five years, the values of Old Sheffield Plate have doubled, and the farseeing buyer of today will guard carefully those pieces he is fortunate to possess today.

The buyer of Sheffield Plate must be a careful and critical purchaser, as the markets are flooded with semi-old and reproduction pieces that are represented to be genuine. Many brand new pieces are being made now with silver edges and tinned backs that at first seem to be Sheffield Plate. But the connoisseur may detect the fraud mainly by the color of the silver, as the old pieces have a bluish tinge caused by the use of alloy, while pieces that have been electroplated are much whiter. Old Sheffield Plate like old silver should be purchased only from reliable dealers, for even connoisseurs are often misled. Many pieces have worn through over a period of years, and have been replated in order to increase their salability. These pieces should be definitely avoided, as any repairing or replating done to an old piece destroys its value as an original.

XVIII

SILVERSMITHING IN AMERICA

IN direct contrast to silversmithing in England and Europe, the trade in America at the beginning was far from profitable. The early New Englanders were hardy people facing arduous tasks in their struggle for existence and they had little use for the luxury of ornamental silver. At no time was any attempt made to imitate the magnificent baronial silver of England and only pieces for particular use were produced. However, the market was considerably bolstered by the needs of the churches. The Pilgrims of course, were very religious and took great pride in their houses of worship so that much of the early American fine plate was for church use.

It was natural that the first pieces should be reproductions of English pieces which the Colonists had brought with them and from this start a natural evolution took place along the lines of the development of the character of the people.

The simplicity and austerity of their lives caused them to prefer in all things purity of form and a fine sense of proportion to elaboration and bulk. This is true of colonial architecture and furniture as well as of silver.

Much of this early American silver was made in New England but New York and Philadelphia were other important centers of silversmithing. Paralleling the English influence on New England silver, New York silver clearly bore a Dutch influence. Whatever there was of Southern silver perished during the Civil War.

In New England, Newburyport harbored some silversmiths but the city of Boston was the real center for the trade in America. It had the advantage of the first start and was the home of the first known American silversmith.

Boston had built up a flourishing trade with England and the colonial possessions in the West Indies. It was the haven of the wealth and the social life of early America and it was quite natural that the greatest market should harbor also the greatest center of production. It is worthy of note that almost no fraudulent practices prevailed among the colonial silversmiths. Also, living conditions being very stable, very little of the plate was destroyed. Practically the only New England pieces that were melted down were those which were in the hands of Southern families during the Civil War.

An Englishman, John Hull, is generally conceded to be the earliest silversmith in America. He was appointed the first master of the first mint in America. This mint was established in Boston in 1652 by the general court of Massachusetts which disregarded the decision of the higher court in London. Colonists had experienced excessive difficulty in securing a sufficient supply of money to carry on local trade. Their complaints and agitation resulted in this decision of the court which in later years was frequently cited as being a deed of defiance against the Crown.

The Colonists had to do with paper currency and the instability of value of this currency stimulated the demand for silver which was a far better investment than paper money of uncertain value. With this stimulated demand, the establishment of the mint and the availability of English and Scotch artisans who had studied the trade abroad, the craft of silversmithing flowered and produced many outstanding silversmiths and a wealth of fine silverware.

The majority of pieces are a vivid reminder of the fact that early Americans did indulge in tippling. Beer and hard liquor accompanied the Pilgrims from England. No business transaction was consummated, no marriage celebrated and no funeral ceremony performed without the company ot spirits. This furthered the production of silver, and tankards, mugs and other drinking accessories are numbered among the best efforts of the Colonial silversmiths. However, the earliest domestic utensil was the spoon, the shape of which underwent many changes from the early "Puritan" types to the early 19th century "Fiddleback." Tea and coffee pots were unknown until the end of the 17th century and few are found antedating 1750. Previous to this though, spout cups are known which were copied from early Chinese models and were undoubtedly the forerunners of tea pots.

Practically the only form of decoration used by American silversmiths was engraving. Chasing and gadrooning are rarely found. The craft flourished until about 1840 when the factories with their machinery for stamping and spinning silver came into general use and the silversmith as a craftsman disappeared.

Many of the early smiths held important civic positions in the community and were generally men of good financial standing. Among the outstanding men who developed the silver trade from its infancy were Jeremiah Dummer, John Coney, John Edwards, and Edward Winslow. They created new styles and pieces, and their fame as superior craftsmen is indelibly associated with Colonial silversmithing. As time went on, the trade became more or less concentrated in the hands of three families: the Burts, the Hurds, and the Reveres. John Burt came to Boston as a young man and was enormously successful, as evidenced by the great value of his inventory. Two sons, Samuel and Benjamin, succeeded him in business, and carried on the traditions of the father in creating many splendid examples. Jacob Hurd, well-known for his military service, enjoyed a brisk business and was finally succeeded by his son, Nathaniel, who eventually became more famous as an engraver of copper plates than as a silversmith.

The most famous American silversmith was Paul Revere, whose works are cherished for their exquisite beauty as well as for the historic association connected with this patriot. His father, originally of French birth, migrated to America where he was apprenticed to John Coney. In 1723, he went into business for himself in Boston, and was so successful that he was able to support a wife and a family of twelve children. Young Paul entered his father's shop at the age of 19, and in the few years that he was connected there, acquired sufficient knowledge and acumen successfully to carry on the business which came to him with the death of his father. Paul Revere, jr., developed great ability as an engraver, which is evidenced by the beautiful crests and armorial designs which adorned many of his pieces. This training enabled him to venture into the realm of copper plating, and eventually this talent caused a great deal of trouble to the Colonies. He frequently published political cartoons in which he derided the British Ministry and these caused no little consternation on the part of the English authorities. One of the most famous pieces of American silver is the magnificent punch bowl ordered by the "Fifteen Sons of Liberty." In this work, Revere reached a degree of excellence rarely attained by any silversmith. The inscription on the side of the bowl is plain-spoken and clearly indicated the feelings of the community at this time: "To the Memory of the Glorious NINETY-TWO Members of the Honorable House of Representatives of the Massachusetts Bay, who, undaunted by the insolent Menaces of Villains in Power, from a strict Regard to Conscience and the LIBERTIES of their Constituents, on the 30th day of June, 1768, voted NOT TO RESCIND."

It has always been difficult to distinguish between the wares of Paul Revere, Sr., and his illustrious son, because in many instances the same maker's marks were used by both.

The Federal, Colonial and state governments did not regulate the craft, set up standards or require date letters. But New York and

Boston each had Societies or Guilds by which the silversmiths themselves regulated their craft and probably other cities also had similar organizations. Baltimore had an assay office with careful supervision by elected silversmiths.

Marks on American silverware consist of the maker's mark which is almost invariably the initials or full name of the maker and occasionally a standard mark. No date letters were used and the dates of pieces can be determined only by other factors, such as engraving, style, etc.

In the collection of American silver one must be careful accurately to identify makers' marks because in many instances English and Irish pieces are misrepresented as American by the removal of all marks except the makers' marks.

SILVERSMITHING IN EUROPE

AN extensive study of European silver reveals one similarly striking fact with regard to nearly all countries; very little of the early plate remains, even though silversmithing on the continent may be traced back as early as the fifth century. The continual struggle for power and existence, plus the dire need for money caused many art treasures to be consigned to the melting pot. Again, the fact that so much of the early plate was made for use in the churches which were in constant fear of destruction, made it necessary to bury a great deal of the silver in the ground for preservation. Sometimes these pieces were not excavated or brought to light for centuries. However, the amount that has been found in this way is so minute compared to the great quantities that were buried, that one stops to wonder why so much more has not been discovered. The book records of the various townships speak of the large quantities of plate made, and yet very little remains to be viewed today.

Unfortunately, there is but little data available regarding the earliest pieces. This is due to the fact that only a few records have survived, and those that have are generally in such a state of decay that they are practically illegible. Although only a little early plate may now be seen in museums, it definitely proves that many magnificent pieces were wrought as early as the eighth century.

SILVERSMITHING IN AUSTRIA

Although it is known that several small towns in Austria had their goldsmiths, Vienna was by far the most important center wherein the art of the metal worker flourished. From the time of Rudolph IV, this city was the permanent residence of the German emperors, and Court Goldsmiths were appointed. It was thought that these smiths were exempt from guild regulations, and consequently, were not compelled to hallmark their wares. Therefore many pieces which were thought to be of Viennese origin cannot be definitely so assigned.

Wenzel Jamnitzer, one of the most famous goldsmiths of the sixteenth century was born in Vienna, but migrated to Nuremberg in 1534. It is here that he built up his reputation for excellent craftsmanship. Many other great silversmiths were apprenticed in

Vienna and surrounding cities, but for the most part they produced their best work in other countries. A few Austrian silversmiths who achieved recognition in their native country are known, including Erhard Efferdinger, identified from his important Gothic monstrance made in 1524, and Marx Kornblum, whose fame results from a few specimens of enamel and metal combination.

Vienna developed rapidly as the social center of the country, particularly during the brilliant reigns of Charles VI (1712-1740) and Maria Theresa (1740-1780). That period brought work that was definitely under the influence of the French craftsmen, as is proved by the many pieces in the Louis XIV style. A specific example of this work is seen in the magnificent gold toilet services made for the Empress by Anton Mathias Domanek. During the eighteenth century a taste for the pieces of English design was noted by the advertisements of a few London goldsmiths in Austria who carried on an enjoyable and rather brisk trade.

SILVERSMITHING IN THE BALTIC STATES

There is definite proof that plate was wrought for several centuries in the Baltic States. But Reval, the capital of Esthonia, and Riga, the capital of Latvia, were the only towns of importance where gold and silver were worked. Hans Ryssenback, who worked in the last quarter of the 15th century, achieved the greatest prominence as a goldsmith. Although it is supposed that many workers resided in Riga during the sixteenth century, only two names have descended to the present time; Hans Urma and Thomas Smallde. Silver made in Riga is easily distinguished from that made elsewhere in the Baltic States because Riga used a town mark as early as the sixteenth century.

No secular plate has survived from Finland although goldsmiths worked there in medieval times. The national museum at Helsingfors has a few pieces of plate from the late eighteenth century which prove the charming quality of the work of the Finnish silversmiths.

SILVERSMITHING IN BELGIUM

At the beginning of the sixteenth century, Antwerp was at the height of its commercial prosperity. Naturally, it was invaded by many of the greatest artists and an enormous quantity of plate was produced there. However, by the end of the seventeenth century, the era of vast wealth was over and Belgium fell victim to a prolonged depression. During the period of 1466 to 1695, many important pieces were created, and as many of the early records are still available, the student of Belgian silver is enabled to get a clear insight to the workings of the smiths and their craft.

Although Antwerp was the center of prosperity, the city of Bruges was by far the most important as the center of artistic activity. Flemish art reached its zenith during the reign of Charles the Bold when many of the world's most famous craftsmen worked in Bruges, but none of the splendid secular plate for which the Flemish goldsmiths were noted remains today. However, some pieces used by the church for daily and festival services have been preserved.

Although there was no definite legislation with regard to silver previous to 1814, many of the early makers used date letters, which have been an invaluable aid in tracing the exact year in which a particular piece was made. Silver in Belgium was made in two qualities; that of 900 fine being shown by the block letter "A" in an irregular shield, and that of 800 fine being denoted by the same letter in a square shield.

It is interesting to note that many of the early Flemish pictures depict objects of silver, and from them we have gleaned much knowledge. In the National Gallery of London hangs the world-famous picture "Taste" done so beautifully by Gonzales Cozues in 1618. The picture shows a cylindrical caster, definitely proving that this article was known in Flanders earlier than in England.

In the city of Antwerp there was one outstanding silversmith, called Hans of Antwerp, but as his maker's mark has never been positively identified, not one actual piece can be said to have been definitely wrought by him.

As early as the fifteenth century, a guild of goldsmiths was organized in Ghent, and this is the earliest note of any such association in Belgium. An outstanding master in this romantic city was Corneille de Bont, who worked in the 15th century.

Many other cities in Belgium produced silver and gold objects at an early date, and among them were the towns of Mons, Liege, and Tournai.

CZECHOSLOVAKIA

The city of Prague was outstanding as the center of art in Czechoslovakia. Under the encouragement and fostering of Premysl Otakar II, the "gold king of the thirteenth century," the art of the silversmith and goldsmith flourished to a high degree. Even to the present time many pieces have been preserved which are recognized as the work of masters, and from which many later artists on the continent copied their designs. However, the silversmiths of Prague were themselves influenced by craftsmen of foreign lands.

Prague was the center for the carving of semi-precious stones and beautiful ornaments and many of these were surmounted by bands of magnificently chased gold and silver. They reveal the highest degree of workmanship, and a limited number of specimens may be seen today in museums.

The only other city in Czechoslovakia noted as a center for goldsmithing, was Olomuc, known today as Olmutz. Pieces have been traced from here as early as 1575, as the workers registered their marks with a town corporation. Although it is definitely known that many smiths wrought their wares previous to this time, no definite marks or pieces are available.

SILVERSMITHING IN DENMARK

No Scandinavian silver dated previous to the thirteenth century has survived, although pieces were made as early as the eighth century. The demand was mostly for pieces of practical use and so artists from other European countries did not settle there to work. The creators of luxurious silver from other countries could find no ready market for their wares in Denmark, and for this reason the majority of articles found pertain to the necessities of life. Much data regarding the life of the silversmith has been obtained from early records, and as early as 1685 the first ordinances governing the production of silver were introduced. During the Thirty Years War vast quantities of plate were buried in the earth for protection against invading enemies, and only recently have numerous pieces been found, thus making the present day collection of early Danish silver more comprehensive.

A distinctly Danish article was the drinking horn. These horns, originally made of whalebone or some other hardy substance by the early settlers in Iceland, were introduced by fur traders and travellers coming to Denmark to purchase their winter supplies. The Danish silversmiths mounted these horns with bands of plain silver, and an object which had theretofore been purely useful became ornamental.

Shortly after the inauguration of horns and other silver drinking vessels, the demand for pieces of more florid taste is noted. From this time silver was executed only of a heavily embossed nature, as the Danish smiths did not possess the skill necessary to indulge in flat chasing. Therefore, Danish silver with contemporary chasing dated prior to 1700 is most valuable. Perhaps ninety per cent of all silver made in Denmark was wrought into drinking vessels, and extravagant ornaments had little vogue.

The name of Magnus Berg is outstanding, as he gained the greatest recognition throughout Europe in his special field of beautifully carved ivory pieces.

Copenhagen was the center of silversmithing in Denmark and pieces from there bear the town mark "in an ellipse, three towers or minarets above the date." The only other town in Denmark where silver was produced was Odense which registered the town mark of "a fleur-de-lys, joined to two spreading leaves in an ellipse."

SILVERSMITHING IN FRANCE

The earliest known French silver dates back to the time of the Roman invasion when silver and gold were used as decorations on horsetrappings. From 588 to 659 a silversmith known as St. Eloi did more to promote the industry than any other man and he is the patron saint of the French goldsmiths. He organized the first guild and secured from the French government permission for this organization to be its own lawmaking body with full privileges. In no other country in the world was a guild formed as early as in France. The French were the first in Europe by several centuries fully to understand and accept the craft of precious metal working. At the time of St. Eloi the craft was practiced only by the priesthood, and it was not until the beginning of the twelfth century that the craft of silversmithing was secularized.

The first statute that required the use of a town mark was enacted in 1275. And in 1313 the first punch of guarantee was introduced, and was denoted by a fleur de lys in a lozenge. The use of the date letter in conjunction with the town mark was introduced in 1416.

With the introduction of the town mark, definite importance was accorded to the industry. When in 1313 the guarantee mark was used, plus the date letter one hundred years later, the actual system of hallmarking silver in France was established. The mark of guarantee was very similar to that used in other countries to denote the actual fine silver content of a piece. During the reign of Louis XII a new office of Farmer of the Reserve was created. This appointee was required to impress his mark next to the maker's mark to show that duty had been charged on the piece. Then, the law required that this Farmer stamp another symbol as proof of the payment of duty. These peculiar punches were used until the duty was abolished. In 1797 the tax was reimposed, but was levied at the time of the imposition of the first stamp, so the discharge mark was eliminated. Inasmuch as the standard of the silver was proved by the same mark, French silver from that date on was only impressed with the symbol of the maker, the town mark and the duty mark.

A splendid piece of early French silver extant today is the beautiful cup of the Kings of France and England. Originally the work of French silversmiths, it was sent as a gift to the King of England, and later returned to France. It was then sent to Spain but was finally shipped to England where it reposes today in the British Museum. It depicts the life of St. Agnes, and is worked in beautifully executed relief.

In recent times the outstanding name in French silver history is that of Odiot who is credited with being the creator of the style known as Empire. Rivalled in excellence only by the Brothers Adam in England, Odiot's designs spread like wildfire throughout Europe and few styles of any period have enjoyed the lasting compliment as did the Empire. Royalty throughout Europe commissioned Odiot to make magnificent services, and much of his silver is known today.

The finest collections of French plate are not to be found in France. The Royalty of Europe and England, eager to own these fine treasures, collected them carefully, and today the most comprehensive collection of French silver in the world is in the possession of Great Britain's Royal family. French silver is ardently sought after by collectors and its value is great. The pieces are beautifully made, finely proportioned and delicately designed. France is second only to England in the excellence of its silversmithing.

SILVERSMITHING IN GERMANY

Today in Germany there is a wealth of early ecclesiastical plate to be seen, dating back to the twelfth century. Although this nation produced gold and silver objects as early as the fifth century, few of these very early efforts have survived. Among the first known pieces of secular plate are the Ewer of Goslin produced in 1477, and the celebrated Luneburg Horn of silver and ivory, made in 1486. These two historical works of art exemplify the characteristic traits of the German silversmith, wherein a wealth of detail and almost an over-profusion of ornamentation are to be observed. Hardly ever is a definite note of simplicity found, and this includes the silver made in Germany today. The influence of the Renaissance is apparent in the goldsmith's art earlier than in any other craft.

This influence was introduced in 1490, and was firmly established by 1520.

The inheritance by the present generation of a great quantity of old German silver can be laid to the fact that this country suffered practically no great losses of plate. The only noticeable disappearance occurred during the Thirty Years War, when hundreds of magnificent pieces were the target for those who invaded to pillage and plunder.

Until 1884, all legislation governing the production of silver was enacted by each separate state of the empire, and hundreds of minor statutes were passed. It is almost impossible to enumerate the individual ordinances, as over five score towns were producing silver in Germany.

Augsburg and Nuremberg were the chief centers of silversmithing. Here the craft of the goldsmith was stimulated by the opulence of the people, as well as by the patronage of ecclesiastics, princes and nobles. The town mark used for Augsburg was "a pineapple erect." Date letters were impressed which have been most helpful in aiding the collector to arrange a chronological list of pieces.

The city of Nuremberg was second only to Augsburg in the quantities of plate produced, and its silver wares were denoted by the letter "N." At first a capital Roman "N" was used, and during the nineteenth century a capital script "N" in a circle was substituted. After 1760 date letters are noted.

Silver in Germany was made of many different standards and each piece was registered and marked accordingly. Today most of the silver manufactured is 800 fine, which is a lesser degree than our own or the English sterling.

Gold and silver tipped horns were used for drinking as early as the days of Caesar. In the years that followed, these are closely identified with the work of the German silversmiths who took the horns of the bison or ulus for these objects. Later on many of the early specimens were bound with silver worked in beautiful detail.

Beakers were very popular during the sixteenth, seventeenth and eighteenth centuries when they were employed as guild cups. Many examples depict Scriptural and classical scenes in high relief.

Among the most unusual articles produced were the ivory, stoneware, amber, and serpentine tankards, invariably mounted with silver. The use of the metal wherever possible clearly proves the definite flair for silver in the Reich.

Double cups, as well as hunting cups in sets of from six to twenty were also made. The double cups with their familiar bosses are distinctly German and were made nowhere else in Europe. They served as household objects as well as things of beauty, for the smaller tops were reserved exclusively for the ladies of the house, while the master consumed his fill from the three-quarter bottoms. These pieces are often referred to as bridal cups, and were the subject of much wagering and amusement in their usage.

Silver objects of every known description are credited to German smiths during the seventeenth and eighteenth centuries. Germany stands alone as the only country in Europe where pieces for purely decorative purposes were produced. The silversmiths frequently modeled animals of massive proportion and it is not unusual to find a replica of a life sized eagle or a small beast. Nautilus shells and ostrich cups met with great favor in Germany, and a few examples which have been carefully preserved may be seen today. Tea services, vases, candelabra, etc., are all products of this age of silversmithing, and probably more plate was exported from Germany than from all the rest of Europe.

In the study of silversmithing in Nuremberg, the name of Wenzel Jamnitzer is preeminent. Often called the Cellini of Germany, he migrated from Vienna in 1534, and continued to produce pieces of rare quality until his death in 1585. He was one of five sons, each of whom lived to create a reputation in the field of art. Jamnitzer often specialized in the production of silver pieces combined with fine enamel, and his works were purchased by collectors throughout Europe. Today, if an example of his work is sold in the open market, the true appreciation of his ability is found in the huge prices realized.

SILVERSMITHING IN HUNGARY

Judging from the number of magnificent vessels unearthed from graves, it is likely that silver was made in Hungary as early as the Middle Ages. The records also tell of rich endowments of plate given to wealthy brides of the day. However, as most of that has perished, the real history of silversmithing in Hungary may be said to start about 1600. As early as the thirteenth century, goldsmiths held important positions in the realm of power, and under the reign of the Anjou kings, they were even granted arms of their own. Today the churches are filled with objects of costly precious metals, showing the early appreciation of beautiful things in Hungary. The goldsmiths' guilds which were formed in each town greatly encouraged the craft, and today the museums are rich in the art that was produced many centuries before.

As evidenced almost everywhere, drinking articles were made in great profusion. However, the most proficient workmen specialized in the production of unusual enamel and gold pieces often combined with colored crystal. Some of the later pieces have been preserved and a visit to the churches in Hungary will quickly prove the high quality of this work.

Goldsmiths were greatly influenced in their designs by the craftsmen of surrounding countries. In the sixteenth century the German trend is noticed, while in Transylvania the silversmiths who were in constant touch with the East displayed definite traits of Oriental artistry. In the South, a definite Turkish manner is found, which combined with the above gives a varied trend in design to the silver of Hungary.

Silver legislation in Hungary commenced at the beginning of the sixteenth century when an ordinance decreed that no maker should sell an unmarked piece. Not only was it necessary for each article to be impressed with the maker's private mark, but after being subjected to a test of quality, it had to be further marked by two fellow workers who would swear under oath as to the silver content. During the seventeenth and eighteenth centuries the hallmark regularly in use was "a castle with central tower, above the numeral 13 in ellipse or irregular outline." In 1836 the word "PESTH" was introduced, and followed in 1866 by the capital Roman "P" which served as a date letter.

SILVERSMITHING IN HOLLAND

Silver was not particularly in general use in Dutch households until about 1850, when a mild wave of prosperity allowed this extravagance. At this time, as in former days, Holland silversmiths specialized in the production of drinking vessels, ewers and basins and a little ecclesiastical plate. It is indeed strange though that tankards were rarely included among domestic pieces.

Early examples of Dutch silver fetch tremendous prices as very few specimens earlier than the fifteenth century have survived. Amsterdam was the center of silversmithing although examples of work are known from the smaller towns, such as Breda, Dakkum, The Hague, Haarlem, Hertagenbisch, Leeuwarden, Rotterdam, Utrecht and Zwolle.

Van Viamen stands out in Holland as the most prominent silversmith. He came from a family famed all over Europe for their accomplishments in art, and a number of beautiful pieces are attributed to this great craftsman. The only other name of prominence

Courtesy S. Wyler, Inc.

Dublin, 1822

TEA SET

Dublin, c. 1730

BOWL

Dublin, 1715

Courtesy S. Wyler, Inc.

PAIR OF BEAKERS

SUGAR   John Irish, Cork, 1750

JUG   Thos. Walker, Dublin, 1718

SALTS   J. Johnson, Dublin, 1⸻

PAIR OF CUPS   *Courtesy S. Wyler, Inc.*   Dublin, 1736, Robert Calder

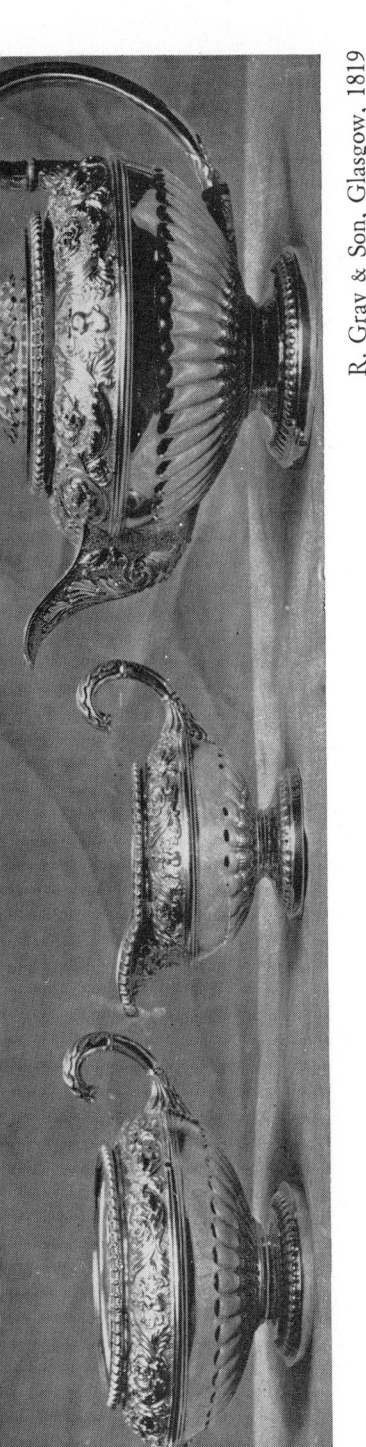

TEA SET   R. Gray & Son, Glasgow, 1819

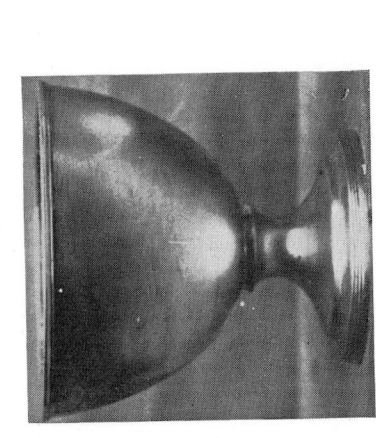

SALTS   J. McKay, Edinburgh, 1810

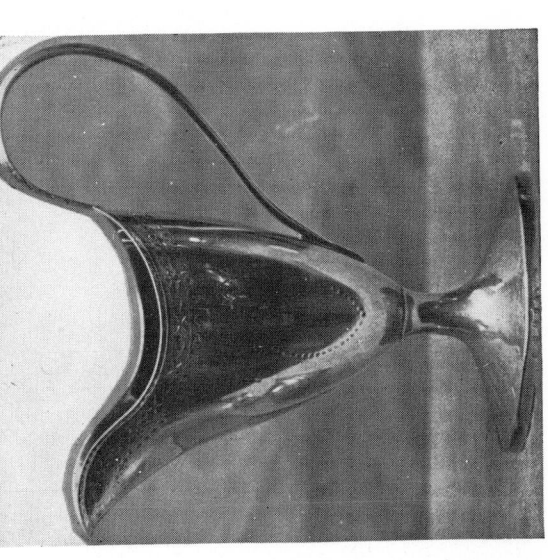

CREAM JUG   James Dempster, Edinburgh, 1790

SUGAR BOWL   Edinburgh, 1784

PAIR OF BEAKERS   Edinburgh, 1776

SHEFFIELD SUPPER DISH   Nathaniel Smith, 180

TEA POT   Paul Revere   Detroit Museum   *Courtesy James Graham, Jr.*

SUGAR BOWL AND CREAM JUG   Paul Revere, Boston   *Courtesy Metropolitan Museum of Art*

Myer Myers, New York, 1760

HEBREW CANDLESTICK

COFFEE POT   Made by F. T. Germain, Paris, (Louis XV) for the King of Portugal

PEG TANKARD   Stavanger, 1812

ITALIAN   16th Centu

DANISH BEAKER   17th Cent.

SILVER-GILT CASKET by Vianen Flemish,
17th Century

PORTUGUESE PERFUME BURNER   18th Cent.

PORTUGUESE EWER AND BASIN   18th Centu

TOBACCO BOX

Amsterdam, 1796

CHALICE

Antwerp, 16th Century

ONE OF SET OF FOUR CANDLESTICKS REPRESENTING
FOUR CONTINENTS
Paris, 1790

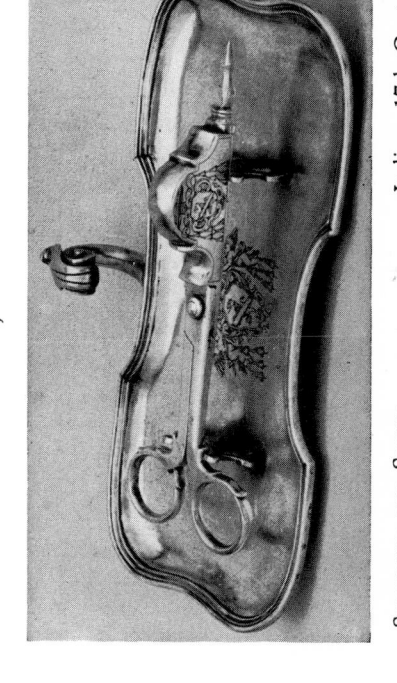

SNUFFERS AND STAND

Italian, 17th Century

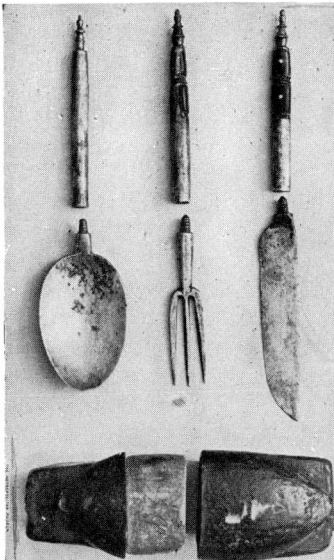

KNIFE, FORK, AND SPOON IN TRAVELING CASE
Spanish, 17th Century

STANDING CUP
Niels Jonson, Copenhagen, c. 1720

COVERED CUP   Fred Kandler, London, 1778

CANDELABRA SUITE   Matthew Boulton, c. 1800

OLD SHEFFIELD SOUP TUREEN   c. 1790   *Courtesy Marshall Field & Co.*

Matthew Boulton, c. 1800

Venison Dish

c. 1785, Coll. Lord Amherst

Sheffield Kettle

c. 1810

OLD SHEFFIELD GLOBE INK STAND   c. 1770

SHEFFIELD WINE COOLER ON PLATEAU

c. 1760

RARE SHEFFIELD GOBLET

c. 1765

RARE SHEFFIELD MACE

OLD SHEFFIELD EPERGNE AND PLATEAU   c. 1810   *Courtesy S. Wyler, Inc.*

CASTER
John Coney, Boston

TEAPOT

Josiah Austin, Charlestown

PLATE

Keonraet Ten Eyck, Albany, 1716

SNUFFER
Cornelius Kierstaede, N.Y.

CANDLESTICKS   Jacob Hurd, Boston, 1702-1758   *Courtesy Metropolitan Museum of A*

SAUCE BOAT   Joseph Richardson, Philadelphia   *Courtesy Metropolitan Museum of*

associated with early Dutch silver is that of Johans Lutma, who was the devoted friend of the great Rembrandt. His portrait done by this celebrated artist is well known.

The town mark used by the city of Amsterdam was "a narrow shield, charged with three saltires in pale, and surmounted by an arch bow." The silver standard was indicated by the "head of Perseus," with the letter "a" on his cap, in a circle. All Holland silver bore the duty mark as well as the stamp of the maker.

SILVERSMITHING IN ITALY

No country in all of Europe was richer in ecclesiastical plate than Italy, but in direct contrast it suffered the greatest losses in secular plate. This was not alone due to the results of conflict and invasion but also to intentional destruction. Many of the later artists, lacking a sufficient quantity of metal were forced to remake earlier pieces.

The Renaissance began and had its first flowering in Italy. The city of Florence was the world's center of art, and students from all over the continent came there to be apprenticed. They had to submit a finished work as an example of their skill, and if accepted, they were then known as full-fledged masters. Some of the most beautiful gold and silver work in the world was made in Italy at this time and goldsmithing was raised to a higher standard than ever known before. Royalty from all of Europe sent to Italy for services to be made to special order, and since time was not an important element, the most magnificent results were achieved. As time progressed, the love of luxury, the desire for elegance and splendor so increased that one finds very few pieces of church plate during the sixteenth century. Rather, the finished articles were pieces of wondrous beauty which graced the halls of those so well able to afford extravagances. Much work in the combination of gold and crystal was produced and the most noted of workers who specialized in this field was Valerio Belli, 1468 to 1546. Of course, the most famous goldsmith of all time—Benvenuto Cellini was an Italian. Very rarely has any artist in his field achieved such a high degree of perfection as was displayed in the works of Cellini. Unfortunately less than a dozen pieces of his work exist today, but it is significant that articles wrought by him command higher prices than those of any other silversmith in the world, regardless of date.

Under the pontificate of Nicholas V, 1447 to 1455, the patronage of the arts really commenced, yet, unfortunately, nothing of the work of the period remains. A decided flair for the improvement of original pieces caused the destruction of many. Many of the world's famous painters and sculptors occasionally tried their hands at goldsmithing, but nothing remains of their efforts.

The first goldsmiths' association in Italy is recorded as early as 1035, while in 1314 the city of Florence introduced legislation protecting the industry. Prior to the consolidation of the numerous small Italian states, each section used its own particular markings. The general laws passed which definitely legalized the production of silver in Italy were not introduced and adopted until 1873.

SILVERSMITHING IN NORWAY

The only silver known in Norway prior to 1400 consisted of a few odd pieces of jewelry and seals, and an occasional silver tipped drinking horn. However, from the year 1425, the craft assumed a real importance and until the end of the fifteenth century it was recognized as a major industry among the arts. The two outstanding centers of silversmithing were Christiania and Bergen, the latter being of far greater importance. A few prominent silversmiths are known from each of these places, from examples of their work which have survived. In Christiania, Romanus Moller and Berendt Platt are noteworthy as the two silversmiths who specialized in the production of pieces reproduced along the styles of the English masters. These pieces are unusual for their extreme simplicity, as most of the early Norwegian silver was rather ornate. In Bergen, the most proficient craftsmen known were Martin Finchenberger and Albert Grath.

The silversmith in Norway specialized for the most part in the production of drinking accessories. Beakers of typical Scandinavian design were made in great profusion and were invariably modeled after the Danish pieces made from horn years previously. Of extreme interest to the student of Norwegian silver is a small two-handled bowl called the "oreskall." This article was made exclusively in Norway and only rarely are examples obtainable. Tankards were by far the most popular pieces fashioned from silver. However, the majority of them were of wood, as only a limited number of inhabitants were wealthy enough to indulge in the luxury of silver. This situation is comparable to the one existing in Scotland, when silver quaiches were made for the prosperous and wooden ones for the peasants.

The city of Stavanger was also a thriving silver center after 1593. Here there was a rather unusual procedure in regard to the legislation on silver. Anders Hansen, a local worker built up a reputation as the outstanding silversmith of the town and ruled the industry for years. However, he accomplished this by political influence, rather than by dint of the quality of the work he produced. In this way he was able to create a monopoly, and in 1789, the records list his name as the only smith known in Stavanger. He even went so far as to disallow the practicing of any other silversmith in the town. He himself introduced the fraudulent practice of impressing his maker's mark on all pieces brought to his shop for repair. The competition offered by Jacob Campbell, a smith who finally secured permission to work in Stavanger, caused the exposure of Hansen.

All Norwegian silver was required to be marked with a maker's mark and a standard stamp. The town mark for Bergen, by far the most flourishing silver center of Norway, was a "mosque or domed building, above seven pellets, in outline."

SILVERSMITHING IN POLAND

The general destruction of art in Poland was deplorable, particularly after the invasions of the Mongols in 1241, 1259, and again in 1287. They effected the wholesale slaughter of the efforts of the earliest Polish artists, to the extent that practically no pieces remain. Poland was producing beautiful silver as early as the year 1000, but, unfortunately, all that has been left to posterity are two silver chalices. One of these bears the date 1166, and is considered to be the finest example of early silver known today. For many years after the Mongolian invasions, art suffered a great depression and very few efforts in any artistic direction were attempted. However, under Casimir the Great, the country again evinced a new interest in silversmithing and many unusual statues and reliquaries were made. The forms of monstrances made during the fifteenth century were dominated by the styles of the Gothic architecture, and this lack of originality is found throughout Polish smithing. Until the middle of the fifteenth century, Bohemian influences are noted, but from that time on the characteristics of the Nuremberg craftsmen were predominant. The dynastic connection between Hungary and Poland may be quickly detected in the similarity of their art, and often when pieces of unmarked silver appeared, it was impossible to distinguish the country of origin.

The Stwasz family in Poland exerted great influence on the decoration of ecclesiastical and secular plate, and their ability as masters of their art was finally recognized when they were appointed as goldsmiths to the Polish court. Krakow, the old capital of Poland, attracted many rich merchants and it became widely known as an important gem center. This naturally caused great prosperity among those displaying artistic talents, and it was in this city that Polish silversmithing reached its greatest heights. Nearly all the plate remaining from these times is ecclesiastical as only those pieces stored in churches escaped destruction in the horrible siege of the city of Krakow in 1655 by the Swedes. Lemberg and Vilna are also known as towns where silver was produced, but neither attained the fame of Krakow. Throughout the political history of Poland and its ever-changing government, the influence of foreign artists on the designs in silversmithing is recognized.

SILVERSMITHING IN PORTUGAL

After the rise of Portugal in the fifteenth century to one of the foremost colonizing powers in Europe, a marked development in the taste of the people is noted. The demand for personal luxuries grew by leaps and bounds and before long a ready market for fine gold and silver was established. Likewise, the churches benefited by this cultural ascent, and houses of worship were filled with beautiful pieces fashioned from costly metals. During the reign of Emanual I, the call for plate increased as Portugal enjoyed greater and greater wealth, and during this time some of the most magnificent objets d'art in all of Europe were produced.

During the Portuguese Empire, 1499-1580, social life in Lisbon is said to have equalled that of Rome. This Golden Age of silversmithing was accompanied by the most intensive appreciation of fine art in the history of the country. Shortly after this, a style of architecture, known as the Arte Manuelina, was introduced which influenced the work of the goldsmiths greatly. Unfortunately, this new trend lacked beauty and the pieces of plate can hardly be called artistic.

No native metal could be mined in Portugal so importation was the only means of supply. Eventually trading became more difficult and this resulted in a natural shortage of silver. As the metal became scarcer, pieces were made of a much thinner gauge, and their appearance also suffered. During the sixteenth century, Portuguese plate was prone to over-ornamentation and resembled the work of the Spanish smiths to such a degree that it was impossible to distinguish between the two in the absence of marks.

The beautiful creations of the two previous centuries were replaced by pieces which bore the influence of foreign silversmiths. However, in 1703, the date of the Methuen treaty with England, the styles of the British silversmiths were reproduced almost exclusively. In Lisbon and Oporto, the two main centers of silversmithing in Portugal, the demand for pieces in the English style progressed to the degree where many of the fraudulent workers punched English hallmarks on their wares.

During the reign of John V, 1706-1750, the most serious destruction of plate in the history of Portugal commenced. His extravagances led to enormous debts and he was forced to melt large quantities of plate to pay for these indulgences. In 1755, the earthquake and resulting fires completed the loss.

The earliest record of the legislation for silver in Lisbon is noted in 1460, while in Oporto the mention of assayers occurs as early as 1570. However, a complete system of hallmarking silver was not established in Portugal until the eighteenth century. The national mark used on gold and silver wares was "A capital Roman 'P' beneath a pellet in arched outline." In Lisbon the town mark adopted was "A capital Roman 'L' beneath a crown, in regular outline." Several other towns in Portugal are known for silversmithing and among these Beja, Broga, Setubal, and Evara are to be remembered.

SILVERSMITHING IN RUSSIA

The Russian art is said to date from the time of Vladimir, 956 to 1015. Although the names of no Russian silversmiths survived from the Middle Ages, that of the famous icon painter, Rublev, is remembered from this period. During the sixteenth and seventeenth centuries the splendor of the Czar's plate was the envy and talk of every visitor to the palace, although most of it was executed by foreign smiths. It was said that although the Russian silversmiths were great copyists they could not create originals. Therefore, most of the designs found in Russia were not the work of their own countrymen. The westernization of Russia by Peter the Great created new tastes in art, so that before long the majority of the typically domestic pieces were discarded. The introduction in 1700 of a system of compulsory hallmarking had a great effect on the industry, particularly in Moscow and St. Petersburg, which were the main silver production centers.

The Russian silversmiths created pieces for practical use which were to be found no place else in the world. The most conspicuous of these was the bratma, which was used as a toasting glass at funerals, for blessings, and at every imaginable function. Often the remains of the deceased were cremated, and the ashes put into the bratma to be buried in the grave. They were fashioned from gold, silver, or precious stones and no wealthy home in Russia was without one. Another typically Russian creation in silver was the kaush, which was a small boat shaped vessel with one handle, used for ladling daily drinks. A small brandy cup, known as a charka was also introduced about the year 1800. The discovery of a product known as niello caused great alteration in the general appearance of the silver pieces. Niello was a variety of black inlay enamel which was used on silver either as a form of decoration or as a means of lettering. The popularity of this alloy has never waned. It is still used at the present time.

Russia contributed the icon to the world of art. This was a beautiful painted piece depicting a Scriptural scene, surmounted by a casing of gold or silver. Icons were made in several styles varying from the rich ones encrusted with precious gems to the peasant icons mounted in copper or some other inexpensive metal.

Although Moscow and St. Petersburg are outstanding as silver centers, other places such as Kaluga, Kazan and Kiow, are known. The town marks used by the main cities are as follows:

Moscow—"A double-headed eagle displayed, holding in his dexter claw a sword, and in his sinister a ball, above the letters MOCK above B.A. in outline."

St. Petersburg—"A double-head eagle displayed, holding in his dexter claw a dagger and in his sinister an orb in outline."

SILVERSMITHING IN SPAIN

Conquest in the New World brought vast wealth to Spain, and again from 1556 to 1590, under the rule of Phillip II, the prosperity of the country increased. Phillip, who was one of the chief monarchs of Christendom, adorned the great Escorial with vast quantities of plate and finely jeweled objects, executed by the leading silversmiths of foreign countries as well as by Spanish craftsmen. Never before had the patronage of the goldsmith in Spain increased so materially. The glory of the Spanish Renaissance was surpassed only by Italy's. But this era, although the most scintillating in Spanish history, has left no traces of its magnificence, though ecclesiastical silver from this time has survived.

The defeat of the Armada in 1588 was a stirring blow to material prosperity, and the art of the goldsmith declined. With the accession to the throne of Phillip III, Spanish power began to wane, and the arts in general deteriorated to the lowest point in the history of the country. The practice of looting treasures of a country by invading enemies is evidenced by the amount of Spanish plate found today in France and England. The soldiers of those countries being sufficiently educated to appreciate fine art, realized that these pieces were more valuable in their original form than if melted down. It is interesting to note that during the eighteenth century, although the Spanish silversmiths were influenced by the influx of French art, the demand was great for typically English table appointments, and so we find cruets, inkstands, candelabra, and other articles of domestic plate made at this time.

In the study of Spanish silver notice must be taken of the huge monstrances used to decorate many of the fine buildings. These custodia, as they were termed in Spain, contained beautifully executed silver and gold statuettes and are of importance for the high quality of the work. Two of the outstanding examples known today were created by Enrique d'Arphe, one for Cordoba in 1513, and the other for Toledo in 1524. His son Antonia, greatly influenced by the style of the Renaissance, produced a most unusual type in 1544 at Santiago. Juan d'Arphe who was the best known of this illustrious family is remembered for the great and important custodia created at Valladolid.

Spanish silver from the fifteenth to the seventeenth century was prone to over-elaboration because the silversmiths worked to special order of the wealthy and noble classes.

Peculiar to Spanish silver history was a shallow dish with a short foot, the shape of which was derived from early Valencian pottery.

As early as the thirteenth century, silversmiths were working at Toledo, Saville, and Burgos, while in the fourteenth century the craft spread to Valencia, Valladolid, Guadalupe, Genoa, and other small towns. The most important center of silver production was Madrid, with Barcelona a close second in the quality and quantity of pieces produced. The filigree work closely related to the Spanish silversmiths was conceived in Barcelona, and work in this design was done later at Cordova and Salamanca. Very little data relative to early Spanish hallmarks is available and it is only through book records that have been preserved, that pieces can be accurately dated or identified.

SILVERSMITHING IN SWEDEN

Silversmithing in Sweden first achieved prominence as an art under the patronage of Charles X and Gustavus Adolphus. It was not until the seventeenth century that the smiths produced pieces of any great importance, and then most of them bear the mark of

German influence. Only the few pieces in filigree design are definitely Swedish. It has been very difficult to date the few early pieces which have survived, since no hallmarks were used until the seventeenth century. Pieces were reproduced from century to century, so one can only surmise the time of their creation. Among the most typically Swedish pieces produced were unusual bridal crowns of silver and gold which held great favor throughout the small villages.

The cities of Gothenburg and Stockholm were the only important centers of silversmithing. The mark adopted by the city of Stockholm was "a maiden's head, affronte, in irregular shield." In 1759 a state control mark which consisted of the arms of Sweden was adopted. This was represented by "three crowns, two and one, in ellipse or inverted trefoil."

SILVERSMITHING IN SWITZERLAND

Swiss domestic silver fell victim to the melting pot in time of war, as did the plate in nearly every other country in Europe. Unfortunately, there is no silver left today that illustrated the important art movement that occurred from 1430 to 1530. Drinking articles were produced here in great quantities as well as many other pieces directly copied from the work of the German silversmiths. Not only were German objects reproduced, but all pieces definitely show the Teutonic influence in design. In 1880 the control of silver was regulated by law, and pieces were made with either of the following standards: the standard of 875 fine was represented by a "bear rampant," while those made of the consistency of 800 bore the mark of a "hen contourne, in ellipse." Zurich, the most prosperous city in Switzerland, was easily the main center of silver production, although seventeen other towns were recorded.

Bear in mind that the marks must be exact. There is often great similarity between marks of widely differing times, places and makers. The marks must also be complete to insure certainty of identification.

FIRST, DETERMINE THE PLACE OF ORIGIN.

If you know this, refer below to the special instructions for that locality and then to the Tables of Hallmarks for that locality. But if you do not know the origin the following *probabilities* may be helpful.

LEOPARD'S HEAD, LEOPARD'S HEAD ERASED: London.

Other possibilities: Leopard's head erased also used by Provinces, 1697-1719. Also Chester used similar markings to London but Chester is noted chiefly for small pieces.

LION PASSANT: English.

THISTLE: Edinburgh.

HARP: Dublin.

FISH AND TREE: Glasgow.

ONE OR TWO MARKS ONLY: American.

Especially if the marks are names or initials. Possibly English Provincial, Scotch or Irish.

"STERLING"; Irish or American.

"COIN," "DOLLAR," "STANDARD," ETC.: American. Possibly Irish.

ORNATE CAPITAL LETTERS WITH CROWN OR FLEUR DE LIS: French.

HAND: Antwerp. Possibly Belfast.

SPREAD EAGLE: German though there are many other possibilities.

If the marks do not indicate the origin perhaps the character, style or workmanship of the piece may give a clue. If not, a process of elimination must be used.

IF YOU KNOW THAT THE ORIGIN OF THE PIECE IS

LONDON. Look for the date letter. Consult the "Marks on London Plate" tables and you will determine the year of manufacture. These tables will also indicate the standard and show what other marks were necessary. The remaining mark will be the maker's mark. Consult the "Index of English, Scotch and Irish Marks" and this will indicate the page on which the maker's mark is listed. Names will be shown for 1697 or later. But maker's names before 1697 cannot be identified though the marks can be verified. Maker's marks may also be found by consulting the "London Goldsmiths Marks" tables for a number of years before and after the date of the piece.

ENGLISH Provincial, Scotch or Irish. If town is known consult the tables for that locality to identify date letter. Then consult "Index of English, Scotch and Irish Marks" for the maker. If town is not known the maker's identification will probably indicate the town. Otherwise a process of elimination is necessary.

SHEFFIELD PLATE. Consult Tables.

AMERICAN. Consult tables which are alphabetically listed according to last names. If mark consists of initials the last letter probably is the initial of the last name.

FRENCH. Consult "French Hallmarks" tables which are arranged according to the character of the marks (Letters, Flowers, etc.)

GERMAN. Consult "German Marks" tables which are in three sections arranged alphabetically by towns (according to the character of the marks). This will give the number of the mark which will be identified in the "Index of German Marks." If you know the town, refer to the proper section. Otherwise, try each section until the mark is found.

OTHER COUNTRIES. Consult "Hallmarks of Other Countries Tables" (arranged according to the character of the marks). This will provide a number which will be identified in the "Index of Hallmarks of Other Countries."

	LEOPARD'S HEAD CROWNED.	DATE LETTER.		LEOPARD'S HEAD CROWNED.	DATE LETTER.		LEOPARD'S HEAD CROWNED.	DATE LETTER.		LEOPARD'S HEAD CROWNED.	DATE LETTER.	LION PASSANT. FROM 1544.
EDW. IV 1478-9			1498-9	(leopard's head)	𝖆	1518-9	(leopard's head)	𝕬	1538-9	(leopard's head)	A	
1479-80	(leopard's head)	𝕭	1499 1500	,,	𝖇	1519-20	(leopard's head)	𝕭	1539-40	(leopard's head)	B	
1480-1			1500-1	,,	𝖈	1520-1	,,	𝕮	1540-1	,,	C	
1481-2	(leopard's head)	𝕯	1501-2	,,	𝖉	1521-2	(leopard's head)	𝕯	1541-2	,,	D	
1482-3			1502-3			1522-3	,,	𝕰	1542-3			
RICH. III. 1483-4			1503-4	,,	𝖋	1523-4	,,	𝕱	1543-4	,,	F	
1484-5			1504-5	,,	𝖌	1524-5	,,	𝕲	1544-5	(leopard's head)	G	(lion)
HEN. VII. 1485-6	(leopard's head)	𝕳	1505-6			1525-6	,,	𝕳	1545-6	(leopard's head)	H	(lion)
1486-7			1506-7	(leopard's head)	𝖎	1526-7			1546-7	,,	I	,,
1487-8			1507-8	,,	𝕶𝕶	1527-8	,,	K	**EDW. VI.** 1547-8			
1488-9	(leopard's head)	𝕷	1508-9	(leopard's head)	𝖑	1528-9	,,	𝕷	1548-9	,,	L	(lion)
1489-90			**HEN. VIII** 1509-10	(leopard's head)	𝖒	1529-30			M	1549-50			M	,,
1490-1	,,	𝕹	1510-1	,,	𝖓	1530-1	,,	𝕹	1550-1	,,	N	(lion)
1491-2	(leopard's head)	𝕺	1511-2	,,	𝖔	1531-2	(leopard's head)	𝕺	1551-2	(leopard's head)	O	(lion)
1492-3			1512-3	,,	𝖕	1532-3	,,	P	1552-3	,,	P	(lion)
1493-4	,,	𝕼	1513-4	,,	𝖖	1533-4	,,	Q	**MARY.** 1553-4	,,	Q	,,
1494-5	,,	𝕽	1514-5	,,	𝖗	1534-5	,,	R	1554-5	,,	R	,,
1495-6			1515-6	(leopard's head)	𝖘	1535-6	,,	S	1555-6	,,	S	,,
1496-7	(leopard's head)	𝕿	1516-7	,,	𝖙	1536-7	,,	T	1556-7	,,	T	,,
1497-8			1517-8	,,	𝖚	1537-8	,,	V	1557-8	,,	V	(lion)

	LEOPARD'S HEAD CROWNED.	DATE LETTER.	LION PASSANT		LEOPARD'S HEAD CROWNED.	DATE LETTER.	LION PASSANT.		LEOPARD'S HEAD CROWNED	DATE LETTER	LION PASSANT
ELIZ. 1558-9	👑	a	🦁	1578-9	👑	A	🦁	1598-9	👑	A	🦁
1559-60	,,	b	,,	1579-80	,,	B	,,	1599 1600	,,	B	🦁
1560-1	,,	C	,,	1580-1	,,	C	,,	1600-1	,,	C	,,
1561-2	,,	d	🦁	1581-2	,,	D	,,	1601-2	,,	D	🦁
1562-3	👑	e	,,	1582-3	,,	E	,,	1602-3	,,	E	,,
1563-4	,,	f	,,	1583-4	,,	F	,,	JAS. I. 1603-4	,,	F	,,
1564-5	,,	g	,,	1584-5	,,	G	,,	1604-5	,,	G	🦁
1565-6	,,	h	,,	1585-6	,,	H	,,	1605-6	,,	h	,,
1566-7	,,	i	,,	1586-7	,,	I	,,	1606-7	,,	I	🦁
1567-8	,,	K	,,	1587-8	,,	K	,,	1607-8	,,	K	,,
1568-9	,,	l	,,	1588-9	,,	L	,,	1608-9	,,	L	,,
1569-70	,,	m	,,	1589-90	,,	M	,,	1609-10	,,	M	,,
1570-1	,,	n	,,	1590-1	,,	N	,,	1610-1	,,	N	🦁
1571-2	,,	o	,,	1591-2	,,	O	,,	1611-2	,,	O	,,
1572-3	,,	p	,,	1592-3	👑	P	🦁	1612-3	,,	P	,,
1573-4	,,	q	🦁	1593-4	,,	Q	,,	1613-4	,,	Q	,,
1574-5	,,	r	,,	1594-5	,,	R	🦁	1614-5	,,	R	,,
1575-6	,,	s	,,	1595-6	,,	S	,,	1615-6	,,	S	,,
1576-7	,,	t	,,	1596-7	,,	T	,,	1616-7	,,	T	,,
1577-8	,,	u	,,	1597-8	,,	V	,,	1617-8	,,	V	,,

	LEOPARD'S HEAD CROWNED.	DATE LETTER.	LION PASSANT.		LEOPARD'S HEAD CROWNED.	DATE LETTER.	LION PASSANT.		LEOPARD'S HEAD CROWNED.	DATE LETTER.	LION PASSANT.
*1618-9	🐆	a	🦁	1638-9	🐆	A	🦁	1658-9	🐆	A	🦁
1619-20	,,	b	,,	*1639-40	,,	B	,,	1659-60	,,	B	,,
1620-1	,,	c	,,	1640-1	,,	C	,,	CHAS. II. 1660-1	,,	C	,,
1621-2	,,	d	,,	1641-2	,,	D	,,	1661-2	,,	D	,,
1622-3	,,	e	,,	1642-3	,,	E	,,	1662-3	,,	E	🦁
1623-4	,,	f	,,	1643-4	,,	ff	,,	1663-4	,,	F	,,
1624-5	,,	g	,,	1644-5	,,	G	,,	1664-5	,,	G	,,
CHAS. I. 1625-6	,,	h	,,	1645-6	,,	H	,,	1665-6	,,	H	,,
1626-7	,,	i	,,	1646-7	,,	I	,,	1666-7	,,	I	,,
1627-8	,,	k	,,	1647-8	🐆	K	🦁	1667-8	,,	K	,,
1628-9	,,	l	,,	1648-9	,,	L	,,	1668-9	🐆	L	🦁
1629-30	,,	m	,,	COMWTH. 1649-50	,,	M	,,	1669-70	,,	M	,,
1630-1	,,	n	,,	1650-1	,,	N	,,	1670-1	,,	N	,,
1631-2	,,	o	,,	1651-2	,,	O	,,	1671-2	,,	O	,,
1632-3	,,	p	,,	1652-3	,,	P	,,	1672-3	,,	P	,,
1633-4	,,	q	,,	1653-4	,,	Q	,,	1673-4	,,	Q	,,
1634-5	,,	r	,,	1654-5	,,	R	,,	1674-5	,,	R	,,
1635-6	,,	s	,,	1655-6	,,	S	,,	1675-6	,,	S	,,
1636-7	,,	t	,,	1656-7	,,	T	,,	1676-7	,,	T	,,
1637-8	,,	v	,,	1657-8	,,	V	,,	1677-8	,,	U	,,

Date	Leopard's Head Crowned	Date Letter	Lion Passant	Date	Britannia	Datl. Letter	Lion's Head Erased	Date	Britannia	Date Letter	Lion's Head Erased	Date	Leopard's Head Crowned	Date Letter	Lion Passant
1678-9	●	a	●	*1697 MCH. 27 TO MAY 29	●	a	●	1716-7	●	A	●	1736-7	●	a	●
*1679-80	,,	b	●					1717-8	,,	B	,,	1737-8	,,	b	,,
1680-1	●	c	●	1697-8	,,	B	,,	1718-9	,, LEOPARD'S HEAD CROWNED	C	,, LION PASSANT	*1738-9	,,	c	,,
1681-2	,,	d	,,	1698-9	,,	C	,,	*1719-20	●	D	●		,,	d	,,
1682-3	,,	e	,,	1699	●	D	●					1739-40	●	d	●
1683-4	,,	f	,,	1700		E		†1720-1	,,	E	,,				
1684-5	,,	g	,,	1700-1	,,	F	,,					1740-1	,,	e	,,
JAS. II. 1685-6	,,	h	,,	1701-2	,,	G	,,	1721-2	●	F	●	1741-2	,,	f	,,
1686-7	,,	i	,,	ANNE. 1702-3	,,	H	,,	‡1722-3	,,	G	,,	1742-3	,,	g	,,
1687-8	,,	k	,,	1703-4	,,	I	,,	1723-4	,,	H	,,	1743-4	,,	h	,,
1688-9	,,	l	,,	1704-5	,,	K	,,					1744-5	,,	i	,,
WM.&MY. 1689-90	●	m	●	1705-6	,,	L	,,	§1724-5	●	I	●	1745-6	,,	k	,,
1690-1	,,	n	,,	1706-7	,,	M	,,	1725-6	,,	K	,,	1746-7	,,	l	,,
1691-2	,,	o	,,	1707-8	,,	N	,,	1726-7	●	L	●	1747-8	,,	m	,,
1692-3	,,	p	,,	1708-9	,,	O	,,	GEO. II. ‖1727-8	,,	M	,,	1748-9	,,	n	,,
1693-4	,,	q	,,	1709-10	,,	P	,,	1728-9	,,	N	,,	1749-50	,,	o	,,
1694-5	,,	r	,,	1710-11	,,	Q	,,	1729-30	●	O	●	1750-1	,,	p	,,
WM. III. 1695-6	,,	s	,,	1711-2	,,	R	,,	1730-1	,,	P	,,	†1751-2	●	q	●
MAY 29, 1696, TO MCH. 27, 1697.	,,	t	,,	1712-3	,,	S	,,	1731-2	,,	Q	,,	1752-3,	,,	r	,,
				1713-4	,,	T	,,	1732-3	,,	R	,,	1753-4	,,	s	,,
				GEO. I. 1714-5	,,	U	,,	1733-4	,,	S	,,	‡1754-5	,,	t	,,
				1715-6	,,	V	,,	1734-5	,,	T	,,	1755-6	,,	u	,,
								1735-6	,,	V	,,				

Date	Leopard's Head Crowned	Date Letter	Lion Passant	Date	Leopard's Head Crowned	Date Letter	Lion Passant		Date	Leopard's Head Crowned	Date Letter	Lion Passant	King's Head
1756-7	(leopard)	A	(lion)	1776-7	(leopard)	a	(lion)		1796-7	(leopard)	A	(lion)	(king)
1757-8	,,	B	,,	1777-8	,,	b	,,		1797-8	,,	B	,,	,,
1758-9	,,	C	,,	1778-9	,,	c	,,		*1798-9	,,	C	,,	,,
1759-60	,,	D	,,	1779-80	,,	d	,,		1799 1800	,,	D	,,	,,
GEO. III 1760-1	,,	E	,,	1780-1	,,	e	,,		1800-1	,,	E	,,	,,
1761-2	,,	F	,,	1781-2	,,	f	,,		1801-2	,,	F	,,	,,
1762-3	,,	G	,,	1782-3	,,	g	,,		1802-3	,,	G	,,	,,
†1763-4	,,	H	,,	1783-4	,,	h	,,	KING'S HEAD.	1803-4	,,	H	,,	,,
1764-5	,,	I	,,	†1784-5	,,	i	,,	(king)	†1804-5	,,	I	,,	,,
1765-6	,,	K	,,	1785-6	,,	k	,,	,,	1805-6	,,	K	,,	,,
1766-7	,,	L	,,	1786-7	,,	l	,,	(king)	1806-7	,,	L	,,	,,
1767-8	,,	M	,,	1787-8	,,	m	,,	,,	1807-8	,,	M	,,	,,
†1768-9	,,	N	,,	1788-9	,,	n	,,	,,	†1808-9	,,	N	,,	,,
1769-70	,,	O	,,	1789-90	,,	o	,,	,,	1809-10	,,	O	,,	,,
1770-1	,,	P	,,	1790-1	,,	p	,,	,,	1810-1	,,	P	,,	,,
†1771-2	,,	Q	,,	1791-2	,,	q	,,	,,	1811-2	,,	Q	,,	,,
1772-3	,,	R	,,	1792-3	,,	r	,,	,,	1812-3	,,	R	,,	,,
1773-4	,,	S	,,	1793-4	,,	s	,,	,,	1813-4	,,	S	,,	,,
1774-5	,,	T	,,	1794-5	,,	t	,,	,,	1814-5	,,	T	,,	,,
1775-6	,,	U	,,	1795-6	,,	u	,,	,,	1815-6	,,	U	,,	,,

	LEOPARD'S HEAD	DATE LETTER	LION PASSANT	KING'S HEAD		LEOPARD'S HEAD	DATE LETTER	LION PASSANT	KING'S HEAD		LEOPARD'S HEAD	DATE LETTER	LION PASSANT	QUEEN'S HEAD
1816-7	(leopard's head)	a	(lion)	(king's head)	1836-7	(leopard's head)	A	(lion)	(king's head)	1856-7	(leopard's head)	a	(lion)	(queen's head)
1817-8	,,	b	,,	,,	VICT. 1837-8	,,	B	,,	(queen's head)	1857-8	,,	b	,,	,,
1818-9	,,	c	,,	,,	1838-9	,,	C	,,	,,	1858-9	,,	c	,,	,,
1819-20	,,	d	,,	,,	1839-40	,,	D	,,	,,	1859-60	,,	d	,,	,,
GEO. IV. 1820-1	,,	e	,,	(king's head)	1840-1	,,	E	,,	,,	1860-1	,,	e	,,	,,
1821-2	(leopard's head)	f	(lion)	,,	1841-2	,,	F	,,	,,	1861-2	,,	f	,,	,,
1822-3	,,	g	,,	,,	1842-3	,,	G	,,	,,	1862-3	,,	g	,,	,,
1823-4	,,	h	,,	,,	1843-4	,,	H	,,	,,	*1863-4	(leopard's head)	h	(lion)	,,
1824-5	,,	i	,,	,,	*1844-5	,,	I	,,	,,	1864-5	Leopard's head as above	i	Lion passant as above	,,
1825-6	,,	k	,,	,,	1845-6	,,	K	,,	,,	1865-6	,,	k	,,	,,
1826-7	,,	l	,,	,,	1846-7	,,	L	,,	,,	1866-7	,,	l	,,	,,
1827-8	,,	m	,,	,,	1847-8	,,	M	,,	,,	1867-8	,,	m	,,	,,
1828-9	,,	n	,,	,,	1848-9	,,	N	,,	,,	1868-9	,,	n	,,	,,
1829-30	,,	o	,,	,,	1849-50	,,	O	,,	,,	1869-70	,,	o	,,	,,
WM. IV. 1830-1	,,	p	,,	,,	1850-1	,,	P	,,	,,	1870-1	,,	p	,,	,,
1831-2	,,	q	,,	(king's head)	1851-2	,,	Q	,,	,,	1871-2	,,	q	,,	,,
1832-3	,,	r	,,	,,	1852-3	,,	R	,,	,,	1872-3	,,	r	,,	,,
1833-4	,,	s	,,	,,	1853-4	,,	S	,,	,,	1873-4	,,	s	,,	,,
1834-5	,,	t	,,	,,	†1854-5	,,	T	,,	,,	1874-5	,,	t	,,	,,
1835-6	,,	u	,,	,,	1855-6	,,	U	,,	,,	1875-6	,,	u	,,	,,

	LEOPARD'S HEAD	DATE LETTER	LION PASSANT	QUEEN'S HEAD		LEOPARD'S HEAD	DATE LETTER	LION PASSANT
1876-7	🐆	A	🦁	👑	1896-7	🐆	a	🦁
1877-8	,,	B	,,	,,	1897-8	,,	b	,,
1878-9	,,	C	,,	,,	1898-9	,,	c	,,
1879-80	,,	D	,,	,,	1899 1900	,,	d	,,
1880-1	,,	E	,,	,,	1900-1	,,	e	,,
1881-2	,,	F	,,	,,	EDW. VII. 1901-2	,,	f	,,
1882-3	,,	G	,,	,,	1902-3	,,	g	.
1883-4	,,	H	,,	,,	1903-4	,,	h	,,
1884-5	,,	I	,,	,,	1904-5	,,	i	,,
1885-6	,,	K	,,	,,	1905-6	,,	k	,,
1886-7	,,	L	,,	,,	1906-7	,,	l	,,
1887-8	,,	M	,,	,,	1907-8	,,	m	,,
1888-9	,,	N	,,	,,	1908-9	,,	n	,,
1889-90	,,	O	,,	,,	1909-10	,,	o	,,
1890-1	,,	P	,,		1910-1	,,	p	,,
1891-2	,,	Q	,,		1911-2	,,	q	,,
1892-3	,,	R	,,		1912-3	,,	r	,,
1893-4	,,	S	,,		1913-4	,,	s	,,
1894-5	,,	T	,,		1914-5	,,	t	,,
1895-6	,,	U	,,		1915-6	,,	u	,,

	DATE LETTER
1916	a
1917	b
1918	c
1919	d
1920	e
1921	f
1922	g
1923	h
1924	i
1925	k
1926	l
1927	m
1928	n
1929	o
1930	p
1931	q
1932	r
1933	s
1934	t
1935	u
1936	A
1937	B

Date	Maker's Mark	Date	Maker's Mark	Date	Maker's Mark	Date	Maker's Mark	Date	Maker's Mark	Date	Maker's Mark	Date	Maker's Mark
1479-80		1500-1		1516-7		1527-8		1536-7		1551-2		1561-2	
1481-2		1501-2		1517-8		"		1537-8		"		"	
1488-9		1503-4		1518-9		1528-9		1538-9		"		"	
1490-1		1504-5		"		"		1539-40		"		"	
1491-2		"		"		"		1540-1		1552-3		"	
1493-4		1506-7		1519-20		1529-30		"		1553-4		"	
1494-5		"		"		1530-1		1541-2		"		1562-3	
"		1507-8		"		1531-2		1543-4		1554-5		"	
"		"		1520-1		"		"		"		"	
"		"		1521-2		1532-3		"		1555-6		"	
1496-7		"		"		"		1514-5		1556-7		"	
"		"		"		"		1545-6		"		"	
"		1508-9		"		1533-4		"		1557-8		"	
1498-9		"		1522-3		"		"		"		"	
1499-1500		1509-10		"		"		"		1558-9		"	
		1510-1		1523-4		1534-5		1546-7		"		"	
		"		"		"		1547-8		1559-60		"	
		1511-2		1524-5		"		1548-9		"		"	
		1512-3		"		"		"		"		"	
		1513-4		1525-6		"		"		"		"	
		1514-5		"		1535-6		1549-50		"		"	
		"		"		"		"		"		1563-4	
		"		"		"		"		"		"	
		"		1527-8		"		"		"		"	
		1515-6		"		"		1550-1		1560-1		"	
		"		"		"		"		"		"	

Date.	Maker's Mark.	Date.	Maker's Mark	Date	Maker's Mark.	Date.	Maker's Mark	Date	Maker's Mark	Date.	Maker's Mark.	Date.	Maker's Mark.	Date.	Maker's Mark
1563-4		1567-8		1569-70		1571-2		1575-6		1577-8		1581-2			
,,		,,		,,		,,		,,		,,		1582-3			
1564-5		,,		,,		,,		,,		,,		,,			
,,		,,		1570-1		,,		,,		,,		,,			
,,		,,		,,		1572-3		,,		,,		,,			
,,		,,		,,		,,		,,		,,		1583-4			
,,		,,		,,		,,		,,		,,		,,			
,,		,,		,,		,,		1576-7		1578-9		,,			
,,		,,		,,		,,		,,		,,		,,			
1565-6		,,		,,		1573-4		,,		,,		1584-5			
,,		,,		,,		,,		,,		,,		,,			
,,		1568-9		,,		,,		,,		1579-80		,,			
,,		,,		,,		,,		,,		,,		,,			
,,		,,		,,		,,		,,		,,		,,			
,,		,,		,,		,,		,,		c. 1580		1585-6			
1566-7		,,		1571-2		,,		,,		1580-1		,,			
,,		,,		,,		,,		,,		,,		,,			
,,		,,		,,		,,		,,		,,		,,			
,,		,,		,,		,,		,,		1581 2		1586-7			
,,		,,		,,		,,		,,		,,		,,			
,,		1569-70		,,		1574-5		1577-8		,,		,,			
,,		,,		,,		,,		,,		,,		,,			
,,		,,		,,		,,		,,		,,		,,			
,,		,,		,,		1575-6		,,		,,		,,			
		,,		,,											

Date.	Maker's Mark.	Date.	Maker's Mark	Date.	Maker's Mark.	Date	Maker's Mark.	Date.	Maker's Mark.	Date.	Maker's Mark.	Date.	Maker's Mark.
1587-8		1593-4		1597-8		1601-2		1605-6		1608-9		1610-11	
"		"		1598-9		"		"		"		"	
"		1594-5		"		1602-3		"		"		"	
"		"		"		"		"		"		"	
"		"		"		"		1606-7		"		"	
1588-9		"		1599-1600		"		"		"		1611-12	
"		"		"		"		"		"		"	
"		1595-6		"		"		"		"		"	
"		"		"		"		"		"		"	
"		"		"		1603-4		"		1609-10		"	
1589-90		"		"		"		"		"		"	
"		"		"		"		"		"		1612-13	
"		"		1600-1		"		"		"		"	
1590-1		"		"		"		"		"		"	
"		1596-7		"		"		1607-8		"		"	
"		"		"		"		"		"		"	
"		"		"		"		"		"		"	
1591-2		"		"		1604-5		"		"		"	
"		"		"		"		"		"		"	
"		"		"		"		"		1610-11		"	
"		1597-8		1601-2		"		"		"		"	
"		"		"		"		"		"		"	
1592-3		"		"		"		"		"		"	
"		"		"		"		"		"		"	
"		"		"		605-6		"		"	
"						1608-9				

Date	Maker's Mark	Date	Maker's Mark	Date	Maker's Mark	Date	Maker's Mark	Date	Maker's Mark	Date	Maker's Mark	Date	Maker's Mark	Date	Maker's Mark
1613-14	TC	1615-16		1618-19	AV	1622-3	ER	1625-6	CB	1629-30	BP	1632-3	D
''	MH	''	WF	''	IC	''	D	1626-7	PI	''	RC	''	IM
''	W	1616-17	IA	''		''	H	''	X	''		''	
''	N	''	RN	''	C	''	IF	''	HS	''	IT	''	CB
''	HB	''	IP	''	RC	''		''	HB	''	CG	''	IG
''	RS	''	IA	''	RW	1623-4	WC	''	RB	''	PG	''	IH
''	IM	''		''	WC	''	IM	''	AH WW	1630-1	TD	1633-4	IB
1614-15	RB	''	RW	''	RC	''	RC	''	BY	''	WM	''	MM
''	RC	''	RC	''	IS	''	EH	''	WS	''	RS	''	
''	BF	''	E	1619-20	E	''	RS	''	WS	''		''	
''	IM FB	''		''	FM	''	TB	1627-8	SW	''	IM	''	ES
''	SO	''	E	''	AB	''	RIS	''	RI	''	IA	''	HB
''	ID	''	IC	''	RK	''	IF	''	WS	''	WC	''	RC
''		1617-18	RW	''	RG	1624-5	IH	''	TB	''	RS	1634-5	RS
''	HM	''	HB	1620-1	IC	''		''	TE	''	RS	''	WM
1615-16	CR	''	IV	''	IM	''		1631-2		''	B	''	PG
''	IR	''	RS	''	IS	''	A	''	TV	''	HM	''	RW
''	MH	''	IC	''	IW WT	1628-9	IO	''	RM	''	WC	''	DW
''	HS	''	RP	1621-2	EL	''	BY	''		''	DW	''	RC
''	IS	''	WC	''	C	''	LE	''		''	WR	''	PB
''		''	IF	''	H	1625-6	IV	''	BY	1635-6		''	F
''	TS	''	H	''	B	''	HS	''	WS	''	C-B	''	LI
''		''	CC	''	R	''	SW	''	C	''	VS	''	RS
''	RD	1618-19	IP	''	C	''	HS	1632-3	DC	''	EH	''	RH
''		''	WR	1622-3	RD	1629-30	WS	''	RB	''	PB	''	RO
''						''	TB			''	TE	''	RS

DATE.	MAKER'S MARK.	DATE.	MAKER'S MARK.	DATE.	MAKER'S MARK.	DATE.	MAKER'S MARK.	DATE.	MAKER'S MARK.	DATE.	MAKER'S MARK.	DATE.	MAKER'S MARK.
1635-6		1637-8		1640-1		1643-4		1649-50		1653-4		1657-8	
"		"		"		"		1650-1		1654-5		"	
"		1638-9		"		1644-5		"		"		"	
"		"		"		1645-6		"		"		"	
"		"		,		"		"		"		"	
"		"		"		"		"		1655-6		"	
1636-7		"		"		1646-7		1651-2		"		1658-9	
"		"		"		"		"		"		"	
"		"		1641-2		"		"		"		"	
"		"		"		"		"		"		"	
"		"		"		1647-8		"		"		"	
"		"		"		"		1652-3		"		"	
"		"		"		"		"		"		"	
"		"		"		"		"		"		"	
"		"		"		"		"		"		"	
1637-8		"		"		"		"		1656-7		1659-60	
"		"		"		1648-9		"		"		"	
"		"		"		"		"		"		"	
"		"		1642-3		"		"		"		"	
"		1639-40		"		"		"		"		"	
"		"		"		"		1653-4		"		"	
"		"		"		1649-50		"		"		"	
"		"		"		"		"		1657-8		"	
"		"		1643-4		"		"		"		"	
"		1640-1				"		"				"	

Date.	Maker's Mark.	Date.	Maker's Mark.	Date.	Maker's Mark.	Date.	Maker's Mark.	Date.	Maker's Mark.	Date.	Maker's Mark.	Date.	Maker's Mark.	Date.	Maker's Mark.
1660-1		1662-3		1664-5		1665-6		1668-9		1670-1		1671-2			
”		”		”		”		”		”		”			
”		”		”		”		”		”		”			
”		”		”		1666-7		”		”		”			
”		”		”		”		1669-70		”		”			
”		”		”		”		”		”		”			
”		”		”		”		”		”		”			
”		”		”		”		”		”		”			
”		”		”		1667-8		”		”		1672-3			
”		”		”		”		”		”		”			
”		”		”		”		”		”		”			
”		”		”		”		”		”		”			
1661-2		”		”		”		”		”		”			
”		”		”		”		”		”		”			
”		1663-4		”		”		”		1671-2		”			
”		”		1665-6		1668-9		”		”		”			
”		”		”		”		”		”		”			
”		”		”		”		”		”		”			
”		”		”		”		”		”		”			
”		”		”		”		”		”		”			
”		”		”		”		”		”		”			
”		”		”		”		”		”		”			
”		”		”		”		”		”		”			
”		”		”		”		”		”		1673-4			
1662-3		1664-5		”		”		”		”		”			

Date.	Maker's Mark	Date	Maker's Mark	Date.	Maker's Mark	Date.	Maker's Mark	Date.	Maker's Mark	Date.	Maker's Mark	Date.	Maker's Mark	Date.	Maker's Mark	Date.	Maker's Mark
1673-4		1674-5		1676-7		1677-8		1678-9		1680-1		1681-2		1683-4			
,,						,,		1679-80		,,				,,			
,,		1675-6				,,		,,		,,				,,			
,,		,,				1678-9		,,		,,				,,			
,,		,,				,,		,,		,,				,,			
,,		,,				,,		,,		,,				,,			
,,		,,				,,		,,		,,				,,			
,,		,,				,,		,,		,,				,,			
,,		,,				,,		,,		,,		1682-3		,,			
,,		,,				,,		,,		,,		,,		,,			
,,		,,				,,		,,		,,		,,		,,			
1674 5		,,		1677-8		,,		,,		,,		,,		,,			
,,		,,				,,		,,		,,		,,		,,			
,,		,,				,,		,,		1681-2		,,		,,			
,,		,,				,,		,,		,,		,,		,,			
,,		,,				,,		,,		,,		c. 1682		,,			
,,		,,				,,		,,		,,		1682-3		,,			
,,		,,				,,		c. 1680		,,		1683-4		,,			
,,		,,				,,		,,		,,		,,		,,			
,,		,,				,,		1680-1		,,		,,		,,			
,,		1676-7				,,		,,		,,		,,		1684-5			
,,		,,				,,		,,		,,		,,		,,			
,,		,,				,,		,,		,,		,,		,,			
,,		,,				,,		,,		,,		,,		,,			
,,		,,				,,		,,		,,		,,		,,			
,,		,,				,,		,,		,,		,,		,,			
,,		,,				,,		,,		,,		,,					
						,,		,,									

Date.	Maker's Mark.	Date.	Maker's Mark.	Date.	Maker's Mark.	Date.	Maker's Mark.	Date.	Maker's Mark.	Date.	Maker's Mark.	Date.	Maker's Mark.
1684-5	WB ★	1685-6	PK	1686-7	R	1688-9	I·IS	1689-90	RL	1690-1	WB	1692-3	IW
"	JW	"	WK	"	T·P	"	EC	"	C·S	"	I·I	"	SC
"	DB	"	BB	"	IC	"	ID	"	T	"	ID	"	R·T
"	N·G	"	BM	"	IC	"	WM	"	H	"	TH	"	GG
"	AV	"	IS	"	I·C	"	WN	"	RE	"	DG	"	NL
"	S	"	TB	"	WC	"	S·D	"	WP	"	AH	"	WE
"	I·I	"	D	"	Y·T	"	OS	"	S·W	"	MH	"	C
"	TY	"	GM	"	DB	c. 1690	IEI	NG	"	IC	"	GF
"	CD	"	AF	"	RI	1690-1	M·S	TE	1691	D	"	IH
"	T	"	IS	"	P	"	I·IS	WB	"	WS	"	LB
"	AH	"	RB	"	CR	"	TV	W·K	"	SD	"	B
"	(monogram)	"	(monogram)	1687-8	RH	"	I·F	ID	"	W	"	WG
"	P	"	HR	"	CO	"	IR	EK	"	BS	"	WH
"	TA	"	SE	"	EG	"	GS	RL	"	S·I	"	TA
"	CS	"	LS	1689-90	RL	"	T·A	RC	"	I·E	"	DG
"	EH	"	WR	"	I·B	"	H·G	T·S	"	IG	"	CA
"	IG	"	M	"	NG	"	D	I·S	"	GM	"	IG
"	RK	"	WLO	"	MH	"	EB	T·L	1693-4	RG	"	IS
"	EO	"	MW	"	T·G	"	WB	TA	"	X·co	"	I·N
"	IS	"	IL	"	FF	"	I·H	TS	"	NG	"	DA
"	GG	"	W	"	IC	"	M·E	WM	"	MH	"	IL
1685-6	D	"	PM	"	HT	"	HH	GM	"	M	"	A
"	WH	1686-7	RS	"	B	"	NB	GN	"	IC	"	HC
"	P·R	"	WM	"	EC	"	DA	TT	1692-3		"	L
"	TZ	"	CK	"	GS	"	I·E	C8			"	DW
												"	ME

Date.	Maker's Mark	Date.	Maker's Mark	Date.	Maker's Mark
1693-4	H·P	1695-6	(mark)	1696-7	T·B
"	R	"	P·M	"	I·B
"	T·K	"	I·H	"	R·W
"	E·T	"	M·B	"	C·C
"	W·S	"	W	"	F
"	R·M	"	S	"	C
"	I·G	"	A·G	"	R·C
1694-5	E·M	"	M·M	"	S
"	I	"	W·K	"	T·B
"	S·T	"	I·D	c. 1696-8	Ga
"	A·N	"	(mark)		
"	R·I	"	I·S		
"	P	"	S·W		
"	F·F	"	M·E		
"	H·B	"	I·S		
"	H·V	1696-7	W		
"	I·S	"	G·M		
"	I	"	I·Z		
"	I·R	"	P		
"	T·A	"	T·B		
"	M·G	"	I·C		
"	W·H	"	I·Z		
"	I·F	"	T·B		
1695-6	R·G	"	L·I		
"	H	"			

Date.	Goldsmiths' Marks and Names.			Date.	Goldsmiths' Marks and Names.			Date.	Goldsmiths' Marks and Names.		
1697	Lawrence	Coles	ent. 1697	1697	Jas.	Chadwick	ent. 1697	1697-8	Jos.	Bird	ent. 1697.
,,	———	Thriscross	,, ,,	,,	Wm.	Gibson	,, ,,	,,	Chas.	Overing	,, ,,
,,	Alexr.	Roode	,, ,,	,,	Name not traced.			,,	Thos.	Brydon	,, ,,
,,	Mathew	West	,, ,,	,,	Thos.	Allen	,, ,,	,,	Thos.	Issod	,, ,,
,,	Jas.	Edgar	,, ,,	,,	Moses	Brown	,, ,,	,,	Robt.	Peake	,, ,,
,,	Andrew	Moore	,, ,,	,,	Danl.	Garnier	,, ,,	,,	Wm.	Scarlett	,, ,,
,,	Edmd.	Townsend	,, ,,	,,	Thos.	Ash	,, ,,	,,	Jos.	Stokes	,, ,,
,,	C.	Williams	,, ,,	,,	,,	,,	,, ,,	,,	Philip	Rolles	,, ,,
,,	Mathew	Madden	,, ,,	,,	,,	,,	,, ,,	,,	John	Fawdery	,, ,,
,,	Lawrence	Jones	,, ,,	,,	Fras.	Archbold	,, ,,	,,	Thos.	Ash	,, ,,
,,	Wm.	Francis	,, ,,	,,	Benj.	Bradford	,, ,,	,,	James	Edgar	,, ,,
,,	John	Hodson	,, ,,	,,	Wm.	Bainbridge	,, ,,	,,	Richard	Syngin	,, ,,
,,	Edward	Ironside	,, ,,	,,	Jno.	Smithsend	,, ,,	,,	Joseph	Bird	,, ,,
,,	? Thos.	Ash	.. ..	,,	———	Wimans	,, ,,	,,	Andrew	Moore	,, ,,
,,	Geo.	Garthorne (probably)	,, ,,	,,	Benj.	Pyne	,, ,,	,,	Joyce	Issod	,, ,,
				,,	Jno.	Shepherd	,, ,,	,,	Isaac	Dighton	,, ,,
,,	Daniel	Garnier (see p. 153)	,, ,,	,,	Frances	Hoyte	,, ,,	,,	———	Wimans	,, ,,
,,	Isaac	Dighton (see p. 155)	,, ,,	,,	Hugh	Roberts	,, ,,	,,	Anthy.	Nelme	,, ,,
,,	Wm.	Gimber	,, ,,	,,	Ed.	Jones	,, ,,	,,	Geo.	Cox	,, 1698
,,	Edwd.	Courthope	,, ,,	,,	Wm.	Brett	,, ,,	,,	John	Cove	,, ,,
,,	Sam.	Hood	,, ,,	,,	Dorothy	Grant	,, ,,	,,	Wm	Bull	,, ,,
,,	Christr.	Canner	,, ,,	,,	Stephen	Coleman	,, ,,	1698-9	Geo.	Garthorne	,, 1697.
,,	Fras.	Garthorne	,, ,,	,,	Jno.	Brassey	,, ,,	,,	Wm.	Mathew	,, ,,
,,	Thos.	Parr	,, ,,	,,	Rich.	Nightingale	,, ,,	,,	Jonath'n	Bradley	,, ,,
,,	Wm. John	Denny & Backe	,, ,,	,,	Geo.	Titterton	,, ,,	,,	Edwd.	Yorke	,, 1705.
				,,	Jn'th'n	Lambe	,, ,,				

Date.	Goldsmiths' Marks and Names.		Date.	Goldsmiths' Marks and Names.		Date.	Goldsmiths' Marks and Names.	
1698-9	Henry	Collins? ent. 1698.	1699/1700	Fras.	Singleton ent. 1697.	1700-1	Phillip	Roker ent. 1697
"	Richard	Nightingale? " 1697.	"	Sam.	Thorne " "	"	Mat.	Madden " "
"	Isaac	Dighton (see pp. 152 and 154) " "	"	Isaac	Davenport " "	"	George	Lewis " 1690
"	Name not traced.		"	Jno.	Chartier " 1698.	"	Henry	Aubin " 1700
"	" " "		"	Sam	Dell " 1697.	"	Rich.	Biggs " "
"	Jos.	Sheene.	"	Pierre	Platel " 1699.	"	Steph.	Edmonds " "
"	Benj.	Bentley " 1698.	"	John	Downes? " 1697.	"	Wm.	Gossen " "
"	Wm.	Matthew " 1697.	"	Isaac	Davenport " "	"	Edm.	Proctor " "
"	Wm.	Fawdery " 1698.	"	?	Gould.	"	John	Tiffin " 1701
"	John	Ruslen " 1697.	"	John	Leach ent. 1697.	"	Alex.	Roode? " 1697
"	Wm.	Scarlett " "	"	Joseph	Ward " "	1701-2	Frans.	Singleton (see p. 156).
"	Jno.	Ladyman " "	"	John	Cory " "	"	Ed.	Gibson ent. 1697
"	Robt.	Cooper " "	"	Richd.	Syngin " "	"	Pierre	Harache " "
"	Lawrence Coles " "		"	Andrew Raven " "		"	Benj.	Watts " 1698.
"	John	Sutton " "	"	John	Laughton " "	"	Sam	Hood " 1697.
"	John	Hely " 1699.	"	Alex.	Roode " "	"	Sam	Jefferys " "
"	Job	Hanks " "	"	Philip	Oyle " 1699.	"	Henry	Green " 1700
"	Jno.	Porter " 1698.	"	John	Broake " "	"	Wm.	Andrews " 1697.
"	White	Walsh " "	1700-1	Wm.	Fawdery " 1700.	"	Thos.	Brydon " "
"	Benj.	Bentley " "	"	Jos.	Stokes as 1697.	"	Wm.	Keatt " "
1699 1700	Wm.	Lukin " 1699.	"	Sam	Wastell ent. 1701.	"	Willo'by Masham " 1701.	
"	Benj.	Traherne " 1687.	"	Jno.	Jackson " 1697.	"	Name not traced.	
"	John	Cory " 1697.	"	Name not traced		"	Wm.	Keatt " 1697.
"	John	Diggle " "	"	Thos.	Jenkins " "	"	Sam	Hawkes " "
			"	David	Willaume " "	"	Fras.	Archbold " "
			"	Ralph	Leeke " "	"	Josh.	Field " 1701.

Date	Mark	Name
1701-2	[GO]	John Goode ent. 1700.
"	[RL]	Ralph Leeke " 1697.
"	[RS]	John Danl. Read & Sleamaker } " 1701.
"	[HV]	Alexr. Hudson " "
"	[CO]	Stepn. Coleman " 1697.
1702-3	[GR]	Henry Greene " 1700.
"	[Sy]	Richd. Syngin " 1697.
"	[EC]	John Eckfourd " 1698.
"	[GA]	Wm. Gamble " 1697.
"	[CR]	Jonath'n Crutchfield " "
"	[Pa]	Humph. Payne " 1701.
"	[GA]	Name not traced.
"	[SA]	Thos. Sadler " "
"	[WA]	Jos. Ward " 1697.
"	[Do]	Jno. Downes " "
"	[Co]	Jno. Cope " 1701.
"	[WA]	Thos. Waterhouse " 1702.
"	[BA]	Wm. Barnes " "
"	[RV]	Abm. Russell " "
"		Jas. Chadwick as 1697.
"	[Co]	Matt. Cooper ent. 1702.
"	[GR]	Hy. Greene " 1700.
"	[Wh]	Name not traced.
"	[AU]	Henry Aubin, see 1700. (earliest ment. 1700).
"	[Fr]	? Fraillon.
"	[LL]	Name not traced.
1702-3	[MA]	Jonathan Madden ent. 1702.
"	[Lo]	Robt. Lovell " "
"	[Co]	Matt. Cooper " "
1703-4	[Ra]	Jno. Rand " 1704.
"	[Je]	Thos. Jenkins " 1697.
"	[GI]	Ed. Gibson " "
"	[AN]	Wm. Andrews " "
"	[FO]	Name not traced.
"	[Br]	J. Broake.
"	[SO]	Soane or Soame.
"	[KI]	Jonah Kirke " "
"	[Pl]	Gabl. Player " 1700.
"	[Sm]	Saml. Smith " "
"	[WI]	Chas. Williams " 1697.
"	[SN]	Jno. Snelling " "
"	[Gr]	Nat. Greene " 1698.
"	[RI]	Name not traced.
"	[WA]	Wm. Warham " 1703.
"	[CH]	Wm. Charnelhouse " "
"	[AR]	Andr. Archer " "
"	[Pe]	Thos. Peele " 1704.
"	[PC]	Wm. Petley " 1699.
1704-5	[St]	Robert Stokes ?
"	[DE]	Wm. Denny " 1697.
"	[LE]	Geo. Lewis " 1699.
1704-5	[SA]	Thos. Saddler ent. 1701.
"	[PE]	Henry Penstone " 1697.
"	[Co]	Jno. Cole " "
"	[EA]	Jno. East " "
"	[Gi]	Jno. Gibbon " 1700.
"	[AD]	Chas. Adam " 1702.
"	[HA]	Geo. Havers " 1697.
"	[MI]	Wm. Middleton " "
"	[HV]	Alex. Hudson " 1704.
"	[Sp]	Wm. Spring " 1701.
"	[CO]	Jno. Cooke " 1699.
"	[BO]	Ishml. Bone " "
"	[FL]	Jno. Fletcher " 1700.
1705-6	[Ti]	Robt. Timbrell " 1697.
"	[FA]	Wm. Fawdery " "
"	[PA]	Samuel Pantin " 1701.
"	[MA]	Jon. Madden " 1702. (see 1702)
"	[LI]	Isaac Liger " 1704. (see below)
"	[PI]	Matthew Pickering " 1703.
"	[FL]	Wm. Fleming " "
"	[Sp]	Thos. Spackman " 1700.
"	[OL]	Mathw. Lofthouse " 1705.
"	[WA]	Saml. Wastell " 1701.
"	[RE]	Josh. Readshaw " 1697.
"	[LI]	Isaac Liger " 1704.

Date.	Goldsmiths' Marks and Names.	Date.	Goldsmiths' Marks and Names.	Date.	Goldsmiths' Marks and Names.
1705-6	Jonah Clifton ent. 1703.	1707-8	Pierre Le Cheaube ent. 1707.	1708-9	Thos. Wall ent. 1708.
,,	Jno. Corosey ,, 1701.	,,	Richard Hutchinson ,, 1699.	,,	Jno. Clifton ,, ,,
,,	Wm. Warham ,, 1705.	,,	Philip Roker ,, 1697.	,,	Richard Clarke ,, ,,
,,	Thos. Corbet ,, 1699.	,,	Benj. Harris ,, ,,	..	John Chartier ,, 1698.
,,	Natl. Lock ,, 1698.	,,	Chr. Atkinson ,, 1707.	1709-10	Jno. W. Stocker & Edw. Peacock } ,, 1705.
,,	John Barnard ,, 1702.	,,	Phil. Rainaud ,, ,,	,,	Jno. Clifton (?)
1706-7	Jos. Barbitt ,, 1703.	,,	Thos. Fawler ,, ,,	,,	Thos. Allen ,, 1697.
,,	Wm. Matthew ,, 1700.	,,	Jos. Smith ,, ,,	,,	Fras. Turner ,, 1709.
,,	Wm. Juson ,, 1704.	,,	Samuel Lee ,, 1701.	,,	Isr'l. Pincking ,, 1697.
,,	Timothy Ley ,, 1697.	,,	Benj. Pyne ,, 1697.	,,	Hy. Greene ,, 1700.
,,	John Backe ,, 1700.	,,	Saml. Wastell ,, 1701.	,,	Laun. Keatt ,, 1701.
,,	Launcelot Keatt ,, 1701.	,,	John Backe ,, 1700.	,,	Jno. Rand ,, 1704.
,,	Benj. Pyne ,, 1697.	1708-9	Mary Matthew ,, ,,	,,	Simon Pantin ,, 1701.
,,	Jacob Margas ,, 1706.	,,	Jos. Bird ,, 1697.	,,	Phil. Rolles ,, 1705
,,	Jno. Ladyman ,, 1697.	,,	Thos. Farren ,, 1707.	,,	See 1702.
,,	Louys Cuny ,, 1703.	,,	Philip Rolles, Jr. ,, 1705.	,,	Wm. Francis ,, 1697.
,,	Jno. Abbot ,, 1706.	,,	Wm. Warham ,, 1703	,,	Andrw. Dalton ,, 1708.
,,	Wm. Spring ,, 1701.	,,	Lawrence Jones ,, 1697.	,,	Ebenezr. Roe ,, 1709.
,,	Jno. Crutcher ,, 1706.	,,	Chris. Riley ,, ,,	..	Thos. Prichard ,, ,,
,,	Wm. Fordham ,, ,,	,,	Alice Sheene ,, 1700.	,,	Hen. Clarke ,, ,,
..	Name not traced.	,,	Jno. Read ,, 1704.	,,	Jas. Wethered ,, ,,
1707-8	Danl. Sleath ,, 1704.	,,	Jno. Bodington ,, 1697.	,,	Richd. Watts ,, 1710.
..	Wm. Fleming ,, 1697.	,,	Wm. Fawdery ,, 1698.	1710-1	Thos. Folkingham ,, 1706.
..	Thos. Burridge ,, 1706.	,,	Henry Greene ,, 1700.	,,	Jno. Smith ,, 1710.
..	John Leach ,, 1697.	,,	Anty. Blackford ,, 1702.	,,	Wm. Hinton ,, 1704.
..	Anthy. Nelme ,, ,,			,,	Geo. Gillingham ,, 1703.

Date.	Goldsmiths' Marks and Names.			Date.	Goldsmiths' Marks and Names.			Date.	Goldsmiths' Marks and Names.		
1710-1	ME	Lewis	Mettayer ent. 1700.	1711-2	PO	John	Porter ent. 1698.	1712-3	Be	Thos.	Bevault ent. 1712.
,,	CO	Ed.	Cornock ,, 1707.	,,	WI	Richard	Williams ,, 1712.	,,	St	Jno. M.	Stockar ,, 1710.
,,	WI	Jno.	Wisdom ,, 1704.	,,	PE	Wm.	Penstone ,, ,,	1713-4	MA	Samuel	Margas ,, 1706.
,,	PE	Wm.	Pearson ,, 1710.	,,	Ie	Ed.	Jennings ,, 1709.	,,	St	Ambrose	Stevenson ,, ,,
,,	TW	Wm.	Twell ,, 1709.	,,	Re	Jno.	Read ,, 1704.	,,	LO	Natl.	Locke 1698.
,,	BE	Jas.	Beschefer ,, 1704.	,,	Me	Lewis	Mettayer (probably).	,,	RO	Hugh	Roberts ,, 1697.
,,	MA	Jacob	Margas . 1706.	,,	CL	Nich.	Clausen ent. 1709.	,,	SL	Gabriel	Sleath ,, 1706.
,,	RO	Jas.	Rood ,, 1710.	,,	Ho	Ed.	Holaday ,, ,,	,,	PA	Mark	Paillet ,, 1698.
,,	KE	Jno.	Keigwin ,, ,,	,,	CO	Aug.	Courtauld ,, 1708.	,,	CO	Henry	Collins ,,
,,	SL	Gabriel	Sleath ,, 1706.	,,	GR	Hen.	Greene ,, 1700.	,,	V-I	Edw.	Vincent (?)
,,	HH	Name not traced.		,,	CH	Jno.	Chamberlen ,, 1704.	,,	LV	Jno.	Ludlow ,, 1713.
,,	MA	Jacob	Margas ,, ,,	,,	DA	Isaac	Dalton ,, 1711.	,,	RO	Gundry	Roode ,, 1709.
,,	GO	Jas.	Goodwin ,, ,,	,,	MA	Wm.	Matthew ,, ,,	,,	MA	Thos.	Mann ,, 1713.
,,	RV	Abm.	Russell (?) ,, 1702.	,,	Ne	Jonthn.	Newton ,, ,,	,,	EW	Thos.	Ewesdin ,, ,,
,,	Ke	Robt.	Keble ,, ,,	1712-3	SU	Thos.	Sutton ,, ,,	,,	LO	Wm.	Looker ,, ,,
,,	SH	Jos.	Sheene ,, ,,	,,	Ra	Jno.	Rand ,, 1704.	,,	BA	John	Bathe ,, 1700.
,,	St	Jno.	Stoskar ,, ,,	,,	LO	Seth	Lofthouse ,, 1697.	,,	IV	Wm.	Juson ,, 1704.
,,	TR	Wm.	Truss ,, ,,	,,	DA	Isaac	Dalton ,, 1711.	,,	LO	Seth	Lofthouse ,, 1697.
,,	Mo	Hezk.	Mountfort ,, 1711.	,,	GI	Ed.	Gibson ,, 1697.	1714-5	TB	Robt. Timbrell & Benj. Bentley }	,, ,,
,,	MA	Isaac	Malyn ,, 1710.	,,	lu	Wm.	Lukin , 1699.	,,	TA	David	Tanqueray ,, 1713.
,,	FL	Jno.	Flight ,, ,,	,,	BA	Richd.	Bayley ,, 1708.	,,	Fa	Joseph	Fainell ,, 1710.
1711-2	PE	Edmd.	Pearce ,, 1704.	,,	RA	Richd.	Raine ,, 1712.	,,	BE	Thomas	Bevault ,, 1712.
,,	GR	Dorothy	Grant ,, 1697.	,,	H	John	Hobson ,, 1697.	,,	Io	Glover	Johnson ,, ,,
,,	EA	John	East ,, ,,	,,	IO	Glover	Johnson ,, 1712.	,,	BO	Mich'l	Boult ,, ,,
,,	BA	Joseph	Barbitt ,, 1703.	,,	Tu	Wm.	Turbitt ,, 1710.	,,	CO	Name not traced.	
				,,	WI	Richd.	Williams ,, 1712.				

Date	Goldsmiths' Marks and Names			Date	Goldsmiths' Marks and Names			Date	Goldsmiths' Marks and Names		
1714-5		Wm. John	England & Vane } ent. 1714.	1715-6		Robt. Hill	ent. 1716.	1717-8		Joseph Ward	ent. 1717.
"		Sam Welder	" "	"		Thos. Holland	" 1707.	"		Edward Barnet	" 1715.
"		Rich'd Green	" 1703.	1716-7		John Holland	" 1711.	"		Chas. Jackson (see 1718 below)	" 1714.
"		Jno. Holland	" 1711.	"		Nat. Roe	" 1710.	"		William Pearson (see 1716)	" 1710.
"		Saml. Hitchcock	" 1712.	"		Jos. Clare	" 1713.	"		Isaac Riboulau	" 1714.
"		Saml. Welder	" 1714.	"		Thos. Mason	" 1716.	"		Edw. Barnet	" 1715.
"		Philip Brush	" 1707.	"		Paul Lamerie	" 1712.	"		Phil. Robinson	" 1713.
"		Josiah Daniel	" 1714.	"		Thos. Ewesdin	" 1713.	"		Thos. Holland	" 1707.
"		Nathl. Bland	" "	"		Jas. Seabrook	" 1714.	"		Jno. Harris	" 1716.
"		Richd. Gines	" "	"		Petley Ley	" 1715.	"		Wm. Street	" 1717.
"		Henry Beesley	" "	"		Phillip Robinson	" 1713.	"		Jas. Smith	" 1718.
"		Henry Miller	" "	"		Joseph Clare (see above and 1719)	" "	"		Thos. Shermer	" 1717.
1715-6		Thos. Allen	" 1697.	"		Anty. Nelme	" 1697.	"		Starling Wilford	" "
"		David Killmaine	" 1715.	"		Geo. Lambe	" 1713.	"		Paul Hanet	" "
"		Fras. Plymley	" "	"		Wm. Bellassyse	" 1716.	"		Thos. Burridge	" "
"		John Corporon	" 1716.	"		David Green	" 1701.	"		Wm. Bellamy	" "
"		Danl. Sleamaker	" 1704.	"		Jno. Guerrie	" 1717.	"		Sam. Welder	" "
"		Humph. Payne	" 1701.	"		Danl. Cunningham	" 1716.	1718-9		Ambrose Stevenson	" 1706.
"		Petley Ley	" 1715.	"		Jos. Bell	" "	"		Wm. Petley	" 1717.
"		Thos. Port	" 1713.	"		Richd. Edwards	" "	"		Paul Hanet	" 1715.
"		Richard Greene	" 1703.	"		Jas. Morson	" "	"		John Farnell	" 1714.
"		Edward Jones	" 1697.	"		Wm. Pearson	" 1717.	"		Chas. Jackson	" "
"		Josiah Daniel (see 1714)	" 1714.	1717-8		Jas. (?) Fraillon	" 1710.	"		Thos. Parr	" 1697.
"		Jas. Goodwin	" 1710.	"		Robt. Kempton	" "	"		Geo. Beale	" 1713.
"		Danl. Yerbury	" 1715.	"		Wm. Penstone	" 1717.	"		Ed. Holaday	" 1709.
"		Geo. Lambe	" 1713.								

Date.	Goldsmiths' Marks and Names.	Date.	Goldsmiths' Marks and Names.	Date.	Goldsmiths' Marks and Names.
1718-9	David Tanqueray ent. 1713. (see 1714)	1719-20	John Gibbons ent. 1700.	1719-20	Joseph Fainell ent. 1710.
,,	Henry Clarke ,, 1709. (see 1709)	,,	Thomas Shermer ,, 1717.	,,	Phyllis Fhillip ,, 1720.
,,	Thomas Mason ,, 1716.	,,	Wm. Darkeratt ,, 1718. (see 1718)	,,	Richard Gines ,, ,,
,,	Thomas Tearle ,, 1719. (see 1719 below)	,,	Edw. Barrett ,, 1715.	,,	Wm. Scarlett ,, ,, (O.S. as before 1697)
,,	John Keigwin ,, 1710.	,,	James Smith ,, 1718.	,,	Mary Rood ,, ,,
,,	John Sanders ,, 1717.	,,	Gabriel Sleath ,, 1706.	,,	Christr. Gerrard ,, ,,
,,	Wm. Fawdery ,, 1697. (as 1705)	,,	Thos. Allen ,, 1697. (2nd Mark)	1720-1	John Edwards ,, 1697.
,,	Wm. Darkeratt ,, 1718.	,,	Thos. Morse ,, 1718.	,,	Thos. Evesdon ,, 1713. (see 1721-2)
,,	Hugh Saunders ,, ,,	,,	Edw. Gibbon ,, 1719.	,,	William Looker ,, ,,
,,	John Bignell ,, ,,	,,	Saml. Smith ,, ,,	,,	Paul Lamerie ,, 1712.
,,	Geo. Gillingham ,, ,,	,,	Jos. Steward ,, ,,	,,	Paul Crespin ,, 1720.
,,	Jno. Millington ,, ,,	,,	Jos. Clare, as 1716-7.	,,	Geo. Lambe ,, 1713. (widow of)
,,	Jno. Lingard ,, ,,	,,	Chris. Gerrard ent. 1719.	,,	William Fawdery ,, 1720.
,,	Do. do. (for O.S.) ,, 1719.	,,	Edmd. Hickman ,, ,,	,,	Henry Millar ,, ,,
1719-20	Thos. Tearle ,, ,, (see 1718-9)	.	Wm. Pearson ,, ,,	,,	Thomas Folkingham ,, ,,
,,	Thos. Langford ,, 1715.		Geo. Brydon ,, 1720.	,,	Petley Ley ,, 1715. (see 1716)
,,	Réné Hudell ,, 1718.	,,	Thos Gladwin ,, 1719.	,,	John Fawdery ,, 1697.
,,	Wm. Spackman , 1714.	,,	Starling Wilford ,, 1720.	,,	Matt. Cooper ,, ,,
,,	Geo. Boothby ,, 1720.	.	John Lingard ,, 1719.	,,	Ann Tanqueray ,, 1720.
,,	John White ,, 1719.	.	John Jones ,, ,,	,,	Chas. Jackson ,, 1714.
,,	John le Sage , 1718.	,,	Paul Hanet ,, 1717.	,,	Sarah Holaday ,, 1719.
,,	Benj. Blakeley ,, 1715	,,	Edwd. Hall ,, 1720.	,,	Hugh Arnett & } ,, ,, Ed. Pocock }
.	Wm. Paradise ,, 1718.	.	Bowles Nash ,, ,,	,,	Name not traced.
,,	Lawrence (?) Jones ,, 1697.	,,	—— Hodgkis ,, 1719.	,,	Thos Bamford ,, ,,
		,,	Phyllis Phillip ,, 1720.		

DATE.	GOLDSMITHS' MARKS AND NAMES.	DATE.	GOLDSMITHS' MARKS AND NAMES.	DATE.	GOLDSMITHS' MARKS AND NAMES.
1720-1	Jno. Bromley ent. 1720.	1720-1	Edw. Feline ent. 1720.	1721-2	Simon Pantin ent. 1717.
"	Benj. Watts " "	"	Jas. Seabrook " "	"	John Wisdome " 1720. (probably)
"	John Bignell " "	"	Jos. Steward " "	"	Jane Lambe " 1719.
"	John Betts " "	"	Henry Miller " "	"	Ed. Turner " 1720.
"	Michl. Boult. " "	"	Geo. Squire " "	"	Abm. Buteux " 1721.
"	Saml. Hitchcock " "	"	Gabl. Sleath " "	"	Saml. Lee " "
"	Thos. Sadler " "	"	Phil. Roker (N.S.) " "	"	Geo. Wickes " "
"	Geo. Boothby " "	"	Do. do. (O.S.) " "	"	Hugh Spring " "
"	Phil. Rolles " "	"	Geo. Brydon " "	"	Mary Rood " "
"	Jno. Hopkins " "	"	Hen. Greene " "	"	Gundry Roode " "
"	Do. do. " "	"	Edwd. Pearce " "	"	Wm. Truss " "
"	Saml. Welder " "	"	Jno. Brumhall " 1721.	"	Do. do. " "
"	*John Penfold " " (probably)	"	Jno. Newton " 1720.	"	Name not traced.
"	Fras. Turner " "	"	Wm. Matthew " "	"	Sarah Holaday " 1719. (see 1720-1)
"	Jas. Morson " "	"	Saml. Lee " "		
"	Jno. Millington " "	"	Henry Clarke " "	"	Joseph Bell ? " 1716.
"	Thos. Folkingham " "	"	Jno. Corosey " "	"	Thos. Evesdon " 1713. (see 1720-1)
"	John Ludlow " "	"	Jno. Farnell " "	"	Edmund Pearce " 1720.
"	Thos. Mann " "	"	Glover Johnson " "	"	Simon Pantin " 1717. (see above)
"	Ed. Jennings " "	"	Wm. Looker " "	1722-3	Bowles Nash " 1721.
"	Do. do. (O.S.) " "	"	Phil. Rainaud " "	"	Edward Feline " 1720. (see 1720)
"	Richd. Watts " "	1721-2	Ed. Vincent " " (probably)	"	Jno. le Sage " 1718.
"	Name not traced.	"	Isaac Liger " "	"	Ed. Wood " "
"	J. Burridge " "	"	Henry Jay " "	"	Benj. Pyne as 1706.
"	Jno. Barnard " "	"	Jos. Clare " "	"	Name not traced.
"	A'brose Stevenson " "	"	M. Arnett & } " " Ed. Pocock }	"	Anth. Nelme as 1716. Edw. Jennings ent. 1720.

Date.	Goldsmiths' Marks and Names.	Date.	Goldsmiths' Marks and Names.	Date.	Goldsmiths' Marks and Names.
22-3	Jno. Bignell ent. 1720.	1722-3	Richard Watts ent. 1720.	1723-4	John Bignell ent. 1718. (see 1720 and 1722)
,,	Natl. Gulliver ,, 1722.	,,	Ed. Dymond ,, 1722.	,,	Geo. Squire ,, 1720.
,,	David Willaume ,, 1720.	,,	Jeremiah King ,, 1723.	,,	Thos. Wall (?) ,, 1708.
,,	Jno. Eckford ,, ,,	,,	Do. do. ,, ,,	,,	Arte Dicken ? or ,, 1720. / John Diggle ,, 1697.
,,	Isaac Riboulau ,, ,,	,,	Wm. Soame ,, ,,	,,	John Motherby (?) ,, 1718.
,,	Pere Pilleau ,, ,,	,,	Do. do. ,, ,,	,,	Sam Hitchcock ,, 1712.
,,	Edw. Wood ,, ,,	,,	John Jones ,, ,,	,,	Wm. Fawdery ? ,, 1720.
,,	Jas. Gould ,, 1722.	,,	Do. do. ,, ,,	,,	Jnthn. Robinson ,, 1723.
,,	Nich. Clausen ,, 1720.	,,	Henry Dell ,, 1722.	,,	Richd. Edwards ,, ,,
,,	Phil. Robinson ,, 1723.	,,	Wm. Owen ,, 1723.	,,	John Owing ,, 1724.
,,	Phil. Goddard ,, ,,	,,	John Gibbons ,, ,,	,,	John Edwards & ,, 1723. Geo. Pitches
,,	Do. do. ,, ,,	,,	Meshach Godwin ,, 1722.	,,	
,,	Natl. Gulliver ,, ,,	1723-4	John East ,, 1721.	1724-5	Richd. Bigge ,, 1700. (probably)
,,	Isaac Cornasseau ,, 1722.	,,	Thos. Farrer ,, 1720.	,,	Richd. Scarlett ,, 1719.
,,	Do. do. ,, ,,	,,	Thos. Morse ,, ,,	,,	David Tanqueray ,, 1720.
,,	Michl. Nicholl ,, 1723.	,,	Aug. Courtauld ,, 1708.	,,	Abm. Buteux ,, 1721.
,,	John Clarke ,, 1722.	,,	Jnthn. Madden ,, 1702.	,,	Meshach Godwin ,, 1722.
,,	Geo. Young ,, ,,	,,	Edw. Peacock ,, 1710.	,,	Humphy. Payne ,, 1720.
,,	Jno. Clarke ,, ,,	,,	Richd. Scarlett ,, 1723.	,,	Paul Crespin ,, ,,
,,	Jas. Fraillon ,, 1723	,,	John Chartier ,, ,,	,,	Jacob Margas ,, ,,
,,	Ed. Dymond ,, 1722.	,,	Arte Dicken ,, 1720.	,,	Fleurant David ,, 1724.
,,	Joseph Adams ? ,, ,,	,,	Paul Lamerie ,, 1712.	,,	Do. do. ,, ,,
,,	John le Sage ,, 1718.	,,	John Jones ,, 1719.	,,	Mathw. Lofthouse ,, 1721.
,,	Philip Brush ? ,, 1707.	,,	Edw. Gibbons ,, 1723.	,,	John Edwards , 1724.
,,	Isaac Cornasseau ,, 1722.	,,	Wm. Spackman ,, 1720.	,,	Edw. Conen ,,
		,,	Jnthn. Robinson ,, 1723.	,,	John Jones ,, 1723.
				,,	W'sc'mbe Drake ,, 1724.
				,,	John White ,,) ,,

Date.	Goldsmiths' Marks and Names.	Date.	Goldsmiths' Marks and Names.	Date.	Goldsmiths' Marks and Names.
1724-5	Jas. Burne ent. 1724.	1725-6	Jacob Margas ent. 1720. (see 1724)	1726-7	Robt. Lucas ent. 1726. (variant of mark of)
,,	Do. do. ,, ,,	,,	Starling Wilford (?) ,, ,, (see 1728 and 1737).	,,	Thos. Evesdon ,, 1713. (see 1720 and 1721)
,,	Saml. Hutton ,, ,,	,,	Edward Feline ,, ,, (see also 1722-1729)	,,	Fras. Nelme ,, 1722.
,,	Do. do. ,, ,,	,,	John Gibbons ,, 1723.	,,	Bern'd. Fletcher ,, 1725.
,,	Ed. Peacock ,, ,,	,,	Edw. Vincent ,, ,, (see 1729)	,,	Thos. Bamford ,, 1720.
,,	John Owing ,, ,,	,,	Thos. Mason ,, 1720.	,,	Robt. Williams ,, 1726.
,,	Peter Simon ,, 1725.	,,	Jas. Gould ,, 1722.	,,	Do. do. ,, ,,
,,	John Gibbons ,, 1723.	,,	John Edwards ,, 1724.	,,	Gawen Nash ,, ,,
,,	Aug. Courtauld ,, 1708.	,,	Geo. Wickes ,, 1721.	,,	Chas. Perier ,, 1727.
,,	Josiah Daniel ,, 1714.	,,	Thos. Clark ,, 1725.	,,	Do. do. ,, ,,
,,	Peter Simon ,, 1725.	,,	Thos. England ,, ,,	,,	Geo. Brome ,, 1726.
,,	John Motherby ,, 1718.	,,	Wm. Scarlett ,, ,,	,,	Peter le Chaube ,, ,,
,,	John Pero ,, 1717.	,,	Peter Tabart ,, ,,	1727-8	Isaac Ribouleau ,, 1720.
,,	Jnthn. Newton ,, 1718.	,,	Do. do. ,, ,,	,,	* Jas. Smith ,, ,,
1725-6	Abm. de Oliveyra ,, 1725.	,,	Mathew Cooper ,, ,,	,,	Edw. Wood ,, 1722.
,,	John Eckfourd ,, ,,	,,	Do. do. ,, ,,	,,	Ed. Cornock ,, 1707.
,,	Josh. Healy ,, ,,	,,	Louis Laroche ,, ,,	,,	Saml. Bates ,, 1727.
,,	Do. do. ,, ,,	,,	John Flavill ,, 1726.	,,	Thomas England ,, 1725.
,,	Robt. Lucas ,, 1726.	1726-7	Name not traced.	,,	Richard Pargeter ,, 1730.
,,	Harvey Price ,, ,,	,,	Wm. Darkeratt ,, 1724.	,,	Matt. Cooper ,, 1725. (see 1725)
,,	John Gorsuch ,, ,,	,,	Richd. Green ,, 1726.	,,	?Andrew Raven ,, 1706.
,,	Wm. Toone ,, 1725.	,,	Benj. Pyne (as before 1697).	,,	Jno. le Sage ,, 1722.
,,	Jos. Bird ,, 1724.	,,	Peter Archambo ent. 1722.	,,	Name not traced.
,,	Hugh Saunders ,, 1718.	,,	Wm. Fawdery ,, 1720.	,,	Sarah Holaday ,, 172.
,,	Paul Hanet ,, 1721.	,,	Wm. Atkinson ,, 1725.	,,	John East ,, 1721.
,,	Fras. Garthorne ,, ,,			,,	Jonah Clifton ,, 1720.

Date.	Goldsmiths' Marks and Names.	Date.	Goldsmiths' Marks and Names.	Date.	Goldsmiths' Marks and Names.
1727-8	Saml. Laundry ent. 1727.	1727-8	Saml. Green ent. 1721.	1729-30	Anthony Nelme ent. 1722.
,,	Edmd. Bodington ,, ,,	,,	Wm. Shaw ,, 1728.	,,	Chas. Martin ,, 1729.
,,	Chas. Kandler & } Jas. Murray } ,, ,,	1728-9	Wm. Darkeratt ,, 1720.	,,	Edwd. Feline ,, 1720. (see 1722 and 1725)
,,	Do. do. ,, ,,	,,	James Goodwin ,, 1721.	,,	Abel Brokesby ,, 1727. (see 1727)
,,	Edw. Bennett ,, ,,	,,	Tim. Ley (as before 1697)	,,	Simon Pantin ,, 1717. (see 1728)
,,	Hester Fawdery ,, ,,	,,	Blanche Fraillon ent. 1727.	,,	George Jones ,, 1724. (see 1735-6)
,,	Thos. Cooke ,, ,,	,,	Isaac Callard ,, 1726.	,,	Name not traced.
,,	Richd. Hutchinson ,, ,,	,,	Name not traced.	,,	Paul Lamerie ,, ,,
,,	Chas. Kandler ,, ,,	,,	James Wilkes ,, 1722.	,,	Ralph Maidman ,, 1730.
,,	Geo. Weir ,, ,,	,,	Peter Archambo ,, 1720.	,,	Richd. Scarlett ,, 1720. (see 1723)
,,	Do. do. ,, ,,	,,	Josh. Holland ,, ,,	,,	Name not traced.
,,	Name not traced.	,,	Simon Pantin ,, ,, (see 1729)	,,	John Jones ,, 1729.
,,	Abel Brokesby ,, ,,	,,	John Millington ,, 1728.	,,	Saml. Margas ,, 1720.
,,	Dike Impey ,, ,, (probably)	,,	Edward Bennett ,, 1727.	,,	Chas. Alchorne ,, 1729.
,,	Benj. Bentley ,, 1728.	,,	Ralph Frith ,, 1728.	,,	Sam. Welder ,, ,,
,,	Mary Johnson ,, 1727.	,,	Do. do. ,, ,,	,,	Benj. Goodwin ,, ,,
,,	I. Wichaller ,, 1728.	,,	Geo. Hodges ,, ,,	,,	Name not traced.
,,	Chas. Hatfield ,, 1727.	,,	Do. do. ,, ,,	,,	Edith Fletcher ,, ,,
,,	Sam. Laundry ,, ,,	,,	John Fawdery ,, ,,	,,	Eliz. Goodwin ,, ,,
,,	Matw. Cooper ,, 1725.	,,	John Montgomery ,, ,,	,,	Jas. Maitland ,, 1728. of the "Grasshopper," Suffolk Street.
,,	David Willaume ,, 1728.	,,	? John Richardson ,, 1723.	,,	Aug. Courtauld ent. 1729.
,,	Danl. Cunningham ,, 1720.	,,	? Wm. Fordham ,, 1706.	1730-1	Paul Lamerie ,, 1712.
,,	Richd. Gines ,, ,,	,,	Starling Wilford ,, 1729. (see 1725 and 1737)	,,	Saml. Jefferys ,, 1697.
,,	Geo. Gillingham ,, 1721.	1729-30	John Tuite * ,, 1721.	,,	Gabl. Sleath ,, 1720.
,,	Chas. Hatfield ,, 1727.	,,	Thos. Tearle ,, 1720.		
,,	Jacob Foster ,, 1726.	,,	Ed. Vincent ,, ,, (see 1725)		

Date.	Goldsmiths' Marks and Names.	Date.	Goldsmiths' Marks and Names.	Date.	Goldsmiths' Marks and Names.
1730-1	Richd. Bayley ent. 1720.	1731-2	Sarah Parr ent. 1720.	1733-4	Aug. Courtauld ent. 1729.
,,	Wm. Belassyse ,, 1723.	,,	Robt. Geo. Abercromby & Hindmarsh } ,, 1731.	,,	Jas. Slater ,, 1732.
,,	Isaac Callard ,, 1726.	,,	Wm. Woodward ,, ,,	,,	Richd. Bayley ,, 1720.
,,	Wm. Petley ,, 1720.	,,	Thos. Causton ,, 1730.	,,	* Henry Herbert ,, 1734. (of the " Three Crowns ")
,,	Perè Pilleau ,, ,,	,,	Etienne Rongent ,, 1731.	,,	Wm. Soame ,, 1732.
,,	Chas. Kandler ,, 1727.	,,	Wm. Darker (see 1731) ,, ,,	,,	Eliz. Buteux ,, 1731.
,,	John White ,, 1719.	1732-3	Richd. Beale ,, ,,	,,	Danl. Chapman ,, 1729.
,,	Anne Tanqueray ,, 1720.	,,	Sam Laundry & Jeffy Griffith } ,, ,,	,,	Lewis Pantin ,, 1733.
,,	? Saml. Laundry ,, 1727. (see also 1727)	,,	Joseph Smith ,, 1728.	,,	Chas. Sprage ,, 1734.
,,	John Chapman ,, 1730. (see 1737)	[,,	Edw. Pocock ,, ,,	,,	Robt. Abercromby ,, 1731. (see 1734)
,,	Samuel Hitchcock ,, ,,	[,,	John Sanders ,, 1720.	,,	Geo. Braithwaite ? earliest ment. 1728.
,,	Jas. Jenkins ,, 1731.	[,,	John Fawdery ,, 1728. (see 1728)	1734-5	Ralph Maidman ent. 1731.
,,	Wm. Justus ,, ,,	,,	Fras. Pages ,, 1729.	,,	Caleb Hill ,, 1728.
,,	Wm. Reeve ,, ,,	,,	? Matt. Lofthouse ,, 1705.	,,,	Lewis Mettayer ,, 1720.
,,	Aaron Bates ,, 1730.	,,	Name not traced.	,,	Wm. Gould ,, 1732.
,,	Aug. Courtauld ,, 1708.	,,	Wm. Lukin ,, 1725.	,,	Robt. Abercromby ,, 1731. (see 1733)
1731-2	John Gamon ,, 1728.	,,,	Fras. Spilsbury ,, 1729. (same mark found in square stamp).	,,	John Newton ,, 1726.
,,	Edwd. Yorke ,, 1730.	,,	Thos. Parr ent. 1732.	,,	Mary Pantin ,, 1733.
,,	Geo. Hindmarsh ,, 1731.	,,	Wm. Matthews ,, 1728.	,,	Richd. Pargeter ,, 1730.
,,	David Willaume ,, 1728.	,,	Jas. Savage ,, ,,	,,	Hugh Arnell ,, 1734.
,,	Wm. Darker ,, 1731.	,,	John Pero ,, 1732.	,,	Alex. Coates & Edw. French } ,, ,,
,,	Thos. England ,, 1725.	,,	Jas. Gould ,, ,,	,,	John Taylor ,, ,,
,,	Jane Lambe ,, 1729.	,,	Geo. Smith R. W. (as 1696). ,, ,,	,,	Wm. Gould ,, ,,
,,	Mary Lofthouse ,, 1731.	,,	Wm. Soame ,, ,,	,,	John Jacob ,, ,,
,,	Thos. Merry ,, ,,	,,	Chas. Gibbons ,, ,,	,,	John Pollock ,, ,,
,,	Jeffrey Griffith ,, ,,	,,	Wm. Shaw ,, 1728.	,,	Jas. Manners ,, ,,
		1733-4	John Eckfourd, jr. ,, 1725.		

Date	Mark	Goldsmiths' Name	Entered
1734-5	[EF]	Edw. French	ent. 1734.
"	[IB]	Jas. Brooker	" "
"	[SH]	Sam. Hutton	" "
"	[WK]	Wm. Kidney	" "
1735-6	[G·I]	Geo. Jones	" 1724.
"	[R·G / T·C]	Richd. Gurney & Thos. Cook }	" 1734.
"	[EB]	Edw. Bennett	" 1731.
"	[KA]	Fred Kandler	" 1735.
"	[B·G]	Benj. Godfrey (see 1739)	" 1732.
"	[GE]	Grif. Edwards	" "
"	[WS]	Wm. Shaw	" 1727.
"	[PB]	Peter Bennett	" 1731.
"	[IW]	John White	" 1724.
"	[AT]	Wm. Atkinson	" 1725.
"	[WY]	Wm. Young	" 1735.
"	[EI]	Name not traced, (see 1729-30)	
"	[FN]	Francis Nelme	" "
"	[I·B]	John Barbe	" "
"	[GH]	Geo Hindmarsh	" "
"	[CH]	Christn. Hilland	" 1736.
"	[D·L]	Name not traced	
"	[H·H]	Henry Herbert (of the "Three Crowns")	" 1734.
"	[LH]	Lewis Hamon	" 1735.
1736-7	[NV]	Name not traced.	
"	[WG]	Wm. Garrard	" 1735.
"	[SW]	Sam. Wood	" 1733-7.

Date	Mark	Goldsmiths' Name	Entered
1736-7	[BW]	Benj. West	ent. 1737.
"	[RB]	Robt. Brown	" 1736.
"	[AH]	Ann Hill	" 1734.
"	[TM]	Thos. Mason	" 1733.
"	[II]	John Jones	" "
"	[IF]	John Fossey	" "
"	[BB]	Bennet R. Bradshaw & Tyrill }	" 1737.
"	[IK]	Jerem. King	" 1736.
"	[TM]	Thos. Mann	" "
"	[DH]	David Hennell	" "
"	[BW]	Benj. West	" 1737.
"	[H·H]	Henry Herbert	" 1734.
"	[HP]	? Harvey Price	" 1726.
1737-8	[IA / MF]	Joseph Allen & Co.	" 1729.
"	[GW]	Geo. Weekes	" 1735.
"	[IS]	Jos. Sanders	" 1730.
"	[SB]	Saml. Blackborrow	" 1720.
"	[TW]	Thos. Whipham	" 1737.
"	[G·H]	Geo. Hindmarsh (see 1735-6)	" 1735.
"	[S·W]	Starling Wilford	" 1729.
"	[IC]	John Chapman (see 1730)	" 1730.
"	[R·W]	Robt. Williams	" 1726.
"	[RB]	Richd. Beale	" 1731.
"	[S·I]	Simon Jouet	" 1723.
"	[T·I]	Thos. Jackson	" 1736.
"	[TG]	Thos. Gladwin	" 1737.

Date	Mark	Goldsmiths' Name	Entered
1737-8	[IB]	John Barrett	ent. 1737.
"	[GB]	Geo. Baskerville	" 1738.
"	[PP]	Philip Platel	" 1737.
"	[ICI]	Jas. Jenkins	" 1738.
"	[GR]	Gundry Roode	" 1737.
"	[IR]	John) Robinson	" 1738.
"	[I·S]	Jas. Schruder	" 1737.
"	[WS]	Wm. Soame	" 1738.
"	[SW]	Sam. Wood	" 1737.
"	[DW]	Denis Wilks	" "
1738-9	[R·Z]	Richd. Zouch	" 1735.
"	[TW]	Thos. Whipham	" 1739
"	[FK]	Fred Kandler	" 1735.
"	[IR]	Jno. Robinson	" 1738.
"	[LD]	Louis Dupont	" 1736.
"	[TR]	Thos. Rush	" 1724.
"	[BB]	Benj. Blakeley	" 1738.
"	[HB]	Henry Bates	" "
"	[PB]	Philip Brugier	" "
"	[WW]	Wm. West	" "
"	[IP]	Fras. Pages	" 1739.
"	[RH]	Robt. Hill	" "
"	[IL]	James Langlois	" 1738.
1739-40	[FK]	Fred Kandler	" 1735.
"	[RB]	? Richd. Bayler	" 1739.
"	[IP]	John Pero (see 1732)	" "

Date.	Goldsmiths' Marks and Names.*	Date.	Goldsmiths' Marks and Names.	Date.	Goldsmiths' Marks and Names.
1739-40	Humphrey Payne ent. 1739.	1739-40	Thos. England ent. 1739.	1739-40	Jessie McFarlane ent. 1739.
,,	Sarah Holaday ,, 1719.	,,	Robt. Lucas ,, ,,	,,	Wm. Justus ,, ,,
,,	Benj. Godfrey ,, 1732. (see 1735)	,,	Ben. Godfrey ,, ,,	,,	Wm. Young ,, ,,
,,	Thos. Whipham ,, 1737.	,,	Do. do. ,, ,,	,,	Jas. Manners ,, ,,
,,	Chas. Hillan ,, 1741.	,,	Gawen Nash ,, ,,	,,	John Harvey ,, ,,
,,	Wm. Kidney ,, 1739.	,,	John Bryan ,, ,,	,,	Chas. Jackson ,, ,,
..	Paul Lamerie ,, ,,	,,	Richard Beale ,, ,,	,,	Thos. Rush ,, ,,
,,	Ben. Blakeley ,, ,,	,,	John Cam ,, 1740.	,,	Thos. Gilpin ,, ,,
,,	Isaac Callerd ,, ,,,	,,	J. Barbitt ,, 1739.	,,	Danl. Chartier ,, 1740.
,,	Jeff. Griffith ,, ,,	,,	Richd. Pargeter ,, ,,	,,	Wm. Shaw ,, 1739.
,,	Thos. Tearle ,, ,,	,,	Marmdk. Daintry ,, ,,	,,	Richd. Gosling ,, ,,
,,	Jnthn. Fossy ,,, ,,	,,	Ed. Bennett ,,, ,,	,,	Fras. Spilsbury ‡ ,, ,,
,,	Paul Crespin ,, ,,	,,	Do. do. ,, ,,	,,	Louis Hamon ,, ,,
,,	John Harwood ,, ,,,	,,	Bennett Bradshaw & Co. ,, ,,	,,	Sam. Hutton ,, 1740.
,,	Richd. Bayley ,, ,,	,,	Thos. Bamford ,, ,,	,,	John Gamon ,, 1739.
,,	Robt. Abercromby ,, ,,	,,	John Eckfourd ,, ,,	,,	Fras. Nelme ,, ,,
,,	Lewis Dupont ,, ,,	,,	Wm. Shaw ,, ,,	,,	Henry Morris ,, ,,
,,	Wm. Hunter ,, ,,	,,	John Jacobs (see 1750) ,, ,,	,,	Thos. Pye ,, ,,
,,	Wm. Gwillim ,, ,,	,,	John Pero (see p. 190) ,, ,,	,,	Jas. West ,, ,,
,,	Geo. Boothby ,, ,,	,,	John White ,, ,,	,,	Jas. Paltro ,, ,,
,,	Edw. Aldridge ,, ,.	,,	Henry Herbert ,, ,,	,,	John Harwood ,, ,,
,,	Wm. Soame ,, ,,	,,	Richd. Zouch ,, ,,	,,	Denis Wilks ,, ,,
,,	Peter Bennett ,,, ,,	,,	Susan'h Hatfield ,, ,,	,,	Philip Roker ,, ,,
,,	Henry Bates ,, ,,	,,	J. McFarlane ,, ,,	,,	Simon Jouet ,,, ,,
,,	John Tuite ,, ,,	,,	Henry Morris ,, ,,	,,	Chas. Clark ,, ,,
		,,	John Luff ,, ,,	,,	John le Sage ,, ,,

DATE.	GOLDSMITHS' MARKS AND NAMES.	DATE.	GOLDSMITHS' MARKS AND NAMES.	DATE.	GOLDSMITHS' MARKS AND NAMES.
9-40	Benj. Sanders ent. 1739.	1740-1	? John Owing ent. 1724.	1742-3	Paul Crespin ent. 1739.
,,	Abm. de Oliveyra ,, ,,	,,	Name not traced.	,,	Jos. Allen & M'decai Fox ,, ,,
,,	Thos. Mason ,, ,,	,,	Do. do.	,,	Robt. Brown ,, ,,
,,	Chas. Martin ,, 1740.	,,	John Roker ,, 1740.	,,	Fras. Spilsbury ,, ,,
,,	Jos. Steward ,, 1739.	,,	Abm. le Francis ,, ,,	,,	Eliz. Tuite ,, 1741.
,,	Geo. Smith ,, ,,	,,	Benj. Gurdon ,, ,,	,,	Anne Craig & John · Neville ,, 1740. (see 1745)
,,	Louis Laroche ,, ,,	1741-2	David Hennell ,, 1739.	,,	Saml. Wells ,, ,,
40-1	John Robinson ,, ,,	,,	James Shruder ,, ,,	,,	Robt. Abercromby ,, 1739.
,,	Griff. Edwards ,, ,,	,,	Eliza Godfrey ,, 1741.	,,	Jas. Montgomery ,, 1742.
,,	John Pollock ,, ,,	,,	Saml. Roby ,, 1740.	,,	Jos. Timberlake ,, 1743.
,,	Jos. Sanders ,, ,,	,,	Geo. Wickes ,, 1739.	,,	Phillips Garden ,, 1739.
,,	Benj. Sanders ,, 1737.	,,	Thos. Farren ,, ,,	,,	Paul Crespin ,, ,,
,,	Wm. Garrard , 1735.	,,	Dinah Gamon ,, 1740.	,,	John Cam ,, 1740.
,,	Gabl. Sleath ,, ,,	,,	John Newton ,, 1739.	1743-4	Dd. Williams ,, 1739.
,,	Richd. Gurney & Co ,, 1739.	,,	Thos Gilpin ,, ,,	,,	Benj. Sanders ,, ,,
,,	Ed. Wood ,, 1740.	,,	Chas Hillan ,, 1741.	,,	? Robt. Abercromby ,, ,,
,,	Chas Bellassyse ,, ,,	,,	John Stewart (?)	,,	Wm. Hunter ,, ,,
,,	Sarah Hutton ,, ,,	,,	Peter Archambo ,, 1739.	,,	Wm. Gould ,, ,,
,,	Ed. Lambe ,, ,,	,,	Jas. Willmott ,, 1741.	,,	Jas. Wilks ,, ,,
,,	Thos. Mercer ,, ,,	,,	John Spackman ,, ,,	,,	Ed. Feline ,, ,,
,,	John Barbe ,, 1739.	,,	Chas Laughton ,, 1739.	,,	Aug. Courtauld ,, ,,
,,	Paul Crespin ,, 1740.	,,	Thos Lawrence ,, 1742.	,,	Geo. Jones ,, ,,
,,	Isabel Pero ,, ,,	,,	Jer'mi'h King ,, 1739.	,,	Jer'mi'h Ashley ,, 1740.
,,	Lewis Ouvry ,, ,,	,,	Benj. Gurdon ,, 1740.	,,	Henry Brind ,, 1742.
,,	Jas. Gould ,, 1741.	,,	Robt. Tyrrill ,, 1742.	,,	Robt. Abercromby ,, 1739.
,,	Edwd. Aldridge ,, 1739. (see 1744)	1742-3	Jno. Gould ,, 1739.	,,	Pere Pilleau ,, ,,

DATE.	GOLDSMITHS' MARKS AND NAMES.			DATE.	GOLDSMITHS' MARKS AND NAMES.			DATE.	GOLDSMITHS' MARKS AND NAMES.		
1743-4		Thos.	Whipham ent. 1737.	1744-5		Jas.	Morrison ent. 1740.	1746-7		Ernest	Sieber ent. 1746.
,,		Name not traced.		1745-6		Benj.	West ,, 1739.	,,		Geo.	Young ,, ,,
,,		Isaac	Duke ,, 1743.	,,		Thos. Wm.	Whipham & Williams } ,, 1740.	,,		Saml.	Meriton ,, ,,
,,		Ed.	Malluson ,, ,,	,,		Ann John	Craig & Neville } (see 1742) ,, ,,	,,		Henry	Herbert ,, 1747.
,,		Geo	Methuen ,, ,,	,,		John	Holland ,, 1739.	,,		Do.	do. ,, ,,
,,		Chas.	Johnson ,, ,,	,,		Ben.	Cartwright ,, ,,	,,		Simon	Jouet ,, ,,
,,		Ann	Farren ,, ,,	,,		Fred.	Kandler ,, ,,	,,		Benj.	Cartwright ,, 1739.
,,		Geo.	Ridout ,, ,,	,,		Wm.	Cripps ,, 1743.	1747-8		Jno.	Sanders ,, ,,
,,		Robt.	Swanson ,, ,,	,,		Fras.	Crump ,, 1741.	,,		Wm.	Gould ,, ,,
1744-5		Wm. Soame or Wm. Shaw	,, 1723. } ,, 1727.	,,		John	Higginbotham ,, 1745.	,,		Richd.	Kersill ,, 1744.
,,		Edwd. Aldridge (see 1740)	,, 1739.	,,		Geo.	Baskerville ,, ,,	,,		Wm.	Williams ,, 1742.
,,		Ed.	Feline ,, ,,	,,		Jas.	Manners, Jr. ,, ,,	,,		Saml. Courtauld (see 1750).	,, 1746.
,,		Lewis	Pantin ,, ,,	,,		? Jer'mi'h King	,, ,,	,,		Jacob	Marsh ,, 1744.
,,		Robt.	Pilkington ,, ,,	,,		John	Swift (probably, see 1754-5) ,, 1739.	,,		Thos.	Carlton ,, ,,
,,		Chas.	Hatfield ,, ,,	,,		Sam	Key ,, 1745.	,,		? John	Eckfourd ,, 1739.
,,		Peter	Archambo ,, ,,	,,		Robt.	Andrews ,, ,,	,,		? Benj. Benj.	Griffin or Gignac ,, 1742. ,, 1744.
,,		John	Quantock ,, ,,	,,		John	Harvey ,, ,,	,,		John	Richardson ,, 1743.
,,		Aymé	Videau ,, ,,	1746-7		Sam	Wood ,, 1739.	,,		Thos.	Parr ,, 1739.
,,		John	Barbe ,, ,,	,,		Jas.	Gould ,, 1743.	,,		M'duke	Daintry ,, ,,
,,		John	Edwards ,, ,,	,,		Wm.	Hunter ,, 1739.	,,		Wm	Solomon ,, 1747.
,,		Wm	Bagnall ,, 1744.	,,		Wm.	Peaston ,, 1746.	,,		Saml.	Herbert ,, ,,
,,		Wm Gwillim & Peter Castle }	,, ,,	,,		Jas.	Morrison ,, 1744.	,,		John	Fray ,, 1748.
,,		Jas.	Smith ,, ,,	,,		Henry	Morris ,, 1739.	,,		Ben.	Cooper ,, ,,
,,		John	Neville ,, 1745.	,,		Jos.	Barker ,, 1746.	1748-9		Edwd.	Medlycott ,, ,,
,,		Thos.	Jackson ,, 1739.	,,		Ed.	Vincent ,, 1739.	,,		John	Wirgman ,, 1745.
,,		Nich's	Sprimont ,, 1742.	,,		Ann	Kersill ,, 1747.	,,		Hmphy. Payne (see 1739)	,, 1739.
								,,		Elias	Cachart ,, 1742.

Date.	Goldsmiths' Marks and Names.	Date.	Goldsmiths' Marks and Names.	Date.	Goldsmiths' Marks and Names.
1748-9	M'decai Fox ent. 1746.	1749-50	Geo. Bindon ent. 1749.	1750-1	John Berthelot ent. 1750.
"	Wm. Grundy „ 1748.	"	Thos. Mann „ 1739.	"	L'r'nce Johnson „ 1751.
"	John Carman „ „	"	John Alderhead „ 1750.	"	Phillips Garden „ „
"	Geo. Young „ 1746.	"	Jas. Tookey „ „	"	Math. Brodier „ „
"	John Barbe „ 1739.	"	Wm. Wooler „ „	"	Fras. Crump „ 1750.
"	Geo. Hunter „ 1748.	"	Geo. Morris „ „	"	Do. do. „ „
"	Phillips Garden „ „	"	Thos. Jeannes „ „	c. 1750-60	W.F [lion] Name not traced.
"	Wm. Shaw „ 1749.	1750-1	John Priest „ 1748.	1751-2	? John Wetherell „ 1743.
"	Eliz. Hartley „ 1748.	"	Chas. Chesterman „ 1741.	"	John Payne „ 1750.
"	Eliz. Jackson „ „	"	Eben. Coker „ 1739.	"	Denis Wilks „ 1747.
"	Eliz. Oldfield „ „	"	John Rowe „ 1749.	"	Fred Knopfell „ 1752.
"	Ed. Dowdall „ „	"	Richd. Gurney & Co. „ 1750.	"	Saml. Taylor „ 1744.
"	Danl. Shaw „ „	"	S. Herbert & Co. „ „	"	P. Werritzer „ 1750.
"	Walter Brind „ 1749.	"	Louis Guichard „ 1748.	"	Thos. Moore „ „
1749-50	Wm. Grundy „ 1743.	"	Geo. Campar „ 1749.	"	Wm. Woodward „ 1743.
"	Dan. Piers „ 1746.	"	Fuller White & John Fray „ 1750.	"	G. & S. Smith „ 1751.
"	Benj. Cartwright „ 1739.	"	Henry Bayley „ „	"	Geo. Morris „ „
"	Paul Crespin „ „	"	John Jacobs (see 1739) „ 1739.	"	Nicks Winkins „ „
"	Name not traced.	"	Saml. Courtauld (see 1747 and 1755) „ 1746.	"	Paul Pinard „ „
"	Jerem'h King „ „	"	Paul Lamerie (see 1729 and 1730) „ 1732.	"	Ed. Doweal „ „
"	Abm. Portal „ 1749.	"	A. Montgomery „ 1750.	"	Thos. Beere „ „
"	Abm. le Francis „ 1746.	"	Michl. Ward „ „	"	Phil. Bruguier „ 1752.
"	Jabez Daniel „ 1749.	"	Geo. Bindon „ 1749.	1752-3	Robt. Cox „ „
"	Wm. MacKenzie „ 1748.	"	John Harvey „ 1750.	"	Lewis Haman „ 1739.
"	Wm. Kersill „ 1749.	"	Thos. Smith „ „	"	Robt. Cox (see above) „ 1752.
"	Andrew Killick „ „			"	Wm. Alexander „ 1742.
"	Henry Haynes „ „			"	John Payne „ 1751.

Date.	Goldsmiths' Marks and Names.		
1752-3	WH	Wm. Homer	ent. 1750.
"	W S P	Wm. Shaw & Wm. Priest }	" 1749.
"	JB	John Berthelot	" 1741.
"	JR	John Richardson	" 1752.
"	DP	Danl. Piers	" 1746.
"	CC	Chas. Chesterman	" 1752.
"	I·C	John Carman	" "
"	RG	Richd. Goldwire	" 1753.
"	PG	Phillips Garden	" 1751.
1753-4	GH	Geo. Hunter	" 1748.
"	DP	Danl. Piers	" "
"	T&W	Turner & Williams	" 1753.
"	RG	Richd. Gosling	" 1739.
"	RH	Robt. Hennell	" 1753.
"	JC	John Cafe	" 1742.
"	AJ	Alex. Johnston	" 1747.
"	FW	Fuller White	" 1744.
"	DW IF	Denis Wilks & John Fray }	" 1753.
"	WB	Wm. Bond	" "
"	TT	Thos. Towman	" "
"	IE	John Edwards	" "
"	GS FC	Gabl. Sleath & Fras. Crump }	" "
"	DCF	D. C Fueter	" "
"	DS	Dorothy Sarbit	" "
"	EA	Edward Aldridge (see 1740 and 1744)	" 1743.
"	IS A	Edwd. Aldridge & John Stamper }	" 1753.

Date.	Goldsmiths' Marks and Names.		
1753-4	TR	Thos. Rowe	ent. 1753.
"	SS	Saml. Smith	" 1754.
"	LL	Simon Le Sage	" "
"	HC	Henry Corry	" .
"	BC	* Benj. Cartwright	" "
"	SB	Sarah Buttall	" "
1754-5	P A P M	Peter Archambo & Peter Meure }	" 1749.
"	RP	? Robt. Perth.	
"	WC	Wm. Cripps	" 1743.
"	I·Q	John Quantock	" 1754.
"	IS	Ed. Aldridge & John Stamper }	" 1753.
"	PG	Phillips Garden	" "
"	IM	John Munns	" "
"	DM	Do'thy Mills	" 1752.
"	JH	John Holland	" 1739.
"	IS	John Steward	" 1755.
"	TC	Thos. Collier	" 1754.
"	HD	Henry Dutton	" "
"	W·B	Walter Brind	" 1749.
"	GB WS	Geo. Baskerville & Wm. Sampel }	" 1755.
"	DPW	Dobson Prior & Williams }	" "
"	D	John Delmester	" "
"	W·I	? Wm. Justus	" 1739.
"	JS	John Swift (see 1745 and below)	" "
"	HM	Henry Miller	ent. 1740.
1755-6	IS	John Swift	" 1739.

Date.	Goldsmiths' Marks and Names.		
1755-6	WS	Wm. Sanden	ent. 1755.
"	LS	Simon Le Sage	" 1754.
"	MF	Magd'n Feline	" 1753.
"	JW	? Thos. Wright	" 1754.
"	S·C	Saml. Courtauld (see 1750)	" 1746.
"	PC	Paul Crespin (see 1749)	" 1739.
"	WB JP	Wm. Bond & John Phipps }	" 1754.
"	WT	Wm. Turner	" "
"	WB	Wm. Bond	" 1753.
"	JJ	Jas. Jones	" 1755.
"	PT	Peter Taylor	" 1740.
"	FV	Fred Vonham	" 1752.
"	SS	Saml. Siervent	" 1755.
"	J·W	John Wirgman	" 1745.
"	RM	Richd. Mills	" 1755.
"	B·B	Benj: Brewood	" "
"	ED	Ed. Doweal	" 1751.
"	RCox	Robt. Cox	" 1755.
"	R·C	Do. do.	" "
"	TB	Thos. Beezley	" "
"	AS	Albert Schurman	" 1756.
"	JR	John Robinson	" 1739.
1756-7	SW	Saml. Wheat	" 1756.
"	PG	Pierre Gillois	" 1754.
"	WR	Wm. Robertson	" 1753.
"	WC	Wm. Caldecott	" 1756.

Date.	Goldsmiths' Marks and Names.	Date.	Goldsmiths' Marks and Names.
1756-7	? Thos. Gilpin ent. 1739.	1757-8	John Schuppe ent. 1753.
,,	Thos. Heming ,, 1745.	,,	Wm. Cafe ,, 1757.
,,	Name not traced.	1758-9	Fras. Nelme ,, 1722.
,,	Mathew Roker ,, 1755.	,,	Saml. Taylor ,, 1744.
,,	Paul Callard ,, 1751.	,,	Wm. Cripps ,, 1743.
,,	John Edwards ,, 1753.	,,	Name not traced.
,,	Wm. Gould ,, ,,	,,	Wm. Shaw & Wm. Priest } ,, 1749.
,,	T. & W. Devonshire Watkins } ,, 1756.	,,	Name not traced.
,,	Ben. Cartwright ,, ,,	,,	John Hague ,, 1758.
,,	Edw. Jay ,, 1757.	,,	Wm. Bell ,, 1759.
1757-8	David Hennell ,, 1736.	,,	Lewis Herne & Francis Butty } ,, 1757.
,,	Joseph Clare ,, 1713. (see 1716)	,,	Jos. Bell ,, 1756.
,,	Eliza Godfrey ,, 1741.	,,	Name not traced.
,,	John Jacobs ,, 1739.	1759-60	S. Herbert & Co. ,, 1750.
,,	W. & R. Peaston ,, 1756.	,,	Fred. Kandler ,, 1739.
,,	Ed. Darvill ,, 1757.	,,	John Delmester ,, 1755.
,,	Robert Innes ,, 1742.	,,	John Perry ,, 1757.
,,	Stephen Ardesoif ,, 1756.	,,	Saml. Wood, 2nd mk. ,, 1739.
,,	Ed. Bennett ,, 1739.	,,	Geo. Ibbott ,, 1753.
,,	John Thos. Kentenber & Groves } 1757	,,	John Perry ,, 1757.
,,	John Frost ,, ,,	,,	Simon Le Sage ,, 1754.
,,	Do. do. ,, ,,	,,	? Walter Brind ,, 1749.
,,	John Chas. Hyatt & Semore } ,, ,,	,,	Wm. Cripps ,, 1743.
,,	Arthur Annesley ,, 1758. (see 1761)	,,	John Hyatt ,, 1748.
,,	Robt. Burton ,, ,,	,,	Henry Bayley (probably).

Date.	Mark	Name	Entry
1759-60	SW	? Saml. Wheat	ent. 1756.
"	SW / IA	Stephen Abdy & Wm. Jury }	" 1759.
"	AB	Alex. Barnett	" "
"	TC	Thos. Congreve	" 1756.
"	TD	Thos. Doxsey	" "
"	WM	Wm. Moody	" "
"	WD	Wm. Day	" 1759.
"	S·E	Saml. Eaton	" "
"	JK	? Jno. Kentenber	
1760-1	R·R	Robt. Rew	" 1754.
"	EW	Edwd. Wakelin	" 1747.
"	CD	Name not traced.	
"	FW	Fuller White	" 1758.
"	AS	Alex. Saunders	" 1757.
"	JM	John Moore	" 1758.
"	CT	C'nst'ne Teulings	" 1755.
"	WH	Wm. Howard	" 1760.
"	GM	Geo. Methuen	" 1743.
"	I·E	John Eaton	" 1760.
c. 1760-1	W·L	Name not traced.	
"	Lee	Jeremy Lee	" 1739.
1761-2	R·R	Richd. Rugg	" 1754.
"	WP	Wm. Plummer	" 1755.
"	FLHB	Louis Fras. Herne & Butty }	" 1757.
"	FBND	Fras. Nicks. Butty & Dumee }	" "
"	WS	Wm. Shaw	" 1749.

Date.	Mark	Name	Entry
1761-2	I·H	John Horsley.	
"	JG	John Gorham	ent. 1757.
"	A·A	Arthur Annesley (see 1757)	" 1758.
"	GH	Geo. Hunter	" 1748.
"	MF	Magdalen Feline	" 1753.
"	TH	Thomas Heming (see 1756)	" 1745.
"	MP	Mary Piers	" 1758.
"	TP	Thos. Powell	" "
1762-3	JJ	Jas. Jones	" 1755.
"	WT	Wm. Tant (probably)	" 1773.
"	WS	Wm. Sampel	" 1755.
"	LB	Louis Black	" 1761.
"	CTW	Thos. Cnas. Whipham & Wright }	" 1757.
"	GI	Geo. Ibbott	" 1753.
"	SD	Saml. Delamy	" 1762.
"	DWI	W. & J. Deane	" "
"	IB	Jos. Bell	" 1756.
"	EA	Edwd. Aldridge & Co.	
"	WD	Wm. Day	" 1759.
"	WWa	Wm. Watkins	" 1756.
"	E*A	Edward Aldridge	" 1739.
"	R‡P	R Peaston	" 1756.
1763-4	RT	Richd. Thomas	" 1755.
"	JD	Tmpsn. Davis	" 1757.
"	EA	Edward Aldridge	" 1739.
"	CTW	Thos. Chas. Whipham & Wright }	" 1758.

Date.	Mark	Name	Entry
1763-4	DS / RS	Danl. Smith & Robt. Sharp }	
"	TWC	T. & W. Chawner (probably).	
"	EC	Ebenezer Coker	"
"	PV	Phil. Vincent	ent. 1757.
"	W·K	Wm. King	" 1761.
"	JB	John Buckett.	
"	IA	John Aspinshaw	" 1763.
"	J·L	John Lamfert	" 1748.
c. 1763-4	NH	Name not traced.	
"	TE / GS	Do. do.	
1764-5	RDH	D. & R. Hennell	" 1768.
"	THRM	? Thos. Hannam Rich. Mills }	
"	CM	Name not traced.	
"	WPRP	W. & R. Peaston (probably).	
"	IWVL	Names not traced.	
"	HSC	John C. Hyatt & Semore }	ent. 1757.
"	AL	Aug. Le Sage	" 1767.
"	TFIM	Thos. J. Freeman & Marshall }	" 1764.
"	AC	Anthy. Calame	" "
"	IAC	J. A. Calame	" "
"	I·I	John Innocent (probably).	
"	WPRP	W. & R. Peaston (see above)	"
"	WC	Wm. Cafe	ent. 1757.
"	ER	Name not traced.	
"	BM	Do. do.	
"	CTW	Thos. Chas. Whipham & Wright }	" 1758.

Date.	Goldsmiths' Marks and Names.		Date.	Goldsmiths' Marks and Names.		Date.	Goldsmiths' Marks and Names.	
1765-6	IWVL	Names not traced.	1767-8	OTBIJ	Thos. Bumfries & Orlando Jackson } ent. 1766.	1769-70	I·K	John Kentenber ent. 1757.
,,	GS	Do. do.	,,	SHHB	S. Herbert & Co. ,, 1750.	,,	AL	Aug. Le Sage ,, 1767.
,,	WC	Wm. Caldecott ent. 1756.	,,	C·B	Name not traced.	,,	EL	Edwd. Lowe ,, 1777.
,,	EC	Eben. Coker (probably).	,,	WA	Wm. Abdy ,, 1767.	,,	WB	Walter Brind ,, 1757.
,,	WIf	Name not traced.	,,	G·F	Geo. Fayle ,, ,,	,,	WG	Wm. Grundy ,, 1748.
,,	ER	Emick Romer ,,	,,	W·T	Wm. Tuite (probably).	,,	SC I·C	Septimus & James Crespell }
,,	BM	Name not traced.	,,	J8	Name not traced.	,,	TI	Thos. Jackson ,, 1769.
,,	R✱P	? R. Peaston.	1768-9	I·P E·W	John Parker & Edwd. Wakelin }	,,	LC GC	Louisa Courtauld & Geo. Cowles. }
,,	IA	John Allen ent. 1761.	,,	I·H	James Hunt ent. 1760.	,,	RR	Robt. Rogers ,, 1773.
,,	SH	Sam. Howland ,, 1760.	,,	T·C W·C	T. & W. Chawner (probably).	,,	JB	John Baker ,, 1770.
,,	GH	Geo. Hunter ,, 1765.	,,	R D S S	Dan. Smith & Robt. Sharp }	1770-1	B·G	Benj. Gignac ,, 1744.
,,	T·C W·C	T. & W. Chawner (probably).	,,	A L	Name not traced.	,,	FH	Thos. Heming ,, ,,
1766-7	LH	Name not traced.	,,	FS	Fras. Spilsbury, Jr.	,,	JA	Jas. Allen ,, 1766.
,,	LC	Louisa Courtauld.	,,	E·T	? Eliz. Tuite ent. 1741. (see 1742)	,,	SC I·C	Septimus & James Crespell } see 1769.
,,	JL	John Lampfert ent. 1748.	,,	WJ	Name not traced.	,,	T·P	? Thos. Powell ent. 1756.
,,	I·L S	John Langford & John Sebille }	,,	EC	Edward Capper (probably).	,,	TA	Thos. Arnold ,, 1770.
,,	MF	Matthew Ferris ,, 1759.	,,	FC	Fras. Crump ent. 1756.	,,	IB	John Baxter ,, 1773.
,,	T·H I·C	Thos. Hannam & John Crouch }	,,	WP JTP	W. & J. Priest.	,,	CW	Chas. Wright.
,,	FC	Fras. Crump ,, 1756.	,,	JL	John Lamfert ,, 1748.	,,	I·B	? John Buckett ,, 1770.
,,	GA	Geo. Andrews ,, 1763.	,,	BB	Benj. Blakeley ,, 1739.	,,	I·L S	John Langford & John Sebille }
,,	TD	Thos. Dealtry ,, 1765.	,,	ID	John Darwall ,, 1768.	,,	G·S	Name not traced.
,,	CM	Chas. Miegg ,, 1767.	1769-70	JN	John Neville (probably).	,,	ER	E. Romer (probably).
,,	DM	Dorothy Mills (probably).	,,	C·H A·G	Chas. Aldridge & Henry Green }	,,	OJ	Orlando Jackson ent. 1759.
,,	T·W	Thos. Wynne ent. 1754.	,,	FC	Fras. Crump ent. 1756.	,,	JW	Sam. Wheat ,, 1756.
1767-8	JR	Jno. Richardson ,, 1752.	,,	GS	Geo. Seatoun.	,,	W·G I·V	John Gimblett & Wm. Vale } ,, 1770.
,,	IWFK	Names not traced.	,,	CW	Chas. Woodward.	,,	I·B	J. Bassingwhite ,, ,,
						1771-2	I·C T·H	John Crouch & Thos. Hannam }

Date.	Goldsmiths' Marks and Names.		
1771-2	TF	Thos. Foster	ent. 1769.
"	DB	David Bell	" 1756.
"	I·S	? Robt. & Jno. Schofield }	" 1776.
"	T·I·D·D	Thos. & Jabez Daniel }	
"	S·B	? Sarah Buttall	" 1754.
"	JA	Jonathan Alleine.	
"	WP	Wm. Penstone.	
"	W·S	Wm. Sheen	" 1755.
"	T·C	Thos. Chawner.	
"	S·H	Saml. Howland	" 1760.
"	A·U	A. Underwood.	
"	CC	Chas. Chesterman	" 1771.
"	EI	Edwd. Jay	" 1757.
"	T·T	Thos. Towman (probably).	
"	WT	Wm. Tuite	ent. 1756.
"	I·R	John Romer	ent before 1773.
1772-3	I·C	John Carter	" "
"	TC	Thos. Chawner	" "
"	E·T	Eliz Tookey	" "
"	WF	Wm. Fearn	" "
"	BD	Burrage Davenport	" "
"	I·A	John Arnell	" "
"	J·S	John Swift	" "
"	P·N	Philip Norman,	" "
"	CW	Chas. Wright	" "
"	P·D	Peter Desergnes or Peter Devese. }	
"	Wa	? Wm. Watkins	" 1756.

Date.	Goldsmiths' Marks and Names.		
1772-3	SS	Henry Hallsworth.	
"	A·F	Name not traced.	
"	I·F	John Fayle	ent. 1772.
"	WE	Wm. Eley (probably).	
1773-4	R·S	Dan. Smith & Robt. Sharp }	ent. before 1773.
"	OI	Orlando Jackson	" 1759.
"	J·H	John Harvey	" 1739.
"	TS	Thos. Smith	" 1750.
"	LV	Name not traced.	
"	A·B L·D	Abr'm Barrier & Lewis Ducornieu }	
"	WS	Wm. Sheen	" 1775.
"	I·D·D	Jabez & Thos. Daniel }	see 1771.
"	BD	Burrage Davenport.	
"	SW	Saml. Wood (probably).	
"	PF	P. Freeman	ent. 1773.
"	MM	Mary Makemeid	" "
"	T·T	Thos. Tookey	" "
"	LD	Louis de Lisle	" "
"	WLB	Wm. Le Bas	" "
1774-5	IS	Jas. Stamp	" 1774.
"	WP	Wm. Penstone	" "
"	E·T	Eliz. Tookey	" 1773.
"	T·E	Thos. Evans	" 1774.
"	IY OI	Jas. Young & Orlando Jackson }	" "
"	I·D	John Deacon	" 1773.
"	TD	Thomas Daniel (probably).	

Date.	Goldsmiths' Marks and Names.		
1774-5	PF	P. Freeman	ent. 1774.
"	WF	Wm. Fennell.	
"	IY	Jas. Young	1775.
"	IS	Jas. Stamp	" 1774.
1775-6	W·T	Walter Tweedie	ent. before 1773.
"	E·C	? Ed. Capper	(see 1776.)
"	WC	? Wm. Cox.	
"	IK	? John Kentish Jas. King or Jas. Kingman }	ent. 1773.
"	WS RC	Wm. Sumner & Richd. Crossley }	" 1775.
"	IY	Jas. Young	" "
"	TL	Thos. Langford (probably)	
"	I·E W·F	? John Easton & Wm. Fearn or Wm. Fennell, etc. }	
"	R·R	Robt. Ross	ent. 1774.
"	MC	Mark Cripps	" 1767.
"	C·W	Chris. Woods	" 1775.
"	RR	Richd. Rugg	" "
"	RI	Robt. Jones	" 1776.
"	G·B M	Geo. Baskerville & T Morley }	" 1775.
"	RP	Robt. Piercy	" "
"	{LD}	Louis Ducomieu	
"	BS	Ben Stephenson	
1776-7	CH	Name not traced.	
"	HS	Henry Sardet,	
"	RP	Robt. Piercy	" "
"	AB	Alexr. Barnet	" 1759.
"	N·D	Nich. Dumee	" 1776.
"	W·G·H C	Geo. Heming & Wm. Chawner }	" 1774.

Date	Mark	Name
1776-7	I·L	John Lautier ent. 1773.
"	I·W / W·T	John Wm. Wakelin & Taylor } " 1776.
"	C·H / A·G	Chas. Henry Aldridge & Green } " 1775.
"	A·C	A. Calame " 1764.
"	E·C	Edwd. Edwd. Capper or Cooke } " 1773.
"	A·L	Aug. Le Sage " 1767.
"	P·R	Phil. Roker " 1776.
"	E·R	Eliz. Roker " "
1777-8	H·G	Henry Greenway " 1775.
"	J·A	Jon'th'n Alleine.
"	R·M / R·C	Robt. & Richd. Makepeace Carter } " 1777.
"	I·H	Joseph Heriot " 1750.
"	W·H	Wm. Holmes " 1776.
"	W·P	Wm. Potter " 1777.
"	W·W / H·C	Wm. Howe & Wm. Clark } " "
"	W·G	Wm. Grundy " "
"	G·N	Geo. Natter " 1773.
"	R·I / I·S	Robt. Jones & John Schofield } " 1776.
"	G·N	Name not traced.
"	T·D	T. Daniel " 1774.
1778-9	H·C / A·G	Name not traced.
"	A·F	Andrew Fogelberg.
"	I·D	J. Denzilow.
"	W·E	Wm. Eley.
"	H·B	Hester Bateman. " 1774.
"	W·H / N·D	Wm. Nichs. Holmes & Dumee } " 1773.
1778-9	N·H	Nichs. Hearnden ent. 1773.
"	E·D	Ed. Dobson " 1778.
"	R·C / D·S / R·S	Rich. Danl. Robt. Carter, Smith & Sharp } " "
"	W·E / G·P	Wm. Geo. Eley & Pierpoint } " 1778.
"	I·D	John Deacon " 1776.
"	C·K	Chas. Kandler " 1778.
"	E·L	Ed. Lowe " 1777.
"	G·R	Geo. Rodenbostel " 1778.
"	T·W	Thos. Wallis " 1773.
1779-80	I·S	John Schofield " 1778.
"	E·F / d	Edith Fennell " 1780.
"	W·G / H·C	Geo. Wm. Heming & Chawner } " 1774. (see also 1781)
"	H·B	Hester Bateman " 1774.
"	T·S	Thos. Satchwell " 1773.
"	T·P / R·P	Thos. & Richd. Payne } " 1777.
"	W·F	W. L. Foster " 1775.
"	E·W / G·F	Wm. Ed. Grundy & Fernell } " 1779.
"	L·C / S·C	Louisa & Samuel Courtauld } " 1777.
1780-1	F·S	Fras. Stamp " 1780.
"	W·G	Wm. Garrard (probably).
"	R / J·M	Jane Rich. Dorrell & May } ent. 1771.
"	I·S	Jas. Sutton " 1780.
"	W·V	Wm. Vincent " 1773.
"	I·M / W·H	Jas. Wm. Mince & Hodgkins } " 1780.
"	T·B / A·H	T. P. Arthur Boulton & Humphreys } " "
"	I·L / I·R	John Langlands & John Robertson of Newcastle } " "
1780-1	H·P	Name not traced.
"	I·P	Joseph Preedy.
"	I·K	John Kidder ent. 1780.
1781-2	T·P / A·H	T. B. Pratt & Arthur Humphreys } " 1773.
"	C·W	Chas. Wright " 1775.
"	R·C	Robt. Cruickshank " 1773.
"	I·C / T·H	John Thos. Crouch & Hannam } " "
"	I·L	Josh. Lejeune " "
"	L·K	Luke Kendall " 1772.
"	G·H / W·C	Geo. Wm. Heming & Chawner } " 1781.
"	W·P / W·W	Wm. Wm. Playfair & Wilson } " 1782.
"	T·D / I·W	Thos. John Daniel & Wall } " 1781.
1782-3	G·S	Geo. Smith " 1782.
"	J·W	John Wren " 1777.
"	G·G	George Giles (probably).
"	A·F / S·G	Andr. Steph. Fogelberg & Gilbert } ent. 1780.
"	R·H	Robt. Hennell " 1773.
"	W·B	Wm. Bayley.
"	N·A / N·A	This mark is A N S A. Name not traced.
"	A·P / P·P	Abm. Peter Peterson & Podie } " 1783.
1783-4	I·L	John Lamb " "
"	I·S / I·B	Jas. Jos. Sutton & Bult } " 1782.
"	W·T	Wm. Tant " 1773.
"	W·B	Wm. Brown (probably).
"	S·B	? Saml. Bradley.
"	A·F / S·G	Name not traced.

Date.	Goldsmiths' Marks and Names.		Date.	Goldsmiths' Marks and Names.		Date.	Goldsmiths' Marks and Names.	
1783-4	EF	Ed. Fennell ent. 1780.	1786-7	SG EW	Saml. Godbehere & Edwd. Wigan } ent. 1786.	1789-90	TW	Thos. Willmore ent. 179..
"	SW	Saml. Wintle ,, 1783.	"	TP·AH	T. Arth. Pratt & Humphreys } ,, 1780.	"	PC	Name not traced.
"	WS	Wm. Sumner ,, 1782.	"	W·S	Wm. Sutton ,, 1784.	1790-1	P·P	Peter Podie ,, 17..
"	W	Name not traced.	"	WR	Wm. Reynolds ,, 1773.	"	TP ER	T. E. Phipps & Robinson }
"	IT	John Townshend ,, 1783.	"		Robt. Hennell as 1782.	"	GS WF	Geo. Wm. Smith & Fearn } ,, 17..
"	TC	Thos. Chawner ,, 1773.	"	HC	Henry Chawner ent. 1786.	"	RH	Robt. Hennell ,, 17..
"	IT	John Tayleur ,, 1775.	"	GG	Name not traced.	"	PB IB	Peter & Jonath'n Bateman } ,, 17..
"	IS	John Schofield ,, 1778.	"	CA	Chas. Aldridge ,, 1786.	"	SD	Saml. Davenport ,, 17..
1784-5	LI	Name not traced.	"	TD	Thos. Daniel ,, 1774.	"	WA	Wm. Abdy ,, 17..
"	BM	Do. do.	"	DD	Danl. Denny ,, 1782.	"	AP	Abm. Peterson ,, 17..
"	CH	Chas. Hougham ,, 1785.	"	WP	Wm. Pitts ,, 1786.	1791-2	WP JP	Wm. Jos. Pitts & Preedy }
"	HG	Hen. Greenway ,, 1775.	1787-8	SM	Saml. Massey (probably).	"	GB	Geo. Baskerville (probab..
"	SA	Stephen Adams ,, 1760.	"	JH	Name not traced.	"	GS	Geo. Smith ent. 17..
"	SG	Saml. Godbehere ,, 1784.	"	WE	Wm. Eley.	"	RS	Robt. Salmon ,,
"	WS	Wm. Simmons ,, 1776.	"	TM	Thos. Mallison ent. 1773.	"	WF DP	Wm. Danl. Fountain & Pontifex } ,, 17..
"	PG	Peter Gillois ,, 1782.	"	DS RS	Danl. Smith & Robt. Sharp } ,, 1780.	"	IB EB	Jas. & Eliz. Bland } ,,
"	RI	Robt. Jones ,, 1778.	1788-9	EI	Edwd. Jay ,, 1773.	"	JL	John Lamb ,,
1785-6	WA	Wm. Abdy ,, 1784.	"	IC	John Carter before ,,	"	TS	Thos. Streetin ,,
"	I·MF	Name not traced.	"	IP	Thc Powell, probably 1770.	"	EB	Name not traced.
"	HV	Do. do.	"	GB	Geo Baskerville (probably).	"	SG RW	Do. do.
"	BL	Ben. Laver ,, 1781.	"	HC	Henry Cowper ent 1782.	1792-3	WL	Do. do.
"	WT	Walter Tweedie ,, 1775.	"	CB	Cornls. Bland ,, 1788.	"	WP IP	Wm. Jos. Pitts & Preedy (see above)
"	TW	Thos. Wallis ,, 1778.	"	TO	Thos. Ollivant ,, 1789.	"	HC	Henry Chawner ent. 17..
"	TD	Thos. Daniel ,, 1774.	1789-90	HB	Hester Bateman ,, 1774.	"	TH	Thos. Howell ,, 17..
"	IK	John Kidder ,, 1780.	"	HG	Henry Greenway ,, 1775.	"	TN	Thos. Northcote.
"	TS	Thos. Shepherd ,, 1785.	"	IT	John Thompson ,, 1785.	"	GS TH	Geo. Thos. Smith & Hayter } ent. 17..
"	AB	Abm. Barrier ,, 1775.	"	IE	John Edwards ,, 1788.			

Date	Goldsmiths' Marks and Names	
1792-3	WF/PS	Wm. Paul. — Frisbee & Storr } ent. 1792.
"	IF	John Fountain " "
"	TG	Thos. Graham " "
"	EI	Edwd. Jay " "
1793-4	I·W/R·G	J. Robt. — Wakelin & Garrard } " "
"	IM	John Moore " 1778.
"	I·S	John Schofield " "
"	PB/AB	Peter & Ann — Bateman " 1791.
"	RM/TM	Robt. & Thos. — Makepeace " 1794.
"	DU/NH	Duncan Urquhart & Naphtäli Hart } " 1791.
"	I·F/I·B	John Fountain & John Beadnall } " 1793.
"	W·F/I·F	Wm. & John — Fisher " "
1794-5	WF	Wm. Frisbee " 1792.
"	I·K	John King " 1785.
"	MB	? Mark Bock (see 1798).
"	F·T	? Francis Thurkle.
"	IR	John Robins ent. 1774.
"	JW	John Wren " 1777.
"	MP	Michl. Plummer " 1791.
"	WF	W. Fountain " 1794.
"	TN/GB	Thos. Northcote & Geo. Bourne } " "
1795-6	RG	Richd. Gardner or Robt. Gaze " 1773. / " 1795.
"	TE	Thos. Ellis " 1780.
"	RM	Robt. Makepeace " 1795.
"	PB/AB	Peter & Ann — Bateman " 1791.
"	TP/AH	T. B. Arthur — Pratt & Humphreys } " 1780.
"	WE	Wm. Eley.

Date	Goldsmiths' Marks and Names	
1795-6	SH	Name not traced.
"	IP/IP	J. & J. Perkins ent. 1795.
"	HN	Henry Nutting " 1796.
1796-7	SP	Name not traced.
"	RH/DH	Robt. & David Hennell } " 1795.
"	IM	John Mewburn " 1793.
"	IBO	Jos. B. Orme " 1796.
"	WEH	Wm. Hall " 1795.
"	HC/IF	Hy. Chawner & Jno. Eames } " 1796.
1797-8	RC	Richd. Crossley " 1782.
"	HC/IE	Henry Chawner & John Emes } " 1796.
"	GC	Geo. Cowles " 1797.
1798-9	EM	E. Morley.
"	IP	Jos. Preedy " 1777.
"	IB	John Beldon " 1784.
"	WE/WF	Wm. Eley & Wm. Fearn } " 1797.
"	GS	Geo. Smith.
"	IH/TL	Jos. Hardy & Thos. Lowndes } " 1798.
"	M·B	? Mark Bock.
"	JE	John Emes.
"	T·D	Thos. Dealtry " 1765.
1799/1800	WP	Wm. Pitts " 1781.
"	WB	Wm. Bennett " 1796.
"	WP	Wm. Pitts " 1799.
"	RC	Richd. Cooke " "
"	AF	Andrew Fogelberg " 1776.
"	IH	John Hutson " 1784.
"	WI	Name not traced.

Date	Goldsmiths' Marks and Names	
1799/1800	IP	Jos. Preedy ent. 1800.
1800-1	P·S	Paul Storr " 1793.
"	I·W/R·G	J. Robt. — Wakelin & Garrard } " 1792.
"	WH	Wm. Hall " 1795.
"	SG/EW/IB	Saml. Ed J. — Godbehere Wigan & Bult } " 1800.
"	TH/IC	Thos. John — Hannam & Crouch } " 1799.
1801-2	RG	Robt. Garrard " 1801.
"	I·P	John Parker.
"	JE	John Emes " 1796.
"	PB/AB/WB	Peter, Ann & Wm. — Bateman } " 1800.
"	GS/TH	Geo. Thos. — Smith & Hayter } " 1792.
"	RH/DH/SH	Robert, David & Saml. — Hennell }
1802-3	IH	John Harris " 1786.
"	DS/BS	Digby Benj. — Scott & Smith } " 1802.
"	HB	Wm. Burwash " "
"	PB/AB/WB	Peter, Ann & Wm. — Bateman } " 1800.
"	AB/GB	Alice & George — Burrows " 1802.
"	CB/TB	Christr. & T. W. — Barker " 1800.
1803-4	B·L	Benj. Laver " 1781.
"	TH	Thos. Holland " 1798.
"	GB/TB	G. & T. Burrows.
"	SG/W	Saml. & George — Whitford " 1802.
"	AJ	Name not traced.
"	IR	John Robins (probably).
"	TR	? Timothy Renou.
"	JA	John Austin.
1804-5	W·P	Wm. Purse.

Date.	Goldsmiths' Marks and Names.		Date.	Goldsmiths' Marks and Names.		Date.	Goldsmiths' Marks and Names.	
1804-5	S·B	Name not traced.	1808-9	TM	? T. W. Matthews.	1812-3	TB	? T. Barker.
"	RB&R	Rundell, Bridge & Rundell.	"	I·C	John Crouch ent. 1808.	"	IS	? John Sanders.
"	GW	Geo. Wintle ent. 1804.	"	E·M	E. Morley.	"	TI	Thos. Jenkinson (probably).
"	RG	Robt. Garrard „ 1802.	"	WE WF WC	Wm. Eley, / Wm. Fearn & / Wm. Chawner } „ „	"	RE EB	Rebecca Emes & / Edwd. Barnard } ent. 1808.
"	I·H	Jos. Hardy „ 1799.	"	HN RH	Henry Nutting & / Robt. Hennell } „ „	"	GS	Geo. Smith „ 1812.
"	HN	Hannah Northcote „ 1798.	"	RC GS	Richard Crossley & / Geo. Smith } „ 1807.	"	MS ES	Mary & Eliz. Sumner „ 1809.
1805-6	DP	Danl. Pontifex „ 1794.	"	W·S	Wm. Sumner „ 1802.	1813-4	IC WR	Jos. Craddock / & Wm. Reid } „ 1812.
"	JE	John Emes.	"	JC	John Crouch „ 1808.	"	PS BRITANNIA	Paul Storr „ 1793.
"	TA	? T. Ash.	1809-10	CH	Chas. Hougham „ 1785.	"	IWS WE	J. W. Story & / W. Elliott } „ 1809.
"	WB RS	Wm. Burwash & / Richd. Sibley } „ 1805.	"	JW	Thos. Wallis „ 1792.	1814-5	SH	Saml. Hennell „ 1811.
"	TS	Name not traced.	"	DW	David Windsor (probably).	"	RE EB	Emes & Barnard „ 1808.
1806-7	RH SH	R̂. & S. Hennell „ 1802.	"	TJ	Thomas Jenkinson „	"	SA	Stephen Adams, junr.
"	PB WB	Peter & Wm. Bateman „ 1805.	"	SJ	Name not traced.	"	W·B	Wm. Bell (probably).
"	JS	John Sanders (probably).	1810-1	TH SH	Do. do.	"	W·E	Wm. Elliott ent. 1810.
"	CF	Crespin Fuller „	"	RC	? Richd. Cooke ent. 1799.	"	IL WA	Name not traced.
"	IS	John Salkeld „	"	BS IS	Benj. Smith & / Jas. Smith. }	"	SH IT	S. Hennell & / J. Taylor } (probably).
"	TR	Thos. Robins „	"	TP ER	T Phipps & / E. Robinson }	1815-6	TP ER JP	Name not traced.
"	WF	Wm. Fountain ent. 1794.	"	SB IB	Name not traced.	"	JE FF	Do. do.
1807-8	TG IC	T. & J. Guest & / Josh. Cradock } „ 1806.	"	TW JH	Thos. Wallis & / Jonath'n Hayne } „ 1810.	"	IP GP	Do. do.
"	PB WB	P. & W. Bateman „ 1805.	"	IC TH	John Cotton & / Thos. Head } „ 1809.	"		Emes & Barnard as above.
"	SW	Saml. Whitford „ 1807.	1811-2	JB	James Beebe „ 1811.	"	RG	Robt Garrard ent. 1801.
"	T·H	Thos. Halford „ „	"	BS	Benj. & Jas. Smith.	"	CR DR	Christ'n Reid & ano'r / of Newcastle „ 1815.
"	BS	Name not traced.	"	WK	Wm. Kingdon (probably).	1816-7	WB	Wm. Burwash „ 1813.
"	JR	T Robins „ „	"	RR	Robt. Rutland ent. 1811.	"	IL	Jas. Lloyd.
"	IWS	? J. W. Storey.	"	SH	Saml. Hennell „ „	1817-8	S SR ILD	Name not traced.
1808-9	I·C	John Crouch „ 1808.	"	DS BS IS	Digby Scott, / Benj. Smith, / Jas. Smith } (probably).			
"	RE WE	Name not traced.						

Date.	Goldsmiths' Marks and Names.		Date.	Goldsmiths' Marks and Names.		Date.	Goldsmiths' Marks and Names.	
1817-8	WB	Wm. Bateman ent. 1815.	1823-4	I·B	John Bridge ent. 1823.	1830-1	TD	Thos. Dexter (probably).
"	M·S	Name not traced.	"	BS	Benj. Smith.	"	RA WS	Name not traced.
"	WC	Wm. Chawner " "	1824-5	TH GH	Thos. & Geo. Hayter " 1816.	1831-2	W·H	" "
"	TR	T. Robins (probably).	"	SC	Name not traced.	,	RH	R. Hennell.
"	WC	Wm. Chawner ent. 1815.	"	R·H	Robt. Hennell.	1833-4	PS	Paul Storr ent. 1793.
"	GP	Geo. Purse.	"	FF	Name not traced.	"	AS JS AS	Adey, Joseph & Albert } Savory " 1833.
1818-9	GW	Geo. Wintle " 1813.	"	WE CE IE	Do. do.	1834-5	N·M	N. Morrison (probably).
"	IW	Joseph Wilson.	"	G·K	Geo. Knight (probably).	"	IF	Jas. Franklin "
"	RG	Robt. Garrard " 1801.	"	WE	Wm. Edwards (").	"	WB	W. Bellchambers "
1819-20	SRID	Name not traced.	1825-6	IC	James Collins (").	"	RP CP	Name not traced.
"	AH	Do. do.	"	GB IB	John Bridge ent. 1823.	"	T·E	T. Eley.
"	HN	Henry Nutting " 1809.	"	RP	R. Peppin (probably).	1835-6	CF	Chas. Fox ent. 1822.
"	WS	Wm. Stevenson (probably).	"	CE	C. Eley (").	"	JCE	J. Chas. Edington " 1828.
"	TI	See 1812-3 above.	"	FH	Fras. Higgins (").	"	CR GS	Reily & Storer (probably).
"	PR	Philip Rundell ent. 1819.	1826-7	I·L H·L C·L	John, Henry & Chas. } Lias ent. 1823.	1836-7	CF	See 1835-6.
1820-1	W·B	Wm. Bateman " 1815.	"	A·B·S	A. B. Savory " 1826.	"	EB EJ	Edwd. Barnard, Edwd. Barnard, jr., John Barnard, & Wm. Barnard } ent. 1829.
"	I·L H·L	John & Henry Lias " 1819.	"	RC	Randall Chatterton " 1825.	1837-8	WE	Wm. Eaton.
1821-2	TB	Thos. Baker " 1815. or Thos. Balliston " 1819.	1827-8	BP	Name not traced.	"	RS	Richard Sibley (probably).
"	IET	? J. E. Terry & Co. " 1818.	"	T·C·S	T. Cox Savory " 1827.	"	GW	George Webb "
"	ICF	? John Foligno.	"	JW	Jacob Wintle " 1826.	"	RG	Robert Garrard ent. 1821.
"	CdCd	An Exeter maker (probably).	"	ME	Moses Emmanuel (probably).	"	MC	Mary Chawner.
"	JA IA	J. & J. Aldous "	1828-9	WS	Wm. Schofield (").	1838-9	WT RA	Wm. Theobalds & Robt. Atkinson } " 1838.
1822-3	PS	Paul Storr "	"	ES	E. S. Sampson (").	"	CR GS	Rawlins & Sumner.
"	WA	William Abdy "	1829-30	JH	Jas. Hobbs (").	1839-40	WB DB	Wm. Bateman & Danl. Ball } " 1839.
"	WT	Wm. Trayes ent. 1822.	"	EE	Edward Edwards.	"	FD	Francis Dexter " "
1823-4	IS	Name not traced.	"	RG	Robt. Garrard ent. 1801.	"	WC	Wm. Cooper (probably).
"	JA	John Angell (probably).	1830-1	CP	Chas. Plumley (probably).	"	IT	Jos. Taylor "

Date.	Goldsmiths' Marks and Names.			Date.	Goldsmiths' Marks and Names.			Date.	Goldsmiths' Marks and Names.		
1839-40	EE	Ed.	Edwards (probably).	1847-8	EE	Eliz.	Eaton.	1864-5	EKR		
1840-1	GL	Name not traced.		1848-9	EJ BW	E. J. & W.	Barnard. }	1865-6	IJK	I. J.	Keith.
,,	TC	Thos.	Cording ,,	,,	RH	R.	Hennell.	,,	R·H	Richd.	Hennell.
,,	GA	Geo. W. Adams	ent. 1840.	,,	JW	Jacob	Wintle (probably).	1866-7	GE GF		
,,	JA JA	J. & J. Aldous.*		1849-50	CTF GF	Chas. T.	Fox & Geo. Fox }	1867-8	GM HD	Macaire &	Dewar.
,,	MC GA	Mary Chawner & Geo. W. Adams } ,, ,,		,,	FD	Frans.	Douglas.	,,	ML HL		
1841-2	JS AS	Jos. & Albert Savory ,, ,,		,,	WRS	W. R.	Smily.	1868-9	AS		
,,	J·L	John Lacy or John Law } (probably).		1850-1	IK	John	Keith.	,,	CS H	Chas. Stuart	Harris.
1842-3	JCE	J. Chas. Edington ent. 1828.		,,	GI	George	Ivory.	1869-70	J EBW J	J., E., W., & J. Barnard.	
,,	R·H	R.	Hennell.	1851-2	EB JB	E. & J.	Barnard.	1870-1	WS	Wm.	Smiley.
,,	WB WS	Brown & Somersall (probably).		1852-3	JE	James	Edwards (probably).	1871-2	HE W	H. E.	Willis.
1843-4	WKR	Wm. K. Reid.		,,	IF	I.	Foligno.	1872-3	RS	Richd.	Sibley.
,,	WB	Wm.	Brown (possibly).	1853-4	EB & JB	E. & J.	Barnard.	1873-4	RM EH	Martin	Hall & Co. of Sheffield.
,,	JA J·A	Joseph & John Angel	see 1844.	1854-5	WR S	W. R.	Smily.	1874-5	JEM GW	Mappin &	Webb.
,,	R·S	Richd. Sibley	ent. 1837.	1855-6	GA	George	Angell.	1875-6	JAR		
1844-5	R·G	R.	Garrard ,, 1801.	1856-7	CTF GF	Chas. T	Fox & Geo. Fox }	1876-7	CFH	Messrs.	Hancock.
,,	JA J·A	Joseph & John	Angel.	1857-8	HW	Henry	Wilkinson of Sheffield.	1877-8	,,	,,	,,
,,	RGH	R. G.	Hennell.	1858-9	J·A	Joseph	Angell.	,,	RJL		
,,	BS	Benj.	Smith (probably).	,,	W·M	W.	Mann.	,,	TJ		
1845-6	ISH	John S. Hunt	ent. 1844.	,,	GR EB	Roberts & Briggs.		1878-9	SS	Stephen	Smith.
,,	CTF GF	Chas. T.	Fox & Geo. Fox }	1859-60	GA	George	Angell.	1879-80	D·H C·H	Hands &	Son.
1846-7	GFP	G. F.	Pinnell.	1860-1	EE JE	Messrs.	Eady.	1880-1	JWD	J. W	Dobson.
,,	H·H	Hyam	Hyams.	,,	CR WS	Rawlins & Sumner.		,,	EYI		
,,	E B & W	E. J. & W.	Barnard.	1861-2	RH	Robt.	Harper.	,,	WIS		
1847-8	IL HL	John & Henry	Lias.	1862-3	RH	Richard	Hennell.	1881-2	FH	Francis	Higgins.
,,	RP GB	R. G.	Pearce & Burrows. }	1863-4	GF	Geo.	Fox.	1882-3	CS H	Chas. Stuart	Harris.
				1864-5	GA	Geo.	Angell.				

Date.	Goldsmiths' Marks and Names.			Date.	Goldsmiths' Marks and Names.		
1882-3	JA JS			1900-1	CCP	C. C.	Pilling.
1883-4	JNM			1901-2	C.K	C.	Krall.
"	J ASM F			1902-3	WC	W.	Comyns & Sons.
"	PW			1903-4	WBJ MBS ND	Edward	Barnard & Sons, Ltd.
1884-5	JRH	J. R.	Hennell.	"	HL	H.	Lambert.
1885-6	JW J			"	J W		
"	CFH	Messrs.	Hancock.	"	JW ECW		
"	J.W. F.C.W	J. F. C.	Wakley & Wheeler.	1904-5	WJ		
1888-9	D&C			1905-6	TB	Thos.	Bradbury of Sheffield.
"	WD			"	A & H	Alstons &	Hallam.
1889-90	CFH	Messrs.	Hancock.	1906-7	C&Cº	Carrington & Co.	
1891-2	EH			1907-8	J&S		
1892-3	E·H			"	LG		
"	WC	W.	Comyns.	1908-9	TH &S	Thos.	Bradbury & Son of Sheffield.
1893-4	SWS	S. W.	Smith & Co. (of Birmingham).	"	HSP LD		
"	ST			"	& WW	Wakeley & Wheeler.	
1894-5	LG CL			1909-10	IMS	John	Marshall.
"	JB ER	Brownell & Rose.		1910-1	SJP	S. J.	Phillips.
"	WBJ	Messrs.	Barnard.	1911-2	CH JW	Thomas & Co., Bond Street.	
1895-6	J.S			1912-3	H&C Ltd	Heming & Co., Ltd.	
"	JNN			1913-4	AP FP	A. & F.	Parsons, (of Edward Tessier).
1896-7	SH & C	W.	Hutton & Sons, Ltd.	"	SG		
1897-8	JBC	Messrs.	Carrington.	1914-5	D&J W	D. & J.	Welby.
1898-9	GG			1915-6	PD H C W	Dobson &	Sons.
1899 1900	EC P	E. C.	Purdee.	"	SJP	S. J.	Phillips.
"	RP			1916-7	LAC	Crichton	Bros.
				1917-8	HSP		
				1918-9	C&R C	Chas. &. Richard	Comyns.

	TOWN MARK.	DATE LETTER.	MAKER'S MARK.	MAKER'S NAME.		TOWN MARK	DATE LETTER.	MAKER'S MARK.	MAKER'S NAME.
ELIZ. 1559-60		A		... .	1583-4	[mark]	k	WR	Wm. Rawnson.
1560-1		B		. . ..	1584-5	[mark]	b	,,	,, ,,
1561-2		C		... ...	1585-6		c		
*1562-3	[mark]	D	RG	Robert Gylmyn.	1586-7		d		... ...
1563-4		E		... ...	1587-8	,,	e	GK	Geo. Kitchen.
1564-5	[mark]	F	M	... ...	1588-9		f		... ...
1565-6		G		... ...	1589-90		g		
1566-7	[mark]	H	H	Christopher Hunton.	1590-1	,,	h	GK	Geo. Kitchen.
1567-8		I		... ...	1591-2		i		... ...
1568-9	[mark]	K	RB / TS / M	Robert Beckwith. / Thomas Symson. /	1592-3	[mark]	k	WR / RG	Wm. Rawnson. / Robt. Gylmyn.
1569-70	[mark]	L	RG	Robert Gylmyn.	1593-4	,,	l	WH	? Wm. Hutchinson.
1570-1		M	♡	Name not traced.	1594-5	,,	m	GK	Geo. Kitchen.
1571-2		N		... ...	1595-6		n		... ...
1572-3	[mark]	O	[mark] / W	John Lund. / William Foster.	1596-7		o		... ...
1573-4		P		... .	1597-8	,,	p	CH	Chris. Harrington.
1574-5	,,	Q	GK	George Kitchen.	1598-9		q		... ...
1575-6	[mark]	R	,,	,, ,,	1599/1600	,,	r	FT	Fras. Tempest.
1576-7		S	TW	Thomas Waddie.	1600-1		s		. ...
1577-8	,,	T		Indistinguishable.	1601-2	,,	t	,,	,, ,,
1578-9		V		... ...	1602-3		u		.. ..
1579-80		W		... ...	JAS. I. 1603-4		w		... .
1580-1		X		... ...	1604-5	,,	x	CH	Chris. Harrington.
1581-2		Y		... ...	1605-6		y		... ...
1582-3	,,	Z	WR	William Rawnson.	1606-7		z		... ...

	TOWN MARK.	DATE LETTER.	MAKER'S MARK.	MAKER'S NAME.			TOWN MARK.	DATE LETTER.	MAKER'S MARK.	MAKER'S NAME.	
1607-8		A	M	John	Moody ?	1631-2		a	SC	Sem.	Casson.
1608-9		B	RC / PP	Robt. / Peter	Casson. / Pearson.	1632-3		b	,,	,,	,,
1609-10	,,	C	FT	Fras.	Tempest.	1633-4	,,	c	RH	Robt.	Harrington.
1610-1	,,	D	PP / ,,	Peter / ,,	Pearson. / ,,	1634-5	,,	d	TH	Thos.	Harrington.
1611-2	,,	E	CH	Chris.	Harrington.	1635-6	,,	e	IT	John	{ Thomason or Thompson.
1612-3	,,	F	FT	Fras.	Tempest.	1636-7		f	RH	Robt.	Harrington.
1613-4		G	PP	Peter	Pearson.	1637-8		g	TH	Thos.	Harrington.
1614-5	,,	H	,,	,,	,,	1638-9	,,	h	RW	Robt. or Richd.	Williamson, Senr. Waite.
1615-6		I	CM / FT	Chris. / Fras.	Mangy. / Tempest.	1639-40	,,	i	FB	Francis	Bryce.
1616-7	,,	K	,,	,,	,,	1640-1		j		...	...
1617-8		L		...	...	1641-2	,,	k	IT	John	Thomason.
1618-9	,,	M	SC	Sem.	Casson.	1642-3	,,	l	TH	Thos.	Harrington.
1619-20	,,	N	PP	Peter	Pearson.	1643-4	,,	m	IT	John	Thomason.
1620-1	,,	O	SC	Sem.	Casson.	1644-5		n		...	...
1621-2	,,	P	PP	Peter	Pearson.	1645-6	,,	o	CM	Chris.	Mangy.
1622-3		Q	,,	,,	,,	1646-7		p		...	...
1623-4		R	RW / D	Robt.	Williamson. / ...	1647-8		q		...	...
1624-5 CHAS. I		S	TH	Thos.	Harrington.	1648-9		r		...	...
1625-6		T	RH	Robt.	Harrington.	COMWTH. 1649-50		s	IP	James	Plummer.
1626-7	,,	U		?		1650-1		t	,,	,,	,,
1627-8	,,	W	IP	James	Plummer	1651-2	,,	u	,,	,,	,,
1628-9		X		...	...	1652-3	,,	v	,,	,,	,,
1629-30	,,	Y	CM	Chris.	Mangy.	1653-4		w		...	...
1630-1	,,	Z	W	Thomas	Waite.	1654-5	,,	x	TW	Thomas	Waite.
						1655-6	,,	y	,,	,,	,,
						1656-7	,,	z	PM	Philemon	Marsh.

Date	Town Mark	Date Letter	Maker's Mark	Maker's Name		Date	Town Mark	Date Letter	Maker's Mark	Maker's Name
1657-8	◉	A	IP	John Plummer		1682-3	◉	A	GG	George Gibson
1658-9	◉	B	,,	,,　　,,		*1683-4	,,	B	WB	Wm. Busfield
1659-60	◉	C	{ WW / IT }	Wm. Waite / John Thomason		1684-5 JAS. II.	◉	C	{ JC / IP }	John Camidge / John Plummer
1660-1	,,	D	IP	John Plummer		1685-6		D	RC	Richd. Chew
1661-2	,,	E	,,	,,　　,,		1686-7	,,	E	IS	John Smith
1662-3	◉	F	{ ,, / GM }	,,　　,, / George Mangy		1687-8	,,	F	IO	John Oliver
1663-4	◉	G	MB	Marmaduke Best		1688-9	,,	G	CW	Chris. Whitehill
1664-5	,,	H	RW	Robt. Williamson		WM. & MY. 1689-90	,,	H	WB	Wm. Busfield
1665-6	,,	I	IP	John Plummer		1690-1		J	RW	Robt. Williamson
1666-7	◉	K	TM	Thos. Mangy		1691-2	◉	K	CR	Charles Rhoades
1667-8	,,	L	MB	Marmaduke Best		1692-3	,,	L	CW	Chris. Whitehill
1668-9	,,	M	PM	Philemon Marsh		1693-4	,,	M	MG	Mark Gill
1669-70	,,	N	TM	Thomas Mangy		1694-5		N	WB	Wm. Busfield
1670-1	◉	O	MB	Marmaduke Best		1695-6	◉	O	CR	Clement Reed
1671-2	,,	P	{ ,, / RK }	Roland ,,　,, Kirby		WM. III. 1696-7	,,	P	WB	Wm. Busfield
1672-3	◉	Q	IT	John Thompson		1697-8	·	Q	IS	John Smith
1673-4	,,	R	MB	Marmaduke Best		1698-9	,,	R		Wm. Busfield as above
1674-5	,,	S	{ RW / TM }	Robt Williamson / Thos. Mangy		1699 1700		S		...　　...　　...
1675-6	,,	T	WM	Wm Mascall						
1676-7	,,	U	HL	Henry Lee						
1677-8	,,	V	WB	Wm. Busfield						
1678-9	,,	W	IP	John Plummer						
1679-80	◉	X	IT	John Thompson						
1680-1	,,	Y	WB	Wm. Busfield						
1681-2	,,	Z	TM	Thos. Mangy						

Year	Town Mark	Britannia	Lion's Head Erased	Date Letter	Maker's Mark	Maker's Name
1700-1	[mark]	[mark]	[mark]	A	GU	Chas. Goldsborough (probably)
1701-2	[mark]	[mark]	[mark]	B	{ Tu / BE	Danl. Turner. / John Bes..
ANNE. 1702-3	,,	,,	,,	C	Bu	Wm. Busfield.
1703-4	,,	,,	,,	D	LA	John Langwith.
1704-5						
1705-6	,,	,,	,,	F	,,	,, ,,
1706-7	,,	,,	,,	G	RH	Chas. Rhoades.
1707-8					LA	John Langwith.
1708-9	,,	,,	,,	δ	{ WI / ma	Wm. Williamson.
1709-10						
1710-11						
1711-2	,,	,,	,,	m	LA	John Langwith,
1712-3						
1713-4	,,	,,	,,	O	,,	,, ,,
GEO. I. 1714-5						
1715-6						
1716-7						

Year	Town Mark	Lion Passant	Leopard's Head Crowned	Date Letter	King's Head	Maker's Mark	Maker's Name
1776-7				A			... ...
1777-8				B			
1778-9				C			... ...
1779-80		[mark]	[mark]	D		HH	J. Hampston & J. Prince }
1780-1				E			... ...
1781-2	[mark]	,,	,,	F		,,	,, ,,
1782-3	,,	,,	.	G		,,	,, ,,
1783-4	,,	,,	,,	H		{ HH / JP	,, ,,
1784-5	,,	,,	,,	J	[mark]	{ HP	Hampston & Prince.
1785-6				K			. ...
1786-7				L			... ...

	Town Mark.	Lion Passant.	Leopard's Head Crowned.	King's Head.	Date Letter.	Maker's Mark.	Maker's Name.		Town Mark.	Lion Passant.	Leopard's Head Crowned.	King's Head.	Date Letter.	Maker's Mark.	Maker's Name.
1787-8	○	○	○	○	A	○	J. J. Hampston & Prince.	*1812-3	○	○	○	○	a	JB WW	James Barber & Wm. Whitwell
1788-9					b		... ...	1813-4					b		... ...
1789-90	,,	,,	,,	,,	c	,,	,, ,,	1814-5					c		... ...
1790-1	,,	,,	,,	,,	d	,,	,, ,,	1815-6	,,	,,	,,	,,	d	,,	,, ,,
1791-2	,,	,,	,,	,,	e	,,	,, ,,	1816-7	,,	,,	,,	,,	e	,,	... ...
1792-3					f		... ...	1817-8	,,	,,	,,	,,	f	,,	,, ,,
1793-4	,,	,,	,,	,,	g	,,	,, ,,	1818-9	,,	,,	,,	,,	g	,,	,, ,,
1794-5					h		... ...	1819-20					h		
1795-6	,,	,,	,,	,,	i	I·B P	,, ,,	GEO. IV. 1820-1			,,	,,	i	,,	,, ,,
1796-7	,,	,,	,,	○	K	,,	,, ,,	1821-2			,,	,,	k	,,	,, ,,
1797-8					l or L		... ...	1822-3					l		... ...
1798-9	,,	,,	,,	,,	M	HP &Co	H. Prince & Co.	1823-4					m		... ...
1799 1800	,,	,,	,,	,,	N	,,	,, ,,	1824-5	,,	,,	,,	,,	n	JB &Co	Jas. Barber & Co.
1800-1	,,	,,	,,	,,	O	HP&C	,, ,,	1825-6	,,	,,	,,	,,	o	BC &N	Jas. Geo. Wm. Barber, Cattle & North
1801-2	,,	,,	,,	,,	P	HP &C	,, ,,	1826-7			,,	,,	p	,,	,, ,,
1802-3	,,	,,	,,	,,	Q			1827-8					q		... ...
1803-4	,,	,,	,,	,,	R	,,	,, ,,	1828-9	,,	,,	,,	,,	r	,,	,, ,,
1804-5	,,	,,	,,	,,	S	,,	,, ,,	1829-30	,,	,,	,,	,,	s	JB GC WN	,, ,,
1805-6	,,	,,	,,	,,	T	,,	,, ,,	WM. IV. 1830-1	○	,,	,,	○	t	JB GC WN	,, ,,
1806-7					U			1831-2		,,	,,	,,	u	,,	,, ,,
1807-8	,,	,,	,,	,,	V	RC JB	Robt. Cattle & J Barber.	1832-3					v		... ...
1808-9		,,	,,	,,	W	,,	,, ,,	1833-4					w		... ...
1809-10		,,	,,	,,	X	,,	,, ,,	1834-5					x		... ...
1810-1	,,	,,	,,	,,	Y	,,	,, ,,	1835-6					y		... ...
1811-2					Z		... .	1836-7					z		... ...

	TOWN MARK.	LION PASSANT.	LEOPARD'S HEAD CROWNED. TILL 1848	QUEEN'S HEAD.	DATE LETTER.	MAKER'S MARK.	MAKER'S NAME.	
VICT. 1837-8	(town mark)	(lion)	(leopard)	(head)	A	JB WN	Jas. Wm.	Barber & North
1838-9	,,	,,	,,	,,	B	,,	,,	,,
1839-40	,,	,,	,,	,,	C	,,	,,	,,
1840-1	,,	,,	,,	(head)	D	,,	,,	,,
1841-2	,,	,,	,,	,,	E	,,	,,	,,
1842-3	,,	,,	,,	,,	F	,,	,,	,,
1843-4	,,	,,	,,	,,	G	,,	,,	,,
1844-5	,,	,,	,,	,,	H	,,	,,	,,
1845-6	,,	,,	,,	,,	I	,,	,,	,,
1846-7					K		....	... ...
1847-8	,,	,,	,,	,,	L	,,	,,	,,
1848-9	,,	,,		,,	M	JB	James Barber	
1849-50	,,	,,		,,	N	,,	,,	,,
1850-1	,,	,,		,,	O	,,	,,	,,
1851-2					P		...	... ...
1852-3					Q		...	... ...
1853-4					R		...	... ...
1854-5					S		.	... ...
1855-6					T		...	.. ...
1856-7	,,	,,		,,	V	JB	James Barber	

Table 1

DATE	CASTLE OVER LION.	DATE LETTER	MAKER'S MARK.
1565-6	[castle]	A	[mark]
1566-7	,,	B	[mark]
1567-8	[castle]	C	} [marks]
1568-9	[castle]	D	[mark]
1569-70	[castle]	E	[mark]
1570-1	[castle]	F	} [marks]
1571-2	,,	G	[mark]
1572-3		H	
1573-4	,,	I	[mark]
1574-5	,,	K	[mark]
1575-6		L	
1576-7		M	
1577-8		N	
1578-9		O	
1579-80		P	
1580-1		Q	
	ROSE CROWNED.		
1581-2	[rose]	R	[mark]
1582-3		S	
1583-4		T	
1584-5		V	

Table 2

DATE (ABOUT).	MARKS.
1590	[marks]
1595	[marks]
1600-10	[marks]
1610	[marks]
1620	[marks]
,,	[marks]
,,	[marks]
1620-40	[marks] TS [marks]
1624	[marks] AH

Table 3

DATE	CASTLE OVER LION.	ROSE CROWNED.	DATE LETTER.	MAKER'S MARK.
1624-5	[castle]	[rose]	A	[mark]
1625-6	,,	,,	B	[mark]
1626-7	[castle]	,,	C	[mark]
1627-8	,,	,,	D	} [marks]
1628-9	[castle]	,,	E	[mark]
1629-30			F	
1630-1	,,	[rose]	G	[mark]
1631-2			H	
1632-3	,,	,,	I	} [marks]
1633-4	,,	,,	K	AH
1634-5	,,	,,	L	[mark]
1635-6	[castle]	[rose]	M	[mark]
1636-7	[castle]	[rose]	N	[mark]
1637-8	[castle]	[rose]	O	} [marks]
1638-9	,,	,,	P	[mark]
1639-40	[castle]	[rose]	Q	[mark]
1640-1	,,	,,	R	[mark]
1641-2	,,	,,	S	[mark]
1642-3	,,	,,	T	[mark]
1643-4			V	

DATE (ABOUT)	MARKS.
1645	(marks)
,,	(marks) AH
1653	(marks) AH
1661	(marks) AH
,,	(marks) WA
1670	(marks) AH
,,	,, ,, (marks) AH
,,	(marks) AH
,,	(marks) AH
1675	(marks) TH
1676	,, ,, (marks) ,,
1679	,, ,, (marks) ,,
,,	,, ,, ,, (mark)
1680	(marks) MH
1685	(marks) TH

	ROSE CROWNED.	CASTLE OVER LION.	DATE LETTER.	MAKER'S MARK.	MAKER'S NAME.
1688	(rose)	(castle)	a	EH	... ...
1689	(rose)	(castle)	b	TH	Thomas Havers.
1690			c		... ...
1691	,,	,,	d	,,	Thomas Havers.
	,,	,,	,,	ID	James Daniel.
	,,	,,	,,	EH	... ...
	,,	,,	,,	LG	... ...
1692			E		... ...
1693			F		... ...
1694			G		... ...
1695			H		... ...
1696	,,	,,	I	ID	James Daniel.
1697	,,	,,	K	PR	... ...
	(rose)	(castle)	,,	EH	... ...

DATE.	MARKS.	MAKER'S NAME.	DATE.	MARKS.	MAKER'S NAME.
e. 1544-98	[RH]	Richard Hilliard.	1600	[X] OZBORN [c]	Richd. Osborn.
c. 1562 / 1607	[RO]	Richard Osborne.	"	" [RH] HERMAN [RH]	R. Herman.
c. 1568-74	I NORTH	John North.	"	[crown]	No maker's mark.
c. 1570	[H]	Henry Hardwicke.	c. 1600	[X] RO	Richd. Osborn.
1570-3	X IONS	John Ions (Jones).	1606	[X] OZBORN	" "
"	IONS	Do. do. do.	c. 1610-20	[X] BW BW a	William Bartlett. (1597-1646).
c. 1570 / 1600	S MORE ✣	Steven More.	1620	" " " b	" "
1571	IN	John North.	"	" [EA]	Edward Anthony (1612-67).
"	IN	Do. do.	"	[X] [FA]	" "
"	[X] X IONS	John Jons.	"	[X] [flowers]	
1572	IW	John Withycombe.	c. 1630	WB [X] WB	Wm. Bartlett (probably).
1575	[X] X IONS [flower]	John Jons.	"	[X] T [hand] T	Anthony mark, &c.*
"	" " " [flower]	Do. do.	c. 1635	IL [X] IL	John Lavers.
"	[X] I " A	Do. do.	"	[X] IP	I. P.
"	" IO " "	Do. do.	c. 1635-8	[X] IL	John Lavers.
1576	I IONS [X] B	Do. do.	c. 1640	[X] [flower] a	... ...
"	VI [X]	... ...	"	[X] HP HP	H. P.
1580	[X] HORWOOD	Wm. Horwood.	"	[IQR] RADCLIFF [X]	Jasper Radcliffe.
c. 1580	[X] I YEDS	John Eydes.	"	[LM] "	L. M.
1582	[X] C ESTON	C. Eston.	"	[R] " "	Jasper Radcliffe.
"	EASTON [dot]	C. Easton.	"	OSBORN "	Richd. Osborn.
1585	[X] BENTLY	— Bently.	"	[X] IL IL IL	John Lavers.
"	[X] HERMAN	R. Herman.	"	[X]	No maker's mark.
1590	[X] ESTON N	C. Eston.			
1592	[X] C ESTON P	Do. do.			

DATE.	MARKS.	MAKER'S NAME.
c. 1640-50	I·E A	{ John Elston / Anthony Tripe
,,	PR X PR ✦	P. R.
,,	X B	Thomas Bridgeman.
,,	⊕ EA	Edward Anthony.
,,	EA	Do. do.
c. 1646-98	X I·F	I. F.
c. 1670	X I·R	Jasper Radcliffe.
1676	X	M. W.
,,	X	— S.
c. 1680	XON IV X	... ...
,,	X	No maker's mark.
,,	,, IS	I. S.
1690	M EX·ON	John Mortimer.
c. 1690	X IS	Daniel Slade.
,,	,, WE	Wm. Ekins.
,,	,, WE	Do. do.
,,	M X	John Mortimer.
,,	❧ 🦁 ⊗	.. ..
,,	IP ⊕ ✦ ✦	I. P. (See Barnstaple, p. 459 infra).
,,	X 🦁 IP	I. P.
1694	EX N ON	Nichs. Browne.
1698	X ✠ ✠ ✠	No maker's mark.

DATE	CASTLE.	BRIT-ANNIA.	LION'S HEAD ERASED.	DATE LETTER.	MAKER'S MARK.	MAKER'S NAME.
1701-2	castle	Britannia	lion	A	CE	J. Elston.
1702-3 ANNE.	castle	,,	,,	B	{ FO	Thos. Foote.
1703-4	castle	,,	,,	C	{ Mu / Au	Hy. Muston. / John Audry.
1704-5	,,	,,	,,	D	Br	Wm. Briant.
1705-6	,,	,,	,,	E	FR	Richd. Freeman.
1706-7	,,	,,	,,	F	RE	Thos. Reynolds.
1707-8	,,	,,	,,	G	{ WI / SA	Richd. Wilcocks. / Thos. Salter.
1708-9	castle	,,	,,	H	PL	Richd. Plint.
1709-10	castle	,,	,,	I	FV	Name not traced.†
1710-1	,,	,,	,,	K	Ri	Ed. Richards.
1711-2	,,	,,	,,	L	{ TR / SW	Geo. Trowbridge. / Ed. Sweet.
1712-3	,,	,,	,,	M	Ri	Ed. Richards.
1713-4	castle	,,	,,	N	SL	Danl. Slade.
1714-5 GEO. I.	,,	,,	,,	O	To: / Mo	—— Tolcher. / John Mortimer.
1715-6	,,	,,	,,	P	TR	Geo. Trowbridge.
1716-7	,,	,,	,,	Q	Sp	Pent. Symonds.
1717-8	,,	,,	,,	R	{ Lo / Sp	Ab'm. Lovell. / Pent. Symonds.
1718-9	,,	,,	,,	S	AR	Peter Arno.
1719-20	,,	,,	,,	T	WO	Andr Worth.
1720-1	,,	,,	,,	V	{ BL / IE	Saml. Blachford / J. Elston.
1721-2	castle	Britannia	lion	W	TS	Thos. Sampson.
1722-3	,,	,,	,,	X	SB	Saml. Blachford.
1723-4	,,	,,	,,	Y	IE	J. Elston.
1724-5	,,	,,	,,	Z	IW	Jas. Williams.‡

Date	Castle	Leopard's Head Crowned	Lion Passant	Date Letter	Maker's Mark	Maker's Name	Date	Castle	Leopard's Head Crowned	Lion Passant	Date Letter	Maker's Mark	Maker's Name
1725-6	●	●	●	a	SB	Saml. Blachford.	1749-50	●	●	●	A	TB	Thomas Blake.
1726-7	,,	,,	,,	b	TS	Thos. Sampson.	1750-1	,,	,,	,,	B	,,	,, ,,
GEO. II. 1727-8	,,	,,	,,	c	JC / PE	Joseph Collier. / Philip Elliott.	1751-2	,,	,,	,,	C	,,	,, ,,
1728-9	,,	,,	,,	d	JE	John Elston, jr.	1752-3	,,	,,	,,	D	WP	W. Parry.
1729-30	,,	,,	,,	e	,, / JS	Do. do. / James Strang.	1753-4	,,	,,	,,	E	DC	Danl. Coleman.
1730-1	,,	,,	,,	f	JB	John Burdon.	1754-5	,,	,,	,,	F	WP	W. Parry.
1731-2	,,	,,	,,	g	PE	Peter Elliott.	1755-6	,,	,,	,,	G	,,	,, ,,
1732-3	,,	,,	,,	h	JC	Joseph Collier.	1756-7	,,	,,	,,	H	TB	Thomas Blake.
1733-4	,,	,,	,,	i	JE	John Elston, jr.	1757-8	,,	,,	,,	I	,,	,, ,,
1734-5	,,	,,	,,	k	SB	Sampson Bennett.	1758-9	,,	,,	,,	K		
1735-6	,,	,,	,,	l	PE	Philip Elston.	1759-60	,,	,,	,,	L	SF	Name not traced.
1736-7	,,	,,	,,	m	JS	James Strang.	GEO. III. 1760-1	,,	,,	,,	M		
1737-8	,,	,,	,,	n	PE	Philip Elston.	1761-2	,,	,,	,,	N		
1738-9	,,	,,	,,	o	PS	Pent. Symonds.	1762-3	,,	,,	,,	O	MS	Mat'w Skinner.
1739-40	,,	,,	,,	p	JB	John Burdon.	1763-4	,,	,,	,,	P		
1740-1	,,	,,	,,	q	JB	Do. do.	1764-5	,,	,,	,,	Q		
1741-2	,,	,,	,,	r	Sy	Pent. Symonds.	1765-6	,,	,,	,,	R		
1742-3	,,	,,	,,	s	IF	Name not traced. J. Freeman?	1766-7	,,	,,	,,	S	RS	Richard Sams.
1743-4	,,	,,	,,	t	JB	John Babbage?	1767-8	,,	,,	,,	T	,,	,, ,,
1744-5	,,	,,	,,	u	,,	Do. do.	1768-9	,,	,,	,,	U	JH	James Holt.
1745-6	,,	,,	,,	w			1769-70	,,	,,	,,	W	TC	Thomas Coffin.
1746-7	,,	,,	,,	x	PS	Pent. Symonds.	1770-1	,,	,,	,,	X	IF	J. Freeman.
1747-8	,,	,,	,,	y	TB	Thos. Blake.	1771-2	,,	,,	,,	Y	RS	Richard Sams.
1748-9	,,	,,	,,	z	JS	Jas. Strang.	1772-3	,,	,,	,,	Z		... ...

	CASTLE.	LEOPARD'S HEAD CROWNED	LION PASSANT.	DATE LETTER.	MAKER'S MARK.	MAKER'S NAME.
1773-4	(castle)	(leopard's head)	(lion)	A	RS	Richd. Sams.
1774-5	,,	,,	,,	B		
1775-6	,,	,,	,,	C	{ TE / WW }	Thos. Eustace. William West of Plymouth.
1776-7	,,	,,	,,	D		
1777-8	,,	,,	,,	E		
1778-9	,,		(lion)	F	,,	Thos. Eustace.
1779-80	,,		,,	G	,,	,, ,,
1780-1	,,		,,	H		
1781-2-3	,,		,,	I	,,	,, ,,
1783-4	,,	KING'S HEAD	,,	K	WP	W. Pearse.
1784-5	,,	(king's head)	,,	L		Thos. Eustace (as 1775-6).
1785-6	,,	,,	,,	M	TE	Thos. Eustace.
1786-7	,,	(king's head)	,,	N	JH	Joseph Hicks.
1787-8	,,	,,	,,	O	,,	,, ,,
1788-9	,,	,,	,,	P	,,	,, ,,
1789-90	,,	,,	,,	q	JP	J. Pearse.
1790-1	,,	,,	,,	r		
1791-2	,,	,,	,,	f	JH	Joseph Hicks.
1792-3	,,	,,	,,	t		
1793-4	,,	,,	,,	u		
1794-5	,,	,,	,,	w		
1795-6	,,	,,	,,	X	RF	Richd. Ferris.
1796-7	,,	,,	,,	y		

	CASTLE.	LION PASSANT.	DATE LETTER.	KING'S HEAD.	MAKER'S MARK.	MAKER'S NAME.
1797-8	(castle)	(lion)	A	(king's head)	RF	Richd. Ferris.
1798-9	,,	,,	B	,,	,,	,, ,,
1799 / 1800	,,	,,	C	(king's head)	JH / WW	Joseph Hicks. W. Welch.
1800-1	,,	,,	D	,,	JH	Joseph Hicks.
1801-2	,,	,,	E	,,	,,	,, ,,
1802-3	,,	,,	F	,,	,,	,, ,,
1803-4	,,	,,	G	,,	TE	Thos. Eustace.
1804-5	,,	,,	H	,,	RF	Richd. Ferris.
1805-6	(castle)	(lion)	I	,,	,,	,, ,,
1806-7	,,	,,	K	,,	,,	,, ,,
1807-8	,,	,,	L	,,	,,	,, ,,
1808-9	,,	,,	M	,,		
1809-10	,,	,,	N	,,	JL	J. Langdon
1810-1	,,	,,	O	,,	WW	W. Welch.
1811-2	,,	,,	P	,,	JH	Joseph Hicks.
1812-3	,,	,,	Q	,,	,,	,, ,,
1813-4	,,	,,	R	,,	GT	G. Turner.
1814-5	,,	,,	S	,,	,,	,, ,,
1815-6	,,	,,	T	,,	,,	,, ,,
1816-7	,,	,,	U	,,	GF	Geo. Ferris.

	CASTLE.	LION PASSANT.	DATE LETTER.	KING'S HEAD.	MAKER'S MARK	MAKER'S NAME.		CASTLE.	LION PASSANT.	DATE LETTER.	QUEEN'S HEAD.	MAKER'S MARK.	MAKER'S NAME.
1817-8			a		GF	Geo. Ferris.	VICT. 1837-8			A		SOBEY	W. R. Sobey.
1818-9	,,	,,	b	,,	,,	,, ,,	1838-9	,,	,,	B		J·O	J. Osmont.
1819-20	,,	,,	c	,,	JH	Joseph Hicks.	1839-40	,,	,,	C		TB	Thos. Byne.
GEO. IV. 1820-1	,,	,,	d	,,	,,	,, ,,	1840-1	,,	,,	D	,,	J·S	J. Stone.
1821-2	,,	,,	e	,,	,,	,, ,,	1841-2		,,	E	,,	RAMSEY	— Ramsey.
1822-3	,,	,,	f		GF	Geo. Ferris.	1842-3	,,	,,	F	,,	SOBEY	W. R. Sobey.
1823-4	,,	,,	g	,,	,,	,, ,,	1843-4		,,	G	,,	,,	,, ,,
1824-5	,,	,,	h	,,	,,	,, ,,	1844-5	,,	,,	H		WRS	,, ,,
1825-6	,,	,,	i	,,	IE	John Eustace.	1845-6	,,	,,	J	,,	,, SOBEY	,, ,, ,, ,,
1826-7	,,	,,	k	,,	GM	Name not traced.	1846-7	,,	,,	K	,,	,,	,, ,,
1827-8	,,	,,	l	,,	JO	J. Osmont.	1847-8	,,		L	,,	WWW	? Williams.
1828-9	,,	,,	m	,,	,,	,, ,,	1848-9	,,	,,	M	,,	J·S	J. Stone.
1829-30	,,	,,	n	,,	JH	Joseph Hicks.	1849-50	,,	,,	N	,,	WRS	W. R. Sobey.
WM. IV. 1830-1	,,	,,	o	,,	,,	,, ,,	1850-1	,,	,,	O	,,	,,	,, ,,
1831-2			P		WS	W. Sobey.	1851-2	,,	,,	P	,,	J·O	J. Osmont.
1832-3	,,	,,	q	,,	J·S	John Stone.	1852-3	,,	,,	Q	,,	,,	,, ,,
1833-4			r	,,	W·P	Wm. Pope.	1853-4	,,	,,	R	,,	IP	Isaac Parkin.
1834-5	,,	,,	s		J·O	J. Osmont.	1854-5	,,	,,	S	,,	,,	,, ,,
1835-6	,,	,,	t	,,	WRS	W. R. Sobey.	1855-6	,,	,,	T	,,	,,	,, ,,
1836-7	,,	,,	u	,,	WW	William Welch.	1856-7	,,	,,	U	,,	J·S	J. Stone.

	CASTLE	LION PASSANT	DATE LETTER	QUEEN'S HEAD	MAKER'S MARK	MAKER'S NAME		CASTLE	LION PASSANT	DATE LETTER	QUEEN'S HEAD	MAKER'S MARK	MAKER'S NAME
1857-8	🏰	🦁	A	👑	J·S	J. Stone.	1870-1	,,	,,	O	,,	..	.. ..
1858-9	,,	,,	B	,,	,,	,, ,,	1871-2	,,	,,	P	,,		., ...
1859-60	,,	,,	C	,,		,, ...	1872-3	,,	,,	Q	,,		... ...
1860-1	,,	,,	D	,,	PO	Name not traced.	1873-4	,,	,,	R	,,		... ...
1861-2	,,	,,	E	,,	JW	Jas. Williams.	1874-5	,,	,,	S	,,		... ...
1862-3	,,	,,	F	,,		... ...	1875-6	,,	,,	T	,,		... ...
1863-4	,,	,,	G	,,			1876-7	,,	,,	U	,,		... ...
1864-5	,,	,,	H	,,		.. ..	1877-8	🏰	🦁	A	👑	JW &Co	J. Whipple & Co.
1865-6	,,	,,	I	,,		... . .	1878-9	,,	,,	B	,,		... ...
1866-7	,,	,,	K	,,			1879-80	,,	,,	C	,,		.. ..
1867-8	,,	,,	L	,,			1880-1	,,	,,	D	,,		.. ..
1868-9	,,	,,	M	,,	H·L	Henry Lake.	1881-2	,,	,,	E	,,		...
1869-70	,,	,,	N	,,		.. .	1882-3	,,	,,	F	,,	WE FD JT	Ellis, Depree & Tucker }

SUPPLEMENTARY LIST OF MARKS OF GOLDSMITHS

Impressed at Exeter, but not illustrated in the preceding tables :—

DATE	MARK.	NAME.	DATE.	MARK.	NAME.
1701	SI	Danie Slade.	1722	PS	Pentecost Symonds.
c 1706	JO	Peter Jouett.	1728	TC	Thomas Coffin.
1707	SS	Thos. Sampson.	1730	IR	John Reed.
1708	WI	Richard Wilcocks.	1732	TC	Thomas Clarke.
1709	SY	Pentecost Symonds.	,,	IS	John Suger.
1710	JP	John Pike.	1741	MM	Micon Melun.
,,	BI	Joseph Bennick.	1771	RB	Richd. Birdlake (Plymouth).
1713	SU	John Suger.	1825	SL	Simon Lery.
1714	AT	Anthony Tripe.	1830	IP	Isaac Parkin.
1717	ZW	Zacariah Williams.	1835	GT	G. Turner & partner (? Son).
1719	BE	Joseph Bennick.	1845	JG	J. Golding (Plymouth).
1721	ER	Edward Richard.	1847	HE	Henry Ellis.
	IM	John March.	1850	IP GS	Isaac Parkin & Geo. Sobey.

DATE (ABOUT).	MARKS.	MAKER'S NAME.
1658		John Wilkinson.
1664		" "
1668		" "
1670		John Dowthwaite.
1672		" "
"		Wm. Ramsay.
1675		" "
"		" "
1680		" "
1684		" "
"		" "
"		" "
1685		Wm. Robinson.
"		" "
1686-7		Eli. Bilton.
1686-8		Wm. Robinson.
1690		" "
1692		" "
1694		Robt. Shrive.
"		Eli. Bilton.
"		" "
1695		Wm. Robinson.
1697		Thos. Hewitson.
1698		" "
1698-9		Eli. Bilton.
1700		" "
"		John Ramsay.
1701		Eli. Bilton.

DATE (ABOUT).	THREE CASTLES.	BRITANNIA.	LION'S HEAD ERASED.	DATE LETTER.	MAKER'S MARK.	MAKER'S NAME.
ANNE. 1702-3				A	Ra	John Ramsay.
1703-4	"	"	"	B	Ba	Fras. Batty.
1704-5	"	"	"	C	Sh	Robt. Shrive.
1705-6	"	"	"	D	Bi	Eli. Bilton.
1706-7	"	"	"	E	" / Yo	" " / John Younghusband.
1707-8		"	"	F	Yo / Fr	" " / J'nath'n French.
1708-9	"	"	"	G	Bv	John Buckle of York.
1709-10	"	"	"	"	Ki	James Kirkup.
1710-11						
1711-2					Bi	Eli. Bilton.
1712-3				C	Ho	Richd. Hobbs.
1713-4					LA	John Langwith.
GEO. I. 1714-5		"	"	D	Fr / Ba	J'nath'n French. / Fr. Batty, jr.
1715-6					Sh	Nathl. Shaw.
1716-7						
1717-8	"	"	"	P	BV	Joseph Buckle.
1718-9	"	"	"	Q	Ba / Ki	Fras. Batty, as above. / James Kirkup.
1719-20	"	"	"	D	Ma Ba / Ca	R. & F. Makepeace Batty. / John Carnaby.
1720-1	"	"	"	E	Wh	Wm. Whitfield.

Date	Three Castles.	Lion Passant.	Leopard's Head Crowned.	Date Letter.	Maker's Mark.	Maker's Name.
1721-2	(castles)	(lion)	(leopard)	a	FB / IR	Fras. Batty, jr. / John Ramsay, jr.
1722-3	(castles)	(lion)	,,	B	RM / I·K	Robt. Makepeace. / Jas. Kirkup.
1723-4	,,	(lion)	,,	C	IF	Jthn. French.
1724-5	,,	,,	,,	D	IC / TP	John Carnaby. / Thos. Partis.
1725-6	(castles)	(lion)	(leopard)	E	IR	Fras. Batty, jr.
1726-7	,,	,,	,,	F	WW / IB	Wm. Whitfield. / John Busfield of York. ?
GEO. II. 1727-8	(castles)	,,	(leopard)	G	I·C	Isaac Cookson.
1728-9	,,	(lion)	,,	H	GB / WW / WD	Geo. Bulman. / Wm. Whitfield. / Wm. Dalton.
1729-30	,,	,,	,,	I	GB	Geo. Bulman.
1730-1	,,	,,	,,	K	WD	Wm. Dalton.
1731-2	,,	,,	,,	L	TG / IF	Thos. Gamul ? / Jon. French.
1732-3	,,	,,	,,	M	TM / IB	Thos. Makepeace. / John Busfield of York. ?
1733-4	,,	,,	,,	N	I·C	Isaac Cookson.
1734-5	,,	,,	,,	O	TP	Thos. Partis.
1735-6	,,	,,	,,	P	GB	Geo. Bulman.
1736-7	,,	,,	,,	Q	WP	Wm. Partis.*
1737-8	,,	,,	,,	R	I·C	Isaac Cookson.†
1738-9	,,	,,	,,	S	WB / IB	Wm. Beilby&Co.
1739-40	,,	,,	,,	T	I·C / R·M	Isaac Cookson. / Robt. Makepeace.
1740-1	(castles)	(lion)	(leopard)	A	S·B / I·K	Stephen Buckle. / James Kirkup.
1741-2	,,	,,	,,	B	WB / IB	W. Beilby & Anor. / Perhaps Jno. Busfield (of York.)
1742-3	,,	,,	,,	C	IC	Isaac Cookson.
1743-4	,,	,,	,,	D	TS / WP	Thomas Stoddart. / William Partis.
1744-5	,,	,,	,,	E	FM	F. Martin (probably).
1745-6	,,	,,	(leopard)	F	TB	Thomas Blackett (probably).
1746-7	(castles)	(lion)	(leopard)	G	IC	Isaac Cookson.
1747-8	,,	,,	,,	H	I·W	John Wilkinson of Sheffield (probably).
1748-9	,,	,,	,,	I	TR	? Thos. Reid of York.
1749-50	,,	,,	,,	K	RG / R·M / TP	R. Gillson (of Sunderland). / Robert Makepeace. / Thos. Partis II. (of Sunderland).
1750-1	,,	(lion)	(leopard)	L	WB	William Beilby.
1751-2	,,	,,	,,	M	WP	William Partis.
1752-3	,,	,,	,,	N	WD / I·B	William Dalton. / Perhaps John Barrett (of Sunderland).
1753-4	,,	,,	,,	O	IC	Isaac Cookson.
1754-5	,,	,,	,,	P	IL / IG	Langlands & Goodriche.
1755-6	,,	,,	,,	Q	IK	John Kirkup.
1756-7	,,	,,	,,	R	IL	John Langlands.
1757-8	(castles)	,,	(leopard)	S	IL / IL	,, ,, / ,, ,,
1758-9	,,			T	R·B	Ralph Beilby.

Year	Three Castles	Lion Passant	Leopard's Head Crowned	Date Letter	King's Head	Maker's Mark	Maker's Name
1759-60	(castles)	(lion)	(leopard)	A		SI	Samuel James.
GEO. III. 1760-8	"	"	"	B		SI / IB	Saml. Thompson. / John Barrett of Sunderland.
1769-70	"	(lion)	"	C		SI / RP	Saml. James. / Robt. Peat.
1770-1	(castles)	"	(leopard)	D		IK / IF / IL	John Kirkup. / John Fearny of Sunderland. / John Langlands.
1771-2	"	"	"	E			
1772-3	(castles)	"	"	F		IC	James Crawford.
1773-4	"	"	"	G		II / IH	John Jobson. / Jas. Hetherington
1774-5	"	"	"	H		WS / IM	Stalker & Mitchison.
1775-6	"	"	"	I		IH·HE / FS	Hetherington & Edwards / Francis Solomon of Whitehaven.
1776-7	"	"	"	K		H·E / IH	Hetherington & Edwards / James Hetherington
1777-8	"	"	"	L		DC	David Crawford.
1778-9	"	"	"	M		IL·R	Langlands & Robertson.
1779-80	"	(lion)	(leopard)	N		DC	David Crawford.
1780-1	"	"	"	O		RP / RS	Pinkney & Scott.
1781-2	"	"	"	P		IL·IR	Langlands & Robertson (as below).
1782-3	"	"	"	Q		IS / BD	John Stoddart. / Ben. Dryden.
1783-4	"	"	"	R		IS	John Stoddart.
1784-5	"	"	"	S	(king)	RP / RS	Pinkney & Scott.
1785-6	"	"	"	T	"	IM	John Mitchison.
1786-7	"	"	"	U	(king)	"	" "
1787-8	"	(lion)	(leopard)	W	"	TG / L&R	Name not traced. / Langlands & Robertson.
1788-9	"	(lion)	"	X	"	C·R	Chrstn. Reid.
1789-90	"	"	"	Y	"	P&S	Pinkney & Scott.
1790-1	"	"	"	Z	"	IM	John Mitchison.

Year	Lion Passant	Three Castles	Leopard's Head Crowned	King's Head	Date Letter	Maker's Mark	Maker's Name
1791-2	(lion)	(castles)	(leopard)	(king)	A	IL / IR	Langlands & Robertson.
1792-3	"	"	"	"	B	R·S	Robert Scott.
*1793-4	"	"	"		C	O / AH	Anth. Hedley.
1794-5	"	"	"		D	MA / GW	Mary Ashworth of Dur. / G. Weddell.
1795-6	"	"	"		E	IR / DD	Robertson & Darling.
1796-7	"	"	"		F	TW / R&D	Thos. Watson. / Robertson & Darling.
1797-8	"	"		(king)	G	GL / JW	Geo. Laws & John Walker.
1798-9	"	"	"		H	CR / IR	Chrstn. Reid. / John Robertson.
1799 1800	"	"	"		I	IR / SC	" " / Sarah Crawford.
1800-1	(lion)	(castles)	(leopard)	(king)	K	IL / TW	John Langlands, jr. / Thos. Watson.
1801-2	"	"	"		L	A·R	Ann. Robertson.
1802-3	"	"	"		M	D·D / CR·DR	David Darling. / Chrstn. K. Reid & David Reid.
1803-4	(lion)			(king)	N	A·K	Alexr. Kelty.
1804-5	"	"	"		O	IL	John Langlands, jr.
1805-6	"	"	"		P	GM	George Murray.
1806-7	"	"	"		Q	TW	Thos. Watson.
1807-8	"	"	"		R	"	" "
1808-9	"	"	"		S	DD / TB	Darling & Bell.
1809-10	(lion)	(castles)	(leopard)	(king)	T	IL	John Langlands.†
1810-1	"	"	"		U	T·W	Thos. Watson.
1811-2	"	"	"		W	D·L / IR·IW	Drthy. Langlands. / Robertson & Walton.
1812-3	"	"	"		X	RP / M&R	Robert Pinkney. / Name not traced.
1813-4	"	"	"		Y	CR / DR / CR	Chrstn. Ker Reid, David Reid, & Chrstn. Bruce Reid.
1814-5	"	"	"		Z	IW	John Walton.

DATE LETTER	KING'S HEAD	LION PASSANT	THREE CASTLES	LEOPARD'S HEAD CROWNED	MAKER'S MARK	MAKER'S NAME		KING'S HEAD	LION PASSANT	THREE CASTLES	LEOPARD'S HEAD CROWNED	DATE LETTER	MAKER'S MARK	MAKER'S NAME
1815-6 A	head	lion	castles	leopard	T·W	Thos. Watson.	1839-40	head	lion	castles	leopard	A	IW	John Walton.
1816-7 B	"	"	"	"	TW	" "	1840-1	"	"	"	"	B	"	" "
1817-8 C	"	"	"	"	C·D	Christ'r. Dinsdale, of Sunderland.	1841-2	head	"	"	"	C	T·W	Thos. Watson,
1818-9 D	"	"	"	"	IR IW	Robertson & Walton.	1842-3	"	"	"	"	D	"	" "
1819-20 E	"	"	"	"			1843-4	"	"	"	"	E		
GEO. IV. 1820-1 F	"	"	"	"	T·W	Thos. Watson.	1844-5	"	"	"	"	F		Lister & Sons (as 1838-9).
1821-2 G	head	"	"	"	"	" "	1845-6	"	"	"	"	G		
1822-3 H	"	"	"	"	"	" "	1846-7	"	lion	castles	leopard	H	GG	Name not traced.
1823-4 I	"	"	"	"	"	" "	1847-8	"	"	"	"	I		
1824-5 K	"	"	"	"	TW	" "	1848-9	"	"	"	"	J		
1825-6 L	"	"	"	"			1849-50	"	"	"	"	K		
1826-7 M	"	"		"			1850-1	"	"	"	"	L		
1827-8 N	"	"	"	"			1851-2	"	"	"	"	M		
1828-9 O	"	"	"	"			1852-3	"	"	"	"	N		
1829-30 P	·	"	"	"			1853-4	"	"	"	"	O		
WM. IV. 1830-1 Q	·	"	"	"			1854-5	"	"	"	"	P		
1831-2 R	"	"	"	"			1855-6	"	"	"	"	Q		
1832-3 S	head	·	"	·	"	Thos. Watson.	1856-7	"	"	"	"	R		
1833-4 T	"	"	"				1857-8	"	"	"	"	S		
1834-5 U	·	·	·	"	W·L	Wm. Lister.	1858-9	"	"	"	"	T		
1835-6 W	··	"	"	"			1859-60	"	"	"	"	U		
1836-7 X		"	"	"			1860-1	"	"	"	"	W		
VICT. 1837-8 Y		"	"	"	T·W	Thos Watson.	1861-2	"	"	"	"	X		
1838-9 Z	"	"	"	"	W·L C·L W·L	Lister & Sons.	1862-3	"	"	"	"	Y		
							1863-4	"	"	"	"	Z		

Impressed at Newcastle from c. 1750 to c. 1880, but not illustrated in the preceding tables :—

MARK.	NAME.	MARK.	NAME.	MARK.	NAME.
GL	Name not traced.	L&SONS	Lister & Sons.	I·M	John Miller.
WF	" "	L&S	" "	CD	Cuthbert Dinsdale.
WB	Mr. Bartlett?	I·B	John Brown.	GL	Geo. Sam. Lewis.
SI	Samuel Jones.	J·B	" "	MY&SONS	M. Young & Sons.
PI	Peter James.	JB	" "	SJ	Simeon Joel.
(cross)	Name not traced.	WS	Wm. Sherwin.	J.C	John Cook.
F·S	F. Somerville or Summerville, Sen., and F. S. Junr.	J·D	James Dinsdale.	RD	R. Duncan of Carlisle.
P·B	Peter Beatch.	JS	Name not traced.	J&IJ	Joseph and Israel Jacobs.
I·T	Name not traced.	CJR	Chrstn. J. Reid.	J·F	James Foster.
R·D	" "	RR	Robert Rippon.	W&JW	Wm. and Jno. Wilson.
R·W	Robt. Wilson.	JS	John Sutler.	TR	Thos. Ross of Carlisle?
D&B	Darling & Bell.	J.W	John White.	TALBOT	A. Y. Talbot of Crook, Darlington.
T·H	Thos. Huntingdon.	DR	David Reid.	TS	Thos. Sewill.
H·B	Hugh Brechinridge.	BUXTON	Wm. Buxton of Bishop Auckland.	IR	Name not traced.
PL	Peter Lambert of Berwick.	I·D	John Deas?	E.JC	" "
CR DR	Chrstn. K. Reid & David Reid.	OSWALD	Robt. Oswald of Durham.	WR	" "
CAMERON	Alexr Cameron of Dundee.	OY	Oliver Young.	E·O	" "
J·R	John Robertson.	IC	John Cook.	RO	" "
		WW&SONS	W. Wilson & Sons.	IH HB	" "
		LP	L. Pedrine of Carlisle.		
		A&S	Alder & Sons of Blyth.		

	DATE LETTER
1864-5	a
1865-6	b
1866-7	c
1867-8	d
1868-9	e
1869-70	f
1870-1	g
1871-2	h
1872-3	i
1873-4	k
1874-5	l
1875-6	m
1876-7	n
1877-8	o
1878-9	p
1879-80	q
1880-1	r
1881-2	s
1882-3	t
1883-4	u

DATE.	MAKER'S MARK, TOWN MARK AND DATE-LETTER.	MAKER'S NAME.
1668	[GO mark]	George Oulton.
c. 1683	[RW] [STERLING] [RW]	Ralph Walley.
"	[NB mark]	Nathanl. Bullen.
c. 1685	[NB] [Sterl:]	" "
"	[NB]	" "
1686-90	[AP] [arms] [helm] [N]	Alexand'r Pulford.
"	[PE] [arms] [helm] [M]	Peter Edwards.
"	[PE] [arms] [helm] [N]	" "
"	[RW] [arms] [helm] [M]	Ralph Walley.
1690-2	[RW] [arms] [helm] [N]	" "
"	[PP] [arms] " " [town]	Peter Pemberton.
"	[PP] [arms] [star]	" "
"	[PP] [arms] [helm]	" "
c. 1692	[PP] [arms] [C]	" "
1692-4	[PP] [STERLING] [STERLING] [C]	" "
1695-1700	[BB] [STERLING] [BB]	Name not traced.
1695	[D]	... ...
1696	[E]	... ...
1697	[F]	... .

DATE.	BRIT-ANNIA.	LION'S HEAD ERASED.	DATE LETTER.	TOWN MARK.	MAKER'S MARK.	MAKER'S NAME.
1701-2	[Britannia]	[lion's head]	A	[shield]	Ri	Richd. Richardson.
ANNE. 1702-3	"	"	B	"	Bi	John Bingley.
1703-4	"	"	C	"	Bu / Bi	Nath. Bullen. Chas. Bird.
1704-5	"	"	D	"	Ri	Richd. Richardson,
1705-6	"	"	E	"	Pe / Ho	Peter Pemberton. Name not traced.
1706-7	"	"	F	"	Ho	" "
1707-8	"	"	G	"	Ro	Thos. Robinson.
1708-9	"	"	H	"	Gr	Name not traced.
1709-10	"	"	I	"	Co	" "
1710-11	"	"	K	"	Ie	" "
1711-2	"	"	L	"	Sa	" "
1712-3	"	"	M	"	Ta	Tarleton.
1713-4	"	"	N	"	Ri	Richd. Richardson.
GEO. I. 1714-5	"	"	O	"	Ri	" "
1715-6	"	"	P	"	Du	Barth. Duke.
1716-7	"	"	Q	"	Ma / Mr	Thos. Maddock. " "
1717-8	"	"	R	"	Ri	Richd. Richardson.
1718-9	LION PASSANT.	LEOP'S HEAD C?	S	"	"	" "
1719-20	[lion passant]	[leopard's head]	T	•	Ri	" "
1720-1	"	"	U	"	Ma	Thos. Maddock.
1721-2	"	"	V	"	Ri	Richd. Richardson.
1722-3	"	"	W	"	Ri	" "
1723-4	"	"	X	"	Ri	" "
1724-5	"	"	Y	"	Ri	" "
1725-6	"	"	Z	"	JM	John Melling.

	LION PASSANT.	LEOPARD'S HEAD CROWNED.	TOWN MARK.	DATE LETTER.	MAKER'S MARK.	MAKER'S NAME.		LION PASSANT.	LEOPARD'S HEAD CROWNED.	TOWN MARK.	DATE LETTER.	MAKER'S MARK.	MAKER'S NAME.
1726-7	(lion)	(leopard)	(town)	A	BP	Benj'n Pemberton.	1751-2	(lion)	(leopard)	(town)	a	RR	Richd. Richardson.
GEO. II. 1727-8	,,	,,	,,	B	BP	,, ,,	1752-3	,,	,,	,,	Borb		
1728-9	,,	,,	,,	C	RR	Richd. Richardson.	1753-4	,,	,,	,,	C	,,	,, ,,
1729-30	,,	,,	,,	D	RP	Richd. Pike.	1754-5	,,	,,	,,	Dord		
1730-1	,,	,,	,,	E	WR	Wm. Richardson.	1755-6	,,	,,	,,	e	,,	,, ,,
1731-2	,,	,,	,,	F		R.R. conjoined as at 1728 above.	1756-7	,,	,,	,,	Forf		
1732-3	,,	,,	,,	G	RR	Richd. Richardson.	1757-8	,,	,,	,,	G	RR	,, ,,
1733-4	,,	,,	,,	H	RR	,, ,,	1758-9	,,	,,	,,	h	RR	,, ,,
1734-5	,,	,,	,,	I	,,	,, ,,	1759-60	,,	,,	,,	Iori		
1735-6	,,	,,	,,	K	RR	,, ,,	GEO. III. 1760-1	,,	,,	,,	Kork		
1736-7	,,	,,	,,	L	,,	,, ,,	1761-2	,,	,,	,,	Lorl		
1737-8	,,	,,	,,	M	RR	,, ,,	*1762-3	,,	,,	,,	m	RR RR	,, ,,
1738-9	,,	,,	,,	N	,,	,, ,,	1763-4	,,	,,	,,	n	RR	,, ,,
1739-40	,,	,,	,,	O	WR	Wm. Richardson.	1764-5	,,	,,	,,	O	RR	,, ,,
1740-1	,,	,,	,,	P	BP	Benj'n Pemberton.	1765-6	,,	,,	,,	P	,,	,, ,,
1741-2	,,	,,	,,	Q	RR	Richd. Richardson.	1766-7	,,	,,	,,	Qorq		
1742-3	,,	,,	,,	R	TM	Thos. Maddock.	*1767-8	,,	,,	,,	R	RR	,, ,,
1743-4	,,	,,	,,	S	RR	Richd. Richardson.	1768-9	(lion)	,,	,,	S	,,	,, ,,
1744-5	,,	,,	,,	T	,,	,, ,,	1769-70	,,	,,	,,	T	B&F	Bolton & Fothergill, Birm.
1745-6	,,	,,	,,	U		... ...	†1771-2	,	,,	,,	U	I.W	Joseph Walley.
1746-7	,,	,,	,,	v		... ...	1773	,,	,,	,,	V	GW / I.D	Geo. Walker. {James Dixon or Jos. Duke.
1747-8	,,	,,	,,	W		Thos. Maddock as above.	1774	,,	,,	,,	W	ID	,, ,,
1748-9	,,	(leopard)	,,	X	RR	Richd. Richardson.	1775	,,	,,	,,	X	GW	Geo. Walker.
1749-50	,,	,,	,,	Y	,,	,, ,,	1775-6	,,	,,	,,	Y	RR	Richd. Richardson, jr.
1750-1	(lion)	,,	,,	Z	RR	,, ,,							

Year	Lion Passant	Leopard's Head Crowned	Town Mark	Date Letter	King's Head	Maker's Mark	Maker's Name
1776-7	[lion]	[leopard]	[town]	a		RR	Richd. Richardson.
1777-8	,,	,,	,,	b		GW	George Walker.
1778-9	,,	,,	,,	c		RR	Richd. Richardson.
1779-80	[lion]	[leopard]	[town]	d		,, / IW	,, ,, / Joseph Walley.
1780-1	,,	,,	,,	e		,,	,, ,,
1781-2	,,	,,	,,	f		GW	George Walker.
1782-3	,,	,,	,,	g		,,	,, ,,
1783-4	,,	,,	,,	h		JA	John Adamson.
1784-5	[lion]	[leopard]	[town]	i	[king's head]	RF / RR	Richd. Richardson. ,, ,,
1785-6	,,	,,	,,	k	,,	JC	J. Clifton or James Conway.
1786-7	,,	,,	,,	l	[king's head]	TP	T. Pierpoint.
1787-8	,,	,,	,,	m	,,	RB	Robt. Boulger.
1788-9	,,	,,	,,	n	,,	IG / RI	John Gilbert. / Robert Jones.
1789-90	,,	,,	,,	o	,,	WH	Wm. Hull.
1790-1	,,	,,	,,	p	,,	WT / WT	Wm. Tarlton. ,, ,,
1791-2	,,	,,	,,	q	,,	IB	James Barton.
1792-3	,,	,,	,,	r	,,	EM	E. Maddock.
1793-4	,,	,,	,,	s	,,	TA	Thos. Appleby.
1794-5	,,	,,	,,	t	,,	TH	Thos. Hilsby.
1795-6	,,	,,	,,	u	,,	TM	Thos. Morrow.
1796-7	,,	,,	,,	v	,,	IA&S	John Adamson & Son.

Year	Lion Passant	Leopard's Head Crowned	Town Mark	Date Letter	King's Head	Maker's Mark	Maker's Name
1797-8	[lion]	[leopard]	[town]	A	[king's head]	GL	George Lowe.
1798-9	,,	,,	,,	B	,,	R·I	Robt. Jones.
1799 1800	,,	,,	,,	C	,,	RG	Robert Green.
1800-1	,,	[leopard]	,,	D	,,	NC	Nicholas Cunliffe.
1801-2	,,	,,	,,	E	,,		Maker's mark indistinct.
1802-3	,,	,,	,,	F	,,	GW	George Walker.
1803-4	,,	,,	,,	G	,,		,, ,,
1804-5	,,	,,	,,	H	,,	I·E	Name not traced.
1805-6	,,	,,	,,	I	,,	N·L	Nicholas Lee.
1806-7	,,	,,	,,	K	,,		,, ,,
1807-8	,,	,,	,,	L	,,	GL	George Lowe.
1808-9	,,	,,	,,	M	,,		Mark indistinct.
1809-10	,,	,,	,,	N	,,	WJ	Name not traced.
1810-1	,,	,,	,,	O	,,	IW	John Walker.
1811-2	,,	,,	,,	P	,,	WP	William Pugh (of Birmingham).
1812-3	,,	,,	,,	Q	,,	A&I	Abbott & Jones.
1813-4	,,	,,	,,	R	,,		,, ,,
1814-5	,,	,,	,,	S	,,	JM	Jas. Morton.
1815-6	,,	,,	,,	T	,,		,, ,,
1816-7	,,	,,	,,	U	,,	HA	Hugh Adamson.
1817-8	,,	,,	,,	V	,,	JA	John Abbott.

	LION PASSANT.	LEOPARD'S HEAD.	TOWN MARK.	DATE LETTER.	KING'S HEAD.	MAKER'S MARK	MAKER'S NAME.
1818-9	(lion)	(leopard)	(town)	A	(king)	JAW	J. Walker.
1819-20	,,	,,	,,	B	,,	V&R	Vale & Co.
GEO. IV. 1820-1	,,	,,	,,	C	,,	I&R	Jones & Reeves.
1821-2-3	,,	,,	,,	D	,,	HVA	Hy. Adamson.
1823-4	,,	(leopard)	,,	E	(king)	MH	Mary Huntingdon.
1824-5	,,	,,	,,	F	,,	JT	John Twemlow.
1825-6	,,	,,	,,	G	,,	JM	J. Morton.
1826-7	,,	,,	,,	H	,,	GL	Geo. Lowe.
1827-8	,,	,,	,,	I	,,	RB	Robt. Bowers.
1828-9	,,	,,	,,	K	,,	TN	Thos. Newton.
1829-30 WM. IV.	,,	,,	,,	L	,,	JH / JH	John Hilsby, L'pool.
1830-1	,,	,,	,,	M	,,	JC	John Coakley.
1831-2	,,	,,	,,	N	,,	JP	John Parsonage.
1832-3	,,	,,	,,	O	,,	TW	Thos. Walker or } Thos. Woodfield }
1833-4	,,	,,	,,	P	,,	RL	Robt. Lowe.
1834-5	,,	,,	,,	Q	,,	RL	Richd. Lucas.
1835-6	,,	,,	,,	R	(king)	IW	John Walker.
1836-7	,,	,,	,,	S	,,	ILS	Jos. L. Samuel.
VICT. 1837-8	,,	,,	,,	T	,,	JS	John Sutters.
1838-9	,,	,,	,,	U	,,	HC	Henry Close.

	LION PASSANT.	TOWN MARK.	DATE LETTER.	QUEEN'S HEAD.	MAKER'S MARK.	MAKER'S NAME.
1839-40	(lion)	(town)	A	(queen)	I&TL	J. & Thos. Lowe.
1840-1	,,	,,	B	,,	I&TL	,, ,, ,,
1841-2	,,	,,	C	,,	HVA	Henry Adamson.
1842-3	,,	,,	D	,,	PL	P. Leonard.
1843-4	,,	,,	E	,,	WS	Wm. Smith.
1844-5	,,	,,	F	,,	RS	Ralph Samuel.
1845-6	,,	,,	G	,,	AB / WG	Adam Burgess. Wm. Crofton.
1846-7	,,	,,	H	,,	JB	J. Burbidge.
1847-8	,,	,,	I	,,	IFW	John F. Wathew.
1848-9	,,	,,	K	,,	CJ	Christr. Jones.
1849-50	,,	,,	L	,,	TW	T. Wilson.
1850-1	,,	,,	M	,,	EK	E Kirkman.
1851-2	,,	,,	N	,,	GW	Geo. Ward.
1852-3	,,	,,	O	,,	TC	T. Cubbin.
1853-4	,,	,,	P	,,	RA / GCL	Richard Adamson. G. C. Lowe. (Manchester).
1854-5	,,	,,	Q	,,	TW	Thos. Wooley.
1855-6	,,	,,	R	,,	AGR	A. G. Rogers.
1856-7	,,	,,	S	,,	JL	John Lowe.
1857-8	,,	,,	T	,,	JM	Joseph Mayer.
1858-9	,,	,,	U	,,	EJ	Edwd. Jones.
1859-60	,,	,,	V	,,	EN	Elias Nathan.
1860-1	,,	,,	W	,,	GR	Geo. Roberts.
1861-2	,,	,,	X	,,	HF	H. Fishwick.
1862-3	,,	,,	Y	,,	HS	H. J. Stuart.
1863-4	,,	,,	Z	,,	FB	Francis Butt.

	LION PASSANT.	TOWN MARK.	DATE LETTER.	QUEEN'S HEAD.	MAKER'S MARK.	MAKER'S NAME.
1864-5	(lion)	(town)	a	(head)	WD	Wm. Dodge.
1865-6	,,	,,	b	,,	IR	John Richards.
1866-7	,,	,,	c	,,	SW	Saml. Ward, Manchester.
1867-8	,,	,,	d	,,	GL	Geo. Lowe, junr.
1868-9	,,	,,	e	,,	HT HT	Henry Tarlton, Liverpool.
1869-70	,,	,,	f	,,	WR	W. Roskell, Liverpool.
1870-1	,,	,,	g	,,	S.Q	S. Quilliam.
1871-2	,,	,,	h	,,	GR	Geo. Roberts.
1872-3	,,	,,	i	,,	RO	Robt. Over.
1873-4	,,	,,	k	,,	TR	Thos. Russell.
1874-5	,,	,,	l	,,	HG	Hugh Green.
1875-6	,,	,,	m	,,	S&R	Samuel & Rogers.
1876-7	,,	,,	n	,,	AC	A. Cruickshank.
1877-8	,,	,,	o	,,	SQ	S. Quilliam.
1878-9	,,	,,	p	,,	GFW	Geo. F. Wright, Liverpool.
1879-80	,,	,,	q	,,	JK	Joseph Knight, Birmingham.
1880-1	,,	,,	r	,,	TP&S	T. Power & Son, Liverpool.
1881-2	,,	,,	s	,,	BN	Benge Nathan.
1882-3	,,	,,	t	,,	WS	Wm. Smith, Liverpool.
1883-4	,,	,,	u	,,	AR	A. Rogers, Liverpool.

	LION PASSANT.	TOWN MARK.	DATE LETTER.	QUEEN'S HEAD.	MAKER'S MARK.
1884-5	(lion)	(town)	A	(head)	NBS
1885-6	,,	,,	B	,,	A.B
1886-7	,,	,,	C	,,	JT&S
1887-8	,,	,,	D	,,	A&M
1888-9	,,	,,	E	,,	W.T
1889-90	,,	,,	F	,,	E.W
1890-1	,,	,,	G	,,	J.W
1891-2	,,	,,	H	,,	T.C
1892-3	,,	,,	I	,,	J.H A.H
1893-4	,,	,,	K	,,	H.W
1894-5	,,	,,	L	,,	J.D W.D
1895-6	,,	,,	M	,,	A.M
1896-7	,,	,,	N	,,	W.N
1897-8	,,	,,	O	,,	H.K
1898-9	,,	,,	P	,,	W.A
1899 1900	,,	,,	Q	,,	T.P.B
1900-1	,,	,,	R	,,	G.N R.H
EDW. VII. 1901-2	,,	,,	A	,,	J.F.
1902-3	,,	,,	B	,,	B.B

MARKS ON CHESTER PLATE.

MARKS ON LINCOLN PLATE.

DATE.	LION PASSANT.	TOWN MARK.	DATE-LETTER.
1903-4			C
1904-5	,,	,,	D
1905-6	,,	,,	E
1906-7	,,	,,	F
1907-8	,,	,,	G
1908-9	,,	,,	H
1909-10	,,	,,	I
1910-1	,,	,,	K
1911-2	,,	,,	L
1912-3	,,	,,	M
1913-4	,,	,,	N
1914-5	,,	,,	O
1915-6	,,	,,	P
1916-7	,,	,,	Q
1917-8	,,	,,	R
1918-9	,,	,,	S
1919-20	,,	,,	T
1920-1	,,	,,	U
1921-2	,,	,,	V

DATE (ABOUT).	MARKS.	DATE (ABOUT).	MARKS.
1560		1640-50	
,,		,,	
,,		,,	
,,		,,	
1569		1642	
c. 1590		1650	
1617		,,	
1624		1650-6	
1628		1660	
1633		,,	
1639		1686	
1640		1690	
1640-50	,,	,,	
,,		,,	
,,		1706	

Year	Lion Passant	Anchor	Date Letter	Kings Head	Maker's Mark	Maker's Name
1773-4	[lion]	[anchor]	A		MB IF	Matthew Boulton & John Fothergill.
1774-5	"	"	B		" "	{ " " , " " }
1775-6	"	"	C		CF	Charles Freeth.
1776-7	"	"	D		"	" "
1777-8	"	"	E		{ RB CF / MB IF }	Richard Bickley, Charles Freeth. Boulton & Fothergill.
1778-9	"	"	F		" "	" "
1779-80	"	"	G		TW	T. Willmore & Alston.
1780-1	"	"	H		...	... ...
1781-2	"	"	I			... ...
1782-3	"	"	K		TW	T. Willmore & Alston.
1783-4	"	"	L		"	" "
1784-5	"	"	M	[kings head]	SP	Samuel Pemberton.
1785-6	"	"	N	"	HH	Henry Holland.
1786-7	"	"	O	[head]	SP	Samuel Pemberton.
1787-8	"	"	P	"	IT	Joseph Taylor.
1788-9	"	"	Q	"	"	" "
1789-90	"	"	R	"	T.W	Thos. Willmore.
1790-1	"	"	S	"	MB	Mathw. Boulton.
1791-2	"	"	T	"	SP	Samuel Pemberton.
1792-3	"	"	U	"	"	" "
1793-4	"	"	V	"	MB	Mathw. Boulton.
1794-5	"	"	W	"	IT	Joseph Taylor.
1795-6	"	"	X	"	IS	John Shaw.
1796-7	"	"	Y	"	TW	Thos. Willmore.
1797-8	"	"	Z	[head]	"	" "

Year	Lion Passant	Anchor	Date Letter	King's Head	Maker's Mark	Maker's Name
1798-9	[lion]	[anchor]	a	[kings head]	TW	Willmore & Alston.
1789, 1800	"	"	b	"	SP	Samuel Pemberton.
1800-1	"	"	c	"	F&W	Forrest & Wasdell.
1801-2	"	"	d	"	IT / TW	John Turner? Thos. Willmore?
1802-3	"	"	e	"	MB	Matthew Boulton.
1803-4	"	"	f	"	IS	John Shaw.
1804-5	"	"	g	"	IT	Joseph Taylor.
1805-6	"	"	h	"	ML / WP	Matthew Linwood. William Pugh.
1806-7	"	"	i	"	JW / C&B	Joseph Willmore. Cocks & Bettridge.
1807-8	"	"	j	"	WP	William Pugh.
1808-9	"	"	k	"	MB	Matthew Boulton.
1809-10	"	"	l	[head]	IS	John Shaw.
1810-1	"	"	m		T&T	Thropp & Taylor.
1811-2	"	"	n		S&S	T. Simpson & Son.
1812-3	"	"	o	[head]	IT / "	Joseph Taylor.
1813-4	"	"	p		C&B	Cocks & Bettridge.
1814-5	"	"	q		L&C	W. Lea & Co.
1815-6	"	"	r	"	"	" "
1816-7	"	"	s		SP / W&K	Samuel Pemberton. Wardell & Kempson.
1817-8	"	"	t		E.T	Edward Thomason.
1818-9	"	"	u		J.W	Joseph Willmore.
1819-20 GEO. IV.	"	"	v		"	" "
1820-1	"	"	w		ML	Matthew Linwood & Son.
1821-2	"	"	x		L&C	Lea & Clark.
1822-3	"	"	y		L&Co	John Lawrence & Co.
1823-4	"	"	z		J.W	Joseph Willmore.

Year	Lion Passant	Anchor	Date Letter	King's Head	Maker's Mark	Maker's Name
1824-5	(lion)	(anchor)	A	(head)	TP / CJ	T. Pemberton & Son. / Charles Jones.
1825-6	,,	,,	B	,,	LV&W / T·S	Ledsam, Vale & Wheeler. / Thomas Shaw.
1826-7	,,	,,	C	(head)	L&Cº / NM	John Lawrence & Co. / Nathaniel Mills.
1827-8	,,	,,	D	,,	U&H / MB / J·W	Unite and Hilliard / M. Boulton & Plate Co. / Joseph Willmore.
1828-9	,,	,,	E	,,	ET / WF	Edward Thomason. / William Fowke.
1829-30	,,	,,	F	(head)	IB / LV&W	John Bettridge. / Ledsam, Vale & Wheeler.
WM. IV. 1830-1	,,	,,	G	,,	TR&S / MB	Thos. Ryland & Sons. / M. Boulton & Plate Co.
1831-2	,,	,,	H	(head)	JW	Joseph Willmore.
1832-3	,,	,,	I	,,	,,	,, ,,
1833-4	,,	,,	K	,,	ES / VR	Edward Smith. / Vale & Ratheram.
1834-5	,,	,,	L	(head)	T&P / WP	Taylor & Perry. / William Phillips.
1835-6	,,	,,	M	,,	GW	Gervase Wheeler.
1836-7	,,	,,	N	,,	FC / J&Cº	Francis Clark. / Joseph Jennens & Co.
VICT. 1837-8	,,	,,	O	,,	T·S / R.E.A	Thomas Spicer. / Robinson, Edkins & Aston.
1838-9	,,	,,	P	(head)	GU / N·M	George Unite. / Nathaniel Mills.
1839-40	,,	,,	Q	,,	N & R	Neville & Ryland ?
1840-1	,,	,,	R	,,	,,	,, ,,
1841-2	,,	,,	S	,,	... ...	
1842-3	,,	,,	T	,,	R.E.A	Robinson, Edkins & Aston.
1843-4	,,	,,	U	,,	ES	Edward Smith.
1844-5	,,	,,	V	,,	N·M	Nathaniel Mills.
1845-6	,,	,,	W	,,	W&ET	Wm. & Ed. Turnpenny.
1846-7	,,	,,	X	,,	Y&W / N·M	Yapp & Woodward. / Nathaniel Mills.
1847-8	,,	,,	Y	,,	,,	,, ,,
1848-9	,,	,,	Z	,,	... ...	

Year	Lion Passant	Anchor	Date Letter	Queen's Head	Maker's Mark	Maker's Name
1849-50	(lion)	(anchor)	A	(head)	N·M	Nathaniel Mills.
1850-1	,,	,,	B	,,	ES	Edward Smith.
1851-2	,,	,,	C	,,	,,	,, ,,
1852-3	,,	,,	D	,,		Nathl. Mills, as 1849.
1853-4	,,	,,	E	,,		... ...
1854-5	,,	,,	F	,,		... ...
1855-6	,,	,,	G	,,	GU	George Unite.
1856-7	,,	,,	H	,,		... ...
1857-8	,,	,,	I	,,		
1858-9	,,	,,	J	,,		... ...
1859-60	,,	,,	K	,,	GU	George Unite.
1860-1	,,	,,	L	,,		... ...
1861-2	,,	,,	M	,,		... ...
1862-3	,,	,,	N	,,		J. H. & Co., as on page 414.
1863-4	,,	,,	O	,,		... ...
1864-5	,,	,,	P	,,	JM&Cº	Names registered after 1850 not disclosed.
1865-6	,,	,,	Q	,,		... ...
1866-7	,,	,,	R	,,		... ...
1867-8	,,	,,	S	,,	JG	... ...
1868-9	,,	,,	T	,,		... ...
1869-70	,,	,,	U	,,		... ...
1870-1	,,	,,	V	,,		... ...
1871-2		,,	W	,,	JT	Crown and 18 instead of lion passant.
1872-3	,,	,,	X	,,		... ...
1873-4	,,	,,	Y	,,		... ...
1874-5	,,	,,	Z	,,		... ...

	LION PASSANT.	ANCHOR.	DATE LETTER.	QUEEN'S HEAD.	MAKER'S MARK.
1875-6	(lion)	(anchor)	a	(head)	TP&S
1876-7	,,	,,	b	,,	,,
1877-8	,,	,,	c	,,	H&T
1878-9	,,	,,	d	,,	
1879-80	,,	,,	e	,,	
1880-1	,,	,,	f	,,	
1881-2	,,	,,	g	,,	
1882-3	,,	,,	h	,,	H&T
1883-4	,,	,,	i	,,	,,
1884-5	,,	,,	k	,,	
1885-6	,,	,,	l	,,	
1886-7	,,	,,	m	,,	
1887-8	,,	,,	n	,,	
1888-9	,,	,,	o	,,	
1889-90	,,	,,	p	,,	N&H
1890-1	,,	,,	q	,,	T.W.D
1891-2	,,	,,	r		N&H
1892-3	,,	,,	s		J·M·B
1893-4	,,	,,	t		SWS
1894-5	,,	,,	u		L.G
1895-6	,,	,,	v		T·H
1896-7	,,	,,	w		H M
1897-8	,,	,,	x		HH&C; JRW
1898-9	,,	,,	y		A&J Z
1899 1900	,,	,,	z		JS SS

DATE.	Anchor.	Lion Passant.	Date Letter.	Maker's Mark.
1900-1	(anchor)	(lion)	a	E & Co L^d
1901-2	,,	,,	b	H·W·E
1902-3	,,	,,	c	I S G
1903-4	,,	,,	d	L & Co
1904-5	,,	,,	e	H & F
1905-6	,,	,,	f	
1906-7	,,	,,	g	
1907-8	,,	,,	h	
1908-9	,,	,,	i	
1909-10	,,	,,	k	
1910-1	,,	,,	l	
1911-2	,,	,,	m	
1912-3	,,	,,	n	
1913-4	,,	,,	o	
1914-5	,,	,,	p	
1915-6	,,	,,	q	
1916-7	,,	,,	r	R & T W
1917-8	,,	,,	s	
1918-9	,,	,,	t	
1919-20	,,	,,	u	
1920-1	,,	,,	v	
1921-2	,,	,,	w	
1922-3	,,	,,	x	
1923-4	,,	,,	y	
1924-5	,,	,,	z	

SUPPLEMENTARY LIST OF ADDITIONAL MARKS OF GOLDSMITHS,

Impressed at Birmingham, not illustrated in the preceding tables.

DATE.	MARK.	MAKER'S NAME.
1776-7	JA&S	Jos. Adams & Son.
1778-9	E·S	Edward Sawyer.
1783-4	S·P	Samuel Pemberton.
1804-5	W	... ...
1806-7	H&Co.	... ...|
1807-8	M	... ...
1811-2	W	... ...
1814-5	J L	... ...
1820-1	T N	Thos. Newbold.
1822-3	S P	... ...
1826	T&K	Geo. Tye & Jas. Kilner.
1832-3	G·T	Geo. Tye.
1876-7	T T & Co	... ...
1862-3	J H & Co	... ...|
1892-3	H W	... ...

Date	Lion Passant	Crown	Date Letter	King's Head (from 1784)	Maker's Mark	Maker's Name
1773-4	lion	crown	C		R·M&C° / SR&C° / MF&Co	Rich'd. Morton & Co. / S. Roberts & Co. / Mat'w. Fenton & Co.
1774-5	"	"	F		GA&C°	Geo. Ashforth & Co.
1775-6	"	"	N		IW&C°	John Winter & Co.
1776-7	"	"	K		W·D	Wm. Damant.
1777-8	"	"	H		TL TL / MF RC	Tudor and Leader. / Fenton Creswick & Co.
1778-9	"	"	S		CS	John Smith ?
1779-80	"	"	A		"	" " "
1780-1	"	"	(letter)		NS&C°	Nath'l. Smith & Co.
1781-2	"	"	D		MF RC	Fenton Creswick & Co.
1782-3	"	"	G		IW&C°	John Winter & Co.
1783-4	"	"	B		DH&C° / IP&C°	Danl. Holy & Co. / John Parsons & Co.
1784-5	"	"	I	(king's head)		" " "
1785-6	"	"	P	"	R·M	Richd. Morton & Co.
1786-7	"	crown	K	"	IP&C°	John Parsons & Co.
1787-8	"	"	T	"	"	" " "
1788-9	"	"	W	"	ITY&C°	John Younge & Sons.
1789-90	"	"	(letter)	"	RS	R. Sutcliffe & Co. (?)
1790-1	"	"	L	"	IP&C°	John Parsons & Co.
1791-2	"	"	P	"	ITY&C°	John Younge & Sons.
1792-3	lion	crown	U	"	IP&C°	John Parsons & Co.
1793-4	"	"	O	"	TL	Thos. Law.
1794-5	"	"	m	"	IG&C°	John Green & Co.
1795-6	"	"	q	"	ITY&C°	John Younge & Sons, as above.
1796-7	"	"	Z	"	GE&C°	Geo. Eadon & Co.
1797-8	"		X	(king's head)	T·LAW	T. Law.
1798-9	"	"	V	(king's head)	SR GC&C°	Saml. Roberts, jr. / Geo. Cadman & Co. }

Date	Lion Passant	Crown	Date Letter	King's Head	Maker's Mark	Maker's Name
1799 / 1800	lion	crown	E	(king's head)	IL&C° / IG&C°	John Love & Co. / John Green & Co.
1800-1	"	"	N	"	GA&C° / IG&C°	Geo. Ashforth & Co. / John Green & Co.
1801-2	"	"	H	"	" / TW&C°	Thos." Watson & Co.
1802-3	(lion)	"	M	"	TL DL / R·M	Thos. & Danl. Leader. / Richd. Morton & Co.
1803-4	"	"	F	"	NS&C°	Nathan Smith & Co.
1804-5	"	"	G	"	IE&C°	Jas. Ellis & Co.
1805-6	"	"	B	"	AG&C°	Alexr. Goodman & Co.
1806-7	"	"	A	"	ITY&C°	J. T. Younge & Co.
1807-8	"	"	S	"	WT&C°	W. Tucker & Co.
1808-9	"	"	P	"	T·B&C°	Thos. Blagden & Co.
1809-10	"	"	K	"	IR&C°	John Roberts & Co.
1810-1	"	"	L	"	" " / GE&C°	Geo. Eadon & Co.
1811-2	"	"	C	(king's head)		John Roberts & Co., as 1809-10 above.
1812-3	"	"	D	"	ST N&H	Smith, Tate & Co. (Nicholson & Holt).
1813-4	"	"	R	"	IKIW&C°	Kirkby, Waterhouse & Co.
1814-5	"	"	W	"	I·L	John Law
1815-6	"	"	O	"	IE&C°	J. Ellis & Co. (?)
1816-7	"	"	T	"	IW	John Watson.
1817-8	"	"	X	"	" " / I&T·S	John and Thos. Settle.
1818-9	"	"	I	"	SCY&C°	S. C. Younge & Co.
1819-20	lion	"	V / U	"	IIC / IKIW&CO / GC&C°	Thos. and Jas. Creswick / Kirkby, Waterhouse & Co. / G. Cooper & Co.
GEO. IV. 1820-1	"	"	Q	"	ST H&T	Smith, Tate, Hoult & Tate.
1821-2	"	"	Y	"	JL	Joseph Law
1822-3	"	"	Z	"	IG&C°	John Green & Co.
1823-4	"	"	U	"	W·B	Wm. Briggs.

	LION PASSANT	CROWN	DATE LETTER	KING'S HEAD	MAKER'S MARK	MAKER'S NAME.
1824-5	lion	crown	a	head	S.C.Y &Co / WB&Co	S. C. Younge & Co. / Wm. Blackwell & Co.
1825-6	,,		b	,,	I&IW &Co	Waterhouse, Hodson & Co.
1826-7	,,	,,	c	,,	BH&H	Battie, Howard & Hawksworth.
1827-8	,,		d	,,	TI NC	T. J. & N. Creswick.
1828-9	,,	,,	e	,,	BH&H	Battie, Howard & Hawksworth. / John Settle & Henry Williamson.
1829-30	,,		f	,,	IS HW	
WM. IV. 1830-1	,,		g	,,	TI NC	T. J. & N. Creswick.
1831-2	,,	,,	h	head	JB	Jas. Burbury.
1832-3	,,	,,	k	,,	S&N / A&O	Stafford & Newton. / Atkin & Oxley.
1833-4	,,		l	,,	T·I NC / WA&Co	T. J. & N. Creswick. / Wm. Allanson & Co.
1834-5	,,		P	,,	I&IW &Co	Waterhouse, Hodson & Co.
1835-6	,,		P	head	H&H	Howard & Hawksworth.
1836-7	,,	,,	q	,,		...
VICT. 1837-8	,,		r	,,	HW &Co	Hy. Wilkinson & Co.
1838-9	,,		s	,,	HW &Co	,, ,, ,,
1839-40	,,	,,	t	,,	SH	Samuel Harwood.
1840-1	,,	,,	u	head	,,	,, ,,
1841-2	,,	,,	v	,,		...
1842-3	,,		x	,,	HE &Co	Hawksworth, Eyre & Co.
1843-4	,,	,,	z	,,	..	.

	CROWN	DATE LETTER	LION PASSANT	QUEEN'S HEAD	MAKER'S MARK	MAKER'S NAME.
*1844-5	crown	A	lion	head	HE &Co	Hawksworth, Eyre Co.
1845-6	,,	B	,,	,,	...	... .
1846-7	,,	C	,,	,,	...	...
1847-8	,,	D	,,	,,	...	...
1848-9	,,	E	,,	,,	...	... .
1849-50	,,	F	,,	,,		Hawksworth, Eyre & Co.
1850-1	,,	G	,,	,,	...	.. ...
1851-2	,,	H	,,	,,	...	... ...
1852-3	,,	I	,,	,,	...	... ...
1853-4	,,	K	,,	,,	...	... .
1854-5	,,	L	,,	,,	...	... ...
1855-6	,,	M	,, ,,	,,	...	... ...
1856-7	,,	N	,,	,,	...	... ...
1857-8	,,	O	,,	,,	...	... ...
1858-9	,,	P	,,	,,	...	... ...
1859-60	,,	R	,,	,,	MH &Co	Martin Hall & Co.
1860-1	,,	S	,,	,,	...	... ...
1861-2	,,	T	,,	,,	...	... ...
1862-3	,,	U	,,	,,	HH	Harrison Bros. & Howson.
1863-4	,,	V	,,	,,	...	... ...
1864-5	,,	W	,,	,,	FBro	Fenton Bros.
1865-6	,,	X	,,	,,	HA	Hy. Archer & Co.
1866-7	,,	Y	,,	,,	RM EH	Martin Hall & Co., Ltd.
1867-8	,,	Z	,,	,,	...	... ...

	CROWN.	LION PASSANT.	DATE LETTER.	QUEEN'S HEAD.	MAKER'S MARK.	MAKER'S NAME.		CROWN.	LION PASSANT.	DATE LETTER.	MAKER'S MARK.	MAKER'S NAME.
1868-9	✦	✦	A	✦	RM/EH	Martin Hall & Co., Ltd.	1893-4	✦	✦	a	JD&S	James Deakin & Sons.
1869-70	,,	,,	B	,,			1894-5	,,	,,	b	JR	John Round & Son, Ltd.
1870-1	,,	,,	C	,,		…	1895-6	,,	,,	c	JD/WD	Jas. Deakin & Sons.
1871-2	,,	,,	D	,,		…	1896-7	,,	,,	d	M&W	Mappin & Webb.
1872-3	,,	,,	E	,,		…	1897-8	,,	,,	e	WF/AF	Fordham & Faulkner.
1873-4	,,	,,	F	,,	IH	John Harrison & Co., Ld.	1898-9	,,	,,	f	HW	Lee & Wigfull.
1874-5	,,	,,	G	,,		…	1899/1900	,,	,,	g	HA	Atkin Brothers.
1875-6	,,	,,	H	,,		…	1900-1	,,	,,	h	W&H	Walker & Hall.
1876-7	,,	,,	J	,,		…	EDW. VII. 1901-2	,,	,,	i	R&B	Roberts & Belk.
1877-8	,,	,,	K	,,		…	1902-3	,,	,,	k	GH	Harrison Bros. & Howson.
1878-9	,,	,,	L	,,		…	1903-4	,,	,,	l		…
1879-80	,,	,,	M	,,		…	1904-5	,,	,,	m		…
1880-1	,,	,,	N	,,		…	1905-6	,,	,,	n		…
1881-2	,,	,,	O	,,		…	1906-7	,,	,,	o		…
1882-3	,,	,,	P	,,		…	1907-8	,,	,,	p		…
1883-4	,,	,,	Q	,,		…	1908-9	,,	,,	q		…
1884-5	,,	,,	R	,,		…	1909-10	,,	,,	r		…
1885-6	,,	,,	S	,,		…	1910-1	,,	,,	s		…
1886-7	,,	,,	T	,,		…	1911-2	,,	,,	t		…
1887-8	,,	,,	U	,,		…	1912-3	,,	,,	u		…
1888-9	,,	,,	V	,,	J·K·B	Hawksworth, Eyre & Co., Ltd.	1913-4	,,	,,	v		…
1889-90	,,	,,	W	,,	WB/JA	W. Briggs & Co.	1914-5	,,	,,	w		…
1890-1	,,	,,	X	,,	RM/EH	Martin Hall & Co., Ltd.	1915-6	,,	,,	x		
1891-2	,,	,,	Y	,,	JD&S	Jas. Dixon & Sons.	1916-7	,,	,,	y		…
1892-3	,,	,,	Z	,,	H·S	Henry Stratford.	1917-8	,,	,,	z		…

SUPPLEMENTARY LIST OF MARKS OF GOLDSMITHS

Impressed at Sheffield, not illustrated in the preceding tables, from 1773 to 1905 :—

DATE.	MARKS.	MAKER'S NAME.
1773	W·H I·R	W. Hancock & J. Rowbotham.
"	WB &Co	W. Birks & Co.
"	T·L / LAW (STER)	T. Law.
"	LAW	" "
"	WB&Co	W. Birks & Co.
"	I·R	J. Rowbotham ?
"	J·L	J. Littlewood.
"	SO	Name not traced.
"	IK&Co	John Kay & Co.
"	JN / WN	J. Nowill. W. Nowill.
1774	I·M	J. Mappin.
"	WM	W. Marsden & Co.
"	SR	S. Roberts.
1775	IR·Co	J. Rowbotham & Co.
"	R·K	R. Kippax.
"	IM&Co	J. Mappin & Co.
1776	T·H	T. Hoyland.
"	IT	J. Tibbitts.
1777	IH Co	J. Hoyland & Co.
"	IH&Co	" "
1778	SW	S. Warburton.
"	DH	D. Holy.
1779	M&T	Madin & Trickett
1780	Y·G&H	Young, Greaves & Hoyland.
"	N·S	N. Smith & Co.
1781	I·D	J. Dewsnap.
1783	S·K	S. Kirkby.

DATE.	MARKS.	MAKER'S NAME.
1784	T·F&Co	T. Fox & Co.
1788	P·S	P. Spurr.
1789	W·J	W. Jervis.
1790	RS	R. Sporle.
1791	I·B	J. Bailey.
"	MF &Co	M. Fenton & Co.
1792	LP &Co	? Luke, Proctor & Co.
1796	GA &Co	G. Ashforth & Co.
1797	CP	C. Proctor.
"	EG	E. Goodwin.
"	IC	J. Creswick.
"	HF&Co	Mark of Henry Tudor & Co.
1798	GG&Co	Goodman, Gainsford & Co.
"	SK&Co	S. Kirkby & Co.
1799	RI	R. Jewesson.
1801	TP	T. Poynton.
1804	(illegible)	Name not traced.
"	IS	J. Staniforth.
1807	W.T&Co	W. Tucker & Co.
1808	IW	J. Watson.
1810	G·W	G. Wostenholme
1811	IS TS	J. Staniforth & Co.
"	RG	R. Gainsford.
1813	I·R	J. Rogers.
1817	RG	R. Gainsford.
1818	B·R	B. Rooke & Son.
"	W·W	W. Wrangham
1820	TJ&NC	T. J. & N. Creswick.
1822	T&IS	T. & J. Settle.

DATE.	MARKS.	MAKER'S NAME.
1822	A·H	A. Hadfield.
1824	CHS	C. Hammond & Co
1825	RG	R. Gainsford.
1828	GH	G. Hardesty.
1829	D&S	J. Dixon & Son.
1833	JM	J. Mappin & Son.
1836	K&W	Kitchen & Walker.
1840	L&M	Lee & Middleton.
"	WK &Co	Walker, Knowles & Co.
1843	W&S	Waterhouse & Co
1844	BW&A	Badger Worrall & Co.
1846	R&S	Roberts & Slater.
1847	P·P &Co	Padley, Parkins & Co.
1853	JC NC	J. & N. Creswick.
1856	WS HS	W. & H. Stratford.
1857	F&A	Fenton & Anderton.
1858	WH	W. Hutton.
"	WS GS	W. & G. Sissons.
1859	MB	Mappin Bros.
"	EM&Co	Elkington Mason & Co.
1861	WWH	W W. Harrison.
1862	W&H	Walker & Hall.
1863	LB	Levesley Bros.
1864	MW&Co	Mappin & Webb.
1866	W& MD	W. & M. Dodge.
1867	J·H·S	J. Slater & Son.
1868	CL TL	Levesley Bros.
1869	AB	A. Beardshaw.
1905	IE &S	Name not traced.

HULL

DATE.	TOWN MARK.	MAKER'S MARK.	TOWN MARK.	MAKER'S MARK.	MAKER'S NAME.
1580	H	PC			Peter Carlille.
1587	IC	H			James Carlille.
1621		IC	RR	HB	" " *
1629	H	RR	H		Robt. Robinson.
1635		RR	"		" "
1638	H	CW	H		Chr. Watson.
1651		IB			James Birkby.
1666		EM			Edwd. Mangie or Mangy. }
				DATE LETTER.	
1666-70		TG		E	Name not traced.
1670-80	"	"		K	" "
"		EM		A	Edwd. Mangie or Mangy. }
1680	"	M			" "
"	"	EM	"	D	" "
1680-97	"	KM	"	E	Kath. Mangy.
"		KM			" "
"	..	EM	"	I	Edwd. Mangy.
1689	"	TH	"		Thos. Hebden.
1690-7		KM			Kath. Mangy.
1697		KM			" "
1706		AB	"		Abm. Barachin.

SHREWSBURY

DATE.	MARKS.
1530	
1560	
"	

LEWES.

c. 1590	
c. 1637	

ROCHESTER

DATE.	MARKS.
1560	
c. 1640	

Sandwich.

BARNSTAPLE

DATE (ABOUT).	MARKS.	MAKER'S NAME.
1568-1601	IC	John Coton.
c. 1570-75	M	Thos. Mathew.
1576	T MATEV	" "
1578	D COTON	J. Coton.
1580	M MATEV	T. Mathew.
"	IC	*J. Coton.
1584	I COTON	" "
c. 1650	I·P	John Peard
1670-80	IP I·P IP	" "
1680	IP	" "
1687	IP	" "
1695	I·P	" "

TRURO

DATE (ABOUT).	MARKS.
1560 1600	
"	R T T
"	" "
1600	
1620	R T T
"	
"	R T T
1630	"

DEVON AND CORNWALL

DATE. (ABOUT).	MARKS.
1576-80	WZ
"	
1580	IN W
? c. 1600	HP
c. 1600-30	IS
"	
"	P·T PT
"	IW
"	IP Fal mo uth
"	
1610	CF CF
1610-50	RA
1630	WR
1641	
1650 1700	M M
1675	IP
1680-5	RA F
1690	DD
1695	
"	I·L
1700	RH B
1715	RP

TAUNTON

DATE (ABOUT).	MARKS.
1645	
,,	,,
,,	
1660	
1676-82	
1689	

LEEDS

DATE.	MARKS.
1650 TO 1702	
,,	,, ,,
1660	
1680	,,
1690	
,,	,,

KING'S LYNN

DATE.	MARKS.
1632	
1635	,,
1640	,,

CARLISLE

DATE.	MARKS.
1571	
1630	
,,	
1670	

GATESHEAD

c. 1680	

LEICESTER

DATE.	MARKS.
1540	
1590	
1600	
,,	
1575 to 1600	
1630	
,,	

PLYMOUTH

DATE.	MARKS.
c. 1600	
1690-5	
1695-9	P IM Britannia
"	IM Sterling
c. 1694	IM Sterling
1698	Rowe Plmᵒ Britan
to	
1700	Row St Ncw Ply

SALISBURY

DATE.	MARKS.
c. 1596	R
"	
c. 1620	H
"	L
c. 1627	IQ
c. 1629	R
"	B

COLCHESTER

DATE.	MARKS.
c. 1723	HUTCHINSON COLCHESTER

JAMAICA

DATE.	MARKS.
c. 1800	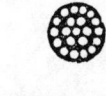

DORCHESTER

Mark of Lawrence Stratford, of Dorchester.	✱ S ✕

SHERBORNE

Mark of Richard Orenge (probably).	
Marks of Richard Orenge.	RO ◯

208

CHANNEL ISLANDS

DATE (ABOUT).	MARKS.
GUERNSEY, c. 1690-1730	
c. 1740	
c. 1750	
"	
"	
"	
JERSEY, c. 1760	
c. 1780	
"	
c. 1790	
c. 1800	
"	
"	
c. 1830	

POOLE.

DATE.	MARKS.
c. 1540	
"	
c. 1560	
c. 1580	
"	
c. 1620	

CALCUTTA.

DATF.	MARKS.
c. 1810	
"	

BRISTOL

DATE.	MARKS.
c. 1730	
c. 1731	
c. 1780-90	

DATE (ABOUT).	MARKS.	DATE (ABOUT).	MARKS.	DATE (ABOUT).	MARKS.

DATE (ABOUT).	MARKS.	DATE (ABOUT).	MARKS.	DATE (ABOUT).	MARKS.	DATE (ABOUT).	MARKS.
1600		1620		1630-5		1640	
"		1623		"		"	
"		1625		"		"	
1600-50		1630		"		"	
1609		"		"		"	
1610		"		"		1640-8	
"		"		1637		1640-50	
"		"		"		"	
"		"		1638		"	
"		"		1640		"	
"		"		"		1650	
"		"		"		"	
"		"		"		"	
"		"		"		"	
1620		1630-5		"		"	
"		"		"		"	
"		"		"		"	
"		"		"		"	
"		"		"		"	
"		"		"		"	
"		"		"		"	
"		"		"		"	
"		"		"		"	
"		"		"			

DATE (ABOUT).	MARKS.	DATE (ABOUT).	MARKS.	DATE (ABOUT).	MARKS.
1650		1674		1680	
,,		1675		,,	
,,		,,		,,	
1658		1677		,,	
1660		,,		1680-5	
,,		1680		,,	
,,		,,		,,	
,,		,,		,,	
,,		,,		,,	
,,		,,		,,	
,,		,,		,,	
1660-70		,,		,,	
,,		,,		,,	
1667		,,		,,	
1670		,,		,,	
,,		,,		,,	
1670-4		,,		,,	
,,		,,		1682	
1674		,,		1684-5	
,,		,,		,,	
,,		,,		,,	

DATE (ABOUT).	MARKS.	DATE (ABOUT).	MARKS.	DATE (ABOUT).	MARKS.
1685		1695		1730	
1687		„		„	
1690		„		„	
„		„		„	
„		„		1730-4	
„		1700		1730-40	
„		„		„	
„		1700-5		„	
„		„		„	
1690-1		1700-40		„	
1690-5		1702		„	
„		1706-9		„	
„		„		„	
„		„			
„		1710		1740	
„		„		1750	
„		1720-5			
„		1720-30		1750-60	
„		1725-30		c. 1760	
„		„			
1690-9		„			
„		1730			
1693					

Date	Maker's Name	Maker's Mark	Town Mark Castle	Deacon's Mark	Deacon's Name
1552-62	Alex. Auchinleck				Thos. Ewing.
1563-4	Henry Thompsone (1561)				James Cok.
1570	(Mark indistinct.)				George Heriot, senr.*
1576	Adam Craige				James Mosman.
1585-6	John Mosman (1575)				John Mosman.
1590-1	Adam Allane, jr. (1589)				Geo. Heriot, senr.*
1591-2	James Craufuird				Do. do.
1591-4	David Gilbert (1590)				Wm. Cok (Cokie).
"	James Craufuird (1591)				Do. do.
1596/1600	Hugh Lindsay (1587)				David Heriot.
1609-10	Gilbert Kirkwood (1609)				Robert Denneistoun.
1611-3	Robert Denneistoun (1597)				David Palmer.
"	George Craufuird, jr. (1606)				Do. do.
1617-9	Do. do.				John Lindsay.
"	John Lindsay (1605)				Do do.
"	George Robertsone (1616)				Do. do.
"	Thos. Thompson (1617)				Do. do.
1617	Hew. Anderson				George Craufuird.
1613-21	Gilbert Kirkwood (1609)				James Denneistoun.
1616-35	George Robertsone (1616)				George Craufuird.
1633	Adame Lamb (1619)				Do. do.
"	Thos. Kirkwood (1631)				Do. do.
1633 (?)	(Mark indistinct.)				Alexr. Reid (probably).

Date	Maker's Name	Maker's Mark	Town Mark Castle	Deacon's Mark	Deacon's Name
1637-9	Jon Scott Adm. (1621)				Jon Scott.
1640-2	Thos. Clyghorne (1606)				Thos. Clyghorne.
1642	Patrick Borthwick (1642)				John Fraser.
1643	Jon Scott (1621)				Do. do.
"	Nicoll Trotter (1635)				Do. do.
1644-6	George Cleghorne (1641)				Adam Lamb.
"	Andro Denneistoun (1636)				Do. do.
"	Thos. Clyghorne (1606)				Do. do.
1644	John Myln or Jas. McAulay				Do. do.
1649	Andro Burrell (1642)				George Cleghorne.
1648-57	Peter Neilsone (1647)				Do. do.
1650	Thos. Scott (1649)				Do. do.
1651-9	Robert Gibsoune (1627)				James Fairbairne.
1657	John Wardlaw (1642)				Do. do.
1660	Edwd. Cleghorne (1649)				Andro Burrell.
1665-7	Wm. Law (1662)				James Symontoun.
"	Andrew Law (c. 1665)				Do. do.
1665	Alexr. Reid				Do. do.
1669-75	Alexr. Scott (1649)				Alexr. Reid (2nd)
1674	James Cockburne (1669)				Do. do.
1663-81	Alexr. Scott (1649)				Edwd. Cleghorne.
1675-7	George Rolland (1675)				Wm. Law.
1677	Alexr. Reid (3rd) (1677)				Do. do.

Left table

MAKER'S NAME	MAKER'S MARK	TOWN MARK CASTLE	ASSAY MASTER'S MARK	DATE LETTER	DATE	ASSAY MASTER'S NAME
Alexr. Reid (1660) / Edwd. Cleghorne (1649) [Adm.]	[monogram]	castle	B	a	1681-2	John Borthwick.
Andrew Law (c. 1665)	AL	,,	B	b	1682-3	,,
Wm. Law (1662)	WZ	,,	,,	c	1683-4	,,
Thos. Yorstoun (1673)	TY	,,	,,	d	1684-5	,,
John Lawe (1661)	IL	,,	,,	e	1685-6	,,
James Penman (1673)	P	,,	,,	f	1686-7	,,
Do. do.	,,	,,	,,	g	1687-8	,,
James Cockburne (1669)	CI	,,	,,	h	1688-9 / WM. & MY. 1689-90	,,
George Scott (1677)	GS	,,	,,	i	1690-1	,,
Wm. Scott (1686)	WS	,,	,,	k	1691-2	,,
James Cockburne (1669)	CI	,,	,,	l	1692-3	,,
Robert Bruce (1687)	RB	,,	,,	m	1693-4	,,
Robert Inglis (1686)	RI	,,	,,	n	1694-5 / WM. III. 1695-6	,,
James Sympsone (1687)	$	,,	,,	o	1696-7	James Penman.
Geo. Yorstoune (1684)	GY	,,	,,	p	1697-8	,,
Alexr. Forbes (1692)	AF	,,	,,	q	1698-9	,,
James Sympsone ? (1687)	[mark]	,,	P	r	1699 1700	,,
(Not identified).	WI	,,	,,	s	1700-1	,,
Thos. Ker (1694)	TK	castle	,,	t	1701-2 / ANNE. 1702-3	,,
Alexr. Kincaid (1692)	AK	,,	,,	u	1703-4	,,
Colin McKenzie (1695)	MK	,,	,,	w	1704-5	,,
Geo. Scott, jr. (1697)	GS	,,	,,	x		,,
Mungo Yorstoun (1702)	MY	,,	,,	y		
Thos. Cleghorne (1689)	[T]	,,	,,	z		
James Sympson (1687) / Patrick Murray (1701)	[S] / [M]	,,	,,			

Right table

MAKER'S NAME	MAKER'S MARK	TOWN MARK CASTLE	ASSAY MASTER'S MARK	DATE LETTER	DATE	ASSAY MASTER'S NAME
Patrick Murray (1701) [Adm.]	[mark]	castle	P	A	1705-6	James Penman
James Tait (1704)	[mark]	,,	,,	B	1706-7	,,
Walter Scott (1701)	WS	,,	,,	C	1707-8	Edward Penman
Wm. Ged (1706)	WG	,,	EP	D	1708-9	,,
John Penman, jr. (1703)	[mark]	,,	,,	E	1709-10	,,
Harry Beathune (1704)	HB	,,	,,	F	1710-1	,,
John Seatoune (1688)	IS	,,	,,	G	1711-2	,,
James Mitchellsone (1706)	IM	,,	,,	H	1712-3	,,
Patrick Turnbull (1689)	PT	,,	,,	I	1713-4 / GEO. I.	,,
Robert Ker (1705)	RK	,,	,,	K	1714-5	,,
Robert Inglis (1686)	RI	,,	,,	L	1715-6	,,
Mungo Yorstoun (1702)	MY MY	castle	,,	MM	1716-7	,,
Thos. Ker (1694)	TK	,,	,,	NN	1717-8	,,
Harry Beathune (1704) / John Seatoun (1685)	HB / IS	,,	,,	N		,,
Chas. Dickson (as 1721) / Chas. Blair (1707)	CB	,,	,,	O	1718-9	,,
Wm. Ure (1715)	WU	castle	EP	PP	1719-20	,,
James Mitchellsone (1706)	IM	,,	,,	P		,,
Mungo Yorstoun (1702) / Alexr. Sympsone (1710)	MY / AS	,,	,,	q	1720-1	,,
Jas. Inglis (1720)	I*I	,,	EP	R	1721-2	,,
,, ,,		,,	,,			,,
David Mitchell (1700)	M	,,	,,	S	1722-3	,,
Chas. Dickson (1719)	CD	,,	,,	T	1723-4	,,
James Clarke (1710) / Colin Campbell (1714)	IC / CC	,,	,,	U	1724-5	,,
Ken'th McKenzie (1714) / Chas. Blair (1707)	KM / CB	,,	,,	V	1725-6	,,
Alexr. Edmonstoune (1721)	AE	,,	,,	W	1726-7 / GEO. II.	,,
Archd. Ure (1715)	AU	,,	,,	X	1727-8	,,
James Taitt (1704)	[mark]	,,	,,	Y	1728-9	,,
Harry Beathune (1704)	HB	,,	,,	Z	} 1729-30	Archd. Ure
Patrick Graeme (1725)	PG	,,	,,	Z		
Wm. Aytoun (1718) / Wm. Jameson (1729)	WA / WI	,,	AU			

MAKER'S NAME.	MAKER'S MARK.	TOWN MARK. CASTLE.	ASSAY MASTER'S MARK.	DATE LETTER	DATE.	ASSAY MASTER'S NAME.
James Anderson (1729) Adm.	[IA]	[castle]	[AU]	A	1730-1	Archibald Ure.
Hugh Gordon (1727)	[HG]	,,	,,	B	1731-2	,,
George Forbes (1731)	[GF]	,,	,,	C	1732-3	,,
John Main (1729)	[IM]	,,	,,	D	1733-4	,,
Edw'rd Lothian (1731)	[E·L]	,,	,,	E	1734-5	,,
John Rollo (1731) (afterwards Lord Rollo).	[IR]	,,	,,	F	1735-6	,,
Hugh Penman (1734)	[HP]	,,	,,	G	1736-7	,,
Alexander Farquharson (1734)	[AF]	[castle]	,,	H	1737-8	,,
James Ker (1723)	[I·K]	,,	,,	I	1738-9	,,
Dougal Ged (1734)	[GED]					
James Ker (1723)	[I·K]	,,	,,	K	1739-40	,,
" " (1737)	..	,,	[GED]	L	1740-1	†
Benr. Oliphant (1737)	[EO]					
Law'ce Oliphant (1737)	[LO]	,,	,,	M	1741-2	†
William Aytoun (1718)	[WA]					
Robert Gordon (1741)	[RG]	,,	[EL]	N	1742-3	†
Edwd. Lothian (1731)	[EL]	,,	,,	O	1743-4	†
Chas. Dickson (1738)	[CD]	[castle]	[HG]	P	1744-5	Hugh Gordon.
Benr. Oliphant (1737)	[EO]	,,	,,	Q	1745-6	,,
John Kincard (1726)	[IK]	,,	,,	R	1746-7	,,
(Not identified.)	[CL]	,,	,,	S	1747-8	,,
William Gilchrist (1736)	[WG]	,,	,,	T	1748-9	,,
Edward Lothian (1731)	[EL]	,,	,,	U	1749-50	,,
Robert Lowe (1742)	[LOW]	,,	,,	U	1750-1	,,
" " " " Benr. Oliphant (1737)	[EO]	,,	,,	W	1751-2	,,
James McKenzie (1747)	[IM]	,,	,,	X	1752-3	,,
James Weems (1738)	[IW]	,,	,,	Y	1753-4	,,
John Edmonston (1753)	[IE]					
Wm. Davie (1740)	[WD]	,,	,,	Z	1754-5	,,

MAKER'S NAME.	MAKER'S MARK.	TOWN MARK. CASTLE.	ASSAY MASTER'S MARK.	DATE LETTER	DATE.
Ker & Dempster.	[K&D]	[castle]	[HG]	A	1755-6
Rbt. Gordon (1741) Adm.	[RG]	,,	,,	B	1756-7
Wm. Taylor (1753)	[WT]				
John Clark (1751)	[CLARK]	,,	,,	C	1757-8
Lothian & Robertson.	[L&R]				
James Welsh (1746)	[I·W]	,,	[THISTLE]	D	1758-9
James Gilsland (1748)	[IG]	,,	[H]	E	1759-60
Alexr. Aitchison (1746)	[AIT]				GEO. III.
Jas. Somervail (1754)	[I·S]	,,	,,	F	1760-1
John Robertson (1758)	[J·R]				
Wm. Dempster (1742)	[W·D]	,,	,,	G	1761-2
" " John Welsh (1742)	[IW]	,,	,,	H	1762-3
John Taylor (1760)	[IT]				
James Hill (1746)	[IH]	,,	,,	I	1763-4
Milne & Campbell ?	[M&C]	,,	,,	K	1764-5
Rbt. Clark (1763)	[RC]				
Wm. Drummond (1760)	[WD]	,,	,,	L	1765-6
John Stirling ? (1757)	[IS]	,,	,,	M	1766-7
Benjn. Tait (1763)	[TAIT]				
Gillsland & Ker.	[G&K]	,,	,,	N	1767-8
Patk. Robertson (1751)	[PR]	,,	,,	O	1768-9
Daniel Ker." (1764)	[DK]	,,	,,	P	1769-70
(not identified.) James Gilsland (1748)	[JB] [IG]	,,	,,	Q	1770-1
Wm. & Jno. Taylor.	[WT] [IT]	,,	,,	R	1771-2
Wm. Davie (1740)	[WD]	,,	,,	S	1772-3
" " Alexr. Gairdner (1754)	[AG]	,,	,,	T	1773-4
James Welsh (1746)	[I·W]	,,	,,	U	1774-5
.. ..		,,	,,	V	1775-6
Wm. Davie (1740)	[WD]	,,	,,	X	1776-7
James Dempster (1775)	[ID]	,,	,,	Y	1777-8
Patk. Robertson (1751)	[PR]	,,	,,	Z	1778-9
James Hewitt (1750)	[IH]	,,	,,	U	1779-80

Maker's Name	Maker's Mark	King's Head	Town Mark Castle	Thistle	Date Letter	Date
W. & P. Cunningham.	W&PC		[castle]	[thistle]	A	1780-1
David Downie Adm. (1770)	DD		"	"	B	1781-2
Fras. Howden (1781)	FH		"	"	C	1782-3
Robt. Bowman (1780)	RB		"	"	D	1783-4
Alex. Edmonston (1779)	AE	[king's head]	"	"	E	1784-5
David Marshall (1782)	DM	"	"	"	F	1785-6
James Dempster (1775)	ID	[king's head]	"	"	G	1786-7-8
Thos. Duffus (1780)	TD	"	"	"	H	1788-9
Alex. Gairdner (1754) / James Douglas (1785)	AG / JD		"	"	J J	1789-90
W. & P. Cunningham.	W&PC		"	"	K	1790-1
Geo. Christie (1791)	GC		"	"	L	1791-2
Alex. Zeigler (1782)	AZ		"	"	M	1792-3
Peter Mathie (1774)	PM		"	"	N	§1793-4
Wm. Robertson (1789)	WR		"	"	O	1794-5
Alex. Henderson (1792)	AH		"	"	P	1795-6
Geo. Christie (1791) / Alex. Spence (1783)	GC / AS		"	"	Q	1796-7
W. & P. Cunningham.	WPC	[king's head]	"	"	R	1797-8
Thos. Duffus (1780)	TD		"	"	S	1798-9
Alex. Graham & Co. ? / W. & P. Cunningham.	AG&C / WPC		[castle]	[thistle]	T	1799 / 1800
John Zeigler (1798)	IZ		"	"	U	1800-1
Fras. Howden (1781)	FH		"	"	V	1801-2
Matt. Craw.	MC		[castle]	"	W	1802-3
Wm. Auld (1788)	WA		"	"	X	1803-4
Simon Cunningham (1800)	SC		"	"	Y	1804-5
(Not identified).	M&R		"	"	Z	1805-6

Maker's Name	Maker's Mark	King's Head	Town Mark Castle	Thistle	Date Letter	Date
R. Green or R. Grierson.	RG	[king's head]	[castle]	[thistle]	a	1806-7
Cunningham & Simpson. (Not identified).	PC&S / D&M	"	"	"	b	1807-8
Do. do. *	IH	"	"	"	c	1808-9
George Fenwick. John McDonald.	GF / IMD	"	[castle]	"	d	1809-10
Robt. Gray & Son (of Glasgow).	RG&S	"	"	"	e	1810-1
Math. Craw.	MC	"	"	"	f	1811-2
Alexr. Henderson.	AH	"	"	"	g	1812-3
J. McKay.,	JM	"	"	"	h	1813-4
Frs. Howden. R. K. (a Perth maker).	FH	"	"	"	i	1814-5
Wm. Zeigler.	WZ	"	"	"	j	1815-6
Js. & Wm. Marshall. Chas. Dalgleish.	J&WM / CD	"	"	"	k	1816-7
J. McKay. Do. do.	JMS	"	"	"	l	1817-8
Redpath & Arnot.	R&A	"	"	"	m	1818-9
J'n'th'n Millidge ?	JM	"	"	"	n	1819-20
Frs. Howden.	FH	"	[castle]	[thistle]	o	GEO. IV. 1820-1
Do. do.	"	"	"	"	p	1821-2
Redpath & Arnot.	R&A	"	"	"	q	1822-3
Alexr. Zeigler.	AZ	[king's head]	"	"	r	1823-4
Marshall & Sons.	M&S	"	[castle]	"	s	1824-5
J. McKenzie ? †	MS	"	"	"	t	1825-6
J. McKay.	JMS	"	[castle]	"	u	1826-7
Leon'd Urquhart.	LU	"	"	"	v	1827-8
(Not identified).	WC	"	"	"	w	1828-9
J. McKay.	JMS	"	"	"	x	1829-30
Do. do.	"	"	"	"	y	WM. IV. 1830-1
Peter Sutherland.	PS	"	"	"	z	1831-2

MAKER'S NAME.	MAKER'S MARK.	KING'S HEAD.	TOWN MARK CASTLE.	THISTLE.	DATE LETTER.	DATE.
Marshall & Sons.	M&S	(head)	(castle)	(thistle)	A	1832-3
Jas. Nasmyth.	JN	,,	,,	,,	B	1833-4
(Not identified).	GB	,,	,,	,,	C	1834-5
Elder & Co.	E&Cº	,,	,,	,,	D	1835-6
J. & R. Keay, of Perth.	R&RK	,,	,,	,,	E	1836-7
McKay.	JMᶜ	,,	,,	,,	F	VICTORIA. 1837-8
.D. (see the Arbroath Marks).		,,	,,	,,	G	1838-9
Jas. Howden & Co.	JH&Cº	,,	,,	,,	H	1839-40
Jas. Nasmyth & Co.	JN&C	,, QUEEN'S HEAD	,,	,,	I	1840-1
Geo. Jameson, of Aberdeen.	GJ	(head)	,,	,,	K	1841-2
Marshall & Sons.	M&S	,,	,,	,,	L	1842-3
.. .. ..		,,	,,	,,	M	1843-4
McKay.	JMᶜ	,,	,,	,,	N	1844-5
.. ..		,,	,,	,,	O	1845-6
D G as Canongate c. 1836 (page 514).		,,	,,	,,	P	1846-7
Marshall & Sons.	M&S	,,	,,	,,	Q	1847-8
Hay.	JH	,,	,,	,,	R	1848-9
Mackay & Chisholm.	M&C	,,	,,	,,	S	1849-50
Do. do.	,,	,,	,,	,,	T	1850-1
.. ...		,,	,,	,,	U	1851-2
		,,	,,	,,	V	1852-3
... ...		,,	,,	,,	W	1853-4
Chas. Robb.	CR	,,	,,	,,	X	1854-5
Hay.	JH	,,	,,	,,	Y	1855-6
(Not identified).	RN	,,	,,	,,	Z	1856-7

MAKER'S NAME.	MAKER'S MARK.	QUEEN'S HEAD.	TOWN MARK CASTLE.	THISTLE.	DATE LETTER.	DATE.
J. & W. Marshall.	J&WM	(head)	(castle)	(thistle)	A	1857-8
Jonthn. Millidge?	JM	,,	,,	,,	B	1858-9
(Not identified).	JU	,,	,,	,,	C	1859-60
Alex. Hay.	A·H	,,	,,	,,	D	1860-1
J. Asherheim.	JA	,,	,,	,,	E	1861-2
R. L. Christie. / J. E. Vernon.	RLC / JEV	,,	,,	,,	F	1862-3
Wm. Crouch.	WC	,,	,,	,,	G	1863-4
D. Blackley. / W. J. McDonald.	DB / WJM'D / RMC	,,	,,	,,/	H	1864-5
Wm. Marshall. / Elder & Co.	WM / DM&G / E&C	,,	,,	,,	I	1865-6
J. Smith or Scott.	JM / JS	,,	,,	,,	K	1866-7
D. & J. Sanderson. / Cockburn & McDonald.	D&JS / COCKBURN	,,	,,	,,	L	1867-8
Geo. Edwards & Son.	GE&S	,,	,,	,,	M	1868-9
J. Hamilton & Son.	JH&SON GEO.ST	,,	,,	,,	N	1869-70
George Laing. / Walter Neil. / Wm. Carstairs. / Carlisle & Watt. / W. Fraser.	GL / WN / WC / C&W / WF	,,	,,	,,	O	1870-1
		,,	,,	,,	P	1871-2
Jas. Aitchison.	AITCHISON	,,	,,	,,	Q	1872-3
J. Johnston. / Jas. Hamilton.	JJ / HAMILTON / JH&Co	,,	,,	,,	R	1873-4
	M&GS	,,	,,	,,	S	1874-5
John Crichton.	J.CRICHTON / JH&C	,,	,,	,,	T	1875-6
M. Crichton.	MC / JG&C					
Robb & Whittet.	R&W / J&WM	,,	,,	,,	U	1876-7
C. or J. Gray.	GRAY	,,	,,	,,	V	1877-8
Mackay & Chisholm.	M&C	,,	,,	,,	W	1878-9
J. Crichton.	J.C	,,	,,	,,	X	1879-80
Hamilton & Inches.	H&I	,,	,,	,,	Y	1880-1
... ...		,,	,,	,,	Z	1881-2

MAKER'S NAME.	MAKER'S MARK.	QUEEN'S HEAD.	TOWN MARK. CASTLE.	TRISTLE.	DATE LETTER.	DATE.
... ...	CS	(head)	(castle)	(thistle)	a	1882-3
Wm. Knaggs.	WK	,,	,,	,,	b	1883-4
Hamilton & Inches.	H&I	,,	,,	,,	c	1884-5
... ...	,,	,,	,,	,,	d	1885-6
Mackay & Chisholm.	M&C	,,	,,	,,	e	1886-7
Jas. Duncan.	JD	,,	,,	,,	f	1887-8
Milne of Aberdeen.	MILNE ABDN	,,	,,	,,	g	1888-9
W. Crouch & Sons.	WC&S	,,	,,	,,	h	1889-90
Hamilton & Inches.	H&I		,,	,,	i	1890-1
J. Crichton & Co.	J&C		,,	,,	k	1891-2
Jas. Duncan.	JD					
Brook & Son.	B&S		,,	,,	l	1892-3
J. Crichton & Co.	J&C		,,	,,	m	1893-4
Lewis Cohen.	L C		,,	,,	n	1894-5
Latimer & Sons.	L&SONS					
Jas. Duncan.	JD					
D. Crichton.	D.C		,,	,,	o	1895-6
J. Crichton & Co.	J&Cº		,,	,,	p	1896-7
McDonald & Horne.	M&H		,,	,,	q	1897-8
J. Hardy & Co.	H&C / C&K					
W. Crouch & Sons.	WC&S		,,	,,	r	1898-9
W. & J. Milne.	W&JM		,,	,,	s	1899 / 1900
Hamilton & Inches.	H&I					
Thos. Johnston.	TJ		,,	,,	t	1900-1
Young & Tatton.	Y&T					
Jas. Robertson.	JR		,,	,,	u	EDW. VII. 1901-2
Brook & Son.	B&S		,,	,,	v	1902-3
... ...			,,	,,	w	1903-4
... ...			,,	,,	x	1904-5
... ...			,,	,,	y	1905-6
... ...			,,	,,	z	1906-7

TOWN MARK. CASTLE.	TRISTLE.	DATE LETTER.	DATE.
(castle)	(thistle)	A	1907-8
,,	,,	B	1908-9
,,	,,	C	1909-10
,,	,,	D	1910-1
,,	,,	E	1911-2
,,	,,	F	1912-3
,,	,,	G	1913-4
,,	,,	H	1914-5
,,	,,	I	1915-6
,,	,,	K	1916-7
,,	,,	L	1917-8
,,	,,	M	1918-9
,,	,,	N	1919-20
,,	,,	O	1920-1
,,	,,	P	1921-2

DATE.	MAKER'S MARK.	TREE, FISH & BELL.	MAKER'S MARK.	DATE LETTER	MAKER'S NAME.		
1681-2	T·M	(head)	T·M	a	Thos.	Moncrur	(1665)
1682-3				b	...	...	...
1683-4	R	(head)	R	c	Robt.	Brook	(1673)
1684-5				d	...	...	...
1685-6	,,	,,	,,	e	Robert Brook		(1673)
1686-7				f	...	...	...
1687-8				g	...	...	...
1688-9				h	...	...	...
1689-90	IS	(head)	IS	i	Jas.	Stirling	(1686)
1690-1	,,	,,	,,	k	Do.	Do.	
1691-2				l	...	...	...
1692-3				m	...	...	...
1693-4				n	...	...	..
1694-5	R	(bell)	R	o	Robt.	Brook	(1673)
1695-6				p	...	...	...
1696-7	R	,,	R	q	Robert Brook		(1673)
1697-8				r	...	...	...
1698-9	WC	(head)	WC	s	Wm.	Clerk	(1693)
1699 1700	R	(bell)	R	t	Robert Brook		(1673)
1700-1	IL	(bell)	IL	u	John	Luke	
1701-2	IL	,,	IL	v	James Luke		(1692)
1702-3				w	...	...	...
1703-4				x	...	...	...
1704-5	IC IL	,, ,,	IC IL	y	Thos. Cumming (1682) John Luke, jr. (1699)		
1705-6	,,	,,	,,	z	Do.	do.	do.

DATE (ABOUT.)	MAKER'S MARK.	TREE, FISH & BELL.	MAKER'S MARK.	LETTER	MAKER'S MARK.		
1706-7	...	...	...	A	...	...	...
1707-8	IL	(head)	IL	B	John	Luke, jr.	(1699)
	,,	,,	,,	D	Do.	do.	,,
1709-10	WC	(IG)	WC	,,	William	Clerk	(1693)
1709-20	IF	(head)	IF		John	Falconer	(1709)
,,	JL	,,	JL		James	Lockhart	(1707)
1717-49	IB	,,	IB		Johan Got-helf-Bilsings (1717)		
1728-31	,,	,,	,,	S	Do.	do.	,,
1725-35	RL	,,	RL	S	Robert	Luke	(1721)
1743-52	IG	(bell)	IG	S	James	Glen	(1743)
,,	GLN	,,	GLN	,,	Do.	do.	,,
1747-60	ST	,,	ST	S	Saml.	Telfer	(1747)
1756-76	D·W	,,	D·W	S	David	Warnock	(1756)
,,		,,		Z	(No maker's mark).		
1757-80	IC	(tree)	IC		John	Campbell	(1757)
,,	JL	(tree)	JL		(Not identified.)		
,,	J·S	(tree)	J·S	,,	Do.	do.	
1758-65	WN	,,	WN		Wm.	Napier	(1758)
,,	B&N	,,	B&N	S	Bayne & Napier.		

DATE (ABOUT).	MAKER'S MARK.	TREE, FISH & BELL.	MAKER'S MARK.	LETTER.	MAKER'S NAME
1763-70	AG	(tree)	AG		Adam Graham (1763)
,,	,,	,,	,,	E	Do. do.
,.	,,	,,	,,	F	Do. do.
1773-80	IT	S	IT	S	James Taylor (1773)
1776-80	M&C	(anchor)		O	*Milne & Campbell.
,,	M&C	(anchor)	M&C	O	*Do. do.
,,	RG	(tree)	RG		Robert Gray (1776)
,,	RG	(tree)	RG	S	Do. do. ,,
1783	T&H	(tree)	T&H		Taylor & Hamilton.
,,	J·Mᶜ	(tree)	J·Mᶜ	,,	James McEwen (1783)
1777-90	WL	,,	WL	,,	Wm. Love (1777)
1782-92	J·W	(tree)	J·W		James Wright (1782)
1785-95	ID	(tree)	ID	S	John Donald (1785)
,,	,,	,,	,,	O	Do. do. ,,
1781 / 1800	MF	(tree)	MF	S	Patrick McFarlane (1781)
1811-3	Mᶠ	(lion rampant)			Archibald McFadyen (1811)

LION RAMPANT.

DATE	TREE, FISH & BELL.	LION RAMPANT.	DATE LETTER.	KING'S HEAD.	MAKER'S MARK	MAKER'S NAME
1819-20	(tree)	(lion)	A	(king's head)	B.SCOTT / M&R	B. Scott. (Not identified.)
GEO. IV. 1820-1	(tree)	,,	B	,,	LFN / JD	Luke F. Newlands (181 / Jas. Downie (181
1821-2	,,	,,	C	,,	RG&S	Robt. Gray & Son (181
1822-3	,,	,,	D	,,	RD	Robt. Duncan (181
1823-4	,,	,,	E	,,	JB	John Bruce (181
1824-5	,,	,,	F	,,	M&S	(Not identified.)
1825-6	,,	,,	G	,,	AM	Alexr. Mitchell (182
1826-7	,,	,,	H	,,	AMᶜᴰ	Angus McDonald (182
1827-8	,,	,,	I	,,	PA	Peter Arthur (180
1828-9	,,	,,	J	,,	EB	Edwd. Bell (182
1829-30	,,	,,	K	,,	JB CO	Jas. Burrell & Co. (182
WM. IV. 1830-1	,,	,,	L	,,	DR	Danl. Robertson (182
1831-2	,,	,,	M	,,		John Mitchell ... (as 1835-6 below).
1832-3	,,	,,	N	(king's head)	RG&S	Robt. Gray & Son (181
1833-4	,,	,,	O	,,	PA	Peter Arthur (180
1834-5	,,	,,	P	,,	DCR	D. C. Rait (183
1835-6	,,	,,	Q	,,	JM	John Mitchell (183
1836-7	,,	,,	R	,,	DCR / JW	D. C. Rait (183 / (Not identified.)
VICT. 1837-8	,,	,,	S	,,	WP	W. Parkins (183
1838-9	,,	,,	T	,,	RG&S	Robt. Gray & Son (181
1839-40	,,	,,	U	,,	,,	Do. do. ,,
1840-1	,,	,,	V	,,	JM	John Mitchell (183
1841-2	,,	,,	W		HM	*Henry Muirhead (183
1842-3	,,	,,	X		HD	*Henry Downs (183
1843-4	,,	,,	Y		DCR	*D. C. Rait (183
1844-5	,,	,,	Z		CB	*Chas. Bryson (183

Date	Tree, Fish & Bell	Lion Rampant	Date Letter	Queen's Head	Maker's Mark
1845-6	[tree/fish/bell]	[lion]	A	[queen's head]	W.B
1846-7	,,	,,	B	,,	R.G &S
1847-8	,,	,,	C	,,	
1848-9	,,	,,	D	,,	J.R
1849-50	,,	,,	E	,,	P.A.Jr
1850-1	,,	,,	F	,,	J&WM
1851-2	,,	,,	G	,,	
1852-3	,,	,,	H	,,	R.G&S
1853-4	,,	,,	I	,,	
1854-5	,,	,,	J	,,	A.M
1855-6	,,	,,	K	,,	R.S
1856-7	,,	,,	L	,,	
1857-8	,,	,,	M	,,	AM&D
1858-9	,,	,,	N	,,	WA&S
1859-60	,,	,,	O	,,	
1860-1	,,	,,	P	,,	
1861-2	,,	,,	Q	,,	
1862-3	,,	,,	R	,,	J.M
1863-4	,,	,,	S	,,	
1864-5	,,	,,	T	,,	
1865-6	,,	,,	U	,,	
1866-7	,,	,,	V	,,	
1867-8	,,	,,	W	,,	
1868-9	,,	,,	X	,,	
1869-70	,,	,,	Y	,,	
1870-1	,,	,,	Z	,,	

Date	Tree, Fish & Bell	Lion Rampant	Date Letter	Queen's Head
1871-2	[tree/fish/bell]	[lion]	A	[queen's head]
1872-3	,,	,,	B	,,
1873-4	,,	,,	C	,,
1874-5	,,	,,	D	,,
1875-6	,,	,,	E	,,
1876-7	,,	,,	F	,,
1877-8	,,	,,	G	,,
1878-9	,,	,,	H	,,
1879-80	,,	,,	I	,,
1880-1	,,	,,	J	,,
1881-2	,,	,,	K	,,
1882-3	,,	,,	L	,,
1883-4	,,	,,	M	,,
1884-5	,,	,,	N	,,
1885-6	,,	,,	O	,,
1886-7	,,	,,	P	,,
1887-8	,,	,,	Q	,,
1888-9	,,	,,	R	,,
1889-90	,,	,,	S	,,
1890-1	,,	,,	T	,,
1891-2	,,	,,	U	,,
1892-3	,,	,,	V	,,
1893-4	,,	,,	W	,,
1894-5	,,	,,	X	,,
1895-6	,,	,,	Y	,,
1896-7	,,	,,	Z	,,

Date	Tree, Fish & Bell	Lion Rampant		Date Letter
1897-8	[tree/fish/bell]	[lion]		A
1898-9	,,	,,		B
1899 1900	,,	,,		C
1900-1	,,	,,		D
EDW. VII. 1901-2	,,	,,		E
1902-3	,,	,,		F
1903-4	,,	,,		G
1904-5	,,	,,		H
1905-6	,,	,,		I
1906-7	,,	,,		J
1907-8	,,	,,		K
1908-9	,,	,,		L
1909-10	,,	,,		M
1910-1	,,	,,		N
1911-2	,,	,,		O
1912-3	,,	,		P
1913-4	,,	,,		Q
1914-5	,,	,,	[thistle]	R
1915-6	,,	,,	,,	S
1916-7	,,	,,	,,	T
1917-8	,,	,,	,,	U
1918-9	,,	,,	,,	V
1919-20	,,	,,	,,	W
1920-1	,,	,,	,,	X
1921-2	,,	,,	,,	Y

1848 TO 1903.

THE DATE WHEN EACH MARK WAS FIRST USED IS NOT RECORDED.

MARK.	NAME.	MARK.	NAME.	MARK.	NAME.
(R in shield)	J. Russell.	(IHH)	J. Hall.	T.SMITH&SON GLASGOW	T. Smith & Son.
WG	W. Gordon.	J.R.&W.L.	J. R. & W. Laing.	TS&S	Do. do.
VL&Cº	V. Levy & Co.	LAING	Do. do.	MF JBM	(Not identified).
SK	D. Sprunt.*	M&M	McIntosh & McCulloch.	A.W.P	A. W. Peden.
JDD	J. D. Davidson.	AB	A. Brown.	R&AA	R. & A. Allen.
M&A	Muirhead & Arthur.	RK	Robt. Kerr.	D.T	D. Todd.
M&A	Do. do.	CCM	C. C. McDonald.	W.S.&Cº	W. Scott & Co.
GA	G. Alexander.	H·L	H. Low.	J.W.	J. Wallace.
JB&S	J. Ballantyne & Son.	J.W	Jas. Weir.	T.W.C	T. W. Crawford.
WR	W. Russell.	WEIR	Do. do.	AWA	A. W. Allison.
WC	W. Corbett.	J.E	J. Easton	W.W	W. Warrington.
A&T	Aird & Thompson.	J.P.C	J. P. Campbell.	MVW	M. V. Wilks.
T.S.&S	T. Smith & Son.	S.&McL	S...... & McLellan.	JM	J. Moir.
TS&S	Do. do.	JHS	J. H. Storer.	K&P	Kerr & Phillips.
R&WS	R. & W. Sorley.	M.G	Mungo Guthrie.	M&A	Muirhead & Arthur.
(RSWS)	Do. do.	H&L	Hamilton & Laidlaw.	A.McD	A. McDonald.
(GE&S)	Geo. Edward & Son.	W.A	W. Allan.	GJEFFREY	G. Jeffrey.
DF·GE	Do. do.	A.L.B	A. L. Boston.	H&M	Hyslop & Marshall.
P&Cº	Parr & Co.	D&M	Duff & Millar.	W.G.T	W. G. Taylor.
GWS	G. W. Stratton.	JADAIR DUMFS	John Adair (Dumfries).	T.M	Thos. Mutter.
KELLY DUBLIN	Kelly & Co., Dublin.	L&Cº	Lawson & Co.	ALEXR&SN	Alexr. & Son.
HOWELL	A. Howell.	(FJR)	J. Riddoch.	JM	J. Mark.
DS	D. Simpson.	D·T	D. Todd.	F&F	Finlay & Field.
GM	G. Mitchell.	D.F.T	D. F. Turnbull.	WP	W. Paul.
J.E.A.	J. E. Ainsley.	J.D	Jas. Douglas.	JP	Jas. Porter.
J.H.&Cº	Jos. Haywood & Co.	TF	T. Fyfe.	GMcP	Geo. McPherson.
P.G	(Not identified).	M&Cº	Mitchell & Co.	T.S.	Thos. Stewart.
WG	W. Gordon.	R.S	Robt. Scott.	JF	J. Fettes.
K.C.B	(Not identified).	SCOTT	Do. do.	D.F	Duncn. Ferguson.
G.E.R	G. E. Rattray.	DCR&S	D. C. Rait & Son.	WVJ	W. V. Jackson.
T.C.G.	T. C. Garstang.	DD	David Dow.	G.J	Geo. Jackson.
D.M.C	D. M. Cameron.	W.J	W. Jenkins.	T.R&S	Thos. Ross & Sons.
DM	D. Munro.	T&W	Thomson & Williamson.	R.T	R. Tennent.
F.&J.S.	F. & J. Smith.	WR	Wm. Russell.	DMcC	D. McCallum.
(ME emblem)	M. Friedlander.	MACFARLANE PARTICK	—— Macfarlane (of Partick).	J.D	John Donald.
M·F	Do. do.	HC	Hector Gollun.	D.S	Danl. Sutherland.
JR	J. Reid.	MW	Mark Wilks & Co.	J.M	Jas. Myres.
JF	J. Ferrier.	J.C	Jas. Crichton.	JB&S	J. Blond & Son.

MARK.	NAME.	MARK.	NAME.	MARK.	NAME.
W.S	W. Semple.	B & M	Brown & Miller.	J.N	J. Neville.
J.D.R	J. D. Reid.	JS	Jas. Simpson.	D&S	Davis & Son.
WR&S	Wm. Russell & Sons.	J.R	Jas. Ross.	LM&Cº	Lorimer, Moyes & Co.
R·MC·I	R. McInnes.	J&Cº	Johnston & Co.	AA	Andrew Allison.
W.&W.LOGAN	W. & W. Logan.	L&L	Lyle & Lock.	AF	A. Ferrier ?
D&M	Duff & Miller.	J.LYᴸ	J. Lyle.	J.MJᴿ	J. Muir, jr. ?
J.S	Jas. Smith.	J.M.B.&C	J. M. Ballantyne & Co.	H.T	H. Tennant.
J.F	Jas. Forrest.	G.D.&Cº	Geo. Drummond & Co.	GD	Geo. Drummond.
J.H.G.	(Not identified.)	M&T	Miller & Thompson.	W&S	Wilson & Sharp, Edinbro.
J.STEVENSUN	J. Stevenson.	AT&S	A. Taylor & Son.	M.BROS	Mitchell Bros.
R&F	Ross & Ferrier.	WM&Cº	W. Miller & Co.	F.N	F. Neville.
R.R	Robt. Ross.	H&I	Hamilton & Inches, Edinbro.	LK	L. King.
WJ	W. Jaffray.	G.W	George White (or Wilson).	RKM	R. K. Muirhead.
W.J	Do. do.	WM	W. Mitchell.	AAP	Anton Pfaff.
PM	Peter Martin.	J.Mᶜᴬ	J. McArthur.	R.LR	R. L. Rawson.
R.B.F.	R. B. Forrest.	RA	Robt. Arthur.	J&AH	J. & A. Howell.
J&AK	Jas. & Andrew Kelly.	R&G	Reed & Garrick.	G&S	Guthrie & Shear.
T&D	Taylor & Downes.	G.T	Geo. Thomson.	TLL	T. L. Leck.
JM&S	J. Muirhead & Sons.	GL	(Not identified.)	DH	D. Howie.
G.I	Geo. Innes.	R.B	Robt. Buchanan.	S&R	Smith & Rait.
SB GG	Barclay & Goodwin.	J.HERON	J. Heron.	ABA	Alex. B. Arthur.
D.S &Cⁱˢ	Dl. Sutherland & Co.	J.MᶜD	J. McDonald.	AW	Alex. Wotherspoon.
JL	J. Laing.	T.F	T. Finlayson.	HD	Hugh Downs.
J&WM	J. & W. Mitchell.	D.T	David Taylor.	J.B	J. Brown.
WA	W. Allan.	TR	Thos. Ross.	AS	A. Sterling.
YOUNG	—— Young.	WB	Walter Baird.	CCC	Colin C. Campbell.
G&W	Gilmore & Watson.	ARS	A. & R. Stewart.	A.L	Alex. Lucas.
L&P	Lindsay & Paisley.	RH	Robt. Hyslop.	MM	M. Michael.
LH	L. Hymens.	LA	Lawrence Aitchison.	W.N	W. Noble
W.C	Wm. Coghill.	WCM	(Not identified.)	J.C.S	(Not identified)
J.Mⁱ	J. McInnes.	W&P	Watson & Pozzie.	JA F	John A. Fetter.
W.S	Wm. Sharp.	D.MᶜD	D. McDonald.	J.F	Do. do.
JMᴳ	J. McGregor.	RD	Robt. Duncan.	R.B.G	(Not identified.)
P&Cº	Panton & Co.	AC	A. Coghill.	RGL	Do. do.
R.L	R. Laing.	T.C	Thos. Chapman.	M&H	Do. do.
T&Cº	Tennent & Co.	MᴷK&Cº	McKenzie & Co.	GL	Do. do.
J&WB	J. & W. Boyd.	WSR	(Not identified.)	W&D	Do. do.
RRK	Robt. Rankin.	L&M	Lorimer & Moyes.	MᶜH&S	Do. do.
J.C	Jas. Crichton.	L.G.&Cº	Leckie, Graham & Co.	R.W.F	Do. do.
		AMC	(Not identified.)	S&R	Smith & Rait.
		G.S.B	Do. do.		

DATE (ABOUT).	MARKS.	MAKER'S NAME.	DATE (ABOUT).	MARKS.	MAKER'S NAME.
1600-25		... ...	1760		(Not identified.)
"		... ...	"		Do. do.
"		... ...	1766-79		Jas. Gordon (1766)
1650		Thomas Moncrur (1649)			Do. do.
"		Do. do. "	"		Do. do.
"		Walter Melvil (1650)	1772-7		Alexr. Thompson (1772)
1660-70		(Not identified.)	1777-8		Jas. Law (1777)
1670-7	WS VS	Wm. Scott (1666)			Do. do.
1672-8	A·G AG	Alexr. Galloway (1671)			Do. do.
1690		(Not identified.)			John Leslie (1782)
1691-7		Geo. Walker (1685)	1782-96		Do. do.
1703		Do. do. "			*Do. do.
1708-14		Geo. Robertson (1708)			Do. do.
1710-20		Do. do. "			Do. do.
1718-27		John Walker (1713)	1783-90		Jas. Smith (1783)
1730	J WALKER	Do. do. "			Do. do.
"		George Cooper (1728)			Do. do.
"		Alexr. Forbes (1728)	1785-95		(Not identified.)
"		George Cooper (1728)	1786 to 1818		Nathl. Gillet (1786)
"		Do. do. "			Do. do.
1734-51	JA	Jas. Abercrombie (1734)			Do. do.
1748-67		Coline Allan (1748)	1790 to 1800		Do. do.
1750		Do. do. "			Do. do.
1763-70		James Wildgoose (1763)	1796 to 1820		James Erskine (1796)
"		Do. do. "			Do. do.
					*Do. do.
					Do. do.
					(Not identified.)

DATE (ABOUT).	MARKS.	MAKER'S NAME.
1800	WB 〓	(*Not identified.*)
	DOUGLAS 〓 〓 ID	J. Douglas (?)
	JA AB 〓	John Allan (1797)
	J.A	Do. do.
	ID 〓 〓	J. Douglas (?)
1800	I·D	Do. do.
TO	GB ABD	(*Not identified.*)
1830	GB AB GB AB	Do. do.
	G.B A B D N	Do. do.
	WJ ABD WJ	Do. do.
	WJ A B D WJ	Do. do.
	A A A	Do. do.
1820	IB ABD	Do. do.
1830	WJ A B D 〓〓	Do. do.
1841	GJ ABDN	Geo. Jamieson
1850	W·W ABDN	(*Not identified.*)
	WW 〓 ABD WW	Do. do.
1871	GS ABD	Do. do.

DATE (ABOUT).	MARKS.	MAKER'S NAME.
1680	VS ABC	Wm. Scott.
1698	VS BAN D	Do. do.
1720	VS 〓 VS 〓	Wm. Scott, junr.
1725	PS 〓 PS BAN	Patk. Scott.
1732-41	PG BAF B	Patrick Gordon.
1750	AS BAF AS	Alexr. Shirras.
1775	BA IA	John Argo.
1780	JA BANF	Do. do.
1785	WB BANF	Wm. Byres.
1795	R IK 〓 B	John Keith.
,,	B IK 〓 H	Do. do.
1800-20	〓 IK F	Do. do.
,,	〓 IK BANF 〓	Do. do.
,,	〓 IK	Do. do.
,,	IK BANF	Do. do.
,,	IK B H	Do. do.
,,	〓 〓 〓	Do. do.
,,	S·A 〓	(*Not identified.*)
1820	GE B	Geo. Elder.
1835	BA 〓 McQ	John McQueen.
1850	WS H B	Wm. Simpson.
,,	,, ,,	Do. do.

ELGIN

DATE (ABOUT.)	MARKS.	MAKER'S NAME.
1728		Wm. Livingston.
1730		E. R.........
1754		James Humphrey.
1760		(E on its back and LN for Elgin). James Humphrey.
1770		... ...
1790 to 1820		Chas. Fowler.
		Do. do.
		Do. do.
		W. F........
1830		Thos. Stewart (see Inverness, p. 549).

CANONGATE

DATE (ABOUT).	MARKS.	MAKER'S NAME.		
1680		...	...	...
"		...	...	...
"		...	...	...
1696		...	...	...
1700		...	...	...
"		...	...	...
1760		...	...	...
1763		...	...	...
1780-90		...	...	...
1790		...	...	...
TO		M. Hinchsliffe.		
1820		...	...	...
		...	...	...
1836		‡David Greig (?)		

MONTROSE

DATE (ABOUT).	MARKS.	MAKER'S NAME.
1670		Wm. Lindsay (probably).
1671		Wm. Lindsay.
		Do. do.
1680-3		Do. do.
1710		... ...
1752		Thos. Johnston.
1788		Benj. Lumsden (admitted 1788).
1811		Wm. Mill (1811)

GREENOCK

DATE (ABOUT).	MARKS.	MAKER'S NAME.
1750		W. L.........
		Jonas Osborne, of Glasgow.
1765		Do. do.
		Do. do.
		Do. do.
		James Taylor, of Glasgow.
1780		G. B.........
		W. C.........
(")		M. C.
1790		B. C.
"		N. H.
1800		J. H.
"		R. N.
"		P. H.
		John Heron.
		Do. do.
1800		Thos. Davie.
		Do. do.
		John Heron.
		J. & G. Heron?
1800 TO 1830		Do. do.
		W. H. T.........
		Do. do.
1820		
"		Peterhead and Greenock mark.

ARBROATH

DATE (ABOUT).	MARKS.
1830	
1838	
1830-9	
"	

THE ARBROATH BURGH SEAL.

DATE (ABOUT).	MARKS.	MAKER'S NAME.
1640	MK INS	M. K......
1643	,, ,, T	Do. do.
1680	MR INS	M. R......
1708	M ,, M	M. L......
1715	M ,,	—— M......
1720	RI INS A	R I......
1730	IB FB ⚜	John Baillie (and another)
,,	I·B EB ▦ A	Do. do.
1740	IB INS X	John Baillie
,,	TB INS	Thos. Baillie
1770	AS INS	Alexr. Stewart
1780	RA C INS	Robert Anderson
1790	AS INS O	Alexr. Stewart, jr.
,,		(No maker's mark.)
,,	H&Cº A	Hamilton & Co.
,,	JA ,, A	J. A.
,,	T&Cº	T. & Co.
,,	AS ☀	Alexr. Stewart, jr.
1800	CJ INS	Chas. Jamieson

DATE (ABOUT).	MARKS.	MAKER'S NAME.
1800	J&N INS	Jameson & Naughton.
,,	MAC MAS ,,	—— Macmas.
,,	DF INS	Donald Fraser.
1810	CJ INS CJ	Charles Jamieson.
,,	,, ,, ,,	Do. do.
,,	J.McR INS	J. McR.
1815	RN INS RN	Robt. Naughton.
,,	RN	Do. do.
1820	AML INS ○ ○	Alexr. MacLeod.
,,	AMcL INS	Do. do.
1830	TS INS	Thos. Stewart.
,,	D·F INS	Donald Fraser.
,,	AS INS	Alexr. Stewart.
1840		... ...
1857	F BROS	Ferguson Brothers.
1880	F&M INVS	Ferguson & MacBean.

DUNDEE   PERTH

DATE (ABOUT.)	MARKS.	MAKER'S NAME.
1628	AL ⚜ AL	Alexr. Lindsay (1628)
1631	RG ⚜	Robt. Gairdine (mentioned 1683)
1643	RG ⚜ RG	Do. do.
1648	RG ⚜ RG	Do. do.,
1667	TL ⚜ TL	Thos. Lindsay (1662)
1722	CD ⚜ CD E	Chas. Dickson (1722)
1730	IS ⚜ IS M	John Steven (mentioned 1764)
1742	AI ,, AI K	Alexr. Johnston (1739)
1764	JS ⚜	John Steven (1764)
1776	WS ,, WS W	Wm. Scott (1776)
,,	,, ,, M	Do. do.
	AC ⚜ C ⚜	Alexr. Cameron (1818)
	EL ,, D ,,	Edwd. Livingstone (1809)
	CAMERON ,, C ,, DUNDEE	Alexr. Cameron (1818)
	RN ⚜ ⚜ ⚜	Robt. Naughton ? (see Inverness, p. 549)
1800	T.S ,, ,,	Thos. Stewart ? (see Inverness, p. 549)
TO	WC ,, ,,	Wm. Constable (1806)
1840	RH S ⚜ ⚜ ⚜ DUNDEE	(Not identified.)
	EL ⚜ EL III	Edwd. Livingstone (1809)
	WK ⚜ ✡	(Not identified.)
	DM ⚜ DM	David Manson (1809)
	DM ,, DM	Do. do.
1809	WY ⚜ D ⚜	Wm. Young (1809)

DATE (ABOUT).	MARKS.	MAKER'S NAME.
1675	WM ⚜ B	W. M......
1680	RG ⚜ B	Robert Gardiner (1669)
1687	RG ⚜ RG	Do. do. do.
1710	WS ⚜ ⚜ S	William Scott, of Banff
1750	H ⚜ 3 ⚜	... ...
1772	IC ⚜ IC ⚜	James Cornfute (1772)
1780	TF ,, TF ,,	T. F......
,,	RK ⚜ RK	Robert Keay (1791)
,,	JJ ,,	J. J.
1791	RK ⚜ RK ⚜	Robert Keay (1791)
1800	WR ⚜ WR	William Ritchie (1796)
1810	IS O ⚜ ⚜ ⚜	John Sid (1808)
,,	R&RK ,, R&RK	R. & R. Keay
1815	DG ⚜ DG ⚜	David Greig (c. 1810)
1816	CM ⚜ CM	Charles Murray (1816)
,,	⚜ S ⚜	(No maker's mark.)
,,	RMcG ,, RMcG	R. McG.
,,	IH ,, IH	I. H.
1820	RG ,,	Robert Greig (1817)
1830	RK ⚜ RK	Robert Keay, jr. (1825)
,,	AM ⚜ AM	A. M......
,,	P ⚜ S ⚜	John Pringle (1827)
,,	,, RK	Robert Keay, jr. (1825)
,,	IP ⚜ IP ⚜	John Pringle (1827)
1830 TO 1850	IK ,,	J. K......
	RD ,,	R. D.....
1856	DG ,,	David Greig, jr.

UNASCRIBED SCOTTISH MARKS

TAIN.

DATE (ABOUT).	MARKS.
1500	
1690	
1700	
,,	
1720	
1730	
1750	
,,	
,,	
,,	
,,	
,,	
1760	
,,	T.COLGAN
,,	
1770	INCE
,,	

DATE (ABOUT).	MARKS.
1780	JW
,,	CF
1790	R&S
,,	AR
,,	LM
,,	F·G
1800	T·H
,,	EW
,,	R·R ,,
,,	R·B ,,
,,	CM
1816	1816 F.D
1800-20	JG
,,	
,,	WV AM

MARKS.
H·R S·B A
H·R TAIN S·B L
A·S TAIN
R·W ,,
W·I. TAIN ,,

ST. ANDREWS.

PG PG

STIRLING.

S

HL

WICK.

JS WICK

	HARP CROWNED.	DATE LETTER.	MAKER'S MARK.	MAKER'S NAME.
CHAS. I. 1638-9	[harp crowned]	A	[VB]	James Vanderbeck,
1639-40	[harp crowned]	B	[JT] / [EC]	John Thornton. / Edwd. Chadsey.
1640-1	,,	C	[JT]	John Thornton.
1641-2	,,	D	[WC]	Wm. Cooke.
1642-3		E		... ...
1643-4		F		... ...
1644-5		G		... ...
1645-6		H		... ...
1646-7	[harp crowned]	I	[B]	John Burke (or John Banister).
1647-8		K		.. .. ..
1648-9		L		.. .
COMWTH. 1649-50		M		
1650-1		N		... .
1651-2		O		... .
1652-3		P		.. .
1653-4		Q		... .
1654-5		R		.. . .
1655-6	[harp crowned]	S	[DP]	Daniel Bellingham.
1656-7	,,	T	[IS]	Joseph Stoaker (or John Slicer).
1657-8		U		... ...

	HARP CROWNED.	DATE LETTER.	MAKER'S MARK.	MAKER'S NAME.
1658-9		a		... ...
	[harp crowned]		[IS]	Joseph Stoaker.
1659-60 {	[harp crowned]	b	[IS]	Do. do.
CHAS. II. 1660-1		c		... ...
1661-2		d		
1662-3		e		... ...
1663-4	[harp crowned]	f	[IS]	Joseph Stoaker.†
1664-5	,,	g	[AR]	Abel Ram.‡
1665-6		h		... ...
1666-7		i		
1667-8		k		
1668-9		l		... ...
1669-70		m		
1670-1		n		... ...
1671-2	[harp crowned]	o	[IS]	Joseph Stoaker.†
1672-3		p		... ...
1673-4		q		
1674-5		r		... .
1675-6		s		
1676-7		t		... ...
1677-8		u		... .

	HARP CROWNED.	DATE LETTER.	MAKER'S MARK.	MAKER'S NAME.
1639-40	[harp crowned]	B	[GG]	George Gallant.

	HARP CROWNED.	DATE LETTER.	MAKER'S MARK	MAKER'S NAME.
1678-9		A		... ...
1679-80	(harp crowned)	B	TB	Timothy Blackwood.‡
			SM	Samuel Marsden.
			IK	James Kelly.
			AG	Andrew Gregory.
1680-1	(harp crowned)	C	,,	Do. do.
			IP	John Phillips.
			WL	Wm. Lucas or Walter Lewis.
1681-2	,,	D	ES	Edwd. Swan.
1682-3	,,	E	IK	James Kelly.
1683-4		F		... ...
JAS. II. 1685-6 7	,,	G	IF	John Farmer.
			IC	John Cuthbert.
			RN	Robert Nevill.
			IH	John Humphrys.
1688 to 1692	(harp crowned)	H	DK	David King.
			RS	Robt. Smith (warden 1701).
		I		... ...
WM. III. 1693-4-5	(harp crowned)	K	IW	Joseph Walker.
			WD	Wm. Drayton.
			WM	Wm. Myers.
			AS	Ant'ny Stanley.
			B	Thos. Bolton.
1696-9	,,	L	IP	John Phillips.
			DK	David King.
			IW	Joseph Walker.
			IH	John Humphrys.
			AS	Anth'y Stanley.

	HARP CROWNED.	DATE LETTER.	MAKER'S MARK	MAKER'S NAME.
* 1699/1700	(harp crowned)	P	EW	Ant'ny Stanley (as 1693-4-5.) Edward Workman.
1700-1	,,	Q	S	Alexr. Sinclair.
* 1701-2	(harp crowned)	R	IW	Joseph Walker.
				... ...
			B	Thomas Boulton.
ANNE. * 1702-3	(harp crowned)	S	B	Do. do.
1703-4	,,	T	,,	Do. do.
1704-5-6	(harp crowned)	R	HM	Henry Matthews.
			IW	Joseph Walker.
1706-7-8	(harp crowned)	S	DK	David King.
			EB	Edward Barrett.
			B	Thomas Bolton.
1708-9-0	,,	T	,,	Do. do. (Maker's mark indistinct)
1710-1-2	(harp crowned)	U	DK	David King. (Maker's mark indistinct)
1712-3-4	(harp crowned)	W	EW	Edward Workman.
			WA	Walter Archdall.
			IC	John Clifton.
GEO I. 1714-5	,,	X	WA	Wm. Archdall.
1715-6	(harp crowned)	Y	IT	John Tuite.†
			IC	John Cuthbert, jun.
			IW	Joseph Walker. David King (as 1706 above).
1716-7		Z		... ...

HARP CROWNED.	DATE LETTER.	MAKER'S MARK.	MAKER'S NAME.
1717-8			Joseph Walker.
			Christr. Thompson.
			Wm. Clarke (of Cork).
			John Hamilton.
			John Savage ?
''			Thos. Parker.
1718-9	''		Erasm's Cope.
1719-20			Henry Daniell.
			John Clifton, jr.
''			John Clifton, sr.
1720-1			John Hamilton.
1721-2	''		Do. do.
			Thos. Sutton.
1722-3	''		John Clifton, sr.
			Edwd. Barrett.
1723-4	''		Robert Harrison.
			Thos. Walker.
			Wm. Duggan.
1724-5			Thos. Slade.
			John Taylor.
			Thos. Bolton.
1725-6	''		Mathw. Walker.
			Michl. Hewitson.,
			Mathw. Walker.
1726-7	''		Noah Vialas.
			Philip Kinnersly.
GEO. II. *1727-8			Robert Calderwood.
			John King.
			Wm. Clarke. (of Cork).
1728-9	''		John Robinson.
			Bolton Cormick.
1729-30			Robert Calderwood.
			John Moore.
			Wm. Archdall.
1730-1	''		David King.

HARP CROWNED.	DATE LETTER.	HIBERNIA.	MAKER'S MARK.	MAKER'S NAME.
1731-2	L			Esther Forbes.
				Erasmus Cope ?
1732-3	''			Anthony Lefebure.
				James Douglas.
1733-4	''		''	Wm. Williamson.
				Charles Lemaitre.
				John Taylor.
1734-5				Wm. Townsend.
				Chas. Leslie.†
				Thos. Williamson.
1735-6	''		''	Barth Mosse.
				Alexr. Brown.
				John Williamson.
1736-7	''		''	John Wilme.
				Andrew Goodwin.
				James Taylor.
1737-8	''		''	David King ?
1738-9	''		''	Samuel Walker.
				Matthew Walker.
1739-40	''		''	Andrew Goodwin.
				Francis Williamson.
				John Walker.
1740-1	''		''	John Moore.
				Alexr. Richards.‡
1741-2-3			''	Isaac D'Olier.
			''	John Laughlin.
				Christr. Locker.
1743-4	''		''	Robt. Holmes.
				John Letablere.
1745	''		''	James Whitthorne.§
				John Moore.
1746	''		''	Jas. Whitthorne. (see 1745).§

	HIBERNIA	DATE LETTER	HARP CROWNED	MAKER'S MARK	MAKER'S NAME
1747	●	A	♔	WW / CF	Wm. Williamson. / C. Fox.
1748	,,	B	,,	WW / WB	Will. Walsh. / Will. Beates.
1749	,,	C	♔	IC / IL	John Christie. / John Laughlin.
1750	,,	D	,,	MB / ID	Mathias Brown. / Isaac D'Olier.
1751-2	,,	E E	●	IP / WR	John Pittar. / William Ring.
1752-3	,,	F	,,	MH	Mich'el Homer.
1753-4	,,	G	,,	WT / AR	Wm. Townsend. / Aléxr. Richards.
1754-5	,,	H	,,	CS	Christr. Skinner.
1757	,,	I	,,	A	Matt'w Alanson.
1758	,,	K	●	DP / MS	Daniel Popkins. / (Not identified.)
1759	,,	L	,,	SW / IP	Saml. Walker. / J'nth'n. Pasley.
GEO. III. 1760	,,	M	,,	RC	Robt. Calderwood.
1761	,,	N	,,	GH / TJ	Geo. Hill. / Thos. Johnston. Do. do.
1762	,,	O	●	X	Matt'w Alanson.
1763	,,	P	,,	DP	David Peter.
1764	,,	Q	,,	WC / WH	Wm. Currie. / Wm. Homer.
1765	,,	R	,,	FI / IC	Francis Jones. / Joseph Cullen.
1766	,,	S	,,	MC IL / F&K	{ M. Cormick & J. Locker. } French & Keating.
1767	,,	T	●	JW / RW	John West. / Richd. Williams.
1768	,,	U	,,	RT / ID	Richd. Tudor. / Jer'm'h D'Olier.
1769	●	W	●	JS / IG	John Shields. / James Graham.
1770	,,	X	,,	IL / CH	John Locker. / Christr. Haines.
1771	,,	Y	●	TK / H	Thos. Kinsela. / John Lloyd.
1772	,,	Z	,,	CT / CM	Chas. Townsend. / Chas. Mullin.

	HIBERNIA	DATE LETTER	HARP CROWNED	MAKER'S MARK	MAKER'S NAME
1773	●	A	●	JW	John Walker.
1774	,,	B	,,	WH / IC	Wm. Hughes. / John Craig.
1775	,,	C	,,	AB / RW	Ambrose Boxwell. / Richd. Williams.
1776	,,	D	●	CT / MW	Chas. Townsend. / Matthew West.
1777	,,	E	,,	HA / DK / SW	Hay Andrews. / Darby Kehoe. / Stephen Walsh.
1778	,,	F	,,	MH / JP	Michael Homer. / John Pittar.
1779	,,	G	,,	II / MK	Jos. Jackson. / Michael Keating.
1780	,,	H	,,	MW / JB	Michael Walsh. / John Bolland.
1781	,,	I	,,	IK / II / TJ	John Kelly. / Jos. Jackson. / Thomas Jones.
1782	,,	K	,,	WW	Wm. Ward.
1783	,,	L	,,	HL / RW	John Laughlin, jr. / Robert Wyke.
1784	,,	M	,,	WT / MW	Wm. Thompson. / Matthew Walsh.
1785	,,	N	,,	CH / WS	Christr. Haines. / Wm. Supple.
1786	,,	O	,,	WJ / L&B	Wm. Johnson. / (Not identified.)
1787	●	P	●	JP / MW	John Pittar.‡ / Matthew West.
1788	,,	Q	,,	MK / IS	Michael Keating. / John Stoyte.
1789	,,	R	,,	WL / RW	Wm. Law. / Robt. Williams.
1790	,,	S	,,	AC / AN	Arthur Clark. / Arthur O'Neill.
1791	,,	T	,,	BT / TJ	Benjn. Tait. / Thos. Jones?
1792	,,	U	,,	RS / WB / IK	Robt. Smith. / Wm. Bond. / James Keating.§
1793	,,	W	,,	MK / JP	Michael Keating. / John Power.
1794	●	X	●	GW / L&B	George West. / (Not identified.)
1795	,,	Y	,,	IL	John Laughlin, jr.
1796	,,	Z	,,	IE / GW / FB	James England. / Geo. Wheatley. / Fredk. Buck.

MARKS ON DUBLIN PLATE

235

	HIBERNIA.	DATE LETTER.	HARP CROWNED.	MAKER'S MARK.	MAKER'S NAME.
1797	(Hibernia)	A	(harp)	J·R	John Rigby. / Geo. West (as 1794.)
1798	,,	B	,,	J·K / J·D	John Keene. / John Daly.
1799	,,	C	,,	L·K WEST / IS	James Keating.† / James Scott.
1800	,,	D	,,	JK / WP	John Kearns. / Walter Peter.
1801	,,	E	,,	IC / JP	Jas. Connor. / John Power.
1802	,,	F	,,	RS / WH	Richd. Sawyer. / Wm. Hamey.
1803	,,	G	,,	O/AN / IB	Arthur O'Neil. / J. Brady.
1804	,,	H	,,	R.B / DE	Robt. Breading. / Danl. Egan.
1805	,,	I	,,	W·D / DM	Wm. Doyle. / (Not identified.)
1806	,,	K	,, (KING'S HEAD.)	S·N / T&W / W·W	Samuel Neville. / Tudor & Whitford. / Wm. Ward.
1807	,,	L	,,	GB	Gust'v's Byrne.
1808	,,	M	,,	C T / I W / SN	Terry & Williams (of Cork). / Saml. Neville.
1809	,,	N N	,,	JJ / RB	Joseph Johnson. / Robt. Breading.
1810	(Hibernia)	O O	(harp)	,,	I·L·B / T·R	Jas. Le Bass. / (Not identified.)
1811	,,	P	,,	,,	C·S / W·N	Chas. Stewart. / W. Nowlan.
1812	,,	Q	,,	,,	HAMY R·S / PM	W. Hamy & R. Smith. / P Moore.
1813	,,	R	,,	,,	WR / J·P	Wm. Rose. / John Pittar.
1814	,,	S	,,	,,	I·S / LAW / I·N	Jas. Scott. / Wm. Law. / John Nicklin.
1815	,,	T	,,	,,	PG / SB	Phineas Garde (Cork). / S. Bergin.
1816	,,	U	,,	,,	DE / RC	Danl. Egan. / Randall Cashell.
1817	,,	W	,,	,,	J·M / WC / NWB	James Moore. / W. Cummins. / Sir N. W. Brady.
1818	,,	X	,,	,,	T·R / I·B	T. Read. / J. Buckton.
1819	,,	Y	,,	,,	ILB WEST	Jas. Le Bass. / Jas. Fry.†
GEO. IV. 1820	,,	Z	,,	,,	JS / EM	J. Salter (Cork). / Edwd. Murray.

	HIBERNIA.	DATE LETTER.	HARP CROWNED.	KING'S HEAD.	MAKER MARK.	MAKER'S NAME.
1821	(Hibernia)	A	(harp)	(King's head)	MW&S / WM / EC	M. West & Sons. / Wm. Morgan. / E. Crofton.
1822	,,	B	,,	,,	I·B / LAW	J. Buckton. / Wm. Law.
1823	,,	C	,,	,,	EP / IF	Edwd. Power. / Jas. Fray.
1824	,,	D	,,	,,	SN / SB	Saml. Neville. / Saml. Beere.
1825-6	,,	E e		,,	WT / R·G	Wm. Teare.? / Richd. Garde (Cork).
1826-7	,,	F	,,	,,	W&Cº / J·S	Ald'm'n West (& Co.). / J. Smith.
1827-8		G		,,	CM / I·R	Chas. Marsh. / J. Read.
1828-9		H		,,	TWY+ / HF / LN	Edwd. Twycross. / Hy. Flavelle. / L. Nowlan.
1829-30 WM. IV.		I I		,,	C·M & M·G	Chas. Marsh. / D. Moulang & W. Gibson.
1830-1		K			S&G / E·J	Smith & Gamble. / Edmd. Johnson.
1831-2		L			R·S / TF / PM	Richd. Sawyer, jr. / T. Farnett. / P. Moore.
1832-3	,,	M	,,	,,	HF	Hy. Flavelle.
1833-4		N N			TM / EJ	Thos. Meade. / Edmd. Johnson.
1834-5		O O			LN / WS	L. Nowlan? / Wm. Sherwin.
1835-6	,,	P P	,,	,,	PW / I·M	P. Weeks? / J. Moore.
1836-7	,,	Q Q	,,	,,	WS / R·G	Wm. Sherwin. / Richd. Garde (Cork).
VICT. 1837-8	,,	R R	,,	,,	IL / S&G	Josiah Low. / Smith & Gamble.
1838-9	,,	S	,,		H&F	Hughes & Francis.
1839-40		T		,,	PW	Peter Walsh.
1840-1	,,	U U	,,	,,	E&JJ / LN	E. & J. Johnson. / L. Nowlan.
1841-2	,,	V	,,	,,	GA	G. Alcock.
1842-3		W		,,	IW / I·L·B	John Warren. / Jas. Le Bass.
1843-4	,,	X	,,	,,	IF / GW	J. Francis. / Geo. West?
1844-5		Y		,,	MN	Michl. Nowlan.
1845-6		Z		,,	JG / II20	J. Gamble. / † Joseph Johnson.

	HIBERNIA.	DATE LETTER.	HARP CROWNED.	QUEEN'S HEAD.	MAKER'S MARK.	MAKER'S NAME.
1846-7	(mark)	a	(harp)	(head)	JJ	Joseph Johnson.
1847-8	,,	b	,,	,,	J·M / T·M	J. Mahoney. / Thos. Mason.
1848-9	,,	c	,,	,,	CC / WL / RS	C. Cummins, jr. / Wm. Lawson. / R. Samuel.
1849-50	,,	d	,,	,,	D&W	Donegan & Co.
1850-1	,,	e	,,	,,	JG / HF	J. Gamble. / Henry Flavelle.
1851-2	,,	f f	,,	,,	IN / AC	Joseph Needham, / Ann Cummins.
1852-3	,,	g g	,,	,,	GARDNER / JS	— Gardner. / J. Smyth.
1853-4	,,	h h	,,	,,	RS / T&W	R. Sherwin. / Topham & White.
1854-5	,,	j	,,	,,	M·K	Michael Keating.
1855-6	,,	k	,,	,,	CC	C. Cummins.
1856-7	,,	l	,,	,,	W·A	W. Atcheson.
1857-8	,,	m	,,	,,	D&W / AJ	Donegan & Co. / Arthur Johnson.
1858-9	,,	n	,,	,,	J·R·N / NEILL	J. R. Neill. / Do. do.
1859-60	,,	o	,,	,,	S·LB	Samuel Le Bass.
1860-1	,,	p	,,	,,	WP / W&IP	Wm. Percival. / W. & I. Percival.
1861-2	,,	q	,,	,,	EP	E. Powell.
1862-3	,,	r	,,	,,	JK / EJ·JJ	J. Keating. / E. & J. Johnson.
1863-4	,,	s	,,	,,	JS	John Smyth.
1864-5	(mark)	t	,,	,,	IS / RYAN&CO	J. Scriber. / Ryan & Co.
1865-6	,,	u	,,	,,	I·W / WATERHOUSE / FM	Jas. West. / Waterhouse & Co. / Francis Martin.
1866-7	,,	v	,,	,,	AH / BRUNKER DUBLIN	A. Hutton. / Thos. Brunker.
1867-8	,,	w	,,	(head)	H·D / WL	Patk. Donegan. / Wm. Lawson.
1868-9	,,	x	,,	,,	E·J / MT	Edmd. Johnson, jr. / Mars. Trench.
1869-70	,,	y	,,	,,	W·L	Wm. Lawson.
1870-1	,,	z	,,	,,	TDB	T. D. Bryce.

DATE.	MARKS.	MAKER'S NAME.
1663-4	(marks)	Abel Ram.
1708-10	(marks)	Philip Tough.
1715-6	(marks)	Wm. Archdall.
1731	(marks)	—— Sutton?
1739	(marks)	Robert Holmes.
1740	(marks)	Will. Walsh. / Jane Daniell.†
,,	,, ,, ,, Su	—— Sutton?
c. 1750	(marks)	

1660	Æ	Andrew Edwards.
1704	AV	Abraham Voisin.
,,	RS	Robert Smith.

1704	IG	John Garrett.
,,	IW	James Walker.

	HIBERNIA.	DATE LETTER.	HARP CROWNED.	QUEEN'S HEAD.	MAKER'S MARK.	MAKER'S NAME AND DATE OF REGISTRATION OF MARK.	
1871-2	⬛	A	⬛	⬛	J.W & R	J. Weir	Wickham. & Rogers.	(1871).
1872-3	,,	B	,,	,,	J.D	John	Donegan.	(1872).
1873-4	,,	C	,,	,,	EGAN CORK	Wm.	Egan & Son (of Cork).	,,
1874-5	,,	D	,,	,,	IC	Ignatius	Cummins.	(1874).
1875-6	,,	E	,,	,,	McD BS	McDowell	Bros.	(1875).
1876-7	,,	F	,,	,,	M'D B	Do.	do.	,,
1877-8	,,	G	,,	,,	W&S	West	& Son.	(1877).
1878-9	,,	H	,,	,,	J R	J.	Redmond.	(1876).
1879-80	,,	I	,,	,,	W&S	West	& Son.	(1879).
1880-1	,,	K	,,	,,	OC &D	O'Connor	& Dillon.	(1880).
1881-2	,,	L	,,	,,	E.JOHNSON / E.J	Edmond Do.	Johnson. do.	(1881). (1882).
1882-3	,,	M	,,	,,	W.C / H.H	Wm. Henry	Carty. Hopkins.	(1881). (1883).
1883-4	,,	N	,,	,,	DM	Danl.	Moulang.	,,
1884-5	,,	O	,,	,,	W&L	Winder	& Lamb.	,,
1885-6	,,	P	,,	,,	F.BS	Frengley	Bros.	(1885).
1886-7	,,	Q	,,	,,	A&CO	Austin	& Co.	(1886).
1887-8	,,	R	,,	,,	MA / JEP	M. Jas. E.	Anderson. Pim.	(1887). ,,
1888-9	,,	S	,,	,,	TB / F.H	Thomas Fredk.	Barton. Hill.	(1871). (1889).
1889-90	,,	T	,,	,,	WQ / J.F	Wm. Joseph	Quinlan. Fray.	(1888). (1889).
1890-1	,,	U	,,		HLS	Henry L.	Stewart (of Limerick).	,,
1891-2	,,	V	,,		S·D·NEILL	Sharman D.	Neill (of Belfast).	(1890).
1892-3	,,	W	,,		H&H / MOSLEY	Hopkins Jas.	& Hopkins. Mosley (Waterford).	(1883). (1892).
1893-4	,,	X	,,		CH / E.J	C. Edmond	Harris (Coventry). Johnson.	(1893). ,,
1894-5	,,	Y	,,		C.H.L / K&G	Chas. Howard Lawson. Kane	& Gunning	(1894). ,,
1895-6	,,	Z	,,		R.D / C.L / C&S	Richard Charles Chancellor	Dillon (Waterford). Lamb. & Son.	(1893). (1895).

	HIBER-NIA.	DATE LETTER.	HARP CROWNED.	MAKER'S MARK.	MAKER'S NAME AND DATE OF REGISTRATION OF MARK.		
1896-7		A		R&W / J·M	Richards	& Walsh.	(1895).
					John	Morton.	(1896).
1897-8	,,	B	,,	G·LTD	Gibson,	Ltd. (Belfast).	(1897).
1898-9	,,	C	,,	R·K / M&C	Robert	Knaggs.	(1898).
1899				RV	Moore	& Co.	,,
					Robert	Valentine.	,,
1900	,,	D	,,	W.J.G / LAWSON DUBLIN	W. J.	Gethings.	,,
					Chas. Howard	Lawson.	(1900).
1900-1	,,	E	,,	L·A·W	Langley Archer	West.	,,
EDW. VII. 1901-2	,,	F	,,	H&T / M·C&D	Henderson	& Thompson (Belfast).	,,
					McCutcheon	& Donaldson (Belfast).	(1901).
1902-3	,,	G	,,	& / W·S	West	& Son.	(1902).
1903-4		H		JEB	J. E.	Byrne (Belfast).	(1909).
1904-5	,,	I	,,	JAMESON	——	Jameson.	,,
1905-6	,,	K	,,	R·LTD	Russell	Ltd. (Manchester).	,,
1906-7	,,	L	,,	A·DUFFNER TIPPERARY	A.	Duffner (Tipperary).	(1907).
1907-8	,,	M	,,	F·S·L·D	Finnegans	Ltd. (Manchester).	(1912).
1908-9	,,	N	,,	E&C	Elkington	& Co. (Birmingham).	,,
1909-10	,,	O	,,	W·E&SNS LTD	W. Egan	& Sons (Cork).	(1910).
1910-1	,,	P	,,	N	——	Neill (Belfast).	(1906).
1911-2	,,	Q	,,	A·H	Youghal Art Metal Works Co.		,,
1912-3	,,	R	,,	FALLER GALWAY	——	Faller (Galway).	,,
1913-4	,,	S	,,	J·M·D	J.	McDowell.	,,
1914-5	,,	T	,,	C·CROMER LIMERICK	C.	Cromer (Limerick).	(1907).
1915-6	,,	U	,,	& / W·W	Wakeley	& Wheeler (London).	(1909).

	HIBER-NIA.	DATE LETTER.	HARP CROWNED.	MAKER'S MARK.	MAKER'S NAME AND DATE OF REGISTRATION OF MARK.		
1916-7		A		W·S	Will	Stokes.	(1910).
1917-8	,,	b	,,	WALDRON SKIBBEREEN	M.	Waldron (Skibbereen).	,,
1918-9	,,	C	,,	JR	Jas.	Ramsay (Dundee).	(1912).
1919-20	,,	D	,,	RS	R.	Sharman.	(1908).
1920-1	,,	e	,,	L·A·C	Crichton	Bros. (London).	(1912).

SUPPLEMENTARY LIST OF MARKS OF GOLDSMITHS,

impressed at Dublin but not illustrated in the preceding tables.

DATE.	MARK.	MAKER'S NAME.	DATE.	MARK.	MAKER'S NAME.	DATE.	MARK.	NAME OF MAKER.
1636	IW	John Woodcocke.	1706	B	Thos. Bolton.	1725-6	MB	Mary Barrett.
1663-4	FC	Francis Coffee or Clifton.	1710	HS	Henry Sherwin.	"	TW	Thos. Wheeler.
1679	E·S	Edward Swan.	1710-2	B	Thos. Bolton?	1726-7	PR	Peter Racine.
1680	E·S	" "	"	(skull)	J. Pennyfather or J. Palet?	1728-9	S+C	... ...
"	LS	Lawrence Salmon.	1712-4	ED	... ...	1729	EF	Esther Forbes.
"	I·S	John Seager.	1715	GS	Geo. Smart.	"	US	Thos. Sutton.
1685	I*P	John Phillips.	"	E+D	Ed. Dowdall.	1730-1	GC	George Cross.
1685-7	IC	John Cuthbert.	1715-6	M	Mark Twelves.	"	GC	Geo. Cartwright.
1696-7	DM	(Not identified.)	1716-7	Z IW	... ...	"	DM	Dorothy Monjoy.
1698	AS+	A. Stanley?	1717-8	WB	W. Bell.	1731	A	Matthew Alanson.
1699	CM P	Cyriac Mallory.	1718-9	T·W	Thos. Walker.	1732-3	EC	Erasmus Cope.
"	GL	George Lyng.	1719-20	AW	Arthur Weldon.	1734	I·G	John Gumly.
1700	AM	Alexr. Mackay.	1720	IR	Thos. Racine.	1735	D	Isaac D'Olier.
1701-2	T·S	Thos. Sumpner.	1722-3	E·F	Ed. Fitzgerald.	1736-7	TM	Thos. Maculla?
"	A|S	.. ..	1723-4	D WS	.. ..	"	AL	Anthony Lefebure.
1702-3	EB	Edward Barrett.	1724-5	PK	Phillip Kinnersly.	"	R·W	Ralph Woodhouse.
"	H	Thos. Hartwell.	1725-6	Sa	John Sale.	"	D S*	... ...
1703-4	D	... ...	"	RP	Robt. Pilkington.	1737-8	I·F	John Freebough.
"	K	David King.	"	MC	Matt. Copeland.			
1706	RF	Robt. Forbes.						

SUPPLEMENTARY LIST OF MARKS OF GOLDSMITHS.

DATE.	MARK.	NAME OF MAKER.	DATE.	MARK.	MAKER'S NAME.	DATE.	MARK	MAKER'S NAME.
1737-8	TD	Thos. de Limarest.	1752	ER	Edward Raper.	1780	HO	Hugh O'Hanlon or Owen Hart?
1740-1	PD	Peter Desenard.	1754	O / R*C	Robt. Calderwood or Cope.	c. 1780	O·C	Owen Cassidy.
"	MR	... ...	"	H*W	Hy. Waldron.	"	AB	Alex. Barry?
"	I·C	Jas. Champion?	1757	M·F	Michael Fowler.	1780-5	BD	Barnaby Delahoyde?
"	PD	... ...	1758	WW	Wm. Williamson.	1785	D·E	Dan. Egan?
"	IL	John Letablere.	"	CS	Christr. Skinner.	1792	MH	Michael Homer?
"	TB	Thos. Burton.	c. 1760	H*W	See 1754 above.	1795	IASK	J. R. Ash.
"	SU	Thos. Sutton.	1762	I·M	John Moore, Jr.	c. 1795	I·W	... ...
c. 1740	HI	? Henry Jago.	1764	ID	John Dawson.	c. 1797	TT	Thos. Tudor.
1743-4	WB	Wm. Bonynge.	"	FI	... ...	1798	IB	John Brooks?
"	R·C	Robt. Calderwood.	1766	RV	Ralph Vizard?	1800	S·T	Saml. Teare.
1745	G·B	George Beere.	1767	W*F	Wm. French.	1800-1	JB	John Bolland.
"	RG	Robt. Glanville.	c. 1767	WT	Wm. Townsend.	"	G&PW	... ...
1746	I·H	John Hamilton?	1768	IW	Jno. Williamson.	1802	JD	John Daly?
"	WF	Wm. Faucett?	"	B·W	Benj. Wilson.	1807	C&W	Clarke & West.
"	B·S	Bart'mew Stokes.	"	A·T	Abraham Tuppy.	"	ÆR	Æneas Ryan.
"	WW	Wm. Walsh.	1769	W·T MC	.. ..	1810	RS	Richard Sawyer.
c. 1750	IT	Joseph Taafe.	"	GH	George Hall.	"	IT	John Teare.
1751	NM	Nathan Murray.	1770	KAR	John Karr.	1811	JK RF	... .. .
"	I*P	J. Pittar.	1776	I·B	... ...	1812	JH	J. Henzell?
"	WB	Wm. Betagh.	1779	IL	John Locker?	"	JK	... ...
			"	MS	... ...	1815	R·W	Richard Whitford.

The marks illustrated below are reproduced from a plate of pewter preserved at the Dublin Assay Office, in which marks in use at various dates, from about 1765 to 1812, have been stamped. The plate contains a number of other marks which it is unnecessary to illustrate here, as they appear in the preceding tables.

MARK.	NAME.		MARK.	NAME.		MARK.	NAME.	
RA	Robt.	Atkinson ?	JSB			WG		
ET			EB			I·T		
RID	Richard &	D'Olier.	CF			WS	Will.	Stafford ?
GM	Jeremiah		IN	Joseph	Nixon.	I·E	John	Ebbs.
JA	John	Austin.	RB	Robert	Breading.	TA		
JC	John	Clarke.	RH			EG		
T·F	Thos.	Farley.				BC		
II	Joseph	Jackson.	JE	Joshua	Emerson.	GN	George Nangle.	
TS			SR	Saml.	Reily (Cork).	IH	James	Hadmill.
W·D	Will.	Digby ?	RL			G·ALLEY	Geo.	Alley.
JK	John	Keene.	GT	Geo.	Thompson.	IK	James	Kenzie.
G&B			JJ	James	Jones.	IA	Jerome Alley ?	
TW	Thos.	Williamson.	PM			I·D	John	Dalrymple.
WB	Will	Beere.	M·CL	Mark	M'Cloughlin.	WS		
TP			WFG	Wm.	Fitzgerald (Limerick).	PS		
JC	John	Coleman.	HL			T M	Thos.	Martin.
MB	Michael Byrne.		IN			WJ	Will.	Johnson.
WP	Walter	Peter.	AN	Ambr'se	Nicklin.	AT	Alex.	Ticknell.
CD	Chas.	Dowdall.	M·N			IO	John	Osborne.
T·C	Thos.	Cooksey.	HM			HN	Henry Nicholson.	
J·J	James	Jones.	NICOLSON	J.	Nicolson (Cork).	RT		
IP			JA			WS		
GW			WK	Wm.	Keene.	S·R	Saml.	Reily (Cork).
CC	Christr.	Clarke ?	JJ	James	Jones ?	H&H	Hopper & Hannay.	
I·W	Jacob	West.	IN			JC		
I·M			LM	La'rence Martin (Kilkenny).		TH	Thos.	Hunt ?
L·A			C·G			GN	George Nangle.	
						PF		

DUBLIN GOLDSMITHS' MARKS, 1765 TO 1812—

MARK.	NAME.	MARK.	NAME.	MARK.	NAME.
LH		WW		FB	Fredk. Buck.
W·H	Will. Hughes?	BT	Benjn. Tait.	ST	Samuel Taylor.
CK		PW	Peter Wingfield.	RC	Randall Cashell?
WG	Will. Gethin?	TA	Thos. Adams.	W·H	Wm. Hannay?
I·T	John Tweedie?	HM		I·C	
R·S	Robt. O'Shaughnessy (Limerick).	TR	Thos. Rourke.	ZL	John Lloyd.
I·H	James Hewitt?	DP		E&B	
IW	John West?	RC	Randall Cashell?	WF	Will French.
JR	J'n'th'n Robinson?	GIBSON	Joseph Gibson (Cork).	W·W	Will Ward.
SLY	Thos. Sly.	GR		AM	Arthur Murphy.
G&P·W		JJ	Joseph Johnson.	W·L	
MS		JC	James Campbell?	R·D	
TE		D·P		BP	
I·M	James Mills?	ID	Isaac Davis?	J·T	
WL	Wm. Law?	MW&S	Matt. West & Son.	I·G	
W·H	Will. Hamey?	I·C	Jas. Connor?	WH	
T·B	Thos. Baker?	B·B		IB	John Bolland?
WF		SINGLETON	—— Singleton.	TSW	
F·R		T·T	Thomas Townsend.		

THE FOLLOWING MARKS, WHICH ARE STAMPED ON A COPPER-PLATE OF LATER DATE, RANGE FROM ABOUT 1813 TO ABOUT 1850.

MARK.	NAME.	MARK.	NAME	MARK.	NAME.
WG		GF		LK	
TK JF		TT		GW WM	
TK		CM		SA	
HL	Henry Lazarus.	IH		JT	John Townsend.
DM		WHT	Wm. H. Townsend.	W·N	Wm. Nelson.
S&W		SB	S. Bergin.	K&F	
J·M &E·M		J·MOORE	James Moore.	RE	
IM	J. Moore.	WC		TO	
BOYLE	—— Boyle.	FM&S		GRAYS	—— Grays.
EM	Edwd. Murphy.	LEE		PG	
		RWS	R. W. Smith.	IS	

DATE.	MARKS.	MAKER'S NAME.	DATE.	MARKS.	MAKER'S NAME.
1662		James Ridge.	1709		Adam Billon.
1663		(Not identified).	1702-29		George Brumley.
1670		Walter Burnett.	1709		John Wigmore.(?)
1673		James Ridge.	1710		Wm. Clarke.
1679		Richard Smart.	,,		Robert Goble.
1680		Samuel Pantaine.	1710-20		John Rickotts
,,		Walter Burnett.	1712		Robert Goble.
,,		(Both marks repeated).	1715-25		Robert Goble, Junr
,,		John Hawkins.	,,		,, ,,
1691		Do. do.	,,		William Clarke
1683		Robert Goble.	,,		,, ,,
1686		Do. do.	1719		Caleb Rotheram
1690		Do. do.	,,		William Clarke.
1692		Caleb Webb.	1720		,, ,,
,,		Robert Goble.	,,		Bernald Baldwin.
1696		Do. do.	,,		
,,		Walter Burnett.	1720-30		
,,		Robert Goble.	,,		} Wm. Newenham
,,		Do. do.	,,		Edward Dunsterfield.
1697		Charles Bekegle.	1720-34		William Newenham
1700		Robert Goble.	,,		,, ,,
,,		Anthony Semirot.	,,		(Not identified—perhaps not Cork).
1705		Robert Goble.	1722		... ...
1709		William Clarke.			

DATE.	MARKS.	MAKER'S NAME.
1724	THO·LILLY STERLING	} Thomas Lilly.
1725-6	R·M STERLING	Reuben Millard.
1730	WN STERLING	Wm. Newenham.
,,	WN STERLING	,, ,,
1730-40	W*B STERLING	William Bennett.
,,	I H STERLING I H	John Harding ?
,,	CR STERLING CR	Caleb Rotheram.
,,	STERLING I·H	John Harding ?
,,	R·G	Robt. Goble, jr. ?
,,	CP CP CP	Christr. Parker.
1720-37	W·MARTIN	William Martin.
,,	W·MARTIN	Do. do.
,,	W·M	Do. do.
,,	R*M	Reuben Millard.
1730-40	WB STERLING WB	William Bennett or Wm. Bentley.
1731	T.BULL	Thomas Bull.
1740	G·H STERLING	George Hodder.
,,	G·H G·H	Do. do.
,,	WB WB	William Bennett or Wm. Bentley.
1740-50	RA	,, ,,,
,,	A·S STERLING	} Anthony Semirot.
1745-70	STARLING G·H	George Hodder.
,,	GH STERLING GH	Do. do.
,,	STARLING GH	} Do. do.
,,	G*H GH GH G·H	Do. do.

DATE.	MARKS.	MAKER'S NAME.
C. 1750	STERLING SB	} Stephen Broughton.
1750-70	R·P STERLING	Robt. Potter.
,,	II I·IRISH II	John Irish.
,,	IH STERLING	Do. do. (?)
1757-80	MD DERMOTT	Michael McDermott.
,,	MD STER	Do. do.
,,	MD STERLING MD	Do. do.
,,	WR ,,	William Reynolds.
,,	WR ,,	Do. do.
,,	WR	Do. do.
,,	WR I STER·N.	Do. do.
,,	,, STERLING	Do. do.
,,	WR	Do. do.
,,	WR WR	Do. do.
,,	WR WR	Do. do.
,,	McD STERLING	Michael McDermott.
,,	MD ,,	Do. do.
1760	L·R STARLING L·R	... ...
,,	IA STERLING IA	... ...
1760-80	WALSH SW STERLING	} Stephen Walsh.
,,	C·B STERLING	Croker Barrington.
,,	SW WALSH STERLING	} Stephen Walsh.
,,	SW STERLING	Do. do.
,,	WALSH STERLING	} Do. do.
,,	SW WALSH STERLING	Do. do.
,,	SW ,,	Do. do.
,,	SM ,,	Stephen Mackrill.

DATE.	MARKS.	MAKER'S NAME.
1760-80	STERLING DMC	} Daniel McCarthy?
,,	DMC STER	Do. do.
,,	STARLING C·B	Croker Barrington.
,,	C·B DOLLAR	Do. do.
1760-85	IH STERLING	John Hillery
1765-95	CT ,, CT	Carden Terry.
1770	IRH STER	John Irish.
,,	TA STERLING TA	... ...
,,	McD Sterling	Michael McDermott.
,,	MD STERLING	Do. do.
1770-88	STER JW STER	} John Whitney (free 1775).
1770-99	IN STERLING	John Nicolson.
,,	IN STERLING	Do. do.
,,	IN ,,	Do. do.
,,	,, NICOLSON	Do. do.
1777-1820	PW STERLING	Peter Wills.
1780	C·T STERLING	Carden Terry.
,,	IH STERLING IH	John Humphreys
,,	I·H ,,	Do. do.
,,	JK STERLING	Joseph Kinselagh.
,,	I·H STERLING	John Hillery.
,,	CT STERLING	Carden Terry.
,,	SC STERLING	(Not identified.)
,,	SR ,,	Samuel Reily.
,,	JSN ,,	Jno. & Sam. Nicolson.
,,	TC STIRLING	} Thomas Cumming.

DATE.	MARKS.	MAKER'S NAME.
1770-80	WM STERG	W. Morrisey.
1770-99	NICOLSON STERLING	John Nicolson.
1777-1810	S·R STERLING	Samuel Reily.
,,	S·R STERLING	Do. do.
,,	SR STERLG	Do. do.
,,	REILY STERLING	Do. do.
1783-95	W·ROE STERLING	} William Roe.
,,	TG STERLING TG	... ...
1786-95	TH STERLING	Thos. Harman.
1787-95	TC STERLG TC	Tim. Conway.
1787	TD STERLING	Thomas Donnallan.
1787-95	JS ,,	John Sheehan.
,,	IG STERLING	Joseph Gibson.
1787-99	R·S STERLING	Richard Stevens.
,,	R·S STERLING	Do. do.
,,	I·S ,, I·S	John Sheehan.
,,	STERLING SHEEHAN	Do. do.
,,	SHEEHAN STERG	Do. do.
,,	SHEEHAN STERLING	} Do. do.
,,	R·S STERLING	} Richard Stevens.
1790-1800	JMcN STERLING	} (Not identified.)
,,	RI STERLING	} Do. do.
1795	WT STERL?	Wm. Teulon.
,,	W·T STERLING	Do. do.
,,	WT STERLING	Do. do.
,,	,, STERL?	Do. do.

DATE.	MARKS.	MAKER'S NAME.
1795		John Supple.
,,	WT / STERLING	William Teulon.
,,	WT STERLING	Do. do.
,,	HSM STERLING	(Not identified.)
,,	WT ,,	William Teulon.
,,	TJB STERLING	(Not identified.)
1791	IW ,,	John Warner
1780-99	,, STIRLING	Do. do.
1795	I.W STERLING	John Williams.
,,	I·W STER	James Warner.
,,	I·W STERLING	Do. do.
,,	I·W STERLG	Do. do.
,,	STERLING / TOLLAND / STERLING	—— Tolland.
1796	I·H STERLING	James Heyland.
,,	RD STERLING	... ...
,,	HEYLAND / STERLING	} James Heyland.
,,	JK STERLING	Jos. Kinselagh.
,,	JMd	... ...' ...
1800	IT TOLEKEN	John Toleken.
,,	TWM STERLING	(Not identified.)
1800-20	GIBSON / STERLING / GIBSON	Joseph Gibson.
,,	WHELPLEY STERLING	John Whelpley.
,,	,, WHELPLY	Do. do.
,,	JC ,, WHELPLY	Do. do.

DATE.	MARKS.	MAKER'S NAME.
1800-20	GIBSON STERLING	Joseph Gibson.
,,	HEYLAND ,,	William Heyland.
,,	,, TOLEKEN	John Toleken.
1795 / 1807	T&W ,,	{ Carden Terry & / John Williams. }
1805	SG STIRLING	Samuel Green.
1805-14	SG / STERLING / SG	} Do. do.
,,	C·T / & / I·W STERLING	Terry & Williams.
,,	T.MONTJOY ,,	Thomas Montjoy.
,,	IN / NN ,,	John & / Nicholas } Nicolson.
1807-21	C·T / I·W STERLING	{ Carden Terry & / Jane Williams. }
1808-20	CORBETT STERLING	Daniel Corbett.
1809-30	JS STERLING	James Salter.
,,	R·G ,,	Richard Garde.
1810	T·MONTJOY STERLING	Thos. Montjoy.
,,	CONWAY / STERLING	} James Conway.
,,	IE STERLING	John Egan.
,,	P·W STERLING	Peter Wills.
1810-20	WS STERLING	—— Steele?
,,	1 SOLOMON STERLING	Isaac Solomon.
,,	IS STERLING	John Seymour.
,,	I·SOLOMON ,,	Isaac Solomon.
,,	F·S ,,	(Not identified.)
,,	PG STERLING	Phineas Garde.
1810-40	IS ,,	{ Isaac Solomon, or / John Seymour.' }
1812	GARDE STERLING	Phineas Garde.
1820	SEYMOUR STERLING	John Seymour.
1820-40	KM ,,	Kean Mahony.
,,	EH ,,	Edward Hawkesworth.
1824	O BRIEN STERLING	Francis O'Brien'
,,	MAHONY / STERLING	} Kean Mahony.
1838	M&B STERLING	(Not identified.)

YOUGHAL

DATE (ABOUT).	MARKS.	MAKER'S NAME.
1620		Morrish Lawless.
„		John Sharpe.
1644		John Green.
1650		Do. do.
1683		Bartholomew Fallon of Galway.
1702		(*Not identified*, but possibly Bartholomew Fallon as above.)
1712		Edward Gillett.
1720	„	Austin Beere.

BELFAST

APPROXIMATE DATE.	MARKS.	MAKER'S NAME.
1780		... ...
„		... ...
1790		*Matthew Bellew ?
1800		... ...
„		... ...

GALWAY

DATE (ABOUT).	MARKS.	MAKER'S NAME.
1648		R. Joyes, sen. (?)
1666-1684		... ...
1695		Richard Joyes.
1700		Do. do.
„		... ...
„		... ...
1720		... ...
1725		Richard Joyes.
1730		Mark Fallon.
„		Do. do.
1743-5		... ...

DATE. (ABOUT).	MARKS.	MAKER'S NAME.	DATE (ABOUT).	MARKS.	MAKER'S NAME.
1710		J. Buck, senr. (?)	1784		Patrick Connell.
1718		Adam Buck.	,,		• Do. do.
1730-40		} Jonathan Buck. (free 1731)	,,		Maurice Fitzgerald.
,,		} Do. do.	,,		Do. do.
1730-62		Do. do.	,,		Do. do.
,,		Do. do.	,,		Thomas Burke.
,,		Do. do.	,,		Do. do.
,,		} Do. do.	,,		Do. do.
1730-75		Joseph Johns.	,,		Do. do.
,,		Do. do.	,,		Do. do.
,,		Do. do.	,,		Matt. Walsh.
1749-50		? Joseph Johns.	,,		Do. do.
1750		} Samuel Johns.	1786		Daniel Lysaght.
1760-85		George Moore.	,,		Do. do.
,,		Do. do.	,,		Do. do.
1768-80		Garret Fitzgerald.	1798		Wm. Ward.
1770		George Moore.	1800		Wm. Fitzgerald.
1780		(Not identified.)	,,		Do. do.
,,		Do. do.	,,		Robt. O'Shaughnessy.
1784		Patrick Connell.	,,		Do. do.
,,		Do. do.	,,		Will. Ward.
			,,		Do. do.
			,,		... ...
			1810-20		Samuel Purdon.
			,,		Do. do.
			1800-13		John Purcell.

UNASCRIBED IRISH PROVINCIAL MARKS.

UNASCRIBED MARKS

DATE (ABOUT).	MARKS.	DATE (ABOUT).	MARKS.
1611		1574	
1650		c.1590	
1652		1660	
1666		1680	
1673		"	
1680		1700	
"		"	
1682		1730	
"		1740-50	
1690		"	
1700		1770	
1705		1780	
1710		1800	
"			
1720			
1720-40			
1726			
"			
1750			
1756			
1760			
"			
1780			
"			
"			

INDEX
ENGLISH, SCOTTISH AND IRISH MARKS

Name of Firm.	Maker's Marks.	Date.
Ashforth G. & Co. ...		1784
Fox T. & Co.	FOX.PROCTOR PASMORE.& Cº	1784
Green W. & Co.	W.GREEN & Cº	1784
Holy D.. Wilkinson & Co.	DANᵗ HOLY WILKINSON & Cº	1784
Law T. & Co. ..., ...	THOˢ LAW & Cº	1784
Parsons J. & Co.	IOHN PARSONS & Cº	1784
Smith N. & Co.	N·SMITH & Cº	1784
Staniforth, Parkin & Co.	STANIFORTH PARKIN & Cº	1784
Sykes & Co.	SYKES & Cº	1784
Tudor, Leader & Nichol-son	TUDOR & Cº	1784
Boulton M. & Co. ...	BOULTON	1784
Dixon T. & Co.	DIXON & Cº	1784
Holland H. & Co. ...	HOLLAND & Cº	1784
Moore J.	Moore MOORE §	1784
Smith & Co.	SMITH & Cº	1784

Name of Firm.	Maker's Marks.	Date.
Beldon, Hoyland & Co. ...		1785
Brittain, Wilkinson & Brownill		1785
Deakin, Smith & Co. ...		1785
Love J. & Co. ... ... (Love, Silverside, Darby & Co.)		1785
Morton R. & Co. ...		1785
Roberts, Cadman & Co.		1785
Roberts J. & S.		1786
Sutcliffe R. & Co. ...		1786
Bingley W.		1787
Madin F. & Co.		1788
Jervis W.		1789
Colmore S.		1790
Goodwin E.		1794
Watson, Fenton & Bradbury		1795
Froggatt, Coldwell & Lean		1797
Green J. & Co.		1799
Goodman, Gainsford & Fairbairn		1800
Ellerby W		1803
Garnett W.		1803
Holy D., Parker & Co. ...		1804

Name of Firm.	Maker's Marks.	Date.
Newbould W. & Son ...		1804
Drabble I. & Co. (...		1805
Coldwell W. ... (...		1806
Hill D. & Co.		1806
Law J. & Son		1807
Butts T.		1807
Green J.		1807
Hutton W.		1807
Law R.		1807
Linwood J.		1807
Linwood W.		1807
Meredith H.		1807
Peake		1807
Ryland W & Son ...		1807
Scot W		1807
Silkirk W		1807
Thomason E. & Dowler...		1807
Tonks Samuel		1807

Name of Firm.	Maker's Marks.	Date.
Waterhouse & Co. ...		1807
Wilmore Joseph ...		1807
Gainsford R.		1808
Hatfield A.		1808
Banister W.		1808
Gibbs G.		1808
Hipkiss J.		1808
Horton D.		1808
Lea A. C.		1808
Linwood M & Sons ...		1808
Nicholds J		1808
Beldon G.		1809
Wright J. & Fairbairn G.		1809
Cheston T		1809
Harrison J		1809
Hipwood W		1809
Horton J		1809
Silk R.		1809
Howard S. & T.		1809
Smith, Tate, Nicholson & Hoult		1810
Dunn G B		1810

Name of Firm.	Maker's Marks.	Date.
Hanson M.		1810
Pimley S.		1810
Creswick T. & J. ,...		1811
Stot B.		1811
Watson, Pass & Co. (late J. Watson)		1811
Lees G.		1811
Pearson R.		1811
White J. (White & Allgood)		1811
Kirkby S.		1812
Allgood J		1812
Allport E		1812
Gilbert J		1812
Hinks J.		1812
Johnson J		1812
Small T		1812
Smith W		1812
Younge S. & C & Co. ...		1813
Thomas S.		1813
Tyndall J		1813
Best H.		1814
Cracknall J.		1814
Jordan T.		1814

Name of Firm.	Maker's Marks.	Date.
Woodward W.		1814
Lilly John	LILLY	1815
Best & Wastidge ...	BEST	1816
Ashley	ASHLEY	1816
Davis J.	DAVIS	1816
Evans S.	S·EVANS	1816
Freeth H.	FREETH / HF	1816
Harwood T.		1816
Lilly Joseph	JOSH LILLY	1816
Turley S.	S·TURLEY	1816
Cope C. G.	COPE	1817
Pemberton & Mitchell ...	PEM BER TON	1817
Shephard J.	SHEP-HARD	1817
Markland W.	W·MARKLAND	1818
Corn J. & J. Sheppard...	CORN & Co	1819
Rogers J.	ROGERS	1819
Hall W.	HALL / §	1820
Moore F.	F·MOORE	1820
Turton J.	TUR TON.	1820

Name of Firm.	Maker's Marks.	Date.
Blagden, Hodgson & Co.		1821
Holy D. & G. ..., ...	HOLY S & Co SHEFFIELD	1821
Needham C.	C NEEDHAM MAKER SHEFFIELD	1821
Sansom T. & Sons	SAN SOM	1821
Child T.	CHILD	1821
Smith I.	SMITH	1821
Worton S.	S WORTON	1821
Rodgers J. & Sons	ROD GERS	1822
Bradshaw J.		1822
Briggs W.		1823
Harrison G.	GH / GH F	1823
Smallwood J.		1823
Causer J. F.	CAUSER	1824
Jones	JONES	1824
Tonks & Co.	TONKS	1824
Roberts, Smith & Co. ...		1828
Smith J. & Son	SMI TH	1828
Askew	A SKEW MAKER NOTTINGHAM.	1828
Hall Henry		1829
Hobday J.	Hob day / Hob day	1829
Watson J. & Son ...		1830

Name of Firm.	Maker's Marks.	Date.
Bishop Thomas... ...		1830
Hutton W.	Hutton Sheffield	1831
Atkin Henry	H A S	1833
Waterhouse I. & I. & Co.	I & I W & Co	1833
Watson W. ..., ...	W WATSON MAKER SHEFFIELD	1833
Dixon J. & Sons	D S / D S / Dixon J / G R DIXON'S IMPERIAL / DIXON SHEFFIELD	1835
Smith J.	JOSEPHUS SMITH	1836
Waterhouse, Hatfield & Co.		1836
Wilkinson H. & Co. ...		1836
Hutton W.	Hutton Hutton	1837
Hutton W'.	H & S	1839
Prime J.	PS / S	1839
Walker, Knowles & Co.		1840
Waterhouse George & Co.	W & Co S	1842
Smith, Sissons & Co. ...		1848
Padley, Parkin & Co. ...		1849

Name of Firm.	Maker's Marks.	Date.
Hutton W.	W H S	1849
Mappin Bros.	MAP BROS	1850
Oldham T.	OLDHAM MAKER NOTTINGHAM	1860
Roberts & Briggs ...	R & B	1860

MISCELLANEOUS MARKS WHICH HAVE NOT BEEN TRACED.

Maker's Marks.	Approximate date of manufacture.
IK	1780-1790
BEST PLATE	1790
DEVER	1790
ALWH GA IH EE	1790-1800
Do.	1790-1800
R J E WESSON MIDLETON & Co	1800-1810
W. B. PINE 352 STRAND	1815-1825
	1815 1825
WILSON	1815-1825
GILBERT LONDON	1840
REGISTERED BY MAPPLE & MELON JAN Y 27 1840 N° 443	1840
R W & W	1840
PAT ENT / PAT ENT	1840
	1850
SALT	1850
	1850
GRC	1850

One date indicates the period, two dates the birth and death.

A

ARON, JOSEPH
Philadelphia, Pa. 1798

BBOTT, JOHN W.
Portsmouth, N.H. 1839   `J.ABBOTT`

CKERMAN, DAVID
New York, N.Y. 1818

CKLEY, FRANCIS M.
New York, N.Y. 1797   `F.ACKLEY`

CTON, GEORGE
New York, N.Y. 1795

DAM, I.
Alexandria, Va. 1800   `JA` `JA` `J.Adam` `I.ADAM`

DAM, JOHN B.
New Orleans, La. 1822

DAM, JOHN
Alexandria, Va. 1829

ADAMS, JONATHAN
Philadelphia, Pa. 1785   `I.ADAM` `J.Adas`

ADAMS, PYGAN
New London, Conn. ..1712-1776   `P·A` `PA` `PA`

ADAMS, WM. L.
New York, N.Y. 1842   `W.ADAMS` `NEWYORK`

ADDISON, GEORGE M.
Baltimore, Md. 1804

ADGATE, WM.
Norwich, Conn. 1767

ADRIANCE, E.
St. Louis, Mo. 1820   `E.ADRIANCE` `ST.LOUIS`

AIKEN, GEORGE
Baltimore, Md. 1765-1832   `G·A` `G.Aiken` `G.Aiken` `G.Aiken` `AIKEN` `G.AIKEN`

AINSWORTH, MICHAEL
Fredricksburg Co., Va. 1755

AITKEN, JOHN
Philadelphia, Pa. 1785   `J.Ritken` `J.AITKEN`

AITKINS, W.
Baltimore, Md. 1802

AKIN, JOHN B.
Danville, Ky. 1850   JOHN B. AKIN DANVILLE KY

ALDIS, CHARLES
New York, N.Y. 1814   `C.ALDIS`

ALEXANDER, A.
Philadelphia, Pa. 1802

ALEXANDER, S. & SIMMONS, A.
Philadelphia, Pa. 1800

ALEXANDER, SAMUEL
Philadelphia, Pa. 1808   `S·ALEXANDER`

ALFORD, SAMUEL
Philadelphia, Pa. 1840

ALFORD, THOMAS
Philadelphia, Pa. 1762

ALLCOCK & ALLEN
New York, N.Y. 1820   `ALLCOCK&ALLEN`

ALLEN, CHARLES
Boston, Mass. 1760   `C·ALLEN`

ALLEN & EDWARDS
Boston, Mass. 1700   `IA` `IE`

ALLEN, JAMES
Philadelphia, Pa. 1720

ALLEN, JOEL
Middletown, Conn. ...,....1787

ALLEN, JOHN
Philadelphia, Pa. 1814   `IA` `IA` `IA`

ALLEN, JOHN
Boston, Mass. ...,.....1691-1760

ALLEN, RICHARD
Philadelphia, Pa. 1816

ALLEN, ROBERT
Philadelphia, Pa. ...,.....1776

ALLEN, THOMAS
Boston, Mass. ...,......1758

ALLISON, PETER
New York, N.Y. 1791

ALSTYNE, JEROMIMUS
New York, N.Y. 1787   `J.Alstyne` `IA` `IA`

ANDERSON, WM.
New York, N.Y. 1746   `WA` `WA`

ANDRAS & CO.
New York, N.Y. 1800   `ANDRAS&CO`

ANDRAS & RICHARD
New York, N.Y. 1797   `A&R`

ANDRAS, WM.
New York, N.Y 1795   `ANDRAS`

ANDREAS, ABRAHAM
Bethlehem, Pa. 1780

ANDREW, JOHN
Salem, Mass. 1747-1791   `I·ANDREW`

ANDREWS, ABRAHAM
Philadelphia, Pa. ...... .1795

ANDREWS, H.
Boston, Mass. 1830

ANDREWS, HENRY
Philadelphia, Pa. 1795   `HA`

ANDREWS, JEREMIAH
Philadelphia, Pa. 1776

ANDREWS, JOSEPH
Norfolk, Va. 1800   `J·ANDREWS` `I·ANDREWS` `NORFOLK` `J.Andrews`

ANDREWS, JR.
Philadelphia, Pa. ..... .1746

ANTHONY, ISAAC
Newport, R. I.
Swansea, Mass.
............1690-1773   `IA`

ANTHONY, J.
Philadelphia, Pa. 1770

ANTHONY, JOSEPH
Philadelphia, Pa. 1783   `J.A` `J·A`

ANTHONY, JOSEPH, JR.
Philadelphia, Pa. 1783-1814

ANTHONY, JOSEPH & SONS
Philadelphia, Pa. 1810

ANTHONY, L. D.
Providence, R. I. 1805

ANTHONY, M. H. & T.
Philadelphia, Pa. 1814

ANTHONY, MICHAEL H.
Philadelphia, Pa. 1810

ANTHONY, THOMAS
Philadelphia, Pa. 1810

ANTHONY, WM.
New York, N. Y. 1800

ANWYL, KENRICK
Baltimore, Md. 1780

APPLETON, GEORGE B.
New York, N. Y. 1820

ARCHIE, JOHN
New York, N. Y. 1759

ARMS, T. N.
Albany, New York 1849

ARMSTRONG, ALLEN
Philadelphia, Pa. 1806

ARMSTRONG, JOHN
Philadelphia, Pa. 1810

ARMSTRONG, WM.
Philadelphia, Pa. 1750

ARNOLD, THOMAS
Newport, R. I. 1739-1828

ARNOLD, THOMAS
Philadelphia, Pa. 1760

ASHMEAD, WM.
Philadelphia, Pa. 1797

ATHERTON, NATHAN
Philadelphia, Pa. 1825

ATKINSON, ISAAC
Philadelphia, Pa. 1825

ATLEE, CHARLES
Philadelphia, Pa. 1837

ATTERBURY, J.
New Haven, Conn. 1799

AUSTEN, DAVID
Philadelphia, Pa. 1837

AUSTIN, BENJAMIN
Portsmouth, N. H. 1775

AUSTIN & BOYER
Boston, Mass. 1770

AUSTIN, EBENEZER
Hartford, Conn. 1782

AUSTIN, EBENEZER J.
Boston, Mass. 1790

AUSTIN, JAMES
Charlestown, Mass. 1780

AUSTIN, JOHN
Philadelphia, Pa. 1802

AUSTIN, JOSEPH
Hartford, Conn. 1740

AUSTIN, JOSIAH
Charlestown, Mass. ...1718-1780

AUSTIN, NATHANIEL
Boston, Mass. 1734-1818

AVERY, JOHN
Preston, Conn. 1732-1794

AVERY, JOHN, JR.
Preston, Conn. 1776

AVERY, ROBERT STAUNTON
Preston, Conn. 1792

AVERY, SAMUEL
Preston, Conn. 1760-1836

AVERY, WM.
Preston, Conn. 1786

AVERY, WILLIS & BILLIS
Salisbury, N. Y. 1820

AYRES, S.
Lexington, Ky. 1805

AYRES, T.
Unknown 1800

B

BABCOCK, SAMUEL
Middletown, Conn. 1788-1857

BACALL, THOMAS
Boston, Mass. 1836

BACHMAN, A.
New York, N. Y. 1848

BACKUS, DELUCINE
New York, N. Y. 1792

BAIELLE, LEWIS
Baltimore, Md. 1799

BAILEY, BENJAMIN
Boston, Mass. 1820

BAILEY, B. M.
Ludlow, Vt. 1824-1913

BAILEY & CO.
Philadelphia, Pa. 1850

BAILEY, EDWARD
Baltimore, Md. 1779

BAILEY, E. E. & S. C.
Portland, Me. 1825

BAILEY, HENRY
Boston, Mass. 1780

BAILEY, JOHN
New York, N. Y. 1762

BAILEY & KITCHEN
Philadelphia, Pa. 1853

BAILEY, LORING Hingham, Mass. 1780	`LB`
BAILEY, ROBERT H. Woodstock, Vt. 1825	`R.H.BAILEY`
BAILEY, SIMEON A. New York, N.Y. 1789	
BAILEY, JOHN Philadelphia, Pa. 1762	
BAILY, WM. New York, N.Y. 1820	`WBAILY`
BAKER Boston, Mass. 1765	
BAKER, ANSON New York, N.Y. 1821	
BAKER, E. New York, N.Y. 1740-1790	`E.BAKER`
BAKER, GEORGE Providence, R. I. 1825	`G.BAKER` `G.BAKER`
BAKER, S. New York, N.Y. 1787-1858	`S.BAKER` `C`
BALCH, EBENEZER Hartford, Conn. 1744	`E.BALCH`
BALCH & FRYER Albany, N.Y. 1784	
BALDWIN & BAKER Providence, R. I. 1817	
BALDWIN & CO. Newark, N.J. 1830	`BALDWIN&CO` `NEWARK`
BALDWIN, EBENEZER Hartford, Conn. 1723-1808	`BALDWIN` `BALDWIN.`
BALDWIN, JABEZ Boston, Mass. 1808	`BALDWIN`
BALDWIN, J. C. Boston, Mass. 1815	`JCBALDWIN`
BALDWIN, JEDEDIAH Portsmouth, N. H. 1793	`J.BALDWIN`
BALDWIN & JONES Boston, Mass. 1813	`BALDWIN & JONES` `BALDWIN & JONES`
BALDWIN, STANLEY-S New York, N.Y. 1820	`STANLEY.S.BALDWIN`
BALL, BLACK & CO. New York, N. Y. 1850	`BALL,BLACK&CO`
BALL & HEALD Baltimore, Md. 1810	`BALL&HEALD`
BALL, HENRY New York, N.Y. 1833	
BALL, JOHN Boston, Mass. 1765	`JOHN BALL.` `JOHN BALL.` `J·BALL`
BALL, S. S. Boston, Mass. 1838	
BALL, THOMPKINS & BLACK New York, N.Y. 1839	`BALL, TOMPKINS & BLACK`
BALL, TRUE M. Boston, Mass. 1815-1890	`W.B` `WBALL` `W·BALL` `W.BALL`
BALL, W. Baltimore, Md. 1802	
BALL, WM. Philadelphia, Pa. 1752	`WB` `W.Ball` `BALL` `BALL` `W·BALL` `WBALL`
BANCKER, ADRIEN New York, N. Y. 1703-1772	`AB` `AB`
BANGS, JOHN Cincinnati, O. 1825	
BARBERET, THEON New Orleans, La. 1822	
BARBIER, PETER Philadelphia, Pa. 1823	
BARD, CONRAD Philadelphia, Pa. 1825	`C.BARD 205 ARCH ST.`
BARD, C. & SON Philadelphia, Pa. 1850	
BARD & HOFFMAN Philadelphia, Pa. 1837	
BARD, J. Philadelphia, Pa. 1800	
BARD & LAMONT Philadelphia, Pa. 1841	`BARD & LAMONT`
BARDEER, CONNARD Philadelphia, Pa. 1831	
BARDICK, GEORGE Philadelphia, Pa. 1790	`G·B`
BARDICK, JOHN Philadelphia, Pa. 1805	
BARDON, STEPHEN Philadelphia, Pa. 1785	
BARIA, WM. New York, N.Y. 1805	
BARNES, ABRAHAM Boston, Mass. 1716	
BARRET, JAMES Norwich, Conn. 1717	
BARRETT, JAMES New York, N.Y. 1805	`J·B`
BARRETT, S. Nantucket, Mass. 1800	★ `S·BARRETT` ★
BARRIER, DAVID Baltimore, Md. 1810	`BARRIER`
BARRINGTON & DAVENPORT Philadelphia, Pa. 1806	`B&D`
BARROWS, JAMES MADISON Tolland, Conn. 1809	`J.M.BARROWS`
BARRY, STANDISH Baltimore, Md. 1763-1844	`SB` `SB` `SB` `BARRY` `Standish` `Barry` `Standish` `Barry` `Barry` `1792`
BARTHOLOMEW, JOSEPH Philadelphia, Pa. 1833	

BARTHOLOMEW, LE ROUX
New York, N. Y. .....1688-1713 — BR BR

BARTHOLOMEW, ROSWELL
Hartford, Conn. ....1781-1830 — RB

BARTLETT, EDWARD
Philadelphia, Pa. 1833

BARTLETT, NATHANIEL
Concord, Mass. ....1760 — N·BARTLETT

BARTLETT, SAMUEL
Boston, Mass. ....1750-1821 — S.B S·BARTLETT

BARTON, ERASTUS
New York, N. Y. 1810

BARTON, ERASTUS & CO.
New York, N. Y. ....1821 — E.B&CO

BARTRAM, WM.
Philadelphia, Pa. 1769

BASSET, FRANCIS
New York, N. Y. ....1774 — BASSETT

BATCHELLOR, N.
New York, N. Y. 1825

BATTELS, A. T.
Utica, N. Y. ....1847 — A.T·BATTELS UTICA

BAY, A. S.
New York, N. Y. 1786

BAYLEY, ALEXANDER
New York, N. Y. 1790

BAYLEY & DOUGLAS
New York, N. Y. ....1789 — DB&AD

BAYLEY, S. & A.
New York, N. Y. 1790

BAYLEY, S. H.
New York, N. Y. 1790

BAYLEY, SIMON A.
New York, N. Y. ....1789 — BAYLEY BAYLEY

BAYLY, JOHN
Philadelphia, Pa. 1755

BAYSSET, JOSEPH
New Orleans, La. 1822

BEACH, A.
Hartford, Conn. ....1823 — A.BEACH

BEACH, ISAAC
New Milford, Conn. 1788

BEACH, IVES & CO.
New York, N. Y. 1820

BEACH, MILES
Litchfield, Conn. ...1743-1828 — MB M·B BEACH

BEACH & SANFORD
Hartford, Conn. ....1785-1788 — B&S B&S

BEACH & WARD
Hartford, Conn. .....1789-1795 — B&W

BEAL, CALEB
Boston, Mass. ....1796 — BEAL

BEAM, JACOB C.
Philadelphia, Pa. 1818

BEAUVAIS, RENO
St. Louis, Mo. ....1850 — R.BEAUVAIS ST.LOUIS

BECHAM
Unknown ....c 1740 — BECHAM

BECK, THOMAS
Philadelphia, Pa. 1773

BECKER, FREDERICK
New York, N. Y. 1736

BECKER, PHILIP
Lancaster, Pa. 1764

BEDFORD, JOHN
Fishkill, N. Y. ....1781 — J·Bedford J·Bedfor

BEEBE, J. W. & CO.
New York, N. Y. ....1844 — J.W.BEEBE J.W.BEEBE & C

BEEBE, JAMES W.
New York, N. Y. 1835

BEEBE, STANTON
Providence, R. I. 1824

BEEBE, WILLIAM
New York, N. Y. ....1850 — BEEBE

BEECHER, CLEMENT
Berlin, Conn. ....1778-1869 — CB CB

BEECHER, C. & CO.
Meriden, Conn. 1820

BELIN, LEWIS
Philadelphia, Pa. 1818

BELKNAP, SAMUEL
Boston, Mass. 1789

BELLIARD, FRANCOIS
New Orleans, La. 1822

BELLONI, LOUIS J.
New York, N. Y. 1835

BELLONI, & DURANDEAU
New York, N. Y. 1835

BENEDICT, A. C.
New York, N. Y. ....1840 — A.C.BENEDICT.

BENEDICT, J.
New York, N. Y. 1830

BENEDICT & SON
New York, N. Y. 1840

BENEDICT & SQUIRE
New York, N. Y. ....1825 — BENEDICT & SQUIRE

BENJAMIN, BARZILLAI
New Haven, Conn. ....1799 — BB B.BENJAMIN

BENJAMIN, BENJAMIN
New York, N. Y. ....1825 — B.B B.BENJAMIN

BENJAMIN, EVERERD
New Haven, Conn. ....1807-1874 — E·BENJAMIN

BENJAMIN, JOHN
Stratford, Conn. .....1731-1796 — I·B I·B

BENJAMIN, SAMUEL C.
New Haven, Conn.   1819

BENJAMIN, SOLOMON
Baltimore, Md.   1817

BENNET, JAMES
New York, N.Y.   1773

BENNETT, JACOB
Philadelphia, Pa.   1839

BENTLEY, THOMAS
Boston, Mass.   1762-1800

BENTSON, PETER
Philadelphia, Pa.   1718

BERARD, ANDREW
Philadelphia, Pa.   1797

BERARD, E.
Philadelphia, Pa.   1800

BERKENBUSH, CHAS. H.
New York, N.Y.   1825

BERRY, WM.
New York, N.Y.   1805

BESLEY, THAUVET
New York, N.Y.   1727

BESSELIEVRE, THOMAS
Philadelphia, Pa.   1831

BEST, JOSEPH
Philadelphia, Pa.   1723

BEVAN, RICHARD
Baltimore, Md.   1804

BERSHING, HENRY
Hagerstown, Md.   1815

BIGELOW & BROS.
Boston, Mass.   . , . , ... 1840

BIGELOW BROS. & KENNARD
Boston, Mass.   1845

BIGELOW, JOHN
Boston, Mass.   1830

BIGGS, JOSEPH
New York, N.Y.   . . . 1830

BIGOTUT, S.
New York, N.Y.   1800

BIJOTAL, SILVIAN A.
New York, N.Y.   1795

BILLING, A.
Troy, N.Y.   1780

BILLINGS, A.
Preston, Conn.   1780

BILLINGS, DANIEL
Preston, Conn.   . . . 1795

BILLON, CHARLES
St. Louis, Mo.   . . . 1821

BINGHAM, JOHN
Newark, N.J.   1664

BINNEAU, THEODORE
Philadelphia, Pa.   1820

BIRD, CONARD
Philadelphia, Pa.   1831

BISSBROWN, THOMAS
Albany, N.Y.   1790

BLACK, JAMES
Philadelphia, Pa.   1795

BLACK, JAMES
Philadelphia, Pa.   1811

BLACK, JOHN
Philadelphia, Pa.   1819

BLACK, WM.
New York, N.Y.   1833

BLACKMAN, FRED'S. S. & CO.
Danbury, Conn.   1811-1898

BLACKMAN, FRED'K STARR
Danbury, Conn.   1811-1898

BLACKMAN, JOHN C.
Danbury, Conn.   1829

BLACKMAN, JOHN STARR
Danbury, Conn. 1777-1851

BLAKSLEE, WM.
Newtown, Conn.   1820

BLAKSLEE, ZIBA
Newtown, Conn.   1790

BLANCHARD, ASA
Lexington, Ky.   1810

BLAUVELT, JOHN W.
New York, N.Y.   1835

BLEASOM & REED
Portsmouth, N.H.   1830

BLISS, JONATHAN
Middletown, Conn.   1800

BLONDELL, ANTHONY
Philadelphia, Pa. 1797

BLONDELL & DESCURET
Philadelphia, Pa.   .   . 1798

BLOWERS, JOHN
Boston, Mass.   1710-1748

BOEHLER, ANDREAS W.
New York, N.Y.   1784

BOEHME, CHARLES L.
Baltimore, Md.   1774-1868

BOELEN, HENRICUS
New York, N.Y.   1684-1755

BOELEN, JACOB
New York, N.Y.   1773

BOELEN, JAMES
New York, N.Y.   1659-1729

BOEMPER, ABRAHAM
Bethlehem, Pa.   1780

BOGARDUS, EVERARDUS
New York, N.Y.   1698

BOGERT, ALBERT
New York, N. Y. ... ... .1815

BOGERT, NICHOLAS J.
New York, N. Y. 1801   `N·BOGERT` `N.J.BOGERT`

BOLTON, JAMES
New York, N. Y. ... .. .1789

BOND, W.
Unknown ... ... C 1765   `WBond`

BONJEAN, VICTOR
New Orleans, La. ... .1822

BONTECOU, TIMOTHY
New Haven, Conn. 1693-1784   T.B. TB.

BONTECOU, TIMOTHY, JR.
New Haven, Conn. 1723-1789   `TB`

BOONE, JEREMIAH
Philadelphia, Pa. , ... .1791   `IBOONE`

BORDEAUX, AUGUSTINE
Philadelphia, Pa. 1798

BORHEK, E.
Philadelphia, Pa. 1835   `E·BORHEK` `STANDARD`

BOSS & KINDELL
New York, N. Y. ... ... .1794

BOSTWICK, ZALMON
New York, N. Y. 1846   `Z·BOSTWICK`

BOSWORTH, SAMUEL
Buffalo, N. Y. ... ... .1835   `BOSWORTH`

BOTSFORD, GIDEON B.
Woodbury, Conn. 1776-1866   `G.B.BOTSFORD`

BOUDAR, JOSEPH
New York, N. Y. 1800

BOUDINOT, ELIAS
Philadelphia, Pa. 1706-1770   `EB` `BOUDINOT` `BOUDINOT`

BOUDO, LOUIS
Charleston, S. C. 1825   `L⸳BOUDO`

BOULLIEN, MOUSIER
Philadelphia, Pa. 1811

BOURDETT, STEPHAN
New York, N. Y. 1730   `SB`

BOUTIER, JOHN
New York, N. Y. 1805   `J.BOUTIER`

BOUTELLE, JAMES
Worcester, Mass. 1787

BOUVAR, JOSEPH
Philadelphia, Pa. 1797

BOWER, C.
Philadelphia, Pa. 1831

BOWNE, SAMUEL
New York, N. Y. 1778   `S:Bowne` `SBowne`

BOYCE, GERADUS
New York, N. Y. 1814   `G.B` `G:Boyce` `G.BOYCE`

BOYCE & JONES
New York, N. Y. 1825   `B&J` `BOYCE&JONES`

BOYCE, JARED
New York, N. Y. 1820

BOYCE, JOHN
New York, N. Y. 1801   `J.B`

BOYD & HOYT
Albany, New York 1830

BOYD, JOSEPH W.
New York, N. Y. 1820   `J.W.B`

BOYD & MULFORD
Albany, N. Y. ... .1840   `BOYD&MULFORD`

BOYD, WM.
Albany, N. Y. 1800

BOYER, DANIEL
Boston, Mass. 1726-1779   `DB` `DB` `BOYER` `Boyer` `BOYER`

BOYER, JAMES
Boston, Mass. 1700-1741

BOYLSTON E.
Stockbridge, Mass. ... .1789

BRABANT, ISAAC
Savannah, Ga. ... .1750

BRACKETT, JEFFREY R.
Boston, Mass. 1840   `JEFFREY R.BRACKET`

BRADBURY, THEOPHILUS
Newburyport, Mass. 1815   `BRADBURY` `Bradbu`

BRADBURY & BROTHER
Newburyport, Mass. ... .1810

BRADFORD, CHARLES H.
Westerly, R. I. ... .Unknown

BRADLEY, ABNER
New Haven, Conn. ...:.1753-1824   `A.BRADLEY`

BRADLEY & BUNCE
Hartford, Conn. ... .1830

BRADLEY, LUTHER
New Haven, Conn. ...1772-1830   `LB`

BRADLEY & MERRIMAN
New Haven, Conn. ... .1826   `B&M`

BRADLEY, PHINEAS
New Haven, Conn. . .1745-1797   `PB` `PB`

BRADLEY, RICHARD
Hartford, Conn. ... .1825

BRADLEY, ZEBUL
New Haven, Conn. ..1780-1859   `Z.BRADLEY`

BRADY, E.
New York, N. Y. ... ... .1825   `BRADY` `E.Brady`

BRADY, WM. V.
New York, N. Y. ... ... .1835

BRAINERD, CHARLES
Hartford, Conn. 1809

BRAMHALL, S.
Plymouth, Mass. ... .1800   `S.BRAMHALL`

BRANDT, A. & C.
Philadelphia, Pa. 1800   `A&CBRANDT`

BRASHER, A.
New York, N. Y. ... .1790   `ABRASHER`

BRASHER & ALEXANDER New York, N.Y. 1800		
BRASHER, E. & CO. New York, N.Y. 1790		
BRASHER, EPHRIAM New York, N.Y. ...1766	EB EB E·BRASHER BRASHER E·B&Cº	
BRASIER, A. Unknown .... Unknown	A·BRASIER	
CLAY, HENRY Philadelphia, Pa. 1799		
CREED, JOHN Colchester, Conn. 1773		
CREED, WM. Boston, Mass. 1750	WB WB WBreed	
BRENTON, BENJAMIN New York, N.Y. 1825	BB BB BB	
BREVOORT, JOHN New York, N.Y. ... 1715-1775	IBV IBV IBV	
BREWER, CHARLES Middletown, Conn. .. 1778-1860	CBrewer C·BREWER C·Brewer C·BREWER	
BREWER & CO. Middletown, Conn. 1810		
BREWER & MANN Middletown, Conn. ... .1803		
BREWSTER, ABEL Norwalk, Conn. 1797	BREWSTER	
BRIDGE, JOHN Boston, Mass. 1723	BRIDGE IBRIDGE	
BRIDGE, JOHN Boston, Mass. 1751	BRIDGE I BRIDGE J·BRIDGE	
BRIGDEN, C. Boston, Mass. 1770	C·B C·B Brigden	
BRIGDEN, TIMOTHY Albany, N.Y. 1813	TB	
BRIGDEN, ZACHARIAH Boston, Mass. 1734-1787	Z·B Z·B Z·B Z·Brigden	
BRIGHT, ANTHONY Philadelphia, Pa. 1739		
BRINKLEY, WM. New York, N.Y. 1802		
BRINTON, GORDON & QUIRK Boston, Mass. 1780		
BRITTON, ISAAC Philadelphia, Pa. 1811		
BRITTON, JACOB Philadelphia, Pa. 1807		
BROADHURST, SAMUEL New York, N.Y. 1724		
BROCK, JOHN New York, N.Y. 1833	I·BROCK	
BROCK, L. New York, N.Y. 1830	L·BROCK	

BROOKHOUSE, ROBERT Salem, Mass. 1750	RB
BROOKS, SAMUEL Philadelphia, Pa. 1793	Brooks
BROTHEARS, MICHAEL Philadelphia, Pa. 1772	
BROWER & RUSHER New York, N.Y. 1834	B&R
BROWER, S. & B. Albany, N.Y. 1810	S&B.BROWER
BROWN, S. D. Albany, N.Y. 1834	
BROWER, WALTER S. Albany, N.Y. 1850	
BROWN, ALEXANDER Philadelphia, Pa. 1840	
BROWN, D. Philadelphia, Pa. 1811	D.BROWN
BROWN, ELNATHAN C. Westerly, R.I. ......Unknown	
BROWN, EBENEZER Boston, Mass. 1793	
BROWN, HENRY Philadelphia, Pa. 1777	
BROWN & HOULTON Baltimore, Md. 1799	
BROWN, JAMES Philadelphia, Pa. 1785	
BROWN, JESSE Philadelphia, Pa. 1813	
BROWN, JOHN Philadelphia, Pa. 1785	J.B
BROWN, LIBERTY Philadelphia, Pa. 1801	
BROWN, ROBERT Baltimore, Md. 1830	R.BROWN R.BROWN R.BROWN R.BROWN&SON
BROWN, SAMUEL C. New York, N.Y. 1850	S.BROWN S.BROWN
BROWN, WM. Albany, N.Y. 1849	
BROWN & SON, R. Baltimore, Md. 1830	R.BROWN&SON
BROWNE & KIRBY Philadelphia, Pa. 1825	BROWN&KIRBY
BROWNE & SEAL Philadelphia, Pa. 1810	BROWNE&SEAL
BRUFF, CHARLES OLIVER New York, N.Y. 1763	C.O.B
BRUFF, JOSEPH Easton, Maryland 1796	IB
BRUFF, JOSEPH Easton, Maryland ...1730-1785	J·BRUFF

BRUFF, THOMAS
Easton, Maryland 1790   T·BRUFF T·BRUFF

BRUSH, EDWARD
New York, N. Y, ...1774

BRYAN, PHILLIP
Philadelphia, Pa. 1802   BRYAN

BUCHE, PETER
New York, N. Y. 1795

BUCHOZ, I. R.
New York, N. Y. 1835

BUCKLEY & ANDERSON
Philadelphia, Pa. 1804

BUCKLEY, J. B.
Philadelphia, Pa. 1807   BUCKLEY

BUDDY, DANIEL
Philadelphia, Pa. 1769

BUEL, ABEL
New Haven, Conn. 1742-1825   AB AB BUEL

BUEL, ADRIEN
New Haven, Conn. 1742-1825

BUEL, D. H.
Hartford, Conn. 1825

BUEL & GREENLEAF
New Haven, Conn. 1798

BUEL, JOHN
New Haven, Conn. 1789

BUEL & MIX
New Haven, Conn. 1783

BUEL, SAMUEL
Middletown, Conn. 1742-1819   S·B

BUICHLE, LEWIS
Baltimore, Md. 1798   LB LB L·B L Buichle

BULL, CALEB
Hartford, Conn. 1840

BULL, EPAPHRAS
Boston, Mass. 1813

BULL, G. W.
East Hartford, Conn. 1840   G·W·BULL

BULL, MARTIN
Farmington, Conn. 1775

BULL & MORRISON
Hartford, Conn. 1780

BUMM, PETER
Philadelphia, Pa. 1814

BUMM & SHIPPER
Philadelphia, Pa. 1819

BUNKER, BENJAMIN
Providence, R. I. 1810

BURDICK, WILLIAM S.
New Haven, Conn. 1810

BURDOCK, GEORGE
Philadelphia, Pa. 1791

BURDOCK, NICHOLAS
Philadelphia, Pa. 1797   N·B

BURGALIE, J. P.
New York, N. Y. 1799

BURGER, DAVID I.
New York, New York 1805   D·I·Burger

BURGER, JOHN
New York, New York ..1786   I·B Burger Burger

BURGER, JOHN
New York, New York 1767   Burger B BB Burger NYork Burger NYORK

BURGER, THOMAS
New York. New York 1805

BURNAP, DANIEL
East Windsor, Conn. ...1791

BURNETT, CHARLES A.
Alexandria, Va. 1793   C·A·B C·A·BURNET

BURNETT & RYDER
Philadelphia, Pa. 1795   B·R

BURNHAM, ROBERT
New York, New York 1790

BURKLOE, SAMUEL
Philadelphia, Pa. 1795

BURNET, SAMUEL
Newark, N. J. 1796

BURNET & RYDER
Philadelphia, Pa. 1795

BURNETT, CHARLES A.
Alexandria, Va. 1793

BURNS, ANTHONY
Philadelphia, Pa. 1785

BURNS, JAMES
Philadelphia, Pa. 1810

BURNS, JOHN H.
New York, New York ...1835

BUROT, ANDREW
Baltimore, Md. 1819

BURR, A. C.
Providence, R. I. 1815   A·C·BURR

BURR, CHRISTIAN A.
Providence, R. I. ...1810   C·A·BURR

BURR, C. A. & CO.
Providence, R. I. 1820

BURR, E. & W.
Providence, R. I. ...1793

BURR, EZEKIEL
Providence, R. I. 1764-1846   E·B E·B E·B E E·BURR E·BURR

BURR & LEE
Providence, R.I. 1815

BURR, NATHANIEL
Fairfield, Conn. ......1698-1784.   NB

BURR, WILLIAM
Providence, R. I. 1793

BURRILL, JOSEPH
Boston, Mass. 1823

BURRILL, SAMUEL Boston, Mass. 1733	SB (SB) S:Burrill S:Burrill (SB)	
BURRILL, SAMUEL, JR. Boston, Mass. ... 1829		
BURRILL, THEOPHILUS New London, Conn. 1736		
BURROWS, WILLIAM Philadelphia, Pa. 1831		
BURT, BENJAMIN Boston, Mass. .. 1691-1745	B•BURT BURT BBURT B•BURT BURT	
BURT, BENJAMIN Boston, Mass. ... 1729-1803	BENJAMIN BURT B•BURT	
BURT, JOHN Boston, Mass. 1691-1745	IB IB I•B I•B I•B I BURT JOHN BURT	
BUSHNELL, PHINEAS Guilford, Conn. 1762	I•BURT I•BURT	
BURT, WILLIAM Boston, Mass. 1726-1752	W.BURT	
BURTON, JACOB Philadelphia, Pa. 1839	SB SB SAMUEL BURT	
BURT, SAMUEL Boston, Mass. 1724-1754	SAMUEL BURT. SAMUEL BURT.	
BUSSEY, BENJAMIN Dedham, Mass. 1757-1842	BB BB	
BUSSEY, THOMAS Baltimore, Maryland 1799		
BUSWELL, JASON Portsmouth, N. H. 1839		
BUTLER, HENRY W. Philadelphia, Pa. 1833		
BUTLER, JAMES Boston, Mass. 1713-1776	IB IB J.BUTLER J.BUTLER	
BUTLER, JOHN Portland, Me. 1765		
BUTLER, N. Utica, New York 1800		
BUTLER, N. H. Philadelphia, Pa. 1837		
BUTLER & LITTLE Portland, Me. 1759		
BUTLER & McCARTHY Philadelphia, Pa. 1850		
BUTLER WISE AND CO. Philadelphia, Pa. 1845	BW&Co	
BUZELL, J. L. Unknown ....C 1750	J.L.BUZELL	
BRYNE, JAMES New York, New York 1789	J.Byrne J.Byrne	
BYRNE, JAMES Philadelphia, Pa. 1784	J.Byrne	

C

CADY, SAMUEL New York, New York 1792		

CADY AND BACKUS New York, New York 1792		
CALDER AND COMPANY Albany, New York 1830		
CALDWELL, E. New York, New York 1800		
CAMERON, ALEXANDER Albany, New York 1813		
CAMMAN, ALEXANDER Albany, New York ...1813	A·C	
CAMOIN Philadelphia, Pa. 1797		
CAMP, ELIAS Bridgeport, Conn. 1825	E·C	
CAMPBELL, CHRISTOPHER New York, N.Y. 1808	CAMPBELL	
CAMPBELL, JOHN W. New York, New York .1814		
CAMPBELL, R. Baltimore, Md. 1824		
CAMPBELL, R. & A. Baltimore, Md. 1835	R.&A.C R&A.CAMPBELL	
CAMPBELL, ROBERT Baltimore, Md. 1819	R·C CAMPBELL.	
CAMPBELL, R. Baltimore, Md. 1824		
CAMPBELL, THOMAS New York, New York 1770	T.CAMPBELL	
CAMPBELL, W. Philadelphia, Pa. 1765		
CANAVILLO, ANTONIO New York, New York 1825		
CANAVILLO, S. New York, New York 1825		
CANDEE & COMPANY, L. B. Woodbury, Conn. 1830	L.B.CANDEE&CO	
CANDEE, LEWIS B. Woodbury, Conn. 1825		
CANDELL, CHARLES New York, New York ... 1795	C·C	
CANFIELD AND BROTHER Baltimore, Md. 1830		
CANFIELD AND FOOT Middletown, Conn. 1798		
CANFIELD AND HALL New York, New York 1805	CANFIELD & HALL	
CANFIELD, SAMUEL Middletown, Conn. 1780-1800		
CANFIELD, SAMUEL Lansingburg, N. Y. 1801	CANFIELD	
CANFIELD BROTHERS & CO. Baltimore, Md. 1850		

CANN, JOHN
New York, New York .   1835

CANON. GEORGE
Warwick, R. I.   .   .   1800   GC GCANON

CANT, GODFREY
New York, N.Y.   1796

CAPELLE, J.
Stt. Louis, Mo.   .   .   1850   CAPELLE St.LOUIS

CARALIN, PIERCE
New York, N.Y.   1804

CARBIN, THEODORE
Philadelphia, Pa.   .   .   .1758

CARGILL   (Noted)

CARIO, MICHAEL
New York, N.Y.   1728

CARIO, WILLIAM
New York, N.Y. 1721   W.CARIO W.CARIO

CARIOLLE
New Orleans, La. 1822

CARLETON, GEORGE
New York, N.Y. 1810   CARLETON

CARLISLE, ABRAHAM
Philadelphia, Pa. 1791   ACarlile

CARMAN, JOHN
Philadelphia, Pa. 1771   IC

CARMAN, JOHN
New York, N.Y. 1800

CARMAN, SAMUEL
New York, N.Y, ...1807

CARPENTER, CHARLES
Boston, Mass. 1807

CARPENTER, JOSEPH
Norwich, Conn. 1747-1804   I-C I-C

CARREL, DANIEL
Philadelphia, Pa. 1806

CARRELL, JOHN & DANIEL
Philadelphia, Pa. 1785   CARREL

CARRIBEC, PETER
Philadelphia, Pa. . , , ...1795

CARROL, JAMES
Albany, N.Y. 1834

CARROLL, JAMES
New York, N.Y. 1825

CARSON, DAVID
Albany, N.Y. 1849

CARSON, THOMAS
Albany, N.Y. 1815   TC

CARSON & HALL
Albany, N.Y. 1813

CARY, LEWIS
Boston, Mass. 1820   L.CARY

CASE, GEORGE
East Hartford, Conn. 1779

CASEY, GIDEON
South Kingston, R.I.   . . .1753

CASEY, GIDEON
Providence, R.I. 1726-1786   G:CASEY

CASEY, SAMUEL
South Kingston, R.I.   1724-1773   S.C S:CASEY S:CASEY

CASHELL, RANDALL, H.
Philadelphia, Pa.   . . .   1807

CASSEDY, ANDREW
Philadelphia, Pa.   . . .1840

CASTON, FRANCOISE
New York, N.Y.   1804

CERNEAU, JOHN
New York, N.Y.   1823

CERNEAU. JOSEPH
New York, N.Y.   . . . :1807

CERNEAU & CO.
New York, N.Y.   . . .   1811

CHADWICK, THOMAS
Philadelphia, Pa.   .   .   1809

CHALMERS, JAMES, Sr.
Annapolis, Md.   1749   IC IC

CHALMERS, JOHN
Annapolis, Md. 1770   IC

CHAMBERLAIN, WILSON
Portsmouth, N.H. 1839

CHAMPLIN, JOHN
New London, Conn. ..1745-1800   I-C

CHANDLER, STEPHEN
New York, N.Y. 1812   CHANDLER

CHANDLESS, WILLIAM
New York, N.Y. 1846

CHAPIN, AARON
Hartford, Conn. 1790

CHAPIN, ALEXANDER
Hartford, Conn. 1838

CHARTERS, JAMES
New York, N.Y. 1844

CHARTERS, CANN & DUNN
New York,, N.Y. 1850   M CC&D

CHASE, J. D.
New York, N.Y. 1820

CHASE & EASTON
Brooklyn, N.Y. 1837

CHASLEY
Boston, Mass. 1764

CHAT, EASTON
Philadelphia, Pa. 1793

CHAT, LE SIEUR
New York, N.Y. 1790

CHAUDRONS & RASCH
Philadelphia, Pa. 1812   CHAUDRONS & RASCH STER.AM

CHAUDRONS, SIMON
Philadelphia, Pa. 1798

CAUDRONS, SIMON & CO.
Philadelphia, Pa. 1807   `SC&Co`

CENE, DANIEL
New York, N.Y. 1786

CERRY, JAMES
Philadelphia, Pa. 1824

CEVALIER, CLEMENT E.
Philadelphia, Pa. 1816

CEVALIER & TANGUAY
Philadelphia, Pa. 1816

CHILDS, GEORGE H.
Philadelphia, Pa. 1828

CHILDS, GEORGE K.
Philadelphia, Pa. 1837

CHITRY, PETER
New York, N.Y. 1814   `P.Chitry` `P.Chitry`

CHITTEN, EBENEZER
New Haven, Conn. 1747   `EC` `EC` `E.CHITTENDEN`

CHITTENDEN, BERIAH
New Haven, Conn. 1787

CHITTENDEN, EBENEZER
New Haven, Conn. ...1726-1812

CHURCH, JOSEPH
New Haven, Conn. 1818

CHURCH, JOSEPH
Hartford, Conn. 1794-1876

CHURCH, RALPH
Buffalo, N.Y. 1832

CHURCH & ROGERS
Hartford, Conn. 1825   `CHURCH & ROGERS`

CHURCHILL, JESSE
Boston, Mass. 1773-1819   `I.CHURCHILL` `CHURCHILL`

CHURCHILL & TREADWELL
Boston, Mass. 1805   `CHUTCHill & Treadwell`

CHURCHWELL, CHARLES
Philadelphia, Pa. 1781

CLAPP, A. L.
New York, N.Y. 1802   `A.L.CLAPP`

CLAPP, PHILIP
New York, N.Y. 1802

CLAPP & RIKER
New York, N.Y. 1802

CLARK & ANTHONY
New York, N.Y. 1790   `CLARK & ANTHONY`

CLARK, ANDREW
New York, N.Y. 1744

CLARK & BRO.
Norwalk, Conn. 1825   `CLARK & BRO. NORWALK.`

CLARK, C. & G.
Boston, Mass. 1833

CLARK, CHARLES
Boston, Mass. 1798

CLARK & COIT
Norwich, Conn. 1820

CLARK, CURTIS
New York, N.Y. 1823

CLARK, GABRIEL D.
Providence, R.I. 1824   `G.D.CLARK`

CLARK, GEORGE, C.
Providence, R.I. 1824   `G.C.CLARK`

CLARK, GEORGE D.
Baltimore, Md. 1826   `G.D.CLARK`

CLARK, HENRY
Philadelphia, Pa. 1813

CLARK, I.
Boston, Mass. 1754   `I·C` `I.CLARK` `I:CLARK` `I.CLARK` `CLARK`

CLARK, I. & H.
New York, N.Y. 1812   `I·&H·CLARK`

CLARK, J. H.
New York, N.Y. 1812   `J.H.CLARK`

CLARK, JOSEPH
Danbury, Conn. 1791   `JC` `J:CLARK`

CLARK, LEVI
Norwalk, Conn. 1801-1875   `CLARK` `NORWALK`

CLARK, METCALF B.
Boston, Mass. 1835

CLARK, PETER G.
New Haven, Conn. 1810

CLARK, RICHARD
New York, N.Y. 1795

CLARK, SAMUEL
Boston, Mass. 1681

CLARK, THOMAS
Boston, Mass. 1783   `T.Clark` `T.Clark`

CLARK, WILLIAM
New Milford, Conn. 1774   `WC` `WC`

CLARKE, JAMES
Newport, R.I. 1734

CLARKE, JONATHAN
Newport, R.I. 1734   `IC` `IC` `J.Clarke` `J:CLARKE` `I.CLARKE`

CLEVELAND, AARON
Norwich, Conn. 1820   `AC` `A·CLEVELAND`

CLEVELAND, BENJAMIN
Norwich, Conn. 1760   `B·CLEVELAND`

CLEVELAND & POST
Norwich, Conn. 1815   `C&P` `C&P`

CLEVELAND, WILLIAM
Norwich, Conn. .. 1770-1837   `WC` `Cleveland`

CLEVELAND, WILLIAM
New London, Conn. ...1770-1837   `WC` `WC`

CLINE, CHARLES
Philadelphia, Pa. . 1829

CLUSTER, ISAAC D.
St. Louis, Mo. . 1850   `I D CLUSTER` `ST.LOUIS.M`

COAN, DANIEL B.
New York, N.Y. 1789   `D·C`

COBB, EPHRAIM
Boston, Mass. 1708-1777

COBURN, JOHN
Boston, Mass. 1765

COBURN, JOHN
Boston, Mass. 1725-1803

CODDINGTON, JOHN
Newport, R.I. . . . 1690-1743

CODMAN, WILLARD
Boston, Mass. 1839

CODNER, JOHN
Boston, Mass. 1754-1782

COE & UPTON
New York, N.Y. 1840

COEN, DANIEL BLOOM
New York, N.Y. 1787

COFFMAN, WILLIAM
Philadelphia, Pa. 1839

COGSWELL, H.
Boston, Mass. 1760

COHEN, BARROW A.
New York, N.Y. 1825

COHEN, WILLIAM
Alexandria, Va., D.C. 1833

COIGNARD, LOUIS
New York, N.Y. 1805

COIT, E.
Norwich, Conn. 1839

COIT & MANSFIELD
Norwich, Conn. 1816

COIT, THOMAS CHESTER
Norwich, Conn. 1812

COLE, ALBERT
New York, N.Y. 1844

COLE, EBENEZER
New York, N.Y. 1818

COLE, JACOB
Philadelphia, Pa. 1785

COLE, JOHN
Boston, Mass. 1686

COLEMAN, B.
Burlington, N.J. 1785

COLEMAN, C. C.
Burlington, N.J. 1835

COLEMAN, JOHN
New York, N.Y. 1814

COLEMAN, NATHANIEL
Burlington, N.J. 1776

COLEMAN, S.
Burlington, N.J. 1805

COLES, JOHN A.
New York, N.Y. 1830

COLEY, SIMEON
New York, N.Y. 1767

COLEY, WILLIAM
New York, N.Y. 1801

COLLET, J. B.
New York, N.Y. 1805

COLLETTE, LAMBERT
Buffalo, N.Y. 1835

COLLINS, ARNOLD
Newport, R.I. 1690

COLLINS & J. W. FORBES
New York, N.Y. 1825

COLLINS, S.
Utica, N.Y. 1840

COLLINS, W. & L.
New York, N.Y. 1830

COLNER, JOHN
New York, N.Y. 1818

COLONEL, JOHN
Philadelphia, Pa. 1804

COLTON & BALDWIN
New York, N.Y. 1819

COLTON & COLLINS
New York, N.Y. 1832

COLTON, LEVI
New York, N.Y. 1825

COLTON, OREN
New York, N.Y. 1818

COLWELL & LAWRENCE
Albany, N.Y. 1850

CONEY, JOHN
Boston, Mass. 1655-1722

CONNELL, M.
Philadelphia, Pa. 1800

CONNING, J.
New York, N.Y. 1840

CONNOR, JOHN H.
New York, N.Y. 1812

CONNOR, JOHN W.
Norwalk, Conn. 1836

CONYERS, JOSEPH
Boston, Mass. 1708

CONYERS, RICHARD
Boston, Mass. 1688

COOK, JOHN
New York, N.Y. 1795

COOK, JOHN
New York, N.Y. 1797-1805

COOK & COMPANY
New York, N.Y. 1797

COOKE, JOSEPH
Philadelphia, Pa. 1785

COOKE & COMPANY
Philadelphia, Pa. 1785

LIDGE, JOSEPH, Jr. oston, Mass. 1770	Coolidge Coolidge	
PER iladelphia, Pa. 1816		
PER, B. ew York, N.Y. 1814		
PER, B. & J. ew York, N.Y. 1810		
PER, FRANCIS W. ew York, N.Y. 1846	F.W.C. N.Y. F.W.COOPER.	
PER, JOHN ew York, N.Y. 1814		
PER, JOSEPH ew York, N.Y. 1770		
PP, JOSEPH ew London, Conn. 1757	J·COPP	
PP, NATHANIEL P. lbany, N.Y. 1834		
RLEY, WILLIAM ew York, N.Y. 1811		
RNELISON, CORNELIUS ew York, N.Y. 1711		
RNELIUS, CHRISTIAN hiladelphia, Pa. 1810	C.CORNELIUS	
RNWELL, N. anbury, Conn. 1776-1837	N.CORWELL	
RNELL, WALTER rovidence, R.I. 1780	CORNELL	
RRIN, JOSIAH hiladelphia, Pa. 1823		
URCELLE, HILAIRE ew Orleans, La. 1822		
UVERTIE, LOUIS ew Orleans, La. 1822	L'COUVERTIE	
VERLY, THOMAS ewport, R.I. 1765	T.COVERLY	
VERLY, THOMAS ewburyport, Mass. . .1730-1800	T·COVERLY	
WAN, WILLIAM D. hiladelphia, Pa. 1808	W.Cowan	
WELL, WM. oston, Mass. 1682-1736	WC WC WC W.C W:Cowell	
WELL, WILLIAM J. oston, Mass. 1736		
WELL, WILLIAM, Jr. oston, Mass. 1713-1761	W:Cowell W.Cowell	
WLES, RALPH leveland, Ohio 1850	COWLES	
X, J. & I. ew York, N.Y. 1844	J&I COX J&I COX	
X, JOHN hiladelphia, Pa. 1818		

CRAFT, STEPHEN New York, N.Y. 1811		
CRAIG, JAMES Williamsburg, Va. 1750		
CRANDALL, BENJAMIN Providence, R.I. . . . 1824		
CRANDALL, BENJAMIN Portsmouth, N.H. 1839		
CRANE, STEPHEN M. New York, N.Y. 1813		
CRANSTON, SAMUEL Newport, R.I. 1684		
CRAWFORD, JOHN New York, N.Y. 1820	J.CRAWFORD	
CRAWFORD, JOHN New York, N.Y. 1815	J.CRAWFORD J.Crawford J.Crawford	
CREW, J. T. Albany, N.Y. 1849		
CRITTENDEN, NEWTON E. Cleveland, Ohio 1839		
CRONE, HENRY Cleveland, Ohio 1780		
CROSBY, JONATHAN Boston, Mass. 1743-1769	JC	
CROSBY, SAMUEL T. Boston, Mass. 1850		
CROSS, WILLIAM Boston, Mass. 1712	WC	
CROUCKESHANKS, ALEX. Boston, Mass. 1768		
CUMMINGS, DAVID B. Philadelphia, Pa. 1811		
CURRIER & TROTT Boston, Mass. 1836	Currier & Trott	
CURRIN, JOSEPH Philadelphia, Pa. 1829		
CURRY, JOHN Philadelphia, Pa. 1831	J.CURRY	
CURRY & PRESTON Philadelphia, Pa. 1831	C&P CURRY&PRESTON	
CURTIS, CANDEE & STILES Woodbury, Conn. 1831	C.C.&S CURTISS·CANDEE & STILES	
CURTIS, DANIEL Woodbury, Conn. 1831		
CURTIS, JOEL Wolcott, Conn. 1810		
CURTIS, LEWIS Farmington, Conn. 1797	L·CURTIS	
CURTIS, THOMAS New York, N.Y. 1835		
CURTIS & CANDEE Woodbury, Conn. 1826		

CURTISS, CANDEE & STILES
Woodbury, Conn. 1825

CURTISS & DUNING
Woodbury, Conn. 1828

CURTISS & STILES
Woodbury, Conn. 1835

CUSHMAN, ISAAC
Boston, Mass. 1823

CUTLER, A.
Boston, Mass. 1820

CUTLER, E.
New Haven, Conn. 1820

CUTLER, J. N.
Albany, N.Y. 1849

CUTLER, RICHARD
New Haven, Conn. 1760

CUTLER, RICHARD, Jr.
New Haven, Conn. 1800

CUTLER, RICHARD & SONS
New Haven, Conn. 1800

CUTLER, SILLIMAN, WARD
New Haven, Conn. 1767

CUTLER, WILLIAM
New Haven, Conn. 1806

CUTTER WILLIAM
Portland, Me. 1823

D

DAGGETT, HENRY
New Haven, Conn. 1763

DALLON, JOHN
Philadelphia, Pa. 1791

DALLY, PHILLIP
New York, N.Y. 1779

DALLY & HALSEY
New York, N.Y. 1787

DANE, THOMAS
Boston, Mass. 1723-1796

DANIEL, PERRY O.
Unknown 1830

DANIELS, CHARLES W.
Troy, N.Y. 1836

DARGEE, JOHN
New York, N.Y. 1810

DARROW, DAVID
New York, N.Y. 1825

DAUBAYSON, VICTOIRE
Philadelphia, Pa. 1820

DAUCE, SIMON
Philadelphia, Pa. 1798

DAVENPORT, JONATHAN
Baltimore, Md. 1789-1801

DAVENPORT, ROBERT
Philadelphia, Pa. 1808

DAVENPORT, SAMUEL
Milton, Mass. 1741

DAVERNE, JOHN
Baltimore, Md. 1799

DAVID & DUPUY
Philadelphia, Pa. 1792

DAVID, JOHN
Philadelphia, Pa. 1736-1794

DAVID, JOHN, Jr.
Philadelphia, Pa. 1792

DAVID, LEWIS A.
Philadelphia, Pa. 1823

DAVID, PETER
Philadelphia, Pa. ...1707-1753

DAVIS & BABBITT
Providence, R.I. 1820

DAVIS & BROWN
Boston, Mass. 1802

DAVIS, E.
Newburyport, Mass. 1775

DAVIS, JOSHUA, G.
Boston, Mass. 1796

DAVIS, PALMER & CO.
Boston, Mass. 1841

DAVIS, SAMUEL
Providence, R.I. 1801

DAVIS, SAMUEL
Boston, Mass. 1813

DAVIS, T. A.
Boston, Mass. 1824

DAVIS & WATSON
Boston, Mass. 1815

DAVIS, WILLIAM
Boston, Mass. 1823

DAVISON, BRAZILLIA
Norwich, Conn. 1765

DAVISON, CHARLES
Norwich, Conn. 1805

DAVY, ADAM
Philadelphia, Pa. 1795

DAWES, WILLIAM
Boston, Mass. 1766

DAWS, R.
Unknown 1800

DAWSON, JOHN
New York, N.Y. 1769

DAWSON, WILLIAM
Philadelphia, Pa. 1763

DEANE, JAMES
New York, N.Y. 1760

DEAS, DAVID
Philadelphia, Pa. 1831

DECKER, J.
New York, N.Y. 1830   J.DECKER

DELAGROW, ANDREW
Philadelphia, Pa. 1795

DELANO, JABEZ
New Bedford, Mass. 1784

DE LAROUX, JOHN
New Orleans, La. 1822   ✳ 🔵 ✳

DELAUNEY, JEAN
New York, N.Y. 1805

DEMILT, ANDREW
New York, N.Y. 1805   DEMILT

DEMMOCK, JOHN
Boston, Mass. 1798

DEMORSY, JEAN
New Orleans, La. 1822

DEMORT, JOHN
New York, N.Y. 1810

DEMORT, LUCIEN
New York, N.Y. 1810

DENISE, JOHN
New York, N.Y. 1798   J:D JD

DENISE, JOHN
Philadelphia, Pa. 1698   IN

DENISE, JOHN & TUNIS
South Kingston, R.I. 1770   J&TD   J&T.D

DENISON, T.
Uknown 1790   T.DENISON

DENNIS, EBENEZER
Hartford, Conn. 1782

DENNIS & FITCH
Troy, N.Y. 1836

DENNIS, GEORGE, Jr.
Norwich, Conn. 1770

DE PARISIEN, OTTO PAUL
New York, N.Y. 1763   OP   OPDP

DE PERRIZANG, OTTO
New York, N.Y. 1786

DE PEYSTER, WILLIAM
New York, N.Y. 1732

DE RIEMER, CORNELIUS B.
Ithaca, N.Y. 1804

DE RIEMER, JACOB R.
New York, N.Y. 1830

DE RIEMER & MEAD
Ithaca, N.Y. 1831

DE RIEMER, PETER
New York, N.Y. 1738-1814   PDR

DESHON, DANIEL
New London, Conn. ..1697-1781   DD

DE SPIEGEL, JACOBUS VAN
New York, N.Y. 1668-1708   I̶V̶S I̶V̶S IVS IVS IVS

DESQUET & TANGUY
Philadelphia, Pa. 1805

DESURET, LEWIS
Philadelphia, Pa. 1799

DEVERELL, JOHN
Boston, Mass. 1764-1813   Deverell

DEVERELL, JOHN
Boston, Mass. 1785

DEXTER, JOHN
Marboro, Mass. 1756

DE YOUNG, MICHAEL
Baltimore, Md. 1816   M·DEYOUNG

DICKERSON, H. & CO.
Philadelphia, Pa. 1815

DICKERSON, JOHN
Morristown, Mass. 1778

DICKINSON, JONATHAN
Philadelphia, Pa. 1794

DICKINSON & ROBINSON
Philadelphia, Pa. 1796

DIMMOCK, JOHN
New York, N.Y. 1801

DIMOND, ISAAC M.
New York, N.Y. 1830

DISBROW, G. E.
New York, N.Y. 1825   G.E.DISBROW NEWYORK

DIXWELL, BASIL
Boston, Mass. 1732

DIXWELL, JOHN
Boston, Mass. 1680-1725   ID

DOANE, JOSHUA
Providence, R. I. 1753   DOANE DOANE

DOBBS
New York, N.Y. 1788

DOBLEMAN, FREDERICK
Philadelphia, Pa. 1813

DOBLEMAN, F. F. G.
Philadelphia, Pa. 1810

DODGE, BENJAMIN
Boston, Mass. 1836

DODGE, EZEKIEL
New York, N.Y. 1792

DODGE, EZRA
New London, Conn. 1787

DODGE, JOHN
New York, N.Y. 1790   J·DODGE

DODGE, NEHEMIAH
Providence, R.I. 1795   N·DODGE

DODGE, SERIL
Providence, R.I. 1765-1803   ☆ S·DODGE ☆

DOLE, D. N.
Portsmouth, N.H. 1805   D·N·DOLE

DOLE, E. G.
Portsmouth, N.H. 1820   [EGDole]

DOLER, DANIEL
Boston, Mass. ....,1765

DONALON, JOHN W.
Boston, Mass. 1823

DONOVAN, WILLIAM
Philadelphia, Pa. 1784   [W DONOVAN]

DONTREMEI, C.
Philadelphia, Pa. 1805

DOOLITTLE, AMOS
New Haven, Conn. ...1754-1832   [AD] [AD]

DOOLITTLE, ENOS
Hartford, Conn. 1781

DORAN, JOHN
Cincinnati, Ohio 1826

DORGY, PETER
Philadelphia, Pa. 1816

DORSEY, JOSHUA
Philadelphia, Pa. 1796   [I·DORSEY]

DORSEY, SAMUEL
Philadelphia, Pa. 1804

DORSEY, SIMON
Philadelphia, Pa. 1820

DORSON, JOSHUA
Philadelphia, Pa. 1802

DOSTER, MICHAEL
Philadelphia, Pa. 1831

DOUGLAS, ALEXANDER
New York, N.Y. 1792

DOUGLAS, CANTWELL
Baltimore, Md. 1799

DOUGLAS, JAMES, W.
Philadelphia, Pa. 1791

DOUGLAS, ROBERT
New London, Conn. 1776   [BD] [RD] [RD]

DOUGLASS & HECKMAN
Philadelphia, Pa. 1837

DOUGLASS, JAMES
New York, N.Y. 1800   [JDouglas]

DOUGLASS, JEREMOTT W.
Philadelphia, Pa. 1790   [Douglass]

DOUGLASS, JOHN
Philadelphia, Pa. 1840

DOUTIEMER, CULE
Philadelphia, Pa. 1791

DOWIG, CHRISTOPHER
Philadelphia, Pa. 1765

DOWIG, GEORGE
Baltimore, Md. 1724-1807   [G·D]

DOWIG, GEORGE
Philadelphia, Pa. 1770   [GD] [GD] [GD]

DOWNES, J.
Philadelphia, Pa. 1770   [J.Downes] [J.DOWNES] [J.Down]

DOWNING, G. R.
New York, N.Y. 1810   [GRD] [N·YORK]

DOWNING & PHELPS
New York, N.Y. 1810   [D&P] [DOWNING&PHELPS]

DRAPER, J.
Wilmington, Del. 1816   [J.DRAPER]

DREWRY, GEORGE
Philadelphia, Pa. 1763   [GD]

DRINKER, JOHN
New York, N.Y. 1835

DROWN, T. P.
Boston, Mass. ..,.....,...1790   [T.P.DROWN] [T P DROV]

DROWNE, BENJAMIN
Portsmouth, N.H. 1800

DROWNE, SAMUEL
Portsmouth, N.H. 1749-1815   [S×D] [S×Drowne]

DROWNE, SHEM
Boston, Mass. 1749   [SD]

DRUMONT, ANTOINE
New York, N.Y. 1808

DUBOIS, ABRAHAM
Philadelphia, Pa. 1777   [AD] [A DUBOIS] [A·DUBO

DUBOIS, A., Sr. & Jr.
New York, N.Y. 1803

DUBOIS, JOSEPH
New York, N.Y. 1790   [J·DUBOIS] [I·DUBOI]

DUBOIS, TUNIS, D.
New York, N.Y. 1799   [T·D·D] [✦] [✦]
                                        [T·D·DUBOIS]

DUBOIS & CO.
New York, N.Y. 1803

DUCHE, RENE
New York, N.Y. 1795

DUCHE & DONARD
Philadelphia, Pa. 1820

DUDLEY, BENJAMIN
Birmingham, Ga. 1768

DUFFEL, JAMES
New York, N.Y. 1801   [I·DUFFEL]

DUHME & CO.
St. Louis, Mo. 1850   [·DUHME·]

DUMMER, JEREMIAH
Boston, Mass. 1645-1718   [ID] [ID]

DU MORTE, JOHN
Philadelphia, Pa. 1796

DUMOURIER, JOSEPH
Philadelphia, Pa. 1816

DUMOUTET, JOHN BAPTISTE
Philadelphia, Pa. 1793   [DUMOUTET] [DUMOUTE

DUNDAS, PRATT
Philadelphia, Pa. 1837

UNKERLY, JOSEPH
Boston, Mass. 1787

UNLEVY, ROBERT
Philadelphia, Pa. 1831

UNN, CARY
New York, N.Y. 1764

UNN, DAVID
New York, N.Y. 1835

UNN & SON
New York, N.Y. 1787

UNSCOMB, DENNIS
New York, N.Y. 1765

UON, H.
Baltimore, Md. 1819

UPUY, DANIEL
Philadelphia, Pa. 1719-1807

UPUY, DANIEL, Jr.
Philadelphia, Pa. 1782

UPUY, JOHN
Philadelphia, Pa. 1770

UPUY, JOHN & DANIEL, Jr.
Philadelphia, Pa. 1783

UPUY & SONS
Philadelphia, Pa. 1784

URAND, JOHN
New York, N.Y. 1835

URANDEAU, JOHN
New York, N.Y. 1835

URGIN, WILLIAM B.
Concord, N.H. 1850

USENBERRY, W. C.
New York, N.Y. 1830

UTEUS, CHARLES J.
Philadelphia, Pa. 1751

UTEUS & HARPER
Philadelphia, Pa. 1755

UVALIER
Unknown ....c. 1800

UYCKINCK, DANIEL
New York, N.Y. 1798

WIGHT, TIMOTHY
Boston, Mass. 1645-1691

E

EAGLES & MORRIS
New York, N.Y. 1799

EAMES, JOSHUA
Boston, Mass. 1828

EASTON. J.
Nantucket, Mass. 1828

EASTON, NATHANIEL
Nantucket, Mass. 1780

EASTON & SANFORD
Nantucket, Mass. 1830

EASTWICK, THOMAS
Boston, Mass. 1743

EATON, TIMOTHY
Philadelphia, Pa. 1793

EAYRES, THOMAS S.
Boston, Mass. 1760-1803

EDGAR, JOHN
New York, N.Y. 1807

EDMECHAT, CLAUDE
New York, N.Y. 1790

EDWARDS, ABRAHAM
Ashby, Mass. 1763

EDWARDS, ANDREW
Boston, Mass. 1796

EDWARDS, CALVIN
Ashby, Mass. 1710

EDWARDS, JOHN
Boston, Mass. 1700

EDWARDS, JOSEPH, Jr.
Boston, Mass. 1707-1777

EDWARDS, SAMUEL
Boston, Mass. 1705-1762

EDWARDS, SAMUEL
Natick, Mass. 1726-1783

EDWARDS, THOMAS
Boston, Mass. 1701-1755

EDWARDS, THOMAS
New York, N.Y. 1731

EMBREE
Unknown ....c. 1790

ELDERKIN, ALFRED
Killingsworth, Conn. 1792

ELDERKIN, ELISHA
New Haven, Conn. 1777

ELDERKIN & STANIFORD
Windom, Conn. 1790

ELLIOTT, JOHN A.
Sharon, Conn. 1815

ELLIOTT, JOSEPH
New Castle, Delaware 1768

ELLIS, LEWIS W.
Philadelphia, Pa. 1837

ELLISON, PETER
New York, N.Y. 1792

ELLSWORTH, DAVID
Windsor, Conn. 1772

ELTONHEAD. THOMAS
Baltimore, Md. 1835

EMERY, STEPHEN
Boston, Mass. 1746-1789

EMERY, STEPHEN
Boston, Mass. 1725-1801

EMERY, THOMAS KNOX
Boston, Mass. 1781-1815

EMERY & COMPANY
New York, N.Y. 1798

ENGLAND, GEORGE
New York, N.Y. 1800

ENGLAND, WILLIAM
Philadelphia, Pa. 1717

ENSIGN
Unknown ....c. 1800

EOFF & CONNOR
New York, N.Y. 1833

EOFF, EDGAR W.
New York, N.Y. 1785-1858

EOFF, GARRET
New York, N.Y. 1785-1858

EOFF & HOWELL
New York, N.Y. 1805

EOFF & MOORE
New York, N.Y. 1835

EOFF & PHYFE
New York, N.Y. 1844

EOFF & SHEPARD
New York, N.Y. 1825

EOLLES & DAY
Hartford, Conn. 1825

EPPS, ELLERY
Boston, Mass. 1808

EQUER & AQUIMAC
New York, N.Y. ... .1816

ERWIN, ANDREW
Philadelphia, Pa. 1837

ERWIN, HENRY
Philadelphia, Pa. 1817

ERWIN, JOHN
New York, N.Y. 1815

ESTEVA, HAYACINTH
New York, N.Y. 1804

ETTER, B.
Unknown .... c. 1780

ETTING, BENJAMIN
New York, N.Y. 1769

EVANS, HENRY
New York, N.Y. .. 1820

EVANS, JOHN
New York, N.Y. 1830

EVANS, ROBERT
Boston, Mass. ......· 1768-1812

EVERITT, JESSE
New York, N.Y. 1811

EVERSTEN, JOHN
Albany, N.Y. 1813

EWAN, JOHN
Charleston, S.C. 1800

F

FABER, WILLIAM
Philadelphia, Pa. 1837

FABER & HOOVER
Philadelphia, Pa. 1837

FAGALER, GEORGE M.
Philadelphia, Pa. 1808

FAIRCHILD, JAMES L.
New York, N.Y. 1830

FAIRCHILD, JOSEPH
New Haven, Conn. ....·...1824

FAIRCHILD, ROBERT
Durham, Conn. 1703-1794

FARIS, CHARLES
Boston, Mass. 1790

FARIS, WILLIAM
Annapolis, Md. 1728-1804

FARLEY, CHARLES
Portland, Me. 1812

FARNAM, HENRY
Boston, Mass. 1799

FARNAM, R. & H.
Boston, Mass. 1807

FARNAM, RUFUS
Boston, Mass. 1796

FARNAM, THOMAS
Boston, Mass. 1836

FARNUM & WARD
Boston, Mass. . ... .1810

FARNHAM & OWEN
Unknown 1810

FARR, JOHN C.
Boston, Mass. 1812

FARRINGTON & HUNNEWELL
Boston, Mass. ...1830

FARRINGTON, JOHN
Boston, Mass. 1826

FAULKNER, J. W.
New York, N.Y. 1835

FELLOWS, ABRAHAM
Newport, R.I. 1826

FELLOWS & GREEN
Maine 1825

FELLOWS, JOHN F.
Portsmouth, N.H. 1824

FELLOWS & STORM
Albany, N.Y. 1839

FENNO, J.
Unknown 1825

FERGUSON, JOHN
Philadelphia, Pa. 1802

ERRIER, JOHN
New Orleans, La. 1802

ERRIS, BENJAMIN
New York, N.Y. 1816

ESSENDEN
Newport, R.I. 1845   FESSENDEN PURE SILVER

EURT, JETER
New York, N.Y. 1731   PF

IELDING, GEORGE
New York, N.Y. 1731   GF

IELDS, SAMUEL
Philadelphia, Pa. 1816

FIELD, JOHN S.
Westerly, R.I.

INCH, HIRAM
Albany, N.Y. 1840

INEWELL, SAMUEL
New York, N.Y. 1835

IRENG, J. P.
Burlington, N.J. 1810   J.P.FIRENG BURLINGTON NJ

ISHER, JAMES
New York, N.Y. 1821

ISHER, THOMAS
Philadelphia, Pa. 1797   T.Fisher T.FISHER TFisher

ITCH, ALLEN
New Haven, Conn. 1808

ITCH, D. M.
New Haven, Conn. 1840   D.M.FITCH

ITCH & HOBART
New Haven, Conn. 1811

ITCH, JOHN
Trenton, N.J. 1769-1875   J.FITCH

ITE, JOHN
Baltimore, Md. 1810   I.FITE

LAGG, JOSIAH
Boston, Mass. 1765

LAGG, JOSIAH, Jr.
Boston, Mass. 1810

LETCHER & BENNETT
Philadelphia, Pa. 1837

LETCHER, CHARLES
Philadelphia, Pa. 1817

FLETCHER & BARDINER
Philadelphia, Pa. 1812   F.&G. F.&G.

FLETCHER, THOMAS
Philadelphia, Pa. 1813   T.FLETCHER PHILAD·

FLING, GEORGE
Philadelphia, Pa. 1749

FLOTT, LEWIS
Baltimore, Md. 1817

FOLLOPPE, A. A.
Boston, Mass. 1808

FOLSOM, JOHN
Albany, N.Y. 1781

FOOTE, WILLIAM
Middletown, Conn.
East Haddam, Conn. 1796

FORBES, ABRAHAM G.
New York, N.Y. 1769   AGF AF N.YORK

FORBES, BENJAMIN G.
New York, N.Y. 1817

FORBES, COLLINS V. G.
New York, N.Y. 1816   CVGF

FORBES, C. V. G. & SON
New York, N.Y. 1835   FORBES & SON

FORBES, G.
New York, N.Y. 1816

FORBES, G. & J. W.
New York, N.Y. 1810

FORBES, GARRET
New York, N.Y. 1808   G.FORBES

FORBES, I. W.
New York, N.Y. 1805

FORBES, JOHN W.
New York, N. Y. 1805   IWF NY IWF NY I.W.FORBES I.W.FORBES

FORBES & SON, C. V. G.
New York, N.Y. 1835   WF WF NEW YORK

FORBES, WILLIAM
New York, N.Y. 1830   W.FORBES NY N.YORK

FORBES, WILLIAM G.
New York, N.Y. 1773   W.FORBES W.G.Forbes WG Forbes WG Forbes W.G.FORBES N.YORK

FORCE, JABEZ W.
New York, N.Y. 1819   J.W.FORCE

FORD, SAMUEL
Philadelphia, Pa. 1797   SF

FOREST, ALEXANDER
Baltimore, Md. 1802

FORMAN, BENONI B.
Albany, N.Y. 1813

FORREST, ALEXANDER
Baltimore, Md. 1802

FORTUNE, ANTHONY
Philadelphia, Pa. 1767

FOSTER, ABRAHAM
Philadelphia, Pa. 1816

FOSTER, G.
Salem, Mass. 1838

FOSTER, I.
Unknown 1761

FOSTER, JOHN
New York, N.Y. 1811   J.FOSTER

FOSTER, JOSEPH
Boston, Mass. 1760-1839   FOSTER I.FOSTER

FOSTER, N. & J.
Newburyport, R. I. 1823

FOSTER & RICHARDS
New York, N. Y. 1815

FOSTER, SAMUEL
Boston, Mass. 1676-1702

FOSTER, THOMAS
Newburyport, Mass........1823

FOURNIQUET, LOUIS
New York, N. Y. 1795

FOURNIQUET & WHEATLEY
New York, N. Y. 1817

FOWLER, GILBERT
New York, N. Y. 1825

FRADGLEY, THOMAS
New York, N. Y. 1797

FRANCIS, JULIUS C.
Middletown, Conn. 1807

FRANCIS, NATHANIEL
New York, N. Y. 1804

FRANCIS, NATHANIEL
New York, N. Y. 1819

FRANCISCUS, GEORGE
Baltimore, Md. 1776

FRANK, JACOB
Philadelphia, Pa. 1793

FRANKS, WILLIAM
Philadelphia, Pa. 1839

FRASER, WILLIAM
Philadelphia, Pa. 1735

FREEBORN, N.
Unknown ....C 1800

FREEMAN, WILLIAM
Philadelphia, Pa. 1839

FREEMANS, J. M. & CO.
Unknown ....C 1800

FRINTH, JAMES
Philadelphia, Pa. 1840

FROBISHER, BENJAMIN C.
Boston, Mass. 1836

FROST & MUMFORD
Providence, R. I. 1810

FROTHERINGHAM, EBENEZER
Boston, Mass. 1756-1814

FRYER, JOHN W.
Albany, N. Y. 1784

FUETER, DANIEL C.
New York, N. Y. 1756

FUETER, DAVID
New York, N. Y. 1789

FUETER, LEWIS
New York, N. Y. 1775

FULLER, ALEXANDER
New York, N. Y. 1811

FURIS, LEWIS
New York, N. Y. 1810

G

GADLEY & JOHNSON
Albany, N. Y. 1849

GAFKINS, J.
Providence, R. I. 1832

GAITHER, GREENBERG
District of Columbia 1834

GALE & HAYDEN
New York, N. Y. 1846

GALE, JOHN
New York, N. Y. 1816

GALE, JOHN .
New York, N. Y. 1819

GALE, JOHN S.
New York, N. Y. 1820

GALE & MOSELY
New York, N. Y. 1830

GALE & STICKLER
New York, N. Y. 1823

GALE, WILLIAM
New York, N. Y. 1816

GALE, WILLIAM, JR.
New York, N. Y. 1823

GALE & SON, WM.
New York, N. Y. ....:..1823

GALE & WILLIS
New York, N. Y. 1840

GALE, WOOD & HUGHES
New York, N. Y. 1835

GALLOP, CHRISTOPHER
Ledyard, Conn. 1790

GALT, SAMUEL
Williamsburg, Va. 1749

GARDINER, B.
New York, N. Y. 1829

GARDINER, BALDWIN
Philadelphia, Pa. 1814

GARDINER & CO.
New York, N. Y. 1836

GARDINER, JOHN
New London, Conn. ...1734-1776

GARDINER, SIDNEY
Philadelphia, Pa. 1810

GARDINER, JOHN J.
Boston, Mass. 1730-1776

GARLLOW, SHAVELIER
Philadelphia, Pa. 1813

GARNER, JOHN
Cincinnati, Ohio 1825

GARRE, S.
New York, N. Y. 1825

ERREN, ANTHONY
Philadelphia, Pa. 1813

ARRETT, P.
Philadelphia, Pa. .... 1811 — P.GARRETT

ARRETT, T. C.
Philadelphia, Pa. 1815

ARRETT, T. C. & CO.
Philadelphia, Pa. ....1815 — T.C.GARRETT & CO

ARRISON, JOHN
New York, N.Y. 1825

ARROW & DORSEY
Baltimore, Md. 1800

ASKINS, J.
Unknown 1760

ASKINS, W. W.
Providence, R. I. ....1830 — WWG

ATHAM, WILLIAM
Philadelphia, Pa. 1802

AY, CHARLES
Baltimore, Md. 1779

AY, NATHANIEL
Boston, Mass. 1664

EE, JOSEPH
Philadelphia, Pa. 1785

EFFROY, NICHOLAS
Newport, R.I. ....1761-1839 — N GEFFROY. GEFFROY N.GEFFROY

ELEY, PETER
Philadelphia, Pa. 1793

ELSTON & CO.
New York, N.Y. ....1837 — GELSTON & CO

ELSTON, GEORGE S.
New York, N.Y. ....1833 — G.S.GELSTON

ELSTON & GOULD
Baltimore, Md. 1819

ELSTON, HUGH
Baltimore, Md. ....1794-1873 — HU.GELSTON GELSTON

ELSTON, LADD & CO.
New York, N.Y. ....1836 — GELSTON LADD & CO

ELSTON & TREADWELL
New York, N.Y. 1836

GEORGEON, BERNARD
Philadelphia, Pa. 1797

GERMON, J. D.
Philadelphia, Pa. 1819

GERMON, JOHN D.
Philadelphia, Pa. ....1782 — I.G

GERRISH & PEARSON
New York, N.Y. ....1800 — Gerrish & Pearson

GERRISH, TIMOTHY
Portsmouth, N. H. ....1753-1813 — TG T.Gerrish GERRISH J Gerrish

GETHEN, JOHN
Philadelphia, Pa. 1811

GETHEN, WILLIAM
Philadelphia, Pa. ....1797 — W.GETHEN

GETTY, JAMES
Williamsburg, Va 1772

GETZ, PETER
Lancaster, Pa. ....1792 — P.Getz

GHISELIN, CESAR
Philadelphia, Pa. ....1695 — CG CG CG

GHISELIN, WILLIAM
Philadelphia, Pa. ....1751 — WG GHISELIN

GIBBS, DANIEL
Boston, Mass. 1716

GIBBS, JOHN
Providence, R.I. ....1798 — J GIBBS

GIBBS, JOHN F.
Providence, R. I. 1803

GIBSON, WILLIAM
Philadelphia, Pa. ....1845 — GIBSON

GIFFING, CHRISTOPHER
New York, N.Y. ....1816 — C.Gifing.N.Y

GILBERT, SAMUEL
Hebron, Conn. ....1798 — SG SG

GILBERT, WILLIAM W.
New York, N.Y. ....1767 — WG N.YORK GILBERT W.Gilbert Gilbert N.York

GILBERT & CUNNINGHAM
New York, N.Y. 1839

GILL, CALEB
Boston, Mass. ....1774-1855 — GILL

GILL, LEAVITT
Hingham, Mass. 1810

GILLEY, PETER
Philadelphia, Pa. 1797

GILMAN, BENJAMIN CLARK
Exeter, N. H. ....1763-1835 — BCG

GILMAN, JOHN WARD
New York, N.Y. ....1792 — I·W·G

GIQUEL, JOHN B. F.
New Orleans, La. 1822

GIRARD, FRANCIS
Philadelphia, Pa. 1817

GIRAUD, HENRY
New York, N.Y. 1805

GIRRAD, HENRY
New York, N.Y. 1805

GIRREAUN, STEPHEN
Philadelphia, Pa. 1785

GIVEN, A.
Albany, N.Y. 1849

GLIDDEN, JOSEPH
Boston, Mass. 1607-1780

GODDARD D. & SON
Worcester, Mass. ....1845 — D.GODDARD & SON

GOELET, PHILIP
New York, N.Y. 1731

GOFORTH, JEREMIAH
Philadelphia, Pa 1700

GOLDTHWAITE, JOSEPH
Boston, Mass. 1706-1780

GOMBACH, JOHN
Philadelphia, Pa. 1802

GOODHUE, D. T.
Boston, Mass. 1840

GOODHUE, JOHN
Salem, Mass. 1840

GOODING, HENRY
Boston, Mass. ...., 1833

GOODING, JOSEPH
Boston, Mass. 1815

GOODING, JOSIAH
Unknown 1810

GOODWIN, ALLYN
Hartford, Conn. 1811

GOODWIN, BENJAMIN
Boston, Mass. 1756

GOODWIN & DODD
Hartford, Conn. . 1812

GOODWIN, H. & A.
Hartford, Conn. ... 1811

GOODWIN, HORACE
Hartford, Conn. 1811

GOODWIN, HORACE & ALLYN
Hartford, Conn, 1811

GOODWIN, RALPH
Hartford, Conn. 1828

GORDON, A. & J.
New York, N.Y. 1798

GORDON, ALEXANDER S.
New York, N.Y. 1795

GORDON, ANDREW
New York, N.Y. 1796

GORDON & COMPANY
Boston, Mass. 1849

GORDON, G.
New York, N.Y. 1800

GORDON, JAMES
New York, N.Y. 1795

GORDON, JAMES S.
Philadelphia, Pa. . .. 1769

GORHAM, JABEZ
Providence, R. I. . . 1792

GORHAM, JABEZ & SON
Providence, R.I. 1842

GORHAM, JOHN
New Haven, Conn. 1814

GORHAM, MILES
New Haven, Conn. ..1757-1847

GORHAM, RICHARD
New Haven, Conn. 1799

GORHAM & THURBER
Providence, R. I. ... .. .1850

GORHAM & WEBSTER
New York, N.Y. .. . ..:1831

GOUGH, JAMES
New York, N.Y. 1769

GOULD, J.
Balimore, Md. 1795-1874

GOULD, JAMES
Baltimore, Md. 1816-1868

GOULD, JOHN
Philadelphia, Pa. 1840

GOULD, STOWELL & WARD
Baltimore, Md. 1840

GOULD & WARD
Baltimore, Md. 1850

GOVERT, JAMES
Philadelphia, Pa. 1802

GOWEN, WILLIAM
Medford, Mass. 1772

GRAHAM, DANIEL
West Suffield, Conn. .. .1789

GRANT, THOMAS
Marblehead, Mass. . . . 1754

GRANT, WILLIAM, JR.
Philadelphia, Pa. . 1785

GRAVELLE, RENE S.
Philadelphia, Pa. .. 1813

GRAVES, THOMAS
Cincinatti, Ohio 1828

GRAVIER, NICHOLAS
New Orleans, La. 1822

GRAY, G.
Portsmouth, N. H. 1839

GRAY, JOHN
New London, Conn. 1692-1720

GRAY, ROBERT
Portsmouth, N. H. 1850

GRAY, SAMUEL
New London, Conn. 1684-1713

GRAY, SAMUEL
Boston, Mass. '1732

GREEN, BENJAMIN
Boston, Mass. 1712-1748

GREEN, JAMES
New York, N.Y. 1805

GREGG, HAYDEN & CO.
New York, N.Y. 1850

GREENE, RUFUS
Boston, Mass. 1707-1777

GREENE, WM. & CO.
Providence, R. I. 1815

GREENLEAF, DAVID
Norwich, Conn. 1737-1800

GREENLEAF, DAVID, Jr.
Hartford, Conn. 1766

GREENLEAF, JOSEPH
New London, Conn. ...1779-1798

GREFFIN, PETER
Philadelphia, Pa. 1801

GRIFFEN & HOYT
Albany, N. Y. 1830

GRIFFEN, P.
Albany, N. Y. 1825

GRIFFING, CHRISTOPHER
New York, N. Y. 1816

GRIFITH, DAVID
Boston, Mass. 1789

GRIGG, WM.
New York, N. Y. ..,......1765

GRIGNON, BENJAMIN
Boston, Mass. 1685

GRIGNON, RENE
Norwich, Conn. 1715

GRIMKE, JOHN P.
Charleston, S. C. 1744

GRISCOM, GEORGE
Philadelphia, Pa. 1791

GRISELM, CAESAR
Philadelphia, Pa. 1700

GRISWOLD, GILBERT
Middletown, Conn. 1825

GRISWOLD, WILLIAM
Middletown, Conn. 1820

GROEN, JACOB MARIUS
(Morrisgreen)
New York, N. Y. 1701

GUERCY, DOMINICK
New York, N. Y. 1795

GUERIN, ANTHONY
Philadelphia, Pa. 1791

GUILLE, NOAH
Boston, Mass. 1701

GUIRNA, ANTHONY
Philadelphia, Pa. 1796

GUNN, ENOS
Waterbury, Conn. 1792

GURLEY, WILLIAM
Norwich, Conn. 1804

GURNEE, BENJAMIN
New York, N. Y. 1820

GURNEE, B. & S.
New York, N. Y. 1833

GURNEE & COMPANY
New York, N. Y. 1820

H

HACKLE, WILLIAM
Baltimore, Md. 1776

HADDOCK & ANDREWS
Boston, Mass. 1838

HADDOCK, HENRY
Boston, Mass. 1836

HADWEN, WILLIAM
Nantucket, Mass. 1816

HAGGENMACHER, J. H. & CO.
Philadelphia, Pa. 1836

HAINES, ABRAHAM
New York, N. Y. 1801

HALL, ABIJAH
Albany, N. Y. 1813

HALL & BROWER
Albany, N. Y. 1830

HALL, BROWER & CO.
Albany, N. Y. 1836

HALL, CHARLES
Lancaster, Pa. 1755

HALL, DAVID
Philadelphia, Pa. 1760-1779

HALL, DREW
New York, N. Y. 1789

HALL, GREEN
Albany, N. Y. 1813

HALL & HEWSON
Albany, N. Y. 1819

HALL, HEWSON &
MERRIFIELD
Albany, N. Y. 1814

HALL, IVORY
Concord, N. H. 1781

HALL & MERRIMAN
New Haven, Conn. 1825

HALL & MERRIMAN
Albany, N.Y. 1825

HALLAM, JOHN
New London, Conn. 1773

HALSEY, JABEZ
New York, N. Y. 1762-1820

HALSTED, BENJAMIN
New York, N. Y. 1764

HALSTED & SON
New York, N. Y. 1799

HALSTRICK, J.
Boston, Mass. 1846

HAM, GEORGE
Portsmouth, N. H. 1810

HAMILL & COMPANY
New York, N. Y. 1817

HAMILL, JAMES
New York, N. Y. 1816   J·HAMILL .N.Y.

HAMILTON, JAMES
Annapolis, Md. 1766

HAMILTON, JOHN
New York, N. Y. 1798

HAMLIN, CYRUS
Portland, Me. 1831

HAMLIN, WILLIAM
Middletown, Conn. 1761   W·H ᴳ WH ᴰ HAMLIN

HAMMERSLEY, THOMAS
New York, N. Y. 1727-1781   TH T·H TH

HANCOCK, JOHN
Boston, Mass. 1732-1772   J·HANCOCK J·HANCOCK J·HANCOCK

HANDLE, JOHN
Philadelphia, Pa. 1839

HANKS, BENJAMIN
Wyndham, Conn. 1777

HANNAH, W. W.
New York, N. Y. 1840   W.W.HANNAH

HANNERS, GEORGE
Boston, Mass. 1697-1740   GH G·HANNERS

HANNERS, GEORGE, JR.
Boston, Mass. 1721-1760   G·H G.H

HANSELL, ROBERT
Boston, Mass. 1823

HARACHE, PIERRE
Williamsburg, Va. 1691

HARDING, N. & C.
New York, N. Y. 1830

HARDING & CO. N.
Boston, Mass. 1830   ← N.H&CO

HARDING, NEWELL
Boston, Mass. 1822   N.Harding NHarding N.HARDING N.H&CO N.Harding&Cº

HARDWOOD, JOHN
Philadelphia, Pa. 1816

HARDY, STEPHEN
Portsmouth, N. H. ...1781-1843   HARDY HARDY

HARLAND, THOMAS
Norwich, Conn. 1735-1807   HARLAND

HARLAND, THOMAS, JR.
Norwich, Conn. 1777

HARPEL, THOMAS W.
Philadelphia, Pa. 1813

HARPER, ALEXANDER
Philadelphia, Pa. ....

HARPER, DAVID
Philadelphia, Pa ....

HARPER, THOMAS W.
Philadelphia, Pa. .... .1813

HARRIS, GEORGE
New York, N. Y. 1802

HARRIS, H.
Albany, N. Y. 1820

HARRIS & STANWOOD
Boston, Mass. 1835   HARRIS & STANWOOD

HARRIS & WILCOX
Albany, N. Y. 1844   HARRIS & WILCOX

HART & BLISS
Middletown, Conn. 1803

HART & BREWER
Middletown, Conn. 1800-1803   H&B

HART, ELIPHAZ
Norwich, Conn. 1789-1866   EH E.HART

HART, JOHN
Philadelphia, Pa. 1776

HART, JOHN J.
New York, N. Y. 1820

HART, JUDAH
Middletown, Conn. 1777-1824   J.HART J.Hart JHART

HART & SMITH
Baltimore, Md. 1816   H&S

HART & WILCOX
Norwich, Conn. 1805-1807   H▾W

HART, WILLIAM
Philadelphia, Pa. 1818   W.HART.

HARTFORD, GEORGE
Philadelphia, Pa. 1794

HARTIN & BARGI
Bound Brook, N. J. 1766

HARTLEY, SAMUEL
Philadelphia, Pa. 1818

HARTMAN, PHILIP
Philadelphia, Pa. 1813

HARVEY, LEWIS
Philadelphia, Pa. 1811   HARVEY.LEWIS

HASCY, ALEXANDER
Albany, N. Y. 1849

HASCY, NELSON
Albany, N. Y. 1849

HASKELL, BARNABUS
Boston, Mass. 1833

HASTIER, JOHN
New York, N. Y. 1726   IH IH IH IH J.

HASTIER, MARQUERIETTE
New York, N. Y. 1771   MH

HASTINGS, B. B.
Cleveland, Ohio 1835   HASTINGS

HASTINGS, H.
New York, N. Y. 1815   H·HASTINGS

HAUGH, SAMUEL
Boston, Mass. 1675-1717   SH

HAVERSTICK, WILLIAM
Philadelphia, Pa. 1781   WH

HAWLEY, NOAH
New York, N. Y. 1816

HAWS, JOHN
Philadelphia, Pa. 1837

HAYDEN & GREGG
New York, N. Y. 1840   HAYDEN & GREGG

HAYES & COLTON
Newark, N. J. 1831

HAYES, W.
Connecticut 1780   WH   W·Hayes

HAYS, ANDREW
Newark, N. J. 1769

HAYS & MYERS
New York, N. Y. 1770   H&M

HEAD, JOSEPH
Philadelphia, Pa. 1798

HEALD, J. S.
Baltimore, Md. 1810   J·S·HEALD   IP

HEALY
Boston, Mass. 1773

HEATH, JOHN
New York, N. Y. 1761   C·HEATH

HEBBERD
New York, N. Y. 1847

HECK, LUDWIG
Lancaster, Pa. 1760   LH

HEDGES, DANIEL
Unknown ....C 1830   HEDGES

HEDGES, DANIEL, JR.
East Hampton, N. Y. ..1779-1856

HEGUENBURG, CHARLES, JR.
New Haven, Conn. 1809

HELME, NATHANIEL
South Kingston, R.I. .1761-1789   HELME   HELME
                                   N·H

HEMPSTED & CHADLER
New York, N. Y. 1811

HENCHMAN, DANIEL
Boston, Mass. 1730-1775   D·H   Henchman

HENDERSON, A. A.
Philadelphia, Pa. 1837   HENDERSON

HENDRICKS, AHASUERUS
New York, N. Y. 1676   AH   A·H

HENRY, FELIX
New York, N. Y. 1815

HEQUENBOURG, CHARLES, Jr.
New Haven, Conn. ... 1760-1851   GH   C·HEQUEMBOURG·JR

HERBERT, TIMOTHY B.
New York, N. Y. 1816

HERILS, FRANCIS
Philadelphia, Pa. 1804

HERON, ISAAC
New York, N. Y. . .1768

HEURTIN, WILLIAM
New York, N. Y. 1731

HEWS, ABRAHAM, JR.
Boston, Mass. 1823   A·HEWS·JR

HEWSON, JOHN D.
Albany, N. Y. 1815

HEYDORN & IMLAY
Hartford, Conn. 1810   H&I

HEYER & CALE
New York, N. Y. 1807   W·B·HEYER & J·CALE

HEYER, WILLIAM B.
New York, N. Y. 1798   W·B·HEYER   W·B·Heyer
                                  W·B·Heyer   H&NJ

HIGBIE & CROSBY
Boston, Mass. 1820   HIGBIE & CROSBY

HILDEBUR
Philadelphia, Pa. 1790

HILL, JAMES
Boston, Mass. 1770

HILL & WADDILL
Petersburgh, Va. 1780

HILLDRUP, THOMAS
Hartford, Conn. 1774

HILLER, BENJAMIN
Boston, Mass. 1687   BH   BH   BH

HILLER, JOSEPH
Boston, Mass. 1745

HILLDRAUP, THOMAS
Hartford, Conn. 1772

HILTON, WM.
Philadelphia, Pa. 1814

HIND, JOHN
Philadelphia, Pa. 1760

HINSDALE & ATKIN
New York, N. Y. 1830   HINSDALE & ATKIN

HINSDALE, EPAPHRAS
New York, N. Y. 1797   HINSDALE

HINSDALE, H.
New York, N. Y. 1831

HITCHBORN, DANIEL
Boston, Mass. 1773

HITCHBORN, SAMUEL
Boston, Mass. 1752

HITCHCOCK, ELIAKIM
Boston, Mass. 1752   E+H   EH

HOBARTH, JOSHUA
New Haven, Conn. 1811   J·HOBART

HOBBS, NATHAN
Boston, Mass. 1792-1868   HOBBS   N.Hobbs

HODGE, JOHN
Hadley, Mass. 1775   `J.HODGE` `HADLEY`

HOFFMAN, FREDERICK
Philadelphia, Pa.   ...1819

HOFFMAN, JAMES M.
Philadelphia, Pa.   1820   `J.M.HOFFMAN`

HOLLAND, LITTLETON
Baltimore, Md.   1804   `L.H.C` `L.Holland` `L.HOLLAND` `HOLLAND` `Holland`

HOLLINGSHEAD, JOHN
Philadelphia, Pa.   1768

HOLLINGSHEAD, WILLIAM
Philadelphia, Pa.   1770   `WH` `WH`

HOLMES, ADRIAN B.
New York, N.Y.   1801   `A.HOLMES`

HOLMES, ISRAEL
Waterbury, Conn.   1793

HOLMES, J.
New York, N.Y. 1816

HOLMES, WILLIAM
New York, N.Y. 1801

HOLSEY, E.
Philadelphia, Pa. 1820   `E.HOLSEY`

HOLTON, DAVID
Baltimore, Md. :....... 1804

HOLTON, JOHN
Philadelphia, Pa. 1794

HOLYOKE, EDWARD
Boston, Mass. 1817   `HOLYOKE`

HOMES, WILLIAM
Boston, Mass. 1717-1783   `WH` `WH` `HOMES` `W.HOmes`

HOMES, WILLIAM, JR.
New York, N.Y. 1742-1825   `WH` `W.H` `HOMES`

HOOD & TOBY
Albany, N.Y. 1849   `HOOD & TOBEY`

HOOKEY, WILLIAM
Newport, R.I. 1750

HOOVER, HENRY
Philadelphia, Pa. 1816

HOOVER, JOSEPH E.
Philadelphia, Pa. 1837

HOPKINS, JESSE
Waterbury, Conn. 1787

HOPKINS, JOSEPH
Waterbury, Conn. 1730-1801   `HOPKINS`

HOPKINS, STEPHEN
Waterbury, Conn. ... 1721-1796   `SH`

HOPPER, SAMUEL
Philadelphia, Pa. 1835

HORN, E. B.
Boston, Mass. 1847

HOSFORD, HARLEY
New York, N.Y. 1820   `HOSFORD`

HOTCHKISS, HEZEKIAH
New Haven, Conn.   1754

HOUGH, SAMUEL
Boston, Mass.   1675-1717   `SH`

HOULTON, JOHN
Philadelphia, Pa.   1797   `HOULTON`

HOUTZELL, JACOB
Philadelphia, Pa.   1801

HOW, DAVID
Boston, Mass.   1790

HOWARD, ABRAHAM
Salem, Mass.   1810

HOWARD, JOHN
Philadelphia, Pa.   1819

HOWARD, THOMAS
Philadelphia, Pa.   1620

HOWARD, WILLIAM
Boston, Mass.   .. 1800

HOWE, GEORGE C.
New York, N.Y.   1810   `GEORGE C.HOWE`

HOWE, OTIS
Boston, Mass. 1788

HOWELL & ARNOLD
Albany, N.Y. 1797

HOWELL, G. W.
Unknown . . . . ..:....... 1790   `G.W.Howell`

HOWELL, JAMES
Philadelphia, Pa. 1802   `J.Howell` `Howell` `J.Howell.`

HOWELL, PAUL
New York, N.Y. 1812   `P.HOWELL`

HOWELL, SILAS W.
Albany, N.Y. 1798   `S.W.Howell` `S.W.Howell`

HOYT, GEORGE B.
Albany, N.Y. 1827   `GEO.B.HOYT`

HOYT, HENRY E.
New York, N.Y. 1820   `HENRY HOYT`

HOYT, S.
New York, N.Y. 1840   `S.HOYT`

HUBBAL
Washington, D.C. 1834

HUERTIN, WILLIAM
New York, N.Y. 1731-1771   `WH` `WH` `WH`

HUGHES & BLISS
Middletown, Conn. 1806

HUGHES, CHRISTOPHER
Baltimore, Md. 1744-1824   `CH` `CH`

HUGHES & FRANCIS
Middletown, Conn. 1807

HUGHES, HENRY
Baltimore, Md. 1781

HUGHES, J.
Middletown, Conn. 1798   `J.HUGHES` `STERLI`

HUGHES, JEREMIAH Annapolis, Md. 1805	J·HUGHES
HUGHES, WILLIAM Baltimore, Md. 1785-1791	W.H
HULBEART, PHILIP Philadelphia, Pa. 1761	
HULL, JOHN Boston, Mass. 1624-1683	IH IH IH IH
HULL & SANDERSON Boston, Mass. 1652	IH RS IH RS IH RS
HUMBERT, AUGUSTUS New York, N. Y. 1818	
HUMPHREYS, RICHARD Philadelphia, Pa. 1772	R·H RH R.Humphrey
HUMPHREYS, THOMAS Philadelphia, Pa. 1814	R·Humphreys
HUNLOCK, BOUMAN Philadelphia, Pa. 1752	
HUNNEWELL, GEORGE W. Boston, Mass. 1836	
HUNT, EDWARD Boston, Mass. 1717	
HUNT, WILLIAM Boston, Mass. 1819	
HUNTINGTON, PHILIP Norwich, Conn. 1770-1825	PH Huntington
HUNTINGTON, ROSWELL Norwich, Conn. 1763	
HUNTINGTON, S. Maine 1850	S·HUNTINGTON
HURD, BENJAMIN Boston, Mass. ...-....1739-1781	B·H
HURD, ISAAC Roxbury, Mass...........1754	
HURD, JACOB Boston, Mass........1702-1758	Hurd Hurd Hurd HURD Jacob Hurd HURD Hurd
HURD, NATHANIEL Boston, Mass. ....-....1730-1777	N·Hurd N·Hurd N·Hurd
HURLBEART, PHILLIP Philadelphia, Pa. 1761	PH
HURST, HENRY Boston, Mass 1665-1717	HH H·H
HURTIN & BURGI Bound Brook, N.J. 1766	
HUSBAND, JOHN Philadelphia, Pa. 1796	
HUSSEY, STEPHEN Maryland 1818	S·HUSSEY
HUSTON, JAMES Baltimore, Md. 1799	
HUTCHINS, JACOB New York, N. Y. 1774	HUTCHINS

HUTCHINS, NICHOLAS Baltimore, Md. 1777-1845	NH J
HUTTON, GEORGE Albany, N. Y. 1799	
HUTTON, I & G. Albany, N. Y. 1799	
HUTTON, ISAAC Albany, N. Y. 1767-1855	HUTTON ALBANY
HUTTON, JOHN New York, N. Y. 1720	H·I I·H
HUTTON, JOHN S. New York, N. Y. ... 1684	
HYDE Newport, R. I. 1730	HYDE
HYDE & GOODRICH New Orleans, N. Y. .. 1810	HYDE & GOODWICH N.O.
HYDE & NEVINS New York, N. Y. 1798	Hyde & Nevins
I	
IAGO, HENRY New York, N. Y. 1745	
INCH, JOHN Annapolis, Md. 1720-1763	II
INGRAHAM, JOSEPH Portland, Me. 1785	
INMAN, BENJAMIN Philadelphia, Pa. 1816	
ISAACKS, MICHAEL New York, N. Y. 1765	
IVERS, B. Unknown ....C 1800	B·Ivers
J	
JACCARD & COMPANY St. Louis, Mo. 1850	JACCARD & CO ST·LOUIS
JACKS, JAMES Charleston, S. C. 1795	
JACKS, WILLIAM Philadelphia, Pa. 1798	
JACKSON, DANIEL New York, N. Y. 1782	DI D·JACKSON
JACKSON, JAMES Baltimore, Md. 1775	
JACKSON, JOHN New York, N. Y. 1731	JACKSON
JACKSON, JOSEPH Baltimore, Md. 1803	J·Jackson J·Jackson
JACOB, GEORGE Baltimore, Md. 1802	G·JACOB
JACOB, MOSES Philadelphia, Pa. 1775	
JACOBS, ABEL Philadelphia, Pa. 1816	A·JACOBS

JACOBS & CO. A.
Philadelphia, Pa. 1820

JANVIER, LOUIS
Charleston, S. C. ...,.,.:...1744

JARVIS, MUNSON
Stamford, Conn. 1742-1824

JENCKES, JOHN C.
Providence, R.I. 1798

JENCKES & COMPANY
Providence, R. I. 1798

JENKINS, JOHN
Philadelphia, Pa. 1777

JENNINGS, JACOB
Norwalk, Conn. 1739-1817

JENNINGS, JACOB, JR.
New London, Conn. 1800

JESSE, DAVID
Boston, Mass. 1670-1705

JOHANNES, JOHN M.
Baltimore, Md. 1835

JOHN
Unknown ....C 1760

JOHNSON & BALL
Baltimore, Md. 1785

JOHNSON, C.
Albany, N. Y. 1828

JOHNSON & GODLEY
Albany, N. Y. 1847

JOHNSON, JOHN
Pittsburg, Pa. 1815

JOHNSON, MAYCOCK W.
Albany, N. Y. 1815

JOHNSON & REAT
Baltimore, Md. 1786

JOHNSON & RILEY
Baltimore, Md. 1786

JOHNSON, SAMUEL
New York, N. Y. 1780

JOHNSON, SAMUEL
New York, N. Y. 1796

JOHNSTON, A.
Philadelphia, Pa. 1830

JOHONNOT, WILLIAM B.
Middletown, Conn. 1766-1849

JONES, BALL & POOR
Boston, Mass. 1840

JONES, E.
Baltimore, Md. 1820

JONES, GEORGE B.
Boston, Mass. 1839

JONES, JAMES
Philadelphia, Pa. 1815

JONES, JOHN
Boston, Mass. 1810

JONES, JOHN B.
Boston, Mass. 1782-1854

JONES, JOHN B. & COL.
Boston, Mass. 1813

JONES, LOWS & BALL
Boston, Mass. 1850

JONES & WARD
Boston, Mass. 1815

JONES, WILLIAM
Marblehead, Mass. 1694-1730

JONES, WILLIAM
New York, N. Y. 1820

JORDAN, PETER
Philadelphia, Pa. 1823

JOUBERT, P.
Philadelphia, Pa. 1807

JUDAH
New York, N. Y. 1774

KAY, AMOS
Boston, Mass. 1725

KEDZIE, J.
Philadelphia, Pa. 1830

KEELER, A.
Norwalk, Conn. ... .1800-

KEELER, JOSEPH
Norwalk, Conn. 1786-1824

KEELER, THADDEUS
New York, N.Y. 1805

KEIFF, JOSEPH
Philadelphia, Pa. 1831

KEITH. T. & W.
New York, N. Y. 1805

KELEY, GRAEL
Boston, Mass. 1823

KELLEY, ALLEN
Providence, R.I. 1810

KELLEY, E. G. & J. H.
Providence, R.I. 1820

KENDLE, CHARLES
New York, N. Y. 1807

KENDRICK, WILLIAM
Louisville, Ky. 1840

KENNEDY, MATHEW
Philadelphia, Pa. 1825

KENRICK, ANWYL
Maryland 1775

KEPLINGER. SAMUEL
Baltimore. Md. 1770-1849

KETCHAM, JAMES
New York, N.Y. 1814

TTELL, THOMAS
arlestown, Mass. 1781   `T·K`

YWORTH, ROBERT
ashington, D.C. 1831   `R·KEYWORTH`

NEY, CANN & JOHNSON
w York, N.Y. 1850   `K.C.∿J.`

NEY & DUNN
New York, N.Y. 1844   `K&D` `K&D`

RSTEADE, CORNELIUS
ew York, N.Y. 1753   `CK` `CK`

RSTEADE, CORNELIUS
ew Haven, Conn. 1722

MBERLY, WILLIAM
w York, N.Y. 1792   `WK` `Kimberly`

G, JOSEPH
ddletown, Conn. 1770

G, THOMAS R.
altimore, Md. 1819   `TRKING`

GSTON, JOHN
ew York, N.Y. 1775

NEY, THOMAS
orwich, Conn. 1786-1824   `TK` `TK`

SEY, DAVID
ncinatti, Ohio 1850   `DKINSEY`

SEY, E. & D.
ncinnati, Ohio 1845   `E.&D.KINSEY`

, BENJAMIN
ew York, N.Y. 1702

PEN, GEORGE
ridgeport, Conn. 1820   `G·KIPPEN`

BY, WILLIAM
ew York, N.Y. 1783

RK, SAMUEL
altimore, Md. 1792-1872   `S.K` `S·Kirk` `Kirk` `S·KIRK` `KIRK`

RK & SMITH
altimore, Md. 1815   `S·KIRK` `SAM·KIRK` `KIRK&SMITH`

RKWOOD, PETER
nnapolis, Md. 1799   `PK`

RKWOOD, PETER
hestertown, Md. 1790

RTLAND, JOSEPH P.
iddletown, Conn. 1796

TCHEN, ANDREW
hiladelphia, Pa. 1835

INE, BARTHOLOMEW
hiladelphia, Pa. ...1837

INE, B. & CO.
hiladelphia, Pa. 1837

EELAND, JOSEPH
oston, Mass. 1698-1760   `I·Kneeland`

AUSE, JOHN S.
ethlehem, Pa. 1805

KRIDER & BIDDLE
Philadelphia, Pa. 1830   `K B`

KRIDER, PETER L.
Philadelphia, Pa. 1850   `P.L.K`

KUCHER, JACOB
Philadelphia, Pa. 1813   `I·KUCHER`

KUMBEL, WILLIAM
New York, N.Y. ...,.....1780

L

LACHAISE, PETER
New York, N.Y. 1794

LADD, WILLIAM F.
New York, N.Y. 1830   `Wᴹ·F.LADD` `NEW·YORK`

LAFORME, ANTOINE
Boston, Mass. 1836

LAFORME, BERNARD
Boston, Mass. 1836

LAFORME, F. J.
Boston, Mass. 1835

LAFORME, VINCENT
Boston, Mass. 1850   **V.LAFORME**

LAINECOURT, STEPHEN
New York, N.Y. 1800

LAKEMAN, E. K.
New York, N.Y. 1800   `E.K.LAKEMAN`

LAMAR, BENJAMIN
Philadelphia, Pa. 1785   `BL` `LAMAR`

LAMAR, MATHIAS
Philadelphia, Pa. 1796   `ML`

LAMESIERE, PETER
Philadelphia, Pa. 1811

LAMOTHE, JOHN
New Orleans, La. 1822

LAMOTHE, PIERRE
New Orleans, La. 1822   `Lamothe` `Lamothe`

LAMPE, JOHN
Baltimore, Md. 1787

LAMSON, J.
Unknown 1790   `J·LAMSON` `J·L`

LANE, AARON
Elizabeth, N.J. 1780   `AL`

LANG, EDWARD
Salem, Mass. ....:1742-1830   `EL` `LANG`

LANG, JEFFERY
Salem, Mass. 1708-1758   `I·LANG` `LANG` `I·LANG`

LANG, RICHARD
Salem, Mass. 1733-1810   `R·LANG`

LANGE, WILLIAM
New York, N.Y. 1844   `·LANGE·`

LANGER, JOSEPH
Philadelphia, Pa. 1811

LANSING, JACOB G.
Albany, N.Y. 1736   `IGL`

LAPEROUSE, JOHN B.
New Orleans, La. 1832

LAROUSSEBIERRE, PETER
New York, N.Y. 1797

LASHING, PETER
New York, N.Y. 1805

LATHROP, RUFUS
Norwich, Conn. 1755

LATRUIT, JOHN P.
Washington, D.C. 1833

LAWRENCE, JOSIAH H.
Philadelphia, Pa. 1817

LAWRIE, ROBERT O.
Philadelphia, Pa. 1840

LEA, SAMUEL J
Baltimore, Md. 1814

LEACH, CHARLES
Boston, Mass. 1765-1814

LEACH, JOHN
Boston, Mass. 1780

LEACH, NATHANIEL
Boston, Mass. 1789

LEACH, SAMUEL
Philadelphia, Pa. 1741

LEACH & BRADLEY
Philadelphia, Pa. 1832

LEACOCK, JOHN
Philadelphia, Pa. 1751

LAYCOCK, PETER
Philadelphia, Pa. 1750

LE BLANC, LEWIS
Philadelphia, Pa. 1815

LEDELL, JOSEPH
Philadelphia, Pa. 1797

LE DORC
Philadelphia, Pa. 1797

LEE, SAMUEL J.
Baltimore, Md. 1815

LEE, S. W.
Providence, R.I. 1815

LEFEVRE, F.
Philadelphia, Pa. 1818

LEFEVRE & GRAVELLE
Philadelphia, Pa. 1811

LEFEVRE, JOHN F.
Philadelphia, Pa. 1806

LEGARE, DANIEL
Boston, Mass. 1688-1724

LEGARE, FRANCIS
Boston, Mass. 1657

LEMAIRE, BAPTISTE
Philadelphia, Pa. 1804

LEMAIRE, MATHIAS
Philadelphia, Pa. 1781

LENCH, PETER
New York, N.Y. 1805

LENDIGREE, M.
New York, N.Y. 1814

LENT, JOHN
New York, N.Y. 1787

LEONARD, S.
New York, N.Y. 1830

LEONARD, SAMUEL
Baltimore, Md. 1786-1848

LEONARD & WILSON
Philadelphia, Pa. 1847

LERET, PETER
Baltimore, Md. 1787

LE ROUX, BARTHOLOMEW
New York, N.Y. 1700

LE ROUX, CHARLES
New York, N.Y. 1689-1745

LE ROUX, JOHN
New York, N.Y. 1723

LESCURE, EDWARD
Philadelphia, Pa. 1822

LE TELIER, JOHN
Philadelphia, Pa. 1770

LETOURNEAUX
New York, N.Y. 1797

LEVELY
Baltimore, Md. 1788

LEVERETT, KNIGHT
Boston, Mass. 1736

LEWYN, GABRIEL
Baltimore, Md. 1771

LEWIS, WILLIAM
Philadelphia, Pa. 1810

LEWIS, HARVEY
Philadelphia, Pa. 1811

LEWIS, ISAAC
Huntington, Conn. 1796

LEWIS & SMITH
Philadelphia, Pa. 1805

LEWIS, TUNIS
New York, N.Y. 1805

LIBBY, J. G. L.
Boston, Mass. 1830

LIDDEN, JOHN
St. Louis, Mo. 1850

LIGHTFOOT, JAMES
New York, N.Y. 1749

LINCH, PETER
New York, N.Y. 1805

NCOLN, A. L.
t. Louis, Mo. .... 1850 — A.L.Lincoln

NCOLN, ELIJAH
Boston, Mass. ...... 1794-1861 — E.Lincoln

NCOLN & FOSS
Boston, Mass. .... 1829 — LINCOLN & FOSS

NCOLN & GREEN
oston, Mass. .... 1810 — L&G

NCOLN & READ
Boston, Mass. .... 1835 — LINCOLN & READ

NDNER, GEORGE
hiladelphia, Pa. 1837

NGLEY, HENRY
ew York, N. Y. 1810

NK, PETER
hiladelphia, Pa. 1811

NTOT
ew York, N. Y. 1762

TTLE, PAUL
ortland, Me. 1760

TTLE, WILLIAM
ewburyport, Mass. ..... 1775 — W.L WL

CKWOOD, A.
ew York, N. Y. .... 1810 — A.LOCKWOOD

CKWOOD, F.
ew York, N. Y. .... 1845 — F.LOCKWOOD

CKWOOD, JAMES
ew York, N. Y. .... 1799 — LOCKWOOD

FLAND, PURNEL
hiladelphia, Pa. 1810

GAN, ADAM
ew York, N. Y. .... 1803 — A.LOGAN

GAN, JAMES
hiladelphia, Pa. 1810

NG, ANDREW
hiladelphia, Pa. . . .1837

NG, WILLIAM
hiladelphia, Pa. . . 1807

NGLEY, HENRY
ew York, N. Y. .... 1810 — H.Longley Longley

OMIS, G. & CO.
rie, Pa. .... 1850 — G.LOOMIS&CO ERIE

RD, BENJAMIN
ittsfield, Mass. 1786

RD, JABEZ C.
ew York, N. Y. ..... 1835 — J.LORD

RD, JOSEPH
hiladelphia, Pa. 1815

RD & SMITH
ew York, N. Y. 1823

RING, ELIJAH
arnstable, Mass. .....1744-1782 — E.Loring. E.Loring

LORING, HENRY
Boston, Mass. ...... 1773-1818 — HL

LORING, JOSEPH
Boston, Mass. ...... 1743-1815 — J.L J.Loring J.Loring J.Loring J.Loring I.Loring

LOUS, ASA
Hartford, Conn. 1792

LOW, BALL & COMPANY
Boston, Mass. 1840

LOW, FRANCIS
Boston, Mass. 1827

LOW, JOHN J. & COMPANY
Boston, Mass. .... 1828 — J.J.LOW&CO

LOW, JOHN S.
Salem, Mass. 1821

LOWER, JOSEPH
Philadelphia, Pa. .... 1803 — LOWER

LOWNER, JACOB
Philadelphia, Pa. 1833

LOWNER, WILLIAM
Philadelphia, Pa. 1833

LOWNES, EDWARD
Philadelphia, Pa. .... 1817 — E.LOWNES E.LOWNES

LOWNES & ERWIN
Philadelphia, Pa. 1816

LOWNES, J. & J. H.
Philadelphia, Pa. 1816

LOWNES, JOSEPH
Philadelphia, Pa. .... 1780 — IL J.Lownes

LOWNES, JOSIAH H.
Philadelphia, Pa. .... 1822 — IHL JHL

LOYER, ADRIAN
Savannah, Ga. 1860

LUCET, JAMES
New York, N. Y. 1802

LULIS, LAMBERT
New York, N. Y. 1804

LUPP, HENRY
New Brunswick, N. J. ... 1783 — H.Lupp

LUPP, PETER
New Brunswick, N.J. 1797-1827 — PL

LUPP, S. V.
New Brunswick, N. J. 1815 — S.V.LUPP

LUSADA, BENJAMIN
New York, N. Y. 1797

LUSCOMB, JOHN G.
Boston, Mass. 1823

LUSSAUR, JOHN
New York, N. Y. 1791

LUZERDER, BENJAMIN
New York, N. Y. 1796

LYELL, DAVID
New York, N. Y. 1699

LYNCH, JOHN
Baltimore, Md. 1761-1848   `I·L` `IL` `JL` `ILYNCH` `I·LYNCH` `J·LYNCH·` `LYNCH` `J·LYNCH` `ID`

LYNDE, THOMAS
Worcester, Mass. 1748-1812   `T·LYNDE`

LYNG, JOHN
Philadelphia, Pa. 1734   `I·L`

LYNG, JOHN BURT
New York, N.Y. 1759   `J·L` `IBL` `LYNG` `N·YORK` `LYNG N.YORK`

LYNN, ADAM
District of Columbia 1796   `A·Lynn` `A·LYNN` `A·Lynn`

LYTLE, R. A.
Baltimore, Md. 1825   `R·A·LYTLE` `IO·I5`

M

MABRID & COMPANY
New York, N.Y. 1787

MACHON, AUSTIN
Philadelphia, Pa. 1759

MAIN, DAVID
Stonington, Conn. 1773

MAINWARING, THOS.
West New Jersey 1664

MARIOT, JEAN C.
New Orleans, La. 1822

MANN, ALEXANDER
Middletown, Conn. 1804

MANNERBACK, W.
Reading, Pa. 1825   `W·MANNERBACK` `READING`

MANNING, DANIEL
Boston, Mass. 1823

MANNING, JOSEPH
New York, N.Y. 1823

MANNING, SAMUEL
Boston, Mass. 1823

MANSFIELD, ELISHA H.
Norwich, Conn. 1816

MANSFIELD, JOHN
Charlestown, Mass. 1634

MANSFIELD, THOMAS
Philadelphia, Pa. 1804

MARBLE, SIMEON
New Haven, Conn. 1777-1856   `S·MARBLE`

MARCHAND, EVARISTE
New Orleans, La. 1822

MARQUAND & BROTHER
New York, N.Y. 1825

MARQUAND & COMPANY
New York, N.Y. 1810

MARQUAND, FREDERICK
New York, N.Y. 1823   `F·M·` `F·MARQUAND`

MARQUARD, ISAAC
New York, N.Y. 1810

MARS, S.
Unknown ....C 1770   `S∴Mars`

MARSH, T. K.
Paris, Kentucky 1830   `T·K·MARSH` `PARIS·K`

MARSHALL, JOSEPH
Philadelphia, Pa. 1818

MARSHALL & TEMPEST
Philadelphia, Pa. 1813   `MARSHALL & TEMPEST`

MARSHALL, THOMAS
Troy, N.Y. 1839

MARTIN, ABRAHAM W.
New York, N.Y. 1835

MARTIN, PETER
New York, N.Y. 1756   `P·MARTIN`

MARTIN, V.
Boston, Mass. 1859   `V·MARTIN` `BOS`

MASI, SERAPHIM
Washington, D. C. 1832

MASON, J. D.
Philadelphia, Pa. 1830   `J·D·MASON`

MATHER & NORTH
New Britain, Conn. 1827   `MATHER & NORTH`

MATLACK, WILLIAM
Philadelphia, Pa. 1828

MAVERICK, D.
New York, N.Y. 1828   `DMV`

MAVERICK, PETER R.
New York, N.Y. 1780

MAYSENHOEDER, C.
Philadelphia, Pa. 1824

MEAD & ADRIANCE
St. Louis, Mo. 1835   `MEAD & ADRIAN` `ST·LOUIS`

MEAD, EDMUND
St. Louis, Mo. 1850   `E·MEAD`

MEADOWS & CO.
Philadelphia, Pa. 1831   `MEADOWS & CO PH`

MECOM, JOHN
New York, N.Y. 1770

MECOM, GEORGE
Boston, Mass. 1836

MERCHANT, J.
New York, N.Y. 1795   `J·MERCHANT`

MEREDITH, JOSEPH P.
Baltimore, Md. 1821   `J·MEREDITH`

MERKLER, JOHN H.
New York, N.Y. 1780   `IHM`

MERRIFIELD, THOMAS V. Z.
Albany, N.Y. 1840

MERRIMAN & BRADLEY
New Haven, Conn. 1817   `M&B`

MERRIMAN, C.
New York, N.Y. 1825

MERRIMAN, MARCUS
New Haven, Conn. 1762-1850   `M` `M` `M·M·` `M·M` `M·M` `M·M`

ERRIMAN, MARCUS & CO. New Haven, Conn. 1817	M.M.&Co
ERRIMAN, REUBEN Litchfield, Conn. 1783-1866	R.MERRIMAN PureCoin R·M
ERRIMAN, SAMUEL New Haven, Conn. .. 1769-1805	S.Merriman
ERRIMAN, SILAS New Haven, Conn. 1760	
ERRIMAN & TUTTLE New Haven, Conn. 1802	
ERROW, NATHAN East Hartford, Conn. 1783	
ICHAELS, JAMES New York, N. Y. 1820	
IKSCH, JOHN MATHEW Bethlehem, Pa. 1775	I·M·MIKSCH
ILES, JOHN Philadelphia, Pa. 1785	
ILHE, STEPHEN Philadelphia, Pa. 1780	
ILLAR, JAMES Boston, Mass. 1832	
ILLARD, GEORGE Philadelphia, Pa. 1816	
ILLER, D. B. Boston, Mass. 1850	D.B.MILLER
ILLER, I. R. Philadelphia, Pa. 1810	I.R.MILLER
ILLER, P. Philadelphia, Pa. 1810	P.MILLER P.MILLER
ILLER, WILLIAM Philadelphia, Pa. 1814	MILLER MILLER
ILLER & SON Philadelphia, Pa. 1833	
ILLNER, THOMAS Boston, Mass. 1690-1745	TM TM
ILNE, EDMUND Philadelphia, Pa. 1757	EM EM E·MILNE
ILNE, F. New York, N. Y. 1800	
ILNE, THOMAS New York, N. Y. 1795	
ILLON, PETER New York, N. Y. 1820	
ILLOUDON, PHILLIPPE Philadelphia, Pa. 1811	
ILLS, EDMUND Philadelphia, Pa. 1785	
ILLS, EDWARD Philadelphia, Pa. 1794	
ILLS, JOHN Philadelphia, Pa. 1793	

MINOTT & AUSTIN Boston, Mass. .1765-1769	Minott Minott IA I.Austin
MINOTT, SAMUEL Boston, Mass. 1732-1803	S·M M S·M Minott Minott Minott
MINOTT & SIMPKINS Boston, Mass. 1769	WS Minott
MINSHALL, WILLIAM Philadelphia, Pa. 1773	
MITCHELL, HARRY Philadelphia, Pa. 1844	MITCHELL
MITCHELL, PHINEAS Boston, Mass. .. .1812	
MITCHELL, WILLIAM Boston, Mass. 1820	W.MITCHELL.
MIX, JAMES Albany, N.Y. 1817	
MIX, VISSCHER Albany, N. Y. 1849	
MOBBS, WILLIAM Buffalo, N. Y. 1835	
MOFFAT, CHARLES H. New York, N. Y. 1830	
MOFFAT, J. L. New York, N. Y. 1815	J.L.MOFFAT
MOHLER, JACOB Baltimore, Md. 1744-1773	I·M
MUNROE, JAMES Barnstable, Mass. 1806	
MONTIETH, J. & R. Baltimore, Md. 1814	MONTEITH
MONTIETH, ROBERT Baltimore, Md. 1814	RM
MOOD, J. & P. Charleston, S. C. 1806	J.&P.MOOD
MOOD, JOSEPH Charleston, S. C. 1806	I MOOD IMOOD JMOOD J.&P.MOOD
MOOD, P. Charleston, S. C. 1806	PM
MOORE & BREWER New York, N. Y. 1835	
MOORE & BROWN New York, N. Y. 1833	
MOORE, CHARLES Philadelphia, Pa. 1804	
MOORE, & FERGUSON Philadelphia, Pa. 1804	MOORE & FERGUSON
MOORE, JOHN C. New York, N. Y. 1844	J.C.M.
MOORE, JOHN L. New York, N. Y. 1835	J.L.MOORE
MOORE, ROBERT Maryland 1778	

MOORE, THOMAS
Philadelphia, Pa. 1805

MORGAN, E.
Poughkeepsie, N.Y. 1810   J.MORGAN POUGH KEEPSIE

MORGAN, JOHN
Philadelphia, Pa. 1813

MORMAGEA, MICHAEL
Philadelphia, Pa. 1816

MORRIS, JOHN
New York, N.Y. 1796

MORRIS, SYLVESTER
New York, N.Y. 1709-1783   SM

MORRIS, WILLIAM H.
New York, N.Y. 1759

MORRISON, ISRAEL
Philadelphia, Pa. ...:....1823

MORSE, DAVID
Boston, Mass. 1798

MORSE, HAZEN
Boston, Mass. 1815

MORSE, J. H.
Boston, Mass. 1792   J.H.MORSE

MORSE, MOSES
Boston, Mass. 1816   M.MORSE

MORSE, NATHANIEL
Boston, Mass. 1709   NM N·M NM

MORSE, STEPHEN
Boston, Mass. 1764   MORSE

MOSELEY, DAVID
Boston, Mass. 1753-1812   DM DMoseley D.Moseley

MOSELEY, JOSEPH
New York, N.Y. 1830

MOSES, JACOB
Birmingham, Ala. 1768   MOSES

MOSES, M.
Boston, Mass. 1830

MOSES, ISAAC N.
Derby, Conn. 1781

MOTT, J. S.
New York, N.Y. 1790   J.MOTT JMOTT J.S.MOTT

MOTT, JOHN & WILLIAM
New York, N.Y. 1789

MOTT, W. & J.
New York, N.Y. 1789   MOTT'S

MOULINAR, JOHN
New York, N.Y. 1744   I.M IM

MOULTON, ABEL
Newburyport, Mass. 1815   A·MOULTON

MOULTON & BRADBURY
Newburyport, Mass. 1796   MOULTON B

MOULTON & DAVIS
Newburyport, Mass. 1824

MOULTON, EBENEZER S.
Boston, Mass. 1796   E.S.MOULTON E.S.Moulton

MOULTON, ENOCH
Portland, Me. 1801   E.MOULTON

MOULTON, JOSEPH, I
Newburyport, Mass. 1680   J·M

MOULTON, JOSEPH, II
Newburyport, Mass. 1757   IM IM IM I·MOULTON

MOULTON, JOSEPH, III
Newburyport, Mass. 1814   J.MOULTON. J.MOULTON

MOULTON, WILLIAM, I
Newburyport, Mass. 1710

MOULTON, WILLIAM, II
Newburyport, Mass. 1720

MOULTON, WILLIAM, III
Newburyport, Mass. 1772   W·M W.MOULTO MOULTON MOULT

MULFORD, JOHN H.
Albany, N.Y. 1835

MULFORD & WENDELL
Albany, N.Y. 1842   MULFORD WENDELL

MULLIGAN, H.
Philadelphia, Pa. 1840   H.MULLIGAN 414 21st ST PHILA

MUMFORD, H. G.
Providence, R.I. 1813

MUNROE, JAMES
Barnstable, Mass. 1784-1879   James Munroe Purel I·MUNROE I.MUNR James Munroe

MUNROE, NATHANIEL
Baltimore, Md. 1777-1861   N.MUNROE N.MUNR

MUNSON, AMOS
New Haven, Conn. 1776

MUNSON, CORNELIUS
Wallingford, Conn. 1742

MURDOCK, JAMES
Philadelphia, Pa. 1779   I.M. J.Murdock

MURPHY, JAMES
Philadelphia, Pa. 1823   J.MURPHY

MUSGRAVE, JAMES
Philadelphia, Pa. 1795   Musgrave

MYER, H. B.
New York, N.Y. 1810   HBMyer

MYERS, ALBERT
Philadelphia, Pa. 1837

MYERS & JACOB
Philadelphia, Pa. 1839

MYERS, JOHN
Philadelphia, Pa. 1773   I·MYERS J.Mye

MYERS, MYER
New York, N.Y. 1723-1795   MM MM Myers Myers

MYGATT, COMFORT
Danbury, Conn. 1763-1823

MYGATT, DAVID
Danbury, Conn. 1777-1822   DM D.MYGATT D·MYGATT

MYGATT, ELY
Danbury, Conn. 1742-1807

MYSENDHENDER
Philadelphia, Pa. 1813

Mc

McCLYMON, JOHN C.
New York, N.Y. 1805

McCONNEL, HUGH
Philadelphia, Pa. 1813

McCONNELLY, H.
Philadelphia, Pa. 1811

McCORMICK, JOHN
Philadelphia, Pa. 1837

McCREA, ROBERT
Philadelphia, Pa. 1785

McDANIEL, PETER
New York, N.Y. 1743

McDONALD, DANIEL
Philadelphia, Pa. 1828

McDONNOUGH, PATRICK
Philadelphia, Pa. 1811

McDONNOUGH, JOHN
Philadelphia, Pa. 1775

M'FADDEN, J. B.
Pittsburgh, Pa. 1840

McFARLANE, JOHN
Boston, Mass. 1796

McFEE, JOHN
Philadelphia, Pa. 1793

McFEE, M.
Philadelphia, Pa. ....—...1769

McFEE & REEDER
Philadelphia, Pa. 1796

McGRAW, DANIEL
Chester, Pa. 1772

McHARG, ALEXANDER
Albany, N.Y. ....—.1849

McINTIRE, JAMES
Philadelphia, Pa. 1840

McINTOSH, JOHN
Ft. Stanwix, Pa. 1761

McKEEN, HENRY
Philadelphia, Pa. 1823

McKLIMENT, JOHN
New York, N.Y. 1804

McLAWRENCE, JOHN
New York, N.Y. 1818

McMAHON, JOHN
Philadelphia, Pa. 1804

McMASTER, HUGH A.
Philadelphia, Pa. 1839

McMULLEN, JAMES
Philadelphia, Pa. 1814

McMULLEN, WILLIAM
Philadelphia, Pa. ....,...1791

McMULLIN & BLACK
Philadelphia, Pa. 1813

McMULLIN, JOHN
Philadelphia, Pa. 1765-1843

McPARLIN, WILLIAM
Maryland 1780-1850

McPHERSON, ROBERT
Philadelphia, Pa. 1831

N

NAGLES, JOHN
Philadelphia, Pa. 1748

NEEDELS, WILLIAM
Easton, Md. 1798

NEVILL, RICHARD
Boston, Mass. 1674

NEUSS, JAN
Philadelphia, Pa. 1698

NEVILL R.ICHARD
Boston, Mass. 1764

NEWBERRY, EDWIN C.
Mansfield, Conn. 1828

NEWHALL, DUDLEY
Salem, Mass. 1730

NEWKIRKE, JOHN VAN
New York, N.Y. 1716

NEWMAN, TIMOTHY H.
New York, N.Y. 1799

NICHOLAS, WILLIAM S.
Newport, R.I. 1785-1871

NICHOLS, BASSET
Providence, R.I. 1815

NICHOLS, WILLIAM S.
Newport, R.I. 1808

NICHERSON, BATY
Harwich, Mass. 1825

NIXON, RICHARD
Philadelphia, Pa. 1820

NOBLE, JOSEPH
Portland, Maine 1823

NORCROSS, NEHEMIAH
Boston, Mass. ....—....1796

NORRIS, GEORGE
Philadelphia, Pa. 1779

NORTH, W. B. & CO.
New York, N.Y. 1823

NORTH, WILLIAM B.
New York, N.Y. 1787-1838

NORTHEE, DAVID I.
Salem, Mass. 1788

NORTHEY, ABIJAH
Salem, Mass. 1775

NORTON, ANDREW
Goshen, Conn. 1787

NORTON, BENJAMIN
Boston, Mass. 1810

NORTON, C. C.
Hartford, Conn. 1820   `C.C.NORTON`

NORTON, SAMUEL
Hingham, Mass. 1795

NORTON, THOMAS
Farmington, Conn. ...1796-1806   `TN` `T.N`

NORTON & PITKIN
Hartford, Conn. 1825   `C.C.NORTON` `&` `W.PITKIN`

NORWOOD, RICHARD
New York, N.Y. 1774

NOXON
Unknown ....c 1800   `NOXON`

NOYES, JOHN
Boston, Mass. 1695   `IN` `IN` `IN`

NOYES, JOSEPH
Philadelphia, Pa. 1719   `IN` `IN`

NOYES, SAMUEL
Norwich, Conn. 1770

NUSZ, FREDERICK
Frederick, Md. 1819   `F.NUSZ.`

NUTTALL, JOSEPH
Maryland 1778

NYS, JOHANNIS
Philadelphia, Pa. 1695   `IN` `IN` `IN`

O

OAKES, FREDERICK
Hartford, Conn. 1825   `OAKES` `OAKES`

OAKES & SOENCER
Hartford, Conn. 1814   `O&S`

OBRIHIM, JOSEPH
Annapolis, Md. 1784

ODELL, LAWRENCE
New York, N.Y. 1830

OERTELT, CHARLES E.
Philadelphia, Pa. 1831

OGIER, JOHN
New York, N.Y. 1791

OGILVIE, GABRIEL
New York, N.Y. 1791

OLIVER, ANDREW
Boston, Mass. 1722   `A·OLIVER`

OLIVER, DANIEL
Philadelphia, Pa. 1805   `D.OLIVER`

OLIVER, PETER
Boston, Mass. 1709   `PO` `PO`

OLIVIER, PETER
Philadelphia, Pa. 1797   `P.O`

OLMSTED, NATHANIEL
Farmington, Conn. 1808   `N.OLMSTED` `W` `P`

OLMSTED, N. & SON
Farmington, Conn. 1847   `N.OLMSTED & SON` `P`

ONCLEBAGH, GARRETT
New York, N.Y. 1698   `B` `GO`

OSGOOD, J.
Salem, Mass. 1817   `J:OSGOOD`

OSTHOFF, ANDREW
Baltimore, Md. 1810   `OSTHOFF`

OTIS, JOHN
Barnstable, Mass. 1703

OTIS, JONATHAN
Newport, R.I. 1723-1791   `I·O` `J.Otis` `Otis` `J.Otis` `OTIS` `J·O`

OTT, DANIEL
New York, N.Y. 1792

OTT, GEORGE
Norfolk, Va. 1806   `G.Ott` `Ott.`

OVERIN, RICHARD
New York, N.Y. 1702

OWEN, JESSE
Philadelphia, Pa. 1794   `OWEN` `JSE OWE`

OWEN, JOHN
Philadelphia, Pa. 1802   `I·OWEN`

Philadelphia, Pa. 1804

P

PADDY, SAMUEL
Boston, Mass. 1659

PAINTER, JOHN
Philadelphia, Pa. 1735

PALMER & BACHLADER
Boston, Mass. 1815   `PALMER & BACHLADE`

PALMER & CLAPP
New York, N.Y. 1823

PALMER & HINSDALE
New York, N.Y. 1815

PALMER, JAMES
New York, N.Y. 1815

PANCOAST, SAMUEL
Philadelphia, Pa. 1785

PANGBORN & BRINSMAID
Burlington, Vermont 1833

PARADICE, WILLIAM A.
Philadelphia, Pa. 1799

PARASET, WILLIAM
Philadelphia, Pa. 1811

PARHAM, WILLIAM
Philadelphia, Pa. 1785

PARIE, JOSEPH
Philadelphia, Pa. 1811

PARISEN, OTTO
New York, N.Y. 1763   `PARISIEN`

PARISIEN, O & SON
New York, N.Y. 1789   `OPDP`

ARISIEN, OTTO W.
New York, N.Y. 1791

ARKER, DANIEL
Boston, Mass. ....1726-1785 **D:P** **D:PARKER** **D.PARKER**

ARKER, GEORGE
Baltimore, Md. ....1804 **G.PARKER**

ARKER, ISAAC
Deerfield, Mass. ....1780 **I·PARKER**

ARKER, RICHARD
Philadelphia, Pa. .:.......1785

ARKER, WILLIAM H.
New York, N.Y. 1835

ARKMAN, C.
Boston, Mass. ....1790 **C.PARKMAN**

ARKMAN, JOHN
Boston, Mass. ....1738 **PARKMAN**

ARKMAN, THOMAS
Boston, Mass. ....1793 **T.PARKMAN**

ARKS, JOHN
New York, N.Y. 1791

ARMELE, JAMES
Durham, Conn. 1763-1828

ARMELEE, SAMUEL
Guilford, Conn. ....1737-1803 **SP** **SP** **S·Parmele** **SP** **S·Parmele**

ARROTT, T.
Unknown ....1760 **T·PARROTT**

ARSONS
Unknown ....1750 **PARSONS**

ARRY, MARTIN
Portsmouth, N.H. .....1737-1807 **PARRY**

ARRY & MUSGRAVE
Philadelphia, Pa. ....1793 **P&M**

ARRY, ROWLAND
Philadelphia, Pa. ....1819 **R·PARRY**

ARSONS, JOHN
Boston, Mass. ....1780 **I·PARSONS**

ASCAL, WILLIAM
Philadelphia, Pa. 1765

ATTERSON, GEORGE
New York, N.Y. 1835

ATON, A.
Boston, Mass. 1850

ATTERSON, JOHN
Annapolis, Md. ....1751 **I·P**

ATTIT, THOMAS
New York, N.Y. 1796

ATTON, THOMAS
Philadelphia, Pa. 1824

AULGREEN, OUOM
Philadelphia, Pa. 1798

AXSON JOHN A.
Philadelphia, Pa. 1810

PEABODY, JOHN
Enfield, Conn. ....1799 **J.PEABODY**

PEALE, CHARLES W.
Philadelphia, Pa. 1765

PEAR, EDWARD
Boston, Mass. ....:.1836 **EP** **EP.**

PEAR & BACALL
Boston, Mass. ....,.1850

PEARCE, WILLIAM
Norfolk, Va. ....1820 **W·PEARCE VA. NORFOLK** **W·PEARCE VA NORFOLK**

PEARSE, SAMUEL
New York, N.Y. 1783

PEARSON, JOHN
New York, N.Y. ....1791 **IP** **J·Pearson** **J·Pearson**

PECK, B.
Connecticut ....1820 **B·PECK**

PECK, LAWRENCE M.
Philadelphia, Pa. 1837

PECK, TIMOTHY
Middletown, Conn. 1786

PEDASY, S.
Philadelphia, Pa. 1810

PEIRCE, JOHN
Boston, Mass. ....1810 **PEIRCE**

PEIRI, JOSEPH
Philadelphia, Pa. 1811

PELLETREAU, ELIAS
Southampton, N.Y. .. 1726-1810 **EP**

PELLETREAU. JOHN
Southampton, L.I. .:......1785

PELLETREAU, MALTBY
New York, N.Y. 1813

PELLETREAU & RICHARDS
New York, N.Y. ....1825 **W.S.P.** **TR**

PELLETREAU & UPSON
New York, N.Y. ....1818 **P&U**

PELLETREAU & VAN WYCK
New York, N.Y. ....1815 **WSPELLETREAU** **SVANWYCK**

PELLETREAU, W. SMITH
Southampton, N.Y. ...1786-1842

PEPPER. HENRY I.
Philadelphia, Pa. ....1766 **H.I.PEPPER** **HIPEPPER** **H.J.PEPPER**

PERKINS. HAUGHTON
Boston, Mass. 1762

PERKINS. ISAAC
Charlestown, Mass. ....1707 **IP**

PERKINS, JACOB
Newburyport, Mass. ..1766-1849 **I·P** **J·PERKINS** **IP**

PERKINS, JOSEPH
Little Rest, R.I. ......1770 **J:PERKINS**

PERKINS. T.
Boston, Mass. ....1810 **T·PERKINS**

PERPIGNAN, PETER
Philadelphia, Pa. 1809

PERPIGNAN & VARNIER
Philadelphia, Pa. 1800

PERRET & SANDOR
New York, N.Y. 1810

PERREAUX, PETER
Philadelphia, Pa. 1797

PERRET, AUGUSTA
New York, N.Y. 1801

PERRY, THOMAS
Westerly, R.I.

PETERS, JAMES
Philadelphia, Pa. 1821

PETERS, R.
Philadelphia, Pa. 1807

PETIT, MATTHEW
New York, N.Y. 1811

PETTIT, THOMAS
New York, N.Y. 1791

PHELPS, CHARLES H.
Bainbridge, N.Y. 1825

PHELPS, JEDEDIAH
Great Barrington, Vt. 1781

PHILIP & YVER
Philadelphia, Pa. ...:....1796

PHILIPS, JASPER D.
Cincinatti, Ohio 1820

PHILLIPE, JOSEPH
Baltimore, Md. 1796

PHILLIPS, JAMES D.
Cleveland, Ohio ....,.....1829

PHILLIPS, SAMUEL
Salem, Mass. 1680

PHINNEY & MEAD
Unknown 1825

PHYFE, WILLIAM
Boston, Mass. ....:1830

PICKERING, CHARLES
Philadelphia, Pa. 1683

PIERCE, HART
New York, N.Y. 1835

PIERCE, JOHN
Boston, Mass. 1810

PIERCE, O.
Boston, Mass. 1821

PIERPONT, BENJAMIN H.
Boston, Mass. 1730-1797

PIERSON, PHILLIP
New York, N.Y. 1798

PINCHIN, WILLIAM
Philadelphia, Pa. 1779

PINTO, JOSEPH
New York, N.Y. 1758

PITKIN, HENRY
East Hartford, Conn. 1834

PITKIN, HORACE E.
Hartford, Conn. 1832

PITKIN, JAMES F.
East Hartford, Conn. 1834

PITKIN, JOHN O.
East Hartford, Conn. .1803-1891

PITKIN, J. O. & W.
East Hartford, Conn. 1826

PITKIN & NORTON
Hartford, Conn. 1825

PITKIN, WALTER
East Hartford, Conn. .1808-1885

PITKIN, WILLIAM J.
East Hartford, Conn. 1820

PITKIN, WILLIAM L.
East Hartford, Conn. ...,..1825

PITKINS, JAMES
Hartford, Conn. 1812

PITMAN, BENJAMIN
Providence, R.I. 1810

PITMAN & DORRANCE
Providence, R.I. ...,,.... 1795

PITMAN & DODGE
Providence, R.I. .,......1796

PITMAN, JOHN K.
Providence, R.I. 1805

PITMAN, SANDERS
Providence, R.I. ...,....1760

PITMAN, WILLIAM R.
New Bedford, Mass. 1835

PITT, RICHARD
Philadelphia, Pa. 1741

PITTMAN, I.
Unknown .....,.,,.....1785

PITTS, A.
Philadelphia, Pa. 1790

PITTS, RICHARD
Philadelphia, Pa. 1741

PLAIN, EDWARD
New York, N.Y. 1835

PLANQUET, GREGORY
New York, N.Y. 1797

PLATT & BROTHER
New York, N.Y. 1820

PLATT, GEORGE W.
New York, N.Y. 1820

PLATT, G. W. & N. C.
New York, N.Y. 1820

ATT, JAMES
New York, N.Y. 1835

ATT, M. C.
New York, N.Y. 1820

INCIGNON, FRANCIS
Philadelphia, Pa. 1796

INCY, PETER
Philadelphia, Pa. 1813

INTE, JAMES
Philadelphia, Pa. 1813

INTE & TANGUY
Philadelphia, Pa. 1818

ISSENOT, N. J.
Philadelphia, Pa. 1806

ISSONIER, FRANCIS
Philadelphia, Pa. 1795

LAND, P.
Philadelphia, Pa. 1837

LGRAIN, QUOM
Philadelphia, Pa. 1797

LHAMUS, J.
New York, N.Y. 1802

LLARD, WILLIAM
Boston, Mass. 1711

NCET, LEWIS
Baltimore, Md. 1800

NS, THOMAS
Boston, Mass. 1789

OR, NATHANIEL
Boston, Mass. 1829

RTER, F. W.
New York, N.Y. 1820

RTER, HENRY C.
New York, N.Y. 1820

RTER & CO., HENRY C.
New York, N.Y. 1830

RTER, I. S.
New York, N.Y. 1850

RTRAM, ABRAHAM
New York, N.Y. 1727

SEY, FREDERICK J.
Hagerstown, Md. 1820-1850

ST, SAMUEL
New London, Conn. 1783

TTER, NILES
Westerly, R.I.

TTER, J. O. & J. R.
Providence, R.I. 1824

TWINE, JOHN
Boston, Mass. 1737

TWINE & WHITING
Hartford, Conn. 1761

POUPARD, JAMES
Boston, Mass. 1751

POUTREAU, ABRAHAM
New York, N.Y. 1726

POWELL, C. F.
Boston, Mass. 1746

POWELSON, CHARLES
Albany, N.Y. 1840

PRATT, HENRY
Philadelphia, Pa. 1730

PRATT, NATHAN
Essex, Conn. 1792

PRATT, PHINEAS
Lyme, Conn. 1747-1813

PRATT, SETH
Lyme, Conn. 1754

PRESTON, S. L.
Philadelphia, Pa. 1830

PRICE, BENJAMIN
Boston, Mass. . . 1767

PRICE, HENRY P.
Philadelphia, Pa. . . 1810

PRICE, JOHN
Lancaster, Pa. 1764

PRIE, P.
Unknown 1780

PRINCE, JOB
Milford, Conn. .. 1680-1704

PURSELL, HENRY
New York, N.Y. 1775

PUTNAM, EDWARD
Salem, Mass. . . . 1710

PUTNAM & LOW
Boston, Mass. 1822

PUTNAM, RUFUS
Albany, N.Y. 1814

Q

QUARITUS, FREDERICK
New York, N.Y. 1835

QUINCY, DANIEL
Braintree, Mass. . . 1651

QUINTARD, PETER
New York, N.Y. 1731
Norwalk, Conn. 1737

R

RABETH, JAMES
New York, N.Y. . . 1835

RAIT, DAVID
New York, N.Y. 1835

RAIT, ROBERT
New York, N.Y. . 1830

RASCH, ANTHONY
Philadelphia, Pa. . 1807

RASCH, ANTHONY & CO.
Philadelphia, Pa. 1820

RASCH, W. A.
New Orleans, La. 1830

RASCH & WILLIG
Philadelphia, Pa. 1819

RAVEE, XAVIER
Philadelphia, Pa. 1796

RAYMOND, JOHN
Boston, Mass. 1775

REED, A. G. & CO.
Nassau, N.H. 1835

REED, ISAAC
Stamford, Conn. 1776

REED, ISAAC & SON
Stamford, Conn. 1810

REED, JONATHAN
Boston, Mass. 1725-1740

REED, LEWIS
New York, N.Y. 1810

REED, O. & CO.
Philadelphia, Pa. 1841

REED, OSMAN
Philadelphia, Pa. 1840

REED, STEPHEN
Philadelphia, Pa. 1846

REEDER, ABNER
Philadelphia, Pa. 1797

REEDER, JOHN
Philadelphia, Pa. 1835

REEVE, G.
Unknown 1825

REEVE, I.
New York, N.Y. 1790

REEVES, ENOS
Charleston, S.C. 1746-1807

REEVES, STEPHEN
Burlington, N.J. 1767

REVERE, EDWARD
Boston, Mass. 1796

REVERE, J. W.
Boston, Mass. 1798

REVERE, PAUL
Boston, Mass. 1735-1818

REVERE, PAUL, Sr.
Boston, Mass. 1702-1754

REVERE, PAUL, III
Boston, Mass. 1795

REVERE & SON
Boston, Mass. 1796

REVERE, THOMAS
Boston, Mass. 1789

REYNOLDS, JOHN
Hagerstown, Md. 1790-1832

REYNOLDS, THEODORE J.
Philadelphia, Pa. 1835

RICE
Unknown ....c. 1780

RICE, HENRY P.
Albany, N.Y. 1815

RICE, JOSEPH
Baltimore, Md. 1784

RICE, JOSEPH T.
Baltimore, Md. 1785

RICE, JOSEPH T.
Albany, N.Y. 1835

RICH, OBADIAH
Boston, Mass. 1836

RICHARD, AUGUSTA
Philadelphia, Pa. 1818

RICHARD, STEPHEN
New York, N.Y. 1828

RICHARDS, SAMUEL
New York, N.Y. 1828

RICHARDS, SAMUEL
Philadelphia, Pa. 1770

RICHARDS, SAMUEL R., Jr.
Philadelphia, Pa. 1793

RICHARDS, STEPHEN
Cohansey Bridge, N.J. 1767

RICHARDS, T.
Unknown ....c. 1800

RICHARDS, THOMAS
New York, N.Y. 1815

RICHARDS, W.
Philadelphia, Pa. 1813

RICHARDS, W. & S. R.
Philadelphia, Pa. 1818

RICHARDS, & WILLIAMSON
Philadelphia, Pa. 1797

RICHARDSON, FRANCIS
Philadelphia, Pa. 1718

RICHARDSON, JOSEPH
Philadelphia, Pa. ... 1711-1784

RICHARDSON, JOSEPH, Jr.
Philadelphia, Pa. 1777

RICHARDSON, JOSEPH & NATHANIEL
Philadelphia, Pa. ... 1785

RICHARDSON, RICHARD
Philadelphia, Pa. 1793

RICHMOND, FRANKLIN
Providence, R.I. 1815

RICHMOND, G. & A.
Providence, R.I. 1815

EWAY, JAMES
ton, Mass. 1789

EWAY, JOHN
ton, Mass. 1813   J:RIDGWAY

UT, GEORGE
York, N.Y. 1745   GR

, JOHAN
adelphia, Pa. 1810

LY, BERNARD
York, N.Y. 1835

S, GEORGE W.
rgetown, D.C. 1805-1810   GR *Riggs* RIGGS
timore, Md. 1810-1840   RIGGS

S AND GRIFFITH
timore, Md. 1816   R&G

S, RICHARD
adelphia, Pa. 1819   RR *Riggs*

R, PETER
York, N.Y. 1802   P.RIKER

R & ALEXANDER
York, N.Y. 1800

ER, MICHAEL
York, N.Y. 1786

TH, ROSWELL W.
wich, Conn. 1826

INS, ELISHA
adelphia, Pa. 1831

S
York, N.Y. 1788

RT, CHRISTOPHER
York, N.Y. 1708-1783   CR

RTS, FREDERICK
ton, Mass. 1770

RTS & LEE
ton, Mass. 1775   R&L

RTS, MICHAEL
York, N.Y. 1786

RTSON, ALEXANDER
adelphia, Pa. 1740

RTSON, ANTHONY W.
adelphia, Pa. 1798

RTSON, ROBERT
adelphia, Pa. 1777

NSON, ANTHONY W.
adelphia, Pa. 1798   A·ROBINSON

NSON, BENJAMIN
adelphia, Pa. 1818

NSON, E.
known 1820   E.ROBINSON

NSON, ISREAL
adelphia, Pa. 1840

NSON, & HARWOOD
adelphia, Pa. 1814

ROBINSON, O.
New Haven, Conn. 1800   O·ROBINSON

ROCKWELL, EDWARD
New York, N.Y. 1825   ROCKWELL ROCKWELL

ROCKWELL, S. D.
New York, N.Y. 1830   S.D.ROCKWELL NEW YORK

ROCKWELL, THOMAS
New London, Conn. 1795   *Rockwell*

RODIER, PETER G.
New York, N.Y. 1825

ROE, WILLIAM
Kingston, N.Y. 1805   W·ROE W·ROE

ROE, W. & STOLLENWERCK
New York, N.Y. 1800   W.ROE & STOLLENWERCK

ROFF
New York, N.Y. 1813

ROGERS, AUGUSTUS
Boston, Mass. 1818

ROGERS, DANIEL
Newport, R.I. 1792   D.R DR D.R D·ROGERS

ROGERS, DANIEL
New York, N.Y. 1835

ROGERS, JOSEPH
Hartford, Conn. 1808   I·R JR I·R I·R

ROGERS & WENDT
Boston, Mass. 1850

ROGERS, WILLIAM
Hartford, Conn. 1801-1873   Wm ROGERS W^t ROGERS HARTFORD

ROGERS, WILLIAM & SON
Hartford, Conn. 1850   WM.ROGERS&S

ROHR, JOHN A.
Philadelphia, Pa. 1807   I·ROHR

ROLLINGSON, WILLIAM
New York, N.Y. 1783

ROMNEY, JOHN
New York, N.Y. 1770

ROOSEVELT, NICHOLAS
New York, N.Y. ...1745-1769   N·R VR

ROOT, W. N. & BRO.
New Haven, Conn. 1850   W.N.ROOT & BROTHER

ROSE, ANTHONY
New York, N.Y. 1755

ROSHORE, JOHN
New York, N.Y. 1792

ROSHORE, & PRIME
New York, N.Y. 1825

ROSS, JOHN
Baltimore, Md. 1756-1798   I·R I·R

ROSS, ROBERT
Frederika, Delaware 1789

ROUND, JOHN
Portsmouth, N.H. 1634

ROUSE, ANTHONY
Philadelphia, Pa. 1807

ROUSE, MICHAEL
Boston, Mass. 1711

ROUSE, WILLIAM
Boston, Mass. 1639-1705

ROYALSTON, JOHN
Boston, Mass. 1770

RULE
Massachusetts 1780

RUSSEL, DANIEL
Newport, R.I. 1792

RUSSEL, JONATHAN
Ashford, Conn. 1770-1804

RUSSELL, GEORGE
Philadelphia, Pa. 1831

RUSSELL, JOHN H.
New York, N.Y. 1794-1798

RUSSEL, MOODY
Barnstable, Mass. 1694

RUSSELIER, PETER
New York, N.Y. 1794

RUTTER, RICHARD
Baltimore, Maryland 1790

RYERSON, LOW
York, Pa. 1760

S

SACHEVERELL, JOHN
Philadelphia, Pa. 1732

SACKETT & WILLARD
Providence, R.I. 1815

SADD, HARVEY
New Hartford, Conn. .1776-1840

SADTLER, P. B. & SON
Baltimore, Md. 1850

SADTLER, PHILIP B.
Baltimore, Md. 1771-1860

SADTLER, PHILLIP P.
Baltimore, Md. 1819

SAINT MARTIN, ANTHONY
Philadelphia, Pa. 1796

SANBORN, A.
Lowell, Mass. 1850

SANDELL, EDWARD
Baltimore, Md. 1816

SANDERSON, BENJAMIN
Boston, Mass. 1649-1678

SANDERSON, ROBERT
Boston, Mass. 1693

SANDERSON, ROBERT, Jr.
Boston, Mass. 1638

SANDERSON, WILLIAM
New York, N.Y. 1799

SANDFORD, ISAAC
Hartford, Conn. 1793

SANFORD, F. S.
Nantucket, Mass. ..,.....1828

SANFORD, WILLIAM
Nantucket, Mass. 1817

SANDOZ & BROTHER
New York, N.Y. 1811

SANDOZ, PHILIP A.
Philadelphia, Pa. 1814

SANDS, STEPHEN
New York, N.Y. 1774

SANFORD, ISAAC
Hartford, Conn. 1785

SARDO, MICHAEL
Baltimore, Md. 1817

SARGANT, ENSIGN
Boston, Mass. 1820

SARGEANT, JACOB
Hartford, Conn. 1761-1843

SAVAGE, EDWARD
Philadelphia, Pa. 1794

SAVAGE, THOMAS
Boston, Mass. 1689

SAVAGE, THOMAS, Jr.
Boston, Mass. 1719

SAWIN, SILAS
Boston, Mass. 1823

SAWIN, SILAS W.
New York, N.Y. 1835

SAWYER, H. L.
New York, N.Y. 1840

SAYRE, JOEL
New York, N.Y. 1778-1818

SAYRE, JOHN
New York, N.Y. 1771-1852

SAYRE & RICHARDS
New York, N.Y. 1802

SCARRET, JOSEPH
Philadelphia, Pa. 1797

SCHAATS, BARTHOLOMEW
New York, N.Y. 1683-1758

SCHAFFIELD, JEREMIAH
Philadelphia, Pa. 1785

SCHANK, GARRET
New York, N.Y. 1791

SCHANK, JOHN A.
New York, N.Y. 1792

SCHOFIELD, SOLOMON
Albany, New York 1815

COT, I.
Albany, N.Y. ....1750 `I SCOT`

COTT, J. B.
New York, N.Y. ....1820 `J.Scott` `J-Scott`

OVIL & KINSEY
Cincinatti, Ohio ....1830 `SCOVIL & KINSEY` `CINCINNATI`

RYMAGEOUR, JAMES
New York, N.Y. 1835

WIND, JOHN
New York, N.Y. 1790

AL, WILLIAM
Philadelphia, Pa. ....1817 `W.SEAL`

ARS, MATTHEW
New York, N.Y. 1835

EBASTIEN, JEANNE L.
New York, N.Y. 1814

EGN, GEORGE
Philadelphia, Pa. 1820

ELKIRK, WILLIAM
New York, N.Y. 1817

ELL, J.
New York, N.Y. 1800

ENEMAND, JOHN B.
Philadelphia, Pa. 1798

EVEIGNES, JACQUES
New Orleans, La. 1822

EVRIN, LEWIS
Philadelphia, Pa. 1837

EXNINE, SIMON
New York, N.Y. ....1722 `SS`

EYMOUR & HOLLISTER
Hartford, Conn. ....1845 `SEYMOUR & HOLLISTER`

EYMOUR, JOSEPH
New York, N.Y. 1835

EYMOUR, OLIVER D.
Hartford, Conn. ....1843 `O.D.Seymour`

HARP, W.
Philadelphia, Pa. 1835

HARP, W. & G.
Philadelphia, Pa. ....1848 `W.&G.SHARP`

HAW, I. A.
Unknown ....1800 `I·A·SHAW` `J.SHAW`

HARRARD, J. S.
Shelbyville, Ky. ....1850 `J.S.SHARRARD`

HAW & DUNLEVY
Philadelphia, Pa. ....1833 `SHAW & DUNLEVY` `PHILA`

HAW, EDWARD, G.
Philadelphia, Pa. 1825

HAW, JOHN A.
Newport, R.I. 1819

SHEETS
Henrico, Va. 1697

SHEPHERD & BOYD
Albany, N.Y. ....1810 `S&B` `SHEPHERD & BOYD`

SHEPHERD, ROBERT
Albany, N.Y. ....1805 `SHEPHERD` `R.Shepherd`

SHEPPER, JOHN D.
Philadelphia, Pa. 1818

SHETHAR, SAMUEL
Litchfield, Conn. 1801

SHETHAR & GORHAM
New Haven, Conn. 1806

SHETHAR & THOMPSON
Litchfield, Conn. 1801

SHEILDS, CALEB
Baltimore, Md. ....1773 `C·S`

SHIELDS, THOMAS
Philadelphia, Pa. ....1771 `T.S` `T.S`

SHIPMAN, NATHANIEL
Norwich, Conn. ......1764-1853 `N·S` `N·SHIPMAN`

SHIVING, GODFREY
Philadelphia, Pa. 1779

SHOEMAKER, CHARLES
New York, N.Y. 1825

SHOEMAKER, JOSEPH
Philadelphia, Pa. ....1798 `J.SHOEMAKER`

SHONNARD, GEORGE
New York, N.Y. 1797

SHOPSHIRE, ROBERT
Baltimore, Md. 1778

SHREVE, BENJAMIN
Boston, Mass. 1834

SIBLEY, CLARK
New Haven, Conn. ...1778-1808 `SIBLEY`

SIBLEY, JOHN
New Haven, Conn. ....1810 `J.SIBLEY`

SIBLEY & MARBLE
New Haven, Conn. ...1801-1806 `S&M`

SILLIMAN, HEZEKIAH
New Haven, Conn. ...1739-1804

SIME & MOSES
Birmingham, Ga. 1768

SIME, WILLIAM
Birmingham, Ga. 1768

SIMES, WILLIAM
Portsmouth, N.H. ....1773-1824 `W·S` `W·SIMES` `W·SIMES`

SIMMONS & ALEXANDER
Philadelphia, Pa. ....1798 `SIMMONS & ALEXANDER.`

SIMMONS, ANDREW
Philadelphia, Pa. 1796

SIMMONS, ANTHONY
Philadelphia, Pa. ....1797 `A.S.` `A.S.` `A·SIMMONS` `A·SIMMONS`

SIMMONS, J.
Philadelphia, Pa. ....1810 `J.Simmons`

SIMMONS, J. & A.
New York, N.Y. 1805

SIMMONS, JAMES
New York, N.Y. 1815

SIMMONS, JOSEPH
Philadelphia, Pa. 1828

SIMMONS, PETER
New York, N.Y. 1816

SIMMONS, S.
Philadelphia, Pa. 1797

SIMPKINS. THOS. BARTON
Boston, Mass. 1728-1804

SIMPKINS, WILLIAM
Boston, Mass. 1704-1780

SIMPSON & BECKEL
Albany, N.Y. 1849

SINGLETON & YOUNG
New York, N.Y. 1800

SIXTE, JOSEPH A.
Philadelphia, Pa. 1837

SIXTE, VINCENT B.
Philadelphia, Pa. 1837

SKATTS, BARTHOLOMEW
Freeman, N.Y. 1784

SKERRET, JOSEPH
Philadelphia, Pa. 1797

SKERRY, GEORGE W.
Boston, Mass. 1837

SKINNER, ABRAHAM
New York, N.Y. 1756

SKINNER, ELIZER
Hartford, Conn.

SKINNER, MATT
Philadelphia, Pa. 1752

SKINNER, THOMAS
New York, N.Y. 1712-1761

SLIDELL, JOSHUA
New York, N.Y. 1765

SLOAN, WILLIAM
Hartford, Conn...........1794

SMITH, DAVID
Philadelphia, Pa. 1778

SMITH, CHRISTIAN
Philadelphia, Pa. 1820

SMITH, EBENEZER
Brookfield, Conn. 1775

SMITH, GEORGE
Philadelphia, Pa. 1831

SMITH, GEORGE O.
New York, N.Y. 1825

SMITH, I.
Boston, Mass. 1742-1789

SMITH & GRANT
St. Louis, Mo. 1850

SMITH, JACOB
Philadelphia, Pa. 1809

SMITH, JAMES
New York, N.Y. 1794

SMITH, JAMES
Philadelphia, Pa. 1807

SMITH, JOHN
Philadelphia, Pa. 1819

SMITH, JOHN & THOMAS
Baltimore, Md. 1817

SMITH, JOSEPH
Boston, Mass. 1742-1789

SMITH, JOSEPH
Philadelphia, Pa. 1804

SMITH, J. & T.
Baltimore, Md. ,..........1817

SMITH, LEVIN H.
Philadelphia, Pa. 1837

SMITH, ROBERT E.
Philadelphia, Pa. 1820

SMITH, SAMUEL
Philadelphia, Pa. 1785

SMITH, WILLIAM
New York, N.Y. 1770

SMITH, ZEBULON
Maine 1786-1865

SOMERBY, ROBERT
Mass. 1794-1821

SNOW, J.
Unknown 1750

SNYDER, GEORGE
Philadelphia, Pa. 1816

SOLOMON, SAMUEL
Philadelphia, Pa. 1811

SONNIER, JOSEPH
Philadelphia, Pa. 1811

SOUMAIEN, SAMUEL
Philadelphia, Pa. 1754

SOUMAIN, SIMEON
New York, N.Y. 1685-1750

SOQUE, MICHAEL
New York, N.Y. 1794

SOWERLT, ANTHONY
Philadelphia, Pa. 1823

SPARROW, HENRY
Philadelphia, Pa. 1811

SPARROW, THOMAS
Annapolis, Md. 1764-1784

SPEAR, ISAAC
Boston, Mass. 1836

ENCER, GEORGE
ssex, Conn. ....:1810

ENCER, JAMES
artford, Conn. 1793

UIRE & BROTHER
ew York, N.Y. ....1846 — SQUIRE & BROTHER OF COIN

UIRE & LANDER
ew York, N.Y. ....1840 — SQUIRE & LANDER

UIRE, S. P.
ew York, N.Y. ....1835 — S.P.SQUIRE

ACY, P.
oston, Mass. ....1819 — P.STACY

ALL, JOSEPH
altimore, Md. 1804

ANIFORD, JOHN
indham, Conn. .....1737-1811 — JS Staniford

ANTON, DANIEL
tonington, Conn. ....1755-1781 — D.Stanton

ANTON, ENOC
tonington, Conn. 1745

ANTON, ZEBULON
tonington, Conn. ...1753-1828 — ZS STANTON

ANWOOD & HALSTRICK
oston, Mass. 1850

ANWOOD, HENRY B.
oston, Mass. ....1818-1869 — HenryB.Stanwood

ANWOOD, J. E.
hiladelphia, Pa. ....1850 — J.E.STANWOOD

ANWOOD, JAMES D.
oston, Mass. 1846

APLES, JOHN J.
New York, N.Y. ....1788 — IIS J.J.S.

APLES, JOHN J., Jr.
New York, N.Y. 1788

. CYR., S. L.
New Orleans, La. 1822

ARR, R.
Unknown ....1800 — R.STARR

ARR, RICHARD
hiladelphia, Pa. ....1813 — R.STARR

EBBINS & CO. E.
New York, N.Y. ....1810 — E.STEBBINS & CO

EBBINS & HOWE
New York, N.Y. ....1815 — STEBBINS & HOWE

EBBINS, T. E.
New York, N.Y. ....1810 — STEBBINS T.STEBBINS

EDMAN, ALEXANDER
Philadelphia, Pa. 1793

EELE, JOHN
Annapolis, Md. 1710

EELE, T. & CO.
Hartford, Conn. ....1805 — T.Steele & Co

STEELE, T. S.
Hartford, Conn. ....1790 — T.Steele

STEPHANIS, GOTHELF
New York, N.Y. 1791

STEPHEN, THOMAS H.
Philadelphia, Pa. 1839

STEPHENS, GEORGE
New York, N.Y. ....1790 — G.S

STEPHENSON, THOMAS
Buffalo, N.Y. ....1840 — STEPHENSON

STEVEN, GEORGE
New York, N.Y. 1719

STEVENS & LAKEMAN
Salem, Mass. ....1825 — STEVENS♥LAKEMAN

STEWART C. W.
Lexington, Ky. ....1850 — C.W.STEWART LEX.KT.

STEWART, JOHN
New York, N.Y. 1791

STICKLER, JOHN
New York, N.Y. 1823

STICKNEY, JONATHAN, Jr.
Newburyport, Mass. ......1798 — I.STICKNEY

STICKNEY, M. P.
Newburyport, Mass. ....1820 — M.P.STICKNEY

STILES, BENJAMIN
Woodbury, Conn. 1831

STILLMAN, ALEXANDER
Philadelphia, Pa. 1806

STILLMAN, BARTON
Westerly, R.I.

STILLMAN, E.
Stonington, Conn. ....1825 — E.Stillman E.Stillman

STILLMAN, PAUL
Westerly, R.I.

STILLMAN, RICHARD
Philadelphia, Pa. ....1805 — R.STILLMAN

STILMAN, WILLIAM
Hopkington, R.I. 1788

STINSON, WILLIAM
New York, N.Y. 1813

STOCKMAN & PEPPER
Philadelphia, Pa. ....1840 — STOCKERMAN & PEPPER

STOCKMAN, JACOB
Philadelphia, Pa. 1828

STODDER & FROBISHER
Boston, Mass. ....1817 — STODDER & FROBISHER

STOLLENWRECK
New York, N.Y. ....1800 — Stollenwerck SB

STOLLENWERCK & BROS.
New York, N.Y. ... .1805 — Stollenwerck & Bros

STOLLENWERCK & CO.
New York, N.Y. 1800

STONE, ADAM
Baltimore, Md.

STONE & OSBORN
New York, N.Y. 1796

STORM, A. G.
Albany, N.Y. 1830   A.G.STORM

STORM, A. G. & SON
Albany, N.Y. 1835

STORRS & COOLEY
New York, N.Y. 1832   S&C

STORRS, N.
New York, N.Y. 1825   N.STORRS

STOUT, J. D.
New York, N.Y. 1850   J.D.STOUT

STOUT, SAMUEL
Princeton, N.J. 1779

STOW, JOHN
Wilmington, Del. 1772

STOUTENBURGH, TOBIAS
New York, N.Y. 1700-1759   TSB   TSB

STOWELL, A., Jr.
Baltimore, Md. 1855   A.STOWELL JR

STRONG, JOHN
Maryland 1778   IS   Stuart   ❋ Stuart ❋

STRONG, WILLIAM
Philadelphia, Pa. 1807

STUART, H.
New York, N.Y. 1808

STUART, JOHN
Providence, R.I. 1737

STUCKERT, ISAAC
Philadelphia, Pa. 1809

STUDLEY, D. F.
Unknown 1830   D.F.STUDLEY.

SULLIVAN, C. D.
St. Louis, Mo. 1850   C.D.SULLIVAN

SULLIVAN, D. & CO.
New York, N.Y. 1820   D.SULLIVAN & Co.

SUPPLEE, JACOB
Philadelphia, Pa. 1791

SUTHERLAND, GEORGE
Boston, Mass. 1810

SUTTON, ROBERT
Boston, Mass. 1820   R.SWAN   R.SWAN

SWAN, B.
Unknown 1825   B.SWAN

SWAN, CALEB
Boston, Mass. 1775

SWAN, ROBERT
Philadelphia, Pa. 1824

SWAN, ROBERT
Philadelphia, Pa. 1799   R.SWAN   R.SWAN
R.SWAN

SWAN, WILLIAM
Worcester, Mass. 1715-1774   WS WS WAN Swan SWAN

SWEETER, HENRY P.
Worcester, Mass. 1768

SYMMES, JOHN
Boston, Mass. 1766

SYNG, DANIEL
Lancaster, Pa.

SYNG, PHILIP
Philadelphia, Pa. 1703-1789   PS PS

SYNG, PHILIP, Jr.
Philadelphia, Pa. 1676-1739   PS ❋ PS PS ❋

T

TABER, WILLIAM
Philadelphia, Pa. 1835

TANGUY, J. & P.
Philadelphia, Pa. 1808

TANGUY, JOHN
Philadelphia, Pa. 1818   I.TANGUY I.TANGU
J.TANGUY

TANGUY, PETER
Philadelphia, Pa. 1810

TANGUY, REPITON
Philadelphia, Pa. 1806

TANNER, JOHN
Newport, R.I. 1740   IT

TANNER, P. G.
Newport, R.I. 1800   P.G.TANNER

TARBELL, E.
Unknown ....c. 1830

TARGEE, JOHN
New York, N.Y. 1799   I.T. IT

TARGEE, JOHN & PETER
New York, N.Y. 1811   I♥PT I&P.TARGEE

TARGEE, PETER
New York, N.Y. 1811

TARGEE, WILLIAM
New York, N.Y. 1807

TAYLOR, GEORGE W.
Philadelphia, Pa. 1824

TAYLOR & HINSDALE
New York, N.Y. 1801   T&H&

TAYLOR, JOHN
New York, N.Y. 1801

TAYLOR & LAWRIE
Philadelphia, Pa. 1841   TAYLOR&LAWRIE

TAYLOR, NAJAH
New York, N.Y. 1793

TAYLOR, N. & CO.
New York, N.Y. 1825   N.TAYLOR&CO

TAYLOR, THOMAS
Providence, R.I. 1727

TAYLOR, WILLIAM
Philadelphia, Pa. 1772

TAYLOR & LAWRIE
Philadelphia, Pa. 1837

TEMPEST, ROBERT
Philadelphia, Pa. 1814

TEN EYCK, JACOB
Albany, N.Y. 1704-1793

TEN EYCK, KOENRAET
New York, N.Y. 1678-1753

TENNEY, WILLIAM I.
New York, N.Y. 1840

TERRY, GEER
Enfield, Conn. 1775-1858

TERRY, JOHN
New York, N.Y. 1820

TERRY, L. B.
Enfield, Conn. 1810

TERRY, WILBERT
Enfield, Conn. 1810

TERRY, WILLIAM
Enfield, Conn. 1785

THAXTER, JOSEPH B.
Highham, Mass. 1815

THEOFILE, WILLIAM
New Orleans, La. 1822

THIBAULT & BROS.
Philadelphia, Pa. 1810

THIBAULT & COMPANY
Philadelphia, Pa. 1797

THIBAULT, FELIX
Philadelphia, Pa. 1814

THIBAULT, FRANCIS
Philadelphia, Pa. 1800

THIBAULT, FRANCIS & FELIX
Philadelphia, Pa. 1807

THIBAULT, FREDERICK
Philadelphia, Pa. 1818

THIBAULT, FREDERICK &
FELIX
Philadelphia, Pa. 1813

THOMAS, CARSON & HALL
Albany, N.Y. 1818

THOMAS, THOMAS
New York, N.Y. 1784

THOMAS, WALTER
New York, N.Y. 1769

THOMAS, WILLIAM
Trenton, N.J. 1775

THOMISON, PETER
Boston, Mass. 1817

THOMPSON, D. B.
Litchfield, Conn. 1825

THOMPSON, WILLIAM
Maryland 1762-1774

THOMSON, ISAAC
Litchfield, Conn. ....,...1801

THOMSON, JAMES
New York, N.Y. 1834

THOMSON, PETER
Philadelphia, Pa. 1835

THOMSON, JAMES
New York, N.Y. 1834

THOMSON, WILLIAM
New York, N.Y. 1810

THORNTON HENRY
Providence, R.I. 1824

TILEY, JAMES
Hartford, Conn. 1740-1792

TINGLEY, SAMUEL
New York, N.Y. 1767

TISDALE, B. H.
Providence, R.I. 1824

TITCOMB, FRANCIS
Newburyport, Mass. 1813

TOMPKINS, EDMUND
Waterbury, Conn. 1779

TOUZELL, JOHN
Salem, Mass. 1756

TOWNSHENDT, THOMAS
Boston, Mass. 1727

TOWNSEND, S.
Unknown 1775

TOWSON, OBADIAH W.
Philadelphia, Pa. 1819

TOWZELL, JOHN
Salem, Mass. 1726-1785

TOY, ISAAC NICHOLAS
Maryland 1771-1834

TOY, JOSEPH
Abingdon, Md. 1748-1826

TRACY, ERASTUS
Norwich, Conn. 1791

TRACY, GORDON
Norwich, Conn. ...,....1767-1792

TRAUX, HENRY R.
Albany, N.Y. 1815

TRIPLER, CHRISTIAN
New York, N.Y. 1794

TROLL, WILLIAM
Philadelphia, Pa. 1810

TROTH, JAMES
Pittsburgh, Pa. 1800

TROTT & BROOKS
New London, Conn. 1798

TROTT & CLEVELAND
New London, Conn. ..1792-1794

TROTT, GEORGE
Boston, Mass. 1765

TROTT, J. P.
New London, Conn. 1769

TROTT, J. P. & SON
New London, Conn. 1820

TROTT, J. PROCTOR
New London, Conn. 1799

TROTT, JOHN PROCTOR
New London, Conn. 1792

TROTT, JONATHAN
Boston, Mass. 1771

TROTT, JONATHAN, Jr.
New London, Conn. 1800

TROTT & SON, JOHN P.
New London, Conn. 1820

TROTT, THOMAS
Boston, Mass. 1701-1777

TRUAX, HENRY R.
Albany, N.Y. 1815

TRUMBUL, RICHARD
Boston, Mass. 1767

TUCKER, DANIEL
Portland, Me. 1781

TUCKER, J. W.
New York, N.Y. 1803

TURNER, JAMES
Boston, Mass. 1759

TUTHILL, CHRISTOPHER
Philadelphia, Pa. 1731

TUTTLE, BETHUEL
New Haven, Conn. 1802

TUTTLE, WILLIAM
New Haven, Conn. 1821

TYLER, ANDREW
Boston, Mass. 1692-1741

TYLER & CO., JOHN H.
Boston, Mass. 1840

TYLER, DAVID
Boston, Mass. 1760-1804

TYLER, D. M.
Boston, Mass. 1810

TYLER, GEORGE
Boston, Mass. 1740-1785

U

UBELIN, FREDERICK
Philadelphia, Pa. 1773

UFFORD, & BURDICK
New Haven, Conn 1814

UNDERHILL, ANDREW
New York, N.Y. 1780

UNDERHILL, THOMAS
New York, N.Y. 1779

UNDERHILL & VERNON
New York, N.Y. 1787

UNDERWOOD, JOHN
Philadelphia, Pa. 1797

V

VAIL, ELIJAH
Troy, N.Y. 1836

VAISSIERE, VICTOR
New York, N.Y. 1816

VALET, PETER
New York, N.Y. 1787

VALLEE, ANTOINE
New Orleans, La. 1822

VAN BERGEN, JOHN
Albany, N.Y. 1813

VAN BEUREN, PETER
New York, N.Y. 1798

VAN BEUREN, WILLIAM
New York, N.Y. 1790

VANDERBURGH, CORNELIUS
New York, N.Y. 1677

VANDERHAN, J.
Philadelphia, Pa. 1740

VANDERHAUL
Philadelphia, Pa. 1740

VANDERSPIEGEL
New York, N.Y. 1701

VANDERSPIEGEL, JACOBUS
New York, N.Y. 1702

VANDERSPIEGEL, JOHANNIS
New York, N.Y. 1687

VAN DYKE, PETER
New York, N.Y. 1684-1750

DYKE, RICHARD New York, N.Y. 1717-1770	
HORN, DAVID Philadelphia, Pa. 1801	
INBURGH, PETER New York, N.Y. 1689-1740	
NESS, & WATERMAN New York, N.Y. 1835	
RIPER, TUNIS New York, N.Y. 1813	
SCHAICK, G. Unknown 1840	
VEGHTEN, HENRY Albany, N.Y. 1760	
VLEIT, B.V. Poughkeepsie, N.Y. 1840	
VOORHIS, DANIEL New York, N.Y. 1779	
VOORHIS & COOLEY New York, N.Y. 1786	
VOORHIS & SCHANCK New York, N.Y. 1791	
VOORHIS & SON New York, N.Y. 1798	
WYCK & PELLETREAU New York, N.Y. 1815	
WYCK, S. New York, N.Y. 1810	
NEY, JOHN Philadelphia, Pa. 1795	
ZIE, JOSEPH Providence, R.I. 1815	
GEREAU, PETER New York, N.Y. 1700-1755	
NON, J. & CO. New York, N.Y. 1798	
NON, JOHN New York, N.Y. 1793	
NON, N. & CO. Charleston, S.C. 1800	
NON, NATHANIEL Charleston, S.C. 1777-1843	
NON, SAMUEL Newport, R.I. 1683-1735	
NON & PARK Pittsburg, Pa. 1815	
ANT, WILLIAM Philadelphia, Pa. 1725	

VILLARD, R. H. L. Georgetown, D.C. 1833	
VINCENT, RICHARD Baltimore, Md. 1799	
VINTON, DAVID Providence, R.I. 1790	
VIRGIN, W. M. Unknown 1830	
VOORHIS, DANIEL VAN New York, N.Y. 1769	

W

WACHNER, F. W. New York, N.Y. 1819	
WADDILL, NOEL Petersburg, Va. 1778	
WAGLIN, THOMAS Philadelphia, Pa. 1837	
WAGSTAFF, THOMAS New York, N.Y. 1791	
WAGSTER, ISAIAH Baltimore, Md. 1776-1793	
WAIT & WRIGHT Philadelphia, Pa. 1837	
WAITE, JOHN Kingstown, R.I. 1770	
WAITE, JOHN New York, N.Y. 1798	
WAITE, W. Unknown 1770	
WAITE, WILLIAM Kingstown, R.I. 1760	
WALDRON, D. New York, N.Y. 1789	
WALKER, GEORGE Philadelphia, Pa. 1797	
WALKER, HANNAH Philadelphia, Pa. 1816	
WALKER, JOHN, Jr. Philadelphia, Pa. 1798	
WALKER, L. Boston, Mass. 1825	
WALKER, WILLIAM Philadelphia, Pa. 1793	
WALKER, W. & S. Phialdelphia, Pa. 1795	
WALLACE, WILLIAM F. Westerly, R.I.	
WALLER, JOHN Philadelphia, Pa. 1804	

WALLIS, THOMAS
Philadelphia, Pa. 1804

WALRAVEN, JOHN
Baltimore, Md. 1771-1814

WALTER, JACOB
Baltimore, Md. ... 1782-1865

WALTON, DANIEL
Philadelphia, Pa. 1808

WALWORTH, DANIEL
Middletown, Conn. 1785

WARD, AMBROSE
New Haven, Conn. 1767

WARD & BARTHOLOMEW
Hartford, Conn. .... .1804

WARD, BARTHOLOMEW &
    BRAINARD
Hartford, Conn. 1809

WARD, BILLIOUS
Guilford, Conn. 1729-1777

WARD & COX
Hartford, Conn. 1811

WARD & GAVETT
Hartford, Conn. 1813

WARD & HUGHES
Middletown, Conn. 1805

WARD, JAMES
Hartford, Conn. 1768-1856

WARD, JOHN
Philadelphia, Pa. 1808

WARD, JOHN
Middletown, Conn. 1805

WARD & MILLER
Philadelphia, Pa. 1822

WARD & RICH
Boston, Mass. 1830

WARD, RICHARD
Boston, Mass. 1815

WARD, SAMUEL L.
Boston, Mass. 1830

WARD, TIMOTHY
Middletown, Conn. 1776

WARD, WILLIAM, Jr.
Guilford, Conn.   1705-1761

WARD, WILLIAM
Litchfield, Conn.   1742-1828

WARDIN, DANIEL
Bridgeport, Conn. 1811

WARNER, A. E. & T. H.
Baltimore, Md. 1805

WARNER, ANDREW E.
Baltimore, Md. 1786-1870

WARNER, ANDREW E., Jr.
Baltimore, Md. 1805

WARNER, CALEB
Portsmouth, N.H. 1784-1861

WARNER, C. & J.
Baltimore, Md. 1825

WARNER, D.
Ipswich, Mass. 1810

WARNER & FELLOWS
Portsmouth, N.H. 1824

WARNER, JOSEPH
Philadelphia, Pa. 1811

WARNER, JOSEPH
Wilmington, Del. 1768

WARNER, JOSEPH P.
Baltimore, Md. 1811-1862

WARNER, SAMUEL
Philadelphia, Pa. 1797

WARNER, THOMAS & A. E.
Baltimore, Md. 1805

WARNER, THOMAS H.
Baltimore, Md. 1780-1828

WARREN, BENJAMIN
Philadelphia, Pa. 1809

WATERMAN, GEORGE
Albany, N.Y. 1849

WATERS, SAMUEL
Philadelphia, Pa. 1790

WATKINS, JAMES
New York, N.Y. 1819

WATLING, JAMES
Philadelphia, Pa. 1837

WATSON & BROWN
Philadelphia, Pa. 1830

WATSON, EDWARD
Boston, Mass. 1821

WATSON, JAMES
Philadelphia, Pa. 1830

WATTS, J. & W.
Philadelphia, Pa. 1829

WATTS, JAMES
Philadelphia, Pa. 1835

WATTS, JOHN W.
New York, N.Y. 1794

WAYNES, RICHARD
Philadelphia, Pa. 1750

WEATHERS, MICHAEL
New York, N.Y. 1794

WEAVER, EMMOR T.
Philadelphia, Pa. 1808

WEAVER, JOSHUA
Westchester, Pa. . 1815

WEBB, BARNEBUS
Boston, Bass. 1762

WEBB & BOON
Philadelphia, Pa. 1785

WEBB, CHARLES
Philadelphia, Pa. 1738

WEBB, EDWARD
Boston, Mass. 1718

WEBB, GEORGE W.
Baltimore, Md. 1812-1890

WEBB, JAMES
Baltimore, Md. 1788-1844

WEBB, ROBERT
Philadelphia, Pa. 1798

WEBSTER, HENRY L.
Providence, R.I. 1831

WEBSTER, HENRY L. & CO.
Providence, R.I. 1842

WEDGE, S.
Baltimore, Md. 1804

WEDGE, SIMON, Sr.
Baltimore, Md. 1774-1823

WEEDER, PELEG
North Kingstown, R.I.

WELCH, JOHN
Boston, Mass.

WELLES, A. & G.
Boston, Mass. .... .1830

WELLES, ANDREW
Hebron, Conn. 1804

WELLES & CO.
Boston, Mass............. 1810

WELLES & GELSTON
New York, N.Y. 1840

WELLES, GEORGE
Hebron, Conn. 1784
Boston, Mass. 1827

WELLES, GEORGE I.
Boston, Mass. ... 1784-1823

WELLES, JAMES M.
New York, N.Y.   1835

WELLS, L. & C.
New York, N.Y.   1798

WELLS, L. & H.
New York, N.Y.   1794

WELLS, LEMUEL
New York, N.Y.   . 1791

WELLS, LEMUEL & CO.
New York, N.Y.   1794

WELLS, WILLIAM
Hartford, Conn.   1828

WENDOVER, JOHN
New York, N.Y.   1694

WENNAM, BARNARD
New York, N.Y.   1789

WENTWORTH & CO.
New York, N.Y.   1850

WEST, BENJAMIN
Boston, Mass.   . 1770

WEST, CHARLES
Boston, Mass.   1830

WEST, JOSEPH
Philadelphia, Pa.   1797

WESTERVELL, JOHN L.
Newburgh, N.Y.   ... 1845

WESTON, BENJAMIN
Philadelphia, Pa.   ..1797

WESTPHAL, CHARLES W.
Philadelphia, Pa.   1802

WHARTENBY & BUNN
Philadelphia, Pa.   1816

WHARTENBY, JOHN
Philadelphia, Pa. 1829

WHARTENBY, THOMAS
Philadelphia, Pa.   1811

WHARTENBY, THOMAS & CO.
Philadelphia, Pa.   1850

WHEATLEY, FREDERICK G.
New York, N.Y.   1805

WHEATON, CALEB
Providence, R.I.   1784-1827

WHEATON, CALVIN
Providence, R.I.   1791

WHETCROFT, WILLIAM
Baltimore, Md.   1735-1799

WHITAKER & GREENE
Providence, R.I. 1825

WHIPPLE, ARNOLD
Providence, R.I. 1825

WHITE, ALFRED
Boston, Mass. 1807

WHITE, AMOS
East Haddam, Conn. ..1745-1825

WHITE, EDWARD
Ulster County, N.Y. 1757

WHITE, GEORGE L.
Cincinnati, Ohio 1822

WHITE, PEREGINE
Woodstock, Conn. ....…....1774

WHITE, PETER
Norwalk, Conn. 1738

WHITE, SAMUEL
New York, N.Y. 1805

WHITE, SILAS
New York, N.Y. 1792

WHITE, STEPHEN
New York, N.Y. 1805

WHITE, WILLIAM
Philadelphia, Pa. 1805

WHITE, WILLIAM J.
New York, N.Y. 1835

WHITE, WILLIAM W.
New York, N.Y. 1835

WHITEMAN, IRA
New York, N.Y. 1761

WHITING, B.
Norwich, Conn. 1755

WHITING, CHARLES
Norwich, Conn. 1725-1765

WHITING, S.
New York, N.Y. 1700

WHITLOCK, THOMAS
New York, N.Y. 1796

WHITLOCK, THOMAS B.
New York, N.Y. 1805

WHITLOCK, WILLIAM H.
New York, N.Y. 1805

WHITON, EBED
Boston, Mass. 1826

WHITTEMORE
Unknown 1736

WHITNEY, AMOS
New York, N.Y. 1800

WHITNEY, E.
New York, N.Y. 1805

WHITNEY, M.
Unknown 1823

WHITNEY & HOYT
New York, N.Y. 1808

WHITON, EBED
Boston, Mass. 1813-1879

WHITTAKER & GREEN
Providence, R.I. 1825

WHITTEMORE, WILLIAM
Portsmouth, N.H. 1710-1770

WICKHAM, DANIEL H.
New York, N.Y. 1835

WILCOX, MICHAEL
Maryland 1772-1799

WILLARD, A.
Utica, N.Y. 1810

WILLARD, JAMES
East Windsor, Conn. 1815

WILLCOX, ALVAN
New Haven, Conn. 1805

WILLCOX, CYPRIAN
New Haven, Conn. 1827

WILLEY, B.
Unknown 1790

WILLIAMS, A. WILLIAM
Washington, D.C. 1829

WILLIAMS, ALEXANDER
Philadelphia, Pa. ..…....1807

WILLIAMS, CHARLES M.
New York, N.Y. 1825

WILLIAMS, DEODAT
Hartford, Conn. 1776

WILLIAMS, JOHN
Philadelphia, Pa. 1793

WILLIAMS, STEPHEN
Providence, R.I. 1799

WILLIAMS, W. A.
Washington, D.C. 1829

WILLIAMS, W. W.
Washington, D.C. 1829

WILLIAMSON, SAMUEL
Philadelphia, Pa. ....1794 `S·W` `SW` `WILLIAMSON`

WILLIG, GEORGE
Philadelphia, Pa. 1819

WILIS, J.
Boston, Mass. 1820

WILLIS, STILLMAN
Boston, Mass. ....1823 `S.WILLIS`

WILLIS, WILLIAM S.
Boston, Mass. ....1825 `Wm S.Willis`   `Opp. Old South`

WILLS, HENRY
New York, N.Y. 1774

WILMOT, SAMUEL
New Haven, Conn. ...1777-1846 `S.WILMOT` `WILMOT`

WILMOT, SAMUEL, Jr.
New Haven, Conn. ...1808-1846 `WILMOT`

WILMOT & STILLMAN
New Haven, Conn. 1800

WILMOT, T. T.
New Haven, Conn. ....1810 `T.T.WILMOT`

WILSON, ALBERT
Troy, N.Y. ..,.,......1834

WILSON, GEORGE
Philadelphia, Pa...........1850

WILSON, H. & CO.
Philadelphia, Pa. ....1815 `H.WILSON&CO`

WILSON, HOSEA
Philadelphia, Pa. ....1812 `H.WILSON` `H.WILSON`

WILSON, HOSEA & CO.
Baltimore, Md. ....1814-1816 `H.WILSON&Cº`

WILSON, JAMES
Trenton, N.J. 1769

WILSON, JOHN
Philadelphia, Pa. ....:1770

WILSON, R. & W.
Philadelphia, Pa. ....1825 `R&W.W` `R&WW` `R&W.WILSON`

WILSON, ROBERT
New York, N.Y. ....1816 `R·W`

WILSON, S.
Philadelphia, Pa. 1805

WILSON, S. & S.
Philadelphia, Pa. ....1797 `S·S.WILSON`

WILSON, THOMAS
Philadelphia, Pa. 1837

WILSON, WILLIAM
Philadelphia, Pa. 1829

WILTBERGER & ALEXANDER
Philadelphia, Pa. 1797

WILTBERGER, CHRISTIAN
Philadelphia, Pa. ....1770-1851 `C.Wiltberger` `C.Wiltberger` `C.Wiltberger`

WINDOVER, JOHN
New York, N.Y. 1694

WINSLOW, EDWARD
Boston, Mass. ....1669-1753 `EW` `EW` `EW` `EW`

WINSOR, WILLIAM
Boston, Mass. 1759

WISHART, ALEXANDER
New York, N.Y. 1808

WISHART, DANIEL
New York, N.Y. 1825

WISHART. HUGH
New York, N.Y. ....1784 `H.WISHART` `WISHART`

WISHART, WILLIAM
New York, N.Y. 1800

WOLCOTT & GELSTON
Boston, Mass. ....1824 `Wolcott & Gelston`

WOLF, JAMES G.
Philadelphia, Pa. 1831

WOLFE, FRANCIS H.
Philadelphia, Pa. ....1829 `F.H.WOLFE` `()` `2`

WOLFE & WRIGGINS
Philadelphia, Pa. ....1837 `WOLFE & WRIGGINS`

WOOD, A. & W.
New York, N.Y. .... 1850 `A&W.WOOD`

WOOD, ALFRED
Unknown ....1800 `WOOD`

WOOD, BENJAMIN B.
New York, N.Y. ....1805 `B.B.WOOD` `B.WOOD`

WOOD & HUGHES
New York, N.Y. ....1846 `W&H` `W&H` `WOOD & HUGHES`

WOOD, J. E.
New York, N.Y. .... 1845 `J.E.WOOD`

WOODCOCK, BANCROFT
Wilmington, Del. ....1754 `B·W` `WOODCOCK`

WOODRUFF, ENOS
Cincinnati, Ohio 1820

WOODRUFF & WHITE
Cincinnati, Ohio 1829

WOODS, FREEMAN
New York, N.Y. ....1791 `Woods` `Woods` `FW`

WOODWARD, ANTIPAS
Middletown, Conn. 1791

WOODWARD, CHARLES
New York, N.Y. 1825

WOODWARD, ELI
Boston, Mass. 1812

WOODWARD & GROSJEAN
Boston, Mass. 1847

WOODWORTH, E.
Unknown 1800

WOOL, JEREMIAH W.
New York, N.Y. 1791

WRIGGIN & CO.
Philadelphia, Pa. 1831

WRIGGINS, THOMAS
Philadelphia, Pa. 1837

WRIGHT, ALEXANDER
Maryland 1776

WRIGHT, JOHN F.
Philadelphia, Pa. 1831

WRIGHT, W.
Unknown 1800

WYATT, JOSEPH
Philadelphia, Pa. 1797

WYER, ELEAZER
Portland, Me. 1768-1848

WYER, ELEAZER, Jr.
Boston, Mass. 1773

WYER & FARLEY
Portland, Me. 1828-1832

WYER & NOBLE
Portland, Me. 1823

WYNKOOP, BENJAMIN
New York, N.Y. 1675-1751

WYNKOOP, CORNELIUS
New York, N.Y. 1724

WYNKOOP, JACOBUS
New York, N.Y. 1765

WYNN, CHRISTOPHER
Baltimore, Md. 1795-1883

Y

YATES, S.
Albany, N.Y. 1810

YATES, S.
Unknown ....c. 1825

YEOMANS, ELIJAH
Hadley, Mass. 1771

YETTONS, RANDELL
Philadelphia, Pa. 1739

YOU, DANIEL
Charleston, S.C. 1744

YOU, THOMAS
Charleston, S.C. 1756

YOUNG, ALEXANDER
Camden, S.C. 1800

YOUNG, EBENEZER
Hebron, Conn. 1778

YOUNG, LEVI
Bridgeport, Conn. 1827

YOUNG, S. E.
Laconia, N.H. 1840

YOUNG, WILLIAM
Philadelphia, Pa. 1761

Z

ZAHM, G. M.
Lancaster, Pa. 1840

ZAHM & JACKSON
New York, N.Y. 1830

NOTE: Most town marks have variable date letters. A mark identical to one shown except for the letter will represent the same town, but a different year.

A

Aix; charge mark; 1781-Revolution.

Paris; charge mark; 1789.

Paris; charge mark; 1681-1684.

Paris; charge mark; 1677-1680.

Paris; charge mark; 1687-1691.

Paris; charge mark; 1684-1687.

Paris; charge mark; 1684-1687.

Paris; charge mark; 1691-1698.

Paris; charge mark; 1672-1677.

Paris; charge mark; 1698-1703.

Paris; charge mark; 1703-1708.

Paris; charge mark; 1708-1715.

Paris; charge mark; 1726-1732.

Arras; town mark.

Paris; charge mark; 1744-1750.

Paris; charge mark; 1715-1717.

Paris; charge mark; 1732-1738.

Paris; charge mark; 1756-1762.

Vicinity of Paris; charge mark; 1781.

Paris; charge mark; 1768-1774.

Paris; charge mark; 1762-1768.

Paris; charge mark; 1738-1744.

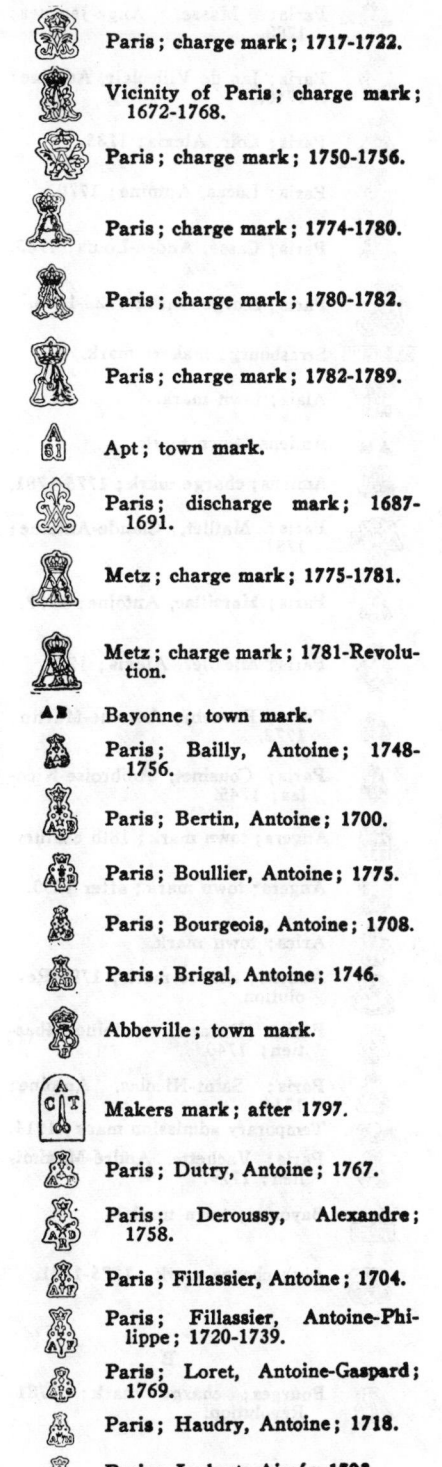

Paris; charge mark; 1717-1722.

Vicinity of Paris; charge mark; 1672-1768.

Paris; charge mark; 1750-1756.

Paris; charge mark; 1774-1780.

Paris; charge mark; 1780-1782.

Paris; charge mark; 1782-1789.

Apt; town mark.

Paris; discharge mark; 1687-1691.

Metz; charge mark; 1775-1781.

Metz; charge mark; 1781-Revolution.

Bayonne; town mark.

Paris; Bailly, Antoine; 1748-1756.

Paris; Bertin, Antoine; 1700.

Paris; Boullier, Antoine; 1775.

Paris; Bourgeois, Antoine; 1708.

Paris; Brigal, Antoine; 1746.

Abbeville; town mark.

Makers mark; after 1797.

Paris; Dutry, Antoine; 1767.

Paris; Deroussy, Alexandre; 1758.

Paris; Fillassier, Antoine; 1704.

Paris; Fillassier, Antoine-Philippe; 1720-1739.

Paris; Loret, Antoine-Gaspard; 1769.

Paris; Haudry, Antoine; 1718.

Paris; Joubert, Aimé; 1703.

Aix; town mark.

 Paris; Masse, Ange-Jacques; 1780.

 Paris; Jan de Villeclair, Antoine; 1750.

 Paris; Loir, Alexis; 1733.

 Paris; Lucas, Antoine; 1770.

 Paris; Cassé, André-Louis; 1763.

 Paris; charge mark; 1722-1726.

 Strasbourg; makers mark.

 Alais; town mark.

 Amiens; town mark.

 Amiens; charge mark; 1775-1781.

 Paris; Maillet, Claude-Antoine; 1781.

 Paris; Marsillac, Antoine; 1777.

 Paris; Micallef, Alexis; 1756.

 Paris; Raveché, Antoine-Martin; 1772.

 Paris; Cousinet, Ambroise-Nicolas; 1745.

 Angers; town mark; 18th century.

 Angers; town mark; after 1750.

 Arles; town mark.

 Amiens; charge mark; 1781-Revolution.

 Paris; Durand, Antoine-Sébastien; 1740.

 Paris; Saint-Nicolas, Antoine: 1714.

 Temporary admission mark; 1911.

Paris; Vachette, André-Maximilien; 1779.

 Bayonne; town mark?

 Aix; charge mark; 1775-1781.

B

 Bourges; charge mark; 1781-Revolution.

 Bordeaux; charge mark; 1781 Revolution.

 Besancon; town mark; 18th cent

 Troyes; town mark.

 Saint-Germain-en-Laye; town mark.

 Paris; town marks; 1765.

 Besancon; town mark; 18th cent.

 Paris; town mark, 1695.

 Rouen; charge mark; 1768-1775.

 Rouen; charge mark; 1775-1781.

 Rouen; charge mark; 1781-Revolution.

 Versailles; charge mark; 1780.

 Bagnols; town mark.

 Bayonne; town mark.

 Paris; Charlié, Brice; 1704.

 Beaucaire; town mark.

 Bordeaux; charge mark; 1775-1781.

 Béziers; town mark.

 Bourges; charge mark; 1775-1781.

 Bordeaux; town mark.

 Bordeaux; town mark.

 Bayonne; charge mark; 1775-1781.

 Bordeaux; town mark.

 Bordeaux; town mark.

Bordeaux; town mark.

Béziers; town mark.

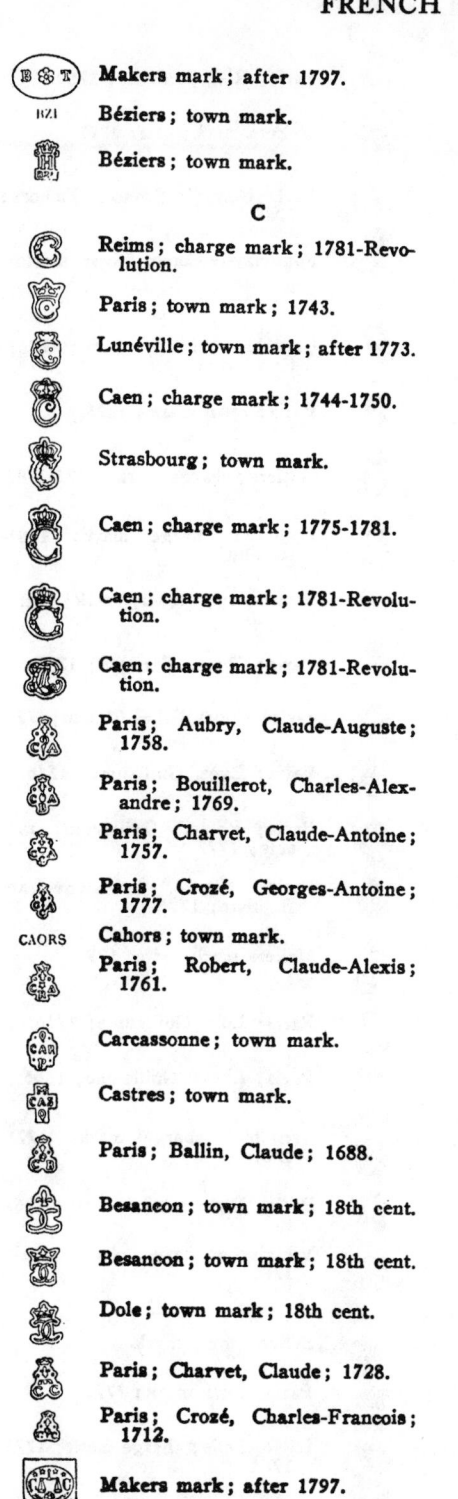

Makers mark; after 1797.

Béziers; town mark.

Béziers; town mark.

C

Reims; charge mark; 1781-Revolution.

Paris; town mark; 1743.

Lunéville; town mark; after 1773.

Caen; charge mark; 1744-1750.

Strasbourg; town mark.

Caen; charge mark; 1775-1781.

Caen; charge mark; 1781-Revolution.

Caen; charge mark; 1781-Revolution.

Paris; Aubry, Claude-Auguste; 1758.

Paris; Bouillerot, Charles-Alexandre; 1769.

Paris; Charvet, Claude-Antoine; 1757.

Paris; Crozé, Georges-Antoine; 1777.

Cahors; town mark.

Paris; Robert, Claude-Alexis; 1761.

Carcassonne; town mark.

Castres; town mark.

Paris; Ballin, Claude; 1688.

Besancon; town mark; 18th cent.

Besancon; town mark; 18th cent.

Dole; town mark; 18th cent.

Paris; Charvet, Claude; 1728.

Paris; Crozé, Charles-Francois; 1712.

Makers mark; after 1797.

Paris; Haudry, Charles-César; 1732.

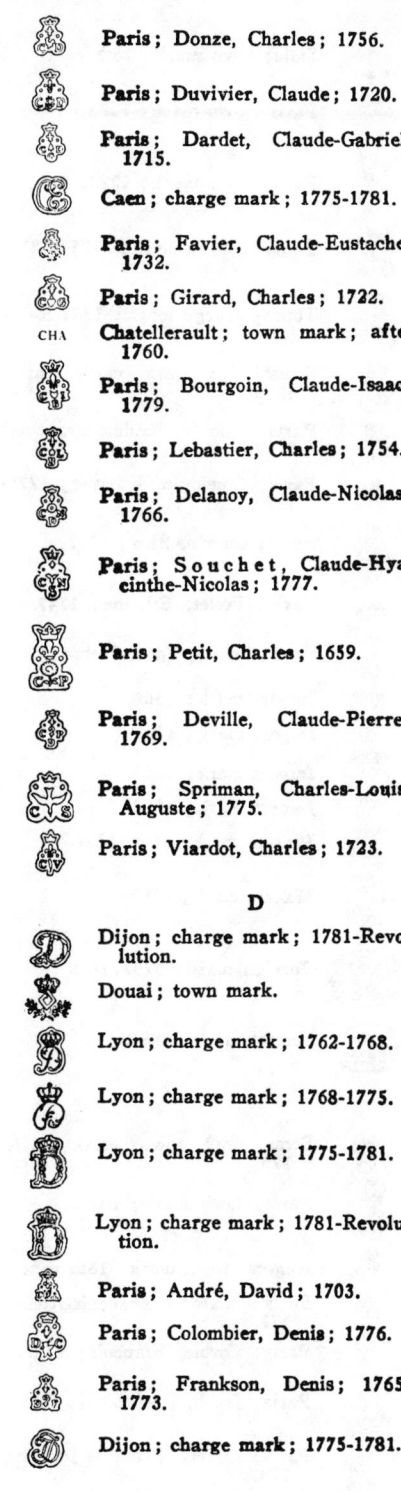

Paris; Donze, Charles; 1756.

Paris; Duvivier, Claude; 1720.

Paris; Dardet, Claude-Gabriel; 1715.

Caen; charge mark; 1775-1781.

Paris; Favier, Claude-Eustache; 1732.

Paris; Girard, Charles; 1722.

Chatellerault; town mark; after 1760.

Paris; Bourgoin, Claude-Isaac; 1779.

Paris; Lebastier, Charles; 1754.

Paris; Delanoy, Claude-Nicolas; 1766.

Paris; Souchet, Claude-Hyacinthe-Nicolas; 1777.

Paris; Petit, Charles; 1659.

Paris; Deville, Claude-Pierre; 1769.

Paris; Spriman, Charles-Louis-Auguste; 1775.

Paris; Viardot, Charles; 1723.

D

Dijon; charge mark; 1781-Revolution.

Douai; town mark.

Lyon; charge mark; 1762-1768.

Lyon; charge mark; 1768-1775.

Lyon; charge mark; 1775-1781.

Lyon; charge mark; 1781-Revolution.

Paris; André, David; 1703.

Paris; Colombier, Denis; 1776.

Paris; Frankson, Denis; 1765-1773.

Dijon; charge mark; 1775-1781.

E

 Dole; town mark; 18th cent.

 Paris; town mark; 1673.

 Paris; town mark; 1721.

 Tours; charge mark; 1775-1781.

 Tours; charge mark; 1781-Revolution.

 Strasbourg; town mark; after 1752.

 Paris; Godin, Edme-Francois; 1747.

 Paris; Gondouin, Etienne; 1778-1786.

 Paris; Guérin, Eloy; 1727.

 Paris; Pollet, Etienne; 1747.

 Paris; Balzac, Edme-Pierre; 1739.

 Import mark; 1864.

 Import mark; 1864.

 Import mark; 1864.

 Import mark; 1864.

 Makers mark; after 1797.

 Makers mark; 1819.

 Foreign mark; 1797/1809.

 Export mark; 1884.

F

 Strasbourg; town mark; after 1752.

 Paris; town mark; 1674.

 Angers; town mark; 18th cent.

 Paris; Caron, Francois-Alexis; 1777.

 Paris; Corbie, Francois; 1777.

 Paris; Jacob, Francois; 1637.

 Paris; Aubert, Francois-Joachim; 1747.

 Paris; Joubert, Francois; 1749.

 Paris; Riel, Francois; 1769.

 Makers mark; after 1797.

 Paris; Germain, Francois-Thomas; 1748.

 Fontenay-le-Comte; town mark.

G

 Grenoble; charge mark; 1781-Revolution.

 Paris; town mark; 1675.

 Poitiers; charge mark; 1775-1781.

 Poitiers; charge mark; 1781-Revolution.

 Strasbourg; town mark; after 1752.

 Paris; Chayé, Germain; 1755.

 Paris; Gouel, Gilles-Claude; 1727.

 Paris; Egée, Guillaume; 1716.

 Paris; Roland, Guillaume Francois; 1777.

 Paris; Gouffé, Guillaume-Jean-Baptiste; 1775.

 Makers mark; after 1797.

 Paris; Loir, Guillaume; 1716.

 Paris; Lucas, Guillaume; 1665.

 Grenoble; charge mark; 1775-1781.

 Paris; Pigeron, Guillaume; 1762.

 Vicinity of Paris; charge mark; 1781.

H

 Salins; town mark.

 Paris; town mark; 1771.

 La Rochelle; charge mark; 1775-1781.

 La Rochelle; charge mark; 1781-Revolution.

Saint-Omer; town mark.

 Paris; Adnet, Henri; 1712.

 Paris; Allain, Henri; 1745.

 Paris; Auguste, Henri; 1785.

 Paris; Debrie, Henri-Nicolas; 1758.

I

 Joinville; town mark.

 Limoges; charge mark; 1775-1781.

 Limoges; charge mark; 1781-Revolution.

 Valenciennes; town mark.

 Paris; Bouillerot, Joseph; 1759.

 Paris; Deharchies, Jean; 1720.

 Paris; Fillassier, Jacques; 1718.

 Commercy; town mark.

 Paris; Josset, Julien; 1767.

 Paris; Bastin, Jean-Nicolas; 1774.

 Paris; Picard, Jean; 1652.

 Paris; Roettiers, Jacques; 1733.

J

 Paris; Anthiaume, Jacques; 1758.

 Paris; Bonhomme, Jacques-Antoine; 1777.

 Paris; Bernier, Jacques; 1781.

 Paris; Besnier, Jacques; 1720.

 Paris; Chéret, Jean-Baptiste-Francois; 1759.

 Paris; Lange, Jean-Baptiste; 1716.

 Paris; Odiot, Jean-Baptiste-Gaspard; 1720.

 Paris; Petit, Julien-Boulogne; 1765.

Paris; Saurin, Jean-Baptiste; 1774.

 Paris; Boudou, Jean-Charles-Marie; 1783.

 Paris; Ducrollay, Jean-Charles; 1755.

 Paris; Morée, Jacques-Charles; 1754.

 Paris; Roquillé-Desnoyers, Jean-Charles; 1772.

 Paris; Ducrollay, Jean; 1734.

 Paris; Debrie, Jacques; 1777.

 Paris; Dubois, Jacques; 1779.

 Paris; Ecosse, Jean; 1705.

 Paris; Famechon, Jacques; 1770.

 Paris; Formey, Jean; 1754.

 Paris; Balzac, Jean-Francois; 1749.

 Paris; Balzac, Jean-Francois, 1755.

 Makers mark; after 1797.

 Paris; Caron, Jean-Francois-Nicolas; 1775.

 Paris; Genu, Jean-Francois; 1754.

 Paris; Garand, Jean-Francois; 1748.

 Paris; Georges, Jean; 1752.

 Paris; Gouel, Jean; 1728.

 Paris; Barriere, Jean-Joseph; 1763.

 Paris; Baudet, Jean-Joseph; 1782.

 Paris; Moillet, Jacques-Joseph; 1742.

 Paris; O u t r e b o n, Jean-Louis-Dieudonné; 1772.

 Paris; Mauzié, Jean; 1723.

 Paris; Quin, Jean-Malquis le; 1735.

 Paris; Roettiers, Jacques-Nicolas; 1765.

 Paris; Pigeon, Jerome; 1705.

 Paris; Charpenat, Jean-Pierre; 1782.

 Saumur; town mark.

 Paris; Pontaneau, Jean-Simon; 1776.

330 FRENCH HALLMARKS

 Paris; Van Conwenberghe, Joseph-Théodore; 1770.

 Paris, Valot, Jean; 1742.

 Paris; Huguet, Jean-Vincent; 1745.

K

 Paris; town mark; 1726.

 Bordeaux; town mark.

 Bordeaux; town mark.

 Bordeaux; town mark.

 Bordeaux; town mark.

 Bordeaux; town mark.

 Bordeaux; town mark.

 Bordeaux; charge mark; 1775-1781.

 Bordeaux; charge mark; 1781-Revolution.

 Lille; town mark.

 Strasbourg; makers mark.

L

 Lyon; charge mark; 1781-Revolution.

 Vesoul; town mark.

 Paris; town mark; 1752.

 Bayonne; charge mark; 1775-1781.

 Paris; Antoine, Léopold; 1706.

 Paris; Taillepied, Louis-Antoine; 1760.

 Paris; Charonnat, Louis; 1748.

 Lucon; town mark.

 Paris; Gabriel, Louis-Emmanuel; 1773.

 Limoges; charge mark; 1781-Revolution.

 Paris; Anthiaume, Louis-Julien; 1779.

 Paris; Gresset, Louis-Joseph; 1781.

 Paris; Prion, Lambert-Joseph; 1770.

 Paris; charge mark; 1780-1782.

 Paris; charge mark; 1782-1789.

 Paris; discharge mark; 1715-1717.

 Versailles; charge mark; 1780.

 Paris; Lenhendrick, Louis-Joseph; 1747.

 Paris; Loir, Louis; 1696.

 Limoges; charge mark; 1775-1781.

 Lunel; town mark.

 La Rochelle; charge mark; 1775-1781.

 La Rochelle; charge mark; 1781-Revolution.

 Paris; Regnard, Louis; 1733.

 Lyon; charge mark; 1775-1781.

M

 Melle; town mark.

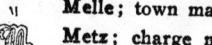 **Metz; charge mark; 1781-Revolution.**

 Paris; town mark; 1775.

 Saint-Malo; charge mark; about 1707.

 Toulouse; charge mark; no date established.

 Toulouse; charge mark; no date established.

 Toulouse; charge mark; no date established.

 Toulouse; charge mark; 1775-1781.

 Toulouse; charge mark; 1781-Revolution.

 Paris; Leroy, Marc-Antoine, Noel; 1769.

 Paris; Berthe, Martin; 1712.

 Mende; town mark.

 Paris; Janety, Marc-Etienne; 1777.

 Paris; Georges, Marie-Gabriel; 1745.

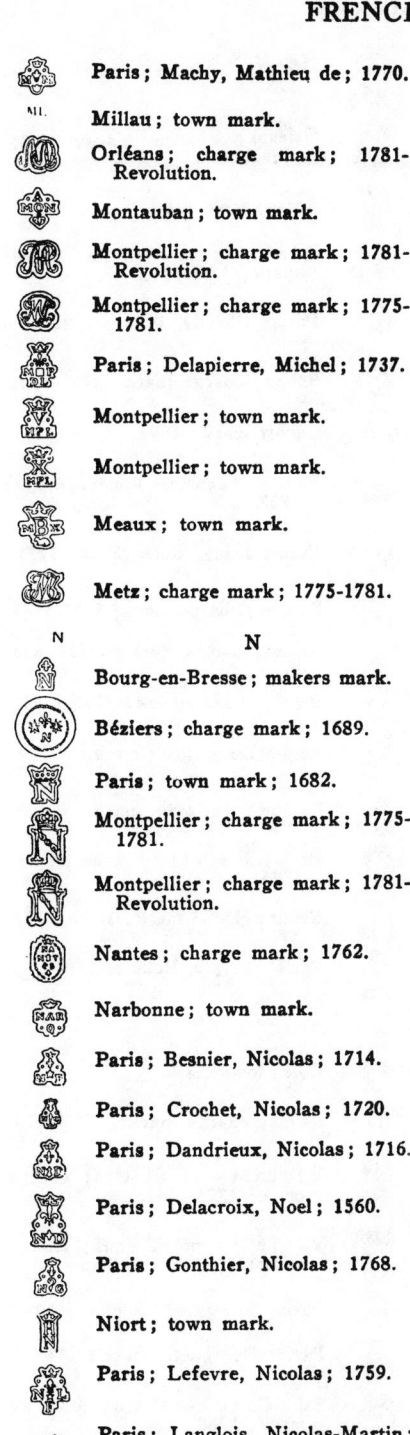

Paris; Machy, Mathieu de; 1770.

Millau; town mark.

Orléans; charge mark; 1781-Revolution.

Montauban; town mark.

Montpellier; charge mark; 1781-Revolution.

Montpellier; charge mark; 1775-1781.

Paris; Delapierre, Michel; 1737.

Montpellier; town mark.

Montpellier; town mark.

Meaux; town mark.

Metz; charge mark; 1775-1781.

N

Bourg-en-Bresse; makers mark.

Béziers; charge mark; 1689.

Paris; town mark; 1682.

Montpellier; charge mark; 1775-1781.

Montpellier; charge mark; 1781-Revolution.

Nantes; charge mark; 1762.

Narbonne; town mark.

Paris; Besnier, Nicolas; 1714.

Paris; Crochet, Nicolas; 1720.

Paris; Dandrieux, Nicolas; 1716.

Paris; Delacroix, Noel; 1560.

Paris; Gonthier, Nicolas; 1768.

Niort; town mark.

Paris; Lefevre, Nicolas; 1759.

Paris; Langlois, Nicolas-Martin; 1750.

Paris; Outrebon, Nicolas; 1735.

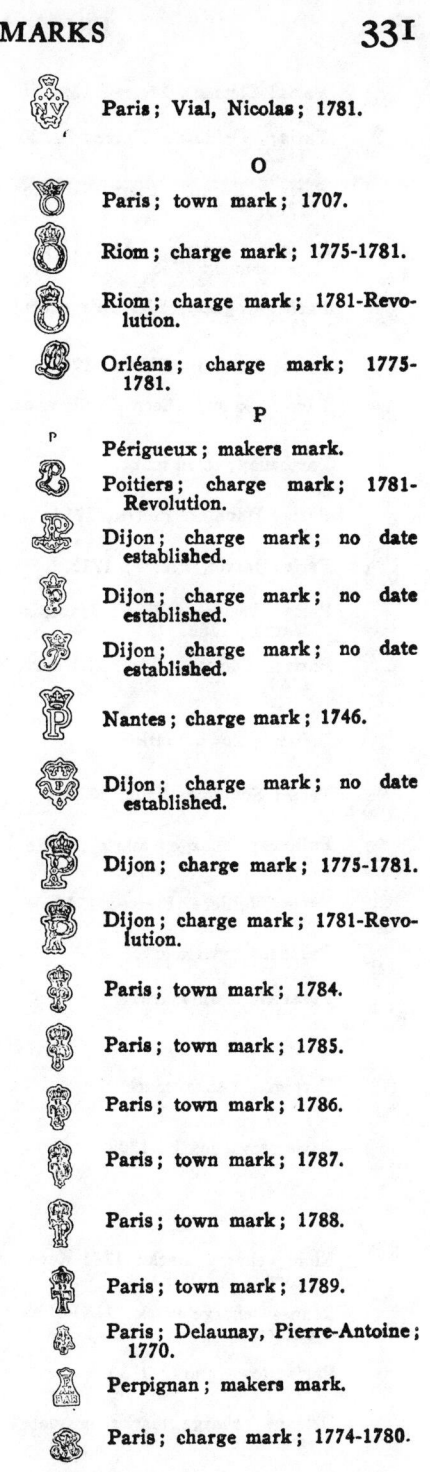

Paris; Vial, Nicolas; 1781.

O

Paris; town mark; 1707.

Riom; charge mark; 1775-1781.

Riom; charge mark; 1781-Revolution.

Orléans; charge mark; 1775-1781.

P

Périgueux; makers mark.

Poitiers; charge mark; 1781-Revolution.

Dijon; charge mark; no date established.

Dijon; charge mark; no date established.

Dijon; charge mark; no date established.

Nantes; charge mark; 1746.

Dijon; charge mark; no date established.

Dijon; charge mark; 1775-1781.

Dijon; charge mark; 1781-Revolution.

Paris; town mark; 1784.

Paris; town mark; 1785.

Paris; town mark; 1786.

Paris; town mark; 1787.

Paris; town mark; 1788.

Paris; town mark; 1789.

Paris; Delaunay, Pierre-Antoine; 1770.

Perpignan; makers mark.

Paris; charge mark; 1774-1780.

Pau; town mark; 18th cent.

Paris; Bourlier, Philippe; 1769.

Paris; Clément, Pierre; 1694.

Paris; Delions, Pierre; 1720-1722.

Paris; Buron, Pierre-Etienne; 1735.

Paris; Garbe, Philippe-Emmanuel; 1748.

Paris; Goguely, Pierre-Francois; 1768.

Paris; Germain, Pierre; 1744.

Paris; Sallot, Pierre-Guillaume; 1750.

Parthenay; town mark.

Paris; Hannier, Pierre; 1716.

Paris; Jarrin, Pierre; 1712.

Paris; Beaulieu, Pierre-Francois-Mathis; 1768.

Paris; Sommé, Pierre-Nicolas; 1768.

Poitiers; town mark.

Paris; Soulaine, Paul; 1720.

Poitiers; charge mark; 1775-1781.

Paris; Valliere, Pierre; 1776.

Pézenas; town mark.

Pézenas; town mark.

Q

Perpignan; town mark.

Paris; town mark; 1709.

R

Riom; charge mark; 1781-Revolution.

Rennes; charge mark; 1781-Revolution.

Paris; town mark; 1733.

Orléans; charge mark; no date established.

Orléans; charge mark; no date established.

Orléans; charge mark; no date established.

Orléans; charge mark; 1775-1781.

Orléans; charge mark; 1781-Revolution.

Arras; town mark.

Vicinity of Orléans; charge mark; 1768-1775.

Paris; Chatria, Rémi; 1724.

Rouen; charge mark; 1775-1781.

Import mark; 1893.

Paris; Auguste, Robert-Joseph; 1757.

Paris; Dany, Roch-Louis; 1779.

Rennes; charge mark; 1775-1781.

Rouen; charge mark; 1781-Revolution.

Riom; charge mark; 1775-1781.

La Rochelle; town mark.

La Rochelle; town mark.

Paris; Ferrier, René-Pierre; 1775.

Reims; charge mark; 1775-1781.

Paris; Turpin, Robert; 1704.

S

Lille; town mark.

Reims; charge mark; 1768-1775.

Vicinity of Chalons; charge mark; 1775-1781.

Vicinity of Chalons; charge mark; 1781-Revolution.

Paris; Boulanger, Simon; 1691.

Paris; Bourguet, Simon; 1740.

Saint-Germain-en-Laye; charge mark; 1780.

Saint-Germain-en-Laye; charge mark; 1780.

Paris; Leblond, Sébastien; 1675.

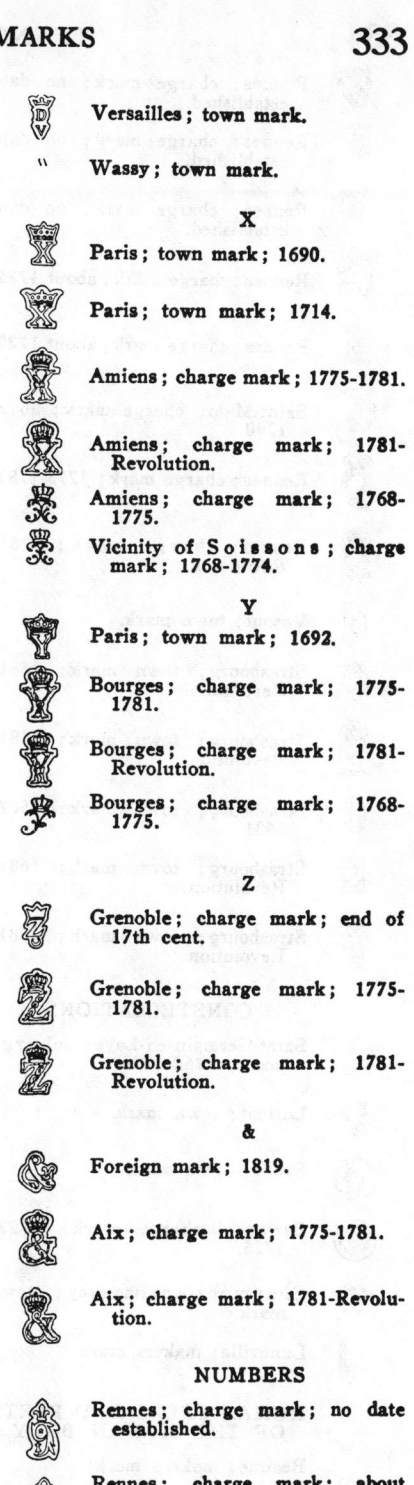

Saint-Omer; town mark.

Saint-Omer; town mark.

Paris; Parisy, Séverin; 1771.

Soissons; town mark.

T

Toul; town mark.
Thouars; town mark.
Tours; charge mark; 1781-Revolution.

Dinan; charge mark; 1759.

Nantes; charge mark; 1744.

Dunkerque; town mark.

Tarascon; town mark.

Paris; Germain, Thomas; 1720.

Toulouse; charge mark; 1775-1781.

Toulouse; charge mark; 1781-Revolution.

Toulouse; town mark; 17th cent.

Toulouse; town mark; 17th cent.

Toulouse; town mark; 18th cent.

Paris; Breton, Thomas-Pierre; 1739.

Tours; charge mark; 1775-1781.

U

Paris; town mark; 1783.

V

Verdun; town mark.

Nantes; charge mark; no date established.

Troyes; charge mark; 1768-1774.

Uzes; town mark.

Paris; Bréant, Vincent; 1754.

Le Vigan; town mark.

Versailles; town mark.

Wassy; town mark.

X

Paris; town mark; 1690.

Paris; town mark; 1714.

Amiens; charge mark; 1775-1781.

Amiens; charge mark; 1781-Revolution.

Amiens; charge mark; 1768-1775.

Vicinity of Soissons; charge mark; 1768-1774.

Y

Paris; town mark; 1692.

Bourges; charge mark; 1775-1781.

Bourges; charge mark; 1781-Revolution.

Bourges; charge mark; 1768-1775.

Z

Grenoble; charge mark; end of 17th cent.

Grenoble; charge mark; 1775-1781.

Grenoble; charge mark; 1781-Revolution.

&

Foreign mark; 1819.

Aix; charge mark; 1775-1781.

Aix; charge mark; 1781-Revolution.

NUMBERS

Rennes; charge mark; no date established.

Rennes; charge mark; about 1680.

Rennes; charge mark; no date established.

Rennes; charge mark; no date established.

 Rennes; charge mark; no date established.

 Rennes; charge mark; no date established.

 Rennes; charge mark; about 1725.

 Rennes; charge mark; about 1730.

 Saint-Malo; charge mark; about 1740.

 Rennes; charge mark; 1775-1781.

 Rennes; charge mark; 1781-Revolution.

 Vesoul; town mark.

 Strasbourg; town mark; 1681-Revolution.

 Strasbourg; town mark; 1681-Revolution.

 Strasbourg; town mark; 1567-1681.

 Strasbourg; town mark; 1681-Revolution.

 Strasbourg; town mark; 1681-Revolution.

CONSTELLATIONS

 Saint-Germain-en-Laye; charge mark; 1768-1774.

 Lorient; town mark.

 Senlis; town mark.

 Paris; discharge mark; 1722-1726.

 Chaumont-en-Bassigny; town mark.

 Lunéville; makers mark.

HUMAN FACES AND PARTS OF THE HUMAN BODY

 Beaune; makers mark.

 Saint-Quentin; town mark.

 Vicinity of Orléans; discharge mark; 1781-Revolution.

 Orléans; town mark; after 1784.

 Toul; town mark; after 1784.

 Rouen; discharge mark; 1781-Revolution.

 Departments; recense mark; 1819.

 Export mark; 1840.

 Export mark; 1840.

 Export mark; 1879.

 Export mark; 1879.

 Export mark; 1879

 Export mark; 1879.

 Export mark; 1879.

 Export mark; 1879.

 Export mark; 1879.

 Departments; standard mark; 1819-1838.

 Metz; discharge mark; 1775-1781.

 Paris; discharge mark; 1780-1782.

 Paris; standard mark; 1819.

 1st standard mark; 1838.

 2nd standard mark; 1838.

 Paris; recense mark; 1819.

 Paris; standard mark; 1819-1838.

Paris; standard mark gold; 1819-1838.

Paris; discharge mark; 1780-1782.

Vicinity of Chalons; discharge mark; 1781-Revolution.

Paris; recense mark; 1798-1809.

Departments; recense mark; 1798-1809.

Paris; recense mark; 1798-1809.

Departments; recense mark; 1798-1809.

Caen; discharge mark; 1775-1781.

Departments; 2nd standard mark; 1819-1838.

Paris; 1st standard mark; 1819-1838.

Paris; 2nd standard mark; 1819-1838.

Vannes; town mark; after 1784.

Sens; discharge mark; 1768-1774.

Dijon; discharge mark; 1781-Revolution.

Orléans; discharge mark; 1768-1775.

Blois; discharge mark; 1768-1775.

Lyon; discharge mark; 1762-1768.

Amiens; discharge mark; 1775-1781.

Paris; garantie mark; 1798-1809.

Departments; garantie mark; 1798-1809.

Paris; garantie mark; 1798-1809.

Departments; garantie mark; 1798-1809.

Departments; garantie mark; 1819.

Meaux; discharge mark; 1672-1768.

Reims; discharge mark; 1768-1774.

Export mark; 1912.

Paris; discharge mark; 1756-1762.

Paris; discharge mark; 1768-1774.

Paris; discharge mark; 1782-1786.

Departments; 1st standard mark; 1819-1838.

Paris; discharge mark; 1768-1774.

Vicinity of Orléans; discharge mark; 1781-Revolution.

Paris; garantie mark; 1819.

Departments; garantie mark; 1819.

Uzes; town mark; after 1784.

Paris, foreign mark; 1819-1838.

Export mark; 1884.

Export mark; 1884.

1st standard mark gold; 1838.

2nd standard mark gold; 1838.

3rd standard mark gold; 1838.

Toulon; town mark; after 1784.

Paris; foreign mark; 1819-1838.

Poitiers; discharge mark; 1781-Revolution.

Bordeaux; discharge mark; 1775-1781.

Paris; garantie mark; 1819-1838.

Departments; garantie mark gold; 1819-1838.

Import mark; 1912.

Import mark; 1926.

Maubeuge; town mark; after 1784.

Departments; recense mark; 1819.

Paris; discharge mark; 1789.

Lyon; discharge mark; 1775-1781.

Tours; discharge mark; 1781-Revolution.

Melle; town mark; after 1784.

Paris; recense mark; 1819.

Saint-Lo; town mark; after 1784.

Senlis; charge mark; 1768-1774.

Versailles; charge mark; 1768-1774.

Saint-Germain-en-Laye; charge mark; 1768-1774.

Montpellier; charge mark; no date established.

Macon; town mark; after 1784.

Departments; garantie mark gold; 1819.

Besancon; makers mark; 15th cent.

Paris; recense mark; 1819.

Vicinity of Orléans; discharge mark; 1775-1781.

Bourges; discharge mark; 1775-1781.

Paris; charge mark; 1744-1750.

Paris; charge mark; 1738-1744.

Riom; discharge mark; 1775-1781.

Tours; discharge mark; 1775-1781.

Bayonne; discharge mark; 1775-1781.

MAMMALS

Paris; discharge mark; 1738-1744.

Paris; discharge mark; 1774-1780.

Avallon; town mark; after 1784.

Rennes; discharge mark; 1781-Revolution.

La Rochelle; discharge mark; 1775-1781.

Gold watch mark; 1819-1838.

Paris; 3rd gold standard mark; 1819-1838.

Pau; town mark; after 1784.

Caen; discharge mark; 1781-Revolution.

Bourges; town mark; after 1784.

Paris; garantie mark; 1819-1838.

Les Sables; town mark; after 1784.

Amiens; discharge mark; 1781-Revolution.

Bourges; discharge mark; 1775-1781.

Rouen; makers mark; 15th and 16th centuries.

Rouen; makers mark; 17th and 18th centuries.

Poitiers; discharge mark; 1775-1781.

Compiegne; town mark; after 1784.

Nantes; discharge mark; 1746.

Metz; discharge mark; 1775-1781.

Recense mark; 1838.

Paris; discharge mark; 1732-1738.

Caen; discharge mark; 1781-Revolution.

Lyon; discharge mark; 1775-1781.

Limoges; discharge mark; 1781-Revolution.

Cambrai; town mark; after 1784.

Gold garantie mark; 1838.

Angouleme; town mark; after 1784.

Riom; discharge mark; 1781-Revolution.

Sedan; town mark; after 1784.

Sedan; makers mark.

Paris; discharge mark; 1750-1756.

Toulouse; discharge mark; 1781-Revolution.

Paris; garantie mark; 1838.

Paris; gold chain mark; 1838.

Departments; gold chain mark; 1838.

Paris; gold mark; 1847.

Alloy mark; 1905.

Departments; 2nd gold standard marks; 1819-1838.

Angers; charge mark; 18th cent.

Valenciennes; town mark.

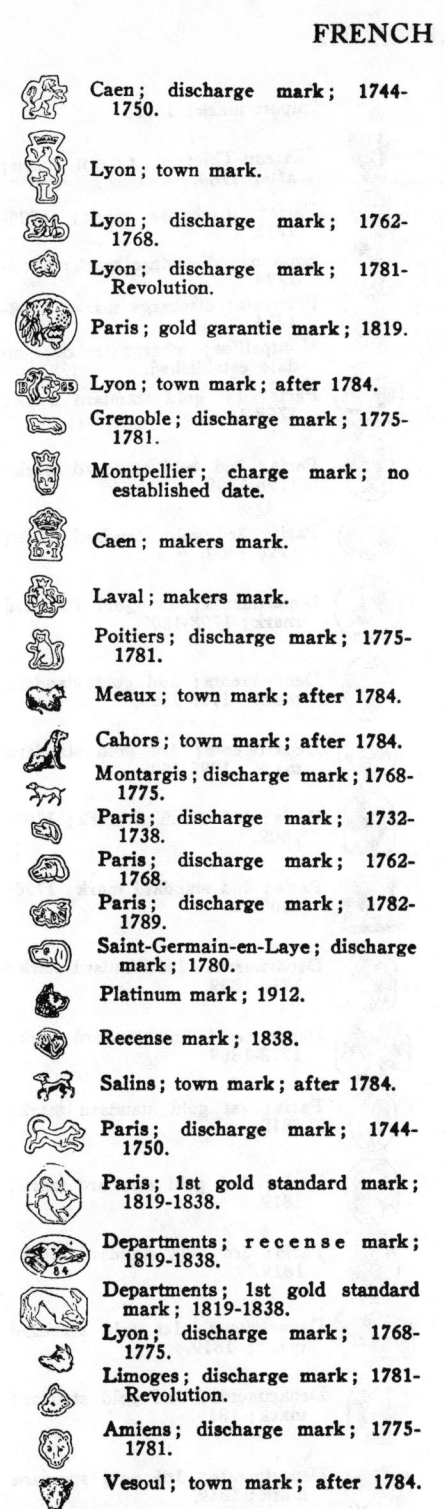

Caen; discharge mark; 1744-1750.

Lyon; town mark.

Lyon; discharge mark; 1762-1768.

Lyon; discharge mark; 1781-Revolution.

Paris; gold garantie mark; 1819.

Lyon; town mark; after 1784.

Grenoble; discharge mark; 1775-1781.

Montpellier; charge mark; no established date.

Caen; makers mark.

Laval; makers mark.

Poitiers; discharge mark; 1775-1781.

Meaux; town mark; after 1784.

Cahors; town mark; after 1784.

Montargis; discharge mark; 1768-1775.

Paris; discharge mark; 1732-1738.

Paris; discharge mark; 1762-1768.

Paris; discharge mark; 1782-1789.

Saint-Germain-en-Laye; discharge mark; 1780.

Platinum mark; 1912.

Recense mark; 1838.

Salins; town mark; after 1784.

Paris; discharge mark; 1744-1750.

Paris; 1st gold standard mark; 1819-1838.

Departments; recense mark; 1819-1838.

Departments; 1st gold standard mark; 1819-1838.

Lyon; discharge mark; 1768-1775.

Limoges; discharge mark; 1781-Revolution.

Amiens; discharge mark; 1775-1781.

Vesoul; town mark; after 1784.

Paris; discharge mark; 1738-1744.

Nantes; charge mark; no date established.

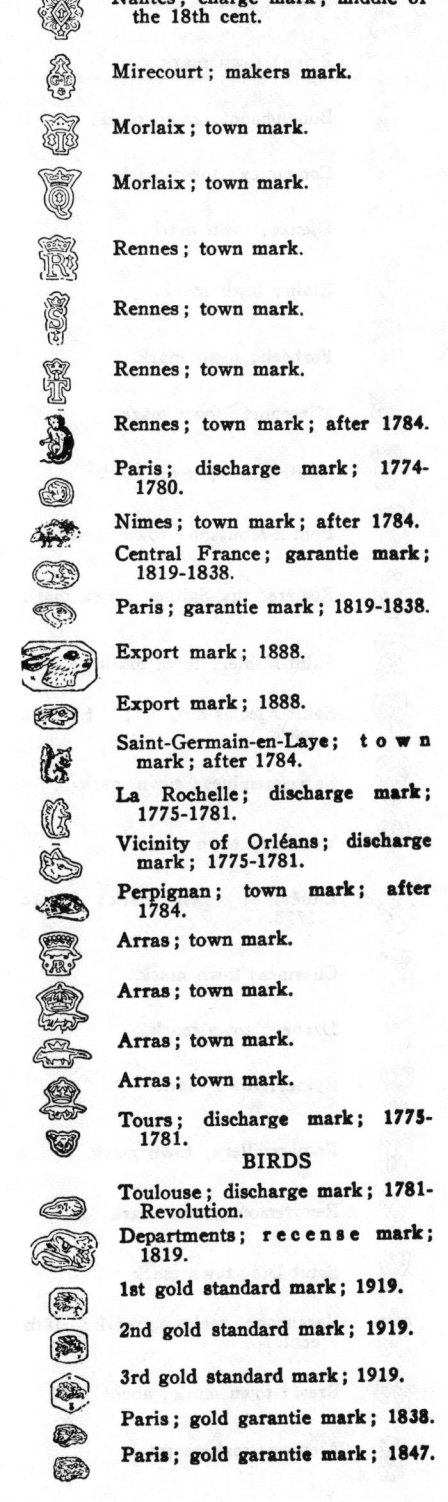

Nantes; charge mark; middle of the 18th cent.

Mirecourt; makers mark.

Morlaix; town mark.

Morlaix; town mark.

Rennes; town mark.

Rennes; town mark.

Rennes; town mark.

Rennes; town mark; after 1784.

Paris; discharge mark; 1774-1780.

Nimes; town mark; after 1784.

Central France; garantie mark; 1819-1838.

Paris; garantie mark; 1819-1838.

Export mark; 1888.

Export mark; 1888.

Saint-Germain-en-Laye; town mark; after 1784.

La Rochelle; discharge mark; 1775-1781.

Vicinity of Orléans; discharge mark; 1775-1781.

Perpignan; town mark; after 1784.

Arras; town mark.

Arras; town mark.

Arras; town mark.

Arras; town mark.

Tours; discharge mark; 1775-1781.

BIRDS

Toulouse; discharge mark; 1781-Revolution.

Departments; recense mark; 1819.

1st gold standard mark; 1919.

2nd gold standard mark; 1919.

3rd gold standard mark; 1919.

Paris; gold garantie mark; 1838.

Paris; gold garantie mark; 1847.

Nancy; makers mark.

 Briey; town mark.

 Bouquemont; town mark.

 Commercy; town mark.

 Dieuze; town mark.

 Etain; town mark.

 Forbach; town mark.

 Mirecourt; town mark.

 Neufchateau; town mark.

 Pont-a-Mousson; town mark.

 Rosieres-aux-Salines; town mark.

 Saint-Mihiel; town mark.

 Saint-Nicolas-du-Port; town mark.

 Sarreguemines; town mark.

 Vézelise; town mark.

 Lunéville; town mark; before 1773.

 Charmes; town mark.

 Darney; town mark.

 Epinal; town mark.

 Rambervillers; town mark.

 Remiremont; town mark.

 Saint-Dié; town mark.

 Besancon; makers mark; 18th cent.

 Brest; town mark; about 1770.

 Alencon; makers mark.

 Import mark; 1893.

 Chateau-Thierry; town mark; after 1784.

 Paris; discharge mark; 1708-1715.

 Soissons; discharge mark; 1768-1774.

 Beauvais; discharge mark; 1768-1774.

Montpellier; charge mark; no date established.

 Paris; 1st gold standard mark; 1798-1809.

 Paris; 2nd gold standard mark; 1798-1809.

 Paris; 3rd gold standard mark; 1798-1809.

 Departments; 1st gold standard mark; 1798-1809.

 Departments; 2nd gold standard mark; 1798-1809.

 Departments; 3rd gold standard mark; 1798-1809.

 Paris; 1st standard mark; 1798-1809.

 Paris; 2nd standard mark; 1798-1809.

 Departments; 1st standard mark; 1798-1809.

 Departments; 2nd standard mark; 1798-1809.

 Paris; 1st gold standard mark; 1819.

 Paris; 2nd gold standard mark; 1819.

 Paris; 3rd gold standard mark; 1819.

 Departments; 1st gold standard mark; 1819.

 Departments; 2nd gold standard mark; 1819.

 Departments; 3rd gold standard mark; 1819.

Paris; 1st standard mark; 1819.

Paris; 2nd standard mark; 1819.

 Departments; 1st standard mark; 1819.

 Departments; 2nd standard mark; 1819.

 Paris; discharge mark; 1750-1756.

 Vicinity of Paris; discharge mark; 1781.

 Paris; gold garantie mark; 1798-1809.

 Departments; gold garantie mark; 1798-1809.

 Paris; gold garantie mark; 1819.

 Paris; gold garantie mark; 1819.

 Departments; gold garantie mark; 1819.

 Departments; gold garantie mark; 1819.

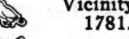 Metz; town mark; after 1784.

 Vicinity of Paris; discharge mark; 1781.

 Versailles; discharge mark; 1768-1774.

 Import mark; 1893.

 Montpellier; charge mark; no date established.

 Morlaix; town mark; about 1740.

 Chartres; town mark; after 1784.

 Toulouse; discharge mark; 1775-1781.

 Lille; town mark; after 1784.

 Trévoux; town mark; after 1784.

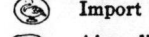 Beaumont-sur-Oise; discharge mark; 1768-1774.

Paris; discharge mark; 1786-1789.

 Import mark; 1893.

Aix; discharge mark; 1775-1781.

 Saint-Martin-de-Ré; town mark; after 1784.

 Saint-Esprit; town mark; after 1784.

Paris; discharge mark; 1726-1732.

Laon; makers mark.

 Angers; charge mark; 18th. cent.

 Aix; town mark; after 1784.

 Laon; discharge mark; 1768-1774.

Pontoise; discharge mark; 1672-1768.

FISH

 Bar-le-Duc; town mark; after 1784.

Beauvais; town mark; after 1784.

Dieppe; town mark; after 1784.

 Southern France; 800 mark; 1819-1838.

 Parthenay; town mark; after 1784.

 Northwest France; 800 mark; 1819-1838.

 Melun; town mark; after 1784.

 Grenoble; town mark; after 1784.

 Paris; discharge mark; 1744-1750.

 Bray-sur-Seine; discharge mark; 1768-1774.

 La Rochelle; discharge mark; 1781-Revolution.

 Dunkerque; town mark.

 Grenoble; town mark.

 Grenoble; town mark.

 Grenoble; town mark.

 Gisors; town mark; after 1784.

AMPHIBIANS AND REPTILES

 Laval; town mark; after 1784.

 Southwest France; 800 mark; 1819-1838.

 Le Havre; makers mark.

 Vitry-le-Francois; town mark.

 Nimes; town mark.

 Nimes; town mark.

INVERTEBRATES

 Abbeville; town mark; after 1784.

 Rennes; discharge mark; about 1730.

Sainte-Ménehould; town mark; after 1784.

 Compiegne; discharge mark; 1768-1774.

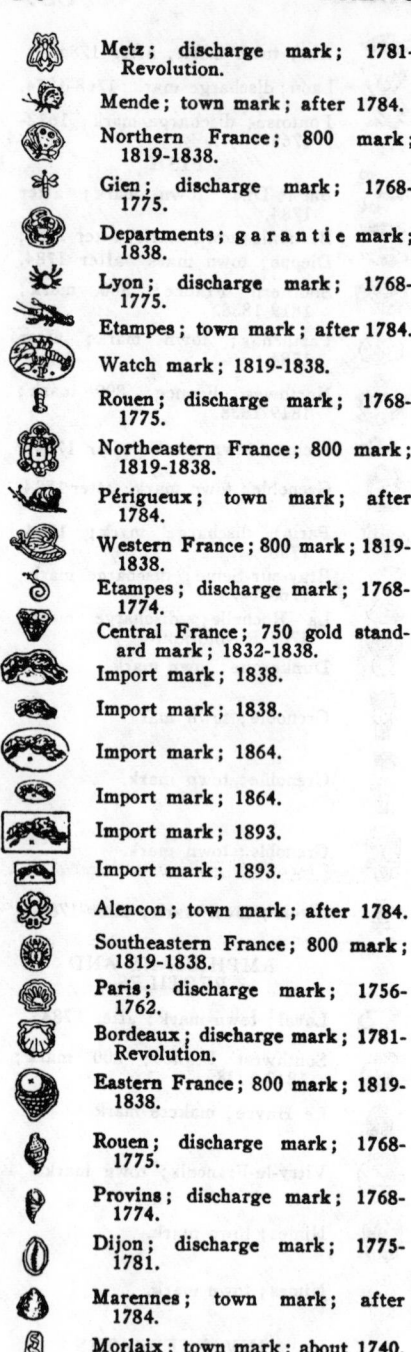

Metz; discharge mark; 1781-Revolution.

Mende; town mark; after 1784.

Northern France; 800 mark; 1819-1838.

Gien; discharge mark; 1768-1775.

Departments; g a r a n t i e mark; 1838.

Lyon; discharge mark; 1768-1775.

Etampes; town mark; after 1784.

Watch mark; 1819-1838.

Rouen; discharge mark; 1768-1775.

Northeastern France; 800 mark; 1819-1838.

Périgueux; town mark; after 1784.

Western France; 800 mark; 1819-1838.

Etampes; discharge mark; 1768-1774.

Central France; 750 gold standard mark; 1832-1838.

Import mark; 1838.

Import mark; 1838.

Import mark; 1864.

Import mark; 1864.

Import mark; 1893.

Import mark; 1893.

Alencon; town mark; after 1784.

Southeastern France; 800 mark; 1819-1838.

Paris; discharge mark; 1756-1762.

Bordeaux; discharge mark; 1781-Revolution.

Eastern France; 800 mark; 1819-1838.

Rouen; discharge mark; 1768-1775.

Provins; discharge mark; 1768-1774.

Dijon; discharge mark; 1775-1781.

Marennes; town mark; after 1784.

Morlaix; town mark; about 1740.

MYTHICAL ANIMALS

Departments; 3rd gold standard mark; 1819-1838.

Paris; 2nd gold standard mark; 1819-1838.

 Bordeaux; town mark; after 1784.

 Import mark; 1838.

 Import mark; 1838.

 La Rochelle; town mark; after 1784.

 Liesse; discharge mark; 1/68-1774.

 Paris; charge mark; 1732-1738.

PLANTS

 Clermont-Ferrand; town mark; after 1784.

 Amiens; discharge mark; 1781-Revolution.

 Alais; town mark; after 1784.

 Draguignan; town mark; after 1784.

 Vicinity of Chalons; discharge mark; 1775-1781.

 Valognes; makers mark.

 Payrat; town mark; after 1784.

 Riom; discharge mark; 1781-Revolution.

 Thiers; town mark; after 1784.

 Rouen; town mark; after 1784.

 Rouen; discharge mark; 1781-Revolution.

 Rouen; discharge mark; 1775-1781.

 Verdun; town mark; after 1784.

 Grenoble; discharge mark; 1781-Revolution.

 Montpellier; charge mark; no date established.

 Paris; discharge mark; 1726-1732.

 Reims; town mark; after 1784.

 Dijon; discharge mark; 1781-Revolution.

 Troyes; town mark; after 1784.

 Vicinity of Chalons; discharge mark; 1781-Revolution.

 Toulouse; discharge mark; 1775-1781.

 Paris; discharge mark; 1789.

 Laon; town mark; after 1784.

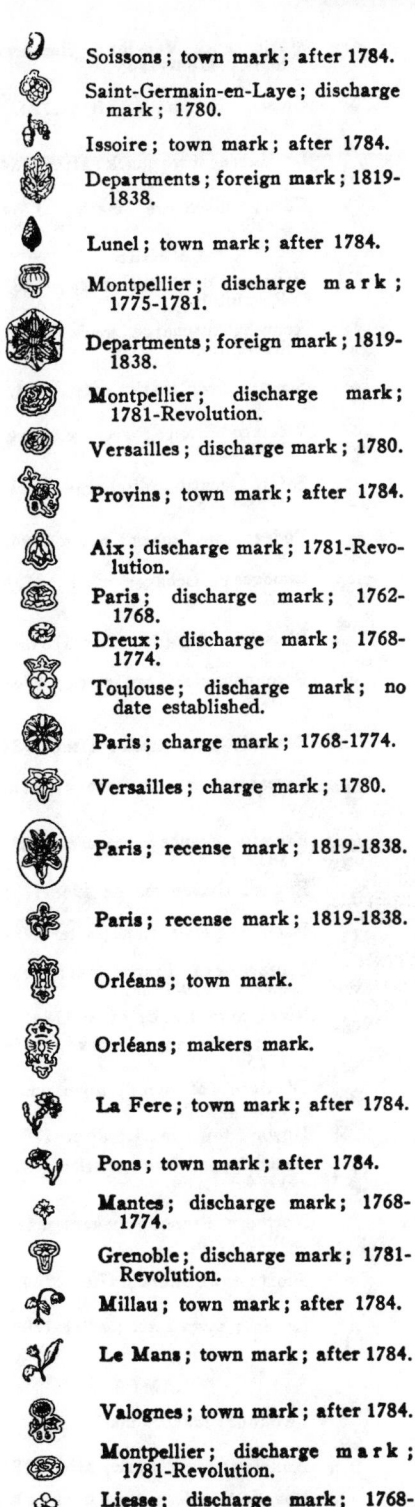

Soissons; town mark; after 1784.

Saint-Germain-en-Laye; discharge mark; 1780.

Issoire; town mark; after 1784.

Departments; foreign mark; 1819-1838.

Lunel; town mark; after 1784.

Montpellier; discharge mark; 1775-1781.

Departments; foreign mark; 1819-1838.

Montpellier; discharge mark; 1781-Revolution.

Versailles; discharge mark; 1780.

Provins; town mark; after 1784.

Aix; discharge mark; 1781-Revolution.

Paris; discharge mark; 1762-1768.

Dreux; discharge mark; 1768-1774.

Toulouse; discharge mark; no date established.

Paris; charge mark; 1768-1774.

Versailles; charge mark; 1780.

Paris; recense mark; 1819-1838.

Paris; recense mark; 1819-1838.

Orléans; town mark.

Orléans; makers mark.

La Fere; town mark; after 1784.

Pons; town mark; after 1784.

Mantes; discharge mark; 1768-1774.

Grenoble; discharge mark; 1781-Revolution.

Millau; town mark; after 1784.

Le Mans; town mark; after 1784.

Valognes; town mark; after 1784.

Montpellier; discharge mark; 1781-Revolution.

Liesse; discharge mark; 1768-1774.

Clermont; discharge mark; 1768-1774.

Melun; discharge mark; 1768-1774.

Crépy; discharge mark; 1768-1774.

Nancy; town mark.

Nancy; town mark.

Paris; charge mark; 1762-1768.

Montpellier; discharge mark; 1775-1781.

Versailles; discharge mark; 1768-1774.

Rennes; discharge mark; 1775-1781.

Dunkerque; town mark; after 1784.

ARTICLES OF CLOTHING

Eastern France; gold 750 mark; 1819-1838.

Bordeaux; discharge mark; 1775-1781.

Limoges; discharge mark; 1775-1781.

Senlis; discharge mark; 1768-1774.

Arles; town mark; after 1784.

Dijon; discharge mark; 1775-1781.

Boulogne-sur-Mer; discharge mark; after 1784.

Bourges; discharge mark; 1781-Revolution.

Poitiers; town mark; after 1784.

Riom; discharge mark; 1775-1781.

Tarascon; town mark; after 1784.

La Rochelle; discharge mark; 1781-Revolution.

Western France; gold 750 mark; 1819-1838.

Strasbourg; town mark; after 1784.

Grenoble; discharge mark; 1775-1781.

Aix; discharge mark; 1781-Revolution.

Southern France; gold 750 mark; 1819-1838.

Vitry-le-Francois; town mark; after 1784.

Marseille; town mark; after 1784.

Rennes; discharge mark; 1775-1781.

Lyon; discharge mark; 1781-Revolution.

Saintes; town mark; after 1784.

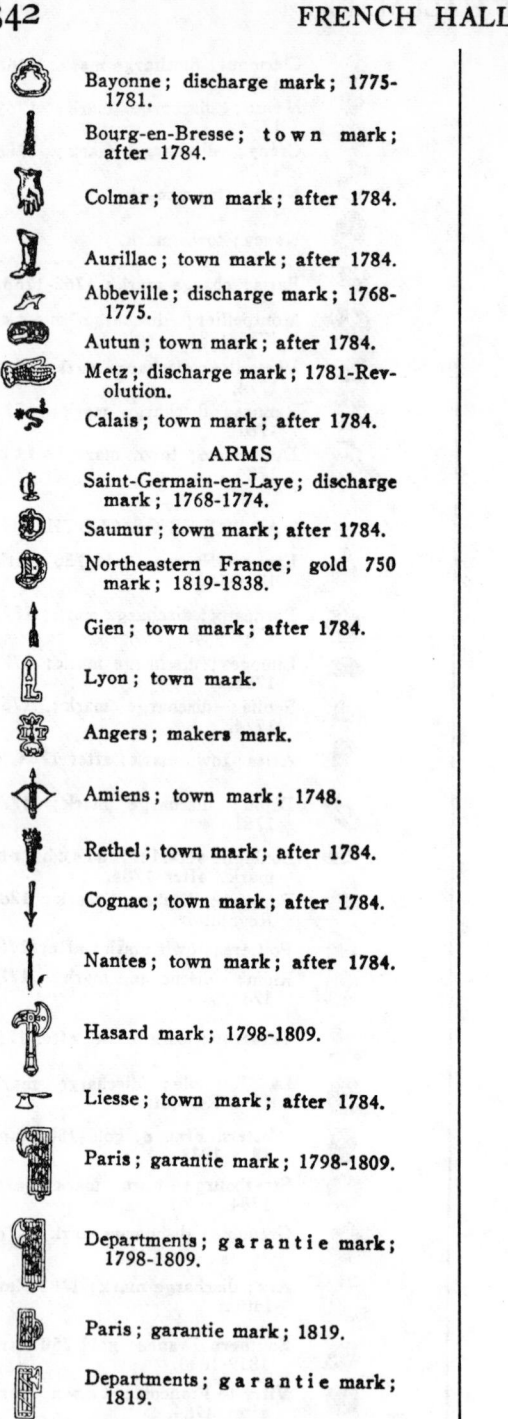

Bayonne; discharge mark; 1775-1781.

Bourg-en-Bresse; town mark; after 1784.

Colmar; town mark; after 1784.

Aurillac; town mark; after 1784.

Abbeville; discharge mark; 1768-1775.

Autun; town mark; after 1784.

Metz; discharge mark; 1781-Revolution.

Calais; town mark; after 1784.

ARMS

Saint-Germain-en-Laye; discharge mark; 1768-1774.

Saumur; town mark; after 1784.

Northeastern France; gold 750 mark; 1819-1838.

Gien; town mark; after 1784.

Lyon; town mark.

Angers; makers mark.

Amiens; town mark; 1748.

Rethel; town mark; after 1784.

Cognac; town mark; after 1784.

Nantes; town mark; after 1784.

Hasard mark; 1798-1809.

Liesse; town mark; after 1784.

Paris; garantie mark; 1798-1809.

Departments; garantie mark; 1798-1809.

Paris; garantie mark; 1819.

Departments; garantie mark; 1819.

Vicinity of Chalons; discharge mark; 1775-1781.

Mézieres; town mark; after 1784.

Marle and Vervins; discharge mark; 1768-1774.

Guise; town mark; after 1784.

Le Havre; town mark; after 1784.

Caen; discharge mark; 1744-1750.

VASES

Poitiers; discharge mark; 1781-Revolution.

Rennes; discharge mark; 1781-Revolution.

Semur; town mark; after 1784.

Western France; recense mark; 1819-1838.

Saint Quentin; discharge mark; 1768-1775.

Rodez; town mark; after 1784.

Limoges; discharge mark; 1775-1781.

Blois; town mark; after 1784.

Péronne; discharge mark; 1768-1775.

Beaune; town mark; after 1784.

Carcassonne; town mark; after 1784.

Eastern France; recense mark; 1819-1838.

Rouen; charge mark; 1768-1775.

Issoudun; town mark; after 1784.

Southeastern France; makers mark; 1819-1838.

Riez; town mark; after 1784.

Roye; discharge mark; 1768-1775.

D'Aligre (Marans); town mark; after 1784.

Noyon; town mark; after 1784.

Beaucaire; town mark; after 1784.

Northern France; makers mark; 1819-1838.

Niort; town mark; after 1784.

Nevers; town mark; after 1784.

LAMPS

Le Mans; makers mark.

Auxerre; town mark; after 1784.

Lons-le-Saunier; town mark; after 1784.

La Fere; discharge mark; 1768-1774.

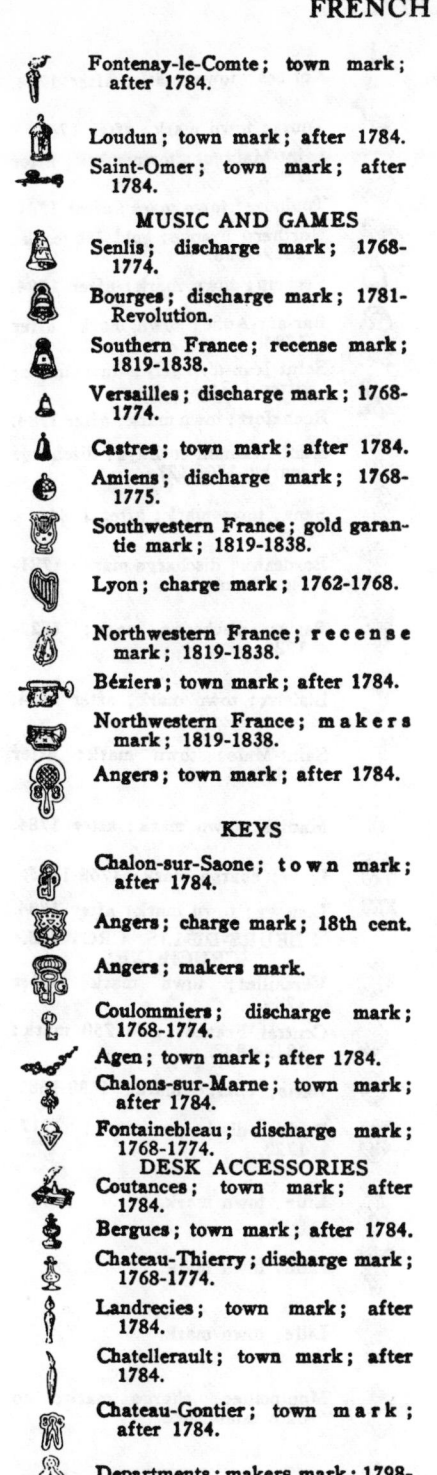

Fontenay-le-Comte; town mark; after 1784.

Loudun; town mark; after 1784.

Saint-Omer; town mark; after 1784.

MUSIC AND GAMES

Senlis; discharge mark; 1768-1774.

Bourges; discharge mark; 1781-Revolution.

Southern France; recense mark; 1819-1838.

Versailles; discharge mark; 1768-1774.

Castres; town mark; after 1784.

Amiens; discharge mark; 1768-1775.

Southwestern France; gold garantie mark; 1819-1838.

Lyon; charge mark; 1762-1768.

Northwestern France; recense mark; 1819-1838.

Béziers; town mark; after 1784.

Northwestern France; makers mark; 1819-1838.

Angers; town mark; after 1784.

KEYS

Chalon-sur-Saone; town mark; after 1784.

Angers; charge mark; 18th cent.

Angers; makers mark.

Coulommiers; discharge mark; 1768-1774.

Agen; town mark; after 1784.

Chalons-sur-Marne; town mark; after 1784.

Fontainebleau; discharge mark; 1768-1774.

DESK ACCESSORIES

Coutances; town mark; after 1784.

Bergues; town mark; after 1784.

Chateau-Thierry; discharge mark; 1768-1774.

Landrecies; town mark; after 1784.

Chatellerault; town mark; after 1784.

Chateau-Gontier; town mark; after 1784.

Departments; makers mark; 1798-1809.

Manosque; town mark; after 1784.

Central France; recense mark; 1819-1838.

Dijon; town mark; after 1784.

WEIGHTS AND MEASURES

Langeac; town mark; after 1784.

Rouen; discharge mark; 1775-1781.

Montauban; town mark; after 1784.

Apt; town mark; after 1784.

Bailleul; town mark; after 1784.

Departments; clocks mark; 1798-1809.

AGRICULTURAL IMPLEMENTS

Pézenas; town mark; after 1784.

Avesnes; town mark; after 1784.

Saint-Quentin; town mark; after 1784.

Southwestern France; recense mark; 1819-1838.

Senlis; charge mark; 1768-1774.

Caen; town mark; after 1784.

Paris; charge mark; 1756-1762.

Bayonne; town mark; after 1794.

Pontoise; town mark; after 1784.

Montpellier; town mark; after 1784.

Limoges; town mark; after 1784.

NAVAL SYMBOLS

Brest; town mark; after 1784.

Saint-Malo; town mark.

Saint-Malo; town mark.

Dinan; town mark; after 1784.

Brest; town mark.

ARCHITECTURE

Noyon; discharge mark; 1768-1775.

Chatillon-sur-Seine; town mark; after 1784.

Tours; discharge mark; 1781-Revolution.

Northeastern France; recense mark; 1819-1838.

Tours; town mark.

Dinan; town mark.

Honfleur; makers mark.

Caen; discharge mark; 1775-1781.

Morlaix; town mark; after 1784.

Aix; discharge mark; 1775-1781.

Calais; discharge mark; 1768-1775.

Joinville and Wassy; town mark; after 1784.

Moulins; town mark; after 1784.

Le Puy; town mark; after 1784.

MISCELLANEOUS

La Charité; town mark; after 1784.

Langres; town mark; after 1784.

Falaise; town mark; after 1784.

Thouars; town mark; after 1784.

Caen; charge mark; 1744-1750.

Southeastern France; gold 750 mark; 1819-1838.

Montargis; town mark; after 1784.

Montereau; discharge mark; 1768-1774.

Luçon; town mark; after 1784.

Valenciennes; town mark; after 1784.

Narbonne; town mark; after 1784.

Grasse; town mark; after 1784.

Besancon; town mark; after 1784.

Guise; discharge mark; 1768-1774.

Dole; town mark; after 1784.

Le Vigan; town mark; after 1784.

Montdidier; discharge mark; 1768-1775.

Montreuil; discharge mark; 1768-1775.

Quimper; town mark; after 1784.

Arras; town mark; after 1784.

Antibes; town mark; after 1784.

Tours; town mark; after 1784.

Saint-Maixent; town mark; after 1784.

Toulouse; town mark; after 1784.

Northern France; gold 750 mark; 1819-1838.

Fécamp; town mark; after 1784.

Bar-sur-Aube; town mark; after 1784.

Saint-Jean-d'Angély; town mark; after 1784.

Rochefort; town mark; after 1784.

Saint-Germain-en-Laye; discharge mark; 1768-1774.

Sens; town mark; after 1784.

Bordeaux; discharge mark; 1781-Revolution.

Paris; discharge mark; 1722-1726.

Lisieux; town mark; after 1784.

Saint-Malo; town mark; after 1784.

Mantes; town mark; after 1784.

Lyon; charge mark; 1768-1775.

Longwy; town mark; after 1784.

FLEURS-DE-LIS. CROWNS. CRUCIFIXES

Versailles; town mark; after 1784.

Central France; gold 750 mark; 1819-1832.

Paris; charge mark; 1680-1681.

Paris; discharge mark; 1717-1722.

Lille; town mark.

Lille; town mark.

Lille; town mark.

Montpellier; charge mark; no date established.

Calais; town mark.

Bolbec; makers mark.

 Languedoc; charge mark; 1700.

 Paris; discharge mark; 1717-1722.

 Paris; discharge mark; 1717-1722.

 Morlaix; town mark; about 1725.

 Paris; discharge mark; 1691-1698.

 Paris; discharge mark; 1687-1691.

 Paris; discharge mark; 1703-1708.

 Paris; discharge mark; 1681-1684.

 Paris; discharge mark; 1681-1684.

 Paris; discharge mark; 1684-1687.

 Paris; discharge mark; 1684-1687.

 Paris; discharge mark; 1698-1703.

 Brest; town mark; about 1720.

 Morlaix; town mark; about 1725.

 Riom; town mark; after 1784.

 Boulogne; discharge mark; 1768-1775.

 Neufchateau; town mark.

 Pont-a-Mousson; town mark.

 Rosieres-aux-Salines; town mark.

 Saint-Mihiel; town mark.

 Saint-Nicholas-du-Port; town mark.

 Sarreguemines; town mark.

 Vézelise; town mark.

 Lunéville; town mark; before 1773.

 Lunéville; town mark; after 1773.

 Charmes; town mark.

 Darney; town mark.

 Epinal; town mark.

 Rambervillers; town mark.

 Remiremont; town mark.

 Saint-Dié; town mark.

 Nancy; makers mark.

 Briey; town mark.

 Bouquemont; town mark.

 Commercy; town mark.

 Dieuze; town mark.

 Etain; town mark.

 Forbach; town mark.

 Mirecourt; town mark.

COATS-OF-ARMS

 Strasbourg; town mark; 1472-1534.

 Strasbourg; town mark; 1434-1567.

 Strasbourg; town mark; 1567-1681.

 Salins; town mark.

 Lons-le-Saunier; town mark.

 Dijon; makers mark.

 Dijon; makers mark.

 Chalon-sur-Saone; makers mark.

Clermont-Ferrand; makers mark.

Toulouse; discharge mark; no date established.

 Trévoux; town mark.

 Trévoux; town mark.

Montauban; town mark.

Montauban; town mark.

 Langres; makers mark

 Tours; makers mark.

 Metz; town mark.

 Metz; town mark.

 Autun; makers mark.

 Dole; makers mark.

 Vesoul; town mark.

 Vesoul; makers mark.

 Bourg-en-Bresse; makers mark

 Toulon; town mark.

 Marseille; town mark

A

27 „A" · 89 „A" · 1293 „A" · 110 A · 1166 A · 1377 A · 1154 · 306 · 185 · 278 · 238 · 108 · 65 · 66 · 67

73 · 110 · 1065 · 1064 · 62 „AB" · 579 AB · 443 · 1146 · 580 A·B · 1001 „ABM" · 20 „ACH" · 21 „ACH" · 982 ACH · 18 ACH · 1012 „ACW" · 936 AD · 597 AD

550 · 948 „AFS" · 947 · 989 · 643 AG · 1005 AG · 508 AH · 1400 · 1312 · 55 „AK" · 1334 · 642 AL · 492 AL · 51 „AM" · 90 „AM" · 675 AM · 522 · 452 AN

840 „AP" · 1447 AP · 380 · 1040 APG · 1325 „AR" · 501 AR · 381 · 54 „AS" · 970 AS · 661 AS · 448 AS · 362 · 1324 · 516 · 1389 · 1388

433 XX · 1436 · 805 · 920 AV · 540 AV · 781 AV · 1313 AV · 520 AV · 641 AV

B

307 „B" · 1294 „B" · 1355 „B" · 1459 „B" · 1085 B · 1106 B · 1088 B

932 · 584 · 412 · 1202 · 1425 · 827 · 1433 · 1332 „CNH" · 1467 „COW" · 731 CP · 1466 CP · 59 · 1411 · 454 · 1446 · 633 CR · 1131 CR

1127 CS · 768 CS · 1004 CSB · 1445 SG · 1220 CV · 1434 CW · 763 CW · 1139 · 1440 · 1016 CXS

D

1296 „D" · 1381 D · 282 · 309 · 241 · 242

243 · 370 „DA" · 370 DA · 370 „D·A·F" · 753 „DB" · 1470 „DF" · 485 DF · 1353 · 1171 DM · 467 · 468 · 1409 DI · 802 DN · 628 DF · 1415 D · 34 · 1077 „DS" · 788 DS · 801 · 360 · 640 DW

439 · 1464 · 496 DZ

E

310 „E" · 1297 „E" · 86 „E" · 31 E · 1142 E · 1157 · 283 · 246 · 245 · 244 · 75 · 809 EA

810 EA · 811 EB · 663 EB · 1217 „ECH" · 1453 „ECS" · 835 ED · 938 ED · 507 · 506 · 1432 EG · 1147 · 1221 EGE · 1011 EGM · 608 „EH" · 502 „EL" · 1398 · 1178 „ERF"

B

1090 B · 1089 B · 693 B · 1091 B · 1095 B · 1356 B · 1473 „B" · 1379 B · 1230 B · 1092 B · 1460 · 1461 · 1378 B · 1084 b · 1086 B · 1098 B·13

1096 · 1103 · 1097 · 1235 · 1238 · 239 · 279 · 280 · 1474 „B" · 375 · 1309 · 566 · 1317 · 587 · 378

84 BDO · 484 BL · 707 · 1448 BH · 903 BH · 1039 BH · 1320 „BIB" · 1315 BK · 432 · 377 BL · 474 BL · 1180 BQ · 679 BS · 891 BS · 386 · 538 „BW" · 537

C

1295 „C" · 1380 · 1155 · 240 · 281 · 602 · 308 · 76 · 109 CB · 453 CB · 944 CB · 1404 · 445 „CCC" · 1417 „CD" · 987 CD · 885 CD · 366 · 398

38 „CF" · 649 CF · 70 CFH · 68 CFS · 1030 CFT · 1037 CGS · 602 CH · 1438 CH · 1126 CH · 429 CH · 623 · 933 „CIS" · 58 „CK" · 682 „CK" · 1451 CK · 949 CKM · 974 CL · 839 CL · 585 CL

1393 „ES" · 803 ES · 1119 ES · 764 EW · 626 „EW"

F

1298 „F" · 421 F · 705 F · 777 F · 1167 F · 1382 F · 1156 F · 1158 · 284 F

311 F · 249 F · 248 F · 247 F · 498 · 940 „FAB" · 858 FAB · 999 FAG · 981 „FAL" · 81 FAL · 83 FAL · 847 „FB" · 1314 „FB" · 899 FCM · 928 FCM · 1047 FD · 1452 FG

100 FG · 1429 FH · 751 · 1007 „FIM" · 878 „FIS" · 1051 FK · 1414 FN · 917 „FRL" · 1482 FS · 646 FS · 853 „FS" · 1135 FS · 1248 „FTI" · 869 F · 1416 F · 594 „FW" · 1179 FW

G

28 „G" · 1384 G · 1383 G · 285 · 251 · 312 G · 250 G · 78 · 22 ACH · 829 GAS · 1125 G · 729 GB · 909 GB · 1144 GB

931 GCD · 1054 GCN · 683 GE · 527 GE · 1321 · 1322 · 1323 · 988 GBC · 736 „GF" · 737 GF · 1022 GFG · 1021 GF · 1335 „GGB" · 1426 GH · 1408 GH

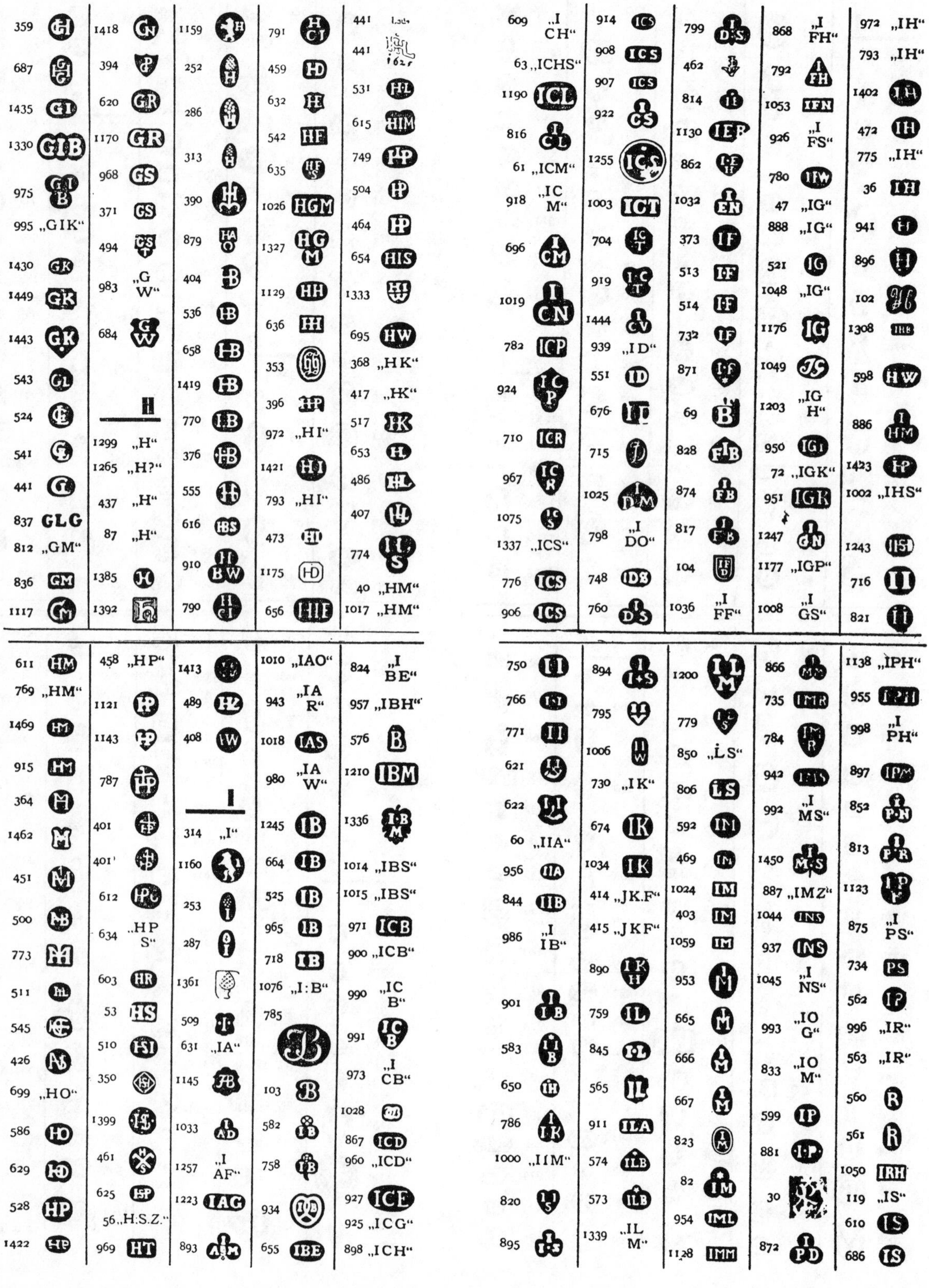
359
687
1435
1330
975
995 „GIK“
1430
1449
1443
543
524
541
441
837 GLG
812 „GM“
836
1117
1418
394
620
1170
968
371
494
983 „G W“
684
H
1299 „H“
1265 „H?“
437 „H“
87 „H“
1385
1392
1159
252
286
313
390
879
404
536
658
1419
770
376
555
616
910
790
791
459
632
542
635
1026
1327
1129
636
353
396
972 „HI“
1421
793 „HI“
473
1175
656
441
441
531
615
749
504
464
654
1333
695
368 „HK“
417 „HK“
517
653
486
407
774
40 „HM“
1017 „HM“
611
769 „HM“
1469
915
364
1462
451
500
773
511
545
426
699 „HO“
586
629
528
1422
458 „HP“
1121
1143
787
401
401'
612
634 „HP S“
603
53
510
350
1399
461
625
56 „H.S.Z.“
969
1413
489
408
I
314 „I“
1160
253
287
1361
509
631 „IA“
1145
1033
1257 „I AF“
1223
893
1010 „IAO“
943 „IA R“
1018
980 „IA W“
1245
664
525
965
718
1076 „I:B“
785
103
582
758
934
655
824 „I BE“
957 „IBH“
576
1210
1336
1014 „IBS“
1015 „IBS“
971
900 „ICB“
990 „IC B“
991
973 „I CB“
1028
867
960 „ICD“
927
925 „ICG“
898 „ICH“
609 „I CH“
63 „ICHS“
1190
816
61 „ICM“
918 „IC M“
696
1019
782
924
710
967
1075
1337 „ICS“
776
906
914
908
907
922
1255
1003
704
919
1444
939 „ID“
551
676
715
1025
798 „I DO“
748
760
799
462
814
1130
862
1032
373
513
514
732
871
69
828
874
817
104
1036 „I FF“
868 „I FH“
792
1053
926 „I FS“
780
47 „IG“
888 „IG“
521
1048 „IG“
1176
1049
1203 „IG H“
950
72 „IGK“
951
1247
1177 „IGP“
1008 „I GS“
972 „IH“
793 „IH“
1402
472
775 „IH“
36
941
896
102
1308
598
886
1423
1002 „IHS“
1243
716
821
750
766
771
621
622
60 „IIA“
956
844
986 „I IB“
901
583
650
786
1000 „IIM“
820
895
894
795
1006
730 „IK“
674
1034
414 „JK.F“
415 „JKF“
890
759
845
565
911
574
573
1339 „IL M“
1200
779
850 „L S“
806
592
469
1024
403
1059
953
665
666
667
823
82
954
1128
866
735
784
942
992 „I MS“
1450
887 „IMZ“
1044
937
1045 „I NS“
993 „IO G“
833 „IO M“
599
881
30
872
1138 „IPH“
955
998 „I PH“
897
852
813
1123
875 „I PS“
734
562
996 „IR“
563 „IR“
560
561
1050
119 „IS“
610
686

#		#		#		#		#	
873	LS	963	„IWG"	80	KM	815	„LK"	291	
685	ISA	964	„IW G"		**L**	415	„LKI"	345	M
1046	ISA			547	L	1405	M	422	M
1052	IS	1023	IWK	1168	L	495	N	822	MAE
719	„ISP"	447	„IZ"	316	Q	772	LR	723	MB
1174	JSW	756	IZ	289	L	1029	LR	711	MB
880	„IT"		**K**	256		727	LS	383	MB
994	ITH	1300	K	290	L	877	„LS"	384	MB
1485	IV	598	K	570	„LB"	424	LS	553	MB
977	„IVG"	457	K	930	LB	1326	LS	505	MB
830	IVG	1161	K	843	LB	702	LW	794	„MDW"
689	IW	288	K	577	LB		**M**	1352	ME
385	IW	254	K	569	L'B	26	„M"		
1319	„IW"	255	K	568	LB	317	„M"	668	MG
688	IV	315	K	85	„LE"	672	M	478	MG
860	IW	423	KE	1483	„LF"	870	„M"	1329	„M GE"
958	IWD	32	KI	402	LH	700	M	692	„M:H"
959	IW D	717	KLD	593	H	1316		601	MH
				549	H	257	M	590	MH
721	MI	662	„MP"	1463	NK	98		262	P
730	MH	1437	„MP B"	430	NL	33		74	P
1465	MI	369	NR	431	NL	1396		1041	„PAG"
789	MK	529	MS	519	NN	1185	OM	945	„PCS"
1412	MI	491	MS	738	NO	41	CR	857	P.D
698	MM	1056	„MU"	372	NT	1391		819	PG
826	„MK"	1441	MW					703	P.G
1057	„ML"	726	MW		**O**			902	„PH"
591	MM		**N**	319	„O"		**P**	1328	PH
105	M·M	318	„N"	293	O	320	„P"	410	PI
882	MM	1162	N	261	O	1301	„P"	595	PI
690	MT	292	N	260	O	512	P	552	PH
691	MM	258	N	230		392	P	647	PD
639	MM	259	N	96		393	P	1115	PH
924	„MV"	564	NF	99		1164	P	713	PHI
488	„MN"	863	NF	95		294		637	PIS
35	„MO"	477	NK	97		263	P	722	PID
37	„PIS"	264		706	„S"	52	„SH"	754	SW
652	PK	265		946	„S"	106	SH	865	
671	„PLD"	1134	S			1027	SHB		**T**
1401	N	266		849	S	471	S	298	„T"
800	PR	77		297		530	S	1305	„T"
765	PR		**R**	1241	S			1387	T
1211	PRW	296	„R"	268		405	S	270	
648	„PS"	322	„R"	460	„SA"			269	
670	PS	1303	„R"	1246	„SA b"	1242	W	218	
778	PS	1116	„R"	997	„SB"	419		324	
834	PST	681	R	1311	SB	1120	S	725	„TB"
861	„PV"	267	R	1035	„SC"	1182	SM	708	TB
613	PW	1340	„RGS"	1124	SC	714	SM	709	T·B
1136	SW	1132	RW	1407	S	724	SI	1442	
	Q		**S**	912	SD	929	SI	497	B
321	„Q"	323	„S"	673	SF	382	S	832	TD
302	„Q"	1304	„S"	1410		1189	SS	1060	„T DI"
677	Q	1386	S	783	S GK	660	SS		
295	Q	1133	S			761	SW		
923			**V**		**W**	1222	„WB"		**Y**
1427	IGW	301	„V"	302	„W"	966	„WD"	304	„Y"
1428	TK	326	„V"	327	„W"	490	WD	329	Y
515	TK	25		627	„W"	1331	„WG"	276	Y
481	TL	271	V	1371	„W"			119	„YS 1549"
984	„T-M"	272	V	1368	W	411	W		**Z**
1431	P	694	„VB"	1366	W	39	„WH"	330	„Z"
1193	T·R	436	VB	1365	W			848	„Z"
1187	R	374	V	1367	W	638	WI	913	Z
1439	TS	113		1370	W	518		277	Z
916	TVG	808	„V·I"	1369	W	1354	W IM	305	Z
373	T	1406	IK	1169	W	728	„WS"	1318	„ZB"
		1390		767	S			420	
	U	1420	VM	274			**X**	413	Z L
325	„U"	440	M	328	„X"			413	„Z.L.F."
299	U	556	·VS·	273		275	X	332	Z
300	U	859	·VSI·	892	„W"	303	X	1338	„ZU Z"

Heavenly Bodies

1		499		2		1165		338
1234	Halb-mond	526		5		370		336
1358		807		3		358		
35		234		4		337		797

Man

46		548		1373		1376		50
								733
831		1372		1375		49		796

Lions

1479	Löwe								
1290		1282		1288		1291		1279	
1292		1281		1278		1285		1280	
1277		1276		1287		1284		1283	
1286		1099		1101		1105		1094	
1289		1102		1104		89ᴬ	Löwe	1394	
1087		1093		1100		588			

Miscellaneous Mammals

1148	1152	1236		1260		353
1149	1153	1240		1262		851
		1479	Pferd			
1150	1239	367		1263		607
		701	Ein Lamm			
1151	1237	921	Lamm	1261		651

Eagles and Miscellaneous Birds

107	„Adler"						
1483	„Adler"	16	1478	442	712
18	13	1232	669	864	Eule
			657		
22	14	1231	755	438
17	15	1233	614	101

Water

445	93	94	92

Plants

428	644	137	153	169
213	122	138	154	170
355	123	139	155	171
356	124	140	156	172
357	125	141	157	173
842	126	142	158	174
532	127	143	159	175
503	128	144	160	176
697	129	145	161	177
533	130	146	162	178
889	131	147	163	179
450	132	148	164	180
449	133	149	165	181
361	134	150	166	182
757	135	151	167	183
	136	152	168	

184	194	203	212	224
186	194ᴮ	204	214	225
187	195	205	215	226
188	196	206	216	227
189	197	207	217	228
190	198	208	219	229
191	199	209	220	231
192	200	210	221	235
193	201	211	222	523
194	202		223	

Scepters and Arms

1253	456	1254	479	352
1483	Szepter			

Utensils

605	1360	1350	1349	1351
	1359			
233	1345	1348	1344	1347
232	1346	1341	1342	739

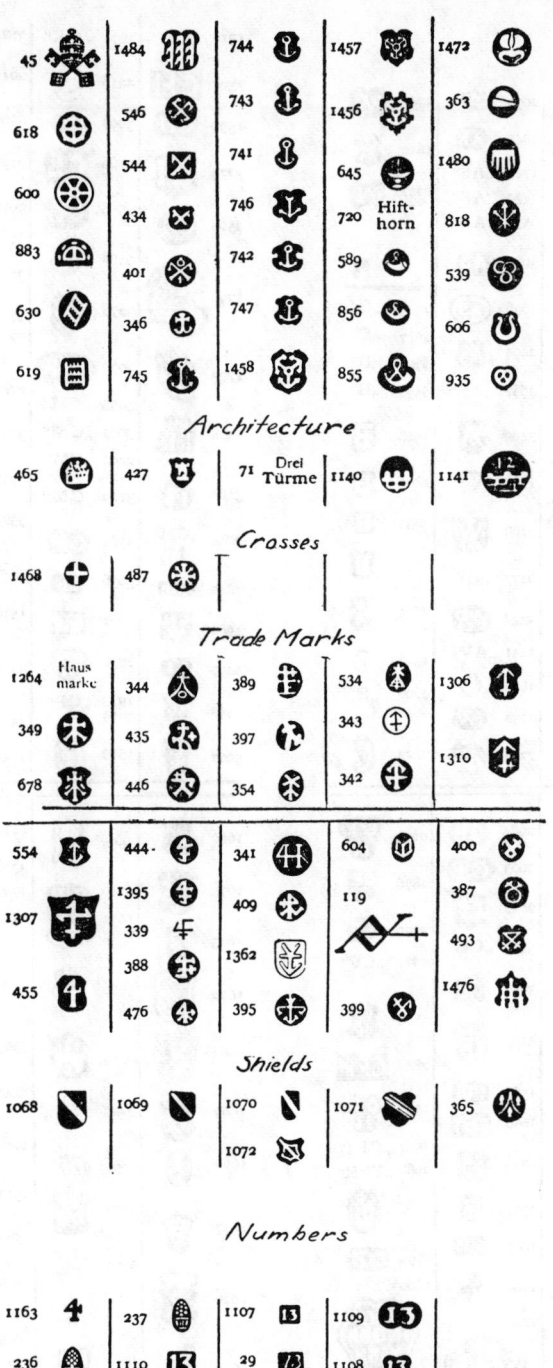

Architecture

Crosses

Trade Marks

Shields

Numbers

A

No.	Label
1687	„A"–„Z"
1851	„A" „Z"
1934	„A" „Z"
3362	„A" „Z"
1696	„A"
2834	A.
2835	A
3017	A
1687	A
3013	A
2513	A
1706	A
2822	a
2697	
2357	
2146	AA
2148	AA
3062	

No.		No.		No.		No.	
3523	„A B"	2878	AI	2099		2240	AW
2392	„A B"	3043	AR	3052	„AIR"	1612	
1966		3117	AK	1743	„AS"	2247	AB
3531	AD	3038		2779	„AS"		
2090	AF	1786	„AK D"	3558	„AS"		
1828	AF	2759	AL	3084	AS		
1967		1588	AL	1636	AS		
1827	AF	2326	AL	2494	AS		
2450	AFL	2102	AM	3557	„AS"		
3559	„A FS"	1862	ANK	3489	A		
1970	AFS	3225	„AN L"	1646	ASI		
1986	AG	3513	AP	3268			
2462 / 2464	„A H"	3515	„A P"	2477			
2324	AH	3514	„A P"	2322	AR		
1578		2746	R	2241	„AW"		
1898				1649			
2877	AI			2238	AV		
				2239	AV		

B

No.	Label
2505	„B"
2617	„B"
2766	„B"
2539	„B"
1526	B
1899	B
2833	B
1852	B
2514	B
1527	B
2206	„B"
2823	C

No.		No.		No.		No.	
2698		3585	„BM"	2955	„C"	2985	CB
2923	B8	2402		2950	C	2063	CB
2455	„Bad"	3306	BNB	2956	C	2842	CB
1504	BB	3496	BP	2951	C	3410	„CB"
1569	BG	1615	„BR"	3255	C	3059	CB
2124	„BF"	2566		2308	C	3183	
2129	BF	1697				1566	CBH
1565	BG	3064	BV	2824	c	1680	CBS
1897	„BH"	2756	„B W"	2683	„C"	2057	„CFI"
2499		2754	BW	3014		2988	„CFR"
2932	BF	2755	BW	1721	t	2727	C
2963	„B K"	2045	BV	2358		1805	CDS
2867	BK 07			2699		1806	CDJ
2866	BK 86			2370		1808	
3057	„BL" „1670"			3615	„CB"	1807	
3058	BL			2038	CB	1865	CH
				3051	CB	2980	CH
				2101	CB	1638	
						1864	CH

C

No.	Label
2683	„C"
3255	„C"
1882	C
2498	C

No.		No.	
2274	CFM	1793	CGM
2876	CES		
2790	CF		
2927	„CF"		
2868	CF 88		
2882	CFH		
1792	CH		
1787			
1790	CGI		
1800			

C·D SCHRO DELS

C·G INGER MANN

Right half

No.		No.		No.		No.	
1916	„CH"	1971	„CK"	3184	„CR"	2204	„CW"
1502	CH	2316	CK	2041	CR	3026	G
1590	CH	3097	CK	2296	CR	2315	„CW"
3274	CH	2880	CL	2192		1797	CWK
2508	CH	2879	CL	2670	„CS"	2787	
		3398	CL	3209	„CS"		
1798	CH	3278		3288	„CS"		
1799		2075	CHK	2175			
		3055	„CM"	1556	CS		
1568	CHD	3087	„CM"	2780	„C.S"		
		2409	„CM"	3122	CS		
3104	CH	3119	„CM"	1913			
2064	„CH M"	2381	CM	3525	„CST"		
1822	CHR	3056	CM	1532	CSI		
1981	GHW	1992	CM	1510	CT		
2497	CI	2776	CMN	2391			
1542		1973 / 3614	„CP"	2418			
3027		1549	CP	1755	„CW"		

D

No.	Label
1624	D
1626	D
2263	D
2309	D
3022	
1722	
1620	„D"
2504	
2700	
1663	
1661	
1664	
1681	
1673	
1678	
1674	

No.	
1659	„D"
3299	„D"
1896	D
1658	D
1659	D
1622	D
1650	„D"
1651	„D"
1621	D
1623	D
2825	D
1853	D
1625	D

No.		No.		No.		No.	
1660		1669		2473	DI	2044	DT
2923				3356	„DIW"	2074	DT
1675		1671		1747	„DK"	2657	DH
1683				1748	„DK"	1937	
1672		1682		1748	„DK"	2765	„D W"
1662		2359		„1629"		2093	
1667		3289		1744			
1680		2860		3203			
1677		2503		„1613"			
1676		2861		„D CW"			
1668		1908		1745	DK		
1679		1909		„DKF" „1617"			
1684		2388		2517	D		
1685		1991		1583	„D M"		
		1915	„DH S"	2404	DM		
				„D GM"			
				3342	DP		
				2893	„DS"		
				3221	„D S"		
				1912	DS		
				1525			
				1910	DS		
				1911	DS		
		2851					

E

No.	Label
1954	E
1949	E
1950	E
1952	E
1951	E
1953	
1518	
1519	
3005	
2813	
2830	
2618	
1874	
1931	
2532	
3256	
1912	
1942	

No.	Label
3113	„E"
1925	
1926	
1933	
1948	
1956	
1935	

No.	Mark	No.	Mark	No.	Mark	No.	Mark	No.	Mark
2761	„EA"	1962	EW	1528	F	2015		2390	FIG
3213	„E.AM"	1961	EW	2284	F	2373		3086	FGM
1928	EC			1523	F	3018	„FAO"	2131	„FH"
2125	ED		„F"	2826	F	3284	„FAR"	2530	FH
1524	EE	2118	Kreuz?	2814	F	2941	FAW	2478	FHV
2668	EE	2310	„F"	1698	F	2294	FB	2940	FIK
		3114	„F"	3006	f	2777	FB	2269	„FIM"
3363	EF	2080	F	1723	f	3528	„FC"	3336	„FK"
1757	EG	2078	F	2152	F	1492	„FCM"	3507	FK
3082	„EH"	2079	F	2010		1491	FCM	3508	FK
2401	EHH	2082	F	2013		3078	FCS	1753	FK
3573	„EI"	2081	F	2619		2751	FD	3553	„FL"
1555	EK	1982	„F"	2741	„FE"			1647	FL
1554	EK	2083	F	2084		2774	FE	2527	FL
1929	EMB	2106	F	2086		2384	„FF"	2297	FLR
3035	EO	3257	F	2085		2395	F	2472	N
3060	ER	2197	F	2360		3046	FF	3504	FO
2070	„E.S.&Co."	1983	„F"			1990	„FG"	3568	„FP"
						3592	„FG"	3526	FP

No.	Mark	No.	Mark	No.	Mark	No.	Mark	No.	Mark
1813	FRS	2174	G	2361	G	3292		1836	„GR"
		2236	G	2218	G	2625	„GH"	3500	„GR"
2930	FS	2235	G	2217	12	1545	„GH"	3090	„GS"
3407	FS	3484	G	2321	„GAW"	2626	GH	3053	GS
2203	FS	3300	G	1834	„GB"	2029	GI	3063	GS
2161	„FSH"	3018	G	2935	CB	3032	G	3551	GS
2760	FW	3007	G	1957	GB	2286	„GK"	2627	GS
2438	FW	3469	G	2518	GB	2223	GL	2849	GS
2529		1724	G	2525	„GD"	3405	GLU	3525	„GST"
2143	FXC	2170	G	2749	GD	2396	G	3587	„GST"
3495	FZ	2620		2285	GE	3497	GL	1592	„G·V"
		2234		2674	GE	2098	„GLK"	2555	„GW"
	G	2162	G	1815	Gebr.S	1740	GM	1594	GW
1688	„G"	2233	G	1818		1739	GM	2938	GW
2249	„G"	2216	G	2954	GE		GMH	3576	„GZ"
2252	„G"	2215		3349	„GG"	1817	Haw	2059	GWS
3115	„G"			1593	„GG"	3479		2541	„GWR"
3259	G			3080	GGB	3305	GO		
				3377	„GP" „1692"				

No.	Mark	No.	Mark	No.	Mark	No.	Mark	No.	Mark
	H	2049	HAS	3199	HD	2538	„HH"		Ao: 1585
1522	„H"	3218	„HAS" Totenschädel	1732	HD	1875	„HH"	1733	
1508	H	2394	„HB"	2139	„HE"	3505	„HH"		
3212	„H"	3414	„HB"	2138	HE			3103	HK
3174	H	2534	HB	1548	HE	2926	HH	2742	„HL"
3597	H	3067	HB	2407	„HE"	3617	HHO	3188	„HL"
1531	H	3598	„HB"	2922	HE	1979	„HI"	2378	„HL"
1707	H	3598	HB	2389	„HF"	2730	HI	2953	IL
2815	H		Hammer	2476	„HF"	1903	HI	1964	IL
2264	H	2445	„HB"	2140	„HF"			2410	IL
2311	H	1546	„HC"	1917	HF	3269	„HI"	2417	HL
1725	h	3068	HP	3307	HG	3223	„HIB"	2397	„HL"
3276	H	2669	„HCH"	3493	„HG"	2939	HB		
3173	„H"	2068	„H.&Co."	2638	HG	2127	„HIH"	2565	HL
2363		3364	HCW	3287	HG	3175	„H"	2422	HB
2368		2981	„HD"	3206	„HH"	1936	H		
2230		3608	„HD"	3049	HH	2040	HS	2423	HB
2564		1900	„HD"	3047	HH	2662	„HK"	1969	HLH
		1901		3048		3102	„HK"		

No.	Mark	No.	Mark	No.	Mark	No.	Mark	No.	Mark
2426	„H·L·P"	2033		3292		2771	HSI	2663	IA
1795	HLS	2250	„HP"			2495	HSI	2198	IA
2453	HM	3600	„HP"	3477		1965	HU	2054	IAB
2433	„HM"	2533	HP			1741	HV	2231	
2856	HM	2435	HP			3399		3400	„I?M"
2857	HM	3603	HP			1635	HW	3406	„IAR"
2850	HM	2862	PA			3081	H.W.		
2888	HM12	3030	HR			2406	HX	2943	IAS
2042	M	3031	HR			3304	NB	3121	„IB"
2199	HN	3482	HR			2200	HZ	3286	„IB"
2036	NB	3483	„HR"	2557	„HS"			2221	IB
2039	RB	3030	HR	3211	„HS"			3041	IB
1557	HOI	3270	HR	2507	HS		I	2630	IB
		1904	„HS"	3185	„I"	1863	IB		
2412	HOI	1641		3418	HS	2836	I	3079	IB
3194	„HO" Turm	2493	HR	2768	HS	3011	I	2429	IB
1582	HOL	2733	HR	3499	HSI	2799	„J"	2624	IB
		3045	HSI	2346		2871	IB94		

2872 IB | 2942 ICL | 2052 IDG | 2194 IF | 3534 IG
3547 IBC | 1639 ICR | 2053 I·DG | 2195 | 3032 „IGB"
1571 IBH | 1637 ICR | 2058 IDK | 2628 „IDS" | 3543 IGB
1553 IBM | 2664 ICS | 2870 IDT | 2454 „IFB" | 2104 IGG
2576 I·B·W | 3076 ICS | 1923 „IE" | 1778 IFB | 3309 IGG
3616 „IC?" | 2665 ICS | 2202 „IE" | 3546 IFC | 2096 IGG
3310 „J.C.B." | 2595 ICS | 1963 IE | 1618 I FF" | 1802 IGG
3089 ICB | 3536 ICS | 2270 IEC | 3094 „IFL" | 2104 I.G.H."
3095 ICB | 3535 ICS | 1619 IEF | 3083 „IFM" | 1570 IGH
1640 ICB | 2076 ICST | 3365 IEH | 3350 IFS | 1597 IGOD
3092 ICB | 3098 ICV | 1567 IEK | 2449 IFS | 1974 IGK
1515 ICD | 2875 ICW | | 2982 IFS | 2269 I·G·M
2239 „ICF" | 3096 ID | 3577 „IES" | 2444 IFW | 3516 IGO
2242 ICF | 2763 ID | 2160 „JF" | 2605 IFW | 1918 I·G·P
1505 ICH | 3215 IRD | 2773 „IF" | 2205 IG | 2246 „JGR"
2680 „I.C.H. 1761" | 2169 IDA | 2925 IF | 3533 IG | 2173 IGR
1572 ICK | | 3345 IF | 3388 „IG" |
 | | | 3502 „IG" |

1810 „IGS" | 3224 „IHS" | 3033 „IL" | 3201 IMF | 3065 „IP"
3554 „IGS" | 3347 IL | 3539 „IMI" | 3601 „JP"
1784 IGS | 2769 II | 3346 IL | 2577 „IMK" | 1872 IP
1819 IGSN | 3567 IIF | 2506 | 3562 IMM | 1742 IP
3544 IGV | 2061 IIH | 2447 ILL | 3621 „JMO" | 2748 IP
3511 IGZ | 1771 | 2885 ILK | 3548 „IMR" | 3604 IP
2962 „IH" | 1779 IIS | 2886 „ILK" „I²" | 2055 IMS | 3344 „IPK"
3520 „IH" | 2968 „JJS" | 2887 | 2065 IMS | 3094 „IPL"
3120 IH | 1734 „IK" | 2509 ILS | 1774 IMW | 1581 „IPR"
3204 „IH" | 3313 IK | 3550 „ILW" | 1773 IMV | 2318 „IPS"
2448 IHD | 2948 | 3542 „IM" | 2062 I·N | 3351 „IR"
2432 | | 1984 „IM?" | 3116 IR
3226 „IHK" | IK | 2961 „IM" | 2468 IN | 2130 „IR"
3290 IHK | 1562 I·K | 2442 IM | 3396 IN | 2767 IR
1803 IH | 2936 IK | 1867 IM | | 1489 IR
2786 IHM | 3054 IK | 1868 IBM | 3397 | 2157 IB
2474 IHP | | 2784 J.M.C. | 1617 IMW | 3564 IR
2037 IRB | 2268 IKB 18 | 3517 „IME" | 1591 IOD | 1575 IR
1796 IHS | 2220 „IL" | 3532 IME | 2678 | 3070 JR
 | 2639 „IL" | | 2444 IOM |

2778 „IR" | 3563 „IS" | 3569 „IW" | 2155 K | L
2623 IR | 3352 IS | 1756 IW | 2672 K | 3260 L
2424 IR | 1655 | 1634 IW | 3196 K | 2990 L
2425 IR | 2516 IS | 3527 „IW" | 1613 K | 2992 L
2594 IRG | 2144 „ISK" | 3394 „IW" | 2839 K | 2995 L
3549 „IRZ" | 2141 ISK | 1785 „IWM" | 2640 „K" | 2991 L
1614 „IS" | 1877 „ISM" | 3524 „IZ" | 1718 K | 2993 L
2955 „IS" | 3066 | 2050 IZ | 2641 „K" | 2994 L
3509 „IS" | 1869 IT | 2874 „IZ" | | 3135 „L"
3571 „IS" | 3093 „ITN" | 1906 „JZ" | 2621 | 1511 L
3072 IS | 3540 „IV" | | 2362 | 1517 L
1861 IS | 2604 IVE | K | | 2827 L
1540 IS | 3538 „IVH" | 2640 „K" | 1760 | 1854 L
2934 IS | 3261 K | 1761 | 3021
2420 IS | 2528 IVHK | 2671 K | 1762 | 1520
2631 IS | 2637 „IW" | | 2030 | 1521 L
2750 „IS" | 2965 „IW" | 2575 IK | 2719 | 2830 „I"
3522 IS | 3217 „IW" 3510 „IW" | 2531 K | 1708 | „e" 1

2622 | 1629 | 3572 LR | 2364 | 2593 M
3003 | 3348 LB | 2427 LR | 2846 | 3537 „MFK"
2998 | 1501 LD | 2770 „LS" | 1544 M | 2267 „MG"
 | 3208 „LD" | 3589 „L.S." | 3530 „MA" | 2843 MC
2996 | 1940 | | 2043 MB | 2792 „MH"
2997 | 2881 LEO | M | 3609 „MB" | 2592 „MH"
 | 3301 IF | 1689 „M" | 1749 MB | 1763 MH
3520 „IH" | 2966 „LH" | 3413 „M" | 1737 | 2320 MH
3120 | | 3384 „M" | 1738 MB | 3123 „MHB"
3204 | 2967 LH | M | 2869 MCH | 2775 „MHR"
2999 | 2855 | 2540 „M" | 1589 MD | 2791 „MI"
3002 | 3283 | 3355 „M" | 1503 MD | 3566 „MI"
 | 2295 LHB | 2726 M | 3555 MD | 1563 M
3000 | 2854 | 2831 M | 3610 MD | 2376 MH
3004 | 2060 | 1699 M | 3579 „ME" | 1632 M
2989 | 1539 LK | 1709 M | 3501 | 2783 „M.I.R."
1628 12L | 3118 | 1571 m | 2984 MS
1627 12L | 2639 „LL" | 1716 m | 1968 MW | 3205 „MK"
 | 3545 „LP" | 3387 | 2219 M

No.	Mark	No.	Mark	No.	Mark	No.	Mark	No.	Mark
2673	MK	1768	NB	1586	NS	3012	q	3220	"P HK"
2526	MKH	2658	NC	1584	NS	3008	q	1558	P HL
3039	M	2399	"NF"	2682	"N W"	1642	PA	3285	"PHM"
2377		2403	NG	1616	NW	2681	PB	2046	PHS
1766	"MR"	2772	"NH"			2629	PB	2047	13 PHS
2323	"MS"	2463	"NH"	**O**		2548	P.B.&C	3222	"PB VA"
3512	"MS"	1902	NH	1701	O	3222		3069	PI
2196	MS	2666	"NIT"	2072		1574	PCG	2659	PI
2983	MS	2782	"NK I"	2721		2788	PE	1781	PI
1780	"MS"	1947	NM	3167	OO	2847	PE	2325	PIF
3516	"MV"	1769	"NM"	2864		2848	PE	2568	"PI S"
3518	"MV"	3282	NM	2865		3088	PG	2567	PIS
3200	"MvB"	2056	NN			3085	PGH	2838	"PH"
3472	"MZ"	1576	NP	**P**				2667	"P.I W"
		1577	NP	1894	P	2661	PH	2789	PK
N		1561	NP	3599	P	2379	PI	2451	"?P.K."
1690	N	1559	"NPI"	2071	"P"	2863		1727	
1700	N	1585	NS	2816	P				
3015	N								
2369	M								

No.	Mark	No.	Mark	No.	Mark	No.	Mark	No.	Mark
2025	M	1550	PR	1509	R	3272	S	1750	S
2858	PS	3042	PR	1550	"R"	2105	S	3214	"SFS"
2027	R	1755	"PZ"	2166	"R"	1551	SDR	2103	SH
3303	PO	2496	PZ	2818	R	1512	S	3219	Anker "SH"
2156	"PP"			3020	R	1513	S	1770	S-B
2319	PR	**Q**		2798	"R"	3611	S	2069	S.H.&Co.
1560	PR	1691	"Q"	2028	R	2828	S	3180	"SI"
1580	PR	1507	Q	1905	RF	1530	S	2745	S
2237	"P·S."	2817	Q	2437	"RG"	1710	S	2097	SK
3077	PS	1702	Q	1633	R	1769	S	3029	SK
3074	PS	3019	9	2920	R	3529	"S"	3044	S
3071	PS	3343	QR	2732	RM	2924	S	2095	SL
2859	PSM			3386	"RT"	2051	SB	2928	"SL"
3575	"P ST"	**R**		2717		2126	SB	1587	SO
3061	"PT"	3195	"R"			1811	"S.BS."	2554	"S OW"
3541	"PV"	1547	R	**S**		1788	SG	1490	SR
3341	PV	3075	R	1538	"S"	2852	D		
		1534	R	1821	"S"	2853			
				2819	"S"				
				2428	S				

No.	Mark	No.	Mark	No.	Mark	No.	Mark	No.	Mark
2762	SS	3016	T	2266		1731	VG	1506	W
1711	T	3096	"TB"			2443	VH	1537	W
3073	S	2023	"TB.fe"	3498		2440	VH	2844	W
1533	St	1514	T	2722	TH	2929	V	3552	"W"
1536	S	2405	DM	2723	TJ	3480	M	2408	W
2553	"SV"	3124	"T W"	2978	F	1535	W		
2764				3413	"VS"	2726	W		
1794	"SW"	2222		3519	VS	2088	W		
3506	SW	1941		1726	VS	2821	W		
3521	S·W	1767	"TL"	2366		2094	VS	3611	"W"
2537	"SZ"	1552	T	2371		3471	vt	3187	Hausmarke "W"
2944	SZ	2757	"TN"			2201	VV	3181	"W"
"ZS"		**Lll. V**		**V**		3277			
2945	SZ	3182	TW	3470	V			3170	
"ZS"		2758		**W**					
I		2158	"TS"	1719	V	1693	"W"	1804	"WB"
1692	"T"	1655		2372		2128	"W"	3207	"WB"
3202	T	1516		1516	CH	2165	W	2134	Wf
2312	T	2747	S	2937	"VE"	1656	"W"	3091	"WH"
2820	T	1914	S	3312	"V G"				

No.	Mark	No.	Mark	No.	Mark	No.	Mark	No.	Mark
1938	W	1978	"WV"	3578	"XB"	**Z**		1758	ZB
2434	WH	3040	"WZ"	1924	"XE"	1695	"Z"		
				3561	XL			1907	
1564	W 10D	**X**		3560	XL	3357	Z		
3308	WL	1703	"X"			2829	Z	1758	"ZR"
3620	"WO"	2832		**Y**					"ZB"
3503	"WR"	3009		1704	Y	1715	Z	2944	"ZS"
2785	WS	1712	X	1705	Y	1720	Z	2945	"ZS"
3280	W	1855	X	1713	Y	3010	Z	1751	ZS
		1694	x	2367		1714		1752	ZS
								1764	Z

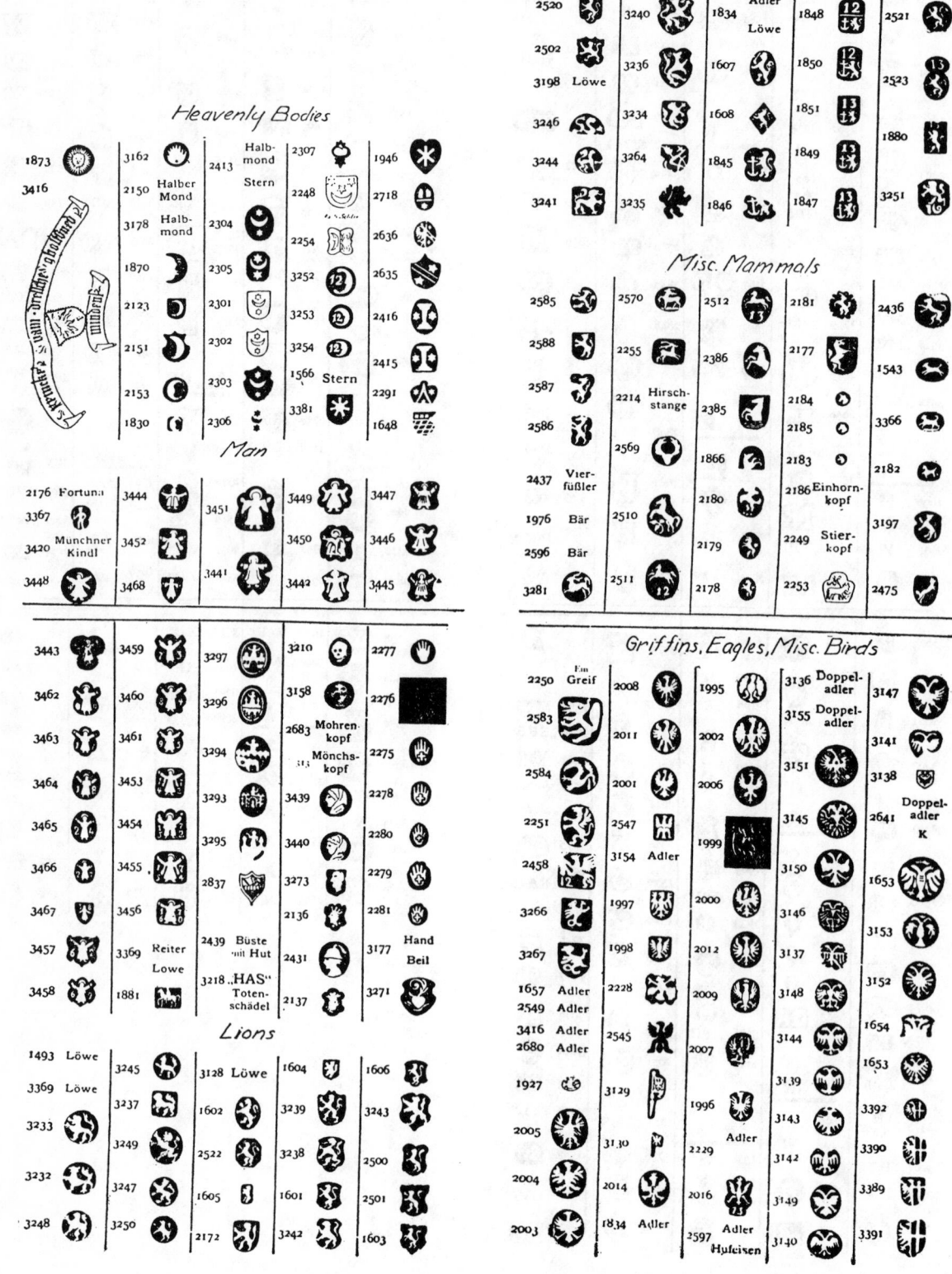

2560   2563   2573   3298   2108

2559   2891 Ein Schwan   2574   1876 Flug „IO"   2117

2841   2073   2110

2948   2383   3186   1878 Flug „12"   2114

2393   2111 Raben-kopf   2115

2562 Adler 49   1541   2118 Raben-kopf   2116

2382   2471   2107   2113

2561 Adler 1 6 4 5   2441   2352   2109   2112

Marine Life and Water

2397 Schlange „PO"   2167 Salm   1529 / 2947 Krebs   2283   2375

Plants

1860 Baum   2643   2648   2651   3179

3192 Baum-strunk   2647   2644   2650   2800 Kleeblatt

2606   2646   2481   2419 Kleeblatt

2290   2649   2481   2958 Dreiblatt 8

2653   2654   2645 / 2652   2289   2489

2491   2488   3487   2374   3165

2490   3279   2515   3172   2288

2492   2612   1644   2430   2293

2483   2613   1645   2744

2484   2615   1643   3166 Rosette   2292

2485   2614   2213   2164   2168 Frucht

2486   2614   3193   2031

2487   2616   1858   2163 / 3275   1859

Crowns, Scepters, and Arms

2713 Krone   2314   2380   2712   2974

1782   2713 Krone 13   2696   3416 Szepter   2971

2677   2691   2705   3263   2976

2676   2693   2704   3265   2972

2675   2692   2711   2970 Ritterhelm   2973

2313   2694 / 2695   2701 / 2708   2975   2969 3 Helme

1977   1666   1670   1665   3037

Implements

2398 Becher (?)   3163   2261   1841   2457

3159   3330   2258   1838   3417

2552 „Gekreuzte Abtstäbe"   3325   2259   1837   2482 Sichel

2986 Gekreuzte Schlüssel   3324   2260   1844   2445 Hammer „HB"

3111 Gekreuzte Schlüssel   3326   2262   1843   2193

3107   3327   2257   1842   3340 Schere

3108   3335   3360   3398 Anker „CL"   3189 Hifthorn

3109   3331   3361   3219 Anker „SH"   3191 Hifthorn

3110   3328   2257   2414   3190 Posthorn

3112 Gekreuzte Schlüssel 12   3332   2892 Kesselhaken   1486   2680 Hufeisen / 3034 Hufeisen,

3337   3168   3164 Anker   1488   1920

3169   3359   1840   1487   3380

3339   3358   1839   1921

  2256   3157 Faß   3160

Architecture

1975 Architekturmarke   2335   2331   2328   2345

3194 Turm „HO"   2334   2336   2341   2356

2987 Torturm   2344   2329   2519   2340

3099   3373   2343   2339   2365

3100   2327   2342   2350   2355

3101   3376   2348   2351

2600 Tor   2347   2349   3375   2353

1985   2330   2338   3374   2354

Crosses

2118 „F" Kreuz?   2159   2906   2145   2800

1943 Andreaskreuz?   2905   3230   2147   2801

3402   2911   3229   2459   2804

3404   2908   2960   2802 Kreuz

1980   2914   2800 Krone

3403 Kreuz   2904   2191   2810   2807

2808	2809	1888	1889	1497
2805	2811	1890	1887	1498
2806	2265	1892	1494	1499
2803	1893	1891	1495	1500
2812	1886	1885	1496	

Trade Marks

20 24 Hausmarke	3395	1939	3338	2091
2026	3023	2089	2979	2729
3607	2714	2735	2122	2731
1857	3176	2736	2411	2092
2720	3393	2724	1958	3485
1959	2716	3028	2715	2737
				2781

Shields and Geometrical Forms

| 2337 | 2333 | 2707 | 2703 | 2709 |
| 2332 | 2706 | 2710 | 2702 | 3408 |

3595	2917	2912	2609	2462
3594	2916	2907	2611	2463
3596	2915	2918	2610	2461
3593	2900		3161	2460
2154	2902	2603	2637	1989
2909	2901	2602	2465	1856
2910	2913	2607	2467	2601
2919	2903	2608	2466	2734
			2464	

A

3638 „A"
4410
3772
3631 „A"
3637 „a"
4540
4438
4187 „AA"
4535
4228
4229
3644 „AD"
4697 „AG"
4531
AI
3838

4675
4677
4149
4150
4660 „AM"
4165
4062
4448
3944
3924 AR
4065 AR
3925 „AR"
4903 „AR"
4480
4778
4212
4099

4100
3978 AS
4189
4456
3656 „ASZ"
4050
4051
4164
3907
3982
4487 „AV"
4637
3920

B

4582 „B"
4411
3773

4802
4884
3632 „B"
3980
3797
3756
3971 „BG"
3972 „BG"
4112
4853 „BK"
4021
4445
4792
4339
4226
3653
4770
4951 „B W"

4952 „BW"
4391
4950 „B W"
4450

C

3774
3633 „C"
4698 „?C"
C
3839
4147
4567
4888
4163 „CD"
4347
4471 „CDH"

4916
4168 CE
4804 „CE O"
4334
3646
4592
4412
3673 „CH"
4266
4117
4267
4639
4915
4324
4233
4259

4699
4076 „CK"
4791
3929
4596 „CK"
4286 „CK"
4079 „CL"
4813 „CL W"
4532
4788
4796
4330
4192
4928
4201
4646
4386

4066 „CS"
4961
4067
4600 „CV"
4361
4595 „CV"
3861
4975 „CW"
4331
4251
3999
4260 „CW"
4245
4261
4648
4982 „CZ"

D

3639 „D"
3775

4403
3634 „D"
3798
4588
4700
3997
3998
4490
4468 „D MB"
4467
4598
3984 „DS"
4270 „DW"
Vogel

E

3776
4620

4542
4674
4587 EB
4308
4500 „EC P"
4679
4074 „EH"
4033
3994
3910 „EL"
4678
3951
4767
4183
4351
4654
4460

F

3777
3799
4871
4599 „FB"
4390
3947
4854 „F.H."
4244
4017
3980
4458
3660
4175
4287
4862 „FK"
4416 „FM"
4793
4248
4063
4064

4309
4421
4420
4419
4422
4870 „FWL"

G

4913 „G"
4932 „G"
3778
4442
4443
4444
3922 „GB"
4200 „GB"
4202
4346 „GB"
4931 „GC C"
4303 „G CG"

4284 „GDW"
4918
3647
4314
4313
4872
4166 „GHB"
4783
3875
3662 „G IN"
4333
4319
4808
4290
4945
4249
4721
4293

3855
4908 „GP"
4787
4262
4049 „GS"
4819 „GS"
4611
4569
4954 „GS D"
3879

H

4493 „H"
3779
4435 „H"
H
3835
4068
4056
4758

3889
4176
4083
4085
4084
4929 „HB"
3876
4089
4090
4091
4092
4917
4096
4093
4095
4094
4774
3853

3890
4682
4057
3995
4108 „HC"
4225
4717
4282
4647
4340
3645
4140 „HD"
4128
3987
4187
4453
4221
4098 HG

4178 HG
4350
4268
4359
4047
4934 „HIB"
4436 „HIK"
4491
4454
4780
4185
4256
3859 HL HL
3657
3981
3905

4132
4781
4782
4645 „HM"
4019
3811 „HM"
4644 „HM"
3862 HM „HM"
4643
4534
4694
4927
4145
4762
3942
4511
4461
4459

4289
4371
3655
4852 „HP"
4608
4638
4354
4861
3932 HR
4126 HR
4137 „HR"
3955
4133
4156 „HR"
4134
4136
4720

4919 „HS"
4111 „HS"
3685 „HS"
4447
4642
3969
4937 „HT"
4059
4060
4223 „HV"
4058
4352
3641
3811
4655
4138 HW
4139 „HW"
4043
4216

4041 HZ	4272	4905 „IE"	4288	4519	4151	N	3764 N	4356 O	4208 PB	
4018 HZ	4613 „IC"	4211 „I·F"	4288	4805 IMW	3975 MM	3684	3758 N	4357 O	3952 PF	
3931	4311	4304	4273	4680 IHS	3976 MM	3686	3768 „N"	4358	4110 PF	
	4205	4725	4301	4814 „INP"	4008 „MN"		3757 N	4318 OF	4790 PH	
4309 „I"	4300 ICB"	4107	4298 INW	4505 „MP"	3687	3769	4214 QH	4862 „PK"?	
4672 „I"	4948 ICP"	4306	4651	4574 IOS	4797 MR		3770	4029 NE	4863 PK	
3780		4501 IFL"	4181 „IK"	3962 NR	3756	4372 NH	4860 OK	3863 „PL"	
3836	4947	4364 IFSI	4120 JR	4143 IP	4981	3784 „N"	4075	4327	4242 „PM"	
4552	4389	4193 IFT	4946 „IK"	4641 IP	4129 RI	3736 N	4363	3669	
4302 IAH	4650 ICS	4462 „IG"	4182 IK	4640 J·P	3654 MR	3939	3756	4203 PR	
4859 IAK	4279 ICW	3926	4585 „JKOR"	4551 IP	4039 MS	3759	4106 NR	4842 OO	4449 PR	
4723 IAS	4122 ID	4935 Stern „IG"	3958 JL	3950 IP	3652 MT	3763	4759 NR	P	4069 „PS"	
4722 IAS	4962 ID	4291 IGH	3959 „IL"	4518 I·P	4612 MV	3822 N	3786 „P"	4070 „PS"	
4695 „IB"	4949	3659 „IGP"	4800 LA	4257 IP	4610 MX	3765 N	4014 ISI	4375 „P"	4071 PS	
3967 IB	4285 DP		4277	4785 IIK	4973	3761 N	4652	4393 „P"	4478 IAS	
4789 IB	4533 IGV	4653 ILW	3904 „IR"	4973 MWA	3767 N	3913	3933	
4795 IB	4553 IDS	3960 IH	4469 „IM"	4806 IR	4280	3766 N	3785 „O"	3912	3934	
4597 „IB"	3991 IE	4360 „IH"	4464 IMF	4217 IR	3760 N	4914 „O"	4455	3935	
3968 IB	3992 IE	4238 IH			3762	4355 O	4451 „PA"	4877 „PTS"	

4153 IR	4724 „ISS"	3813 PO	4034 „LO"	3849	4061	3814 W	4275 SW	3989 SR	4171 „TW"	
4218 IR	3917 IT	4271 K	4408 LO	4148 MB	4119	4387 „RZ"	3928	4657	4121	
4086 IR	4798 IN	4271 K	4179 LR	3804 ·M·B·		Q	S	4118 SG	4930	
3661 IR	4362 IV	3909 R	4142 „LT"	3806 MB	3787 „Q"	3789 „S"	4938 „SI"	U	
	4719	L	4177 LT	3993 MB	4580	4536 „S"	4104	3791 „U"	
4665	4609 W	3782 „L"	3963 Ir	4097 MD		4537 „S"	3870	3790 „T"	
4154 IR	4799 M	3810 L	4186 IV	3744 „ME"	4629	4538 „S"	4082 T	V	
4307 IRK	4353 IWV	4328 L	M	3979 ME	4509 „S"	4199 S	4670 T	3792 „V"	
4974 IS	4299 „IWW"	4329 L	3783 „M"	3979 „ME"	R	4527 S	4105	4671 T	4481 „V"	
3986 IS	4505 „I2L"	4659 „M"		4483	4803 S	3918 T	4794 V	
3974 IS	3678 IZ	4310 LAL	3658 M	3949 MF	4622	4470 „SIA"	4180 TD	4816 V	
4073 IG	K	4936 „LB"	4841 M	3949 „MF"	4484	4617	3943 SK	4417 „TE"	
3985	4673 „K"	4476 „LD"	4812	4463 MF	4482	4222	3756	4432	
4976 „ISB"	3781 K	4760	4489 MF	4526	4676	4174 „TH"	4728	
4466 „ISG"	4666 K	4818	4109 MH	4485	4525 S12	4209 TT	4731	
4465	4784 K	4028 IH	4562	4488 MH	3788 „R"	4498 „SA"	4933 „THD"	4733	
4963 ISM	4004 K	4885 LI	3846 „M"	4452	4020 „R"	4236 „SB"	4446 SP	4082 „TL"	4732	
3643	3856 KB	3668 LK	4775	4037	4702 R	4904 „SB"	3936 S	4246 „TR"	4735	
	3857 KB	4909	3845	4232 RR	4227 SBF	3961 S	4081 S	4487 VA	
							4207 S		

4372 „VH"	4851	4881 „W 12"	4044	4960
3906 „VK"		4876 „13 W"	4022 WZ	4964
4953 „VPT"	4801		4024	
4457	3635 „W"	4943	4026 „WZ"	3800
W	4517	4539 „WD"		4768
3793 „W"	4253 „W"	3988	X	4769
4870 „W"	4312	4206		4958 PROB AUGSBURGER
4878 „W"	3670	4294 „W IW(?)"	3794 „X"	
4169 „W"	3832	3966	Y	4965
4332		4428	3795 „Y"	
4955	4807	3854	Z	4966
4855	4188	4305 „WS"	3796 „Z"	4255 „ZH"
4867	3965	4388	3636 „Z"	4023 ZM
4868	4584	4402 „WV"	4959	4195 „ZM" / 4025
4001	3956	4401	4957	4027 „ZM"

Misc. Mammals

4437 Tier?	4630	4627	4901	4269
4727	3964	4624		4516
4379 Wolf	4701		4894	4515
4383		4911	4900	4159
	4510			4969
4384	4625	4912	4897	4237
4385	4618			4087
4590	4615	4619	4899	4231
4080	4616	4910	4898	4323
4243	4623	4880 Stierkopf	4219 Schaf	4365
3824	4628	4902		4263
4321 Hirschstangen	4621		4895	4887
4631	4626		4003	

Heavenly Bodies

4892 Halbmond	4696	4197	3681	3880
4508 Stern, Mond	4690	4220	3680	3884
Ringe	3841	4718	3682	3818
4509 Rose / Halbmond	4131 / 4130	4278	4040	3882
4006	3888	4250	3880 / 3881	3683 / HICKEN

Man

4283	4667	3828	

Lions

3665 Löwe?	4381	4315	4869	3921
4376	4382	4821	4146	4968
4337 Löwe				
4499	4856 Löwe	4504	3834	3675 Tatze

Griffins, Eagles, Misc. Birds

4486 Greif / 4475 Adler / 4891 Adler	4714	4710	4424	4326 Hahn
4320 Adler	4716	4705		3957
4322 Adler		4708	4425	4196
4838	4715	4707	4336 Adler	4141
4522	4712	4706	4427	4247
4839	4523		4882	4577
4704	4713	4406	4971	4579
3677	4711	4407	4972	4578
			4687 Schwanenhals	3871
4524	4709	4423	4295	

Marine Life

4101	4703	4492 Fische	4687 Muschel	3945
4591		4167	4160	4005

Plants

4235	4530	3817	3864	3927
4135	4757	4756	3865	

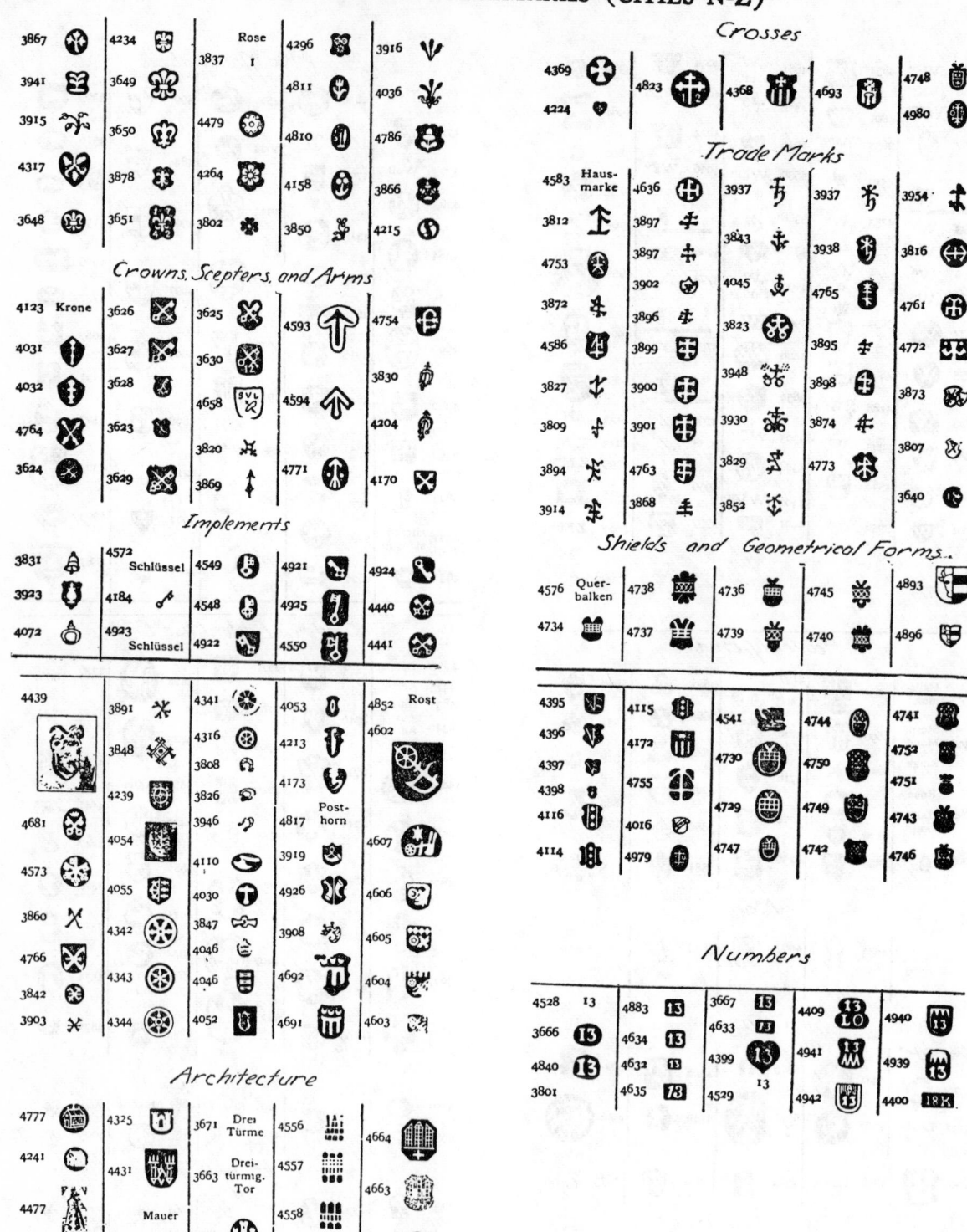

1086. 1618
1087. 1626
1088. 1639
1089-1092. 17.-18. cent.
1093. 18. cent.
1094. 18. cent.
1095-1096. beginning of 18. cent.
1097-1098. middle of 18 cent.
1099. end of 18. cent.
1100-1101. 18.-19. cent.
1102-1105. 18.-19. cent.
1106. 1830
1107-1108. 18. cent.
1109-1110. early 19. cent.

BAUTZEN

1140-1141. 18. cent.

BERLIN

1148. second half 17. cent.
1149-1150. first half 18. cent.
1151-1152. since 1735 or earlier ?
1153. since 1735 or earlier ?
1154-1158. second half 18. cent.
1159-1160. 18.-19. cent.
1161-1162. 19. cent.
1163-1164. 18.-19. cent., changing with the years or masters
1165-1169. 18.-19. cent., changing with the years or masters
1171. Daniel Männlich, 1676-1701
1199. Christian Lieberkühn, 1738-1764

BEUTHEN/ODER

1230. about 1732
1231-1232. about 1736-1770
1233. about 1775

BIBERACH

1235-1236. 17. cent.
1237. middle of 18. cent.
1238. middle of 18. cent.
1239-1240. 18.-19. cent.

BRAUNSBERG

1260. about 1684
1261-1262. about 1740
1265. late 18. cent.

BRAUNSCHWEIG

1276. end of 16. cent.
1277. 16.-17. cent.
1278. 17. cent.
1279. second half 17. cent.
1280. about 1680-1690
1281. end of 17. cent.
1282. about 1690
1283. about 1695
1284-1285. about 1695-1700
1286. about 1705
1287-1288. beginning of 18. cent.
1289-1290. about 1750
1291-1292. about 1790-1800
1313. Adam Wagner, 1675-1681

1315. Berendt Knop(f), 1686
1324. Andreas Seitz, 1692-1709 ?
1327. Herman Georg Mirus, 1699
1330. Gottfried Johann Boden, 1709

BREMEN

1342. 17. cent.
1343. about 1650
1344-1345. about 1690
1346. 17.-18. ? cent.
1347. about 1700
1348. about 1720
1349. about 1750
1350. about 1800
1351. 19. cent.
1358. M. H. Wilkens, founder of the business M. H. Wilkens & Sons, 1782-1869

BRESLAU

1365. from 1542 till 1553
1366. from 1553 till early 17. cent.
1367. early 17. cent.
1368. middle of 17. cent.
1369. second half of 17. cent., till after 1721
1370. from before 1737 till about 1740
1372. with 19 different variations, end of 17. cent., till 1842
1373. since about 1710
1375-1376. since 1843
1377. 1710-1712
1378. 1712-1721
1379. 1721-about 1727
1380. about 1727-1737
1381. 1737-1745
1382. 1746-1758
1383. after 1758-about 1760
1384. about 1761-1776
1385. 1776-about 1791
1386. 1839-1849
1387. 1849-1861
1391. Oswald Rothe, 1503-1522
1392. Andreas Heidecker, 1509-1533
1399. Hans Schönaw, 1567-1608 or Hans Strich, 1582-1616
1400. Augustin Heyne, 1571-1601
1401. Paul Nitsch, 1573-1609
1402. Joachim Hiller, 1573-1613
1404. Caspar Bendel, 1575-1599
1406. Veit Koch, 1580-1619
1407. Christoph Stimmel, 1584-1627
1408. Georg Hoffmann, 1586-1609
1410. Friedrich Schoenau, 1598-1627
1411. Caspar Pfister, 1598-1635
1413. Hans Volgnadt, 1605-1622

1414. Fabian Nitsch, 1602-1630
1421. Hans Jachmann, 1638-1685
1425. Christian Mentzel, 1668-1699
1426. Gottfried Heintze, 1673-1707
1428. Thomas Kuntze, 1683-1716
1429. Gottfried Heyner, 1682-1716
1430. Gottfried Körner, 1685-1722
1434. Christian Winckler, 1690-1706
1435. Gottfried Ihme, 1691-1737
1438. Christian Heintze, 1701-1732
1439. Tobias Schier, 1702-1733
1440. Carl Wilhelm Hartman, 1706-1729
1441. Michael Wissmar, 1715-1746
1442. Thomas Beyl, 1719-1758
1444. Johann Christoph Vogel, 1722-about 1742
1448. Benjamin Hentschel, 1732-1774
1449. George Kahlert the younger, 1732-1772
1451. Christian Kretschmer, 1734-1758
1455. Karl Friedrich Korok, 1835-1858

BRIEG (SILESIA)

1456. end of 16. cent.
1457. 16.-17. cent.
1458. 17. cent.
1459. since 1685 and 18. cent.
1460. about 1740
1461. about 1745
1463. Nickel Knobloch, 1578-after 1596

BRUSHSAL (BADEN)

1448. 17. and 18. cent.

BÜTZOW (MECKLENBURG-SCHWERIN)

1472. 16. cent.
1473. 17. and 18. cent.
1474. 19. cent.

BUNZLAU (SILESIA)

1478. about 1750

CHAM (BAVARIA)

1480. end of 17. cent.

CRAILSHEIM (WUERTTEMBERG)

1484. 17. cent.

DAGEBUELL

1486-1487. 17. cent.
1488. 17.-18. cent.

DANZIG (Free State)

1494. 17. cent.
1495. 17. cent.
1496. 17. cent.
1497. second half of 17. cent.
1498. 17.-18. cent.
1499-1500. 17. and early 18. cent.

INSPECTION MASTERS

1501. 1730, 38, 44
1502. 1731, 37
1503. 1732, 41
1504. 1734, 43, 47, 53
1505. 1735
1506. 1737 or 42, 46, 54
1507. 1740
1508. 1745, 49, 59
1509. 1748, 56, 62, 66
1510. 1752, 58, 64
1511. 1755, 61
1512-1213. 1757, 65, 69
1514. 1758, 64
1515. 1760.
1516. 1763, 67
1517. 1768, 72, 86, 90
1518. 1770, 74
1519. 1770, 74
1520-1521. 1771, 75, 79
1522. 1773, 77
1523. 1778, 82, 84
1524-1525. 1781, 85, 91, 95
1526-1527. 1789, 93, 97
1528-1529. 1792, 96, 1800, 04, 08
1530. 1799, 1803
1531. 1801, 05
1532-1533. 1814, 18, 19
1534. 1829-33, 36
1535. 1834, 35, 37-39
1536. 1840, 45, 50, 51
1537. 1841-44, 46-49
1549. Christian Paulsen I, 1630-1650
1556. Christian Schubert, 1644-1651
1557. Hans O p h a g e n , 1648-1701
1560. Peter Rohde 2nd, 1654-1677
1567. Ernst Kadau(w) 2nd, 1674-1690
1571. Jacob Beckhausen, 1678-1704
1572. Conrad Jacob Keseberg, 1679-1722
1594. Christian Pichgiel, 1681-1700
1575. Johann Rohde 2nd, 1684-1720
1578-1579. A n d r e a s Haidt, 1686-1721
1580. Peter Rohde 3rd, 1688-1717
1584-1586. Nathanael Schlaubitz, 1690-1726
1587. Siegfried Oernster, 1691-1735
1596. J o h a n n Gottfried Sclaubitz, 1 7 3 3 - 1766

DARMSTADT

1601. (16. till) 17. cent.
1602-1603. 17.-18. cent.
1604. about 1700
1605. about 1800
1606. 18.-19. cent.

1607-1608. 19. cent.
1609-1611. 18.-19. cent.

DEMMIN (POMMERN)

1620. "D with crown"

DESSAU (ANHALT)

1621. 17. cent.
1622-1623. 18. cent.
1624-1625. 18.-19. cent.
1626. 19. cent.
1627. 18. cent.
1628-1629. 18.-19. cent.
1630-1631. 19. cent.

DILLINGEN

1643-1644. first half of 18. cent.
1645. second half of 18. cent.
1646. Anton Simon Lang, 1723-1753
1647. Franz Lang, 1753-1785

DINGOLFING

1648. end of 17. cent.

DONAUWOERTH (BAVARIA)

1653-1653a. 16.-17. cent.
1654. 18. cent.

DRESDEN

1658. 16.-17. cent.
1659. 17. cent.
1660-1662. first quarter of the 18. cent.
1663-1664. 1722-1725
1665. 1730
1666. 1737
1676. 1739
1668-1670. middle of 18. cent.
1672-1678. third quarter of 18. cent.
1679-1680. end of 18. cent.
1681-1686. 19. cent.

DATE LETTERS

1687. 1702
1688. 1708.
1689. 1713.
1690. 1714.
1691. 1717.
1692. 1720.
1693. 1722
1694. 1723 or 1747
1695. 1725
1696. 1726
1697. 1728
1698. 1731
1699. 1737
1700. 1738
1701. 1739
1702. 1741
1703. 1747
1704-1705. 1748
1706. 1750
1707. 1757 ?
1708. 1760 ?
1709. 1761
1710. 1767
1711. 1768
1712. 1771
1713. 1772
1714. 1773

1715. 1773 ?
1716. 1785
1717. 1793
1718. 1808
1719. 1818
1720. 1822
1721. 1825
1722. 1826
1723. 1828
1724. 1829
1725. 1830
1739. Georg Mond, 1599-1623 ?
1751-1752. Zacharias Schlosser, 1624-1654 ?
1756. Jakob W a t z k y , 1641-1679 ?
1764. Zacharias Schlosser, 1646-1676 ?
1768. Niclas Bille, 1676-1687 ?
1773-1774. Johann M i c h a e l W i n c k e l - mann, 1690-1724 or Johann Michael Wecker, 1716-1749
1788-1789. Samuel Gaudig(ch), 1717-1759
1790. Christian Gottlieb Irminger, 1719-1749
1800. Carl Gottlieb Ingermann, 1 7 3 6 - 1774
1805-1808. Carl David Schrödel, about 1762
1812-1813. Friedrich Reinhard Schrödel, 1 7 5 6 - 1796
1814. Johann Christian Neuber, 1752-1808
1815-1816. brothers Schrödel, about 1770
1817-1818. Gotthelf M o r i t z Hauptvogel, 1768-1810 ?

DUESSELDORF

1837-1838. 17. cent.
1839-1844. 17.-18. cent.
1845-1851. 18. cent.

DATE LETTERS

1852-1853. beginning of 18. cent.
1854-1855. 18. cent.

EINBECK

1874. first half 17. cent.

ELBERFELD

1880. end of 19. cent.

ELBING

1885. 1647-end of 17. cent.
1886. a b o u t 1657-1728, perhaps-1772
1887. 1698-1705
1888. 1705
1889. 1708-1744
1890. 1742
1891. 1743-1753
1892. 1792-1797, perhaps 1777-1811
1893. beginning of 19. cent.

2280-2281. 18. cent.
2282. early 19. cent.
2293. 17. cent.

HALLE / SAALE

2301. 16. cent.
2302-2303. 17. cent.
2304-2305. 17.-18. cent.
2306-2307. 18. cent.

ANNUAL LETTERS

2308. 1710
2309. 1711 ?
2310. 1713
2311. 1715
2312. 1 ? ? control mark
2313. 1728-1769 ?
2314. 1786-1808 ?
2319. Peter Rockenthin, 1645-1663
2324. early 18. cent.
2325. early 18. cent.
2326. 1749-1765

HAMBURG

2327. end of 16. cent.
2328. 16.-17. cent.
2330-2333. early 17. cent.
2334-2349. middle of 17. cent.
2350-2356. late 17. cent.
2357-2362. 17.-18. cent.
2363-2364. early 18. cent.
2365-2367. middle of 18. cent.
2368-2369. late 18. cent.
2370-2372. early 19. cent.
2373. "Hamburger" watchmaker
2382. 17. cent.
2383. master mark
2395. Frederick Frederichs, 1628-1767
2396. Gregorius Lambrecht, 1628-1672
2401. Heinrich Eickhoff, 1628-1708
2405. Dietrich Thor Moye, 1633-1652
2409. 1662
2415. 1648
2417. first half of 17. cent.
2422. Lambrecht, 17. cent.
2424. Juergen Richels, 1664-1711
2427. Leonhard Rothaer, 1671-1698 ?

HAMELN

2457. 17. and 18. cent.
2458. 18. cent.

HAMMELBURG

2459. early 18. cent.

HANAU

2460. about 1600
2461. 16.-17. cent.
2462. (Old-Hanau) 17.-18. cent.
2463. (New-Hanau) middle of 18. cent.
2464. (Old-Hanau) 18. cent.
2465. 18. cent.

2466-2467. 18.-19. cent.
2468. 19. cent.
2469. standard mark
2475. Johann Benedict Fuchs, 1724-1747

HANNOVER, CITY

Hannover-Altstadt
2483. 1640
2484. 1644
2485. 1663
2486. 1665
2487. 1670
2488. 1686
2489-2491. early 18. cent.
2492. middle of 18. cent.
2493. Hans Rhaders, 1627-1644
2494. Andreas Scheele (Scheilen), 1638-1675
2495. Hinrich Saedeler, 1665

Hannover-Neustadt
2500-2501. 17.-18. cent.
2502. 1726
2503-2504. about 1700
2505. 1726
2508. master mark

Hannover-(King's Court)
2510-2512. 18. cent.
2513-2514. 18. cent.
2515. gold stamp. 18. cent.
2516. Joachim Sander, 1680
2517. master mark
2518. master mark

HAYNAU (SILESIA)

2519. about 1708

HEIDELBERG

2520. 17.-18. cent.
2521-2522. 18. cent.
2523. 18.-19. cent.

HEILBRONN

2533. middle of 17. cent.
2534. early 18. cent.
2535-2536. 19. cent.
2542. Peter Bruckmann, 1805-1850

HILDBURGHAUSEN

2557. 17. cent.

HILDESHEIM

2559. 16. cent.
2560. 17. cent.
2561. 1645
2562. 1649
2563. 1705
2567-2568. P. J. Syring, 1726

HIRSCHBERG

2569. 18. cent.
2570. 18. cent.

ILMENAU (SACHSEN)

2573. 17. cent.
2574. about 1700

INGOLSTADT ?

2583. 15. cent.
2584. 15.-16. cent.
2585. 17. cent.
2586-2587. 17. cent.
2588. 18. cent.

INSTERBURG

2596. about 1677

JAUER (SILESIA)

2601. about 1693
2602-2603. early 18. cent.

JULIUSBURG (SILESIA)

2606. about 1707

KARLSRUHE (BADEN)

2607-2611. after 1806

KASSEL

2612. before 1658
2613-2614. 17. cent.
2615. 17.-18. cent.
2616. 18. cent.
2618-2622. 18. and 19. cent., connected with annual letters

KAUFBEUREN

2635. 16. cent.
2636. 18. cent.

KIEL

2643. 15. cent.
2644. 16.-17. cent.
2645-2649. 17. cent.
2650-2653. 18. cent.
2654-2655. 19. cent.
2661. 1695
2662. 1698
2665. 1714

KITZINGEN (BAVARIA)

2671. about 1595
2672. 18.-19. cent.

KOBLENZ (RHINE PROVINCE)

2675. 17. cent.
2676-2677. 18. cent.

KOELN

2691-2693. 16. cent.
2694-2697. 16.-17. cent.
2697-2700. second half of 17. cent.
2702-2706. first half of 18. cent.
2707-2708. middle of 18. cent.
2709-2712. end of 18. cent.
2767. Johann Ruetgers, 1700-1744 ?
2798. Ernst Riegel from Muenchen, 1907-1912

KOENIGSBERG (PRUSSIA)

2800. 1684-1703
2801. 1704-1716
2802. 1714 and later

2803. 1754-1761
2804. 1760-1772
2805. 1760-1770
2806. 1780-1790
2807. 1784-1786
2808. 1788-1800
2809. 1800-about 1830
2810. for more than 6 oz. silver, only 1815
2811. about 1830-1860
2812. 19. cent.

Annual letters

2813. 1693
2814. 1694
2815. 1696
2816. 1703
2817. 1704
2818. 1705
2819. 1706
2820. 1707
2821. 1709
2822. 1713
2823. 1714
2824. 1715
2825. 1740
2826. 1742
2827. 1747
2828. 1754
2829. 1761
2830. 1766 or 1772
2831. 1773
2832. 1784
2833. 1788
2834. 1818
2835. 1843
2846. Andreas Meyer from Nuremberg, 1608-1647
2847-2848. Paul Eckloff, 1612-1646
2854-2855. Lorenz Hoffmann from Nuremberg, 1659-about 1684
2856-2857. Johann (Hans) Meyer, 1662-1688
2858-2859. Peter Schoenermark, 1665-1703
2860-2861. David Doehring, 1670-1696
2862-2863. Peter Andreas Haendel (Hendel), 1671-1699
2863-2865. Otto Schwerdtfeger, 1685-1713
2868. Christian Friedrichs, 1688-1708
2869. Michael Christian Hetsch 1st, 1695-1721
2870. Johann Daniel Tamnau 1st, 1696-1732
2877-2878. Andreas Junge 1st, 1710-1757
2879-2881. Christian Leo, 1734-1771
2884. Christoph Philipp Hartung, about 1777-1800
2885-2888. Johann Leopold Kaewerstein, 1790-1812

KONSTANZ

2900. about 1557
2901-2905. 16.-17. cent.
2906-2909. early 17. cent.
2910-2911. middle of 17. cent.
2912-2913. end of 17. cent.

2914-2917. 18. cent.
2918-2919. 19. cent.

KULMBACH

2950-2951. 16.-17. cent.

LANDSBERG

2960. 17.-18. cent.

LANDESHUT

2966-2967. 18. cent.

LANDSHUT

2969. 15. cent.
2970. middle of 16. cent.
2971. 16. cent.
2972. 1723
2973. 1751
2974-2975. middle of 18. cent.
2976. end of 18. cent.
2982. Joseph Ferdinand Schmid (1), 1741-1790
2983-2984. Martin Spitzelberger, end of 18. cent.
2985. Caspar Bettinger (Pettinger), 1780-1794

LAUBAN

2986. inspection mark

LEER (EAST FRESLAND)

2989. end of 18. cent.

LEIPZIG

2990-2991. 16. cent.
2992. 16. perhaps 17. century too
2994-2996. 17. perhaps 18. century too
2997. 17.-18. cent.
2998-2999. early 18. cent.
3000-3003. 18. cent.
3004. end of 18. cent.

DATE LETTERS

3005. 1587-89
3006. 1588-90
3007. 1589-91
3008. 1597-99
3009. 1626-28
3010. 1627-29
3011. 1635-37
3012. 1641-43
3013. 1650-52
3014. 1656-58
3015. 1662-64
3016. 1668-71
3017. 1675-77
3018. 1682-84
3019. 1692-94
3020. 1693-95
3021. about 1711
3022. about 1725
3032. Elias Geier, 1589
3038. Andreas Kauxdorf, 1618-1669
3039. Melchior Lauch, 1622-1665
3042. perhaps Peter Richter, 1633

3043. Augustus Richter, 1633
3044. Sebald Krumbholz, 1634-1656
3045. Hans Scholler, 1642
3049. master mark, 1800
3053. Gottfried Schmidt, 1667-1681
3054. Joachim Krumbholz, 1669
3066. Johann Paul Schmidt, 1683-1703
3084. perhaps Andreas Schroeder, 1700
3085. Paul Gottfried Haussmann, 1732

LEUTKIRCH

3099. 16. cent.
3100-3101. 17. cent.

LIEGNITZ

3107. 16. and 17. cent.
3108. early 17. cent.
3109-3110. end of 17. cent.
3111. 17.-18. century (crossed keys in a square)
3112. about 1720 (crossed keys with 12)

ANNUAL LETTERS

3113. 1729 ?
3114. 1730
3115. 1731

LUDWIGSBURG

3129-3130. 19. cent.
3131. 19. cent.
3132. date letter

LUDWIGSLUST

3135. 19. cent.

LUEBECK

3137. 15. cent.
3139. 1501
3140. 1507
3141. early 16. cent.
3142. 1540
3143. middle of 16. cent.
3144. second half of 16. cent.
3145. 16.-17. cent.
3146. 1622
3147. 1631
3148-3151. middle of 17. cent.
3152-3153. 18. cent.
3154. 1828-1831
3155. 1831-1834

LUENEBURG

3232-3234. 15.-16. cent.
3235-3238. first half of 16. cent.
3239. middle of 16. cent.
3240. second half of 16. cent.
3241-3244. second half of 16. cent.
3245-3248. 16.-17. cent.
3249-3250. about 1650
3251. beginning of 17. cent.

3252-3254. beginning of 19. cent.
3255. 1790-1828
3256-3257. 19. cent.

MAGDEBURG

3293. 1622
3294. 1666.
3295. 1667
3296. end of 17. cent.
3297. early 18. cent.
3298. 17.-18. cent.
3299-3300. end of 17. cent.

MAINZ

3324-3325. 16. cent.
3326. 17. cent.
3327. late 17. cent.
3328. early 18. cent.
3329-3330. 1761 and later.
3331. 1765-1769
3332. 19. cent.
3333-3334. 19. cent.
3335. mark of the arch-bishop

MANNHEIM

3357. 17.-18. cent.
3358. 1717
3359. 1727
3360. 1737-1766
3361. 1775

MARIENBURG

3373. 17. cent.
3374. 17.-18. cent.
3375. 17. cent. ?
3376. 19. cent.

MARIENWERDER

3380. 18. cent.

MARKDORF

3381. 17. cent.

MEININGEN

3384. 1688

MEISSEN

3387. inspection mark

MEMMINGEN

3389-3390. middle of 16. cent. perhaps earlier
3391-3392. 17. cent.

MERGENTHEIM

3402. inspection m a r k, time not sure
3403. about 1700
3404. late 18. cent.

MERSEBURG

3408. 1661
3409. 18. cent.

MUEHLHAUSEN

3417. 1618

MUENCHEN

3439. 15.-16. cent.
3440. 16.-17. cent.

3441-3443. second half of 17. cent.
3444-3447. about 1700
3448-3452. early 18. cent.
3453. 1742
3454. 1752
3455. 1754
3456. 1760
3457. 1762
3458. 1769
3459. 1773
3460. 1784
3461. 1795
3462. 1800-1820
3463. 1815-1822
3465. 1820-1835
3467. 1835-1850
3468. 1840-1860
3507. Franz K e s s l e r, 1664-1717
3516. J o h a n n Georg Oxner (1), 1677-1712
3533-3534. Joseph Grossauer, 1718-1755, perhaps Ignaz Gruenewaldt, 1745-1764
3567. Ignaz Franzowitz, 1765-1813

MUENSTER

3593-3594. 16. cent.
3595-3596. 17. cent.

NAUMBURG

3623. 16.-17. cent.
3624-3625. 17. cent.
3626. 1684
3627-3630. 18. cent.

ANNUAL LETTERS

3631. A 1700
3632. B 1701
3633. C 1702
3634. D 1703
3635. W 1720
3636. Z 1723
3637. 1724
3638. 1748
3639. 1749

NEISSE

3648. 1604
3649. 1610-1614
3650. about 1700
3651. 1742

NEUSTADT on the HARDT

3666. 18. cent.
3667. 19. cent.

NEUSTADT on the SAALE
3671. about 1750

NOERDLINGEN

3677. 17. cent.

NORDEN
(PROVINCE HANNOVER)

3680-3681. 18.-19. cent.
3682. 19. cent.
3683. 19. cent.

NORDHEIM

3684. 1660

OLD-NUREMBERG

3686. inspection mark
3678. about 1600

NUREMBERG

3757. 1550-1600
3758-3759. 1550-1650
3760. 1600-1660
3761. 1600-1700
3762-3763. 1600-1700
3764. 1640-1675
3765-3766. 1650-1700
3767. 1700-1750
3769. 19 cent., earlier
3770. 19. cent., later
3771. 19. cent.

Assayer marks

3772. 1766-perhaps 1769
3773. 1769-1773 ?
3774. 1773-1776 ?
3775. 1776-1780 ?
3776. 1780-1783 ?
3777. 1783-1787 ?
3778. 1787-1790 ?
3779. 1790-1794 ?
3780. 1794-1797 ?
3781. 1797-1800 ?
3782. 1800-1804 ?
3783. 1804-1808
3784. 1808
3785. 1808-1811 ?
3786-3796. early 19. cent.
3797-3800. middle of 19. century and perhaps also later
3801. 19. cent.
3839. Christoph Jamnit-zer, 1592-1618
3856-3857. Kaspar B a u c h, 1541-1583
3878. Christoph Linden-berger, 1546-1580
3880. Christoff R i t t e r (le) 1st, 1547-1598
3881. Christoff R i t t e r (le), 2nd, 1 5 7 7 - 1616
3882. Jeremias R i t t e r, 1605-1646
3899-3900. master mark, 17. cent.
3912-3913. Paulus D u l n e r, 1552-1596
3919. Caspar Widmann, 1554-1590
3923. J a c o b Froehlich, 1555-1579
3928. E r h a r d Scherl, 1556-1593
3962. M a r t i n Rehlein, 1566-1613
3966. Wolff Loescher, 1568-1591
3969. H a n n s s Straub, 1568-1610
4002-4003. Hans P e t z o l d, 1578-1633
4004. Heinrich J o n a s, 1579-1605
4017. F r i e d r i c h Hille-brandts, 1580-1608
4029. Nicolaus Emmer-ling, 1582-1606
4031-4032. Hans Keller, 1582-1609
4033. Eustachius Hoh-man, 1682-1612
4054-4055. H a n n s s Beut-mueller, 1588-1622
4070-4071. P e t e r Sigmundt, 1608-1624

STADTAMHOF
4573. 1767

STETTIN
4577. 16.-17. cent.
4578. 18. cent.
4579. gold 18. cent.
4580. 18. cent.

WERNIGERODE and STOLBERG
4590-4591. 18. cent. (stag for Stolberg, fish for W.)

STRALSUND
4593-4594. 17. cent.

STRAUBING (BAVARIA)
4602. tin (1614)
4603-4606. second half of 16. cent.
4607. middle of 18. cent.

STUTTGART
4615. end of 16. cent.
4616. middle of 17. cent.
4617. end of 17. cent.
4618-4619. about 1700
4620-4621. about 1700-1760
4623-4624. 18.-19. cent.
4625-4629. 19. cent.
4632-4635. 19. cent.

SUHL
4657-4658. 17.-18. cent.

TILSIT
4663. 18. cent.
4664. beginning of 19. cent.

TORGAU
4670. 16.-17. cent.
4671. 17. cent.
4672-4673. 17. cent.

TREBNITZ
4681. 17. cent.

TUEBINGEN (WUERTTEMBERG)
4690. 16.-17. cent.
4691. beginning of 17. cent.
4692. 17. cent.
4693. 18. cent.

TUTTLINGEN (WUERTTEMBERG)
4701. about 1660
4702. about 1660

UEBERLINGEN (BADEN)
Inspection marks
4704-4706. end of 16. cent.
4707-4709. 16.-17. cent.
4710-4713. 17. cent.
4714-4716. 18. cent.

ULM
Inspection marks
4728-4729. 16. cent.
4730. 16.-17. cent.
4731-4736. 17. cent.
4737-4744. 17.-18. cent.
4745-4752. 18. cent.
4784. Johann Adam Keinlin the older, 1651-1691 ?
4787. Georg Preg, 1658-1691

URACH
4816. about 1700
4817. 17.-18. cent.

VELBURG
4821. 18.-19. cent.

VERDEN
4823. 17. cent.

VILLINGEN
4838. 15. to 16. cent.
4839. 18. cent.
4840. 18. cent.

WAREN
4851. 18. cent.

WEILHEIM
4857. 17.-18. cent.
4858. 18. cent.

WEIMAR
4867-4868. 17. cent.
4869. end of 17. cent.

WERTHEIM
4882. about 1660
4883. 19. cent.

WESEL
4887. 16. and also 17. cent.

WISMAR
4893. end of 16. cent.
4894. beginning of 17. cent.
4895. 1694, probably since 1686
4869. end of 17. cent.
4897. beginning of 18. cent.
4898. about 1730-1748
4899. about 1736-1746
4900. middle of 18. cent.
4901. end of 18.-beginning of 19. cent.
4902. 19. cent.

WITTENBERG
4906. middle of 17. cent.

WOLFENBUETTEL
4910. 1668.
4911. 17. cent.
4912. 17.-18. cent.
4913. 1707
4914. 1714.

WORMS
4921-4922. 16.-17. cent.
4923. 17. cent.
4924-4925. 17. to 18. cent.

WUERZBURG
4939. early 18. cent.
4940-4942. 18. cent.
4943. early 18. cent.

WURZEN
4955. 18. cent.

ZERBST
4957. 1696
4958. about 1700
4959. 1723
4960. 1752

ZITTAU
4964. 1710
4965. 1731
4966. about 1750

ZWEIBRUECKEN
4968. 18. cent.

ZWICKAU
4971. 16.-17. cent.
4972. 17. cent.

FRAUSTADT
4979-4980. 17.-18. cent.

A

No.	Label	No.	Label	No.	Label	No.	Label	No.	Label
	"A"	5060		6086 b) / 6128	"A"	6353	"A"	6369	
5257	"A"	9534		6174 / 6791	"A"	5805		6544	
8176		8710		6453		8722			
8181 / 8319	"A"	6016		6455		6527		6527	
8321 / 8333 / 8340		5968		7633		6357		6538	
9520		7501		6290	"A"	6383		6511	
9115		8592		6449		6396		6521	
5007		7111		6459		5553		6472	
5006		7175		6461		5961		6470	
5363		7187		6463		6502		6423	
9597	"A"	7201		9454		5160		6490	
7217		7219		6027	"A"				
7877		7220							
7880		9454							
7863		8763	"A"ₓ						
5100									
9500									

No.	Label	No.	Label	No.	Label	No.	Label	No.	Label
6474		7860		5960 B	"A 87-"	6969		5493 B	"AD"
				6084	"AA"	7959			
6495		7861		9154 A		7084	ABD	5785	"AD"
						9063		5811	"AD"
6451		7862		6236		7085		7918	
		6555				ABV			
6515		7963	"AI"	6232		9499		5417	
		7962	"AI"	7246				5468	"AD"
6534		5004		7892		8883		7945	
6506		5005		6084 / 8621	"AB"	7518		DOMANEK	
6479		7873		9585	AB	7075		6704	
				5733	"AB"	6629	"AC"	5642	"AE"
6499		9240	"A 6"	7770		9094		5440	
5161	"A"	9241	"A 6"	7233		6096		8032	
	"A"	9264	"A 7"	7420					"A Ev(O)RA 7"
6292		9265	"A 7"	7686		5792	"ACB"	7293	AF
		9306	"A 8"	6026		5788	"ACR"	8808	"AF"
7859		9307	"A 8"			7358	"A R C"	5415	"AF"
		9382	"A 10"			7950		6781	"AF"

No.	Label	No.	Label	No.	Label	No.	Label	No.	Label
5531	"AF"	8798	"AK"	6278		8820	"Annoni"	7421	
7930		7818	AK	8846		8653	"AO"	7236	
9386	"AF K"	9450	AK	5768	"AM"	5692	"AP"	5963	
5451	"AG"	9331		8623		8709		8718	ASB
7351	"AH"	8609	AK						
9507	AH	8671		5979		7405		6668	
8824	"AH"		ÅKERMAN	5974	"AM"				
		7768		5169		9176	PE FEZ	8672	"A.STAF-HELL"
7636	ASH	7767	AL			7336		8676	"ÅSTRÖM"
8366	AH 1727	8397	AL		A:MANZ			9528	
5815	"AI"	6651		5975	"AM G"	7337			
7961	"AI"			8845				7281	
7675		5679	A 1769		"A MOLL"	5958			
6666		7015		5720	"A N"		AQVIS	8710 b)	
			ALBERTI	5080					
9248	"AI A"	6487		9154 B		5577		5646	"AT"
6628 a)	"AIV"	8659	ALM		AN ARFE	5682	"AR 84"	5472	
6693		6687	"ANC"	5832 / 8876	"ARGENT"	7887			
		9157	A Lopcz	5991 / 5992	"AN-GERS"	5684		7082	"AΘENAI"

B

No.	Label	No.	Label	No.	Label	No.	Label	No.	Label
7889		8364		5362	B	8026	"B"	6042	"B"
				5554	B				
7890				8343	B	9580	B	8789	
7891		6277		7502	B	6397		8790	
		5964		5366	B			8791	
7283				6063		6859		8783	
7711			B			6855			
7711			"B"	6076				8784	
7721		8182 / 8188 / 8341	"B"	7176		6424		8785	
9463		6344		7161		5174		8786	
7893				5549		5172		8787	
7894		5548		7215		5176		8788	
6759		7107		7341 / 8748 / 8843	"B"	6054	"B"	7481	
6760		7194		9327 / 9328	"B"	5194	"B?"	9429	
6458				5295	"B"	5202	"Bet..."		
7895		5242						7569	
6760		7167		7749	"B"	6770		9234	
8644				6041	"B"				
7819		7164		8027	"B"	6340		9323	

9324	5535 „B D"	9075	**C**	9403		
7836 „B 4"	5654 „D B H" 1708	7841	5637 „C"	5273		
5376 „BA"		6055 BOR	8220 8222 8228 8271 „C"	7205		
9101 BA	9135 BER	7478 „B P?"	8383 8390 „C"	7049 „C" 7070 „C"		
9100 BR	8684 „BERGS"	7784 BP	9325 „C"	7834 „C" 7837 „C"		
9104 BR	7361 „BERS"	9538 BP		8749 „C" 9326 „C"		
9102 BA	8654 „BFR"		7195	6005		
9105 BR	6072 B	7470 BP	7573	6291		
9103 BR	8838	7771 BREVIG	5364	7776 „C"		
9098	8951 „BH"		7739	7777 „C"		
BARDA	9246 B	9456 B	5056	8031 „C"		
9096 BR ROK	8606 B		6972	8227 8393 „C"		
9097 BARK NONA	5133 BK	9123	6109	8390		
7479 BB	6084 „BI"	BVRG	6384			
7470	6768	9090 B.V	5550	6398		
7477 „BC"	5132 „BK"	9371 BW	5097	6094		
6059	6034 „BK" 5401 „BM" 8885 „BM"	7765 B	9440 „C" 7503 C			

6090	9131 CA2TE	8221 „C C" 8385	9133	7179		
5200	9330 u. 7894	6045 „CC"	9181	7743		
8392		6044 „CC"	9180	8018		
8393 A	8895 CB	8384	8388 „CG"	6628		
5277 B	8435 CFB	6044	6669	6279 „CI M"		
6293 „C"	8939	6152	5734	8984		
9276	7248	5821 „C.C.T"	9548	5752 „CK"		
6804 „C 5"	8358	6674 „CD"	5681 „C H"	9513		
6192 „C 6"	7476	8922 CD	7527 CH	9550		
9252 „C 7"	7289	9054 CD	7921 CH	8013 CL		
9253 „C 7"			9050 „CH"	8014 CL		
7775	6650	8944 CD	7288 CH	7773		
7876 „CA"	8610	7526 C Dey	9088	7581		
9130 IRD	8375	6092	9072	9525		
9187 CAM POS		9142	9588			
6710	6779	CBA RONA	7635 9522	9281		

6319	6757	6744	8593	6938		
6698	7949	9523	6139	6425		
9599		9473	7504 D	9263 „D 1"		
5607	9196		6223 „D" 6268 „D"	9305 „D 2"		
5779 „CM"	9134	5105	6850 „D" 7986 „D"	9381 „D 4"		
7511	7362 „COZ"	5678 „C.WER"	7989 „D" 8750 „D"	7359 „DA"		
7470	5715 „C P" 7254 „CP"	9477	6939	5656 „D B" 1688		
5778 „CMF"	7617		D	6315 „D"	5663 „D B" 1708	
5776	8726 „C·P·A"		„D"	6356 D	6974 DB	
5777	7019 „CR"	6678 „D"		5410 „D B"		
9577	9509 CR	5635 „D"	5319 D	8082		
	5331 „CR"	5272	5507 D	5404 „DC"		
9088 „CM K"	7160		6399 D	8915 „DCC"		
9575	9571 CR	7170 D	5071 D	7958 D.D 8909 „DD" „P"		
6252	9483 CR	9239 „D"	5075 A	5773 „DE"		
8074	7280 CR	7600 D	6206 D	8604		
7939 CN	5638 CRO 6956 7729 C3	5551	6202 D	6349		

5402 DFL	7938 B	7810 „E"	7206	7051		
9288 DG	7285 D·L	8189 bis 8192 „E"	5505	6946		
9497	5736 „DO"	8322 8347	7188	6412		
7411 D.G.	„DOUBLE"	8352		6426		
8350 DH	5134 „DP" 5675 „DP" 1747	5844	9404 E			
6986 BH		7211	5973 „E" 6010 „E"	7567		
6987 BH	5659 DSK 170?	5002	6050 „E" 6194 „E"			
8617	5660 „DSK" 1720	5367 E	6245 „E" 6828 „E"	7811		
9073 RH	5406 „DT"	7976 „E"	7977 „E" 7978 „E"	7971		
6991	5636 DUC	7640	6947	7344 „E 1"		
6992	7522 DVH	5052	8034 „E"	7789 „E 3"		
6993	6124 DW	5072	9581 EA			
5676 DH 1747	8836 DW 6122 DW	7168	5552	9446 EB		
5482 „DI"	7845 DW	7505		7383		
6135	9126 „DX"	5523	6400 E	7387		
5197 DIC	E	5845		5771 „EG"		
7763 DK	„E"	5046	6947	7290		
7937 B	5843 „E" 6442	7216	7055	8953 „E?GO"		

Top-left section

5324 „EH"	9514	F	8420	7368		
6120 EH	5842 6442 7414 „ET"	8193 8195 8197 8354 8855	8394	6401		
8351 EH	8098 „ET"			5472	5066	
8840	6614 ET	7987 „F"	8597	6413		
8841 „EK"	6958 „ET"			9304 „F1"		
8812 „EL"	6958	5614	7364 „F"	9308 „F 1"		
5384 „EM"	5908 ET	5365	7988 „F" 8751 „F" 9238 „F" 9242 „F" 9243 „F"	9380		
8998 EMG	5909 ET	6002		9391 „F 3"		
9195 EN 3150			6955	9262 „F 4"		
6019	6957 „ETR"	9468	6954	6153		
6015	8033	5610	5399 „F"	8650 „FB" 8796 „FB"		
	9193 avan		6346 „F"			
6684	8839 „EW"	5609	9553	8884 FB		
6117 „ES" 8625 „ES" 9256 „ES"	8344 EW	5611	6370	9089 FD		
7330	8665 „EWS"	5612	6360	7302 FB ND		
9095 ESTOR GA	5889 „EXP" 583 M			6669 „FC?" 6709 „FC"		

Bottom-left section

6629 FC	8965 „FIR"	6681 8071	7687	7802 „G" 7802 „G" 8752 8778 „G" 8753 „g"
5714 „FCF"	9374 FK	„F.P.H."	6276 G	
5719 „FCM"	5381	7885 7886	8037 „G"	7797
5718	7286	9127 „FRA DIS"	7801 „G"	
7347 „FF"	7924 FL	8969 „FRT"		8359 „G"
8796 „FF"	7271	8628	5053	
5664 FF 1719	7301	7418	7169 G	6347
5198 „FG"	5389 „FM"	6658	7109 G	8204 „G"
6482 „FH"	9587 „FM"	5534 „FV"	9551	5269 G
5324 „FH"	7940 FO	7927	9487	6358 G
5721 „FH G"	9197	G	6162	5073 G
8645 „FHK"		„G"	5472	5271
9569	FOEN RIOZ	7799 „G" 7967 „G" 8356 „G"		
9124 „F (I)"	5666 FOW	8198 „G" 8203	5492	6371 G
6691 FJ	5667 „FOW 173?"		7174	5067
5288	7425 FP	7601		
8855 „F?IB?"				

Top-right section

6799	7388 G.B.S	7925 G	6771 „GRM"	7812 „H"
6795	7242	5123	8641	8206 8213 8215 8367
8036	5396 „GC"	8950	9595	„H"
6427	7943 GCM	8983 „GIS"	7935	8371 8372 8374
8872 „G" Schlüssel-bart(?)	7807 „GD"	7307 GK	7847	
8775 „G" Schlüssel-ring	8941	5387 „GL"	7868 7869	6001
9598 GV	5394 „GD"	9481	9311	7196
7823 „G 2"	5388 „GD B"	6189	8954	7212
7824 „G 2"	7410 GDC	5409	8795 GT	7574
9216 „G 3"	7407 GGC	5408 „GL"	7480 GV	
9217 „G 3"	7392 7356 „GM"	8787		8369
7356 „GA" 6737 „GA G"	7469	6663	5662 „GVH"	5437
5831 Garni 5661 „GB"	8924	6158	5746	5425
7310 GB		6536 „GP"		8370 „H"
7389	7470	6971	H	8587
7408 GBAC	9132	7746 GR KEUR	7791 „H"	8594
	GVMN	8858	7099 „H"	8360 „H"

Bottom-right section

7162	6842	7267	5880 „HF" 6153 „HF"	8952
8216 „h"	6838	5818	8837	5743 HIS
8214 „h"		„HA"	IWP	8683 „HK"
6033 „H" 6101 „H" 6167 „H" 6806 „H"	6428	8363 AB	7261 HG	9298
6879 „H" 6962 „H"	7816 „H 1"	7624 „HAD?"	5373	8615
7800 „H" 7803 „H" 7805 „H"	7790 „H1" 7817 „H 1"	5820 „HB"	9087 HGO	6040
5226	7345 „H 2"	9070 IB	9003 „HH"	8800 „HL"
	7346 „H 2"	8084	9442	9515
6372	9259	5135	7309 HH	5582 „HLH"
6385 „H"	8016	ICB	5787 „HHG"	9556 HZS
6361 „H"	6674 „HA" 6767 „HA" 6766 „HA"	7623 CB V	9603	8611 „HM" 6240 „HM"
6402	7266	5232	8821	7514
5074	6685	9049 9048	9505	9495
7263 H	6674	9466		9335
		8988		
	7993 HFISIG	9052	8433 „HN"

8637 „HN"

7250 (HS mark)

7740 (mark)

6348 (mark)

6717 (IAR mark)

5378 „IH" B

5812 „IH"

7349 „IH"

6027 (mark)

5657 „IK" 1697

7234 (IM mark)

6674 „JOR" A

5403 „IP"

5148 (mark)

9125

„HONDA"

9384 „HT"

8218 „I"

6354 (mark)

7350 (IAW mark)

7225 (IH mark)

6715 (mark)

7593

7594 „IL"

8632 „JL"

5807 „IL"

7252 (IMFB mark)

7956 „IM H"

6180 „IP"

6714 „IP" b)

8651 „HP"

8636 „HP"

8935 (HV mark)

7207 (I mark)

6403 (mark)

5653 „JB"

8643 „JB"

6815 IAB

7229 (mark)

6752 (mark)

7947 (II mark)

7313 (mark)

8445 „JP"

9412 (IP mark)

9552 (IP mark)

9332 (IP mark)

9475 (M mark)

7663 (II mark)

6386 (mark)

6187 (mark)

8801 (IB mark)

8811 (IB mark)

7295 (mark)

8866 (mark)

5119 (mark)

7533 (IL mark)

9249 „I MK"

9408 (mark)

9554 (HR mark)

5658 „HR 04"

7677 (HVB mark)

8096 „HW"

9385 „HW"

9428 (mark)

7554 (mark)

6183 (mark)

8802 (IB mark)

8639 (IB mark)

8925 (IM mark)

5665 (JH 1723 mark)

5795 „IIO"

5680 „IIS"

7516 (mark)

5668 (ML29 mark)

7730 (IP mark)

7299 (JP mark)

8999 (HR mark)

7228 (HW mark)

8663 (HW mark)

5988

6082

6144 „I"

6297

7821

7825 „J"

8758 „J"

6414 (mark)

6429 (J mark)

8620 „JB"

9536 (JB mark)

9051 (mark)

5120 (HK mark)

5680 „IIS"

7524 (IL mark)

7957 (IW mark)

7946 (IW mark)

7Ὁ.4

5405 „IP"

6662 (M mark)

8817 (HS mark)

9373 (HS mark)

9405 (I mark)

7568 (mark)

9536 (JB mark)

8642 (JB mark)

5785 „I HR"

5391 „IK"

8437 „IK"

5650 „IK"

9591 (ILM mark)

5686 „IM"

8616 (IN mark)

5669 (INR 1723 mark)

5260 (JP mark)

9485 (ISI mark)

7115 (i mark)

5774 „IA"

5187 (IA mark)

9606 (B mark)

7314 (mark)

7948 (IM mark)

7101 „INS"

7101 „INVS"

7244 (IP mark)

5325 „IP"

8099 (ISI mark)

6626 „I"

7817 „I"

7189 (i mark)

9605 (AB mark)

6716 „JB"

5588 „IHS"

9593 (IK mark)

5131 (M mark)

5471 „IO"

8432 (IPB mark)

9035 (IS mark)

7213 (mark)

8598 (I mark)

8856 (IAC mark)

6254 (mark)

6630 (IHS mark)

6121 (IK mark)

5769 „IK"

9383 (IM mark)

6994 (O mark)

7300 „I OM"

8989 (IIS mark)

8217

8378 „J"

5063 (VI mark)

7423 (JAG mark)

8060 JAR

6705 (mark)

5688 (II mark)

8017 (MI mark)

6180 (IK mark)

7257 (IM mark)

5786 „I OM"

6180 „IPK"

7519 (mark)

6683 (mark)

8380 „IE"

6147 „IE"

7015 (IFB mark)

6808 „II"

6941 (K mark)

8805 (mark)

9503 (IC8 mark)

6985 (E mark)

7014 (IFB mark)

5766 „IG"

5825 (mark)

6765 (mark)

7531 (ICH mark)

7247 (IE mark)

7235 (mark)

8652 „K"

8857 (IBC mark)

6999 (ICR mark)

7954 (E mark)

6689 (IF mark)

6536 (mark)

6680 (IR mark)

7279 (JS mark)

7249 (mark)

7181 (mark)

6349 (B mark)

6708 (JB mark)

5418 „ID"

8337 (ID mark)

9517 „J.E."

6231 (IFD mark)

6697 (mark)

5687 „IBD"

9179 „I BENA BENTE"

8373 (ID mark)

6148 „IE"

6771 JFF

6996 (IGB mark)

5791 „I GD"

7243 (IR mark)

5783

5648 / 5649

6652 (mark)

9461 (mark)

9566 (IEB mark)

6695 (mark)

6699 (mark)

5790 „IGD"

5648 „IS"

8634 „IS"

6701 (mark)

6724 „IE B"

6735 (JF mark)

5521 „IGE"

8662 „JS"

7312 (ISH mark)

7806 (mark)

7653 (K mark)

8901 (mark)

I-BOSSARD

5188 „IDC"

5793 „IDK"

5753 „IE K"

7010

7520 (IGF mark)

9388 (IS mark)

7744 (K mark)

5590 (mark)

6716 „JB P."

8862 „ID M."

7308 (IET mark)

5705 „J.F"

5257 „JFS"

9583 (IFS mark)

7844 (IGG mark)

9290 (IS mark)

9531 (B mark)

5589 „K"

8589 K

6373 (mark)

7444 „IC"

5677 „IC"

9338 „ID P."

6700 (mark)

8612 (mark)

6275 (IGH mark)

9337 „IG L."

8794 (IS mark)

7523 (IST mark)

7824 „K"

7190 (K mark)

5068 (mark)

6196 (IC mark)

7529 (ID R mark)

8822 (mark)

8813 „IFB"

6722 „JF B."

8336 (JJ mark)

9372 (IG T mark)

5685 „IGS"

7951 (IS mark)

7953 (ISW mark)

5398 „IT"

8219

8223

8226

8229 „K"

7208 (K mark)

6057 (mark)

8016 „ICB"

7528 (ID R mark)

5114 „IG"

6147 „IG"

6280 „IG"

8657 IG

9527 (IGZ mark)

3147 IH"

7304 (JS mark)

7305 (JS mark)

9188 (IU LORI CO mark)

8232

8379

8391 „K"

7191 (K mark)

6061 (mark)

7534 (ICB mark)

5651 (IE mark)

7012 (IFB mark)

7253 (IS mark)

8823 (KV mark)

8381 „K"

6851

9214 „K"

9218 „K"

6940 (mark)

6430

7282 „KA"

7287 „KA"

9420 „KB"

5371 „K"

„D"

7510 KH

6180 „KI"

8137 KIOV

6180 „KIP"

7016 KIRSTEIN

7008 KRUG

L

„L"

9215 „L"

8233

8238
8240
8241
8242
8244
8401
8403
8405
8406
8408 „L"

5048

7182

7689

9273

5361

6208

8595

7741

6017

8243 „l"

8239 „l"

7462 „L"
7465 „L"
8754 „L"

6953

8045 „L"

5426

6374

8042

8038

9273

6431

5399
5402

8040

8044

8041

9602

7275

5400 „L AD"

5332 „LB"

9213 13 Adler „LB"

5081

5470 „L·D"

6179 „l.d."

7042

9155 „lcon"

9158 LEONI 13

6653

5471 „L·F"

8809 „LF"

7040 L GUI TOU

7674

6218 L·H

8422

6761

6646

6541

6546

6547

6688 „LL"

7073

6653 LL

5386 „LM"

6227 „L.M."

8816 M

6176 LM

5823 LM

8399

9136

6714 „LR"

8996 „LR"

L.M.HOLM

LORP

5819 „LR"

7917 LR

6679 LR

6714

7970 „LT"

5395 „LT"

7447 „LV"

9137 LVIS

7933 LW

7931 LW

7932 LW

5411 „LW" A

7006 LZ

5747

9177 LZNA

6840

6204

6844

6021

5229

8043

7512

M

„M"

5450 „M"
5744 „M"
6342 „M"
8624 „M"
8842 „M"

8245 bis 8251 8253 8254 8424 „M"

7379 h „M"

7198

5615

5180 M

7466 „M"

6230

5192 B „M"

5521

5275

8590

6238

8596

6225 „M"
6307 „M"
7467 „M"
7578 „M"
5322 „M?"

9601 M

8991 „M"

9590

6350

6375

6387 M

7416 MAC

6404 M

5075 B

6359 M

7032 M

7036 M

6432

7044

6216 1760

5576 „M" B

8602 M3

9225 „M 5"

9224 „M 5"

6220 „MA"

7315 MA

7416 MAC

9164 „MAIO RCA"

9166 „MAI ORCA"

9165

8022 Vicnna

9116

MARTIN

8608 „MB"

8607 MB

9254

6665

6665 M*B

7808 „MB H"

5249 M

5412 M·D

5781 „MD"

7356 C 7394 „MDA"

7589 „ME"

8701 NE

8605

6756

9501 MF

8073

9255

8688 „MHB"

5737 „MHH"

9469 M

5745 „M I"

6770 M JG G"

7582 MK

9310 „MK"

7515 MK

7944 „ML" h)

6185

5587 „MM"

5673 „MM 175?"

8835 MN

5250 „MO"

8252 „MO"

8062

6323

6249

8834 MZ

5459 „MP"

7809 „MP"

7764 MP A

8613 MP

6263

7486 MP

6259

8059 MR

9573 MRH

5377 „MS"

7393 „MS"

7470 E

7209

5748 M

5149 A M

9161 1712 MVNOZ

6250

6234

N

„N"

„N"

7963 B

8255 bis 8263 H

8426

8430

8436 H

8439

5049

5613 N'

8618 „N"

5317

7171

7209

5054

8335 N

N

5998 „N"
8755 „N"
8756 „N"
8916 H „N"

7406 N B

9223 „N 2"

7024

„N"

5064 N

6405 N

6376 N

5069 N

6257 N

6261 N

9299

7985 13 N

7398 B „NA"

7409 NA

7404 NA

7402 NAP 716

7399 NAP

7403 NAP 120

7401 NAP 702

7400 NAP

7398 B NAP

7398

8614

8398 NB

5128 MB

6667

7397 B NTC

9189 „NCA (L)AD?"

8437 „NH"

6285

5414 ND

6627 ND

8409 „N.Dahl"

5696 NE

5695

5697 „NEV"

5671 NF

7884 R

6346 „NG"

7926 NS

5382 „NG"

6726

7412 „NSC"

6725 NG

8997 „NHM"

8666 NL

5491 NL

7374 NT

8923

8434 NO

6283 NA

6284 NAP

6979 NR

6980 NR

6981 NR

6982 NR

8963 NR

„NR D"

7638

7178 NS

7292 NS

7210

7656

7192 O

7733 NB

9544 NS

9464 NB

5525 „NV?"

8918 W

8919 W

8920 W

„O"

5011

5008

5010

8264 8323 bis 8328 8440 „O"

O

O

7691 O

7610 S.XVII .7608

7774 „O"

7576

6588 O

6406 O

7541

5224 O

6830

6834

6415 O

7632

8851

7659 O

7178 O

7210 O

7656 O

6772	7992 OS	7122	6407	9296 „P 3"		6797	Q	8266 „R"	5062	6857
5009	9174	7120	6389	9297 „P 3"		6178 „P. t."	„Q"	7184	6390	6130 Lilie
8395 O3	8345 Ow			9342 „P 4"		9540	7183	5151	6317	6131 „RF"
9121		5443	5427 5433	9343 „P 4"		7705 „PV 1610"	7692	6975		7311
	P	6801	6133	8103 „P 10"		7706 „P.V. 1611"	8685	5057	6321	8814 „RH"
8365 OF	9401 „P"	7604	6137	9221 „P 11"		7707 „P.V. 1612"	7670	6836	6417	5616
8690 „OHB"	7199	9434	6433	9430		7697 „P V"	8599	6823	6434	9074
6994	7180	8757 „P"	6416	7273		7698 „P V 1606"	5070	6975	9415 „R 4"	6703
9511	9489	9402 „P"	6436	8648 „P·A·H"		7700 „P V 1607"	6408	5001	9416 „R 4"	7230 „RL"
8415 „O.L"	8265 „P"	6950	6439 40	5959		7699		9272 „R"	9286 „R 6"	5704 RM
8416 OLD	9312 P	8068 „P"	6441	6529		7701 „P V 1608"	6363	6355 „R"	7232 RB	6671
8414 OLA	9312 P	8068	6441	6252 „PB"		7726		5707	6658 RB	6819
6988	8066 P	5061	7011	5251 „PB"		7704 V 1610	R	6377	7269 RC	6861
9118 „OO"	8067		6973	8807 PB			„R"		7738 RD	6832
8065	7764	8729	9421 „P 1"	8622 PB		8719 PW	9271 „R"	6409	6675 „RDC"	6815 O A
6310 OR	9313	6362	9368 „P 2"	8674 Halbmond		5772 PWP	8267 „R"	6364	7303 „R D H H"	7440 „ROMA"
	5424		9369 „P 2"	„PB"						

6729	6690 GE	9564	5106 „PM"	6786 PP „EYA"		6023	7827 „S"	7172	7785	8975
5653	9400	8633 „PIZ"	6743 „PMB"	8844 „PR"		9125 „RONDA"	7848 „S"	8167	6435	8976
5390 „PC"	5374 „PF"	9247	6721 „PM B"	8660 „PR"		S.307 „RS"	7828	8170	6942	8977
6730 „P C"	6674 F&B	9274 PK	6740 6741	5094		6105	7780	7829		5708 „SA"
5292 „PC"	5452 „PG"	7627 PK	5822 „PM G"	5093		5152	7831		6103	9043 SA
6758	6659 „PG"	7455 PL				7251 RS	7830	8279 „)"	6107	5644
7417 PD	6655 „PG"	7276 PL	6253	8063		7030	7693 S	8284 „)"	5397 „S"	7043
9413 PD	7769 PGA		9275 „PN"	9444 P9R		9122 „RS" „A??"	7833 S	5482 „S" 7050 „S" 8759 „S"	„S"	7045 SAMSON
8891 PD	8689 „PH"	7272	5608	8083		S	7832 S	8075		7045
6712 PD	5689 PH	7277	6983	8669 „PS"		„S"		6943	9365	8658 „SAUTER"
	9452		7356 „PP"	7306 PS		S.121 „S"	7177 S		9366 SA	8061
6645 PDN	9546 PH	6197	7356 7395 7934 „PP"	6977 PS		7836 „S" 8949 „S"	5050	5225	9367	8061 SB
7702 „PDVF 1608"	8630 PH	6880 „PLS"	6786 „PP"	5088 „PS"		5767 „S"	7781	6378	9504	7297 SC
9119 DRO	8723 PH	7041 TOV	6852	7607 „PS"		8268 8273 8275 8277 8280 8281 8283 8285 8288 „S"	5142 S		8972	7296 SC
9120 PGDNO	7265	6198 EV	7356 „PPA"	5780		8291 8442 8443 8694	7202 S	6391	8973	9427
	6673 „PJB"	5407 „P M"	7298 P·A·M	6998 PS			7203 S	5318	8974	8931 „SCH" 6774

Upper left quadrant

No.		No.		No.		No.		No.	
7772		8655	"SICKMAN"	7294		7452	SUL	8008	
8803		5743	"SIH"	5076	"ST"	7453	SUL	8010	
8804		7970	"SK"	5253	"ST"	7454	SUL	8102	
8097	"SG"	7274				9287		7185	
5617		8619	"SL"	8670	STAF HELL	9004		7688	
6871		9607		7003	STAHL			7057	
6869		7992	"SO"	5710		7284		6418	
5784	"SH"	6874	SOM	7450		9579	SW	7222	
8085	SH	9162	SOPU ERTA	8463	"Stockholm"	8638	"SY"	8591	
8086	"SH"	6020	"SP"	7007	STRAVS			8431	
9542		7437	"SP"	8678	"STRÖM"	8005	"T"	8361	
8852		5645		5672	STS 1756	9375	"T"	6068	"T"
5775	"SI(?)"	7439	"SPQR"	9425		8292	"T"	6115	"T"
6039		7438	"SPR"	7451	SUL	8298	"T"	6214	"T"
8410	SIB	5717	SR	7455	SUL	8696		7063	"T"
		9407	SR			7571		8760	"T"
		5090				8009		8964	"T"
		6880	S*S D			8007		5298	"T"
								5518	"T"

Upper right quadrant

No.		No.		No.		No.		No.	
8305 / 8306 / 8309 / 8313		5536		5127	"VE"	5127			W
6343	"V"	5076	"V"	7842		7804	"VR"		"W"
7572		6366		7483		7826	"VR"	8304 / 8307 / 8308 / 8310	
9198	"V"			7919		9329	"VR"	8312 / 8314 / 8316	"W"
7651		6392		8818		9244	"VR"	8702 / 8711 / 8712 / 8713	
5522		6380		7477		7990	"VR"		
7163		7555		7840		8991	VRI	5770	"W"
7165		6419		7883				7613	
7173		5076	17 V 49	7881				5058	
7186		5245	"V"	9057	VHB	7882		7668	
7557		5782	"VA"	7517	VHK	5368		8601	
8362		9178	"VAENA"	7676		9076		7000	
6813	"V"	5083	"VC"	8629				7001	
9199	"V"	5091	"VC"	7678		7923		8712	"W"
7487		9558				5248	"VW"	5145	"W" mit Krone
		5436	"VD"	9138	"vm"	9020			

Lower left quadrant

No.		No.		No.		No.		No.	
5520		7260		7259		9173	"TOL"	7200	
5516		8680		8680	"THOME"	7020		7204	
6365		8064		7258		7021		7664	
6410		8917	"TE"	9529		7022		7193	
6379		6610		7264		7023		5182	
7461		5902		9370		7053		7166	
9437		5900		7034		5667		8600	
9220	"T 2"	6608		5385	"TM"	9562	"TP"	8697	
9423		7241		7038		5652	"TS"	6411	
9424		7245		5392	"TM"	7507		8092	"U 1"
9191		6989	"TF"	5670	TMW 1723	6123		8093	"U 1"
5372	"TB"	8960		9175				8396	U 3
8819	"T·B"	7888		6625				8717	U n
6974	"TB. fe"	5378	"T G"	7024	TOI			8080	"U 4"
		6657				8299		8094	"U 5"
		7268	"TH"			8303 / 8697 / 8700	"U"	7066	"V"

Lower right quadrant

No.		No.		No.		No.		No.	
5816		7857		7256	WS	5981		8318	"Y"
5817		8024	"Warsavie"	7255	WS	5977		7690	"Y"
8992		9336	WB	7291	W·W	6944		7625 / 7626	"Y"
8994		6984	"WD"			6420		7080	"Y"
8993		5655	"WF S 169?"		X	8890		9426	
9002		8646	HK	6312	"X"	8914	"XID"	6381	
7851				7095	"X"	9334		6394	
7850		7270	WI	5047		9192		6070	
7852		5724 / 5725	Wiborg	5059			Y	6074	
		7002	WIRZ	5055			"Y"		
7849		9608	W&O	5510	"X"	6182	"Y"	5545	
		7915		7096		8317 / 8715	"Y"		
7853		7240	WR	6945		5183		5543	
7854		8626	WRK	6367		7570			
7858		8627	WRK	6393		5274	"Y"	6421	

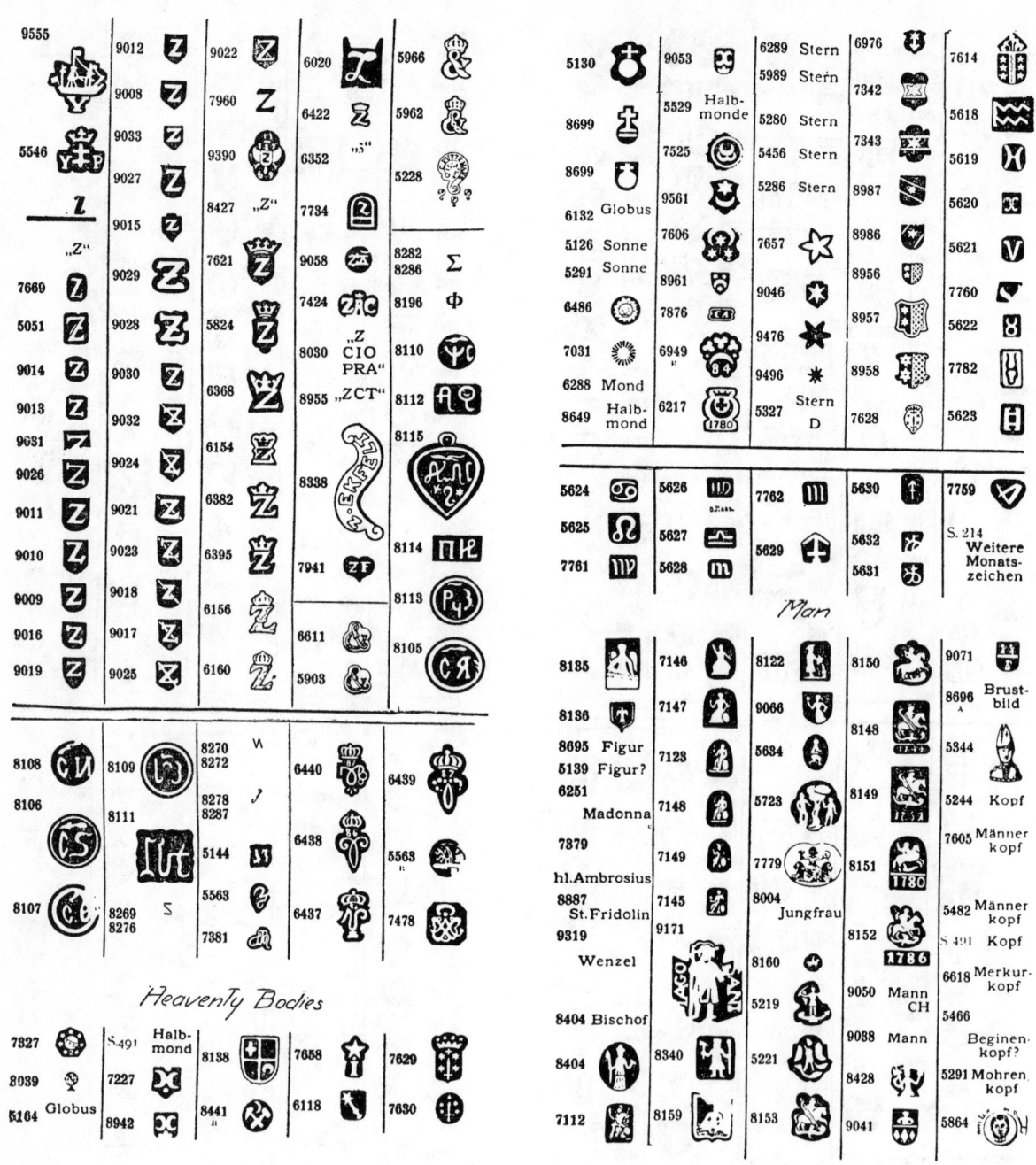

Heavenly Bodies

Man

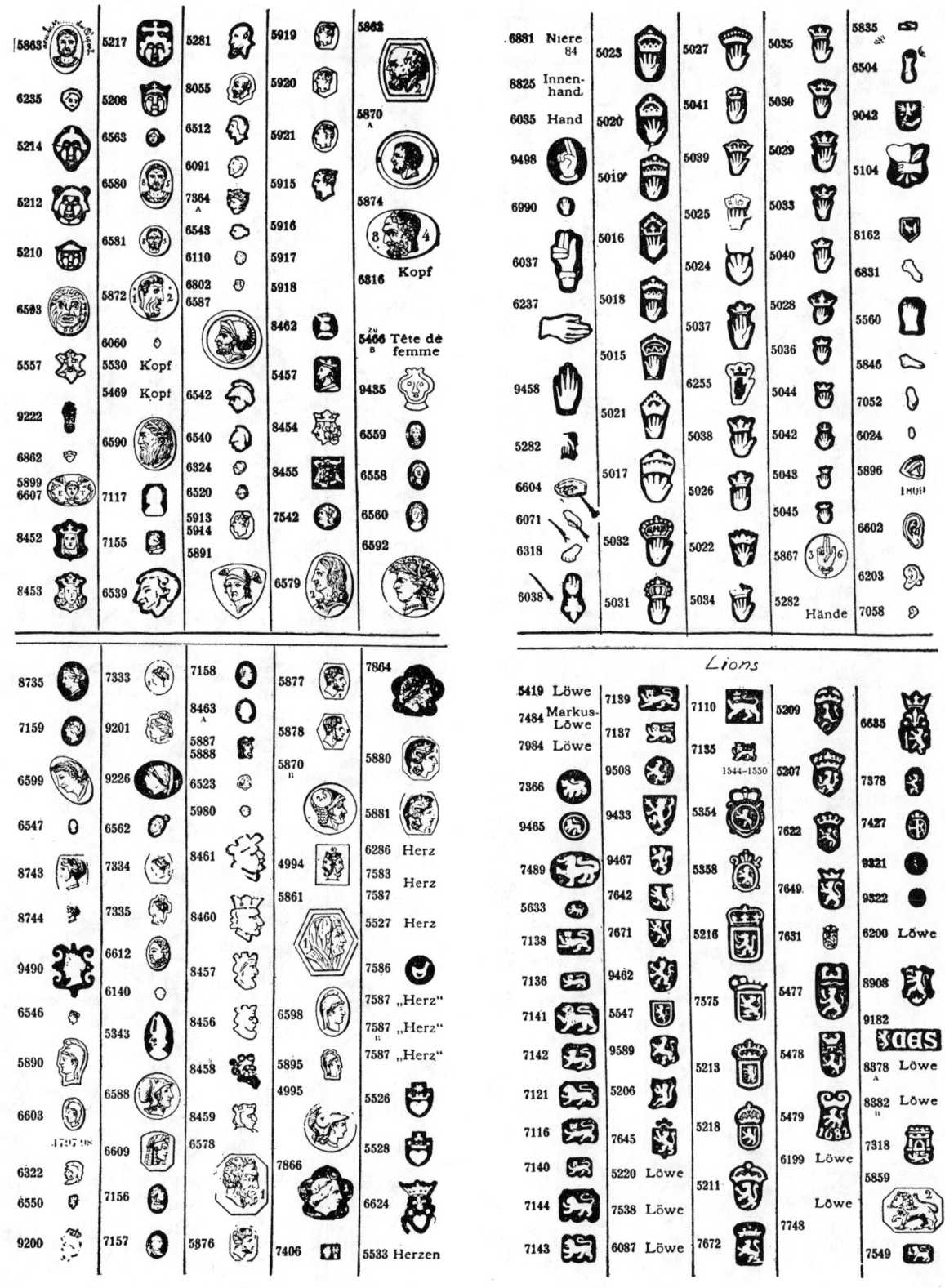

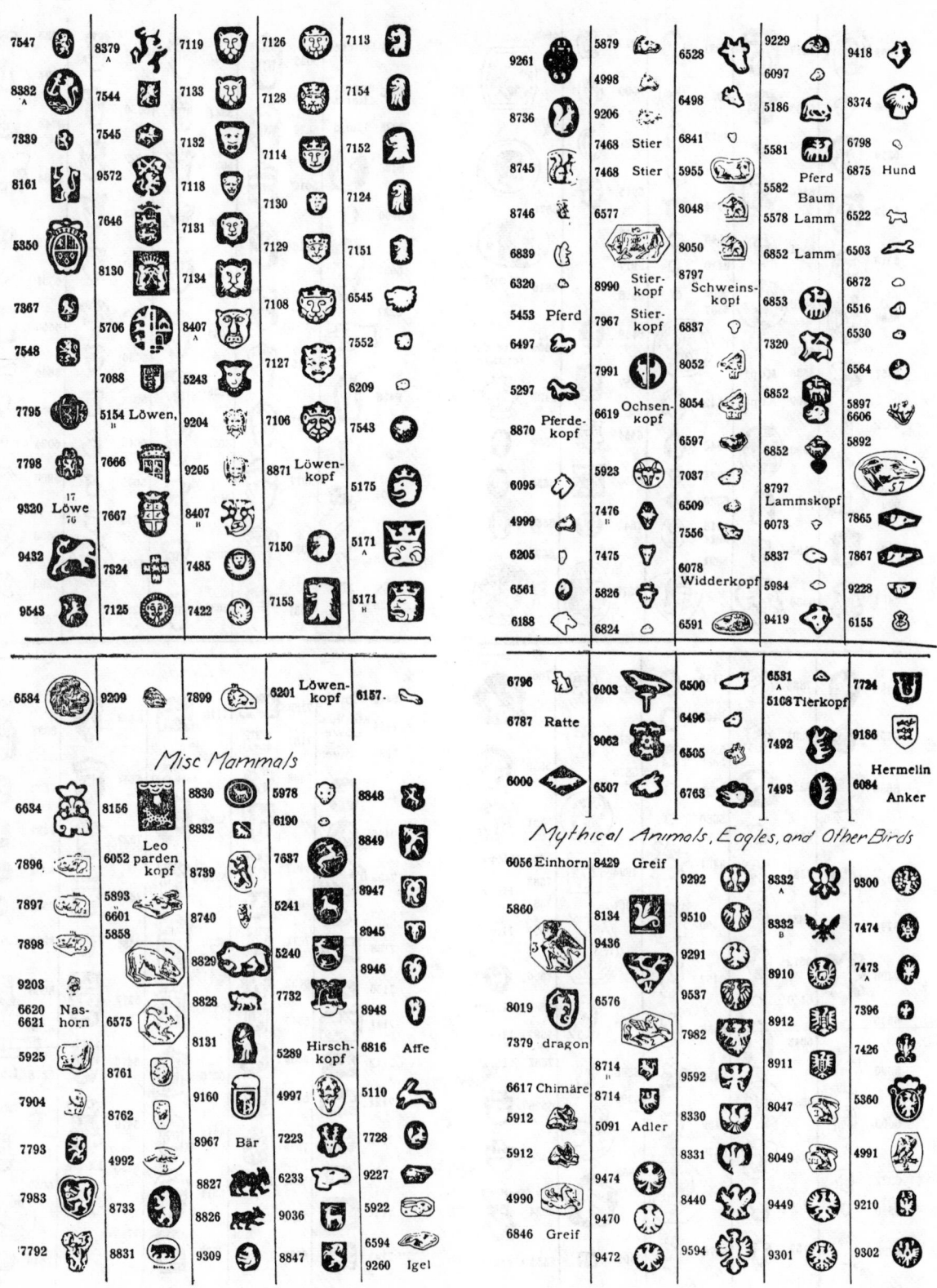

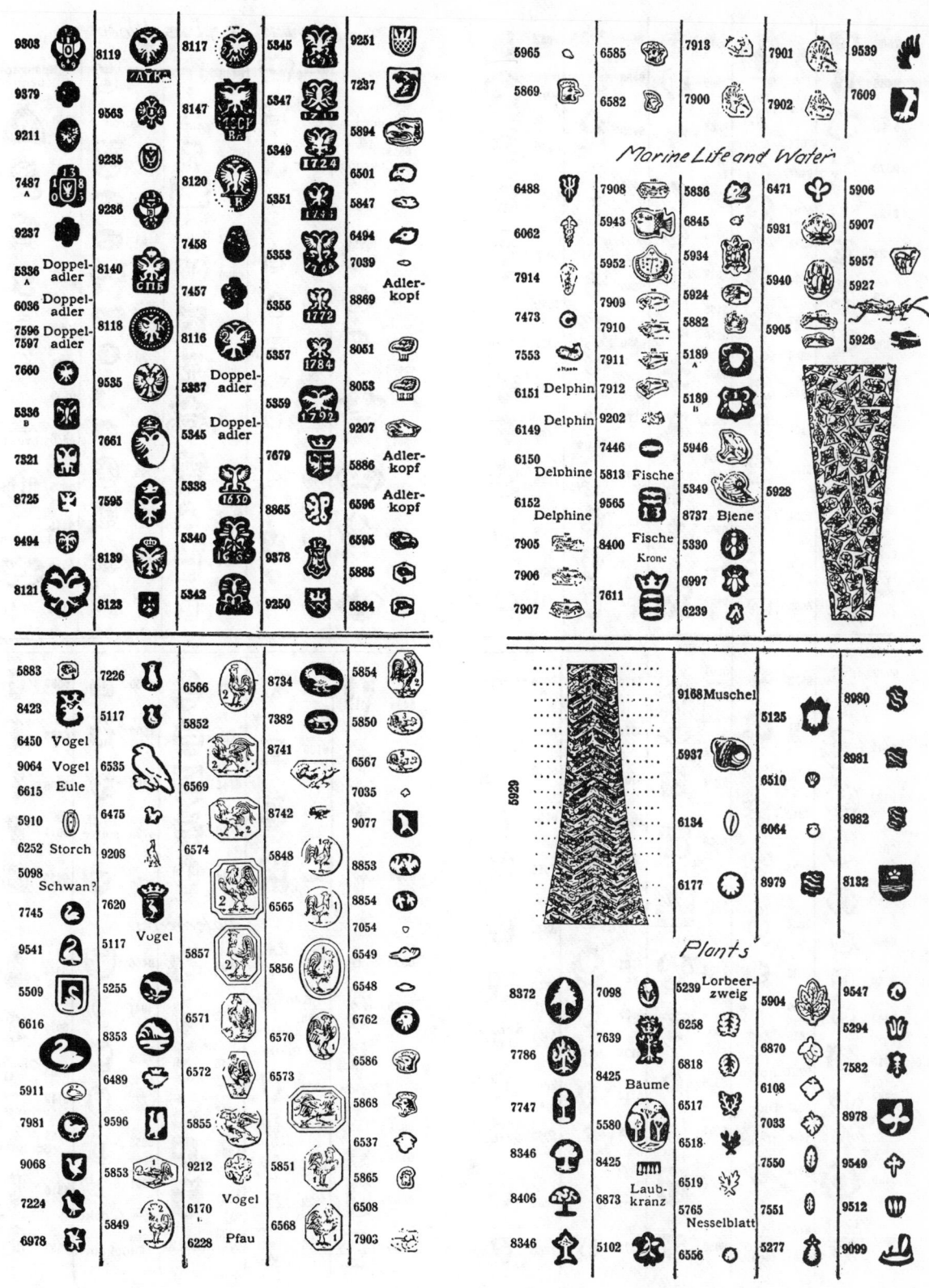

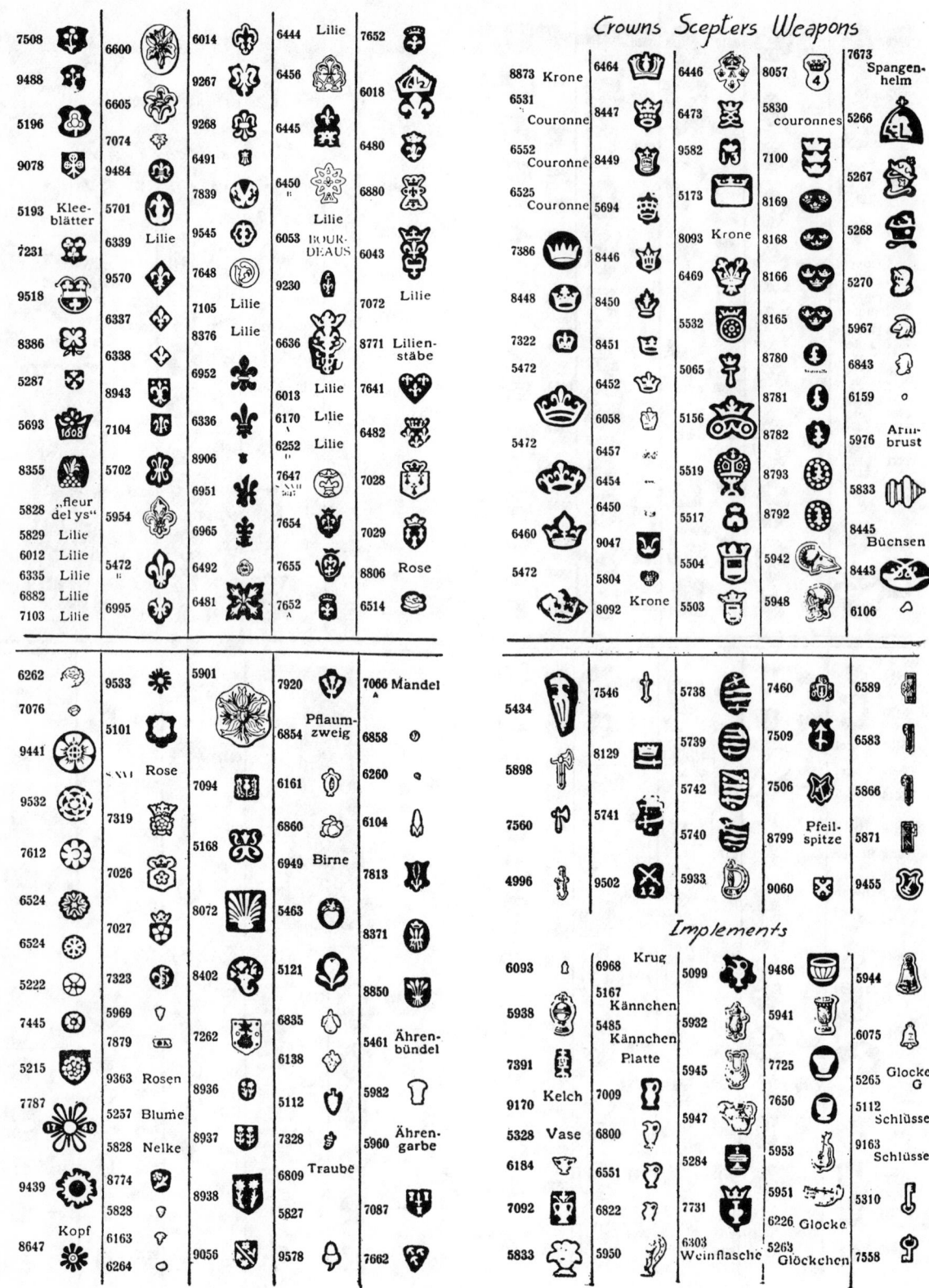

Top left block

5307 | 8874 Schlüssel-stiel(?) „G" | 7998 | 6111 Uhrschlüssel | 9387 | 13
5308 | 5732 Schwert Schlüssel | 7644 | 6856 | 5246 Rost
9506 | 8694 | 7433 | 6272 | 6513
5750 | 5730 | 7434 | 6273 | 6153 Sensen
— | 5731 | 7436 | 6271 | 5230
5751 | 9431 | 7432 | 6270 | 9040
5994 Schlüssel | — | 7431 | 9034 | 5256 Striegel
— | — | 7499 | 7490 | 9443
5312 | 8968 | 7500 | 7491 | 9453
5314 | 7997 | 7498 | 9600 | 9069
8720 | 8930 | 7496 | 5293 | 5433
5316 | 8412 | 7497 | 8704 | 8021
8721 | 8411 | 7495 | 8703 | 8436
— | 8412 | 7494 / 7435 | 8705 | 7086 / 7443

Top right block

6006 Stuhl | 7238 | 7025 Triumph-wagen | 6089 Pflug-schar | 5456
6181 Trag-korb | 6256 Destillier-Apparat | 5930 | 6696 | 5472
6028 Vogel-bauer | 7380 | | 9580 |

Architecture

5200 B Haus / 5195 Haus | 9445 | 7750 | 7535 | 7371
7093 | 7090 | 7751 | 5514 | 9398
8727 | 7056 | 9397 | 7370 | 8101
8728 | 8133 | 9395 | 5441 | 9399
6029 Turm / 7316 Turm / 8005 Turm / 6287 Turm / 5278 Turm | 9194 | 9394 | 5442 | 8025
5935 | 5472 | 9396 | 7369 | 7340 Türme
9480 | 7753 | 7749 B Turm | 5515 | 9451
8438 H | 7752 | 9316 | 7372 | 9482
| 8438 A | 9316 | 7373 | 9258

Bottom left block

8146 | 5113 | 7579 | 9280 | 6207
8145 | 5810 | 5449 | 5290 Post-horn | 6820
8143 | 5579 | 5279 Hammer | 7643 | 8125
8141 1746 | 7488 | 5136 | 7922 | 7843
8142 1760 | 7091 | 8940 | | 9067 Rinke
9144 | 5838 | 8441 Hämmer | 5936 | 5158 Brillen-zeichen
6085 Drei-master | 5840 | 9364 | 8158 | 5159
5711 | 5839 | 8921 | 6553 | 5165 Brillenz.
5713 | 5841 | 7059 Maurer-kelle | 6794 Turban | 5157
8711 | 4993 | 8843 | 6077 | 6022
5712 | 6240 Baßgeige | 5103 | 6833 / 6186 / 6136 | 5939
7994 | 5095 | 7846 | 6146 | 5956
7326 | 5490 | 5166 | 6119 Hand-schuh | 5993 Ball-schläger
7089 | 7329 / 7580 | 8341 | 5834 / 6219 Schleife | 6046 Kork-zieher / 9045

Bottom right block

5589 Türme / 7083 Türme / 8418 Türme | 8859 | 5603 | 8377 Türme | 9317 Stadtmauer
7317 | 9219 | 5705 Drei Türme / 5604 | 8089 Tor | 9038 Gitter
7097 | 9568 | 5596 | 8012 | 9277 „Pyra-mides"
9567 | 9598 1725 | 5593 1639 | 8090 | 8126
8367 | 5597 1721 | 5594 | 9156 | 9257
7981 | 5599 1711 | 5592 | 8091 | 9278
7982 | 5601 1763 | 5595 | 9340 | 9279
8418 | 5600 1736 | 5606 | 9341 | 5509
9339 | 5605 | 5591 | 5585 | 5314 Staut-mauer
8124 | 5576 | 9318 Staut-mauer | 9604
5439 | 5602 1767 | 5591 | 9315 1686 | 7972
8860 | 8011 Stadttor | 9417 | 7973 / 9516 / 7815

7814   9277 „Saulen"   5963   5129   9169 Grab

Crosses

5756	5154	8900	9557	7598	
5192	6754	9086	9283		7599
9478	6753	croix	9284	étoile	
9559	6246				7561
9438	5137	8959	9285		
5014	6829 / 8747 / 8833	7469 Kreuz	9231		7562
5013	8764	7471			
9524	8765		9282	7563	
5758	9457	9491			
9584			5544	7564	
5759	8391				
5760	8955	9044	5542	7566	
5299	8772	9085	5541	7565	

8894	9526	5339	6887	8913	
8767	7788		6886	9377	
8769	9574	5346	6901	9376	
8768	9576			7602	
8766	5754	5348	6884	5283	
8770	5757		6890		
6227 Schild	5755	5352	6892	7239	
7605 Pfahl	9007			9479	
7608	7736	7685	6897	8702	
	7737	7686	6889		
8899	9586	6888		8907	
5422	7472	6891	7681	9190	
5421	9092	6885	7684	8861	
5421	7856		7683	6083 2Punkte	
5423	6482	6894	7682	7397	
				8730	
5642 3 Pfähle Kreuz	7665	6900	5259	7754 Sieben Punkte	

Trade Marks

8631 Hausmarke	8707	9519	9460	7513	
6967	7722	9037	5700	5493	
9471		6970	7221	9289	
	9493	8706			
8721	9447	5643	8708	9459	
5086	9448	9492	5641	5698	

Shields and Geometrical Forms

5192 Wappenschild	5341	9080	5309	9270	
6713		7723	5315	9269	
6882	8889	9059		6226 Schild	
9061	9082	9233	5356	8933	
6808	9083	7870		8932	
7712	9084		7855	8970	
6883	9005	5311	9294	8971	
7727	9081	5313	9295	8905	

Numbers

6780 Zahlen	7616	8 E	6100 13	6899	6922
6780 Zahlen	6817		6221 13	6895	6913
8903 0,900			5970 13* / 5971 13*		
			8995 13	6905	
7463	6821			6930	6923
7559	9093 „9 D"		7794 13	6931	6909
7618 2/Z	7384	11	7820	6934	6910
7871	6222	12	7796		6921
	5972	12*		6933	6924
7619	7757	12	6898	6932	6919
	5257		6893	7459	
6793 „3 P"	7875				6916
7735	8867		6918	6920	6914
8056	7974		6902	6912	
7835 „B 4"	7979 „12·| / 7980 „13·|	6896		
8095 „U 5"	8020 „13"		6915	6917	6908
6328 8 / 6866 8	9330 „13"				

6911	[mark]	7758	[20]	6165	42	6295	63	6008	76
		7878	[mark]	6327	43	6790	64	6877	76
6906	[mark]	8173	.20 K"	5997	47	7068	64*	6788	77
				6114	49		64	6959	78
				6812	49	5444		6125	79
6903	[mark]	6936	20 K	6325	50			6031	79
				5555		5162	..64"	6211	80
6907	[mark]	8650	..21 K"	5255	..50"	5168		6780	..80"
						6961	..65"	5524	81
6904	[mark]	6049	23	5556	..51"	5077	[65]		
		8172	..23 K"			6127	..66"	6789	81
9582	[mark]	6047	24			6242		6805	81
		6048	25	5227	[mark 31]	5257	..67"	6193	82
		6086	27					6960	82
7975	[mark]	7048	29			6213	67		82
		6086	30	6296	52	6304	68	5446	
8421	[13N]	6067	31	6326	52	6171	69	6126	..83"
		6086	31	7069	53	6243	69		
6098	14	6267	32	5995	55	6305	71	8023	[84]
6099	14	6827	33	6244	55				
6280	15	7046	33	6306	56	5163	[mark 71]	5079	[84]
8603		7047	34	6112	56(57)?	5169			
[15 Löd]		6065	35	6810	56*(?)			8157	[84*]
		7062	35	5996	57	5320	..72"	5276	..85"
6849	16			6173	57	6172	..72"	5294	..85"
6081	17			6803	59	7079			
6847	17	7375	[mark]			5078	[mark 72]	6212	..85"
6848	17			5256	..60"				
6079	18	6066	36	6009	60	5321	..73"	7755	[87]
6080	18	6166	36	6113	60	6007	73	5524	87
		6265	37	6294	60	6865	73		
8174	..18 K"	6266	38	6811	60*	6876	73 (?)	7077	87
		6825	38	6878	60*	5987	75	6863	88
6935	18/6	6826	39	5468	61	6030	75(?)	5985	90
		7060	40	7067	61*(?)			5428	..96"
6143	19	6164	41	6032	62*	5445		5437	
6141	20	7061	41	5147	..63"		76		
6142	20								

7385	[91.]	7078	94	6927	[Xld 129]	9293	[H/56]	7872	
		6864	95			5257	1760	[mark]	
		6191	96					7464	[1805]
5447	91	5986	98	6928	[Xld 129]	5703	[1763]	7874	
		7756	[99]			7870	[1774]	[1824]	
5429	[mark] 91	6926	[Xld 129]	6929	[IId 129]	7958	[793]	8902	.[1891]
5437									

Note that the marks shown on pages 373-387 are of all European countries except Germany. They have been classified according to character only, no distinction being made as to locality. However, they have been numbered according to locality and indexed accordingly, so that the marks of any locality may be ascertained by consulting the index first and then referring to the marks.

Numbers 5823-7081 are French marks and 7083-7324 are English marks. These are more completely and more specifically listed in the special tables for those countries.

5032. 1645-46
5033. 1651-52 ?
5034. 1663
5035. 1663-64
5036. 1666-67
5037. so or similar 1669-70 or 1687-88
5038. 1672-73
5039. so or similar 1686-87 or 1706-07
5040. 1688-89
5041. 1738-39
5042. 1767
5043. about 1767
5044. 1772
5045. 1784
5046. 1507-08
5047. 1524-25
5048. 1537-38
5049. 1539-40
5050. 1544-45 or 1552-53 ?
5051. 1551-52 or 1558-59 ?
5052. 1563-64
5053. 1565-66
5054. 1574-75
5055. 1581-82
5056. 1588-89
5057. 1606
5058. 1606-07
5059. 1607-08 ?
5060. 1610-11 or 1611-12
5061. 1625-26
5062. end of 17. cent.
5063. 1641-42
5064. 1645-46
5065. 1651-52 ?
5066. 1663
5067. 1663-64
5068. 1666-67
5069. 1669-70
5070. 1672-73
5072. 1685-86 or 1686-87
5073. 1687-88
5074. 1688-89
5075a. 1706-07
5075b. 1738-39
5076a. 1743-44 or 1745
5076b. 1745-49
5076c. 1749-17??
5077. 1765
5078. 1772
5079. 1784
5080. government assayer Arnold Nyst since 1869
5081. assayer Ch. Lemaire since 1869

ATH (AETH)

5154a. 1671, in changing shield f o r m till 1788
5154b. second half of 18. cent.

OUDENAARDE

5156. about 1660
5157. 1618
5158. since 1655 and to the beginning of the 18. cent.
5159. 1771
5160. city mark early 18. cent.
5161. about 1775
5162. 1764
5163. 1771

(BRUGES)

5171a. beginning of 16. cent.
5171b-5172. about 1613, perh. 1622
5173-5174. about 1623
5175-5176. about 1660
5177. 1536-1560
5178. 1560-1584
5179. 1584-1595
5180. 1595-96
5181. 1608-09
5182. 1621-22
5183. 1630-31
5184. 1632-33
5185. 1742
5189a. Jan Crabbe, master after 1587 or
5189b. Jan Crabbe, master after 1604

BRUSSELS

5206. 15. cent.
5207-5208. beginning of 16. cent.
5209-5210. 1545 and middle of 16. cent.
5211-5212. 1553
5213-5215. about 1660
5216-5217. beginning of 18. cent.
5218-5221. 1750- about 1760
5222. since about 1760
5223. 1553
5224. 1618 ?
5225. 1624-25
5226. 1663 or perhaps 1670
5227. 1751
5228. government assayer Ch. Puttemans since 1868
5229. assayer Lelièvre since 1868

COURTRAI

5259. middle of 17.- late 18. cent.
5260. government assayer Philippeu s i n c e 1869

DINANT

5263. 1750

GHENT

5266b. about 1482
5267. second half of 16. cent.
5268-5269. about 1660
5270-5271. about 1722
5272. 1482
5273. 1557
5274. 1660
5275. 1722-26
5276. 1785

GRAMMONT

5299. about 1662

LOUVAIN

5307. late 15. cent.
5308. about 1500
5309-5310. about 1650
5311-5312. about 1712
5313-5314. about 1714

5315-5316. 1772 and 1773
5317. late 15. cent.
5318. about 1675
5319. about 1712
5320. 1772
5321. 1773

LIÈGE

5336a. 15. cent.
5336b. middle of 16. cent.
5337. 1612-1650
5338-5339. 1650-1688
5340-5341. 1688-1693
5342-5343. 1693
5344. interregnum mark, 1694, 1744, 1764, 1784
5345-5346. 1693-1705
5347-5348. 1711-1723
5349-5350. 1724-1743
5351-5352. 1744-1763
5353-5354. 1764-1771
5355-5356. 1772-1784.
5357-5358. 1784-1792
5359-5360. 1792-1797
5361. probably 1551
5362. 1745
5363. 1764
5364. or "G" 1774 or 1778
5365. 1777
5366. 1785
5367. 1788
5368. 1620-about 1640

MALINES

5421a. about 1500
5412b. 1513-37
5421c. about 1675
5421c. about 1718
5422. 1790
5423. 1791
5424. 1527-28
5425. 1592-93
5426. 1619-20
5427. 1719-20
5428. 1790
5429. 1791
5434. Jean van Campenhoudt, 1762-1791

MONS

5439. end of 15. cent.
5440. 1608-1693
5441. 17. cent.
5442. 1766
5443. about 1686
5444. 1764
5445. 1776
5446. 1782
5447. 1791

NAMUR

5477. 1505
5478. 1520
5479. 1682

NIVELLES

5490. 16. cent.
5491. 17. cent.
5492. about 1525

TERMONDE

5503. about 1713 ?
5504. about 1727

BOLOGNA

7339. 18. cent.
7340. 1811-1817
7341. inspection mark Vatican City since 1817

BOLZANO

7342. 1708
7343. middle of 18. cent.
7344. 1824-1866
7345. 1866-1872
7346. since 1872

FERRARA

7364a. 17.(?) cent.
7364b. 1815

FLORENCE

7366. 16. cent.
7367. 17.-18. cent.
7368. 18. cent.

GENOA

7369. 16. cent.
7370. 17.-18. cent.
7371. (1)720-(1)768.
7372. end of 18. cent.

LUCCA

7378. 17. cent.

MILAN

7379b. beginning of 16. cent.
7379c. middle of 16. cent.
7379d. 17.-18. cent.
7380. 1810
7381. control mark
7382-7386. master marks with comarks

MANTUA

7391. 17. cent.

MODENA

7396. 17. cent.

NAPLES

7379a. silver since 1380
7379b. gold since 1380
7398a. about 1400
7398b. 16. cent.
7399. 17. cent.
7400. 17??
7401. 1702
7402. 1716
7403. 1720
7404. 1736
7405. 1782
7406a-7406b. probably also Naples 17.-18. cent.

ASSAYER MARKS

7407. about 1700 ?
7408. about 1702
7409. about 1716
7410. about 1720
7411. about 1736
7412. about 1742

PALERMO

7426. 17. cent.

PARMA

7427. 17. cent.

ROME

7431. 17. cent.
7432-7433. end of 17. cent.
7434. 17.-18. cent.
7435. 18.-19. cent.
7436. 18.-19. cent. for gold
7437-7438. sterling, 1358-1398
7439. Bolognese standard 1508
7440. Caroline-silver 1508

SULMONA

7451. 13. and 14. cent.
7452. 14. cent. till 1406
7453. 1406-middle of 15. cent.
7454. middle of 15. cent. till ??

TRIESTE

7457-7459. 18. cent.
7460. 1805
7461. 1805
7462. 1807/09 and 1824/66
7463-7464. gold 1805
7465. 1806/07
7466. 1866-1872
7467. since 1872

TURIN

Inspection marks
7468a. 1597
7468b. 1597
7469a. since 1678
7469b. 17. cent.
7470a-7470e. 18. cent.
7471-7472. 18. cent.
7473a-7476a. about 1750
7476b. 18. cent.

VENICE

7484. 15.? cent.
7485. 17.-18. cent.
7486. 16.-18. cent.
7487a. silver since 1805
7487b. silver since 1805
7488. since 1810

LATVIA

BAUSKA

7489. inspection mark 18. cent.

GOLDINGEN

7490. 18. cent.
7491. 18.-19. cent.

MITAU

7492-7493. 17. cent.

RIGA

7494. 16. cent.
7495-7496. about 1600
7497-7498. 16.-17. cent.
7499-7500. 18. cent.

7501. 1749-56
7502. 1756-60.
7503. 1760-64
7504. 1764-68
7505. 1768-80
7514. Heinrich Meyer, 1654-1694
7516. Juergen Linden, 1674-1688
7517. Heinrich von Koelln (Kollen, Coeln), 1679-1693
7520. Joh. Georg Eben, 1703-1710
7524. Johann Abrahamsohn Lamoureux (Lamore), 1719-1744
7526. Christoffer Dey, 1729-1748
7528-7529. Johann Dietr. Rehwald, 1738-1759
7531. Joh. Christian Henck, 1750
7532. Michael Kresner the younger, 1758
7533. Joh. Friedrich Lamoureux, 1763-1797
7534. Joh. Christoph Barrowsky, 1771-1790

MEMEL

7535. mark 18. cent.

NETHERLANDS

7542. silver, since 1852
7543. gold, since 1852
7544. silver standard
7545. silver standard
7546. silver standard
7547. gold standard
7548. gold standard
7549. gold standard
7550. gold standard
7551. gold standard
7552. gold standard
7553. taxes mark till 1909
7554. inland
7555. import till 1909
7556. import till 1909
7557. since 1909
7558. export
7559. gold

AMSTERDAM

7561. about 1566
7562. 16.-17. cent.
7563. about 1606
7564. about 1608
7565. 1655
7566. about 1694
7567-7569. 18. cent.

ANNUAL LETTERS

7570. 1566
7571. 1608
7572. 1609
7573. 1655
7574. 1694
7575. 1696 and later
7576. old mark 1807

BOLSWARD

7595. mark 1725

BREDA

7598. 15.-16. cent.
7599. 16.-17. cent.
7600. 1595 or 1694

DORDRECHT

7608-7610. inspection marks with annual letters

ENKHUIZEN

7611-7613. inspection marks with annual letters

GOUDA

7614. 16. cent.

GRONINGEN

7616-7617. Cornelis Papinck,
7618-7619. master marks

THE HAGUE

7620. inspection mark
7621. inspection mark with annual letter
7622. 17. cent.

HAARLEM

7628. about 1700
7629-7630. 18. cent.
7631. middle of 18. cent.
7632. 1807

HERZOGENBUSCH

7639-7641. Aert van Muers, 1607

HOORN

7643. about 1640

LEIDEN

7644. 17. cent.

LEEUWARDEN

7645. 17.-18. cent.
7646. 1695
7652a-7652b. Johannes Lelij, 1695
7654-7656. Garbijnus van der Lelij, 1731

MAASTRICHT

7657. end of 18. cent.
7658. end of 18. cent. with annual letter

MIDDELBURG

7659. 1726
7660. middle of 18. cent.
7661-7664. inspection marks

ROTTERDAM

7665-7667. 18. cent.
7668-7669. 18. cent.
7670. 18.-19. cent.
7671. 18. cent.
7672. 18.-19. cent.

SNEEK (PROVINCE FRIESLAND)

7679. about 1770

UTRECHT

7681. about 1614
7682. 17. cent.
7683. about 1710
7684-7686. 18. cent.
7687. 1602
7688. 1614
7689. about 1650
7690. 1733 ?
7691. 1748 ?
7692. 1775 ?
7693. 1775 ? or 1802 ?

VLISSINGEN (PROVINCE ZEALAND)

7731. inspection mark

ZIERIKZEE

7734. 1600
7735. 1700

ZWOLLE

7736. 17. cent.
7737. 1721
7738. about 1726 and later
7739. 17. cent.
7740. about 1721
7741. about 1726

NORWAY

BERGEN

inspection marks
7750. 1784
7751. 1799
7752. 1812
7753. 1820
7754. 1844 (seven dots without the tower)

ANNUAL LETTERS

7755. 1787
7756. 1799
7757. 1812
7758. 1820
7759-7762. monthly marks
7763. Dimar Kahs, assayer 1763-1789
7764a-7764b. Mathias Pettersen, assayer 1796-1812
7765. Peter Michael Blytt, assayer 1812-1821

BREVIK

7771. 1779

FREDRIKSSTAD

7772. about 1687

LARVIK

7773. about 1746

OSLO (formerly CHRISTIANIA)

7774. end of 16. cent.-1624
7775. 1624
7776. 1712 ?-1781
7777. 1782-after 1814
7778. since about 1820

7779-7781. assayer mark second half of 19. cent.
7782. monthly mark April-May

SKIEN

7785. about 1781

STAVANGER

7786. first half of 18. cent.

TRONDKJEM

7787. 1746

AUSTRIA

BREGENZ

7788. about 1732
7789. since 1824
7790. 1866-68, as Vienna
7791. since 1868

GRAZ

7792. end of 16. cent.
7793. 1678
7794-7795. 1732 and 1743
7796. 1764
7797. 1778
7798. 1800
7799. 1778-1800
7800. 1807-1866
7801. 1866-1872
7802a. since 1872
7802b. since 1922
7804. 1807-1824
7805. 1810-1824

HALL (TIROL)

7810. since 1809
7811. 1809 ? 1824-1866
7812. 1866-1868

INNSBRUCK

7814. end of 17. cent.
7815. 17.-18. cent.
7816. 1868-1872
7817a. since 1872
7817b. since 1922

KLAGENFURT

7820. 1801
7821. 1807-1866
7822. 1866/67
7823. 1868-1872
7824a. since 1872
7824b. since 1922, law 1921
7825. 1806/07
7826. 1811-1824

SALZBURG

7827. 1494
7828. 16. cent.
7829. end of 16. cent.
7830. 1638
7831. 1662
7832-7833. 16.-17. cent.
7834. 1807/09
7835. 1866-72
7836a. since 1872
7836b. since 1922
7837. since 1806/07

SCHAERDING

7846. about 1600
7848. since 1781

VIENNA

Inspection marks
7849. 1524
7850. middle of 16. cent.
7851. end of 16. cent.-1674
7852. 16.-17. cent.
7853. 1675-1696
7854. 1675-1696
7855. 1699 till 1736
7856. silver 1737-1806
7858. silver 1764-1795
7859. silver 1807-1810
7860-7861. silver 1810-1866
7862. silver with changing annual letters 1819-1866
7863. 1866-1872
7864-7865. 1866-1872
7866-7867. since 1872
7868-7869. for all Austria-Hungary
7870. gold from 1774
7871-7872. gold 1791-1824
7873-7874. gold 1824-1866
7875-7877. silver
7878-7880. gold
7881-7882. 1807-24
7884-7886. 1809-10
7887. 1810-1824
7888. 1810-1824
7889. import 1866-68
7890. import 1868-1872
7891. import gold 1868-1872
7892. import since 1872
7893. import gold since 1872
7894. import silver 1902-1921
7895. import gold 1902-1921
7896-7904. standard mark
7905-7915. import

WIENER—NEUSTADT

7960. 1807-1866
7962. 1866-1872
7963a. 1872-
7963b. since 1922

POLAND

GRAUDENZ

7967a. 17. cent.
7967b. 18. cent.

KRAKOW

7971. 1807-09
7972-7973. 1809-1835
7974. 1835-1866
7975. 1859
7976. 1866-1872
7977. since 1872
7978. 1806-07
7979-7980. standard mark

LEMBERG (LWOW)

7983. 1694
7984. 18. cent.
7985. 1787-1806
7986. 1807-1866

7987. 1866-1872
7988. since 1872
7989. 1806-07
7990. 1811-1824

LISSA (LESZNO)

7991. second half of 18. cent.

LOMSHA

7994. 1781

POSEN (POZNAN)

7997-7998. 17.-18. cent.

THORN (TORUN)

8007-8009. 17. cent.
8010. 18. cent.
8012. 1760-1780
8017. Jakob Jenny, 1704-1749
8018. Johann Christian Broellmann, 1700-1719

WILNA (WILNO)

8025. 16.-17. cent.

PORTUGAL

BEJA

8026. 18. ?-19. cent.

BRAGA

8027. 1800-1881

COIMBRA

8031. 17. cent.

EVORA

8033. 1740
8034. 18.-19. ?

GUIMARAES

8036. 1790
8037. 19. cent.

LISBON

8038. 1688
8039. 1700
8040. 17.-18. cent.
8041-8042. 18. cent.
8043. 1780
8044. 18, cent.
8045. 19. cent.
8047-8050. on bigger implements
8051-8054. on smaller implements
8055. for ancient implements
8056-8057. export since 1891

PORTO

8065. about 1600
8066-8067. 17. cent.

ROUMANIA

SIBIU

8080. since 1872

CLUJ

8089. 16. cent.
8090. 16.-17. cent.
8091. 1833
8092. 1866-1872
8093. since 1872

KRONSTADT

8094. 1866-1872
8095. since 1872

TEMESVAR

8101. 1838
8102. 1866-1872
8103. since 1872

RUSSIA

8105-8110. about 1700
8116-8121. 1727-1740
8122-8126. 1741-1762

ASTRACHAN

8129. 1771

IRKUTSK OR TOBOSK

8130. 1774, 1776

JAROSSLAWL

8131. 1756, 1767

KALUGA

8132. 1797, 1799

KAMJENEZ-PODOLSK

8133. 1857-61

KASAN

8134. 1763, 1797

KIEV

8135. about 1794
8136-8137. 19. cent.

KOSTROMA

8138. 1834-1878

LENINGRAD (ST. PETERSBURG)

Inspection mark
8139-8140. about 1730-40
8141. about 1740-50.
8142. about 1760-80
8143. about 1780-1800
8144. 1808
8145. about 1810-1820
8146. about 1820-1880

MOSCOW

8147. 1734-41
8148. 1747
8149. 1751
8150. 1778

8151. 1780
8152. about 1782-1787
8153. about 1790-1801
8154. 1816-1843
8155. beginning of 19. cent.

PSKOW (PLESKAU)
8156. 1771, 1791

TULA
8157. 19. cent.

TWER
8158. 18. ? cent.

WELIKI-USTJUG
8159. beginning of 19. cent.

WITEBSK
8160. 1873

WLADIMIR
8161. 1763

WOLOGDA
8162. 18. and 19. cent.

SWEDEN
8165. s i n c e 1752, but since 1912 only for gold
8166-8167. silver since 1912
8168. import mark since 1912 only for gold
8169-8170. import mark since 1912 for silver
8176-8328. Town Marks

ARBOGA
8330-8332a. 17.-18. cent.
8332b. about 1771
8333. since 1860 ?
8334. 1733/34, 1757/58
8335. 1771

ASKERSUND
8340a. about 1742-1765
8340b. since 1860

BORAS
8341a. 18. cent.
8341b. since 1860 ?
8342. 1694, 1718, 1742
8343. 1743 ? 1760 ?

EKSJOE
8346a. 17. cent.
8346b. 18. cent.
8347. since 1860 ?
8348. 1730, 1773

ENGELHOLM
8351. 1722-1775
8352. 1860 ?

FALKENBURG
8353. 1809-1825
8354. 1860 ?

FALUN
8355a. about 1768
8355b. since 1860 ?

GAEVLE
8356. 17.-19. cent.

GOETEBORG
8358. first half of 18. cent.
8359. since 1812
8360a. 1693 and 1717
8360b. 1724
8361. 1735
8362. 1737

HAELSINGBORG
8367a. 1702-1739
8367b. 1860 ?

HAERNOESAND
8369-8370. 18. and 18.-19. cent.

HALMSTAD
8371a. 17.-18. cent.
8371b. since 1860 ?

HEDEMORA
8372a. 18. cent.
8372b. since 1860 ?

HUDIKSVALL
8374a. 18. cent.
8374b. since 1860 ?

KALMAR
8379a. 17.-18. cent.
8379b. since 1860 ?

KARLSHAMN
8381. about 1714
8382a. end of 18. cent.
8382b. 18.-19. cent.
8383. since 1860 ?

KARLSKRONA
8384. 17. and 18. cent.
8385. since 1860 ?
8386. 1733 ?

KARLSTAD
8390a. m i d d l e of 18. cent.
8390b. since 1860 ?

KOEPING
8391a. m i d d l e of 17. cent.
8391b. since 1860 ?

KRISTIANSTAD
8392. 17. and 18. cent.
8393a. 18. and 19. cent.
8393b. since 1860 ?
8394. 1764

8395. 1820
8396. 1826

LAHOLM
8400. 17.-18. cent.
8401. since 1860 ?
8405. since 1860 ?

LIDKOEPING
8404a. beginning of 18. cent.
8404b. 18. and 19. cent.

LINDESBERG
8406a. 18. cent.
8406b. since 1860 ?

LINKOEPING
8407a-8407b. end of 18. cent.
8408. since 1860 ?

LULEA
8411. middle of 18. cent.
8412a-8412b. beginning of 19. cent.
8413. since 1860 ?

LUND
8418a. 18. cent.
8418b. 18. and 19. cent.
8419. since 1860 ?
8420. 1764
8421. about 1764

MALMOE
8423. 17.-18. cent.
8424. since 1860 ?

NORA
8425a. about 1760
8425b. about 1840-1850
8426. since 1860 ?

NORRKOEPING
8427. 17.-18. cent.
8428. 18. cent.
8429. 17. (?) and 18. cent.
8430. since 1860 ?
8431a. 1754
8431b. since 1759

NORRTAELJE
8436a. early 19. cent.
8436b. since 1860 ?

NYKOEPING
8438a. 18. cent., after 1730
8438b. early 19. cent.
8439. since 1860 ?

OEREBRO
8440a. after 1750
8440b. since 1860 ?

SCHAFFHAUSEN

8945. 16. cent.
8946. 17.-18. cent.
8947-8948. 18. cent.
8949. since 1893

SION

8956. 16. cent.
8957. 17. cent.
8958. 18. cent.

STANS (CANTON UNTERWALDEN)

8968-8969. Franz Remigius Trachser, 1724-1752

SURSEE CANTON (LUCERNE)

8970-8971. 17. and 18. cent.
8972. beginning of 17. cent.
8973-8975. 17.-18. cent.
8976. about 1680
8977. 1707

THUN

8986-8987. 17. cent.

URI

8990. inspection mark

VEVEY

8992. 16. and 17. cent.
8993-8994. 18. cent.
8995. 18. cent.

WINTERTHUR

9002. 18. cent.

ZOFINGEN, CANTON ARGAU

9005. 18. cent.

ZURICH

9007. 1545
9008. 1563
9009. 1563, 1564, 1565
9010. 1608
9011. 1621
9012-9013. early 17. cent.
9014. about 1629
9015. 1631
9016. 1633
9017. 1638
9018. 1642
9019-9029. 17. and 18. cent.
9030. 1667
9031. 1674
9032. 1752
9033. 1779
9037. Abraham Gessner, 1571-1613
9051-9052. Hans Jacob Holzhalb, 1634-1657

ZUG

9080. 1584
9081. 1620
9082. 17. cent.
9083-9084. 18. cent.

SPAIN

9092-9093. since 1881

AGUILAR, PROVINCE CORDOBA

9094. 17. cent.

ASTORGA

9095. 16. cent.

BARCELONA

9096. 14.-16. ? cent.
9097. 15. cent.
9098. 15. cent.
9099-9100. 15.-16. cent.
9101. 16. cent.
9102. late 16. cent.
9103. 16. (also 17. ?) cent.
9104-9105. 16. (also 17. ?) cent.

CERVANTES, PROVINCE LUGO, or CERVERA, PROVINCE LERIDA

9133. 15.-17. cent. ?

CORDOBA

9134. 15. cent.

MADRID

9160. 18. cent.

PALMA MALLORCA

9164. 15. cent.
9165. 15.-16. cent.
9166. 16. cent.

TOLEDO

9173. 16. cent.
9174. about 1600
9175. 17. cent.

VALENCIA

9178. 16. cent.

VALLADOLID

9179. Juan de Benavente, 1565-1609

ZARAGOZA

9180. 14. and 15. cent.
9181-9182. 16. cent.

JUGOSLAVIA

ZAGREB

9198. 1866-1872
9199. since 1872

BELGRADE

9200-9203. gold 1882-1919
9204-9207. silver 1882-1919
9208. import gold
9209. import silver

LAIBACH (LJUBLJANA)

9210. 18. cent.
9211. 1802
9212. 1806
9213. 19. cent.
9214. 1807/08 and 1824-66.
9215. 1866/68
9216. 1868/72
9217. since 1872

NEUSATZ (NUVI SAD)

9219. inspection mark
9220. 1866-1872
9221. since 1872

RAGUSA (DUBROVNIK)

9222. 17. or 18. cent.
9223. 1866/67
9224. 1868/72
9225. since 1872

CZECHOSLOVAKIA

9226. standard mark 1-4
9227-9229. standard marks
9230. import mark silver

ALTSOHL (ZVOLEN)

9231. 1657

BRUNN (BRNO)

9233-9234. till 1646
9235. 1683
9236. 1769
9237. 1806
Official marks
9238. 1807-1866
9239. 1866-1868
9240. 1869-1872
9241. since 1872
9242. 1806/07
9243. 1810-1824
9244. 1811-1824

EGER (CHEB)

9250. 17.-18. cent.
9251. beginning of 18. cent.
9252. 1868-1872
9253. since 1872

HOTZENPLOTZ (OSOBLAHA)

9257. 1769

(HUNGARIAN) HRADISCH

9258. 1608
9259. 1769

IGLAU (JIHLAVA)

9260. 1548-beginning of 18. cent.
9261. 1769 (-1776).
9262. 1807-1866
9263. 1866-1868
9264. 1869-1872
9265. since 1872

KASCHAU (KOSICE)

9267. 16. cent.
9268. 17.-18. cent.

BIBLIOGRAPHY

"English Goldsmiths and Their Marks"—Sir Charles James Jackson. Macmillan and Co. Ltd. London, 1921.

"History of Old Sheffield Plate"—Frederick Bradbury. Macmillan. 1912.

"Der Goldschmiede Merkzeichen"—Marc Rosenberg. Berlin, 1928.

"American Silversmiths and Their Marks"—Stephen G. C. Ensko. New York, 1927.

"Les Poinçons de L'Orfèvrerie Française"—Louis Carré. Paris, 1928.

"Guide de L'Amatur d'Orfèvrerie Française"—Louis Carré. Paris, 1929.

"Domestic Silver of Great Britain and Ireland"—Edward Wenham. Oxford University Press. London, 1931.

"Old English Silver"—William W. Watts. E. Benn, Ltd. London, 1924.

"Old Silver of Europe and America"—Edward Alfred Jones. B. T. Batsford, Ltd. London, 1928.

"Chats on Old Silver"—Arthur Hayden. T. F. Unwin Ltd. London, 1915.

"English Domestic Silver"—Charles C. Oman. A. C. Black Ltd. London, 1934.

"Matthew Boulton"—H. W. Dickinson. Cambridge University Press. London, 1937.

"Paul de Lamerie"—P. A. S. Phillips. B. T. Batsford, Ltd. London, 1935.

"American Silversmiths and Their Marks II"—Stephen G. C. Ensko. New York, 1937.

"Early American Silvermarks"—James Graham Jr. New York, 1936.

"American Church Silver"—Museum of Fine Arts. Boston, Mass., 1911.

"American Silver"—Introduction. R. T. H. Halsey. Museum of Fine Arts. Boston, Mass., 1906.

"American Collector"—New York, 1936 and 1937. Various.

GENERAL INDEX